D1737641

WOLVES OF SUMMER

BOUND TO THE FAE · BOOKS 1-3

EVA CHASE

Wolves of Summer: Bound to the Fae - Books 1-3

1 in the Bound to the Fae Box Sets series

First Digital Edition, 2022

Cover design: Story Wrappers

Case character art: Jo Painter

Ebook ISBN: 978-1-990338-89-2

Hardcover ISBN: 978-1-990338-90-8

CAPTIVE OF WOLVES

BOUND TO THE FAE #1

CAPTIVE OF WOLVES

BOUND TO THE FAE #1

CHAPTER ONE

Talia

I can always tell when they've come to steal my blood. It's only those times that my captors arrive all together, the three hulking men-who-aren't-men marching into the room that holds my cage.

When they enter on their own to shove food and water through the bars or to change my toilet bucket, they have a curt, preoccupied air as if paying me any attention bores them. The group effort gets them excited. They always come in chuckling and giving each other hearty smacks on the shoulders, congratulating themselves on a job well done before they've even done it.

Or maybe it's mostly done already. I have no idea what they want my blood for or how large a part of those activities it is.

All I know is that while my entire existence here is awful, these days are the worst.

The second I hear their merry voices on the other side of the door, my fingers clench around the scratchy fabric of my wool blanket. Every nerve in my body clangs to propel myself away from the threat. But the farthest I can go is the corners of my cage, which isn't anywhere at all.

It'll be over faster the more cooperative I am. And my one chance at ever getting *out* of this awful existence depends on me tamping down on my dread enough to focus all my attention on listening.

As my captors walk in, my fingers keep clutching the blanket. It's the only protection I have against their harsh gazes and sneers. They can't be bothered to go to the trouble of clothing me, but they don't want me coming down with a chill either. I'm valuable enough to be kept alive but not remotely comfortable.

The man at the head of the bunch gazes down at me where I'm crouched on the hard metal floor of the cage, his nose wrinkling in undisguised revulsion. It must stink in here—*I* must stink, considering I can't remember the last time they bothered to even hose me off. I've lived in filth for so many years I can't tell anymore.

As far as I've been able to tell, that man—the one with hair as brilliantly yellow as the petals of a sunflower and ears that rise to inhuman points—is the leader. Yellow doesn't do much other than watch and order the others around. But he's the one who unlocks my cage. I have to concentrate on him.

The second of my captors, the one with the rotund belly and heavy feet, goes to the plain cupboard that's the room's only other furnishing. I think of him as Cutter because of his role in this ritual. He gets out the little ivory-handled knife and a glass vial. My skin twitches in anxious anticipation.

The third of the men bends down beside the cage until he's almost at my level. His lips curl into a grin that looks cut into his ruddy face. He isn't burly like the other two but all sharp angles, from the tips of his ears to the toes of his narrow boots to the tufts of his blueish white hair that poke from his scalp like icicles.

I'm uncomfortably familiar with Ice's angles. Occasionally he gets bored enough with whatever else his life consists of to saunter in here and "play" with me. He'll poke and prod until he forces out a gasp of pain.

They have a rule about injuring me—I've heard them talk about it. Nothing that could jeopardize my life is allowed. Ice has made a hobby out of discovering all the ways he can torment my body without causing any tangible damage.

Not surprisingly, he's always the one who volunteers to pin me down.

I could make it even easier for them. I could sprawl out on my belly the way they'll want me positioned so he has no reason to shove me down. But he'll push me around anyway, and whatever small fragment of pride I've somehow held onto balks at the thought of prostrating myself quite that willingly.

Yellow leans forward. Black tattoos in unfamiliar symbols mark all of their bodies, but he has the most, several on his arms and neck, one poking from his hairline at his temple. A twisting line from one stretches across his chin all the way to his lips.

He's going to say the word—the word that spills from his mouth with a resonance that prickles down my spine. The word that opens the door.

The word I have to learn.

He rests his hand on the latch. His lips part, and the sounds slip out fast and sibilant, one blending into the next. "*Fee-doom-ace-own.*"

That's what it sounds like to my pricked ears, anyway. That's what it's sounded like since I realized some kind of magic holds my cage closed and that the word is the key, although it took several attempts before I was sure of each of the syllables. I replay everything I've heard my captors say over and over in my head, searching for meanings beyond the obvious that might offer a helpful clue to ending my torment, but that word is the one I've returned to the most.

I'm still not *really* sure of it, or I'd be able to say it properly, wouldn't I? Just how much does his voice lilt upwards with the "ice" bit? How long does he stretch out the "o" in "own"?

What am I missing?

I might be missing the capacity to work any kind of magic word at all, no matter how well I say it. In the back of my head, I know that, not any flaw in my concentration, could be the problem. Because these *aren't* really men, and they have powers beyond anything I understood before they threw me in this cage. He says the word quietly and quickly, but I don't think he's all that worried about me overhearing it.

He doesn't think I could use it. But it's all I have.

He unhooks the latch. The hinges squeak as the door swings open.

The cage is barely big enough for me. When I'm sitting, I can touch the bars overhead without raising my arm completely. Standing is out of the question. But the doorway is large enough for Ice to squeeze through. There's just enough space for him to grab me by the back of my neck and slam my face against the floor.

Pain radiates through my skull. He clambers on top of me with his pointy knees digging into my calves and the spikes of his elbows jabbing my ribs. His weight bears down on my back, squashing most of the air from my lungs until I'm on the verge of suffocating. He grinds one of those elbows into the tender spot just below my shoulder blade, and I catch my lower lip between my teeth.

I hate the whimper that slips out of me anyway. I hate his fingers burrowing into the hollow between my cheek and my jaw to press my face even harder against the grubby metal. I hate that he knows exactly how to take me from discomfort to agony in the space of a breath.

I hate the jagged snicker that tells me how much he loves it.

There are easier ways they could position me, but this one is more fun for them.

A jolt of adrenaline shoots through my veins, more panic than anything else, and I have to clamp down hard to smother the urge to thrash against Ice's hold. There is no escaping him. I know that. And the one time I tried, when I didn't know very much yet, the man on top of me repaid me in spades for the one kick I landed to his gut. He grasped my foot and twisted his hands, and the bones snapped in an explosion of pain.

That pain has never quite gone away. They didn't let the fractures heal right—a little extra security against me running away. I can't really walk in this cage, but any time I put weight on that foot, a dull ache spreads through it. Extra security and a constant reminder of the consequences of fighting back.

I have other ways of defying them that they can't see. I pull all the way back into my mind, into the depths where the pain is only a distant buzzing, into an imagined vision of the world they wrenched me from. It isn't a part of that world I ever experienced in real life, but one I dreamed about traveling to someday back when I could have dreams that large.

Before me lies a broad pool of turquoise water surrounded by weather-sculpted rock. Brilliant sun beams down to glitter off the ripples. I would drift in that pool, embraced by gentle warmth, gazing up at the clear blue sky…

Cutter lets out a raspy sound of amusement. "Can we have her arm already?"

Ice leans his weight onto his left elbow in a way that nearly dislocates my shoulder. The spike of pain shatters the illusion I've formed in my head. As he yanks my other arm toward the open door, I grit my teeth, but a little cry seeps out anyway. He snickers again. I squeeze my eyes shut, tears leaking out despite my best efforts.

Cutter doesn't revel in the process, but he doesn't appear to have any objection to his companion's antics. Without another word, he slices the knife into my wrist.

It's a shallow stinging, mostly drowned out by the cacophony of hurts already coursing through my body. From the glimpses I've gotten of the vial, they only take a few teaspoons. He pinches the flesh and then ties a thin bandage over the wound with a perfunctory tug to fix it in place.

Cutter straightens up. Ice pushes off me, knocking my head against the metal floor once more for good measure. When he's clambered out, Yellow shuts the cage door and voices his magic to lock it.

Normally, this is when they'd leave. Instead, Ice peers down at me, folding his arms over his chest. The light glittering off the pale, spiky tufts on his head turns them even chillier-looking.

"She barely responds anymore," he says. "It makes this rather tiresome."

Cutter shakes his head. "Only you would wish for a fight."

"I'm only saying that while we have her, we might as well make use of her for some entertainment in between more vital matters."

"What did you have in mind?" Yellow asks as if he doesn't really care about the answer. He's eyeing the vial rather than me, with a triumphant gleam in his eyes.

Ice rubs his jaw, showing the tattoo that spears across his knuckles. "We could give her the run of the castle. Make it more of a chase."

Hope flickers to life in my chest despite the throbbing of my ribs. I might not even need to make the magic work to get my chance. If I could get that much closer to—

His sneering voice cuts through my thoughts. "Of course, I'd break her other ankle to ensure she can't get far without our say so. She can crawl around the place like the vermin she is."

My blood freezes, a wave of hopelessness dousing the flare of hope in an instant. *No.* Fleeing this place with one unsteady leg

would be hard enough. Escaping without the use of either… They might as well cage me within my body and swallow the key.

"Let me think on it," Yellow says in the same distracted tone. "It is something of a waste putting her to use so infrequently. Perhaps she could polish the floors while she's down there."

He's really considering it. I bite back the scream that's trying to bubble up my throat.

"Sleep well, dung-body!" Ice calls over his shoulder to me, and they all laugh as they head out.

A shiver runs through my limbs. Within moments, I'm shaking so hard I can't get a hold of myself. I roll onto my side and pull my knees up to my chest, gulping air and groping for control.

I can't let it happen. I can't. I can't. I'd rather be dead.

But they won't let me take that escape either.

Listen. I have to listen to that magic word again. Listen and then try, oh please, oh please…

I close my eyes and reach back to the turquoise pool I pasted into my scrapbook of wonderful places years ago, when I was still a kid. I can't quite conjure up the warble of the breeze over the water or its warm caress against my face, but gradually, my shudders peter out.

Over time, I've built an extensive imaginary world inside my head. Along with the exotic locations from my scrapbook, I summon up scenes from favorite movies: mine, sweeping fantasy epics of heroic adventures, and the ones Mom always loved, comedies where everyone speaks in arch remarks and often with British accents. In the long stretches of when I'm left alone, I fantasize about stepping into those stories, joining conversations with comments that sound just as valiant or smart. It stops my brain from turning into mush with boredom.

If it weren't for that pretend world, this existence would probably have reduced me to a mess of vague thoughts, shudders, and pain by now. I run my fingers down my side to my right hipbone, to the tiny mottling of scars there. One for each year I've been able to mark, digging my ragged fingernail into my skin until it bled. Eight altogether.

How many more years lie ahead if they shackle me to a ruined body and set me to work? Will I even be able to drift away inside my head in between the worst parts, or will I lose even that make-believe escape?

Another shiver ripples through me. I force myself to breathe slow and steady. The chance isn't gone yet. I have to focus on that and not on the terrors that might lie ahead.

As I uncurl myself, I reach toward the ceiling of my cage. I might not be able to walk in here, but I've kept myself strong however I can. Gripping the bars, I heft myself up and down, over and over, until a different sort of ache burns through my muscles.

It isn't comfortable, but there's something satisfying about knowing I still have some small say over what my body is put through. It helps that the exertion makes it hard to think about my future, now even more precarious than before.

I'm bicycling my legs in an attempt to work those muscles too when the sound I've been waiting for reaches my ears. The muffled but audible thud of what I assume is the building's front door carries all the way to this room.

I flip into a crouched position, keeping most of my weight on my good foot. My captors never say much around me, but from the snippets I've gathered over the years, I've gotten the impression they have to leave this place to complete their plans. I don't know who else might live in the building other than the three of them, but to the best of my knowledge, no one else here has ever seen me. Even if I run into another inhabitant, they might not realize I'm meant to be a prisoner.

If I want to regain my freedom, this is my best opportunity. Possibly the last opportunity I'm ever going to get.

I just have to say that strange word right.

I tip so close to the cage door that my forehead brushes the bars. Fixing my eyes on the latch, I dredge up my memory of my captor's lilting pronunciation. My voice comes out in a whisper. "Fee-doom-ace-own."

When I reach through the bars to rattle the latch, it doesn't budge. I'm *sure* I said it exactly the same way Yellow did. But then, I've felt that way dozens of times before.

"Fee-doom-ace-own," I say at the latch, letting my voice rise, shifting my inflection. "Fee-doom-ace-own. Fee-*doom*-ace-own. Fee-doom-ace-*own*! Come on!"

My heart is pounding. I grasp the bars and gather my composure. It's not just being trapped in here that I'm scared of. I'm also scared of what will happen if I *do* get out. What I might face beyond this room. What my captors will do to me if they catch me. Every time I've tried this, that terror lurks right behind my resolve.

I can't let the fear stop me. I *can't*. Nothing could be worse than what I'll face if the sharp-edged man gets his way.

Thinking about dragging myself around this place with its bone-white floors and walls, scrubbing them clean, enduring jabs and kicks all day long, my soul recoils. That tropical pool I dream about is out there somewhere. Even if it feels like a fantasy now, it's a place as real as this one. Wouldn't it be worth anything to get there?

I'll scream at the lock until I'm hoarse if that's what it takes. I can do this. I have to.

I train my gaze on the lock and pull all my determination into my lungs. "Fee-doom-ace-own. *Fee*-doom-ace-own. Fee-*doom*-ace-own. Fee-doom-ace-own!"

The final incantation crackles over my tongue like an electric shock. The hairs on my arms jump to attention, my mouth goes abruptly dry—and the latch twists beneath my desperate fingers.

I'm so startled I nearly choke on the little saliva I have left.

Breath held, I apply more pressure, and the latch turns all the way. The door squeaks open at my nudge. The way is clear.

I'm *free*. Of the cage, at least. Oh my god.

In that first moment, my body locks in place. I clench my jaw and tug the scratchy fabric of my blanket around me in a makeshift cloak. I ease out through the opening, first my head and shoulders, then a shuffling step—

A thump and a shattering sound reverberates through the room's ceiling, and I flinch. Panic seizes me.

They've come back. They've come back early, and they're angry.

The thought has barely passed through my head before voices filter through the door. Terror blanks my mind. On pure instinct, I yank the cage's door closed and throw myself to the back of the space, huddling under the blanket in case something in my expression or my pose will give away what I've accomplished.

There's a scuffling noise outside, which isn't what I'd expect. Then footsteps tramp in, accompanied by those voices—but now that I can hear them more clearly, I don't recognize the speakers.

"Phew. Whatever they were keeping in that cage, they obviously didn't believe in cleaning up after it." That voice is buoyant with more warmth than I've ever heard any of my captors express. He must take me for just a heap of blanket, nothing living in here right now. I will my body to stay utterly still.

It doesn't sound as if he's *bothered* by the fact that my captors would have been keeping something in this cage. Even if he seems friendlier than them, that doesn't mean he's any kinder. Who are these people? What are they doing here?

"This doesn't look like a room where they'd be keeping their notes stashed," he goes on. "Or... how did Sylas put it? 'Apparatus'?"

The voice that answers is dryly melodic but equally male. "If only Aerik and his cadre had been kind enough to leave detailed instructions posted in their front hall. It appears they're just as irritating in this as they are in every other way."

"I suppose it *is* their big secret."

"Let's not have any sympathy for the devils, now. Come on, we may as well have a look in this cabinet while we're here."

I'm still tensed, motionless, under the blanket, but the fabric has fallen so that one fold gives me a sliver of a view into the room. A man strides into view, tall with ample brawn filling out his simple tee, dark auburn hair sprouting above his broad, boyish face. As he inspects the cabinet, his eyes gleam so avidly I assume the first voice was his.

He doesn't look menacing, despite all that powerful bulk, and his ears are smoothly rounded at the top, but my gaze catches on the black symbols inked on his skin. One follows the curve of his bicep; another partly encircles his wrist. Symbols like the tattoos all three of my captors display.

My body goes even more rigid than it already was. Whoever he is, he must be one of them. A man-who's-not-a-man. A monster in human-like skin.

The other man saunters up beside him: even taller and equally brawny in his high-collared shirt, his tawny hair rumpled into artful disarray. Where the first man gives off an eager, youthful energy, this one is all languid, muscular poise. With the angle of his face, I can only see the corner of his smile—and an ear with a low but obvious point at its peak.

"Well, now we know where they keep some of their empty glassware and linens. No papers in there?"

The boyish one leans in to paw through the contents. "Doesn't look like it." He sighs and swivels on his heel with no diminishing of his upbeat energy. "So much for that. Let's see what else they've stashed down here in the basement."

The poised one holds up his hand. The edge of a tattoo spirals up across the heel to his palm. "Just a moment. There's something…" He inhales audibly and turns—toward me.

I stop breathing completely. I am a rock. A bundle of rags. A lump of nothingness that should be of no interest to anyone.

My silent pleas have no effect. The man's nostrils flare, and he stalks toward my cage with a purposefulness that turns my gut to water.

CHAPTER TWO

Talia

With the intruder standing right in front of my cage, I can only make out one leg in trim midnight-blue slacks through the small gap in the folds of my blanket. My body screams out for me to sink into the hard metal floor, away from him —as if I wouldn't have done that years ago if I could.

Please, no. I was so close. Just leave, leave me alone, let me flee.

My heart is thudding so hard it nearly drowns out his dry voice.

"With all the foul smells in here I almost missed it. Take a good, deep breath, little brother, and tell me what your nose tells you."

The other one sucks in a breath. My own breath quivers over my lips, as shallow as I can keep it.

"There's a hint—like the tonic." The boyish one's voice vibrates with excitement. "And... human." Another breath. "Female?"

Oh, no. What do I do now? The cage door—it isn't even locked. I released the magic on the latch. Horror crawls through me with a betraying twitch of my arm.

"Human, female, and awake, though in what state beyond that I can hardly guess. It would appear this cage is still in use after all." There's a rustle of fabric as the poised man drops into a crouch. "Get our glorious leader. He should be here for this."

Footsteps thump as the other one dashes away. An ache has formed at the top of my throat. It's taking all my strength to hold my body in place, frantic tension clutching every muscle.

The way these men have talked, I don't think they like my captors very much. What does that mean for me? What are they going to do to me?

They could be better than the monsters who stole me… or they could be worse. And even *better* wouldn't necessarily mean *good*. Right now, all I'm sure of is they're cutting off my last chance at escape.

The man speaks in a lower, smoother tone. "Hello in there. Why don't you come out and let us have a look at you? Can you even understand me?"

As long as he thinks I can't, I have an excuse not to respond. I stay where I am.

More footsteps thump into the room—at least a few sets. How many of these intruders are there?

A rich baritone resonates through the room with a note of total authority. "What's the fuss about, Whitt? We can't be sidetracked by Aerik's vulgar hobbies."

"I don't think this is a sidetrack—I think this is *the* track, straight to our goal. Perhaps they have this servant assist them in making the tonic. There's a whiff of it in here."

"All the whiffs I'm catching are putrid," a fourth voice says, this one sharp and grating. It reminds me so strongly of the man who pinned me down less than an hour ago that I flinch.

There's a pause, and then I sense someone else crouching by the cage. "No, Whitt's right. Can she speak?"

"I don't know," says the poised one who's apparently named

Whitt. "This is all we've gotten out of her so far: a very adept impression of a crumpled blanket."

"Well, we don't have time to wait for her to warm up to us. Let's see what we've got in here."

The latch clicks; the hinges squeak. My body clenches up, my fingers digging into the coarse fabric, but of course that doesn't stop him. A powerful tug on the blanket pulls it partway off me, exposing my bare back and legs to the room's cool air.

It's too much. Panic flashes through me, and without any conscious intention, I'm snatching at the blanket, wrenching it toward me, kicking out with my legs. My good foot smacks a solid arm. I jerk back against the bars of the cage, my pulse hammering —oh god, am I going to have my ankle shattered by *these* monsters?

The man with the resonant voice just… laughs. Not my captors' jeering snickers, but a deep guffaw as if he's a little impressed along with his amusement. "We've got a fighter," he says. "Pitiful thing. Come on now, we just need to talk."

And I'm supposed to believe that? I let the fabric tumble away from my face so I can see what I'm fighting against and find myself staring into a pair of mismatched eyes set in brown skin.

The man who's leaning through the cage door looms even larger and brawnier than the first two, like a grizzly among lesser bears. He carries a mark of at least one violent battle. His right eye, fixed on me, is a dark brown as rich as his voice. The other shines milky white, bisected by a pale, jagged scar that cuts from his hairline across the eyelid to halfway down his cheek.

Thick waves of coffee-brown hair fall to his massive shoulders, but don't quite obscure the steep points of his ears. Curving black lines of tattoos creep up his neck from under his shirt collar. More darken his forehead and the edges of his jaw. Every inch of his being emanates power.

The sense washes over me that if he wanted to, he could maul any of my captors to shreds without suffering more than a few scratches. Possibly all three of them at the same time.

I don't stand a chance.

"There we go," he says evenly. "Answer a few questions about your masters, and we'll leave you alone. We're not here to hurt you."

Someone behind him makes a rough noise. The boyish man-who's-not-a-man peers over the grizzly's shoulder. "Somehow I'm thinking Aerik and them don't have the same qualms."

"It's none of our concern," the sharp-voiced man says from somewhere beyond my view. "Let dung-bodies wallow in dung. We need to know about the tonic."

"Hush," the grizzly says without looking back, quiet but firm. His attention stays on me. "What do they have you do for them, little scrap? Something like cooking? Can you tell us about it?"

My voice stays locked at the back of my mouth. I don't want to tell them anything, but I'm not sure I could even if I did want to. There's a lump as big and hard as a fist lodged in my throat.

"It appears she's dumb in more ways than one," the sharp voice says. "Drag her out and make her show us."

I can see just enough of the poised one—Whitt's—face to watch him roll his pale eyes. "Right. Fantastic plan. Take the creature that's already terrified mute and terrify her more. That'll definitely open her up."

"There are other ways we could open her up," the other snaps.

The grizzly slashes his broad hand through the air, its back dappled with another tattoo. "Enough." As the others fall silent, his gaze roves over me. Even with the blanket, even though he only has one eye to inspect me with, I feel utterly exposed.

"Ignore them," he says to me. "This is just between you and me. Your masters let you out sometimes, don't they? They bring you to another room—somewhere they're mixing things or bottling things? I only need to know where, and then we're gone. We'll see that you forget we were ever even here."

I do want them gone. Gone so I can scramble out of here before those "masters" return. But I have no idea what he's talking about. My captors never let me out, and I've never heard them talk about cooking anything.

My throat is still closed, but I manage to shake my head, willing him to understand. Willing him not to be angry. I don't have what they want. I can't help them with whatever they're searching for.

"No?" He frowns, which turns his already intimidating face fierce. My pulse lurches. "Do they bring something in here for you to help them with?"

I shake my head again, not quite restraining a shiver at the same time, and the blanket slips over my arm. The grizzly glances down at my wrist, and even though he was crouching there unmoving before, somehow he goes even more still.

Before I can react, his hand shoots out to grab my arm just below the bandage. He yanks it toward him. A yelp jolts out of me.

I try to scramble backward, but there's nowhere to go, and his fingers grip me tightly. He pulls my wrist level with his nose. His eyes widen.

"Please," I say, my voice stretching so thin on its way up my constricted throat that it's barely a whisper.

He doesn't seem to hear. Still clutching my arm, he turns toward his companions.

"She doesn't smell like the tonic because they put her to work on it. She smells like it because she *is* it."

The one called Whitt guffaws. "She *is* the tonic? She hardly looks fit to be bottled."

The grizzly glowers at him and jerks my arm up higher. "They bled her today. The scent is clear as anything. *This* is their wretched secret ingredient."

Through the panic and my scattered thoughts, the pieces click together. What they're searching for is the same as the reason the other monsters take my blood. They aren't going to leave me alone. They're here for *me*.

What fresh hell will they drag me into?

The moment that question crosses my mind, my body is already reacting. I flail and thrash, hitting out with every limb, a piercing wail wrenching out of me. *No, no, no. No more. Not when I was so close.*

"Shut her up!" one of them says.

The grizzly is already heaving me toward him, blanket and all. His powerful arms squeeze me against him, trapping my arms. The smacking of my knees against his thighs doesn't make him so much as blink. His hand claps over my mouth, and a scent like earth and woodsmoke fills my nose with my next frantic breath.

As I squirm and kick, voices volley around us.

"This isn't what we planned for. We weren't supposed to be taking prisoners."

"If she's what we need, then she's our new guest of honor. Let's get her out of here fast, before she makes such a stir the neighbors catch on."

"Snap her neck—that would do the trick."

Panic blares through me with a shriller edge. I struggle twice as hard, as hopeless as it feels. The grizzly hefts me up in his arms like I'm weightless, one arm dropping to catch my legs, and then I'm bundled tight against him, barely able to move. I swing back my head, one of the few parts of me not clamped in place, and my skull slams into my kidnapper's jaw.

He lets out the faintest of grunts, his grip not loosening in the slightest. "Kill her, and there goes the supply. We'll take her—now. But we need her pliant to get her out of here unnoticed. August, the blanking grip."

"But—"

The next word is a snarl. "*Now.*"

I wriggle in his hold like a fish wrapped in a net, my head

whipping back and forth, but it's not enough. The man with the warm, boyish face steps up beside the grizzly and presses his hand to the crook of my neck. As he says a quiet but emphatic word, his thumb and forefinger pinch and squeeze—and my awareness snuffs out into blackness.

CHAPTER THREE

Sylas

The moon is on the rise. Even with it hidden beyond the oaks and pines around us, I'm aware of every fraction of its journey to scale the horizon. The prickling energy of its full-faced state carries on the warm evening breeze alongside the green and musky scents of the forest and the beasts that live in it. Once, the ghostly impressions beyond regular sight that sometimes seep through my deadened eye show a glimpse of it like a translucent afterimage superimposed against the shadows.

Far too soon, that round white circle will be completely exposed in the darkening sky. With every passing minute, its energy niggles deeper into my bones.

I don't like it. I don't like the turn our mission took or how much time we had to spend departing Aerik's fortress with our unexpected cargo. I thought we'd be hurrying off with a sheaf of papers or a notebook or two, ideally after downing a vial of the tonic. We'd have moved faster and had more advantage of stealth in our wolfish forms. We wouldn't have needed to worry about that moon.

But there were no vials remaining in the fortress. Aerik and his pack must have taken this month's entire batch to distribute. And while our cargo isn't much more than a slip of a creature, she's still significantly more unwieldly than a book.

Aerik and his cadre will know someone broke in. The pottery Kellan smashed—accidentally, he said, but the bastard can be fastidiously careful when it suits *him*—would have told the story well enough even if we weren't absconding with an entire human girl they were keeping locked away. The last thing I want is to add our names to that story. No one can know it was Sylas and his cadre who stole the secret of the tonic, not until we've decided exactly how we're going to leverage that secret in our favor.

So, we had to make awkward use of one of the faded pack member's wheelbarrows and some hasty concealment spells, and now we're tramping through the forest an hour later than we were meant to be returning to our carriage. Which means we're an hour closer to the moment when the full moon's energy overwhelms us completely.

There's no telling what we might do then. Whether we'd spare the girl or savage her or misplace her in the woods. Whether we'd rage deeper into the woods or back out into the open fields where Aerik's pack might spot us on their return. If we don't make it away from this foray in time, we'll manage to fall even farther in standing than we already have, and that catastrophe will be on my shoulders too.

August is carrying the girl now, slung over his shoulder, still limp from his magic-enhanced touch. With her ratty blanket wrapped around most of her scrawny form, she bears an uncomfortable resemblance to a sack of bones—and a half-empty one at that. The pink ridges of scarring that mottle one of her knobby shoulders bear testament to a more brutal savaging than the cut on her wrist some time in her past—a savaging that appears to have come with a gouging of wolfish fangs.

This is the key to Aerik's surge in prestige, to all the favor he's curried in the past several years, and he's treated her with less dignity than I'd subject my worst enemy to. Starved, hunched, and filthy, mute with fear at the very sight of us...

I can't shake the image of my first glimpse of her eyes, the pale green of newly budded leaves but bloomed wide with terror, so striking in her sallow, sunken face.

A rat would deserve better treatment, and humans are leagues closer to fae than any rodent. I'd amassed a great deal of disgust for Aerik's methods already, and I believe tonight has just doubled it in magnitude.

Not all of my companions would agree with me on the measure of humans compared to rodents, though. Kellan stalks behind August with his silvery gaze lingering on the slumped girl, his expression like that of a cat planning to pounce on a mouse. I've kept our home free of human servants to spare them from his inclinations, but clearly that's only given him plenty of time to stockpile his antagonism toward those who turn so quickly to dust.

He notices my gaze and gives me the bitterest of wolfish grins. "So much riding on a piece of dung. No wonder Aerik kept the secret so very quiet."

"I expect it had more to do with the fact that the blustering prick relished lording his mysterious cure over the rest of us," Whitt remarks in his careless way. He strides along with an air of total nonchalance, but I can scent a hint of stress from him.

I doubt it's the coming of the moon that worries him, though all of my cadre will be able to sense it as well as I can. He's never been overly concerned about the shifting of our natures—which I suppose makes sense, considering he earned the nickname "Wild Whitt" well before that wildness became inescapable. He has no shortage of pride, though. He won't like the idea of our raid being discovered and the disgrace that would follow any more than I do.

Even Kellan's chuckle manages to sound bitter. "Still, imagine having to keep this stinking creature around for years, having to handle the pathetic thing before every full moon, always needing to be so *careful* with it so as not to lose the rotting source of their claim to glory." His lip curls with disgust aimed in a very different direction from mine. "The only proper use for a dung-body—"

"The only proper use for your *mouth* right now would be to take in enough breath to pick up your pace," I interrupt, keeping the edge in my voice firm rather than acerbic. He *is* a member of my cadre, and I am his lord, and I will not swat him across the head as if he were a sulking whelp, as much as I might sometimes be tempted to.

I owe him more than that, and may I never forget it. He certainly never will.

Clearly I will have to keep an eye on him when it comes to the newest—if temporary—member of our household, though. So far, Kellan hasn't overtly disobeyed a direct order. He knows there'd be no room for leniency there. But he has appeared to enjoy finding ways to maneuver around my obvious intentions, increasingly so in the past few years.

In consideration of his circumstances and our history, I've allowed him all the patience I can, but there are limits. There may come a point when he'll regret trying me.

The bloated orb of the moon will be easing its thickest span above the horizon now. We have perhaps fifteen minutes before the change comes. As long as we're on our enchanted ride and away, it won't matter. The secure hold I conjured with the thing to ensure we didn't damage our bounty is large enough to hold the girl.

We must be almost upon the carriage. I'm running low on the landmarks I made note of to guide our way—

Whitt has sauntered farther ahead. He halts, his head jerking around to scan a small clearing—a clearing that's familiar and too empty for comfort. An annoyed breath hisses through his teeth.

"Our ride appears to have conveyed itself without us."

I curse under my breath. I know the true names of every family of tree in this wood and any other; I can talk a seed into a sapling; but while I've lived so far from the Heart of the Mists, my magic has dwindled. All it would take is for some other nearby fae with greater reserves calling for a vehicle, and my hold on the conjured carriage would falter.

August swings around, a shadow crossing his normally cheerful face. "How are we going to get back? We're still too close, and the moon—"

"I know." I swivel, taking in the forest. "I can fashion another carriage." It might take a minor sacrifice after all the power I've already expended this evening, but a bit of skin is nothing compared to the vengeance Aerik will want to rain down. "I just need to find a juniper."

None of that specific tart scent reaches my nose. There is nothing I can use close by. A fresh wave of the full moon's prickling energy washes through my body, making my thoughts twitch. Soon I'll lose my ability to control them—to control all of me— altogether. My jaw clenches.

"Let's move!" I bark, and lope through the trees at a faster pace, drawing lungfuls of air through my mouth. If I can catch even the slightest hint of juniper to direct my way... I train my dead eye as intently as my whole one, willing it to offer some fleeting image that might help, but all it catches on is a shimmering echo of the carriage racing away through the forest as it must have done not long ago.

A shiver runs through my body, nearly making me stumble. My muscles aren't just prickling now but coiling in anticipation. My skin tightens, and an ache runs through my gums where my fangs are on the verge of springing forth.

The change is coming on faster, stronger, than ever before. That's the story of our wretched lives, isn't it? Even if I slammed into a juniper right this instant, I'm not sure I could hold onto my awareness long enough to work the necessary spell.

A growl is building in my throat, and my shoulders are itching to bow. In a matter of moments, I'll be nothing but a mindless beast.

The wrongness of our malady stabs through me. I am Sylas once of Hearthshire, lord of my lands even if those lands aren't much better than a dung heap these days, and I succumb to no one.

No one except my own raging beast erupting out of me to meet the moon.

I wheel toward the others. August has stumbled with a ragged grunt. He bends, his back shuddering, the girl slipping from his grasp. Her bandaged wrist falls toward the ground, and one solid thought anchors me in the midst of the storm rising within.

I didn't want to do it this way. We don't even know what she is or how she is it. But none of that will matter if we lose ourselves to our beasts tonight.

With the last bit of conscious will I have in me, I throw myself to August's side, raise the girl's hand to my lips, and nick her forefinger on my sharpening teeth.

The merest bead of her blood seeps into my mouth, sharp and metallic with that odd glimmer of resin-y brightness that I recognized from Aerik's tonics. The second it touches my tongue, the furious clouds rolling through my mind dissipate. The contractions in my muscles release. My fangs retreat.

I am myself again—fully, gloriously myself, like stepping out of searing heat into the cool spray of a waterfall. I could roar with joy.

But I don't, because I have my cadre to think of. I grasp August's shoulder and press the girl's split fingertip into his mouth. His breath hitches halfway into a snarl. He gazes up at me with startled, awed understanding lighting in his face.

Whitt pitches forward, his body shaking. He lurches into a tree trunk. I scoop up the girl's horrifyingly meager weight and stride toward him. It takes a few seconds, his head thrashing from side to side as his skull stretches, for me to get a grip on his jaw tight enough to be sure he won't chomp her whole hand off. I maneuver the nicked finger between his lips.

With the taste of her blood, he sags onto the ground, his features reverting to their usual configuration. He takes a deep gulp of the night air and laughs with abandon.

Kellan has collapsed into the dirt, his limbs bending into their wolfish alignment, his face now fully canine. As I approach, he snaps at me, staggering up on four legs. His body isn't quite finished reshaping itself though, and his balance is off. I swipe a smear of the girl's blood across my own finger, catch his muzzle in mid-sway, and dab the miraculous substance on his tongue.

He finishes his shift, but with alert awareness in his darkening eyes. His wolf stretches and shakes out its body, and then he rears up to transform back into a man. He stands there staring at the girl in my arms with an expression that looks as revolted as it does elated.

Yes, I will definitely need to keep a tight leash on him around the human.

Whitt has picked himself up, brushing grit from his clothes. He's ogling the girl too, but in his case it's only open amazement.

"By all that is dust. To halt the change right in the middle of it —it barely took a second—" He shakes his head with another laugh. Then something in his face shutters again. "What *is* she? How in the lands did Aerik find this treasure?"

"I expect we'll get more answers from her back at the keep," I say. "We must get the entire measure of the situation before we decide how to proceed from here."

Kellan's lips curl into a grin that can only be described as vicious. "I don't give a rat's ass what she is. There's no way the arch-lords can dismiss a gift like this."

August's head jerks around. "Who says we're offering her to the arch-lords just like that?"

I tuck the girl's limp body over my shoulder much as he did before and raise my other hand. "We aren't doing any offering or gifting or anything else until we understand what we're dealing with. And for that, we need to get home. Whoever finds me a juniper first gets the last of yesterday's roast."

That both shuts them up and sets them stalking off in different directions. I adjust the girl in my grasp, the sap-like note of her scent teasing my nose again.

She's a treasure, all right—a prize beyond imagining, and a complication far more immense than I'd made any preparations for.

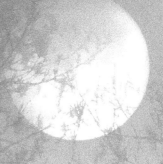

CHAPTER FOUR

Talia

The first thing I'm aware of is the drape of a soft sheet over my shoulders. My head is nestled in a fluffy pillow. Fresh summer-sweet air grazes my cheek.

The sensations are so familiar and yet not that my mind jars to a halt around one thought: it was all a dream. No, a nightmare. An excruciating, seemingly endless nightmare that I've finally woken up from into my actual bed in my actual bedroom, and any second now Mom will rap on the doorframe and ask whether I want waffles or French toast for Saturday breakfast, and Jamie will leap onto the bed and insist I help him with some tricky level in his latest video game, and everything will be perfectly, blissfully *normal*.

Then I open my eyes.

I find myself gazing up at a ceiling that's nothing at all like my ceiling back home. It looks as if it's made out of the kind of vibrant, polished wood you'd expect from floors in some old but posh mansion, rings and whorls showing faintly in the chestnut-brown grain.

And it's not just the ceiling. I ease my head to the side and take in the rest of the room. The walls and, yes, the floor gleam with the same wood, other than a finely woven rug that covers a patch beside the bed.

I *am* lying in a bed, one with posts of a darker wood carved with intricate fern leaves, a spruce-green sheet covering me to my shoulders, a blanket in the same hue woven with silver embroidery folded at the foot. Matching curtains in a heavy fabric hang on either side of a window. Sunlight streams through it across the rug and one corner of the bed.

I blink and blink again, dizzy even though I've barely moved. I'm not home, but I'm not in my cage. Is *this* a dream? A startlingly real one that my captors will shock me out of at any moment with the clink of a glass of lukewarm water or a dish of jumbled food scraps hitting the floor? How—? Where—?

The memories of my last waking moments rush into my head in a flood. Opening the cage—the unexpected noises. The four unfamiliar men-who-aren't-men gathering around my cage, questioning me… threatening me. Dragging me out.

Did *they* bring me here? Why would they put me in a room like this? Why did they want me at all? They were looking for something—something about a "tonic." That must have been what my captors were putting my blood into. Why anyone wanted that tonic, especially enough to steal me away over it, I still have no idea.

The monsters who've kept me all this time won't be happy about my disappearance. I remember how loud the leader yelled at the sharp-edged one the time early on when he wasn't so careful with his torments and I spent a day retching up everything in my stomach. *She's not here to be your* toy. *We need her alive. Find something else to play with before you destroy everything we've gained.*

I recovered from those injuries, and the sharp man resumed his playing after a short period of penance, but it was always clear:

having me alive was important. *Having* me was important, period. And now they don't.

What will they do to steal me back?

Different images flash through my mind. Shudders of color and sounds blot out the room around me. Scarlet on dusky green, a scream, a fleshy tearing noise, the stars swaying overhead—

When I'm aware of my body again, it's trembling, my breath coming in short pants. My heart is racing as if I've just run a mile full tilt. I feel like I might vomit now.

I roll over and press my face into the pillow. It's real. A delicate lavender scent tickles into my nose. I send my mind off to another of the photos I printed off of a landscape I dreamed of visiting one day—a vibrant green landscape with little hills rising in whorls like miniature castles—until my breaths and my pulse even out. Then I dare to open my eyes again.

How can I think about the future when I don't even understand my present? The simple act of breathing bewilders me. When was the last time I tasted outside air rather than the stale, lifeless stuff in the room that held my cage?

At least eight years, by the scars on my hip. Eight years since I breathed fresh air. Eight years since I felt sunlight. Eight years since I set eyes on anything outside.

I've accomplished the first of those things. A desperate urge grips me to achieve the other two before anyone can come and take them away from me all over again.

I push myself to the edge of the bed and discover in the process one more thing that's different: I'm wearing clothes for the first time in forever. A loose, sleeveless nightgown hangs on my emaciated frame, the fabric thin but smooth. When I swing my legs over the edge of the bed, the narrow band of lace at the hem gathers around my knees.

Someone put this on me, maybe one of the strangers who dragged me from my cage. It's hard to feel embarrassed about that when the alternative would have been lying here naked. Some person here cared enough to restore a bit of my modesty.

Out of nowhere, tears prick at the corners of my eyes. I blink hard and inhale deeply, my fingers curling around the edge of the mattress.

The bandage on my wrist is gone too. I study my arm for a moment without quite processing what I'm seeing before my thoughts catch up.

The cut where my captors took my blood—it's gone. The skin is sealed over, only a faint pink line where it used to be. How…?

There are too many questions I can't answer. I lift my gaze toward the window again. That one goal I can achieve on my own.

My skinny calves and feet jut from beneath the nightie's hem, the right foot with its unnatural crook in the middle. I haven't stood up in over eight years either. The thought of trying right now makes my pulse stutter. Thankfully, the window is close enough that I can reach the nearer curtain without leaving the bed.

I tug the heavy fabric farther from the frame. There are two panes of glass, one raised almost level with the other, letting the breeze whisper in. I lean forward to get a better view.

For the first several seconds, the sunlight is so dazzling it whites out my vision. It falls across my face and paints my skin with warmth. As my eyes adjust, my cheeks pinch with an unexpected movement of my mouth.

I'm smiling. How long has it been since I last did *that*?

Based on the view, I must be on at least the second floor of this strange wooden building. Beyond the window, fields mottled with green and a sicklier yellow stretch out toward a darker mass of trees. To my right, a dozen or so small structures dot the field. I'm not sure whether to call them houses, although I can make out doors and windows. The outer shells of the buildings look like massive stumps with the bark filed smooth, rising to a curving peak as if some immense giant came by and twisted off the rest of the tree.

The sun I found so bright is only just coming up. Its rays sear the forest's treetops.

East. That way must be east.

It'd be a lot more useful to know that if I had any idea which direction my real home lies in.

The sound of footsteps carries through the opposite wall of the bedroom. My heart bashes against my ribs, and I shove myself all the way back onto the bed without thinking, propelled by a surge of panicked adrenaline.

My hands skitter across the sheet, but I can't see anything around that I could use to defend myself if I needed to. Other than the bed with its covers and the window, there's only a small table on the other side of the bed that holds an empty ebony bowl and a tall wardrobe too far away for me to reach in time.

A man opens the door and walks in, coming to a stop just inside. It's the one I thought of as a grizzly bear with the scar through his left eye. He somehow looks even bigger than before, his massive frame nearly as tall and broad as the doorway he passed through.

He's wearing similar clothes to those I've seen on my captors, his grass-green shirt showing a hint of chest and the snaking line of a tattoo behind the lacing at its V neck, the sleeves loose from the shoulders to partway down his forearms where they narrow to grip his wrists, his black slacks fitted to his muscular thighs and calves.

A leather sheath hangs from his belt, the glinting hilt of a dagger protruding from it. My fingers tense around the sheet instinctively, as if the weapon makes any difference when he could do more than enough damage with those fists and feet.

He shuts the door behind him with a nudge of his heel, his mismatched gaze trained on me. Even though his left eye is clouded over, I get the impression it's watching me just as much as the uninjured one. My shoulders hunch, my legs pulling closer to my body, as if I can shrink away from his scrutiny.

"We might as well start at the beginning," he says in the low, resonant voice I remember. "What is your name?"

I stare at him. In more than eight years, my captors never bothered to ask that question. It never mattered to them. Before, in my old life, I must have told people my name dozens of times, but I'm out of practice, and giving it up now feels somehow perilous. Why does he want it?

The man frowns. He walks to the end of the bed and rests his hand on one of the posts. The black lines of the tattoos that creep up from under his sleeve and up his neck across his jaw remind me that he's not really a man, no more than the ones who shoved me into their cage were.

"Do you understand me?" he asks, measuring out the words more slowly.

I nod automatically, just a brief dip of my head before I catch myself with another flicker of panic. Should I have acknowledged that? Was I better off if he thought I couldn't?

He takes another step, and my body cringes against the headboard. The man takes in the movement with his pensive gaze and stops where he is. He lowers himself so he's sitting on the edge of the bed right by the footboard, turned toward me, leaving a few feet between us.

He's only slightly less intimidating closer to my level.

"You're scared," he says—a statement, not a question.

A hysterical giggle claws at my throat. *Ya think?* Jamie would have said, with all his eight-year-old impertinence, if someone made a ridiculously obvious observation.

"Why don't I start then?" The man leans against the bedpost behind him with no hint of impatience. "I'm Sylas, originally of Hearthshire, and this is my keep. You won't find yourself in a cage here. I just have some questions to ask to give me a better sense of your situation."

He could be lying. But if it matters enough to him, he could probably also find ways of forcing the answers out of me—ways much more unpleasant than this. A longing trickles up through my chest—a longing to clutch at this moment of relative peace and normalcy, however brief it might be.

I open my mouth. My tongue tangles. How long has it been since I last spoke—an actual conversation, not just a single word or a cry prodded out of me?

Finally, I work a fragment of my voice from my throat. It comes out in a raspy whisper. "Talia. My name. It's Talia."

As I say it, it no longer feels like giving up but reclaiming something my captors never quite managed to tear away from me. I am Talia McCarty. I'm a human being, not—not vermin, or whatever else the monsters called me. It's easier to hold onto that certainty here in actual clothes sitting on an actual bed with sunlight streaming past me.

"Talia," Sylas says, rolling the name off his tongue as if tasting each syllable. In his resonant baritone, it sounds lovelier than I ever thought of it before. Important. Like I'm not just a human being but a figure of acclaim. "Can you tell me how you ended up in that cage in Aerik's fortress, Talia?"

Fortress. Like *keep*, it sounds like a word from a fantasy movie, not the reality of my childhood. But then, the reality of my childhood didn't include men who could change into beasts or magically sealed locks, either.

How did I get into that cage? The icy splashes of memory flicker in the back of my mind, but I manage to stay focused on what's in front of me. I don't have to go back there to answer.

My voice still refuses to rise above a whisper, but I don't force it. "They attacked me. Bit my shoulder." Of its own accord, my hand rises to the ridges of scar tissue there. "I was out, walking in the woods, after my family had gone out for dinner. They looked—they looked like huge wolves, and then they didn't. They took me... like you did... and when I woke up I was in the cage."

"I apologize if our actions reminded you of that time. We had to make haste to ensure we weren't caught and forced to leave you there."

I'd appreciate the apology more if I knew what he and the other men he was with plan on doing with me. They talked about me too much like the ones who put me in that cage—like I was something they wanted to use.

And here comes the part where he gets at that purpose. He tips his head, the sunlight picking up a hint of deep purple in the thick, coffee-brown waves of his hair, and indicates my now-sealed wrist. "We healed your most obvious wounds as well as we could. They were taking your blood. How often?"

"I don't know. I think it was weeks apart. I lost track of time pretty quickly."

"Of course. And the rest of your days there? It doesn't appear they treated you all that well."

"No." My back stiffens. The words tumble out before I can catch them. "Are they—are they going to know you took me? If they come here—"

Sylas holds up his hand. "They shouldn't know, but even if they figure it out, I have no intention of letting them throw you back in that wretched cage. Aerik is mostly talk and not much action. If he dares to try me, he'll regret it." He grins, baring fierce white teeth.

I don't know whether I should believe him, but he seems sure of himself. I suck my lower lip under my own teeth for a moment and realize I haven't answered his question. "The rest of the time, mostly they left me alone except to bring a little food and water. And to change the toilet bucket."

"Did they ever tell you what they wanted your blood for?"

I shake my head. "They didn't really talk to me."

"All right. What of your life before that? Were you already here, in the Mists, or did they take you from the human lands?"

My words fail me for a few heartbeats. "The Mists? What's that?"

I guess my confusion is answer enough. Sylas's mouth twists. "The land of the fae. Where you are now. You had no knowledge of us before the attack, I take it."

"No." *Fae*. Like faeries? My mind dredges up an image of Tinkerbell, but the man in front of me is about as far from that little pixie as I am from Batman. He doesn't have much in common with Santa's elves or the seven dwarves either.

"You had an ordinary human life, then?" he asks. "Parents, school, playing in the park, that sort of thing?"

He must be able to tell just looking at me that I'd have been taken as a child. If I've counted the years right, I'm barely out of my teens. "Yes," I murmur, too much anguish balling at the base of my throat just with that one word of acknowledgment.

"No experiences before your kidnapping that stand out as unusual?"

"I—I can't think of any."

My fingers are starting to ache where they're clutching the sheet. Maybe Sylas notices. He stands, smoothly but so swiftly my heart skips a beat.

"I think that's enough talk for now. We should get some food and drink into you before you waste away before my eyes."

My stomach pinches, but I've had enough experience since my kidnapping to clarify, "Nothing that... does funny things to my head or my body. Just normal food?"

Sylas's expression turns so perceptive I wonder if that mismatched gaze can pierce right into my mind and see the ways my captors chose to muddle me when it suited them. "Ordinary food only. And perhaps you'd like the use of a proper toilet as well."

Yes, that would be helpful if I don't want to soil these nice sheets—well, any more than my unwashed body already has.

He beckons for me to follow him. My limbs balk, but only for an instant. I'm not sure what's going on here, and I'm even less sure of where *here* is than I was before our conversation, but even if Sylas is like my captors in some ways, he's giving every indication of being gentler. And I know what state I'll end up in if I try to refuse to eat completely.

I ease off the bed and brace my feet against the floor. As I put my weight on them, a faint ache spreads through the warped one. Keeping more of my balance on my good side, I manage a few wobbly steps.

But it's been too long since I really walked. For all my attempts at keeping my strength up, there are muscles I didn't reach—muscles I need to hold me up.

Sylas is just opening the door when a tremor runs through my legs. I try to tense them, but it's too late. They give beneath me, sending me toppling onto my hands and knees. The twist of my foot with the fall sends a sharper needle of pain through my ankle.

I scramble to right myself, and Sylas is there, grasping my arm firmly but carefully to help me up. Having that huge, powerful frame so close to me is nearly overwhelming. I don't think it's just my unworked muscles to blame for my unsteadiness now.

His gaze has fallen to the floor. "Your foot. Is that from before, or did Aerik's men injure it?"

"It was them. So I—so it'd be harder for me to run away."

He makes a gruff sound that's unnervingly growly and reassuringly disgusted at the same time. Easing me around, he takes my hand and sets it on his elbow. "Put as much of your weight on me as you need to."

The muscles in his arm are even more solid than I expected, flexing as I adjust my grip. Heat floods my face. But what's he going to do if I refuse—sweep me up like he did from the cage and carry me to my meal? No, I can handle this.

As I limp beside him into the hall, a snicker carries from behind us. Sylas's head swings around at the sound.

Another man, one I didn't see last night, peers at me, his eyes glittering silver in his pale face. When he speaks, I recognize that sharp voice as the one who suggested they kill me rather than deal with my struggles.

"So the dung-body is a cripple as well. Wonderful."

"Move along, Kellan," Sylas commands.

The other man brushes past us without further comment, but his words linger. The icy fear that Sylas's calm presence started to melt solidifies in my gut all over again.

This place may be prettier and more luxurious than my cage, but who's to say it's any safer?

CHAPTER FIVE

Talia

*I*t turns out faeries have toilets. Or at least, these faeries do.

After Sylas helps me to the room he calls a "privy" and the heat of approximately a thousand suns has burned across my face with embarrassment, I manage to convince him that I can make my way to the porcelain throne without assistance. And I do, grasping the sink for balance as I leverage myself over.

Of course, neither the sink nor the toilet are actually made out of porcelain. They're more of a shell-like material with a pearly sheen on the inside. I can't see any pipes. Is there a fae sewer system, or will my pee be washed away by magic?

It's easier letting my mind puzzle over silly things like that rather than to dwell on the contempt in the silver-eyed man's voice when he talked about me.

This setup sure beats a bucket, even if the details are odd. Rather than toilet paper, I find a wicker box full of leaves. I try to dampen one at the sink and give myself a bit of a wipe-down everywhere I can reach, though it doesn't feel all that effective. Then I splash more water on my face.

The room has no mirror, but maybe that's a good thing. If I could see how bedraggled I must look, I'd feel ten times more awkward walking back out.

Sylas leads me down a spiral staircase that's the same polished wood everything in this keep appears to be built out of. I cling to his elbow as little as possible, which is still quite a lot. He doesn't remark on my shakiness—or anything else, for that matter—but I catch him eyeing my feet in apparent contemplation. Do I even want to know *what* he's contemplating about them?

There is one question I can't hold back, as nervous as I am about the answer. When we reach the bottom of the stairs at one end of a wide, wood-lined hall, I glance up at him and gather my courage.

"Why did you bring me here? I mean, what—what are you going to do with me?"

Sylas considers my face now, his expression so unreadable I can't tell whether he's annoyed or amused by the question. "I was planning on getting you full of breakfast," he says. "We're almost at the dining room."

That isn't what I meant, as I'm sure he knows, but before I can figure out how to demand a proper response—and whether it's worth the risk that he'll turn those fierce white teeth on me rather than offering one—another of my rescuers-slash-kidnappers from yesterday pokes his head from a nearby doorway.

It's the man with the broad boyish face, which splits with an eager smile. Now that I've got a better look at him, I'm struck by his eyes. The sharp-voiced man, the one Sylas called Kellan, might have a silver sheen to his irises, but this guy's are pure gold, as radiant as that smile of his, both warm and utterly inhuman.

"You're up!" he says with the same buoyant energy I saw before. "Perfect. I was just about to serve the meal."

Then I notice the spatula he's brandishing and the apron draped over his muscular frame. Apparently he's also the one making our breakfast. Smells drift from the room behind him: creamy and meaty, buttery and doughy. My stomach gurgles loud enough that I suspect the whole keep can hear it.

The eerily gorgeous guy widens his grin. "And it sounds like you're ready for it."

My lips part, but I don't know what to say.

Sylas motions to me. "Her name is Talia. Talia, this is August of my cadre. I wouldn't typically have any of them working the kitchen, but we're in short supply of staff."

"And I like doing it." August twirls the spatula in his fingers and waves it at me. "If this isn't the best breakfast you've ever had, I'll keep trying until I get there."

It's guaranteed to be the best breakfast I've had in more than eight years, as long as Sylas was telling the truth about no funny business with the food. My throat's still closed up, but I tip my head in acknowledgment, and somehow August's smile grows even wider. It doesn't quite reach his eyes, though. They've crinkled at the corners with a shimmer of something almost sad…

It's probably pity. My face flushes again, but pity is better than contempt, at least. "Thank you," I manage to say, though still in the whisper I'm having trouble breaking my rusty voice out of, so I'm not sure whether the attempt makes me seem less pathetic or more.

Maybe I should be encouraging these men to see me as pitiable if it means they keep offering me comfy beds and extravagant breakfasts. They want something from me just like my former captors did. If they think I'm strong enough to withhold it, who's to say they won't change their approach to something harsher?

Sylas guides me on down the hall, and August pauses partway through turning back toward the kitchen, taking in my limp. His gaze jerks to Sylas, the shine in his eyes flaring with fury so suddenly I flinch.

"Is she still hurt?" he demands, the muscles in his shoulders coiling.

"Her foot," Sylas says. "It's an old injury Aerik's people dealt, healed badly. And I expect she's simply become unused to walking, given the size of the cage they had her in."

"Mangy beasts," August mutters with a hint of a snarl.

Sylas claps a hand to his companion's shoulder. "They don't have her anymore. Settle yourself down, and let's have that breakfast."

Still muttering under his breath, August stomps off into the room. It appears that everyone takes Sylas's orders. He said this was *his* keep. And that August was part of his—

"What's a cadre?" I ask as we continue down the hall.

Sylas peers down at me from his great height as if bemused that anyone could be unaware. "All lords have a cadre—it's our inner circle, our closest advisors and comrades in arms. For now, mine will be the only folk you have for company. Better not to involve the rest of the pack when the matter involves some… discretion."

Because the more people who know I'm here, the more chance it'll get back to this Aerik—the one with the sunflower-yellow hair who commanded my other captors, I assume? But I'm more struck by another part of his wording. *Pack.*

My legs lock. My hand tightens on the silky fabric of Sylas's sleeve, wanting to both grip harder for balance and to shove myself away. I knew they weren't really men, but I didn't know for sure they were *that* much like the others.

My whisper comes out with an additional quaver. "You're wolves too."

Sylas has stopped next to me. I thought of him as a grizzly before, but his predatory, brawny self-assurance could fit one of those massive wolfish monsters just as well. Whose claws slashed through his one eye?

His other, dark eye holds my gaze. "We're fae. All of the Seelie can shift from man into wolf as it suits us." He touches his chest. "The animal belongs to us; it does not consume us. How much of a beast any of us becomes is a matter of personal choice."

I'm guessing he'd put himself above my captors on that scale. That doesn't mean there's nothing beastly about him at all. Just standing here with his attention focused on me makes the hairs on the back of my neck rise.

If he's a predator, there's no world where I wouldn't come across as prey.

An acidic voice that's quickly becoming familiar reaches us from farther down the hall. "Except when it isn't."

Kellan is leaning against a doorframe, his silver gaze as cold as before. He isn't quite as beefy as the others, but his lean frame still exudes plenty of power—and animosity. It doesn't strike me as a good sign that he must be part of Sylas's "inner circle" too.

I've lost too much of the thread of the conversation to know what he's referring to, but Sylas's expression darkens. "Are you here to eat or to complain?" he asks.

The other man shrugs, swiping a hand over his sleek hair, which is a shade of orange so pale you'd think most of the color had been wrung out of it. He stalks into the room he was standing by, and, joy of all joys, we follow him.

The keep's dining room stretches long enough to hold a table for twenty under two chandeliers that look like coiled branches sprouting from the ceiling. They're not lit now, their jeweled leaves twinkling in the glow from the broad windows opposite us. Someone has already set out silverware, plates, and goblets for five around one end of the table.

Sylas takes the head of the table so automatically I can tell that's where he always sits. When he gestures for me to sit kitty-corner to him, Kellan's lips curl in disdain.

"We're to be faced with the dung-body through the whole meal? Not what I want to rest my gaze on if I'm going to keep my appetite. There are plenty of other seats, all of them grander than she should expect."

August barrels into the room then holding a platter on each hand and two more balanced on his bulging, tattooed arms. "If you're so concerned about the view, maybe you should head to the other end and spare her having to look at your ugly mug." He sets down the platters with a series of clinks.

Kellan bares his teeth. "I think you forget *your* position here, whelp."

August bristles with a flash of his eyes, and Sylas holds up both hands, one toward each of them. "Enough. I prefer that she sits near me. The rest of you can take a chair wherever you'd like in consideration of that." He shoots a pointed look at Kellan. "Ideally without any more commentary."

Kellan glares at his lord, but he sinks down at one of the places already set—thankfully the one that's farthest from me.

August grabs the seat beside me. "Where's Whitt? This is usually the one morning out of the month when he's up at a normal hour."

"Last night was hardly a typical night," Sylas says. "And I have no intention of waiting on his whims. Dig in."

I'm already ogling the dishes August laid out. Saliva pools in my mouth. If I'm not careful, in a second I'll be drooling.

One platter is heaped with flat, circular patties that look kind of like small hamburgers but smell like sausages. Another holds little boiled eggs that are robin-blue even without their shells, which give off a delicately appetizing zesty scent. The third offers a rainbow of cut fruit, much of which I can't recognize in colors as vibrant as gems, and the fourth ornate pastries twisted into five-pointed stars, the crisp dough so airily puffy I half expect them to start flaking under my gaze.

I don't know where to start. The men reach for the serving utensils and load their plates. When the long-tined fork is free, I take a sausage and then a scoop of fruit and a pastry that appears to have melted chocolate in the hollow at its center.

August motions toward my plate. "There's lots for everyone. Take as much as you want."

Just what I already have looks like a feast. As I look at it, my stomach knots. I'm not used to proper meals anymore—and I'm not exactly relaxed about this whole situation, either.

"I don't know how much I can manage when I got used to... not much," I murmur.

"Aerik's crew obviously didn't feed you right, but we'll fix that. After all that, you are a wee mite."

"We could even say a dust mite," says a breezy, melodic voice from behind me. The fourth of yesterday's men strolls into view and flops his well-built frame down in the chair across from me.

By daylight, Whitt's light brown hair looks sun-kissed, the rumpled strands veering upward at their varying angles as if to embrace the sky. Or maybe, given his attitude, to goad it.

His gaze barely flits over me, and then he's stabbing at the sausages, tossing several onto his plate with a few flicks of his wrist. His presence doesn't leave me as cold as Kellan's, but my muscles tense more all the same.

"She can't help how she is," August declares, and pats me on the arm. "Go ahead. Eat, even if it's only a little."

So much emphasis has been placed on how much food I consume that my stomach has clenched twice as tight as before. But I do need to eat before I get any more light-headed.

I cut off a chunk of one of the sausage patties and nibble at it tentatively. A savory flavor made richer by a subtle mixture of herbs seeps over my tongue, and my mouth starts watering again. It's delicious. I haven't tasted anything this good in ages. I haven't tasted anything that tasted like *food* in almost a decade.

No blurring or tingling effect muddles my senses. As Sylas promised, the herbs mustn't hold any magical properties. I stuff the rest of the bite into my mouth, and the next thing I know, the entire sausage has disappeared from my plate. My stomach still aches, but more of that is tension than hunger now.

August grins at me, obviously taking my speeding devouring as a compliment to his cooking, and glances around at the others. "So, I take it we haven't gotten any—" He cuts himself off and hesitates with a hint of chagrin. When he speaks again, I can tell he's changing the subject. "I was going to hunt before lunch. Any particular meat the rest of you are keen on today?"

Was the first thing he meant to say something he didn't want to mention around me?

Whitt waggles his fork. "Since you're taking requests, let's have a buffalo. Or elephant. I've always wondered what those taste like."

Sylas makes a dismissive sound at the joke—at least, I assume it's a joke. Who knows what animals roam around this place for fae men to hunt? "I wouldn't mind some venison," he says.

August nods, and the table lapses into a silence that doesn't feel totally comfortable. It could be they always sit here, awkwardly quiet, while they eat, but it seems more likely that my presence has thrown a wrench into their typical flow of conversation. What is there they'd want to talk about that it'd be a problem for me to know?

Not the kind of thing you can ask even in the best of circumstances.

Gradually, I swallow morsels of a melon-like fruit that tastes close to honeydew. The third is enough to transform the ache in my stomach into a sensation of fullness. I've already eaten twice as much as my former captors ever offered me in one meal. I sip from my goblet, which turns out to be full of a lightly bubbly liquid with a raspberry-esque flavor, and clasp my hands together in my lap beneath the table.

As deftly as Sylas dodged my question, I still need to know what's going on here. It doesn't matter how scared I am of the answer. Am I a guest, or am I a prisoner?

For a few minutes, I watch the food disappear from the fae men's plates, working up my courage. "Thank you for the meal and getting me away from the place with the cage and... everything," I say finally, willing my thready voice a little louder. "It's been years since they took me away. If I wanted to go home—"

Kellan interrupts me with a bark of a laugh. His voice is chilling. "Go home? You can wipe that idea out of your mind forever, pipsqueak."

"*Kellan*," Sylas says, his growl turning those two syllables ominous. He turns his mismatched gaze on me. "We'll treat you as a guest, but you will stay here for now. It'll take some time to decide how to best handle the situation. I stand by my word that Aerik and his pack won't lay one more claw on you."

All right. It's not really a surprise, but his words still echo through me with an icy quiver. However generous any of these men might be with me, I've traded one set of captors for another.

I *am* better off, though, aren't I? I'm not locked in one corner of a room behind immoveable bars. This keep must have a door to the outer world somewhere, and the outer world, even if it's some sort of faerie realm, must have gateways to the world I came from. I just need to find out how to get there so I'm not wandering aimlessly at the mercy of whatever monsters come across me next, and then I can escape after all, better fed and rested than I'd have been fleeing from my previous captivity.

If I ask for any of the information I need now, I'll tip them off to what I'm thinking. Instead, I incline my head as if in acceptance and take another sip of my drink.

Kellan's silvery gaze lingers on me. Is that suspicion in his eyes? I have the urge to shrink inside my skin.

He wrinkles his nose. "If the sight of her wasn't bad enough, the stink alone should consign her to the upper reaches."

"Thankfully, that's solved easily enough." Sylas points his knife at Whitt. "You've demolished at least twice your share of breakfast already. Go run our guest a bath."

CHAPTER SIX

Whitt

Run our guest a bath. As I turn on the faucet, I repeat the command in my head in exactly the mocking tone I was tempted to toss it back in our glorious leader's face. Not a request but an order, as if I'm a servant and not cadre. Presumably this is August's fault. His frolicking around in the kitchen has convinced Sylas we should all play staff.

Water hisses from the tap. I drop a towel on the tiled floor next to the gleaming tub, since Heart help us if the mite could manage to find even that on her own. Where are the clothes Sylas dredged up for her from who in the lands knows where?

I'd rather not know. I prefer to think as little as possible of what relations our lord might or might not be having with beings of the female persuasion, human or otherwise.

That turn takes my mind in a darker direction than my initial silent heckling. I find the bundle of human-made fabric, rougher even at its best than what the fae can spin but I suppose more familiar to our "guest," and leave it next to the towel. As I step back, I pull a flask out of one of my vest's many pockets.

It's important to always have lubrication on hand should one want to grease one's mood.

I toss back a shot's worth of faerie absinthe. It burns in the best way going down. Before it's even hit my stomach, the edges of my annoyance have smoothed with a tickling glow.

It's less the alcohol that provides the lube than the cloying fruit this beverage was made from. If that scrap of a human took one bite of the peach-like globes, she'd find herself attempting to walk on her hands and gulp grass for dinner without any idea she was behaving at all oddly.

My being relegated to a servant's task is Kellan's fault the most, really. Even when he was merely a visitor in Sylas's domain, you could always tell where he'd recently passed by from the terrorized glaze that came over the human servants' eyes even while under their enchantments—and the fact that one or two of them was liable to go missing if he was around long enough. A pity he wasn't Aerik's brother-by-marriage instead. They clearly share some inclinations.

But no, he's our problem. Here in our new abode with that mangy prick as a permanent fixture, it's no wonder Sylas has declared collecting servants from beyond the Mists to be "too much trouble." And with the pack so dwindled and beaten down, our benevolent benefactor hardly wants to add to their burden other than a few tasks here and there.

None of that bothers me overly so except when the burden falls on my shoulders instead.

The bath full, I shut off the water and wipe my hands of the chore. When I step into the hall, August is just helping the girl up the staircase. I turn on my heel away from them and take a deep inhalation, absorbing the lingering scents.

Sylas has come by too—on his way to his study, no doubt. He

tends to go there when he'd rather not be disturbed, but disturbing people is a particular talent of mine.

I amble over and knock—as a courtesy, and because he is my lord and I'd rather keep my throat intact, thank you very much.

"Come," the rumbling voice says.

Sylas's study is one of the grandest rooms in the keep, naturally, since it's fit for a lord. I'll never say he doesn't have decent taste in décor. As I prowl in, I tamp down any envy I might otherwise feel over the expanse of that hawthorn-wood desk, twice as large as the one in my own office of sorts, or the liquor cabinet against the wall with its assortment of rare vintages left over from our great exodus.

Would keeping my dishonorable emotions in check be easier or harder if I didn't have to admit our lord has filled the role quite capably? It's impossible to say. As we all do, he has his weak points, but on the measure of things he's as tremendous a lord as anyone could ask for.

Sylas glances up at me from where he's sitting behind the desk, a journal full of notations open in front of him. "What is it, Whitt?" He doesn't need to stand and show off his full height to convey the authority we both know he holds over me—over this entire place. Everything from the command in his tone to his imperious gaze gets the message across.

I prop myself against the bookcase next to the door and aim a smile at the oldest of my younger half-siblings: the only offspring who ever mattered to our father.

"I was merely wondering what the delay is about. It's not like you to dilly dally. We know how the girl can be used—we experienced the power of her blood ourselves last night. You've been waiting for a chance like this for decades. We invaded Aerik's domain specifically to *get* that chance. Why not turn her over to the arch-lords straight away and claim our reward?"

Sylas considers me thoughtfully, as if he thinks I should be able to put the pieces together on my own. Out of everything, this side of him, measured and penetrating, irks me the most.

My half-brother's passions can be as fiery as those of any of our summer kin, but he always keeps an even temper with me. It feels like a judgment—as though he's determined that I'm so volatile he can't afford to be anything but steady with me. As though I'm fragile along with that volatility, and the wrong word or gesture might send me spiraling beyond my control into some action that'll harm me more than him.

It would irk me less if there wasn't a tidbit of truth hidden in that assessment. But I do have enough awareness of the important lines not to cross them… most of the time.

"We've experienced it," he says. "The arch-lords haven't. They won't be able to test our claim until the next full moon. And given our circumstances, I'm not inclined to trust them to take our word for it."

He might have a point there. All the same— "I could smell the same essence as in the tonic from her small wound even through the stink in that room. We give her arm another little nick, and they can't miss it."

"It may not be enough. They know—"

Another knock on the door interrupts him. When Sylas calls out, it's both Kellan and August who peer in.

Kellan notes my presence with a narrowing of his eyes, as if he thinks I'm there on some untoward purpose. I wish that I *could* scheme with our lord against the jackass. The closest I've come—the closest Sylas would ever allow—was a series of stealthy discussions on the matter of whether, given the prick's clear and growing discontentment, it would be more generous or insulting if Sylas gave him full leave to seek a place in a different pack should he wish to.

The trouble is, as much as I suspect Kellan might wish to, there aren't likely to be any packs of anywhere near the standing he'd accept who'd accept *him*. His reputation is the most tarnished of all of us by virtue of proximity to the initial offense, as he no doubt realizes. And perhaps he wouldn't wish to anyway, since he must know there's no lord other than the kin-of-his-mate who'd tolerate his unruliness even to the small extent Sylas has.

In the end, Sylas did extend the offer, and Kellan declined. But for all he professed to want to continue serving in this cadre, his disposition has become even more insolent since. Apparently, despite our lord's best efforts, he did take it as an insult.

"We need to speak about the girl," he says in that obnoxiously tart voice of his.

"It appears we do." Sylas motions for the new arrivals to close the door. "Whitt was just advocating that we cart her straight to the arch-lords."

A flicker of surprise crosses Kellan's face, which gratifies me for the second before he opens his mouth again. "I agree. She's the leverage we wanted—we have to make use of her, not waste our time coddling the creature."

I like my stance less now that he's joined me there. If he thinks that's a good idea, maybe it isn't one after all.

August glares at me as if I've betrayed him somehow, his shoulders coming up. He has already taken up doting on the mite, and my youngest half-brother has about as much rein on *his* temper as a jockey who's toppled off a runaway horse.

"As soon as we approach the arch-lords, Aerik will know we're the ones who stole her," he says. "They'll probably find some way to take credit for it—the arch-lords might even hand her back to them so they can throw her back into that cage and keep brewing their tonic. Then all we are to them is thieves."

Oh, we're much more than that. I don't think it'll help the situation to go over our extensive list of crimes in the arch-lords' eyes, though.

Kellan rounds on him. "What do you suggest we do then? Put

her up in our keep as if it's some fancy hotel while we all cater to her whims?"

A furious light flares in August's eyes. "Getting enough food into her to bring her back from the verge of starvation and taking her first bath in who knows how many years aren't *whims*," he growls. "If you suggest we put her in a cage like they did, I—"

Sylas stands with a rasp of the chair legs against the floor that shuts August up. Even Kellan draws up short. The newest member of our cadre might like to bitch at all of us, but there are lines he doesn't cross too, no matter how closely he might toe them.

"There's no point in arguing about it—from either perspective," Sylas says in his laying-down-the-law tone. "It makes no sense that a random human girl could have this kind of power. We don't understand how she came to be that way or how else she might be connected to the wildness. Are there others like her? Is there a way to replicate the effect she has without needing her at all?"

Kellan lifts his nose haughtily. "Is that your main concern: finding a way to return the feeble thing to her 'home'?"

Sylas manages to keep his glower restrained, but there's no mistaking it for what it is. "Are you so caught up in your scorn for humans that you can fail to see she's hardly a permanent solution to our problems, for the same reasons you scorn her? What are we supposed to do years from now when she succumbs to old age and we're still here with the moon and its inevitable waxing?"

The absinthe is still bubbling through my veins headily enough that I barely catch my laugh at how taken aback Kellan looks. His mouth closes into a sour line, so I ask the necessary question.

"What are you proposing we do with her in the meantime, exactly?"

Sylas spreads his hands. "We have four weeks until the next full moon when we could demonstrate her usefulness to the arch-lords. Until then, we treat her well enough that she'll trust us, we find out what we can from her, we observe her, and at the same time we

evaluate how to balance the fallout of Aerik's potential anger—and how we might avoid it entirely. It should be simple enough. From what I've observed already, I don't imagine she's going to ask for much."

"We could speed all that along with the right wine and a charm or two," Kellan says. "Magic her into telling the truth or at least into total compliance."

"No. I don't think she's purposefully hiding anything from us— she's even more bewildered by all this than we are. And she's hardly a threat. We simply need to find the right questions to get at the answers we need. Controlling her with magic might make her *less* inclined to open up if it reminds her of her treatment at Aerik's hands. She's already recoiled at the idea of being presented with intoxicating food." Our lord folds his arms over his chest. "We'll treat her as we should any respected guest."

The other man's lips curl back. "You can hardly expect me to pamper—"

"I *expect* you to steer clear of her if you can't control yourself enough to avoid terrorizing her, kin-of-my-mate," Sylas says sharply. "We want to open her up, not tear her down. But you can leave that to the rest of us."

Kellan looks as if he's bit back a grimace, but he says nothing more, just ducks his head in acknowledgment. Then he marches out with an audible huff.

August turns to our lord. "How do you think Aerik found her to begin with?"

Sylas rubs his jaw. "From what she was able to tell me about her capture—and from that scar on her shoulder—it sounds as though Aerik and his cadre roamed into the human world while caught up in the wildness and came across her. When they attacked her, the taste of her blood must have woken them from their madness. Which gave them enough wherewithal to decide to bring her back with them so they could make more use of her."

"And torment her at the same time." August's eyes flash again. "We *can't* let her fall back into their hands."

"I agree with you completely on that. You don't need to worry about it."

"They'll be sniffing around for her," I can't help noting. "It's quite the prize to lose."

Sylas gives me a grim smile. "And we'll deal with that eventuality when it comes for us. Now…" He taps the notebook lying on his desk. "I'd like to return to my reading, if you don't mind."

His reasoning makes sense, but I'm not sure I like the vehemence with which he's expressed it. I saw how carefully he handled the girl last night, how quickly he attended to her needs this morning. Whatever flaws our glorious leader has, one of them is definitely an over-inflated sense of honor, especially when it comes to the vulnerable. We wouldn't be putting up with Kellan's impudence otherwise.

It won't do any of us any good if he softened to the poor thing as much as August has—or more.

Sylas will hardly appreciate my saying that to his face, though, so I motion to August, putting on an innocent tone. "Come on, Auggie. I believe I might smell something burning. Did you leave the stove on?"

My little brother's eyes widen. I don't smell anything of the sort, so he couldn't have either, but simply saying it sends him hustling out of the room and down the hall. My lips quirk with mild amusement. He can pay me back for the trick with a tussle later.

I shut the study door firmly on the way out. As I head toward the staircase myself, my gaze roves to the bathroom door behind which our "guest" is still washing. My ears prick.

No sounds of water moving against a body reach me. Has she finished already? I'd have thought she would need at least an hour to scrub all the accumulated grime from her skin.

Or is she up to something else entirely?

I stalk down the hall and grip the handle with the ease of centuries' practice in stealth. The latch and the hinges don't make the slightest sound as I ease the door open a sliver.

She isn't in the bath, but she's by it. Sitting on an overturned wooden box—the one for tossing used towels into—her elbow leaning over the lip of the tub. With her back to me, there's no chance of her seeing me. What is she *doing*?

Her hand dips into the tub with a faint sloshing of the water and lifts out the sponge I left for her. She brings it to her calf to rub the pale skin there, her leg canting to the side. The sight of her foot, of the unnatural slant to the bones there, triggers my understanding.

She was too weak and too lame to scramble into the tub on her own, or at least she thought it was too much of a risk to try and possibly slip, bang her head, and drown herself. Apparently she was also too embarrassed to say as much to August when he showed her to the room or to call for help if she realized it later.

Kellan was wrong about that much. This one is hardly demanding pampering.

Without the nightgown or the blanket from last night, her emaciation is even more evident. Beneath the fall of her dark, tangled hair, her shoulder blades jut like a hatchling's featherless wings. The segments of her spine form a picket fence down the center of her back; the angles of her hips are nearly as sharp as the nub of her chin.

And yet there's a delicate grace to her movements that I find myself appreciating, as if she were one of those intricately sculpted twig puppets one of the court craftswomen used to construct for the shows that entertained me in my childhood.

No, more alive than that. A gamboling fawn, perhaps.

The thought slips through my head, and I yank myself back from the door, shutting it as silently as I opened it. I shake those images from my head. August will be out there hunting deer on Sylas's request for our luncheon. We *snack* on fawns.

The last thing I need is to find myself admiring one.

I stride away before anyone can notice I've lingered here. Even after I throw back another gulp of absinthe, my hands curl into fists.

I wish we had found nothing more than a recipe in Aerik's fortress. Or a rare toadstool. Or a vat of nauseating chemicals.

Anything other than a human girl with grass-bright eyes and a frailness she tries to hide.

CHAPTER SEVEN

Talia

The knock comes just as I'm squirming into the blouse left for me on the bathroom floor. I spin around, my feet skidding on the wet tiles. Even with my hand on the edge of the tub for support, I nearly fall.

The blouse's thin fabric drifts to my thighs. The clothes are a little too big on me, the waist of the jeans threatening to slip over my hips, but I've become so skinny I'm not sure what size *would* fit.

"Yes?" I say, managing to push my voice above its now-standard whisper.

Sylas's commanding baritone carries through the door. "If you're finished with your bath, I'd like to speak with you."

Oh. I look at the floor, blotchy with dirty puddles I didn't feel right trying to sop up with the fluffy white towel, and run my fingers into my hair, which is damp but still full of knots I couldn't untangle. Not that the latter should matter. The man-who's-not-a-man on the other side of that door has seen me much worse off. At least now I'm reasonably clean, with a light floral scent from the soap clinging to my skin.

I take a sniff of my arm, weirdly giddy at the proof that I'm no longer a stink-fest, and brace myself in case he's angry about the puddles. "You can come in." Like he really needs my permission.

Sylas strides into the room and stops a few feet from me, eyeing the floor with a puzzled expression.

"I'm sorry," I say quickly, clutching the side of the tub. "I tried not to make a mess, but…"

His gaze snaps to me—to my face and then to my arm taut as it balances me. His mouth tightens.

"You couldn't get into the water. I should have realized. My apologies. The next time—we have a sort of sauna in the lower chambers, with a small in-ground pool you could use instead. It has steps."

He expects me to be here long enough that I'll take multiple baths. It's hard to know what to make of that when I have no idea how often faeries generally bathe.

I glance around. Better not to make myself any more of a nuisance than I already have while I am here, while he's being kind to me. "If there's a mop, I could clean it up—"

He shakes his head before I can finish. "I'll see that it's taken care of. I have something for you that should make getting just about anywhere *other* than into the bath easier for you."

He steps closer, holding out his hands, and that's when I register the object he's brought me. It looks like a snapped off branch, nearly as thick as my wrist, blunt at the narrower end and spreading into a shallow crescent at the thicker end. The crescent is polished smooth, but the rest of the surface is covered in bark.

Sylas turns the branch-staff-thing so the blunt end touches the floor and stands it next to me, studying it. Then understanding clicks in my head.

"It's a crutch?" I say.

CHAPTER SEVEN

Talia

The knock comes just as I'm squirming into the blouse left for me on the bathroom floor. I spin around, my feet skidding on the wet tiles. Even with my hand on the edge of the tub for support, I nearly fall.

The blouse's thin fabric drifts to my thighs. The clothes are a little too big on me, the waist of the jeans threatening to slip over my hips, but I've become so skinny I'm not sure what size *would* fit.

"Yes?" I say, managing to push my voice above its now-standard whisper.

Sylas's commanding baritone carries through the door. "If you're finished with your bath, I'd like to speak with you."

Oh. I look at the floor, blotchy with dirty puddles I didn't feel right trying to sop up with the fluffy white towel, and run my fingers into my hair, which is damp but still full of knots I couldn't untangle. Not that the latter should matter. The man-who's-not-a-man on the other side of that door has seen me much worse off. At least now I'm reasonably clean, with a light floral scent from the soap clinging to my skin.

I take a sniff of my arm, weirdly giddy at the proof that I'm no longer a stink-fest, and brace myself in case he's angry about the puddles. "You can come in." Like he really needs my permission.

Sylas strides into the room and stops a few feet from me, eyeing the floor with a puzzled expression.

"I'm sorry," I say quickly, clutching the side of the tub. "I tried not to make a mess, but…"

His gaze snaps to me—to my face and then to my arm taut as it balances me. His mouth tightens.

"You couldn't get into the water. I should have realized. My apologies. The next time—we have a sort of sauna in the lower chambers, with a small in-ground pool you could use instead. It has steps."

He expects me to be here long enough that I'll take multiple baths. It's hard to know what to make of that when I have no idea how often faeries generally bathe.

I glance around. Better not to make myself any more of a nuisance than I already have while I am here, while he's being kind to me. "If there's a mop, I could clean it up—"

He shakes his head before I can finish. "I'll see that it's taken care of. I have something for you that should make getting just about anywhere *other* than into the bath easier for you."

He steps closer, holding out his hands, and that's when I register the object he's brought me. It looks like a snapped off branch, nearly as thick as my wrist, blunt at the narrower end and spreading into a shallow crescent at the thicker end. The crescent is polished smooth, but the rest of the surface is covered in bark.

Sylas turns the branch-staff-thing so the blunt end touches the floor and stands it next to me, studying it. Then understanding clicks in my head.

"It's a crutch?" I say.

He nods. "Not quite tall enough, I think. I had to estimate from memory." His fingers close around the top of the crutch, a few soft syllables slip from his mouth, and before my eyes, the branch *grows*. Just a couple of inches, so it's the perfect height to fit under my armpit.

More magic. How much can he do with it? Suddenly I'm remembering the houses I saw from the bedroom window that looked like twisted-off tree stumps. Did the fae *grow* those homes rather than build them?

Sylas is waiting for me to try out his gift. I'm pretty curious too. I tuck it under my arm, ease some of my weight onto it, and take a few tentative steps away from the tub.

The crutch's base stays steady on the floor, and my damaged foot doesn't ache at all when I don't need to fully press down on it. I wouldn't want to get too used to this thing, since who knows how long I'll be able to keep it, but for now it'll at least allow me to walk around the keep without needing to cling to the furniture or my new captors.

I'm already that much closer to making my escape, and I have the man who brought me here to thank.

And I should actually do that. I give him a cautious smile, not sure how much gratitude he'll need to be satisfied. "Thank you. I really appreciate it."

Sylas offers a restrained smile, so I guess that was enough. A trace of humor gleams in his dark eye. "It benefits us as well, not needing to act as your crutch ourselves."

I wet my lips, hesitating over my next question. "So, it's okay, then? If I wander around this place a bit?"

"Nothing within the keep should pose a danger. Any rooms we'd prefer to keep private will be locked. All I ask is that you stay inside. Aerik and his cadre, perhaps his whole pack, will be on the hunt for you. We can't risk anyone seeing you."

Because then he and *his* cadre would lose me. But it's hard to resent that when he's just granted me so much more freedom than I've had in years.

I drag in a breath and find I have the courage to push a little harder. "You need something from me—like they did. Something to do with my blood?"

I can see Sylas withdraw behind that tattooed, square-jawed face with its vicious scar. The hint of warmth that was there an instant ago vanishes. He called himself a lord, and it shows in both the sternness of his gaze and the lifting of his posture.

"Don't trouble yourself about that," he says. "All you need to know is that we won't treat you the way they did. Would you like to begin your explorations now?"

Part of me would, but a larger part wilts with exhaustion at the thought of tackling more of the winding hallways. I need to figure out where the main door is and what else this place holds, but right now, I'm ready to crash. The exertion of moving around even this much must be getting to me after all that time in the cage.

"I think—I think I'd just like to rest for a little while," I say.

"Of course. Let me see you to your bedroom."

The room I woke up in is around the corner from the privy where the hall splits, two doors down to the left—important details to remember. Sylas lets me walk in unaccompanied.

I stop on the threshold, taking in the brighter sun flooding through the window and the warmth it brings, the sweet smells of wildflowers and hay drifting in on the breeze, and the spread that's been laid out for me on the table next to the bed: a wooden comb, a hand mirror framed in silver, and a goblet that, I determine as I meander closer, is full of water. A large pitcher sits on the floor next to the table in case I want to refill that or, I guess, the ebony bowl for a quick wash.

This is mine. I mean, it's not, and it's technically a prison cell besides, but I can't smother the tickle of possessiveness, giddy as my enjoyment of the soap smell on my skin, that runs through my chest. I lean my crutch against the wall and flop onto the bed, my lips curling into a smile as I surrender to the coziness of the covers.

It's dark, so horribly dark. Hands grasp at me. A knee jabs my back. A snicker reverberates through my ears. The cold bite of a knife slices into my skin—

And I wake up, gasping and shuddering, sitting bolt upright in my new bed.

It isn't dark at all. The sunlight no longer slants through the window, but an indirect glow fills the room. Nothing's restraining me; nothing's cutting me. Still, it takes several breaths before my pulse stops rattling in my chest at its panicked pace. Sweat has glued my blouse to my back.

I barely remember the dream, only that I was back there, back in the cage, and the bars seemed to be closing in on me as if to crush me completely…

I'm not there anymore. Maybe I'm not totally sure of this new place or what I'm going to face here, but at least I'm not *there*.

Outside my window, a pinkish tint is streaking through the clouds. It must be evening. My stomach gurgles, reminding me that after my first real breakfast in ages, I've gone and slept through lunch. Have I missed dinner too?

I grope for the crutch Sylas made for me—more for his convenience or mine, it's hard to say—and swing myself onto my feet. The muscles in my legs only wobble a little on my way to the door. As I grasp the knob, a quiver of panic shoots through me. Will it even open?

But it does, turning easily in my grasp. I tug the door open, and the smell of roasting meat carries from the staircase to greet me. Oh, yes, I'd like some of that.

It takes me twice as long as a normal person to lurch down the stairs, but I do it all on my own, so I'll count that as a win. Someone—August, I assume—is humming a buoyant melody in the kitchen, utensils clinking against the cookware. The dining room is empty. I'm even a little early for the meal.

No time like the present to get in some of that exploring, then. Ignoring the tension that twists around my gut with each limping step I take, I head farther down the hall. Sylas said I could feel free to wander. I'm not breaking any of his rules.

I'm just figuring out where I *would* go about breaking them when I'm ready to.

With the dimming of the natural light that appears to seep down through slits at the edges of the ceiling, orbs mounted along the walls have lit up with a flame-like flicker. The amber glow leads the way to a branching of the hall in two directions, just like upstairs. To my right, I find a grand entrance room, with even more orbs beaming along the walls and across the vaulted ceiling. A red-and-gold rug spills across the floor to the broad wooden door striped with reinforcements of gleaming brown metal.

Bronze, I think. Like my cage. Faeries are supposed to be repelled by iron, aren't they? I guess that must be true, and they use whatever other metals they have available instead.

I shuffle along the rug, wincing inwardly at each muffled tap of my crutch. The hall is quiet; no one's around. There's no one here to see me grip the handle on that door and tug.

It doesn't budge—not when I heave it up and down, not when I haul it toward me or shove at it. The door is locked in some way I can't see the mechanism to, which means I can't *un*lock it.

Of course Sylas wouldn't leave it up to me and my accepting of his orders. He gave me those orders, and he also made sure I can't leave whether I want to or not.

I swivel around to make the trek back toward dinner. I've only taken one step in that direction when a lean figure skulks out of the hall, stopping at the edge of the entrance room.

Kellan's silvery eyes glitter as they settle on me, and every inch of my skin prickles in alarm. "What do you think you're doing all the way over here, little mousey?" he asks.

"Sylas—Sylas said I could explore the keep," I stammer. "I was just taking a look around."

"Were you now? Such a coincidence you immediately looked at the front door."

I cling to my crutch, a tremor racing through my legs, but I manage to raise my chin. "It *was* just a coincidence. I don't want to go out there and get caught by the monsters who had me before."

There's enough truth to the statement that it comes out with more confidence than I'd even hoped for, but Kellan doesn't look convinced. He stalks toward me, baring his teeth in a grin that's nowhere near friendly.

"We aren't stupid, pipsqueak—me least of all. And let me disappoint you now. There's magic binding that door and the one at the back, more power than a dung-body like you could ever contend with. You're stuck with us."

He looms over me, still grinning, and I can't stop myself from cringing backward in a cower. His grin stretches. His eyes spark. For a second, I think he's going to say or do something worse. Then he flattens his mouth and whirls with a snap of his flowing vest.

"August went to call you for supper. You'd better come quickly. Who knows how much time you have before we make a supper out of *you*."

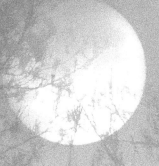

CHAPTER EIGHT

Talia

The next morning's breakfast is an even quieter affair than the first one, mainly because Whitt doesn't make any appearance at all. With Kellan eyeing me ominously from across the table, I gulp down a small portion of juicy bacon and hash browns with an unusual licorice-like flavor as quickly as I can and then excuse myself.

On my way back to the stairs, my eye catches on a movement beside me. A small mirror hangs on the wall in a gleaming frame, the wood so polished it could almost pass for brass. My face stares back at me, my eyes too big in my pale, sunken face, my hair a dark bird's nest around it. I look like a wraith from one of those horror movies my friend Marjorie started cajoling us all into watching when we were ten.

Does Marjorie still love freaky thrillers? What is she even doing now? She must have graduated high school, maybe college too. She could have a job, her own apartment. She could be married for all I know.

All those possibilities feel as distant from my reality as if they're a movie in themselves. As if I've been stuck in suspended animation, the rest of the world moving on without me while I drifted unknowing beyond time itself.

Maybe that's not totally inaccurate either, but I hate looking like the prison escapee I technically am. If I could wash every trace of the last eight years away with the gurgle of bathwater down a drain, I would. Leaning on my crutch, I tug at a particularly stubborn clump of knots with my other hand.

August comes out of the dining room and catches me at it. "Having trouble with those?"

"I don't know if they're ever going to come out," I admit. The comb one of the fae men left on my bedside table is the first one I've seen in years, and it wasn't up to the job. Maybe I'd have to shear my head to the scalp and start over. The thought of looking even more like an invalid makes me cringe.

It shouldn't matter, but it does. I'm already vulnerable enough without adding to that impression. And it'd be yet another thing my former captors stole from me, if far from the worst.

The awareness of the much more wrenching losses I've suffered rolls through me, suffocating me like my dream yesterday. For a moment, my mind blanks out under the weight of it. When I get a hold of myself again, my skin has gone clammy and my hand is clutching the crutch so tightly my knuckles ache.

August is watching me with a deer-in-the-headlights expression that sits oddly on his broad face, his muscles tensed and his golden eyes alight but his stance uncertain. "Do you want me to try to help you with your hair?" he asks after a moment's hesitation. "We all have different areas of magic we take to most naturally, and one of mine is all things bodily. I could check out your foot too."

All things bodily. That's why he was the one Sylas called on to knock me out when they dragged me from my cage. I still don't know how much I should be grateful for that—how much it was a rescue versus being thrown from the frying pan into a fire I haven't yet uncovered the full extent of.

But he's been the kindest to me out of all four of my new captors, and I'm never going to get the answers I need if I hide away in my bedroom until that fire is licking at my bedposts. I suck in a deeper breath, willing away the jitters, and nod. "Okay. Thank you."

His usual warm enthusiasm comes back into his face and his voice. "Thank me when we see how much I can actually do for you. Come on—the parlor has good light."

"The parlor" turns out to be an alcove off the kitchen where a few well-padded armchairs—less ornate than most of the furniture I've encountered in the keep—squat in a semi-circle around a matching footstool and a coffee table of pale wood. Big windows look out over a garden of unfamiliar plants in neat rows and a cluster of trees bearing vibrant globes of fruit.

Beyond the orchard, more fields stretch out toward thick forest. In the distance on the left-hand side, spires of peach-colored stone jut high above the tree-tops, dotted with patches of clinging lime-green shrubs. It looks like the kind of awe-inspiring landscape I'd have printed off for my travel-planning scrapbook.

The thought of those long-lost dreams squeezes my throat. I wrench my gaze away.

A door leads out to the garden, simpler and less imposing than the big one in the entrance room. Seeing it, an itch runs through my arms. It doesn't seem likely that Sylas would have protected the front door so carefully but neglected this back one—Kellan even said there was a back one that was magically sealed—but at least I know for sure there's more than one way out.

August motions for me to sit on the footstool and hunkers down on the edge of the chair behind me so he can examine my hair. His fingertips graze my shoulders, warm and gentle.

"Let's see… I should be able to convince at least some of these knots to unwind themselves."

He says a word in that melodious tone all the fae seem to use when casting their magic, and a tickle of energy passes over my scalp. His fingers keep moving through the strands of my hair with only the faintest of tugs. A wisp of heat from his breath grazes my neck. By the time he asks me to turn so he can work on the waves that frame my face, my pose has mostly relaxed. I can't say I feel *safe*, but I'm reasonably sure I'm not in imminent danger while he's next to me.

When August has worked over both sides, he leans back to consider his handiwork. "The ones higher up weren't so bad, but near the bottom there were a lot of strands twisted pretty tight. I couldn't get them all free without breaking some. I could remove those completely?"

I have the abrupt, ridiculous thought that the lower span of my hair is one of the few things I have left from my time in the real world, before faeries and cages. But maybe I'd feel better having it closer to the chin-length bob from when I was twelve and had no idea any of this existed?

"All right," I say. "Just as long as it doesn't end up with big chunks missing or something." Before the words have even finished tumbling out, my face flushes. I'm not really in a position to be making demands.

August just chuckles. "I may not be a trained barber, but I can manage to do a better job than that."

He goes into the kitchen and comes back with what appears to be a large carving knife. My back stiffens automatically. August halts a few feet away, holding the knife with the tip pointing at the floor. "It's an enchanted blade—it'll cut where I need it to in an instant. I promise I'll be careful."

He looks so hopeful that I'll let him finish his work, so eager to reassure me, that I manage to nod. If he wanted to stab me, he could have done it the moment we walked in here, no need for some complicated subterfuge about fixing my hair.

And he's telling the truth. He lifts the hair from my back with another brush of his fingers and slices through the strands so swiftly that I feel nothing but the patter of what remains hitting my shoulder blades. When I glance back, he's got about four inches of tattered tangles in his hand. At least for the few moments before he murmurs another magical word, and they burst into flames. I flinch, but the fire is already gone, my hair only a sprinkling of ashes that August tosses away.

"It's better not to have your hair lying around—it can be used for enchantments and things," he says, as if reminding me of something I should already know, and offers me an easy smile. On him, the gesture doesn't seem to be hiding ulterior motives like so many of the other grins that've been aimed at me since I got here. "Swivel all the way around, and I'll tackle that mis-healed foot of yours."

He'd better not be planning on using the carving knife on *that* part of my body.

I do as he asked, and he picks up my warped foot by the heel to rest it on his knee. It's bare where it protrudes from the leg of my jeans—the fae men didn't bother to give me socks or shoes. A subtle discouragement from attempting to make a run for it or simple oversight since they knew they weren't letting me outside anyway?

August slips his thumb over the lump of misshapen bone, one side of his mouth slanting downward. His light touch doesn't wake up the usual ache. Then he lifts his gaze, his golden eyes darkened with regret so tangible it sends an unexpected flutter through my chest.

"The injury happened quite a while ago?" he asks.

"About eight years," I say, my voice falling back into its previous whisper. "As well as I've been able to keep track."

"Feet are difficult as it is—a lot of little bones that have to fit together just right. I'm not sure I have the skill that I could have set them properly even a week afterward. Now that the pieces have had so much time to fuse together and settle into their new form… It's easier to mend something than to break it apart once it's combined into something new—that would be like trying to magic a cake back into flour and eggs. I'm afraid I'd hurt you worse."

"That's okay." I hadn't really believed he'd fix *that*, I realize. Would Sylas even want him to? The faerie lord gave me the crutch rather than asking August to check the bones. Maybe he could tell from a glance it was too complicated a task, or maybe he doesn't want me recovering *quite* that much.

But I don't think August would have offered up the possibility if he hadn't planned to help if he could. As far as I can tell, he's more disappointed than I am.

"Why are you being so nice to me?" I blurt out, and then snap my mouth shut, my cheeks flaring hotter than before.

August blinks at me. "Why wouldn't I be?"

I grope for the right words. "I just mean—no one else here was offering to fix my hair or my foot… or anything." Even Sylas was brisk and business-like about the crutch. Whitt has barely bothered to pay attention to me at all, and I could do without the attention Kellan has directed my way.

August sets down my foot. "I wasn't needed for anything else, and you shouldn't have to go around uncomfortable if I can change that easily enough. It's bad enough what Aerik and his cadre put you through."

That doesn't explain why he's been so much friendlier than the others, but I guess it's a reasonable explanation. Before I can decide whether to prod further, he reaches out and gives one of my newly trimmed locks a playful but still gentle tug. Tipped toward me like that, his knees nearly touch mine—his unsettlingly handsome face is less than an arm's length away.

My pulse flutters again, this time with a quiver of heat that's not embarrassment.

"We could do something else with your hair," he offers. "Cut more off, change the color—whatever you like. Take you farther away from everything you've had to endure."

I kind of like that idea, and it's a welcome distraction from the new sensations spreading through my body. Mom always said I could dye my hair when I got older. Well, I'm older now, aren't I?

I tamp down on the hysterical giggle that bubbles up my throat at that justification and manage to say, "Another color—I think that would be good."

He gestures to the windows. "Whatever you like. I've got plenty of materials to bolster my magic."

Any color I want? Thinking of my captor with the sunflower-yellow hair and the purple tint in Sylas's, I have to assume even the natural range for fae coloring isn't as restricted as it is for humans.

A memory pops into my head so suddenly it jerks at my heart. A few months before I was taken, I saw a singer whose name I can't remember anymore in a music video, her hair neon pink, and became desperately determined to emulate that look. It seemed like the height of coolness.

I've got no one here to impress with my style and probably using my preteen sensibility for guidance isn't the best idea ever, but it would be a tribute to my old life. The one I was meant to have. And I definitely wouldn't look like a horror movie wraith like that.

"Can you make it pink?" I ask.

August grins. "Absolutely. Wait right there."

He gets up and bounds out into the garden, but not so swiftly that I miss the indecipherable whisper as he opens the door. Yeah, it's got a locking spell on it too. Damn it.

As he crosses the garden to the fruit trees, I can't help watching his muscular stride, taking in the blatant strength of that brawny body and the eager energy with which he carries it. It's a combination that's more appealing than I want to admit.

He isn't just a man. He untangles hair with a word and conjures flames from his hands. He can turn into a wolf—one of those huge, vicious wolves like the one that left the ring of scars on my shoulder.

August has just passed out of sight amid the trees when Whitt strolls into the kitchen, dressed in an indigo housecoat of what looks like satin with gold embroidery along the cuffs and hems. If he's surprised to find me there, he doesn't show it.

"Hmm," he says. "I came to get some breakfast, but it looks like August has been busy. Are you lunch?"

I wince, but the remark is too flippant for me to take it seriously, the total opposite of Kellan last night when he threatened to have me for supper. Whitt's eyes glint as he watches my reaction, and I'm gripped by the urge to play something other than the trembling captive just this once.

"At this point, I don't think I've got enough meat on my bones to make much of a meal," I say.

Surprise flashes across Whitt's face. My pulse hiccups with the fear that I've made a mistake, but then he barks a laugh.

"We'll see how you turn out after a few weeks of August's cooking, then," he says in the same offhand tone, grabbing a couple of pastries and a heap of bacon out of a basket at the back of the counter and dropping them onto a plate. He saunters out without another word.

The tension from the brief encounter releases from my limbs with a tremor, but at least he's not around to see how much it took out of me to produce that single retort.

August hustles back inside with a couple of glittering fruits that look like rubies in the shape of pears and a handful of bell-like magenta flowers that bob in his hand even when he comes to a stop, as if they're drifting in their own innate breeze. "It'll just take a moment," he promises me.

He dumps his entire haul into a bowl and mashes it together with the energetic pounding of a pestle. He adds a little water from the kitchen faucet, mashes some more, and brings the gloopy mess over to me. "Ready?"

My heart has started thumping as if this was a perilous mission rather than a makeover, and it seems abruptly absurd that this linebacker of a man is going to deliver a dye job, but I've come this far. "Ready," I agree, willing my voice not to shake.

He has to sit even closer to me to work the gloop into my hair, his fingers massaging my scalp and spreading the concoction down through the strands, which still fall to about an inch past my shoulders. When he speaks one of those hushed, melodic words to enhance the dye's effects, his breath washes over my neck again. The fluttering heat returns to my chest, traveling lower in my belly in a way I'm not sure I like.

There's no chance he's feeling anything like that about *me*. I'm a pitiful prisoner he's trying to make himself feel better about keeping locked away.

I don't want to enjoy the tender press of his fingers. I don't want to like him at all.

Whatever his reasons, he *is* being nice to me—extraordinarily nice. Maybe there's a way I can take advantage of that so I can get away from here and all these unwanted feelings ASAP.

I didn't want Whitt looking at me like I was pathetic, but I suspect August is more likely to cooperate if I play up the pitifulness with him. I'm nervous enough about broaching this subject that my voice comes out wavery without any need to feign it.

"August… can I ask you something?"

He kneads more of the dye into a patch of hair at the back of my skull and then eases it out through the rest of the strands there. "Of course. What is it?"

My hands ball in my lap. "I know the reason this Aerik guy kept me and the reason you all wanted me too has something to do with my blood. What's so—what's so special about it? I just want to understand why all this has happened to me."

My words break toward the end. Suddenly I'm choked up, through no act, just honest emotion.

What could possibly have been worth all the other blood spilled, the screams that echo in my memory, the years crouched in that filthy cage? Or maybe to faeries it doesn't need to be all that big a deal to justify that kind of violence.

August's hands have gone still. He pauses for a moment, and then he says, in a more subdued tone than usual, "We don't really understand it either. We only know what it does."

"And what's *that*?"

He inhales slowly. "I think I heard Sylas tell you that we can transform into wolves?"

I nod, suppressing the cringe accompanying the images that rise up in my head. "He did."

"Well, it used to be, a long time ago when I wasn't even of age yet, that the shift was always under our control. It felt right to let our wolves out under the full moon, but we didn't *have* to, and we were just as much ourselves if we did. Then that started to change. We would shift even if we didn't want to. And when we did, on those full-moon nights, our wolves would go wild."

"Wild?"

"Savage." August grimaces. "Nothing in us but the urge to fight and destroy. Like some kind of curse, but we have no idea what might be responsible or how. And the wildness has taken over us for longer and more violently as the years passed. These days, the full moon makes us more like monsters than wolves."

Another memory flits through my mind: hulking, furred shapes lunging out of the shadows. Monsters, indeed.

"That's awful," I say, restraining a shudder.

"It is. But for most of the Seelie, the ones with a decent amount of favor among our peers, it hasn't been so bad for the last several years. Aerik started selling a tonic that if drunk would either prevent the wildness or halt it if it'd already taken over, clear the folk's heads. And as far as we can tell, the key ingredient in that tonic was the blood they were stealing from you."

"Oh." The word falling from my lips is utterly inadequate, but I don't know what else to say. "Has anything else ever helped stop the curse?"

He shakes his head. "Nothing we've ever found or heard of."

A chill spreads through my chest, eating up any heat that remained from August's closeness. I'm the key to taming a savage sickness that has taken over the fae—the only cure they have. How could they ever consider letting me go?

And even if I manage to make an escape, what lengths will they go to in order to get me back?

CHAPTER NINE

Talia

On my way down the hall that evening, my reflection catches my eye again. I can't help stopping and goggling as I have several times already at the magic August did with my hair.

And it really is magic in every sense of the word. No human dye job could ever have worked like this. Somehow the pink hue sank into my dark brown in a way that lets the natural variation come through without diminishing the vibrancy of the new color. It's a deep, rich pink just a few shades shy of purple, and if I didn't know that humans don't grow hair like this, I'd believe it sprouted out of my head that way.

I still look gaunt, my skin sallow, but the vivid waves elevate those flaws from sickly to something luminous, almost as otherworldly as the fae men who brought me here. That's pretty magical in itself. It makes me feel just a tiny bit more powerful than I did before, but a tiny bit matters a lot when you started with nothing.

As I head to my room upstairs, the sound of lilting music reaches my ears. Curious, I clomp along with my crutch to follow it —down the hall in the opposite direction, to where a narrow arched window overlooks the fields to the south.

Beyond the fields and the low, rolling hills beyond them in this direction, the sun has sunk below the distant forest, leaving only a ruddy glow in the dusky sky that's a close match to my new hair. A brighter illumination lights the field at the outskirts of the cluster of stump-like houses. Amber orbs float like immense fireflies around rugs spread out on the grass amid platters of food and goblets of what from the general vibe must be wine.

Several men and women lounge on cushions scattered across the rugs. Others sway beneath the orbs in time with the tune played on a misshapen guitar by an elegant man with fingers that look a joint longer than they ought to be. Laughter rises up as loud as the music.

One couple is kissing, pressed up against a nearby tree. Another two sprawl between cushions at the edge of the festivities, the woman straddling the man in an embrace so intimate my face heats as I avert my gaze.

These must be members of the larger pack—the faeries who live in those houses. The flickering light falls on one familiar face: Whitt, the rumpled strands of his sun-kissed hair catching the glow as if they contain their own internal sun, his hand raised in a toast. He says something with a grin, and another wave of laughter carries through the gathering.

He's entirely lit up with a radiant energy I don't remember seeing when I've encountered him in the keep. It's impossible not to notice how striking these fae men are in general, but watching Whitt right now, I forget how to breathe.

That's how faeries trick mortals in the tales about them, isn't it? Dazzle them with beauty and wonders so they don't realize just how much the fae are stealing from them at the same time.

Still, I can't tear my eyes away.

A creak of the floor makes me startle. I jerk around as fast as my warped foot allows, my body tensing defensively even though I don't see how I could have been doing anything wrong.

That turns out to be the right reaction anyway. Kellan stands in the shadows of the hall, his lips curled into a smile so cruel you'd think someone cut it into his face with a blade. My fingers tighten around the stem of my crutch.

"Enjoying Whitt's revels from afar, maggot meat?" he says. "That's as close as you'll ever get to them."

I swallow hard. What does he want? "I'm fine staying in here," I say in that pathetic whisper. I can't seem to propel my voice louder around him, not with his silvery eyes fixed on me like blades in themselves.

"Such a docile little lamb." He takes a step closer, and my spine goes even more rigid. "Or perhaps a clown, with that ridiculous cataclysm the whelp has made on your head."

As much as I'm fighting not to react, my cheeks burn. All I want is to get away from him, but he's standing between me and my bedroom. Between me and the entire rest of the keep, really. He has me cornered here at the end of the hall, and with that growing awareness, my breath comes short with panic rather than awe.

He prowls even closer. I think the glint in his eyes might be a sort of pleasure alongside the maliciousness. He licks his lips, making no effort to hide the motion of his tongue, and I'm sure of it then. He wants exactly what he's getting: me, trapped and terrified, at his mercy. He's simply enjoying testing how much he can scare me.

Because he wouldn't *actually* hurt me, not while Sylas has said they're going to keep me safe here. Right?

Under Kellan's cold stare, I can't summon much faith in that pledge.

My heart is thudding, and I just barely hold my body back

from trembling. Will he let me get out of this stand-off if I try? I *have* to try—the panic as he closes in is already dizzying me.

I fumble for words, lurching forward with my crutch as I do. "I'll get out of your way. I was just going to bed."

I limp past him as quickly as I can, sticking close to the wall. Kellan watches me go, folding his arms over his chest, his gaze pickling over my skin.

"That's right. Run, little dung-body. Enjoy your lavish bed while you can. You won't have it much longer."

I stumble into my bedroom and slump against the closed door. My limbs aren't just trembling but shaking now, so hard I might vomit. When I close my eyes, images flash behind my eyelids: the bronze bars of my cage, the haughty faces sneering down at me, the gleam of the blade that dug into my wrist.

I'm not there anymore. I'm not there. I remind myself of that over and over in my head, but my body isn't convinced.

My body knows that all I've done is traded up for a prettier cage and jailors with nicer manners. Well, most of them.

I let myself sink to the floor and summon different images in my mind. The Egyptian pyramids, rising ancient and sublime out of the desert under a scorching sun. The dawn glow filtering green through the thick bamboo stands in a forest near Kyoto. Picture after stunning picture from my collection. There's still a chance I'll make it to those places someday.

Gradually, the tremors fade away. I'm still wobbly as I shuffle over to the bed, but I make it there without falling.

The full moon must be weeks away. I have time before any of these wolfish fae *need* my blood. I've already found out so much more than I knew before.

I've just got to hope that they don't change their minds about how much freedom they're allowing me—or about keeping me to themselves to begin with—before I discover everything I need to.

The bedcovers settle around me, cocooning me in feathery softness. As I tug them closer, the lavender scent in my pillow tickles into my nose. My breath evens out, and sleep pulls me under.

The next thing I'm aware of is a cold, hard surface beneath me. I'm slumped against it, unable to move. Too *weak* to move. Like I've refused to eat or drink for days and even thinking about lifting my arm is exhausting, let alone doing it. I can't find the energy to so much as stretch my fingers.

Then someone is grasping my jaw with bruising force, wrenching my mouth open. Sharp eyes glint beneath spikes of blueish-white hair.

A cloying, viscous liquid flows over my tongue. I sputter and gag, but I'm too weak to push at the hand, too weak to spit the stuff out. My survival instincts kick in against my will, and I swallow, swallow, swallow until my head spins with the magicked wine and my lips are sticky with fruit pulp.

It courses down my throat and into not just my stomach but my lungs—I'm drowning. Gasping, gurgling. Muscles wasted and slack. Helpless, so helpless—

Suddenly I'm sprawled on grass in a forest clearing. The stars whirl overhead. My little brother calls my name, his voice wavering through the twilight. I blink, and I see him silhouetted in the distance, Mom and Dad on either side of him, coming this way.

No, no, they can't. The monsters are coming.

But my body won't move, no sound will travel up my throat. When I called out to them before, I thought I was fighting, struggling to survive, but all I did was give everything up.

Just one word. One cry of warning. A cold sweat breaks out across my skin, my lips part a fraction of an inch—

Claws slash from the darkness, carving screams in their wake. Not again, not—

A hand grasps my arm, and I yelp, thrashing. Thrashing… against the soft sheet tangled around my legs.

I wheeze, my lungs constricted with panic, my pulse thundering in my ears. The air tastes like lavender and wildflowers. Moonlight streams through the gap in the curtains —in my bedroom, or the room that's my bedroom for now, at least.

And the hand still gripping my arm, carefully but firmly, belongs to the massive man sitting beside me on the bed, his milky scarred eye even more eerie in the dimness.

"You were having a nightmare," Sylas says, his voice slow and measured, as if talking to a young child. "You were crying out. There's no easy way to wake from one like that."

No, I didn't wake easy at all. As my eyes adjust to the faint moonlight, I make out a fresh scratch on his unscarred cheek where my fingernail must have caught him when I lashed out.

He heard me in distress and came to shake me out of it, and I *attacked* him. My heart stutters all over again. What consequences am I going to face for that mistake?

My voice wobbles as it spills out. "I'm sorry. I didn't mean—I didn't realize—"

"The dream followed you out," he says, calmly enough that the alarm clanging through me starts to dull. "They do that sometimes. Are you all right now?"

A laugh catches in my throat. How can I possibly be *all right*, even now that I'm awake? But I know what he means.

"Yes," I say. My body is catching up with reality, the panic falling away. "Thank you. It was… awful."

I expect him to get up and leave. Did I wake him up with the noises I was making—oh, crap, did I wake *all* of them up?

But Sylas doesn't appear to be in any hurry to get back to his own bed, if he was even already in it when the nightmare hit me and not burning the midnight oil on whatever it is he does when he's not kidnapping human girls and making crutches for them. How much do fae even need to sleep?

He sets down my arm but stays where he's sitting, close enough that my knee tingles with the proximity of his hip even though it isn't quite touching me. His dark eye studies my face. "What did you dream about?"

A shiver runs through me, just remembering. The memory of my family sends an ache through my chest so sharp I know I can't talk about that. But the rest…

"When the other fae—Aerik and whoever—had me," I say. "There was a point when I gave up. I didn't think I'd ever get away from them, and I just wanted to die. So I refused to eat or drink anything… But it didn't work. When I got weak enough, they forced things down my throat. I couldn't stop them. I couldn't do *anything*. Not even die. It was… the worst I ever felt."

Sylas nods. "I can see how that would be."

I swipe my hand across my mouth. A prickling sensation has formed behind my eyes, but I don't want to cry in front of him. He's seen me in a bad enough state without adding to it.

"I decided that if I had to live, I'd better make sure I was strong enough to do something with that life, even if it wasn't much. I couldn't stand staying completely helpless like that. So I kept eating, and when I could move I did, just to work my muscles a little. Just… just in case." My shoulders tense. "I dreamed it happened all over again—the weakness, the way they force-fed me. That's all."

"They never should have treated you that way," Sylas says firmly. "Some of my fae kin may be pitiless, but I promise you it's far from all of us." He pauses. "Aerik and his men—the wolves that attacked you in your world—were they the first wolves you'd seen roaming? Had you ever seen *them* before that night?"

Does he think they might have planned the attack? I knit my brow, thinking back across the seemingly endless stretch of captivity. My sense of my life before has gone vague and dreamlike, as if *it* was only a happy illusion conjured in my sleep, but I know I'd remember seeing *wolves* wandering around town. It was a pretty small town, but hardly some tiny settlement in the wilderness.

I shake my head. "No. Nothing like that. The biggest animals I remember seeing even when we'd go for hikes are raccoons and one time a porcupine."

"Do you recall ever noticing a raven nearby? Or perhaps a wild rat?"

"There were crows sometimes, but I don't think ravens. They're bigger, right? And we had a wild mouse get into the house a few years before... but definitely no rats." I glance up at Sylas. "Why specifically those?"

He gives me one of his restrained smiles. "I can't help wondering if there was some fae influence in how you came to be as you are. We Seelie have the wolf in our nature, but there are also the Unseelie of the winter lands, who become ravens, and the rats of the Murk... who are better not dealt with at all if one can help it." He moves to get up. "I shouldn't be troubling you with these matters when you need your sleep."

"It's all right." I rub my arms, willing away the last flickers of uneasiness from my nightmare. "Thank you for coming in. I'm glad I didn't have to spend any more time in that dream."

"No doubt you will find yourself there again. Nightmares like to inflict our worst memories on us. If I can, I'll make sure you don't stay in any of them too long."

He turns toward the door, and I wonder abruptly how he speaks with so much confidence on the subject. What kinds of nightmares has *he* had?

I don't think he'll answer that, but him coming to me, helping me, was an opening. One I have to grasp hold of however I can, just like I grasped the bars of my cage to build up the strength in my arms.

"Are you usually awake at night?" I venture. I need to know when my new captors sleep if I'm ever going to escape.

I'd hoped the question would sound innocent enough, but Sylas's expression turns even more opaque than before. "Don't you worry yourself about me, little scrap."

He says the nickname kindly enough, but the rest like a command, not a mere suggestion. Before I can respond, he's already striding out of the room, closing the door behind him.

I sit there in the dark for several minutes, too wound up to even consider trying to sleep. My body slowly relaxes, but another question grips me, one I can answer for myself.

I slip off the bed and limp across the room, leaving my crutch so the tapping won't give my movement away. My balance teeters, and a muted throbbing wakes up in my warped foot by the time I reach the door, but traveling around the keep over the last couple of days has steadied my legs enough that I at least don't fall.

I curl my fingers around the polished wooden knob and twist it ever so gingerly.

It only moves a smidgeon before it catches. I can't turn it any farther, and when I give it the gentlest of tugs, I can tell the door won't budge.

The faerie lord wouldn't let me stay trapped in a nightmare, but that hasn't stopped him from locking me in my room at night.

My mouth has gone dry. I focus on the knob, remembering that moment in my cage when I released the lock. The syllables I practiced so many times before they worked tickle across my tongue with no thought at all. I cling to the fear winding through me and murmur the word with every bit of emotion I can muster. "*Fee-doom-ace-own.*"

The knob doesn't budge. I repeat the magic word again, and again, and then stop, afraid if I keep it up someone will hear me.

Who knows how many different kinds of locking magic there

are? Sylas hasn't treated me like my former captors did in any other way, so why would I assume he'd use the same spell to hold me in?

It'll be open during the day. I'll still have chances. But as I shuffle back to the bed, my heart has sunk with an all-too-familiar sense of hopelessness. I close my hands into fists against it.

I made it out of that cage, and I'll make it out of here too. I just have to keep believing that.

CHAPTER TEN

Talia

When I peek into the kitchen halfway through one afternoon, August is already in a flurry of motion throwing together some kind of epic dinner. Catching sight of me, he beams without slowing down his preparations. "My favorite new assistant! Come in. I've got something for you to stir."

Over the past few days, I've found myself gravitating here more and more often, as if drawn by August's typical clatter like a bee to nectar. The auburn-haired fae man with his human-like ears and his warm smiles has always waved me in eagerly. Nothing appears to make him happier than sharing the secrets of one recipe or another with me—not that I'm likely to use those anytime soon, seeing as most of them involve ingredients I'm pretty sure the grocery store back home won't offer, like cat's milk and hummingbird eggs.

He's the only one of my new captors who makes me feel like I really am a welcome guest and not a prisoner.

Today, I'm soon perched on my usual kitchen stool with a bowl wider than I am propped on my knees and a long wooden spoon clutched in my hand. The dough I'm mixing is a weird combination of sticky and sloshy, but it gives off a sweetly spicy smell that makes my mouth water.

"What's this going to become?" I ask.

"You'll just have to wait and see," August says with a sparkle in his golden eyes. "I promise you'll enjoy it."

"I want to eat it already."

He laughs. "It won't taste half as good before it's baked." He pauses, studying me with sudden concern. "Are you hungry? I can get you a snack."

The thing that appears to make August second-happiest is watching me devour his cooking. Every meal where I manage to consume closer to a full serving—though still nothing like the amount these men-who-aren't-men eat—he perks up a little more. And every day, I have a little more energy of my own.

I'd have thought it'd be in their best interests to keep me weak, but August doesn't seem to think so, and Sylas isn't stopping him. I don't know what to make of that.

"No, keep going with your dinner prep," I say. "I'm not really hungry—this just smells so good."

"And I haven't even added the malvia sugar yet," he says, whatever that is. "I'd make these things more often if they didn't take so long to bake. Easier when I have help, though." He flashes another smile at me and goes back chopping up root vegetables of an odd pale blue color. "It'll need another five minutes stirring, but if your arm gets tired, I can jump in. Just let me know."

As I continue turning the batter, I glance around the kitchen. It's twice as big as my bedroom, which is pretty big in itself, with three ovens, two islands—one massive and one narrow—and pots and pans of all shapes and sizes dangling from vine-like ceiling fixtures. "It seems like this kitchen is meant to have a whole team working in it."

"Sylas modeled it on the one we had in Hearthshire. We had a full staff there. Back then, I really just noodled around in the kitchen when they didn't need it…"

He trails off with a hesitant note, as if he's not sure he should have said that. That might mean it's important. Sylas said something about Hearthshire, didn't he? I can't remember exactly what.

"Why did you move here?" I venture. I *do* remember the fae lord indicating that it was unusual for August to be doing the cooking—for them not to have staff. I haven't seen anyone in the keep other than him and the three members of his cadre since I arrived here. Whatever work the rest of the pack does, it happens outside these walls.

August sweeps the chopped veggies off the cutting board, his stance uncharacteristically awkward. "Unfortunate circumstances. But we've made the best of things here."

A typically vague answer, the kind I get whenever I ask anything at all prying. I suck my lower lip under my teeth to worry at it. He was willing to open up a bit about my role here, but that involved me directly—and he wasn't keen on talking even about that.

I have to understand how everything works in this place, where we are and why and all the rest, if I'm going to have a real hope of being anything more than a walking blood dispenser. But it's going to be obvious if I prod too much. I veer back to what seems like a safer subject, hoping I'll get another opening.

"Have you always liked to cook then, even though you wouldn't normally need to?"

August nods, his usual energy coming back into his movements and the gleam in his eyes. "I've mostly trained in fighting, to defend Sylas and the pack if it comes to that. Thankfully there's not much call for combat most days." He shoots me a lopsided grin. "But everyone always needs food, and just about everyone appreciates food that's well made. I like knowing I always have something to contribute."

I glance down at the batter I'm still stirring, struck with an unexpected pang by how much I relate to that sentiment. Isn't that exactly why *I* keep volunteering to pitch in rather than sitting back and simply observing, which I know he'd happily let me do? I want to show I can give something back.

"That makes sense," I say.

"I came by it pretty naturally." August sets a frying pan on one of the stoves. "With all the physical training, I was constantly getting hungry between meals and scrounging around in the kitchen. But even as a kid, I wasn't satisfied with just a piece of bread and cheese, so I hassled the head cook until she taught me some of her tricks. In some ways, it's kind of like warfare, figuring out which elements will come together and cooperate or clash."

I never would have thought of cooking like that. "I'm glad you did learn. With the food you make, I don't think anyone could *not* get their appetite back quickly."

He laughs. "Then my plan is working. Here, give that a couple more whirls and it should be done."

I put my elbow into the last few stirs, the batter thicker against the spoon now, and try to think of what else I might ask him. Before I land on anything, Sylas strides into the kitchen through the back door.

I'm not sure I'll ever *not* be intimidated by the giant of a man with his mane of purple-brown hair and intense, mismatched eyes. My pulse hiccups and my mouth snaps shut before his gaze has even settled on me.

"August is putting you to work, is he?" he says.

The other man leaps to snatch the bowl from me, giving his lord a hasty but respectful bob of his head. "I just thought—since she likes hanging out in here anyway—"

"It's fine," I say quickly. "I'm happy to help out." It does feel good to be doing something useful. Something that's actually me *doing* it and not just a part of my body being stolen away.

Sylas considers me as if he can see that unspoken thought, but he doesn't remark on it. He gestures me up and toward him in the parlor area. "There's another way you can be of use. Come sit with me."

I can't exactly deny him, even if I'm less sure of his good intentions than August's. I walk over, confident enough with my crutch after a few days of practice that it's more an amble than a lurch now. At another motion from Sylas, I sink into one of the armchairs. He pulls another up closer to me and sets a bag of waxy fabric on the coffee table next to us.

"What am I doing?" I ask, fighting the urge to shrink into myself with his powerful form so close. He might rule here, which means he's the one keeping me captive, but he hasn't hurt me. So far.

He takes a sprig dotted with tiny orange leaves from the bag. "I've gathered some of my medicinal herbs from the garden. I'd like to test and see if you have any reaction to them. Just on your skin, nothing that should affect you too strongly if you do react."

That doesn't sound like a huge imposition. But— "Why?"

"You're obviously not a typical human being," he says evenly. "I'm curious to see how else that might bear out and whether it could allow us to determine what exactly makes you unique."

Why my blood can cure this wild curse the fae are suffering from and no one else's can. If he figures that out, would that mean they might be able to replicate the cure without needing me? I'm all for *that* possibility. And the more helpful I am, the more helpful these men will hopefully become when I'm asking more of my questions.

Obediently, I stretch out my arm, bare beneath the sleeve of my T-shirt. I rest it on the arm of the chair, the skin on the underside somehow even paler than the rest, nearly translucent. Blue veins crisscross the delicate bones. August's incredible meals have started filling me out from my half-starved state, but it hasn't been that long. I'm still thin enough that I want to wince, seeing myself.

Sylas moves methodically, so different from August's enthusiastic vigor. He crushes a few of the orange leaves between his thumb and forefinger and then rubs the paste that forms onto my skin just below my wrist. He waits, observing. "Do you feel anything unusual?"

I shake my head. "Nothing I wouldn't expect to."

After a little longer, he wipes the herb off, studies the faint pink spot it left on my skin, and hums low in his throat. It mustn't be anything all that exciting, because rather than spend any more time on that reaction, he retrieves another sprig from his bag, this one bushy as a squirrel's tail—if squirrels came with lavender fur.

That stuff sends a faint stinging sensation through my skin when Sylas applies it. He has me describe the feeling, wipes it off, examines the slightly darker pink mark, and rubs a cool gel onto it that absorbs the sting. Apparently that wasn't anything unexpected either. He immediately moves on.

We've gone through five herbs, none of them provoking any response that holds Sylas's attention for more than a few seconds, before I gather the courage to find out if my cooperation has earned me any of *his* cooperation in return.

"August said the four of you haven't always lived here."

Sylas pauses and looks from me to his cadre man. August ducks his head and throws himself even more energetically into stuffing the roast he's working on now. "August seems to have a habit of mentioning things he doesn't need to," the fae lord says, his tone mild but low enough that there's a hint of reproach in it anyway.

Is Sylas upset that August told me as much as he did about the curse? I didn't mean to get him into trouble. "I— He didn't say very much," I add quickly. "But you said something when I first got here, about somewhere called Hearthshire… That's where you used to live?"

The lord's mismatched gaze comes back to me, and my skin prickles with the impression that he's again seeing a lot more than I said. Then he chuckles, a deep rolling sound that's only a tad less unnerving than if he growled. "The little scrap listens well. Why do you want to know about Hearthshire?"

I can't exactly tell him that I'm hoping someone will slip up and offer a tidbit that'll aid my eventual escape. But I have other, more innocent reasons I can give that are still true.

"I've been living in your world for years, and I don't know anything about it. I haven't *seen* anything of it except the room my cage was in and this keep. I can't help… being curious."

"We were gone from Hearthshire long before you came to the Mists," Sylas says, returning his attention to his herbs. "Long before you were even born, from the looks of you. It's better for all of us if we look forward instead of back."

I can't really argue with that. "What do you see looking forward?" I ask instead.

A small smile curls the lord's lips. "Better things, if we're wise in how we make our moves. I'll take care of that, one way or another."

He doesn't look me in the eyes as he says it, training his gaze on my arm and the bright green herb he's rubbing into my skin now. A shiver creeps down my back.

I'm going to be a part of those moves—and it's hard to believe that the way I end up fitting into their plans will be better for *me* in the long run.

CHAPTER ELEVEN

August

"Just one more tartlet?" I implore, waggling the pastry at Talia. "Otherwise I'll think today's baking wasn't up to snuff."

The human gives me that hesitantly fierce look, as if she knows I'm not being serious but isn't quite confident enough yet to call me on it. At the same time, her lips twitch with a smile, and the blush I adore more every time I see it brings color to her wan cheeks.

Knowing that she's comfortable enough with me by now that she trusts I won't really push the issue—that she can take my urging her to eat her fill in the friendly spirit with which I mean it rather than as a threat—fills my chest with warmth. In just a week, she's come a long way from the skittish, cringing girl who could barely speak above a whisper. I'd like to think I can take at least a little credit for that.

I can definitely take credit for the softness that's starting to fill out her features and frame, smoothing out the harsh angles of starvation. Since the first morning when she picked at her breakfast like a mouse, she's worked up to what I think must be close to a human-sized meal. After so many years without any humans around, my frame of reference is shaky.

"I'm full, I promise," she says, setting her hand on her still-concave belly, her voice quiet but clear. "You're going to give me a stomach ache."

"All right, all right." I grin at her and pop the pastry into my mouth instead.

"Let's not give her the impression we're trying to fatten her up for the slaughter," Whitt drawls from across the dining table.

I can tell he's teasing, but Talia's obviously not as sure of him. Her shoulders tense with a restrained flinch. Then she shoots me a swift little smile as if to reassure me that she knows that's not my intention, and a swell of affection rushes through my chest.

She's been through so much. When I think of Aerik and his cadre, of the state in which they kept her and the cage we found her in, of the reactions that show just how much they traumatized her, anger hazes my mind. I want to storm right back into their fortress and tear the lot of them apart. I *would* rend them into pieces if giving into that desire wouldn't screw over my own cadre. But if Aerik or his people ever set foot on our territory...

My fingers curl, my claws prickling beneath the tips. I focus on Talia's bright green eyes and the strikingly rich pink I transformed her hair into, and the fury recedes. She's been through so much, and yet she can find the space to care how I might take my older brother's hassling. The hard part is stopping myself from gazing at her for too long.

As Kellan has clearly noticed. He bares his teeth in a sneer where he's sitting next to Whitt. "Yes, let's all become mudlickers and organize our lives around *her*."

My hackles rise again, but Sylas shoots me a sharp look, and I manage to hold my tongue. It's only through our lord's grace that I haven't already ripped the mangy asshole's throat out.

Sylas stands, the meal done, and I get up to collect the plates. He motions to Whitt. "I would see you in my study now."

Whitt dips his head. "I can barely contain my excitement." Despite his sarcasm, he follows our lord out without hesitation.

One of his runners came by the keep this afternoon. News about the Unseelie incursions, maybe? Have they launched another assault?

I clench my teeth, holding in my impatience that Sylas doesn't yet consider me astute enough to add something to the larger strategy discussions. How am I supposed to learn enough to have something to contribute if I'm shut out?

This isn't the time to campaign for more responsibility, though. Sylas is still deciding how we're going to handle Talia and *her* unique contributions to our situation. He's taken in what I've had to say about that. I have to be ready to speak up for her again if I need to.

It doesn't matter how important she is to us—she still deserves better than to be passed around like a bargaining chip. I can't let other concerns distract me and then fail her.

This time I won't let the worst happen.

I carry the dishes to the sink I've already filled with hot water and fermented shearvine juice. Within an hour in that potion, all the bits of food still clinging to the ceramic surfaces will have dissolved. I lope back to the hall, passing through the kitchen doorway just as Kellan swipes his foot toward Talia and knocks her crutch out from under her.

Talia squeaks and tumbles onto her knees. Kellan looms over her, his laugh so vicious she winces, and every thought in my head blanks out beneath a roar of fury.

I hurl myself at the other man, the roar bursting from my throat. My fist slams into the side of his head before he's had a chance to turn fully around.

Kellan staggers backward, catches himself, and springs at me with a snarl. I land a punch on his jaw, but he manages to knee me in the gut. I dodge another blow and leap at him again, conscious of nothing but the thunder of my pulse and the rageful red tinting the edges of my vision.

He *attacked* her, that poor slip of a thing not even half his weight with no means of defending herself, and he is going to pay.

My teeth twinge as they lengthen into fangs; my shoulders start to hunch with the instinct to unleash my wolf. I can fight in either form, but the animal is faster, freer. Kellan slashes at my face with fingertips already sprouting claws—

—and a force larger than either of us rams between us, shoving us apart.

Sylas plants himself there with his arms spread, one hand gripping my shoulder and the other Kellan's. The growl I was about to let out dies in my throat under my lord's scrutiny.

"Get a hold of yourself," he barks, and jerks his head around to level his glare at Kellan too. "Both of you. Are you my cadre, or are you whelps barely off their mother's teat?"

My muscles are still clenched with anger, but the flare of adrenaline is already tapering off. A sickly sense of shame trickles through me. And I was just bemoaning that he doesn't invite me into his higher strategy discussions. Small wonder.

"He hurt Talia," I say, because if I'm going to be shamed, Kellan is owed at least as much. "Kicked her crutch away so she'd fall. I was—"

"Defending her?" Sylas fills in with a dark rumble in his voice. He tips his head toward the stairs. "It doesn't appear she's appreciated your attempt all that much."

I glance past him, and my heart plummets. Talia has scrambled over to the foot of the steps. She's crouched there, a pose not so different from when we found her in Aerik's cage a week ago, her expression as terrified as it looked then. She holds her crutch braced in front of her like a shield. She's *trembling*, her breath coming in shallow gulps.

The shame that gripped me before is nothing compared to what rolls over me at that sight. We rescued her from fae who acted like monsters toward her, I've been doing everything I know how to help her heal—and what could she see me as after that display of violence but a monster just like them, ready to snap the second he's angered?

I would never lash out at you like that, I want to tell her. *You have nothing to fear from me.* But why in the lands should she believe me?

"Talia," Sylas says gently, "you're in no danger. The fighting is over. I'll deal with these two. No one will hurt you."

Her hands squeeze tighter around the crutch, but she nods in acknowledgment, her breath catching and then starting to even out.

Sylas's tone softens even more. "Do you need me to help you upstairs? I think you'd best retire to your room for the night."

She holds still for a few more seconds, getting her trembling under control, and then pushes herself upright with a shaky determination that makes my heart ache twice as much as before. "I —I think I'll be all right," she whispers.

"I'm glad to hear it. I'll see that you're not disturbed."

She bobs her head again and limps away up the steps, her crutch wavering in her anxious grasp. I feel every fall of her feet like an additional jab of guilt.

When she's out of view, our lord lowers his arms and turns back to Kellan. His voice comes out taut with the anger *he* knows how to control. "I told you to leave her be."

"She wasn't hurt," the other man says dismissively. "I was merely reminding her not to get too cozy around here, since this whelp seems to be doing everything he can to spoil her."

Sylas's voice drops even lower. "Just this once, because surely the kin-of-my-mate would never ignore a direct command, I'll assume you forgot that I specifically said we *want* her to be comfortable so that she'll cooperate in every way we need. To make sure the message sticks this time, I'd have you attend to her in some way to make up for it, but I suspect seeing you is the last thing she'd like right now. The upstairs lavatory could use a good scrub, though."

Kellan draws back. "You're not actually—"

"*Someone* needs to take care of it, and I'd rather not risk anyone else from the pack seeing our guest for the time being. Get to it, and don't let me find out you've been terrorizing the little scrap again."

Kellan's mouth tightens into a grimace, his displeasure obvious, but he turns tail and stalks up the stairs without another word.

Sylas rounds on me. "It's bad enough we can't rein in the wildness one night out of a month without you giving yourself over to it when there's no moon to blame. However you may feel about Kellan, he *is* your cadre-fellow. Every disagreement can't turn immediately into a brawl, or we'll make more broken bones than decisions."

"I know." I lower my head. "He's been picking at her so much, and then seeing him menace her physically as well—I had too much anger building up, and it burst out."

"I don't fault you for defending her. Just attempt it with words next time before bringing out the fangs and the claws. Go for a run. Let out that energy and clear your head. And do that again the next time you notice tensions building inside."

"Yes, my lord."

It's less punishment than Kellan faced—barely any punishment at all. As I head to the back door to follow his orders, my shame over disappointing him fades quickly.

What doesn't fade is the image of Talia's frightened face, the way she gripped her crutch as if she thought she might have to fend us off with it. I bow down over the grass beside the garden, the change rippling through me with a rush of exhilaration the way it's meant to be when our wolves come out, but my stomach stays knotted.

How many times has Kellan pulled stunts like that when none of us were close enough to catch him? How long will it be before his hostility turns even more brutal?

I don't think he'd kill Talia knowing what having her alive means to all of us, but I wouldn't put it past him to injure her, possibly even badly, and count on begging forgiveness. It's hard to imagine Sylas actually kicking him out of the cadre over an offense against a human.

But she shouldn't have to live in fear of him... of all of us.

I look toward the orchard, my mind already traveling past it to the fields and forest beyond. Maybe I can find her a real means of protecting herself—just enough to spare her the worst of his malice.

I stretch my wolfish limbs and set off at a trot toward the edge of the Mists.

CHAPTER TWELVE

Talia

Taking an afternoon nap is becoming a habit of mine. I've started staying up into the early hours of the morning, watching from my window and listening to the footsteps and door clicks that seep through the walls, forming a picture of the fae men's comings and goings. The nap gives me a chance to catch up on the missed sleep. My body doesn't seem to appreciate it, though. I'm always groggy when I wake up.

I rub my eyes in the warm sunlight and scoot to the edge of the bed where I left my crutch. I've gotten used enough to walking that my bad foot only twinges a bit when I put my weight on it. Since I can't count on always having the crutch when I need it—as Kellan went out of his way to prove a couple of days ago—I'm trying to lean on it as little as possible. I use it for balance more than anything until my foot starts outright aching from the pressure of walking.

I've also been working on moving silently. It's clear that faeries have keen ears—like wolves, I guess. Sylas came barreling down the stairs to intervene the second August collided with Kellan the other day.

Stealth isn't easy with the wooden end of the crutch bracing against the hard floor. I set it down as carefully as I can manage, make sure it's steady before taking a step, and lift it straight up so it doesn't scrape the floor. I'm going to need to rely on it more when I'm ready to get out of here so that my feet themselves don't make too much noise with my uneven gait. No matter how I try, my warped foot catches on the ground a little every time I raise it.

Along the hall and down the stairs, I only slip up with the crutch and tap it on the floorboards once. Not bad. I'm getting there. Considering that I still have no concrete idea how I'm going to get past the locks or find my way out of the fae world afterward, I've got plenty more time to practice.

I expect to find August in the kitchen. As I slip through the doorway, my body tenses just slightly in anticipation. An image flickers through my head: his face twisted with fury, his fist hurtling at Kellan's face, his animalistic roar ringing through the hall.

He was protecting me. I know that. I know it, and my pulse still stutters when I remember how he looked and sounded in that moment.

He's been so sweet to me, but he's no more a man than the others. He has one of those monstrous wolves inside him. I can't ever forget that.

Scary as that might be, it doesn't change the fact that I find him *less* scary than his companions. The kitchen remains my favorite hangout spot.

There's no sign of his dark auburn hair or well-built body in the room right now, though. I'm about to head back out when a clinking sound reaches my ears. As I glance around, Whitt emerges from the pantry that's just off the cooking area.

His sun-kissed hair is in typical disarray, his stride as jaunty as ever, but his high-collared shirt and trim slacks look more rumpled than I'm used to, as if he's slept in them. Maybe he has. There was another party outside the keep last night, one I could still hear strains of music and laughter from until I finally let myself sleep. He didn't emerge for breakfast *or* lunch today.

When he catches sight of me, he cocks his head. There's a glaze to his eyes as if he's not quite seeing me after all.

"Are you all right?" I find myself asking, even though on the scale of scary Whitt is definitely at the upper end. He's never been mean to me like Kellan, but he hasn't ever been *nice* either.

He makes a humming sound and brandishes a bowl of something he must have grabbed from the pantry. "I will be. Perfect hangover cure."

Something that counteracts the effect of faerie-world intoxication? That could come in handy. A shiver runs through me with the memory of the pulped fruit my former captors shoved into my mouth when they wanted me particularly compliant.

"What is it?"

Whitt ambles over to the parlor and flops into one of the chairs with a leg casually draped over the padded arm. "Much too precious a delicacy for a mite like you," he declares, warmly enough. "You wouldn't know what hit you."

My body balks for a second before I force myself to limp over. I haven't really talked with Whitt before—maybe I should have tried. He might not go out of his way to be friendly, but he seems pretty free with his words. Maybe he'd tell me some of the things the others are keeping secret. Especially while he's hung over.

"I've survived all the faerie food I've eaten so far," I remind him.

He hums again and takes a swig from the bowl, which I can now see holds a syrupy liquid a slightly lighter shade of pink than my hair. He swirls the rest against the sides of the bowl and scrutinizes me with eyes the same bright blue as the ocean under a beaming sun. A perfect match for his hair, not so much for his temperament.

"You want a taste, do you?" he says, a sly glint lighting in those eyes. "I suppose that sort of boldness should be rewarded."

I sink into the chair next to his, and he hands me the dish. It's like an oversized mug in his broad hands; in mine, it's more like a mixing bowl. I raise it to my lips and manage to take a sip without spilling it down my chin.

The syrup coats my tongue, lighting up a giddying warmth everywhere it touches. It's fruity and sweet—so sweet my gums tingle—but rich at the same time. I'm overwhelmed by the flavor in an instant, and at the same time I want to gulp and gulp until I've filled myself to the brim with it.

"Oh, no, you don't, my overeager friend." Whitt snatches the bowl back from me before I can pour more into my mouth. He takes another swig and grins at me, looking a little giddy himself. "I'm sure you never had anything half that delectable back in your own world."

I think of cotton candy at the summer fair, of sugar cookies at Christmas, of crème-filled chocolate eggs left by the supposed Easter Bunny. If all those flavors were somehow combined into one, it would almost reach the wonder of that pink stuff.

Instead of answering, I hold out my hands. "Could I have a *little* more?"

Whitt chuckles and passes the bowl back. I take a bigger swallow than could really be called "a little" before he pulls it out of my grasp. "Watch you don't drown yourself in that, mite."

My head tips back against the cushioned chair, the warmth swelling from my belly all the way to the tips of my fingers and toes. Why get hungover if you could just have this "cure" to begin with?

My thoughts spin around that question and bounce off another consideration of cures. My head feels heavy when I lift it to look at Whitt. "I'm a cure. Not for hangovers. For going wild when it's a full moon."

"Indeed you are." He winks at me and throws back the rest of the syrup. "Wouldn't want to try the hair of the dog approach there. A pity we can't package you up in the pantry so easily."

Hair of the dog. I've heard that expression before—from my parents, way back when?—but I don't remember what it means, if I ever knew. The entire contents of my head have started spinning now, but it's an exhilarating sensation, like whirling around on a merry-go-round.

I cling onto the thread I'd meant to pursue, pulling the words from my mind as if they're unravelling from a spool. "You talked about a tonic—you could keep a tonic in the pantry. Why didn't you just keep using that? Why did you come looking for me?"

"Oh, we didn't know it was you we'd find. We just wanted our own means of making the tonic. Aerik didn't often share with us, you see. We're somewhat out-of-favor with most of our Seelie brethren. And he did enjoy holding that over our heads. No more!"

"Because of me?"

"One way or another." Whitt tosses the empty bowl onto the coffee table and stretches in the chair, more cat-like than wolfish in that moment. A very large cat that could sprout claws just as sharp. "No more living on the fringes of the Mists, human drudges just around the corner. No more half-sized keep for a home. No more dwindling pack. As soon as our lord and master gets on with sorting it all out."

A bit of an edge has crept into his flippant tone, but my attention has stuck on something else. The fringes of the Mists? Humans just around the corner? Are we *close* to the regular world here, then?

I want to ask that, but when I open my mouth, all that tumbles out is a breathless laugh. My mind isn't just whirling but soaring now—I'm suddenly sure that if I reached up I could brush my fingers over the ceiling. The colors of the chairs with their leafy patterns are so vibrant they make me want to cry for awe. Am I even still sitting in one or am I floating?

"You *did* like that syrup, didn't you?" Whitt says with a laugh of his own. "Feed you on this every day, and you'd be happy enough."

In some distant part of my brain, it occurs to me that this isn't normal. It isn't right. No regular food or drink would give me this giddy, soaring sensation. It might not be the cacophony of sounds and color that the pulpy mash put me through, but this—Whitt's hangover cure—it's plenty intoxicating in itself.

I can't quite bring myself to care, though. I reach upward, in the grips of the notion that if I just angle my arms right, I can flap them and fly off the chair like a bird.

Whitt leans toward me, his bright blue eyes sparkling, the same pleased glow in his face that I saw when I watched him at his party the other night. "What are you trying to do, little birdie?"

"I don't know," I say, and giggle so hard my ribs vibrate with the sound. "Is this what you have all those parties for? To float like this?"

"Something like that. Don't fly too far now."

"No. That wouldn't be good. I might hit my head on the ceiling." I giggle even harder. My gaze latches on his face, smiling and so bright. "You're beautiful. Are all faeries beautiful?"

His glow diminishes at that comment, as if the act of pointing out his breathtaking looks drains some of the power from them. His mouth tightens. Is he mad at me? I didn't mean to make him mad.

I was supposed to be asking him about something—about the Mists. About fringes. They moved here from a long way away. Here is close to humans.

Is it close to home? What is home, even? I've lived in Fae Central for almost as many years as I had where I was meant to be.

For some reason, that realization provokes another laugh. My head lolls in the other direction.

Whitt tsks, his good humor seeming to return. "Never did meet a mortal who could handle their—"

"*Whitt*," a voice growls, cutting through the glittery vibe of the moment with a tone so dark it might as well throw a shadow over us.

I crane my neck around and squint to focus. Sylas strides into the pantry, glowering at Whitt and then moving to my side. He looms over me, a mountain of a man. I clap my hand over my mouth, since he's obviously not happy about something, but a giggle leaks past my palm anyway.

"What have you done to her?" he says. "I told you she didn't want anything inebriating."

"She changed her mind," Whitt replies. His voice has gone strange, with a tone I don't think I've ever heard before. Flat and brittle, as if it might snap if he speaks just a little more forcefully. "She practically begged me for a taste, I assure you."

"Did she know what she was asking for?"

Whitt is silent for a few seconds. "It didn't hurt her any. She's loving it. It wasn't any of the harsher stuff."

"That's not your call to make."

Sylas descends on me and scoops me up in his arms. "I'm fine," I tell him, unable to stop myself from grinning. "It was *de*licious. Now I can fly!"

"I think we'd better fly you up to bed so you can sleep this high off safely, little scrap." He tucks me against his broad chest and gives Whitt one last glance. "Stay here. I've got more to say about this."

Being carried in his arms feels even closer to soaring. The heat of his chest encircles me, and the flex of those solid muscles against my body sends a deeper tingling through me.

He's looking after me like he always does. My fiercely stalwart protector. I want to lean into him, drink in the rich earthy smell that wafts off of him and lick that smoky tang off his neck. Mmm.

I shift against Sylas, and he adjusts me so his corded neck is just out of reach. Spoilsport. Instead, I watch the ripples in the wood grain on the ceiling flow by. "I'm not tired. I don't need to sleep."

"Then you can just rest until you do need to. I'll bring your dinner up."

"Not hungry either. That syrup filled me right up."

"I can see it did." His tone is dry. I don't think he's angry at me. A jolt of panic shoots through me at the thought that he could have been angry, even though I've just decided that's not the case. Everything is backwards and upside down.

But my body is still light as air. My thoughts bubble around in my brain like fizz in champagne.

"I was trying to be friendly," I tell Sylas.

"Of course you were."

We're in my room—I don't remember the door opening, but here's the bed and the window with the sun beaming outside. Sylas shuts it. No flying that way. Not a good idea anyway. I snicker to myself.

Sylas sits me down on the edge of the bed and steps back. The loss of contact sends a pang through me. "Are you going? I didn't mean—if I made a mistake—"

He chuckles. "If you did, it's a mistake most of us make at least once."

"Not you."

"Even me. Let's not get into the time I got myself fully drunk on duskapple wine when I was a whelp even smaller than you are. I grew a whole new orchard of emeraldfruit trees before one of my tutors caught me."

I blink at him in disbelief. "You were *never* smaller than me."

That declaration provokes an outright laugh. "It *was* a very long time ago. And to answer your question, I'm not going quite yet. I came looking for you because I made something for you. I'll show you now, but we can go over it again tomorrow if the instructions don't stick. All right?"

"You made me a present?" I peer at him, aware that my smile has turned goofy. "You're very generous for a kidnapper."

Sylas's mouth twitches in the other direction, some of his humor fading. He holds up a strange wooden contraption only a little bigger than his hand, like thin branches curved together to form a sort of cage—although you couldn't keep anything in it, the "bars" are too far apart.

I tip my head, taking it in. "What's that for?"

"Your foot. The crutch isn't an ideal solution. You attach this brace around your calf, and it'll offset some of the pressure so you can walk with less pain using just your two legs." He pauses. "Not something anyone could steal or kick away."

Like Kellan. In my current state, that terrifying moment feels centuries ago. Still, the idea of walking steadily without the crutch appeals to me even in my daze.

I swing my feet against the side of the bed. "Show me how to put it on?"

Sylas slides the device over my ankle, talking me through each step as he centers my foot on thin, padded slats across the bottom and tightens bark-like strips around my thin calf. They grip my skin but hardly weigh on it.

I stand up and take a few experimental steps. My body sways, but I think that's from the giddy dizziness. With the extra support, my warped foot holds me up just as well as the good one.

I spin around and stagger. Sylas catches my arm to keep me from falling. Still watching out for me, making sure I don't get hurt. I want to hug him, but his expression sobers me enough that I don't try.

"It'll take some time for the muscles in your leg to adapt," he says. "And your foot may still hurt, especially if you're on it for a long time. But the brace will help."

"Thank you." I peer down at the contraption and then up at him. The question spills unguarded from my lips. "Why are you helping me like this when you don't really want me going anywhere?"

Sylas's face darkens. "We may have use of you, but that's no reason to torture you. Make what you can of what you're given." He gives me a careful nudge toward the bed and leaves without another word.

Abruptly, even through my joyful lightness, I find myself wondering whether he even likes me.

CHAPTER THIRTEEN

Sylas

n my way to my study after a twilight run, I pause outside the girl's bedroom. With my ears pricked, I can make out the soft rise and fall of her breath even through the door, rhythmic but not slow enough to indicate she's sleeping.

She's often still awake when I come by and cast the magic that locks this door. I can imagine it must be difficult to sleep when she can clearly sense her situation here remains precarious. There's no way I can reassure her of her fate when I'm not sure of it yet myself.

Why should I even want to reassure her? The security of my pack and our chance to redeem ourselves in the arch-lords' eyes come before concern for any human. If the image of her vivid green eyes, turned more vibrant in contrast with the striking hue August added to her hair, lingers in the back of my mind even when she's not in front of me, I can blame that easily enough on my long dry spell. She might be a scrap of a thing, but there's a loveliness to her delicate form that I can't deny.

Taking lovers from among our dwindled pack poses too much

risk of adding tensions where there are enough already. My cadre has stolen off beyond the Mists from time to time to sate their lustful hungers with mortals, but I've held myself back from indulging in even that brief satisfaction. I thought it would be a distraction. Now it seems the lack of indulgence may become a distraction in itself, too much pent-up hunger.

Better I don't even enjoy *looking* at Talia. Any desire I develop for her will only interfere with my decision-making. I'll have to find my own chance to go on the prowl.

The thought sends an unwelcome pang through me, as if I owe any faithfulness to one long gone from this world. I shake off the sensation and murmur the spell word over the door knob.

I called a meeting before I went for my run. August arrives at my study at five minutes before the hour, typically over-eager. Kellan stalks in exactly on time, his way of keeping to the letter of the law while making it clear he won't give me a shred more respect than he has to. Whitt ambles in a few minutes late with an air of nonchalance as if he hasn't realized, smelling faintly of absinthe.

I can tell his carelessness is feigned. His shoulders give him away, stiffening just slightly as he crosses the threshold, as if bracing for a scolding. In the hazy afterimages that filter through my dead eye, a ghost of his form bows its head beseechingly—so unlike the man that I know that it's not a reflection of any past dealings we've had.

Perhaps it's an exaggerated echo of his apology yesterday when I laid into him for sharing his edible entertainment with the girl. Perhaps my eye sees some future in which he'll have more to apologize for.

That's a disturbing thought if there ever was one. Criticism tends to roll off Whitt like water off a duck. What could he possibly do that even he would feel he needed to kowtow for forgiveness?

There's no way of knowing what the fleeting impression means.

It's gone before I can study it, as always. I focus on what I can see in the here and now with my unmarred eye.

"You've all had some time to interact with the girl," I say, sweeping my gaze over my cadre. "Some of you in more… acceptable ways than others. I feel it's time we go over what we've learned and see what picture we can piece together from it."

Whitt props himself against the side of one of my armchairs. "Well, as we saw yesterday, she responds to cavaral syrup like any regular human would. I haven't observed anything differently from afar either."

August glares at the other man before turning to me. "I haven't seen any signs that there's anything otherworldly about her either. Other than the effect of her blood under the full moon, I'd say she's fully human."

"Perhaps we should test her blood under other circumstances and see what comes of that," Kellan suggests with a narrow, predatory smile. "There are plenty of other body parts she could spare that we could sample as well."

August's muscles bunch as if to spring, but I remind him of his obligations with the clearing of my throat. That doesn't mean I'm going to let Kellan's remark go unchecked, though.

The trouble is, he isn't entirely wrong.

"We will not be mangling the poor thing's body in any way beyond how Aerik has already harmed her," I say with the full force of a lord's command. "If we need to sample her blood, we'll do it as painlessly as possible."

August's head jerks toward me. "You can't really mean we're going to—"

I hold up my hand to halt him. "She's a mystery—a mystery that must be investigated. If her blood can affect us in other ways, and we present her to the arch-lords without determining that, we could undermine our position or even cause some catastrophe down the line. As I said, we won't hurt her."

He stirs restlessly but manages not to argue. "You tested those herbs on her skin—did you see anything from that?"

I shake my head. "I haven't observed anything that would suggest she has other innate powers. If I hadn't experienced the effect of her blood myself, nothing would indicate to me that she's anything other than a perfectly ordinary human girl."

Well, "ordinary" isn't quite the word for her. To have withstood the abuse Aerik's cadre subjected her to for all those years and still have fought like she did when I first plucked her from their cage— to be making her tentative steps toward exploring this place rather than staying huddled in her room in a quivering ball—there's an extraordinary resilience to her soul. It hints at so much more to be discovered. Perhaps *that* is why her face lingers in my mind.

She certainly can't be considered a mere cowering victim.

"I think you haven't pushed her hard enough," Kellan tosses out. "Dabbing her with herbs in between feasts. And this one, coddling her in the kitchen like she's a pet puppy." He jabs his thumb toward August. "There's no reason for an 'ordinary' dung-body to have the power to affect us like that. Either she isn't all human, or she's had some sort of magic worked on her."

"If she has, she doesn't know about it," I say. "You can't push knowledge out of a being if it's not there to begin with."

"You can push it from her dust-destined body. Terrify her and see what comes out when she's provoked enough. Aerik and his lot left her to languish, but who knows if they ever really came down on her." Kellan's eyes flash. "You complained that I wasn't following your orders, but all I want to do is test her to find out what you claim to want to know. Or do you not really want answers after all, my *lord?*"

He puts such a disdainful sneer on the title that my lips itch to draw back in a snarl. Instead, I take a step toward him, my chin high and shoulders flexed, reminding him that I'm more powerful than him in more than just name. "Your 'test' resulted in nothing more than putting her into a state of panic. Or did you make some useful observation you haven't bothered to share?"

Kellan tenses, but he holds his ground and my gaze. Oh, he is getting bolder with his defiance. "You haven't given me the opportunity to pursue my approach further. It seems you value this dung-body over your own pack—over your cadre. Most would see that as an absolute failure of rule."

I do snarl then, my voice coming out in a growl. "If you're unhappy with my leadership, I've already made it clear that you may find yourself another lord at any time, kin-of-my-mate."

"I'd be happy to show you the door if you've been having trouble finding it," Whitt pipes up, ever cavalier.

"Threatening rather than facing up to your failures. How impressive of you," Kellan snaps back at me.

"It wasn't a threat. It was a statement of fact. Here is another one—one you should heed. I rule this keep and this pack, and I will not be insulted to my face or have my orders disregarded without consequence. The bond between us can be broken, Kellan, and if *you* break it, you'll have no one to blame but yourself for the result."

We stare each other down for a few seconds. A glimmer dances in Kellan's eyes that's so wild I'd almost think he's caught in the full moon's light. With a twist of my gut, I brace myself for the worst, but to my relief, he lowers his gaze. He dips his head just enough to indicate he's recognizing my authority.

Recognizing it only by a thread, though. I don't like how close he's coming to forcing my hand. I swore I'd do right by him, that I'd give him the best life I was capable of offering, but if his behavior outright threatens the stability of the cadre, I can't give him a pass.

Does he think I will? Or is he simply testing just how close he can get to that line so he can stay right on the other side of it?

In that moment, I'm not sure which would be worse.

"You *are* soft on the girl," he says, still keeping his head bowed. "The crutch, and now this brace for her foot?"

"I explained my reasoning before," I reply. "The more comfortable she feels, the more she'll cooperate. If you hadn't interfered, I might have asked for a sample of her blood to test already and had her willingly offer it, no torment necessary. *You're* letting your enjoyment of the torment cloud your judgment."

He says nothing more, but his denial radiates from his stance. He probably thinks blood gained through torment will serve us better.

And he might not be entirely wrong. Did I need to share that brief story of my childhood follies with the girl? Does it niggle at me more than it should when I see her off-balance?

Surely she's earned at least that much respect when we're asking so much from her, though.

I can't see anything more to be gained from this discussion. I motion toward the door. "It sounds as though we've covered all our observations and made our stances clear. Let us continue to observe, and I will take additional steps as I see necessary. If you wish to test the girl in some way, you pass it by me before taking action. Are we understood?"

My cadre gives me a round of murmurs of agreement. Kellan hurries out, muttering something inaudible under his breath. As August moves to follow him, I hold him back.

"You returned from roaming late these last two nights. It's not like you. Have you found some new venture to occupy your time?"

My eyes are keen, and August is too much of a novice at the art of deception to completely suppress the flicker of guilt that crosses his expression. Whatever it is he's been up to, he thinks I won't approve.

"I've just been restless," he says. "I took some long runs to work out that extra energy, like you suggested."

I hadn't expected him to take runs so long he hadn't returned when I finally took to my bed. Is there more to it than that, or is his guilt simply at the memory of how he lost control of his temper toward Kellan—and the fact that he needs to put that much effort into avoiding doing so again?

It would be much easier to fulfill my role if being lord came with the power of telepathy as well. But I've known August since he was a literal whelp, and I trust he wouldn't do anything he believed could harm the pack. Whatever he might feel guilty about, it's of a personal nature. I can be benevolent enough not to pry… for now.

"If anything should come up that you believe I should know, don't hesitate to come to me," I say.

He nods and lopes out—perhaps to take another of those runs.

Whitt heaves himself away from the chair with a chuckle under his breath. When I aim a sharp look at him, he gives me one of his wry smiles.

"For such a little mite, she's certainly opening the fault lines wide, isn't she?"

Then he saunters into the hall, leaving me stewing over how much truth there might be to that statement.

CHAPTER FOURTEEN

Talia

The knock comes just as I'm pulling my blouse over my head. Thankfully the rest of me is already dressed, other than I haven't fit the wooden brace around my leg yet. I tug the hem of the shirt down to the waist of my jeans and sit up straight at the edge of the bed. "Yes?"

"May I come in?"

Even if I didn't recognize August's mellow voice, I'd have guessed it was him simply from the fact that he asked first. It's not as if this is really *my* room.

"Of course," I say, and find I don't know what to do with myself.

August has never visited me in my bedroom before. He walks in with unusual hesitance, as if I might yell at him to get out despite what I said. As scary as he was when he attacked Kellan, he's never been anything but cheerful and considerate with me. That's probably why seeing his handsome face sends a flush over my skin like it does so often these days.

He might be kind to me, but he follows Sylas's orders. He's helping keep me prisoner. How can I have a crush on him? Apparently I'm still twelve somewhere in my head. Delayed development due to emotional isolation. That's totally a thing, right?

Labeling it as some kind of delusion doesn't make the effect go away, though. I just have to make sure I don't start *acting* like a swoony preteen. If I will the tickling heat away from my face, can I make it leave?

It was bad enough that I started throwing compliments at Whitt and snuggling into Sylas when I was drunk on that syrup. What would I have done if I'd run into August in that state?

"Are you already serving breakfast?" I ask. The typical kitchen smells haven't come trailing after him this morning. My head is still a bit muggy from my late night monitoring the sounds of the keep —I woke up earlier than I'd have liked, in the grips of a nightmare not quite loud enough to bring Sylas to my door.

"Oh, no, I'll be getting right on that as soon as I've talked to you." August smiles and shuts the door behind him, glancing back at it as if worried someone will notice.

A chill runs down my back. I can't forget that I barely know him. That he's fae, not human. That there's no way for me to be sure he'll be consistent in his kindness even when he's following his own conscience.

I curl my fingers into the bed covers, ready to shove myself onto my feet if I need to. But August doesn't make any aggressive moves. He walks closer, his smile slanting in a way that looks more sad than anything, and reaches into the satchel slung over his shoulder. He… winces? And then pulls out a small leather pouch closed off with a drawstring.

He tosses the pouch onto the bed next to me as if he can't get it out of his hand quickly enough. Even though it lands a couple of feet from me, I flinch.

"Sorry," August says quickly. "It's hard for me to handle that, even contained in the leather. It was hard getting it at all." He laughs a little sheepishly, running his hand through his dark auburn hair.

The pouch lies there on the duvet motionless. I eye it to make sure it isn't going to sprout little fangs or spew out spiders or some other horrible thing, and then I glance back at August. "Why? What's in it?"

"Salt." His mouth twists again as if even the word bothers him. "I had to go to the human world to get it. It and iron are the only two materials toxic to fae."

I was right about the metals then, but I don't know what to make of this gift. I pick up the pouch and tug it open with careful fingers.

It does indeed hold a teaspoon or two of chunky salt crystals, the mineral scent mingling with the musk of the leather when I lean close. My brow furrows. This doesn't make any sense.

"Why are you giving this to me?"

August ducks his head, a shadow darkening his golden eyes. "I don't trust Kellan. He's already pushing the boundaries, and he's made it clear he likes harassing you. There isn't enough salt in there to really hurt him, but if he comes after you, if you think he might hurt *you*, toss that in his face while you call for help, and it should get him to back off long enough for one of us to get to you and stop him."

It takes a moment for the full import of what he's said to sink in. He's giving me something that I could use against him and his colleagues. He's putting my security over his loyalty to his cadre and his lord—only in a small way, but more than it would ever have occurred to me to hope for.

I'm abruptly ashamed of my nervousness at his behavior. He was acting shifty on my *behalf*, not against me.

He raises his head to meet my eyes again, and I can't tune out the flutter that passes through my chest. He's earned that affection, fair and square.

"Thank you," I say. "It really means a lot. I guess…" I have to keep the pouch somewhere the others won't notice, but where I can easily grab it. I tuck it into the hip pocket of my jeans, making sure it's out of sight but with the cord right where a hasty finger could snag on it.

August clears his throat. "I also wanted to apologize. For the other day, with Kellan. I don't regret stepping in, of course, but I shouldn't have leapt straight into a fight. I was so angry, seeing him treat you like that—but then I scared you even more. That's the last thing I would have wanted to do."

He sounds so torn up about it that I immediately believe him. Without thinking, I scoot forward so I can reach for his hand. A flicker of surprise crosses his face, but he squeezes my fingers, and the longing to have him wrap his arms right around me, to envelop me in his protective intent, floods every other thought from my mind.

It takes me a second to find my words again. "It's okay. I know you were only trying to help." I'm not sure I was really scared of him in that moment or just tangled up in the memories of the wolves I faced before, the violence of that past encounter echoed in the fight in front of me.

August grips my fingers a little tighter and then lets them go. "Still. I won't let it happen again."

The pouch forms a soft pressure against my hip. He got it from the human world—from the world where I belong. The one I have to get back to.

After he's made a gesture like that, it feels like a betrayal to ask the question rising in my throat. But I have to know. "Whitt mentioned that the keep is on the fringes of the Mists. Did you have to go very far to get to the human world?"

"It wasn't any trouble getting there," August says. "The harder part was finding a bit of salt in a situation where I could grab it without having to come in too close contact. But that didn't take too long either." He beams down at me, his stance relaxed now that he's gone through with his minor mutiny and received my gratitude. "Things are hard enough for *you* without having to worry about that jackass tormenting you."

If I can get out of here, what Kellan wants to do with me won't matter anyway. I run my tongue along the backs of my teeth, searching for a way I can ask exactly which direction the human world is in and whether there's any special procedure to getting out of the Mists that won't tip him off to my hopes.

Maybe if I come at it in a roundabout sort of way…

"Whitt made it sound like it's a bad thing, living on the fringes," I say. "Like things haven't been so great for you since you moved."

August's eyebrows rise. "Look who's got the big mouth now. Yeah, we've had some troubles."

"But what's so bad about the fringes? I mean, if it lets you get to the human world quickly whenever you need something there…"

"As you've probably noticed, a lot of fae don't have the highest opinion of humans, so being close to them isn't seen as a good thing. What everyone wants is to be close to the Heart of the Mists. It's the source of our magic, and the closer you are to it, the more of that power you absorb. Living out here, after a while we can't work our magic quite as well."

The Heart of the Mists. There's a reverence in the way he says it that sends a tingle over my skin, as if the name itself holds a kind of power. I make a show of glancing around. "Where is the Heart compared to here?"

August waves his hand to the south. "We always build our fortresses so the main door faces it. In theory, that makes it easier for the power to reach us."

So, that means the farthest fringes—and the human world

beyond them—must be to the north. I smile at him, grateful and relieved despite the guilt nibbling at my gut underneath. "You must miss being closer to it."

"I do, but—it couldn't be helped. Sylas is doing his best to make things right. Kellan is always grouching about it, as if he wasn't even more involved in—"

August snaps his mouth shut before the rest of that sentence tumbles out. He makes an apologetic grimace. "You don't need to worry about that either. And, you know, I'm not the only one looking out for you. Sylas doesn't want you harmed either."

The faerie lord has done a lot more for me than any prisoner should really accept. I look down at the brace leaning against the end of the bed. My chest constricts with a sudden wave of emotion.

"Maybe he doesn't, but none of you would let me leave if I wanted to, would you."

I say it as a statement, not a question, and August obviously can't deny it. His expression clouds, his hands stirring restlessly at his sides as he searches for a response.

He doesn't confirm my comment, but at least he doesn't completely change the subject. "I guess you have family back there that Aerik stole you from."

Splashes of red on green flicker through my mind. My heart is suddenly thudding. I grip the edge of the bed and swallow hard. Stole me from them—that's one way of putting it.

"Yes." My voice comes out quietly, an uneasy tension coiling through my ribs. Who *will* I be running back to when I get my chance to escape?

Mom and Dad and Jamie are long gone. There was my aunt and uncle and the baby they had on the way—God, that kid will be eight years old by now—but they lived the next state over, if they're even still in the same town. I never knew their exact address. We only saw them a few times a year. My grandparents on Dad's side lived on the west coast, and only visited over the Christmas holidays. I'm not sure what city they live in. I don't even know their first names. And Mom's parents were all the way over in Greece. I only met them twice.

Of course, I'm coming at this all wrong. I'm twenty now, not twelve. Twenty-year-olds don't need family to take them in. They're supposed to get jobs and their own places to live, like adults do.

Thinking about all that makes my pulse thump even harder. I drag in a breath, and August steps close enough to grasp my shoulder tentatively before drawing his hand back just as quickly. "I'm sorry. I didn't mean to upset you now either."

"No, it's just—It's a lot to wrap my head around." I touch my pocket. "I really do appreciate the protection. And you just talking with me. That makes everything easier."

His smile returns, so pleased my heart aches at the sight. "Do you want to come help me whip up some breakfast? You're my best assistant."

I manage to laugh. "I'm not sure how high praise that is when it seems like I'm your *only* assistant." My insides still feel all tangled up. I inhale again, right to the bottom of my lungs. "I'll be down soon. I need a minute or two, if that's all right?"

"Of course, absolutely." He bobs his head to me and lopes out of the room with typical exuberance.

I find myself gazing toward the window—toward all that open space I still haven't gotten to experience, even though I'm so much more "free" than I was in my cage. What's going to be waiting for me in the world Aerik's cadre ripped me from more than eight years ago? What am I going to do once I get there—how am I going to *explain* any of what I've been through? If I say I was kidnapped by faeries, everyone will think I'm insane.

It doesn't matter. That's the world where I belong—the world where men-who-aren't-men won't be fighting over how to use my blood. I'll be able to figure things out one way or another. I just have to get there.

And now I know which direction to run in.

I strap the brace around my calf the way Sylas showed me, take a few testing steps to make sure it's secure, and then head out. I don't feel quite as steady as I did with the crutch, but the independence of not needing to hang on to an entire other object makes up for it.

Walking slowly, I feel no more than a slight pressure around my muscles, and the wooden strips across the base produce only a faint scuffing sound. I'll have to practice until I can eliminate that altogether.

As I come up on the bend in the hall, my balance wobbles. I catch myself with a hand against the wall—and an urgent voice filters through the door just behind me.

"Our forces managed to push them back, but there were a lot of Seelie losses. They're getting cleverer with their tactics."

My body goes rigid. I don't recognize that voice. It doesn't belong to any of the four men who've appeared to be the keep's sole inhabitants. I thought Sylas wanted to prevent anyone else from seeing me and possibly tipping off my former captors.

But maybe he's making arrangements for whatever he's going to do with me next, and that means setting aside a little of that caution.

What forces were pushing back who? It sounds like some kind of battle. I stay in place, my ears straining to make out the response.

Whitt's dry voice answers, terse in a way I've never heard before. "Has there been any recognition of our pack's contributions?"

"No mention of us so far. It's been pretty chaotic. I'm not sure how well they're keeping track of who's joined the patrols anymore."

Whitt lets out a sharp sigh. "Hang in there as well as you can. We're all worse off if those Unseelie bastards gain more ground. Is there anything I could send you back with that might give you an advantage, from what you've observed?"

"No, nothing so far."

"Well, if anything comes up, reach out to me at once and I'll see it done. Our lord will be glad for any chance of winning some glory in the conflict. You're dismissed."

Dismissed—the stranger is about to leave the room? My nerves jump, and I lurch farther away so clumsily my foot brace scrapes against the floorboards.

If I had proper use of both my feet, this would be where I'd make a dash around the corner to the stairs. But I don't, and I can only imagine the racket the wooden slats would make if I attempted a sprint—if I even manage to run rather than fall flat on my face after a few steps. I scramble forward as quickly as I can while keeping my balance, but I've barely moved when the door flies open.

Whitt storms out. He grabs my arm, yanking me around to face him. His ocean-blue eyes remind me more of a tsunami now, his fingers grasping painfully tight.

"What are you doing skulking outside my study?"

My mouth opens and closes. I can't seem to work any sound from my throat. "I—I—"

"Don't give me that wide-eyed act. I know you were out here listening."

He tugs me toward him, his grip pressing into my muscles exactly where Aerik's man used to clamp down as he readied to cut my wrist. The breath shudders out of me.

"Well?" Whitt demands, but I've lost my words completely. He glowers down at me. "If you're going to sneak around here like a crook, maybe it's time Sylas locked you up in that bedroom permanently."

A sharper surge of panic blares through me. To be shut off from the rest of the keep—to lose so much of the little freedom I've regained— What other punishments will they inflict on me? Maybe they'll think I don't deserve any better than a cage after all.

I gulp for air, trying to recover my voice, but my chest has constricted too tightly. A flood of cold washes through my body. My heart batters against my sternum. I'm suffocating like in that dream.

Help, I want to say. *Help, I'm drowning.* But I can't force my vocal cords to form the words—and I'm not sure Whitt would care anyway.

CHAPTER FIFTEEN

Whitt

The dust-destined girl twitches in my grasp like a rabbit in a snare. As shudders wrack her body, her wide eyes stare at me, so hazed with terror I'm not sure she's even seeing me. Her breath wheezes in her throat.

My fingers tighten around her arm, holding her from collapsing now. Is she having an attack of some physical ailment? Or are these dramatics just a way to get herself out of trouble now that I've discovered her lurking outside the room that holds my most closely guarded secrets?

It doesn't really matter which it is. If Sylas finds us like this, it's me he'll lay into for frightening her, even though *she's* the one who violated my privacy in my own blasted home. As if I'm not even owed one *room* to conduct my work as I see fit—meddling with my affairs—wretched female looking to gain any advantage—

I tamp down on my fury as well as I can. Heart take me, I don't have the patience for dealing with this, but I'd better find it before our glorious leader rains down twice as much on me.

And I'll work on finding it somewhere he isn't likely to stumble on us, thank you very much.

I tug the girl to the next door down: my bedroom. Better she see that space, as much of a mess as it no doubt is—I honestly don't know; I have better things to do than pay attention to the state of my bedcovers—than my office. Most important items in the office are tucked away or unintelligible to her human understanding, and Ralyn is long gone through the secret passage that allows direct transit between the room and outside, but I'd rather not take any chances. I hadn't expected to find this mite lurking nearby in the first place.

My bedchamber turns out to be in an even worse state than I would have predicted. Discarded shirts and slacks litter the floor, and the blankets slump over the side of the bed in a rumpled waterfall of fabric. One of my pillows has made it all the way to the other end of the room, and sitting on that pillow is a crumb-scattered plate I really should get around to taking back to the kitchen at some point. A couple of goblets rest nearby, one of them tipped on its side in a thin, sticky puddle of evaporated wine.

Perhaps it's been a tad too long since my periodic, manic tidy sessions.

At least the space doesn't outright smell, other than a fair tang of fermented fruit that some might consider almost pleasant. Not that my unintended guest appears to be in any state to draw judgments. She's still gasping, one hand pressed to her chest over her heart, the arm in my grasp shaking. Her heart is racing loud enough that I can hear its beat without even leaning close.

She really is terrified. If this is an act, it's a better one than I've seen any evidence she's capable of. I'd started to think she was made of stronger stuff than this. A couple of snappy remarks were enough to send her into a total meltdown…?

My mind trips back over the words I said, and understanding hits me. I threatened to have her locked in her room—shut away in one small space where she can't speak to anyone, can't even pretend she's an actual guest here. That bedroom Sylas gave her is leagues above the hospitality Aerik offered, but perhaps the suggestion of being caged at all was too much. And I did grasp hold of her rather brusquely on top of that.

It wasn't a huge offense, but there aren't many fae who'd come out of years of torment with their minds unscarred, let alone mortals.

My stomach twists, torn between shame over making myself an Aerik-like figure and irritation that I have to deal with this problem at all. If Sylas had just shipped the girl off to the arch-lords and let them decide what to do with her in the first place—

But she is here—he wants her here—so I must play with the hand I'm holding.

"Hey." I pitch my voice as low and soothing as I can manage, bending down so I'm on her level. What would Sylas say to calm her down? Or August—he's gotten awfully chummy with the mite. Let's see if I can channel my inner over-eager whelp.

"It's all right," I go on. "Nothing awful is going to happen to you right this minute. You startled me. We can talk about it—you can explain."

Talia sinks down until she's sitting on the floor. Tremors keep running through her body, but at least the wheezing is tapering off. It occurs to me that having her wrist still in a death-grip probably isn't helping the situation. I release her arm, hesitate, and give her an awkward pat on the back. "There, there. You've got nothing immediate to worry about. Everything in here is fine."

The statements ring hollow in my ears, but the girl's shoulders come down a little. To outright lie diminishes a fae's connection to the Heart of the Mists, so I avoid it as much as possible, but I do have quite a lot of practice at speaking around the truth in convincing ways.

She blinks at me, her eyes really focusing on me for the first time since the panic hit her. Another shudder shakes her scrawny frame. She braces her hands against the floor and drags in a deep breath.

"I—I'm sorry," she says. "I just—I couldn't help it—I couldn't *breathe*—"

I stay crouched across from her and cock my head. "But you can now. All's well that ends well?"

A shocked laugh tumbles out of her, so she must be nearly recovered. She rubs her hand over her pale face and into that shock of deep pink hair. It's the sort of vibrant hue you'd typically only see on the purest-blooded of fae. On a human, as natural as August has made it look, it's incongruous.

And yet I can't stop the memory rising up of that face lit with laughter the other day in the parlor, how lovely it became in the giddy glow of the cavaral syrup. Maybe if I gave her some more of that, she'd calm down faster, and I could enjoy that recklessly gleeful side of her again…

I clamp down on that thought and shove it away before it can even fully slip through my consciousness. She's not here for me to *enjoy* her in any way. I shouldn't even want to.

When the girl looks up at me, it's with an expression as if she still thinks I might toss her into a locked room and throw away the key—or perhaps even hit her. I wince inwardly. Did I really come across that vicious?

"I was listening," she admits, her shoulders hunching. "I heard a voice I didn't recognize, and I was confused, so I was trying to figure out what was going on. I only caught a little of the conversation."

I don't think Ralyn and I mentioned anything particularly sensitive. Nevertheless— "None of us here will take kindly to eavesdropping—not even Sylas would be pleased about it."

She nods. "Are you—are you going to tell him? Honestly, it's the first time. There's just so much about this place I still don't understand…"

The muddled little mite. I have to admit that if *I* were in a similar situation, I'd be listening at every door I could. She is resourceful and determined, even if her traumatized emotions sometimes get the better of her.

In some ways her bewilderment is Sylas's fault, for keeping her here while still holding her at a distance. How could she know what to make of us? So far we've barely decided what to make of her.

Thank the lands that soon enough she won't be our problem anymore.

"We can keep this first transgression between ourselves," I say, forming as firm an expression as I could manage. I'm not so practiced at that—usually I leave the authoritarian posturing to our lord. "But only this once. If you want to know something, you *ask*, and if we don't deign to answer, you weren't meant to know it. If I catch you spying again, I can't give it a pass as a mistake. Clear?"

She nods again, more vigorously this time, her stance slumping with relief. "Completely clear." Then she pauses. "Can I ask—who *were* you talking to?"

I almost guffaw at the balls on this smidge of a girl. I definitely will need to keep a closer eye on her while she's in our midst. "I can tell you that it was an expected visitor—by Sylas as well as myself—and while he'd mean you no harm anyway, I'm ensuring he never encounters you. That's all you're going to get. Now come along. You've got most of the keep to scamper around in still—you don't need the use of my rooms on top of that."

As I direct her to the door, her gaze darts around the bedroom, really taking it in for the first time. She's wise enough not to remark on the overall state of disarray. Good girl.

She scurries dutifully off toward the stairs. I pull my gaze away before I'm inclined to admire the slim curves that her body is shaping into or the deftness with which she's adapted to that brace on her foot. No doubt she's off to canoodle some more with August in the kitchen. There are several words I could say about his decisions in that regard, but it's not my place when it hasn't caused any real trouble *yet*, so I can manage to keep them to myself for now.

The encounter has left an uncomfortable edginess in my nerves, though. I'm in no mood to saunter downstairs and make small-talk around the table, which is all we *can* make with our "guest" looking on. I hadn't really wanted to be up this early to begin with, but duty called, and now I'm too awake for the bed to have any appeal.

Instead, I prowl back into my study, push aside the sliding bookcase, and speak the word to open the hatch only Sylas and I can access. I step into the narrow chamber on the other side, secure the shelves and hatch in place, and head down the tight spiral of steps.

At the base, another word magically unseals the door. I duck out, stretch my lips, and let my wolf spring forth.

The joy of how naturally my beast emerges from my skin at times like this only makes the memories of the wrenching transitions under the full moon more horrible in contrast. I set off at a trot, soaking in the warm breeze tickling through my fur and the banquet of scents my wolfish nose picks up even more easily than when I'm a man. I make a full circuit of our territory every day. It can't hurt to take it in earlier than usual this once.

A few of the faded pack members are already up and about. As I travel past their cluster of houses, they tip their heads respectfully to me. I eye the buildings, going over my mental tally of who remains and who I've sent to join the arch-lords' border patrols. Can we spare anyone else?

We need to keep some good fighters among us, of course. A pack that becomes too weak begins to look like prey to those with a hunger for conquest, and I happen to know through my contacts that there are at least a couple of lords who've eyed our domain.

Not because they want this fringe-land, but because Sylas has a reputation for being a powerful leader if no longer the official prestige, and it'd elevate anyone's status to say they cowed him.

The fact is, we can't send a large enough force to the arch-lords for them to be all that impressed anyway. They're as likely to see our meager contribution as a sign of how far we've fallen rather than how dedicated we are to their cause. No, our best bet will be if Ralyn or one of the others abroad susses out a strategy none of the others have picked up on. Wits can win the day as easily as strength if we use them right.

Or Sylas could present the gift of the girl, and then we wouldn't *need* to prove ourselves so much in other ways.

I pass into the forest, where the shadows drape the ground with patches of cool and the scent of pine fills my nose. I test it periodically for any taint of an intruder. About halfway through the stretch of woodland, I catch another wolfish whiff, but it's a familiar one—one of our sentries.

One of ours, and loping toward me. I veer off course to meet her and pull myself back into my regular form so we can speak.

As the sentry comes into view between the trees, she does the same. It's Astrid, gray-haired and wiry in both forms, her face just beginning the transition from wrinkled to wizened. She's getting to the point where I'd have pulled her off sentry duty so she can spend more time resting her old bones if I didn't know she'd sooner slash my face off than accept.

Astrid has fought in more skirmishes than I have, and she intends to fight alongside us until those bones give out completely. She wouldn't still be here otherwise.

"Is there trouble?" I ask.

She lets out a short huff. "Not yet, but I can smell the start of it. One of the Copperweld cadre was sniffing around the borders, wanting to know if we've had any human girls come wandering onto our territory. I told him no, but he looked as if he'd have made his own investigations if I hadn't showed my teeth."

Copperweld—that's Aerik's domain. My back tenses. "Good that you did," I say. "A lost servant is no excuse for them to intrude on our territory. If a human does ramble this way, let the keep know first."

She bobs her head in acknowledgment and slips back into the shadows, leaving me twice as uneasy as before.

Aerik's cadre is making inquiries all the way out here already. Do they specifically suspect us, or are we simply an easy target, one they had less concern about offending with their attempted imposition?

Either way, it amounts to the same thing: the mite is now bringing yet more trouble down on all our heads.

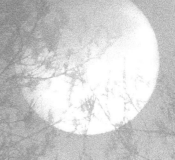

CHAPTER SIXTEEN

Talia

*A*fter another of August's extravagant dinners, Sylas catches my elbow on my way out of the dining room.

"Come with me?" he says with the inflection of a question but the air of a command.

As he leads me down the hall, my pulse kicks up a notch. Did Whitt mention my eavesdropping to the fae lord after all—is he going to rebuke me in some way he doesn't want his cadre to see?

Sylas doesn't show any sign of anger or disappointment, striding along in his usual powerful, assured way. I can tell he's keeping his speed in check so that I don't fall too far behind. The brace on my foot taps against the floor as I hustle along, not wanting to seem like I can't keep up.

When he heads down the steps to the keep's basement, a deeper prickling races beneath my skin. I haven't been down there except for a few baths in the small sauna room with its hot-tub-like pool. The thicker shadows and the cooler air that seeps through the wood make me uneasy, and when I pushed myself to explore a little farther once, I found the few other rooms along the hall were locked.

Not tonight. Sylas opens a door farther down from the sauna and motions me in. Two steps inside, I stop in my tracks, staring.

It's not that the contents of the room are so alien. No, what's startling is how familiar they are: a flat-screen TV, a shelving unit of DVDs, a device I don't fully recognize but can identify as some kind of game system. The shelves at the other side of the room are stuffed with paperback and hardcover books in regular human-style bindings. Sure, the wooden shelves and the unit holding the TV look as if they've grown right out of the walls rather than being constructed by regular means, and the long, curving sofa that stretches through the middle of the room is upholstered with what looks like woven willow leaves, but still. I haven't seen this much evidence that the world I remember really does exist since I was torn from it.

Tears I can't suppress spring to my eyes. I inhale slowly, trying to steady myself, and propel myself toward the sofa. "This is—why do you have all this stuff?"

One corner of Sylas's mouth turns up with apparent amusement. "We fae enjoy a variety of entertainment. If we can bring humans themselves over, why not their amusements as well?"

"I just—I wouldn't have thought—" I'm not sure I have the words to explain how bizarre it is imagining the imposing faerie lord chilling out in front of the latest Hollywood flick. If I found them, I'm afraid they'd end up coming out in a way that offends him.

"It's mostly August who plays the games," Sylas says, ambling past the TV. "Helps him work out some of his aggressive impulses. We have to replace the controllers rather more frequently than I'd prefer."

It's not difficult to imagine the exuberant fae man perched on the sofa with controller in hand, whooping in triumph as he kicks digitized ass in a fighting game or sports simulation. My own mouth twitches into a smile.

"What part of this collection is yours?"

Sylas motions to the DVDs. "Mostly the movies. A… past associate of mine introduced me to human cinema."

I step closer, peering at the spines. Some of the titles I don't recognize—movies that must have been from well before my time or that came out after I was stolen away—but others jump out at me. *Mean Girls. Zoolander. 17 Again. Legally Blonde.* They stir up memories of surfing through Netflix on sleepover nights.

I glance at Sylas, unable to stop my eyebrows from rising. "You like the comedies, huh?"

Is there a hint of embarrassment in his smile now? He laughs with a casual shrug. "I have enough drama and combat in my life here. It's fascinating how humans can make an entire story where nothing happens that really matters, and everyone ends up with what they deserve, happy or not."

Maybe *I* should be insulted by that assessment of my species' efforts, but I find it too funny that he likes watching this stuff at all. The comment spills out unthinking. "You'll have to catch me up on some of the good recent ones."

Sylas gives me a measured look as if trying to decide whether I'm serious. I can't really tell whether I am myself—it's impossible to picture sitting next to this regal giant of a man while he laughs at some slapstick joke and tosses back a handful of popcorn. Does he sit through the comedies with nothing more than one of those restrained smiles? Or maybe he does loosen up now and then… though that doesn't mean he'd want me seeing him like that.

In the end, he chooses not to address my remark at all. "Any time you'd like to relax in here, just let me, August, or Whitt know and we'll open the room for you. I thought you might need more to keep you occupied beyond acting as kitchen servant."

"I really don't mind helping with the cooking," I say quickly, in case he's gotten the idea that August pressured me into that job somehow. The faint pressure of the pouch of salt in my pocket makes me feel extra defensive of the younger man. Then I pause. "Why do you keep this room locked at all?"

Sylas's lips twitch again, but this time it looks like he held back a grimace. "Kellan has some strong opinions about anything to do with humans, as you've undoubtedly observed. He wouldn't go out of his way to damage what we've collected here, but if he happened to wander in when he's in the wrong sort of mood—it's easier to simply ensure that set of circumstances never occurs."

Then I'll be safe from that brute in here too. I'm liking this setup more and more. For however long I'm still staying in the keep, at least.

That last thought brings a gloom over me. I sink onto the sofa and pick up a video game magazine someone—August?—left tucked into the crease by the arm. My gaze skims over the computer-generated warrior on the cover, the bold headlines—and snags on the date of the issue beneath the title.

For a second, I just stare at it, my body rigid. Sylas looms closer, frowning. "Is something the matter?"

"How long ago is this magazine from?" I ask, my voice sounding distant to my ears.

"A moon or two ago," Sylas says, which I guess means a month. "You look as if something about it disturbs you."

"No—I mean, sort of—" An awkward laugh spills out of me. "I just didn't realize how long it's been. I was trying to keep track of the years while I was locked up in that cage. I thought I had. I thought it'd been only eight. But it's actually been nine."

I'm twenty-one, not twenty. Three hundred and sixty-five more days than I counted have passed since I lost my home.

It shouldn't be a big deal. What's one more year in the grand scheme of things? But the knowledge hits me like a punch to the gut.

Where did I miss it? How warped had my sense of time become while Aerik held me prisoner that I didn't catch on that it'd been far too long?

Sylas sits carefully on the sofa a couple of feet away from me. "I'm impressed that you managed to keep track even if not totally accurately," he says. "How did you determine the passing of the years?"

I twist a strand of my hair around my finger, pulling tight as if the sting in my scalp will offset the horror of those memories. "There was a night pretty early after they took me when I heard all this howling, loud enough that it reached all the way to the room with my cage. The next day the men said something about how they were glad they only had to bother with "it" once a year. And then it was ages, I almost forgot, until it happened again. I figured if it's something you all do once a year, then it was a way I could keep track."

"That was important to you."

I shrug, my head drooping. It seems like such a minor victory now that it's almost silly. "It was one small way I could hold on to *something* I understood. Knowing how long it'd been, how old I was… I was afraid I'd forget, so I marked myself as well as I could."

I hesitate and then ease down the waist of my jeans to where the thin scars mark the skin over my hipbone. Eight of them where there should be nine. "I must have been so exhausted on one of those nights I slept right through the howls. What is that racket all about, anyway?"

"The Wild Hunt," Sylas says. "You judged right—we take it up once a year. It's a sort of holiday, a celebration… The arch-lords race through the human world on horseback and the rest of the Seelie follow in our wolf forms. For some, it's the only time they venture among humans at all—a chance to snatch up new servants or whatever else they might want that they can't find here."

Servants they maybe treat only slightly better than Aerik and his cadre did me? Or that they treat *worse*, because those servants have no special blood to grant them a tiny respite? I shudder.

Sylas looks away. When his gaze returns to me, it's as solemn as I've ever seen it. His voice comes out even lower than usual, deep and grave.

"Our kind doesn't generally *hate* humans. Kellan is not the norm, and neither is Aerik. Many mortals live among us for a long time, mingle with our families, find some sort of place in our domains that they're satisfied with. August's mother was fully human, you know."

I'm startled by that revelation only for an instant. Suddenly all the kindnesses the other man has shown me makes a lot more sense.

"But mostly you—the fae—bring us here to be servants and things like that?"

He tips his head in acknowledgment. "I can't say the norm is to see humans as equals either. In most cases, your people are simply a means to an end."

"Like animals. Something you can own."

"Yes. Which isn't hate or hostility. It's just…" He sighs as if he's not sure how to finish that sentence. "But I have seen plenty of suffering too, and I don't wish to perpetuate that."

"You've given me a lot," I have to acknowledge. "You got me away from Aerik."

"But I'm also keeping you here, when no doubt the realms of the fae are the last place you'd prefer to linger."

He pauses and then turns to face me more fully. "Talia, I don't expect you to like what I'm doing or to approve of it. If there was a way that I could ensure security for my people without your presence, I'd escort you back to your home this second. But my entire pack depends on me, now more than ever, and this 'curse' affects all my Seelie brethren as well. With so much on the line, I can't let you go without more answers. But I promise I will give you whatever comforts I can to ensure you're *not* suffering, and that any decisions I make, they're not made lightly."

Something about that statement brings a lump into my throat. I hate that I'm still a prisoner, and I'm frightened of what's to come when he makes those decisions… but right now, at least, I'm not frightened of him. How could I tell him that my life should matter more to him than his own and that of all the people counting on him?

It does mean something that what happens to me matters to him at all, even if not as much as those other things.

"All right," I say, a rasp creeping into my voice.

He studies me. "In light of that, there's one request I'd make of you that I know you may recoil from. If we're to find another cure that works so that we can release you without losing that boon, I need to understand everything I can about your blood. I'd like to take a sample from you to test."

I flinch automatically, a jolt of panic racing through me—a rush of images: elbows and knees pinning me down, blue-white hair and daffodil-yellow, a glinting blade, the slice into my wrist. My lungs start to constrict like they did when Whitt made his threat the other day, but Sylas has spoken so calmly and gently that the sensation doesn't turn completely suffocating.

Closing my eyes, I travel away in my head to a bamboo forests and sublime mountains. After a few gulps of breath, my thoughts stop spinning.

He asked, rather than just taking. He's *not* like my former captors. And if he can figure out some alternate cure by studying my blood, then both our problems will be solved.

"Okay," I whisper.

Sylas's smile comes back, though the edges of it look pained. "You're made of strong stuff, little scrap. I thought I might put a movie on now—perhaps there's something in my collection you're familiar with?—and that would help take your mind off the procedure."

Is that why we're really here? I can't argue against his strategy. My gaze has already shot to the stack of movie cases, starving for something from home. "That sounds good."

As I get up to consider my options, a sharper awareness cuts through the muddle of my momentary panic. Sylas has opened up a lot. I should use this chance while he's feeling particularly generous to find out more that *I* need to too.

"You have a lot," I say as casually as I can manage. "I guess when you're close to the human world here, it's pretty easy to go back and forth?"

"It certainly wouldn't be much trouble if there's anything missing that you'd particularly like to see."

That's not quite what I'm trying to get at. I worry my lip under my teeth, pretending to be absorbed by the movie selection. "I wouldn't want you to have to waste your magic or whatever just getting me a movie."

The fae lord hums dismissively. "The boundaries aren't so solid as to need an enchantment to breach them. On the fringes, one can slip from one world to the next without even meaning to if one isn't careful."

Then I could slip through too, all on my own. Relief settles in my chest alongside a twinge of guilt at manipulating the conversation to my own ends. Of course, I doubt he'd have admitted that fact if he thought there was any chance at all that I could escape the keep to make use of the information.

"I think this one will do it," I say, pulling out a superhero parody Mom and Dad took me and Jamie to see in the theater not that long before Aerik ripped me away from my life.

Sylas pops the disc into the player, and I find myself frozen on the sofa, caught in a surge of more conflicting emotions than I can pick apart. The act of watching the movie is familiar and *right* but so distant from what I've been living through for almost a decade. I remember jostling with Jamie trying to grab the seat closest to the center of the row and Dad jokingly threatening to banish us to the back of the theater. The echo of salty, buttery popcorn laces my mouth.

It's a bittersweet distraction, but it does stop me from flashing back to my grimy cage. Sylas dabs a clear salve on my wrist to numb the skin, and I keep my eyes fixed on the TV screen as he cuts a small nick into my skin. I don't even check what he's collecting the blood in. It's barely enough time for the movie's characters to crack a few jokes and flub a heroic rescue, and then he's murmuring a spell over my arm that seals the skin, a kindness Aerik never bothered with.

"Thank you," the fae lord says, getting up. "I'll let you watch the rest of the film in peace. The door will lock behind you when you leave."

He brushes his hand over my hair in a gesture just shy of a caress, and that brief contact brings my awareness crashing back to the present with a flutter of my pulse. I watch him go, feeling abruptly tingly and wondering if I wouldn't have rather he stayed and watched with me.

I don't end up finishing the movie. It doesn't take long before the bitterness of the associations overwhelms any sweetness. Even in a superhero fantasy version of reality, there are far too many reminders of all the things I've lost that I might never get back.

When I emerge from the room, the keep is quiet. I creep up the two flights of stairs, practicing the steps that provoke the least noise from my foot brace. Singing voices filter through the walls; Whitt must be hosting another of his revels.

I *am* starting to feel a little more at peace, if not overjoyed with my situation, when I turn the corner and Kellan appears, his icy silver eyes glittering.

My heart stutters. I stumble backwards instinctively—not far enough. Kellan marches right up to me without hesitation and shoves me into the wall. He pins me there, glaring down at me, but with a smirk twisting his lips that shows he's as much delighted as he is angry.

"Going to cry for help, maggot meat?" he snarls under his breath, the light in his eyes almost feverish now. "We can find out how quickly one of my claws will slice out your tongue."

My body trembles. I grasp at the wall, wanting to make sure that when he lets me go—*if* he lets me go—I won't collapse. "Please. I just want to go back to my room."

"Hmm. Think you're so safe in there, do you? I could open that door if I wanted to. Imagine the fun we'd have then."

He bares his teeth and kicks my bad foot—not hard enough to break the brace but enough to send a lance of pain through the sinews. I gasp, and the stairs creak at the far end of the house.

Kellan jerks away from me and stalks off with his chin lifted haughtily.

I slump against the wall, hugging myself as if my heart might explode from my chest if I don't hold it in. No, I can't stay here. What if he comes back?

It's only when I've staggered into my room, gasping to fill my lungs, that I remember the salt. I could have used it, could have forced him to back off.

But would that really have helped anything? I'd have shown my hand, he'd demand that Sylas take it away from me, and I think Sylas would agree, even if he laid into Kellan for harassing me too. I've got to hold onto that gift until I *really* need it, until it's my only chance.

As I shake off my daze, I find myself staring blankly at the doorknob. What Kellan said about being able to unlock it comes back to me. It's magic that holds me in overnight, of course. Why would fae bother with keys when magic is something I can't steal?

But maybe…

I can't test the idea yet. I crawl into bed and tuck the covers around me, the shivers not quite subsided. My foot keeps aching. The ghost of Sylas's affectionate touch lingers on my hair, but the memory of Kellan's assault stays with me much more vividly.

It doesn't matter how kind some of these fae men are. They all want to use me in one way or another, it's only a matter of how painfully. I *have* to get out of here.

Time slips by. I might doze a little in the quiet of the keep. Then there's the faintest of footsteps outside my door. Someone stops to cast their magic.

After they've left, I count to one hundred in my head, and then do it again, and then again, just to be sure. When I'm convinced that whichever of my captors bespelled the lock must be long gone, I peel off the covers and limp across the room to the door, fishing the leather pouch out of the jeans I didn't bother to take off.

I pour the salt into my hand and press it against the fixture just below the knob. I hold it there until the coarse grains have bitten into my palm. Then I brush them back into the pouch and ever-so-carefully twist the knob.

It turns. I inch the door open a fraction of an inch, just enough to be sure, and hastily close it again. My heart thumps, but not with panic this time.

I can get past the locks. I can open the doors and leave the keep. I know which direction it is to the human world, and that if I go far enough, chances are I'll stumble into it.

There's nothing left to stop me but my captors themselves. I can't go while Whitt is partying with the pack outside—someone's bound to notice me, no matter how drunk or high they get. But he rarely gathers them two nights in a row.

Tomorrow... Tomorrow I could be free.

CHAPTER SEVENTEEN

August

The rain rattles against the parlor windows, blurring the landscape beyond them into a watercolor painting. It's a summer downpour, though, not a refreshing shower. With the panes closed, the air inside the keep has gotten uncomfortably humid.

My muscles itch to be active, but my wolf doesn't fancy a run in that muddy chaos. I roll my shoulders and head down the hall instead.

Kellan is prowling back and forth near the stairs, his mouth set in an even sourer scowl than usual. He catches my eye.

"We could be done with days like this if our 'lord' would get his head out of his ass. Much more of this, and I'll think that head's gone as soft as a rotten fruit."

My stance tenses, my jaw clenching. I manage to hold myself back from a growl. I *can* keep my temper, as much as this asshole tests it.

"If that's the way you feel, go ahead and bring it up with him, and we'll see how soft he is about that," I retort instead.

There's a feral air about him that I don't like at all. In the dim hallway, his eyes shimmer like coins through murky water. "You won't fight me over it because you know I'm right. Someone's got to make him see this dawdling is only going to screw us all over."

He's trying to provoke me. I don't need to dignify that statement with any response at all. It's true that it only rains like this on the fringes of the summer realm; in Hearthshire, we never had to deal with more than a pleasantly mild shower. But his solution isn't right at all. He wants to present Talia to the arch-lords like she's a doe cut down on a hunt. And he'd clearly like to take a few bites out of her first.

I turn my back on him and jog down the stairs to the basement, where I find the girl herself, poised stiffly just beyond the staircase. When she looks at me, the anxiety shining in her gaze sparks a rage twice as blazing.

"Did he chase you down here?" I demand.

Talia flinches, and I mentally cuff myself across the head for my tone. I still have to be careful how I let my aggression out around her. A beast is scary to witness no matter who its anger is aimed at.

I will my voice to even out and my balled hands to open. "If he's been hassling you again, you can tell me about it. Sylas will get him in line."

I hope so, anyway. Kellan's talk lately has been creeping too close to mutiny for my comfort. If he doesn't like his lot here, why doesn't he go back to the two-faced family he came from?

Because there's nothing but crumbs left of them, and he thinks he deserves better.

"Nothing's happened today," Talia says, which makes me wonder what's happened other days that I haven't witnessed. She did look as if she was limping more than usual this morning. "Is he gone yet? I just—I thought I'd go to the entertainment room after breakfast, but obviously I couldn't open the door, and when I was going to come looking for you or Sylas, Kellan was hanging around near the top of the steps…"

She doesn't need to explain why she didn't like the looks of that situation. I let out my frustration in a rough breath. "He's still up there, but I can open the room for you. And make sure the coast is clear before you head back upstairs."

"Thank you. But—were you going to use the room?"

So worried about imposing when we're the ones who've essentially imprisoned her in the keep. I offer her a reassuring smile. "Not at all. I was going to work out my urge to punch Kellan's face in a way that won't get me in trouble with Sylas. I've got a… what would you call it? A small gym down here."

Talia brightens much more than I'd have expected at that information. The eagerness in her expression takes her from pretty to stunning so abruptly my breath catches. I glance away for a second to make sure I don't come across as leering.

"For exercising?" she says. "Can I—can I see it?"

I grin back at her. "Sure. Allow me to give you the tour."

She follows me down the hall in the opposite direction from the sauna. I watch her steps from the corner of my eye, but not just to appreciate her slender form. She's *definitely* favoring her once-broken foot more than she normally is.

My fingers curl into fists. Maybe I won't plant one of those in Kellan's face, but Sylas can't complain about me informing him that the asshole must have been harassing Talia again.

Sylas asked me to keep the gym locked because there's equipment in here he wouldn't want Talia getting her hands on unsupervised—we use the space for combat training as well as pure exercise—but I can't see how she'll get into any trouble with the swords and daggers while I'm here. They're all shut away in the cupboard at the far end of the room anyway.

As we walk in, the lantern orbs in the corners of the ceiling light up with their orange glow. Talia blinks at them, still awed by the magic that's so ordinary to me. How ridiculous is it that she's spent so much of her life in our realm yet gotten to experience so little of what it can offer?

I want to see how her eyes would widen and her lips part in amazement if I took her out to the lunar tree grove to watch the flowers bloom and sing by moonlight. Or to the Shimmering Falls, where the water glitters like crystal and tastes sweet as fresh honey. I want to pull metals from the earth and show her how I can talk them into forming a blade or a bracelet.

But it isn't safe to let her leave the keep—for her or for us. And maybe that longing is beneath me. Whitt would scoff at me for being so keen to please *anyone*, especially a human girl.

I beckon for Talia to follow me all the way into the room. A thick layer of moss covers most of the floor, providing a firm enough surface for aerobic exercise and sparring with enough cushioning that no one's likely to break any bones if they take a hard fall. I like the rich loamy scent it adds to the air and the feel of it under my feet, dense but springy.

A leather punching bag dangles in one corner, the material mottled with thinning patches. That piece of equipment gets a lot of use. On the opposite wall, branches form bars at varying heights. Next to them rests a stack of metal weights. It's probably a good thing the weapons cabinet is closed, come to think of it, because I'm not sure Talia would have quite as enthusiastic a reaction to the space if she caught a glimpse of all those killing blades and the target dummy that's definitely seen better days.

She walks up to the wall with the bars and grasps one that's well above her head. I'm about to warn her not to strain herself when she hefts herself up, curling her back and legs so she can rest her feet on the bar's underside. Wiry muscles I hadn't realized were quite that strong stand out in her slim arms. She tips her head back to smile at me upside down, her hair streaming like a pink flame, and then flips back around, careful in her landing.

"Good to know I haven't lost the basics from lack of practice," she says. My surprise must show on my face, because a blush colors her cheeks. "When Aerik had me—I didn't want to let myself get too weak. I'd exercise as well as I could using the bars on the ceiling of the cage. I don't know how useful those muscles are for anything other than dangling off of bars, but…" She shrugs as if embarrassed to have admitted that much.

"Arm and shoulder strength like that can help you with a lot," I say quickly. "I'm impressed. You should have told me sooner you needed a workout space."

Her blush deepens. "It wasn't—I mean, it didn't seem as important— It's been amazing just getting to walk around, so I guess I was more focused on that." She waves toward the rest of the room. "Don't let me stop you from whatever you were going to do. Unless you wanted to use the bars?"

"No, go ahead, that's not where I'd usually start anyway."

As I meander toward the punching bag, I can't help watching her a little longer. Determination sparks in her eyes as she grips the bar again. There's no mistaking the enjoyment she gets out of putting her body to work. It warms me, seeing that. Thinking about how she managed one small act of resistance even while battered and starved in that filthy cage.

The small curves of her breasts rise beneath her shirt with the stretch of her arms, and a headier sort of warmth, one I don't let myself look at too closely, travels down my chest to my groin. I jerk my gaze away and train my attention on the punching bag. Now I've got more than one kind of energy I need to work out of my system.

It only takes a minute or two for me to shed the distraction of her presence and fall into the familiar groove of punches and side-steps. I weave one way and another, sometimes focusing only on the angle of my strikes and the force of the impact, and sometimes picturing Kellan's sour face and letting my fists fly with some of that pent-up aggression.

As I intensify the workout, I tug off my shirt like I typically do so it doesn't end up a sweaty mess. The perspiration that breaks out as I pummel the bag some more cools my skin. I've worked a satisfying burn into my arms and chest when I finally step back and take a breather.

Talia is still standing by the bars, but she's stopped her own exercises. I glance at her, worried that my violent display might have frightened her even when directed at an inanimate object.

When our gazes meet, the emotion in her eyes isn't anything like terror. No, there's a hunger in the dilation of her pupils—one I can taste a moment later in a faint musky tang that carries through the air between us.

She yanks herself around to grasp the bars again, flushing so darkly even her neck has reddened. A matching flush washes through me with a flare of my own desire. My wolf stretches within me, roused by the urge to stalk right over there and pull her into a kiss, dig my fingers into that vibrant hair, taste the sweat that shines on her skin. She's such a tantalizing mix of sweetness and strength...

By sheer force of will, I hold myself back. She might welcome the advance. She finds me attractive—I've sensed it in her bodily reactions as we've worked together in the kitchen, when I came to her with my offering of salt the other night. But no doubt she isn't sure what to do about it or even if it'd be safe for her to try to do something, considering she can't have had much experience in that area before Aerik stole her from her world.

The one small mercy she's had in the midst of so much torment is the result of more disdain: Aerik's pack has always recoiled from the idea of sexual relations with humans. They sneer at those who take on mortals as lovers—and those like me who are the direct result of a coupling like that. It appears the most intimate of violations is the one indignity they didn't subject her to. The problem is, it wouldn't necessarily be all that much safer for her to act on her desires with me.

The human lovers of the fae tend to meet dire ends. I should know.

The chill of that long-ago horror winds through my lust, dampening its heat. As much as my blood stirs at the thought, I can't offer Talia what she wants, what *I* want, especially when she's barely had a chance to explore what that even is.

If she builds enough courage to make her own advances, though... Heart help me, I'm not sure I could resist.

I heave another blow at the punching bag, but my fist glances off the side in my distraction. Is there a way I can make sure the attraction between us never reaches that point? A way that she could release her hunger just as I'm letting loose my aggressions into this sack of leather? A possibility rises up in my mind.

If I have the chance, I have to at least try—for both her sake and mine.

CHAPTER EIGHTEEN

Talia

In what I intend to be my last evening in the faerie realm, dinner centers around a large roast bird that looks like an elongated turkey, which August calls a "flame pheasant." I've got to say that his cooking means there'll be a few things I'll miss about this bizarre supernatural world. The pheasant's meat has a rich, smoky flavor that's so delicious I find myself licking the leftover juices off my fork.

For dessert, he serves bronze-skinned apples carved so they appear to be blooming out of rings of crisp pastry, topped with a dollop of cream. Be still my heart. I'd already planned on stuffing myself as full as I could tonight, since I don't know how long I'll need to find my way back to the human world—or how long it'll take me to secure myself another meal once I do—but I'd have gorged myself tonight anyway.

August had a few apples left over in the kitchen after his carving and baking. As I lean back in my chair, savoring the caramel-sweet aftertaste lingering in my mouth, I consider asking him if I can take one up to my room. I could say I sometimes wake up in the middle of the night hungry, and I know he'd jump at the chance to get more nourishment into me. Then I'd have a little food to bring on my uncertain journey.

But Kellan's gaze pauses on me more than once with its usual cold glint. I've never asked for more food after a meal before. I should have thought of that, established a pattern—now any deviation from my normal routine could rouse suspicions.

I'll be okay. *Someone* in the human world will have to be willing to help me… right?

Will I even come out in the same town I was taken from? There's no reason to assume I will. What if I end up in some country where I can't speak the language? Or hundreds of miles from civilization in the Amazon jungle or the Antarctic tundra? I dreamed of traveling to epic landscapes like those, sure—but with proper preparations and supplies. Stranded with nothing but the clothes on my back and a permanently injured foot, it'd be less an adventure and more a catastrophe.

My pulse thumps faster. I get up, letting the rasp of the chair legs against the floor cover my shaky inhalation. Whatever happens, I'll figure it out. I have to try. If I stay here, I'm pretty much guaranteed to meet an even worse fate, aren't I?

August has already swept around the table to clear the dishes. He meets me in the hall with a playful little bow, so attentive in his enthusiasm that I can't suppress a pinch of guilt at the huge secret I'm keeping from him. Maybe he'll be glad when they wake up and find me gone, though. He's doing what he feels he has to, but he obviously doesn't like that they're keeping me captive.

"Shall we descend to the sauna?" he asks.

Oh, right, this is a bath night. I hesitate, but it isn't as if I can make my escape yet anyway. From what I've gleaned about their schedules, the four fae men won't all retire to their bedrooms until the early hours of the morning. A soak in the hot water might even do me some good. Since Kellan's assault yesterday night, my foot's still aching more than usual.

"Of course." I give him my best everything-is-perfectly-normal smile and walk with him down the stairs to the basement.

My bathing routine requires a bit of an awkward arrangement. After my difficulties with the tub upstairs, Sylas didn't want to risk that I might lose my balance on the slippery floor and injure myself with no one around to hear me call for help. So, while I take my bath in the little in-ground pool, August sits on a chair behind a folding screen he set up, giving me most but not all of my privacy.

Sometimes it's nice having someone to talk to, and I've wobbled on the slick tiles enough times to appreciate the security of the measure too. But when my thoughts take a darker turn, his presence only reminds me of how much I *am* still a prisoner, as much as we might like to pretend otherwise.

Inside the sauna room, August dips his head to me and takes his spot behind the folding screen. I sit on a stool to take off the wooden foot brace and then peel off the rest of my clothes. Steam floats through the small room, condensing on my bare skin. I drag it into my lungs, some of the tension I've been holding in easing in the humidity's embrace.

Gripping the edge of the pool, I limp down the steps. Now that I've gotten used to the brace, I can't ignore how uneven my gait is without it. Sylas has aided my escape without even realizing it. I just hope someone in the human world will be able to look at it and figure out how to construct something similar for when my current one wears out or breaks.

The water closes around me all the way up to my chin, hot enough to melt even more of my uneasiness. It holds a slight salty scent, but not enough that it stings if I rub my eye with a wet hand. I tip my head back, my hair floating around my shoulders like pink seaweed. The currents propelled by the jets beneath the surface of the water tickle across my waist.

For a few minutes, I drift in pure indulgence. Then I grab the soap from its dish near the steps and get to work on the actual washing. The bar gives off a welcoming smell like a summer forest with all the vegetation at its most vibrant, and it lathers quickly between my hands.

I massage the bubbles into my hair down to the roots, dunk my head several times to rinse it out, and then rub every other inch of my skin. I'm never again giving anyone the opening to claim that I stink if I can help it.

I'm business-like about it, my awareness of August's presence never fading, but when my fingers brush over my breasts, a quiver of giddy sensation runs through my chest. Closing my eyes against it doesn't help one bit. The memory rises up of seeing August in the basement gym this morning—of the sculpted muscles flexing beneath his sweat-damp skin, the power with which he wielded them, his rhythmic breaths in time with his movements. The look in his eyes when he caught me watching him, their golden gleam turning molten.

More heat than I can blame on the water courses through me now, leaving me dizzy. I suck in the steamy air.

"Are you all right?" August calls from behind the screen. The genuineness of his concern only puts me more off-balance.

"Yes," I say, and grope for something to steer my wayward mind in a less provocative direction. "I— Sylas told me your mother was human."

There's a momentary silence and then a startled but not offended chuckle. "He did, did he? Did that surprise you?"

I consider. "I don't think I know enough about fae to have any idea whether that's a surprising thing."

"It's not—not really." His chair squeaks, and I picture him leaning back in it. "Pure fae are essentially immortal when it comes to old age, but the trade-off is they struggle to have kids. So ages ago, when one or another got a hankering for an heir, sometimes they'd steal away a pretty lady or handsome gentleman to help with that process. At this point, I doubt there's any of us that haven't got at least a bit of human blood in there somewhere, even if some turn up their noses at the thought."

"But that's not the only way fae have kids," I say. "Sylas and Whitt and Kellan—they didn't have a human parent, did they?" I'm assuming Sylas would have mentioned as much instead of just August's if they had.

"It isn't the only way," August agrees. "Now that there's been so much intermingling, it's not even all that common. The faded fae— which is most of us, with blood that's already quite mixed—don't have as much trouble producing children. And now and then those pure enough to be called true-blooded manage it despite the odds. That's why Sylas is a lord and Whitt and I aren't. Our father had him with his soul-twined mate, both of them true-blooded, so Sylas is as well. Whitt and I came from lesser dalliances."

Hold on a second. "You're all *brothers*?" They do have similar builds, and they're all gorgeous in their own ways, but they have such different coloring the possibility never occurred to me.

August laughs. "He didn't mention that part, then? Yes, we're half-brothers. Well, all of us except Kellan. That's typically how a lord forms his cadre—with his faded siblings and sometimes those of his mate…"

He trails off into a sudden silence, as if realizing he might have said too much. I watch the surface of the water ripple in front of me. "If Kellan's not related to Sylas, why did he include *him*?"

"They are related, in a way," August says evasively. "Why are you asking all this, Talia? You don't have to— I mean, none of us would force you to… end up in a situation like that."

His energetic voice has turned abruptly awkward. A situation like what—like getting pregnant by one of them? Is *that* what he thinks I'm wondering about?

My cheeks burn, but a flutter passes through my belly. Now I *am* thinking about it—about the act that gets women pregnant, anyway. About what it'd be like to have August touch me, take me as a lover. So much for finding an unprovocative subject.

"No," I stammer. "I wasn't—I wasn't thinking that. Not that way."

Perfect. Now that begs the question of how I *was* thinking about it.

Before I can find the words to dig myself out of the hole I've unwittingly tumbled into, August clears his throat. When he speaks, his tone is as gentle as I've ever heard it. "It's all right. What you've felt, what you've wanted. Totally natural impulses for any living creature to have, fae included."

Does he *know* about the kindling of desire I've experienced when he's around? Oh, that's a silly question, isn't it? If I could pick up on some sign of those desires being returned when I've got no experience with those urges at all, how obvious must mine have been to him? Augh. Maybe I should drown myself to avoid any further embarrassment.

"We don't have to talk about it," I mumble.

"I didn't want to put you on the spot. I just—" He draws in an audible breath. "It might be easier for you if you have another way of… addressing those feelings, without me or anyone else involved. And from what I understand, the pool is a rather good place for that."

Despite my mortification, curiosity nips at me. My voice comes out even quieter. "What do you mean?"

"I gather the jets can be, ah, very stimulating to females, if you place yourself so the water moves between your legs."

If my face was burning before, it's a wonder it doesn't outright incinerate now. At least August sounds equally—and adorably, damn it—self-conscious about the subject. And I can't help wondering how he found out this fact about "females." How many women has he brought down here, fae or otherwise?

I don't actually want the answer to that question.

Possibly the only sensible thing to do would be to climb out of the water and scrub this entire conversation from my mind as thoroughly as I can. But with his words, a tingling has shot through the sensitive parts at the apex of my thighs, and I can't help wavering.

This is my last night among the fae—or at least, if I don't make it, it's my last night with anywhere near this kind of freedom. I don't have anywhere else to go just yet. Why *shouldn't* I take advantage of this moment, do something that's insensible— something that might be very enjoyable if the clamoring of my bodily instincts can be trusted.

August doesn't think there'd be anything wrong with it. He wouldn't have suggested it otherwise.

I move through the water to one of the circular protrusions that shoots a stream of water into the pool. When I'm standing in front of it, the current strikes the top of my belly. I ease closer and hook my elbows over the edge of the pool to pull my body upward.

The jet ripples down my belly and hits the sensitive folds below. A bolt of sensation races through me, so intense a gasp tumbles from my mouth.

And it doesn't stop. The intensity builds, pleasure swelling from that spot down through my hips and up to my chest with every passing second the pressure continues. I've never felt anything this *good* in my life.

I grip the tiles harder, my head slumping forward. I want to hold on tight; I want to let go. I'm not sure which of those impulses even makes sense.

The heady surge of sensation seems to reach its peak. It continues radiating through me with the lick of the current against my sex, gripping me with a demand I don't know how to fulfill. I need *more*. There's something just beyond my reach. My whole body quakes with the longing, but I have no idea how to get there.

The need is desperate enough to cut through my embarrassment. My voice comes out hoarse. "August, I— I don't know— It's not enough—"

He manages to piece together that frantic jumble well enough to figure out what I'm asking. "You could add your hand?" he suggests, low and rough, as if he's as affected as I am.

I shift my weight so one elbow can hold me up and dip the other arm beneath the water. My fingertips glide over the spot just above my folds, and my body lights up as if I've struck a match inside me. Oh, yes, that's it.

I press against my hand, my breath spilling over the tiles, my hips straining to reach that higher peak I haven't yet discovered but can sense lies so, so close. The pleasure blazes through me faster.

Closing my eyes, I find myself imagining August is standing in the warmth of the water beside me, that it's *his* hand stroking over me. His fingers exploring this tender part of me.

The thrill of that idea sweeps me to even greater heights. My breath shudders. I rub myself with a little jerk, the current still gushing against me, and it's like a firework erupts from within. It bursts through my body, shocking a cry from my throat and quivering across every nerve.

In the aftermath, I sag against the pool wall. The bliss fades, but echoes of it still ripple through me. I feel wrung out with delight, all that urgency released—and yet a pang rises up inside me with the desire to do it all over again.

Did the release make the feelings August was trying to help me work through better or worse? I can't tell. But, oh, I don't think I can say I regret it either way.

"Talia?" August says tentatively, bringing my attention out of my body. How long have I been floating there, reveling in the moment?

I lift my head and drop my feet to rest them on the pool floor. "I'm fine. I'm… good."

That simple statement must convey a lot more than just the words, because August's response comes out so heated it sends a tingle straight to my core. "I'm glad to hear that."

He must have heard a lot. I made at least a few sounds during that... interlude, or whatever I should call it.

A fresh flush creeps across my cheeks, but it's not quite as intense as before. Apparently I've burned through some of my capacity for mortification.

I glide through the water to the steps and clamber out. While I towel myself off and dress, August stays behind the screen, but every particle of my body is aware of him there. Everywhere fabric grazes my skin, new tingles race through me.

He was on the other side of the room, he couldn't even see me, but somehow it feels as if he really was right there with me, boosting me to pinnacles of pleasure I'd never imagined.

When I'm dressed and strapped into my foot brace, I tug at the hem of my shirt, anxious about looking him in the face after all that. "I'm done."

August steps out, his eyes smoldering the moment they meet mine. For a second, I can't breathe.

He walks over to me like he's stalking his prey. I brace myself automatically, but I find I'm not actually scared of him. Even if I should be.

He stops a couple of feet away, his muscles flexing with restrained power. If anything, his gaze has only gotten more intense. I'm caught in his golden stare. It doesn't feel like such a bad place to be. A flicker of my earlier giddiness returns, coursing through me from head to toe.

August licks his lips, and my gaze follows the movement. "I thought giving you an outlet would make resisting easier," he says in that same low, strained tone. "It turns out I was wrong. You have no idea how badly I want a taste of you—just *one*."

As if the words are a magnet tuned to me, my body sways

toward him unbidden. His control snaps with a groan. He cups my face and captures my mouth, the scorching press of his lips setting off a rush of sensation even more intoxicating than anything I summoned alone.

It can't be more than a few seconds of that dizzying paradise before he wrenches himself away, his hands dropping to his sides. I just barely restrain myself from snatching after him to yank him back.

"Just one," he says again, as if trying to convince himself. He inhales deeply and seems to get a grip on himself. "Maybe I should let you go on upstairs by yourself."

Yes. This can't be anything more than it just was. But I don't want him to think he's violated me in some way, especially when this might be the last chance I have to clarify that.

"Thank you," I say, as emphatically as I can, holding his gaze with a fervent smile so he knows I mean for everything.

As I slip out of the room and head to the stairs, it occurs to me that the list of things I'll miss about this place has just gotten longer.

CHAPTER NINETEEN

Talia

I sit with my back against the wall next to the bedroom door so I can hear the comings and goings in the hall as clearly as possible. In the afternoon, I napped as long as I could to make sure I wouldn't inadvertently fall asleep now, but I still have to jerk myself into alertness a couple of times when my eyelids start to droop.

When footsteps pause outside, I hold my breath. There's a murmur so faint I can't make out the word, and then whoever that was moves on. The door must be locked now—until I put my salt trick to use.

I was right that Whitt wouldn't be hosting another party tonight, but I'm guessing he's the one who takes the longest coming up to the bedrooms. I'm shuffling my feet against each other to keep me awake when the final set of footsteps finally reaches my ears, rounding the corner to the rooms where the fae men sleep.

Of course, going to bed doesn't necessarily mean dozing off just yet. I wait longer, anticipation buzzing through my nerves, my pulse already hiccupping.

I'll only get one chance. One chance, with no idea what really awaits me once I leave the keep. What if Aerik or someone from his cadre is prowling around out there? What if I stumble out of the Mists into a human war zone?

I press my hands against the floor to steady myself. Whatever happens, happens. All I can do is take it one step at a time. I *can* do this.

When the keep has been silent for long enough that my skin starts to itch with impatience, I wait a few minutes more. Then I ease onto my feet. The fae might have good hearing, but surely a few small sounds won't be enough to wake them.

The salt crystals hiss into my hand. I push them against the knob like before, and a quiver of energy darts through me. A few of the crystals crumble into a dust so fine I can't see it after it falls from my hand.

I snatch the rest back against my palm. When I peek at the salt, it looks like I've lost almost half of the meager amount I started with. Counteracting the magic must damage the crystals in the process.

What if this isn't enough to get me through the outer door too?

I drag in a shaky breath and fight off the suffocating sensation rising through my chest. I won't know until I try.

After dropping the remaining salt into the leather pouch for safe keeping, I edge the door open so slowly the hinges don't make the slightest squeak. I close it behind me, knowing that the appearance of me still being inside could buy me vital minutes or even hours if one of my captors walks by, and head for the staircase with carefully even steps. My fingers squeeze the pouch tight.

As I make my slow, measured way down the hall, the foot brace only rasps faintly against the floorboards a couple of times. Both moments make my heart lurch, but its thudding is the only answering sound I hear. No one stirs in the other rooms.

The stairs are trickier to handle silently. I grip the bannister and lower my warped foot first, making sure it's stable, and then set my sturdier foot down beside it. I probably look like a toddler taking her first steps, but about a century later, I'm finally on the main floor.

I'd thought I'd slip out through the back door, which I've studied plenty of times from the kitchen and which is closer to both the stairs and my eventual destination. But when I try the kitchen door, I find that's locked too—maybe to ensure I don't go scavenging for butcher knives in the middle of the night?

I hesitate outside it, clutching the pouch of salt, and then push away. I can't risk using up what power the crystals still contain getting into the kitchen and then not making it outside from there. The front door it is.

The evening's bath might have soothed the pain in my foot a little, but by the time I reach the expansive entrance room, an ache has already formed right where the bones are set wrong. Maybe I should have brought the crutch for extra support, but I can't risk going back for it now.

I'm not letting myself think about how much farther I might need to walk, or how much more my foot might hurt by the end of all this. I won't think about anything except getting past that door.

Once I'm away from the keep, at least I can vary my gait a little without worrying so much about keeping quiet. If I get to the forest past the fields to the north where I'll have some shelter, I might even find a branch I can use in place of the crutch.

I creep across the thick rug through the darkness. As I reach the broad door, I pour the last of the salt out of the pouch. I press it against the handle, willing it to work.

The crystals fragment against my skin, powder drifting from my grasp and wisping away. When I tug on the handle, it gives. My spirits leap, a smile stretching my mouth. I pull harder, my eyes fixed on the crack where the fresh night air will flood in over me—

A body hurtles at me, crashing into my side and slamming me to the floor. My head smacks the boards at the edge of the rug. Pain splinters through my skull, and a yelp of surprise and agony bursts from my lips for an instant before a heavy hand slaps against my mouth. Sour breath spills over my face.

"Thank you, little dung-body," Kellan snarls under his breath, barely visible above me other than the manic silvery sheen in his eyes. "Thank you for proving me right. We'll see how much you like the results, won't we?" He grins, a faint glint catching on teeth partly curved into fangs.

The hard weight of his body crouched on top of me sends me spiraling back to the times when my former captors would pin me down as brutally as they could manage. My lungs seize, panic hazing my vision. My limbs start to flail, but Kellan rams his elbow into my ribs, leaving me gasping. He wrenches both my arms off to the side under his free hand. The knobs of his knees dig into my thighs.

Claws prickle against my wrists and over my cheek where he's clamped down on my mouth. He digs them in deeper, enough that a cool trickle of blood seeps over my skin. His eyes flash brighter. His mouth opens wide, fangs growing, jaw extending—and a pounding of feet from down the hall jerks his attention away.

His grip prevents me from turning my head to see, but there's no mistaking Sylas's voice. "Get off her, Kellan. *Now.*"

"This piece of maggot-meat was about to walk right out that door, Sylas," Kellan says. "*That's* what she thinks of all the effort you've put into your hospitality." He raises his hand from my mouth and curls his fingers. "Let's make sure she doesn't have anything like a chance again. I think I'll start by scratching out those eyes and then snap off both her feet for good measure."

A wordless wail tears from my throat. I whip my head to the

side, squeezing my eyes shut, feeling his muscles shift and the air brush my face as he swings his clawed hand—

With a lurch, his weight falls off me. There's a growl and a snapping of jaws, bodies thudding against the floor.

My eyes pop open to see two huge wolves now wrestling each other on the floor just a few feet away—the one now on top dark furred with one eye scarred through, the one attempting to heave him off paler and leaner.

I shove myself backward, but there isn't very far to go. My shoulder hits the wall. I flinch, the panic tightening around my lungs, the lack of air dizzying me.

The Sylas-wolf lunges for the Kellan-wolf's neck, but Kellan twists away at the last second and slashes his lord's muzzle. They roll, Kellan getting the upper hand only for a moment. A second later, Sylas hurls him back against the floor. Blood flecks the paler wolf's fur. Like the blood—like the blood—

I clutch myself, longing for an image of a peaceful landscape to retreat into, unable to tear my attention away from the chaos before me.

But it's almost done. This time, Sylas manages to jam his paw against the underside of Kellan's chin. His claws rake bloody lines down to the other wolf's throat. With a ripple of his body, he's a man again, holding the struggling wolf down with his still-clawed hand like a vise around Kellan's neck, a feral glimmer in his unmarred eye. A jagged cut slices across his temple, bisecting one of his tattoos.

"*Yield*," he demands, half growl, half bellow. "Yield, and you can leave with your life. By the Heart, Kellan, don't force my hand. You know Isleen would never have wanted this."

Kellan glares up at him, his teeth still bared, holding his wolf form. His muscles tense. He has to be able to see he's beaten, doesn't he?

Maybe he does. Maybe he just doesn't care.

His wolf appears to go limp as if in submission. Sylas starts to release his choke-hold—and Kellan flings his body to the side. Not slashing out at the larger man. No, he whips his head around, his fangs and claws aimed at *me*.

One paw scrapes across my ankle, smashing the thin slats of the brace into splinters and carving through my flesh. Agony spikes up my leg. I heave sideways on my shaking limbs, not fast enough to outpace those gaping wolfish jaws descending on me.

But I don't have to outpace them. Sylas springs, grabbing Kellan's throat and slashing through the jugular with one powerful stroke.

Blood gushes down the beast's chest. Kellan slumps onto the floor inches from my feet. His life flees him with a grotesque gurgle and a twitch of his furry limbs.

In another shudder, he's shifted back into the man with the sallow orange hair and silvery eyes. Those silvery eyes don't gleam at all now. They just stare dully at me, unblinking, while a scarlet puddle spreads across the floor beneath his head.

I push myself farther away, along the wall toward the door, a tremor wrenching through me. He's dead. Completely and utterly dead. My stomach lists queasily.

I've never watched anyone die before.

He died—because Sylas killed him. The fae lord kneels over the other man, his chest heaving. His claws retract into his bloody hands. He can't seem to tear his eyes away from his former comrade, his face stiffening in a mask of horror.

He slit his cadre member's throat for *me*. To save me from being mangled by those fangs and claws.

As my stomach lurches again, a draft of cool air licks over my arm. My gaze slides from Sylas to the front door, which is standing ajar. Darkness and the rustle of the breeze over the fields beckon from beyond it.

I could still make a run for it. I'm bleeding and my brace is broken, my pulse is thundering and my breath still coming short, and maybe Sylas would give chase—but I have some kind of chance. For all I know, I might stumble out of the Mists into the human world just a few feet from this building.

Staring at the sliver of freedom, my body recoils.

I could dash out there into darkness and uncertainty, into a realm where every other being I meet might happily throw me back in a cage, chop me up, or worse—and if I'm lucky, scramble beyond it to a world I don't know how to even start belonging to. Or I could stay here, with the only people who've shown me any kindness in nine long years. With the man who just killed one of his own rather than see me blinded and hobbled.

How can I really say I'll be safer out there than Sylas has just proven I am within these walls? Whatever his reasons for detaining me, he won't allow this prison to destroy me, no matter how much *he* has to sacrifice.

And it was a sacrifice. When I look at him again, his anguish is still plain on his face. I'm not sure how much he actually *liked* Kellan, but he definitely didn't like killing him. To the very last, he tried to avoid that ending.

But when push came to shove, he chose me.

My head swims, exhaustion and emotion welling up inside me. Then a determined impulse pierces the rest, driving me onward.

I half-limp, half crawl around Kellan's limp body to come up beside Sylas. His head has drooped as he reaches to shut his comrade's eyes. I hesitate and then extend a shaky hand to touch his shoulder. My voice comes out in a raw whisper. "I'm sorry."

The fae lord's gaze jerks to me. He blinks at me, looking momentarily, unnervingly dazed. A furrow creases his brow. He opens his mouth, and I have the sense that he's summoning his voice from deep down inside.

"*You* have nothing to be sorry for."

"I'm sorry you had to—I'm sorry it ended up like this."

His mouth twists, not a smile but maybe a shadow of one. "It was a long time coming. The worst you did was speed it up a little."

He hefts himself to his feet, and for the first time I notice the other men in the room. August and Whitt come up to join their lord. They must have been here all along—they'd have heard my cry and the scuffle at the same time Sylas did. They hung back while he decided what justice to deal out, as I guess he would have wanted.

Sylas considers the partly open door and the leather pouch that fell from my hand next to it. "I don't suppose you'd enlighten me as to how exactly you removed the magical seal from the lock?"

I suck my lower lip under my teeth. That's not just my secret but August's too.

The sight of the pouch must tip the younger man off, though, and he's loyal enough to own up. "It must have been—I didn't think—I was only trying to give her a way to fend off Kellan after he kept harassing her—"

Sylas turns his impenetrable stare on August. "Just spit it out. What did you do?"

August winces. "Salt. I gave her salt. Only a little."

Whitt lets out a hoarse guffaw. Sylas's lips pull back with a hint of a snarl, but his voice stays even. "We'll deal with that blunder later. For now, we'd best prepare our cadre-fellow for his final send-off."

CHAPTER TWENTY

Talia

They perform the funeral indoors in the same room where Kellan met his end. From snippets of overheard conversations I'm not totally included in, I gather that isn't typical, but Sylas thinks it's best not to reveal Kellan's death to the rest of the pack just yet because of the questions it would provoke.

Thin morning sunlight streams from narrow skylights in the vaulted ceiling. Sylas and his remaining cadre stand around Kellan's body, wrapped now in a thick gray shroud in the middle of the space. The leafy fronds of a fern-like plant circle the corpse, their cut stems giving off a pungent herbal odor. The blood that spilled by the door—his and mine—has been wiped from the floorboards.

No one asked me to witness this ceremony. I could have stayed in my bedroom or tucked myself away in the parlor as if it wasn't happening. But I can't shake the gnawing awareness that Kellan died at least in small part because of me. My presence pushed him over whatever edge he'd been teetering on into territory Sylas couldn't accept; my escape attempt brought those tensions all the way to the surface.

I might have thought of him as a monster; I might not be the slightest bit sad that he's gone, but I won't pretend away his death or my role in it. The others should know I'm not that much of a coward. Sylas should know how much I really do recognize his grief.

I stayed here rather than running, and I still think that was the best choice I could have made, but I don't want the fae lord to regret it. I'm still not sure exactly what last night's events are going to mean for me going forward. For now, I'm here, watching from the far side of the entrance room, present but not participating.

Sylas, standing by the head of the corpse, lets his powerful baritone carry through the air. "As lord and cadre-fellows to Kellan of Oakmeet once Thistlegrove, we honor the last of his time in this world and convey him to his end. He has stood with us in combat and never shied away from a threat."

"He was generous with his advice whether it was wanted or not," Whitt contributes, earning him a sharp look from the fae lord.

The tense set of August's jaw suggests he's having trouble coming up with anything at all positive to say for his colleague. "He was firm in his convictions," he says finally, his mouth slanting closer to a frown.

It's a good thing I'm not expected to speak. I'm not sure a compliment like *He had a way with insults* or *He really knew how to terrify a girl* would go over well in this context.

Sylas lifts a sparkling goblet. "As kin to my mate, I recognize him as family and send him off as family. May the summer sun embrace him with all its warmth."

My gaze flies to his face. Kin to his *mate*?

August said Kellan wasn't related to Sylas like he and Whitt are —that he had another reason for joining the cadre—but if Sylas has a mate, where is she? Why hasn't anyone mentioned her?

Why does something drop out of the pit of my stomach at the thought? It isn't as if he ever—or I ever wanted— Maybe he's set off some of the same feelings August has in me, but I wouldn't have expected them to lead anywhere. I don't think I'd even hope for it to.

Would I?

Sylas drizzles a shimmering liquid from the goblet over the shroud. The fabric lights up for a few seconds before swallowing the glow.

Whitt and August bend down and move several of the fronds so they cover Kellan's body from his feet to his shoulders. Then they step away. Whitt backs up to the front door, where he leans against the doorframe, pulling a flask from his pocket. August drifts backward until he comes to a stop beside me.

Sylas begins to walk in a slow circuit around the body, rhythmic words falling from his lips in a language I don't recognize. It sounds like magic, like an incantation. A shiver prickles down my back.

"Is this what it's always like?" I murmur to August. "Or do cadre members get special funerals?"

"I believe the ceremony is essentially the same as this, other than we'd usually conduct any funeral outside," August replies in a matching low tone. "Sylas would know better than I do. Most of it is the lord's responsibility. This is actually the first funeral I've participated in as cadre, and I only watched one before that when I hadn't yet received my place."

I can't help glancing up at him, startled. I've gathered that the fae men are much older than they look, and with all the aggression I've already witnessed among faerie kind, it's hard to imagine he's experienced so little death in his life so far.

August must be able to guess my thoughts. He grimaces. "Did you assume we kill each other left and right? I haven't been a very good model of fae decorum."

"No, I just— Two deaths doesn't seem like very many in

general." In my mere twelve years in the human world, I'd already been to one funeral—for my great-grandmother who passed on when I was seven.

"I told you we can essentially live forever. So taking a life—the life of a fellow fae—through violence is a much more serious matter than it is for humans. You're likely stealing not just decades but centuries. Most fights end just before a killing blow. The victor requests a yield, and the loser offers it up, usually with specific consequences attached."

"Sylas asked Kellan to yield," I say, remembering last night's skirmish with unsettling clarity.

August nods. "It's the only honorable way. If Kellan had given his yield last night, Sylas probably would have banished him from this domain. Most would take banishment over death. He could have ended up gathering stragglers into a lordless pack of his own or found another lord willing to take him in for his services."

But Kellan hated me so much that he was willing to die just to take one last stab at wounding me. My throat closes up. No wonder Sylas looked so agonized afterward. For all I know, Kellan is the first person—the first fae—he's *ever* had to kill.

And he did it for me. A human, a girl he's barely known two weeks—an interloper who'd been in the process of *betraying* him.

How can I make sure he never regrets an act as colossal as that?

August touches my shoulder, just briefly. That fleeting contact is enough to stir a rush of heat into my skin despite the dread creeping through my chest. My mind jolts back to yesterday's other unexpected event—to the pool and August's voice encouraging me to find my pleasure, to the blaze of his kiss afterward.

He didn't want to do anything more than that—he wasn't going to let himself. Maybe that's why he pulled his hand back so quickly just now. I think I hear a hint of a rasp in his voice when he speaks next, but maybe it's sympathy rather than desire.

"You can't blame yourself for what happened. Kellan knew what he was doing. He knew he was acting against Sylas's orders. He made that choice."

But you could also say I forced the issue to a head.

"I hope Sylas didn't get too angry with you about the salt," I venture. And how does August feel about my use of that salt?

If he saw my escape attempt as a betrayal of his trust, he doesn't show it. "It was nothing I wasn't prepared to face when I got it for you." He pauses. "I can see why you'd have wanted to leave, but… I'm glad you changed your mind."

"I am too," I say quietly. At least, I think I am.

I hug myself, and the brush of my arms against my torso wakes up other memories, other feelings that shouldn't have any place at a funeral. I'm too aware of August's presence beside me. Not knowing what to do about the shift in our relationship only makes me more uneasy.

I squash the emotions down, but it's possible they're what spurs the other question that's been tickling through my mind, though I'm too uncertain to phrase it quite as a question. "Sylas said Kellan was the kin of his mate."

August hesitates. "Yes," he says. "Half-brother. He was originally part of her cadre as Whitt and I am to Sylas, but after the trouble that brought us here, without her, Sylas offered to take him on. He thought it was only right."

The weird twinge that ran through me earlier returns. "His mate was banished—she was sent somewhere they can't be together?"

"Ah, no. It's not my place to get into it. Sylas will tell you if he decides to. I'll just say that hers would have been my first funeral as cadre if we'd had her body to conduct it."

That's horrible, but what's even more horrible is that some part of me is *relieved* she isn't still out there somewhere.

My gaze returns to Sylas, who is still chanting, kneeling beside the shrouded body. Does it make things better that Kellan wasn't a man he necessarily would have chosen for his cadre if it hadn't been for awful circumstances, or worse, because he's killed not just a member of his cadre but the half-brother of a woman I assume he loved and already lost?

Just thinking about it makes my stomach ache.

Sylas says a few final words and extends his hands over the body. A light bursts through the fabric, a golden aura so bright I gasp. As it contracts, the fronds, the fabric, and the corpse beneath shrink too, until there's nothing left of Kellan at all—nothing but a pool of cloth and a gleaming gem nestled in its folds.

Sylas picks up the gem, which fits perfectly in the hollow of his palm. When the sunlight catches on it, it beams as if it's a miniature sun in itself. I have trouble associating Kellan's soul with anything that beautiful, but I guess that's what all fae are made of, deep down at their core.

No wonder they would sneer at humans whose bodies turn into dirt and dust.

"What will he do with the jewel?" I ask August.

"Kellan will have given him instructions about where he'd want his essence laid to rest. I'd guess probably in his family's original domain, Thistlegrove. It isn't theirs anymore, but lords are obliged to honor those kinds of requests—when Sylas has an opportunity to journey that way." August exhales as if shedding a great weight. "Well, it's done now." He turns to me, his gaze traveling over my body to the ankle he bandaged just hours ago. "How's your leg?"

The slash of Kellan's claws dug too deeply into my flesh for August's magic to fully seal it. It took the wrapped fabric packed with some of Sylas's medicinal herbs to stop the bleeding completely. "It's still a little sore," I say. "But a lot better since you worked your magic on it."

"I should make sure the gauze doesn't need changing."

He crouches down beside me, his fingers gliding over the wrapped fabric as he examines it. Heat courses up over my skin, and I think a gleam of desire passes through his golden eyes, but he doesn't look up at me or make any further move.

What happened between us that once, he obviously doesn't mean it to happen again. It *was* only a kiss, even if it feels like much more than that.

Sylas marches over to where we're standing, his attention fixed on August. Something in his stride and the intensity in his expression sends an uneasy ripple of recognition through me, though I can't say why. "Does her wound require more attention?" he asks.

"Not yet, from what I can tell," August says. "The binding of the flesh I managed appears to be holding."

"Good. Let's proceed with care." Sylas steps closer, his gaze rising to meet mine, and just for an instant, something flashes through his unscarred eye. A flicker of heat in the darkness that solidifies my sense of recognition.

The way he stalked over just now reminded me of how August approached me yesterday by the pool: predatory and possessive. That flicker wasn't far off from the searing look the younger man gave me before he kissed me.

It's gone now, though, only grim weariness left. Maybe I imagined it, or maybe it was merely concern because of my injury. I am still an object of value here, even if Sylas sees me as a person in my own right who's worthy of protection, more than just a means to an end.

"I'll construct another brace for you," he says. "Assuming you found the first one suitable?"

"Yes," I say, my gut knotting at the much less pleasant memory of how that first one was broken. "It helped a lot. But you don't have to go to any trouble—I still have the crutch—"

He waves off my concerns before I've even finished expressing them. "It's a small thing to offset the fate you nearly met last night."

We haven't talked about what led to that horrifying moment—

about my attempt to escape—other than Sylas replacing the magical lock on the front door and confirming I had no more salt to break the spells. He hasn't pushed the subject, and I'll admit I've been nervous about bringing it up myself. What if he's angry with me underneath all his authoritative poise?

I do want to make one thing clear. "Have you had any luck with testing that sample of blood you took from me? If you need more to try other things—anything I can do to help you figure out how it works…" And how that effect might be replicated, so I'm no longer such a precious commodity as well as a person…

"I'll let you know if anything comes of it or if I require more from you," Sylas says, in a tone that indicates he hasn't discovered anything all that useful yet.

Disappointment winds through my ribs, but I raise my chin against it. I might want the fae lord's protection, but I don't think it'll help my situation if I take on too much of the role of a victim.

Sylas taps my jaw with the lightest of caresses, and I'd swear another flicker of heat unfurls in his one dark eye. "You should get yourself some rest, little scrap. I don't imagine you had much last night. August, I need to speak with you."

The younger man hurries to follow his lord down the hall, shooting me a quick, reassuring smile over his shoulder. I swallow hard. He'd better not be getting into even more trouble over how *he* protected me.

Whitt sweeps across the room a moment later. He pauses by me, observing me watching his two comrades. His teasing voice comes out with more edge than usual. "Plotting which of us to off next, mite?"

I wince and hug myself tighter. "I didn't—Even with Kellan, I never wanted—"

A glint dances in Whitt's blue eyes, coolly amused and maybe a little unsteady. Not really how I'd expect a man to look minutes after putting a close colleague to rest. I remember the flask I saw him retrieving. Is he even sober?

He isn't even a *man*. None of them are. I have to keep remembering that, no matter what else happens.

"We like you more than we liked him," he says with a chuckle. "That isn't saying much, so I wouldn't let it go to your head."

As he saunters off, my stomach sinks. What if I made the wrong choice, staying here?

If I did, I don't think there's any taking it back now.

CHAPTER TWENTY-ONE

Talia

When night falls, I'm wide awake. I must have dozed too much during the day between restless tossing and turning in my bed.

I sit by my bedroom window for a while, watching the fields and the forest beyond sink into almost total darkness. The moon is nothing but a thin sliver. Just past the halfway point before it's full again.

Whitt's last snarky remark echoes through my head. I flop down on the mattress, hoping that my body will take the hint and relax, but my heart keeps thumping a little too fast. My thoughts flit through my mind like nervous birds in an undersized cage.

Kellan is gone, but he was never the real threat. The real threat is the power of my blood and what using that power could mean for Sylas and his pack.

Maybe it won't be so bad if I stay here. If I made it back to the human world, I'd be starting over from scratch anyway—no friends, no close family, no full education, no money. All the dreams I had will be even more out of reach than when I was twelve. My life there could be pretty awful.

The keep has plenty of space for me to roam around in; I've been able to keep myself entertained. I get to gorge myself on three fantastic meals every day. The atmosphere could be outright peaceful without Kellan's harassment. We might even get to the point where Sylas feels comfortable letting me go with them outside during the night when it's less likely anyone will spot me.

I'd take that living situation over not living at all any day. He could collect a little of my blood once a month as he needs it, as gently as he did that once…

But as soon as the cadre starts distributing that "cure" beyond the keep, Aerik will catch on, won't he? He'll know they must be the ones who broke into his fortress and ran off with me. If he can prove it, will he be able to reclaim me? I don't know how faerie laws work.

And it's not just about having the cure. Sylas wants to regain the status he lost, to return his pack to a better home closer to the Heart of the Mists. Can he do that while keeping me, or will he have to turn me over to these arch-lords and let them treat me however they like?

I trust him not to let anyone abuse me while I'm under his roof, but can I be sure he wouldn't hand me over to someone he knows might be cruel where he doesn't have to witness it?

The memory of the way he looked at me this morning, the momentary heat in his gaze, swims up through those uneasy questions. Fae men *can* find me desirable. August made that much clear, even if he didn't want to follow through on his interest. I've felt Sylas's body against mine before—I know how thrilling his powerful presence can be. Thinking about him now, a tingle forms between my legs where the jet and my own fingers stroked the sensitive folds to so much satisfaction yesterday.

What if I gave him a little more incentive to keep me around? Showed him I'm willing to not just cooperate with his tests and rules but to become his lover as well? Obviously he'd never become as devoted to me as he must have been to his former mate, but every bit of affection I can encourage in him is one more reason for him to hold on to me rather than send me away.

As I turn the possibility over in my mind, more tendrils of warmth unfurl low in my belly. My understanding of the actual act of sex comes mostly from the awkward health classes in middle school and a book my parents gave me after a hasty version of "The Talk." I know which parts come together and all that. It's hard to imagine sharing my body like that with… well, anyone, let alone Sylas with his massive frame.

But everything about my time here tells me he'd be careful with me. He wouldn't want to hurt me.

I might even enjoy it.

Once the idea has taken hold, I can't shake it. I roll one way and the other on the bed and finally sit up.

Only a glimmer of starlight shines through the window. The room is so dark I can barely make out the door.

It's probably locked. I wouldn't be able to go to his bedroom anyway. I'll just walk over there and show myself that, and maybe then I'll be able to set aside these thoughts until at least tomorrow.

I pad across the floor on my bare feet, my nightgown teasing across my lower thighs. The trek sends my mind tumbling back to last night, to gripping the knob like I am now and to all the stress and pain that came after.

My throat squeezes shut. I close my eyes, just holding onto the door.

Tonight can't be like that. Kellan is gone—as gone as any living thing can be. And I don't have any more salt. I'm going to twist the knob, and nothing will—

It turns in my grasp, smooth and silent. I'm so startled I let go, and the latch clicks back into place. Staring at the knob, I swivel it again, and it releases just like before.

They didn't lock me in tonight. Is that Sylas's way of repaying the trust I showed him by staying—giving me free run of the keep even while they're sleeping? I can't imagine he overlooked that security measure by accident this soon after I broke past it once.

Now that I know I *can* go through with my plan, I'm suddenly a whole lot less sure of it. I ease the door open, and then I stand there peering into the hall for several heartbeats, not quite able to convince my feet to move. The thoughts that brought me to this point rise up again. More heat pools between my legs.

The unlocked door is a gift. It could almost be an invitation. I think I'm more likely to regret ignoring it than accepting it.

I slip into the hall and make my slow, limping way toward the other end where my captors have their bedrooms. I noted them in my explorations before—at least, the ones that opened at my curious nudge. Whitt's was locked to me until he pulled me into it in the middle of my panic attack the other day; Kellan's I never saw at all, not that I'd want to.

Sylas and August never bothered to secure theirs, I guess thinking there was nothing in there they needed to hide. It was easy to tell which was which even with my quick peeks. Sylas's had larger, grander furniture in vibrant rosewood, everything neatly in its place, while August had clothes hanging from the bed posts, and the air held a whiff of fresh baking that must have carried with him from the kitchen.

Sylas's room remains unlocked. The soft rumble of his sleeping breath travels through the darkness. With the curtains drawn over his window and only faint light seeping from the hall behind me into the room, I can only make out the vaguest shape of his bed and his large form beneath the covers. The distinctive scent that reaches my nose, like rich earth and woodsmoke, tells me I'm in the right place.

My pulse starts to race. Where do I go from here? Can I really just walk right up to him and…?

It seems I can. My feet carry me to the massive bed—it's got to be at least half again the size mine is, and mine's already the biggest bed I've ever slept in. This one is high, too. I rest my hands on the edge of the mattress, my eyes adapting as much as they can to the darkness, watching Sylas's sleeping body sprawled down the middle of that expanse.

Maybe I could just curl up next to him and see what he'd like to do with me when he wakes up? My coming here should be a pretty clear proposition. I have the feeling I'll make a fool of myself if I try to express my intentions in words.

I turn to heft myself onto the bed ass-first, roll to lie on my back—

A muscular arm shoves me down into the mattress with much more force than I was prepared for. A squeak slips from my throat. Sylas stares down at me, braced over my body with his arm clamped across my chest, so close the fall of his wavy hair grazes my cheek.

My lungs have only just started to clench in panic at being pinned when his expression shifts from defensive to confused. As his brow furrows, he sets his hand beside me and pushes himself higher, still peering at me. I can't shake the sense that his ghostly scarred eye sees just as much as the dark whole one.

"Talia?" he says, his baritone thickened by the sleep I've woken him from but his gaze now fully alert. "What are you doing?"

His entire body is still hovering over me, its heat teasing through my nightgown and over my skin. His knees feel almost scorching where they've settled on either side of my thighs. I can see enough in the darkness to tell he isn't wearing anything from the waist up. His shoulders and chest are all sculpted muscle, even more impressive than when hidden under his shirts, the stark black lines of his tattoos swirling and twining across his brown skin.

A weird shivery tingle races down through my belly. I can't tell whether I'm more terrified or turned on. Every nerve is quivering with the knowledge that this man is dangerous, and I'm definitely not half as scared as I should be.

"I—I thought—" I manage to force my voice out of its timid whisper. "I thought you might like some… company."

Even with my awkward phrasing, the insinuation clearly isn't lost on him. He blinks, the furrow in his brow deepening, but the heat I saw before sparks in his unscarred eye before he tamps down on it.

"And why did you decide to offer that company *now*, like this?"

I open my mouth and close it again. It'll hardly work to win his affection by telling him that's what I'm attempting to do. Even thinking of putting it into words makes me feel duplicitous, as if I was doing something slimy.

I don't know what to do other than ignore the question entirely. Tentatively, I raise my hand to touch the side of his chest. His skin is surprisingly smooth over all that hard-packed muscle, and it seems to flare with heat the second I touch it. "You don't like me?"

The way he closes his eyes with a strained grimace suggests *that* isn't the problem. When he looks at me again, it's like a flame is dancing in the dark iris. He keeps his voice steady, but there's a roughness to it that wasn't there before.

"I like you just fine, little scrap. But I don't think this is about liking. Your fate doesn't depend on you submitting yourself to my whims—is that understood? I'll do as right as I can by you regardless of whether you warm my bed, and I always intended to do so."

I guess my motivations weren't so difficult to figure out. I wet my lips, and Sylas's gaze tracks the motion. His attention, the closeness of his body, and his obvious attraction are making me dizzy in a way that's nearly as intoxicating as Whitt's drugged syrup.

"We could still… do something…"

I must sound so naïve. He lets out a sound that's halfway between a chuckle and a groan and pushes off me, settling onto the bed a couple of feet away. "Go on back to your room, Talia. If this is what you really want, for your own sake and not out of fear, you can come back another time when you're sure of that."

I swallow hard against a swell of emotion. The fact that he's sending me off for my own good, even when he's not at all disinterested, extinguishes any fear I still had in me, leaving only the embers of my desire. A desire I'm clearly not going to see fulfilled tonight, thanks to the way I went about it.

But lying there next to his warmth, his smell twined around me and every inch of the stately room speaking of his authority here, I have trouble convincing myself to limp back to my lonely, spartan room. The conviction sweeps through me with so much certainty it takes my breath away: as long as I'm near him, no one can really hurt me.

"Could I stay here?" I venture. "I won't bother you." The bed has more than enough room for both of us. We could lie at opposite ends and barely brush fingertips with our arms outstretched.

Sylas offers another ragged chuckle and runs his hand through his hair. "Are you attempting to test my self-control? I told you—"

From somewhere inside me, I find the bravery to interrupt. "I really mean just to sleep. I—It feels safer in here than in my room." Although that's an awfully selfish reason to impose on his privacy, isn't it? A flush burns across my cheeks. "It's okay. I'll—"

I move to push myself off the bed, and Sylas catches my wrist. When I glance back at him, there's something so haunted in his gaze it squeezes my heart.

Whatever emotion that was, he masters it a moment later. He drops my arm and shifts farther across the bed, leaving more room for me. "Fine. Only to sleep. Just keep your hands to yourself."

The hint of a growl in his voice sends another of those giddy shivers through me. I lay my head down. "Thank you."

When I drift off, it's with a vision of his hands moving over me like the currents in the pool's water.

CHAPTER TWENTY-TWO

Sylas

I wake up painfully hard. The scrap of a girl isn't even close enough to touch, tucked under the sheet at the far end of the bed with her head nestled in my other pillow, but the memory of her lithe body beneath me has been floating through my head all night. That and her scent: woodsy and sweet but not syrupy, like maple sap that hasn't been simmered to tameness.

I want to drink it off her skin. I want to watch those delicately green eyes dilate with pleasure.

I'm going to explode right here in the bed if I don't rein in thoughts like that.

She's so deeply asleep that she doesn't stir as I get up. I pause by the door to my en-suite lavatory, taking in the softness of her face in sleep, the contrast of the pale skin with the deep pink hair falling around it.

She must have meant it when she said she felt safe in here. With me. She sounded as if she meant it, but the words were so jarring I couldn't fully accept them.

A bittersweet pang echoes through my chest, but it does nothing to diminish the erection tenting the fabric of my drawers. If I *am* going to be safe for her in every possible way, I'd better take care of that.

I lock the lavatory door, because I'm not sure I could control my hunger if she wandered in while I'm in the middle of satisfying these urges, and turn on the water in the shower alcove. It thrums through the pipes and rushes over me in a hot stream. I comb it through my hair and let it cascade over my body, and then I bring my hand to my throbbing cock.

I'm keyed up enough that just that first touch sends a bolt of pleasure through my loins. Bracing my other arm against the wall, I bow my head to the shower spray still raining over me and grip myself firmly.

As I build up a rhythm, stroking from head to base, I can't help picturing Talia kneeling before me. Her pink hair slicked back from her face. Her perfect Cupid's bow lips wrapping around my erection. Her tongue slicking a heady line along the underside of my cock while she gazes up at me in a haze of desire.

Would she cringe if she knew I was thinking of her that way? I can't believe she understood just what she was offering last night, hesitant and stuttering. That mouth has never taken a cock into it; no part of her has been so penetrated.

But she wasn't *un*willing. Regardless of how well she understands carnal acts, there was no mistaking the tang of arousal she gave off while I loomed over her.

I want to do right by her, to make up for the horrors she's been subjected to under Aerik's roof and now mine. But Heart help me, I want to take her too, so badly the memory of her gasp when I first caught her last night sends me careening right over the edge, balls clenching, semen spurting against the wall.

I haven't come this hard in ages.

Afterward, I don't feel quite as unburdened as I was hoping. My cock softens, but a knot of lustful tension remains coiled behind my groin. My chest still tightens at the thought of walking back into my chamber and seeing her in my bed.

Well, there's one way to douse most of my lingering desire. I switch the tap to cold and let an icy torrent pour over me until even my bones are chilled.

The frigid deluge leaves me fully alert and focused. I dry myself briskly, pull on fresh drawers and my dressing gown, and start toward the door.

I'm still a few strides away when my ears pick up a sound that stops me in my tracks. It's the slightest intake of breath but with a husky note that shoots straight to my groin.

As I stand there motionless, the sounds that follow draw a picture that quickens the blood in my veins all over again. A rustle of fabric. A whisper of hair against a pillow. A murmur of a groan, muffled as if against a bitten lip.

The fire inside that I tried so hard to expel and then extinguish flares up all over again. My wolf rears its head, urging me on with its animal appetites.

I walk to the door and push it open. When my gaze falls on Talia, she's lying still beneath the sheet, her head tipped to the side, her expression innocent. But the faint daylight that spills around the edges of my curtain reveals a deep blush in her ivory cheeks.

My dead eye conjures a ghostly image that swims over her face for a moment: those same features turned wanton with a carnal hunger. A thicker tang of arousal scents the air. As I breathe it in, I lose my grip on the vast majority of my good intentions.

I prowl over to my side of the bed, holding her gaze. The words roll scorching over my tongue. "And what have you been up to, my little human?"

Her eyes widen. Her own tongue flicks across her lips, and by all that is dust, I'm hard again. "I—Nothing," she stammers. "I just woke up."

I sit down and reach across the mattress to slide my hand under the sheet. My fingers curl around her arm. Tugging by the elbow, I raise it to bring her fingers level with my nose.

Her cheeks flame hotter when she realizes what I'm after, and her arm twitches as if to yank away. I've already gotten the whiff I expected, the musk of the slickness that must be seeping from her sex. I raise my eyebrows at her as if to say, *Care to try again?*

I wouldn't have thought her face could turn any more red, but it's nearly as bright as her hair now. "I was only— I woke up, and I felt so… wanting, and I thought maybe if I took care of it myself— I didn't know how quickly you'd be back."

She was taking the same tack I did. Not quite so inexperienced in these pleasures as I assumed, it seems. I wonder if it would have worked any better for her than it has for me. It's taking every shred of control I have left not to lick those fingertips and then bury my face between her legs to see how much more of that exquisite nectar I can draw out of her.

"And where did you learn how to do that?" I ask teasingly, not really expecting much of an answer.

Talia wets her lips again. "August showed me."

With a skip of my heart, my vision goes red. Every instinct in my body clangs with the need to claim and defend what is *mine*. My lips are already curling back from my teeth, fangs emerging, before I catch hold of myself enough to register the anxiety flickering across the girl's face.

I manage not to outright snarl, but the question comes out plenty harsh as it is. "He did *what*?"

She flinches, and seeing that, I suppress a little of my burst of temper under the shame of scaring her.

"It—it was in the pool," she says, her voice falling into the whisper that was all she could manage when we first found her. "He just told me how I could use the jets and my hand… He didn't even watch or anything—he was behind the folding screen the whole time."

That doesn't explain why he was making suggestions like that in the first place. That impertinent whelp—I'll cuff him across the head so hard his ears ring for a week.

I inhale slowly, settling my inner animal as well as I can for the girl's benefit, not August's. My voice comes out still fierce but not quite as curt. "Is that all?" Did she come here last night planning to act out what he's already shown her? My gums itch to set my fangs free.

She lowers her eyes. "He kissed me. Only once, and only very quickly. He made it sound like he didn't think he should have done even that."

Another snarl rises in my throat. He *shouldn't* have done it. And he never bothered to mention his partial seduction of our convalescent guest to me? In that moment, the transgression angers me more than his secret gift of salt.

And I'm man enough to admit that some part of that anger is because I now have to ask this question: "Was it him you were thinking of when you touched yourself?"

Her gaze darts back up to meet mine. Her face, paler after my display of ire, flushes all over again. Her answer slips out so soft it's barely a murmur. "No. I was thinking about you."

The rest of my fury crumbles away under a wave of triumph, more than I'd have expected to feel over one tiny human girl. No, not a girl, not really. She's a woman coming into her own, bit by careful bit now that she has the room to find herself—and this woman wants me, with every beat of her racing pulse.

She still carries so many wounds, old and more recent. There's still so much she hasn't yet experienced. The passion I'm capable of might scare her as much as my anger did. But I can make her mine as much as anyone should while she's in this state.

I let go of her arm, unable to tear my gaze from her bright green eyes. "Show me."

She blinks. "What?"

I tip my head toward her body, desire roughening my tone. "Show me how you would pleasure yourself."

Her lips part, and for a second I think she'll refuse in embarrassment. Then, ever so slowly, she tucks her hand back under the sheet. From the corner of my eye, I track its movement down her torso, but my gaze stays fixed on her face. She stares right back at me, clearly still nervous, but with a gleam of excitement as well.

I can mark the exact moment she finds the perfect spot between her legs. Her eyelashes quiver, and she sucks in her breath with a little hitch. Her head pushes farther into the pillow instinctively.

My renewed erection strains against my drawers, but this is for her, not for me. This is to give her a taste of the reality of whatever she's imagining, of what she pictured happening last night.

All the same, I intend to relish every moment.

I bend over and brush my lips to her soft cheek. The essence of her, that wild sap-sweet smell, floods my nose, enflaming my hunger. I kiss a gentle path from her cheek to the crook of her jaw, with the slightest nibble of the tender skin there.

Talia arches farther back with a gasp that's almost a whimper. I tease my mouth down the side of her neck, tasting her with a swipe of my tongue. Her breath breaks into shaky little pants that make me want to unleash my desire and devour her like a beast.

No. She is mine, and I'll treat her like the precious being she is.

As I continue to attend to her neck, I glide my hand over the silky fabric of her nightgown to cup her breast. My fingers trace a lazy circle around the small mound. She trembles at my touch, her hips shifting needily beneath the sheet. More of her delectable musk laces the air.

When I skate my thumb over her nipple, I earn my first full

moan. She turns her head toward me, seeking me out. No force in the lands could stop me from claiming her lips.

I kiss her deeply, reveling in the tart sweetness of her mouth, in the invigorating sounds that course from her mouth into mine as my thumb urges her nipple into a stiffened peak. Skies above, there's so much I want to teach her about the pleasures her body is capable of.

I drop my mouth to her collarbone, slicking my tongue across the delicate ridge and grazing my fingers over her chest to her untended breast. Her hips are rolling now as if grappling with the hand between her thighs.

"Take yourself all the way," I say against her skin. "Find your pinnacle, Talia."

Her groan sends a violent throbbing through my rigid cock. "I—I can't seem to get there."

Oh, my lovely innocent. I nibble my way along the edge of her scarred shoulder, back up her neck, until I reach her earlobe. "Are you aching to be filled? Dip those eager fingers right into your slit."

A gasp that's almost startled leaves her lips, but I can tell from the motion of her arm that she's following my command. Her eyes roll up, a strangled sound following them. "*Oh.*"

"That's right. Give yourself over to it."

I'm not sure I've ever seen a vision quite as erotic as this nearly untouched woman chasing her release. The flush in her cheeks is only delight now, no embarrassment, and her irises flare so brilliantly they put emeralds to shame. I ease down her body to draw one of those pert nipples into my mouth through her nightgown. A cry shudders out of her.

"I still can't— Would you help me?"

Her voice is so fraught with need there's no way I could deny her request, even if I wanted to. I trail my hand down her arm to where her own hand is pressed tight to her pussy, the heel of it by her clit and two of her fingers curled inside her channel. Watching her expression, I apply a hint of pressure over her clit, and then a little more, my thumb stroking over the inside of her thigh where the slickness of her arousal has spread.

That small assistance is all it takes to carry her over. Talia closes her eyes and opens her mouth. With a choked cry, her head jerks back against the pillow. Her whole body quakes against mine with the force of her orgasm.

As her shudders subside, her hand goes slack beneath mine. I raise my arm to collect her against me, wanting her to be sure of me in the aftermath as well as in the act itself. She ducks her head under my chin. In her silence, her fingers drift over the collar of my dressing gown.

"This isn't why—" she starts, and hesitates. "I haven't done anything for *you*."

"Don't worry yourself about that," I say, ignoring the ache in my groin. "I got plenty of enjoyment out of this interlude." Once she's left, another shower will *definitely* be in order.

Talia looks up and scoots against me to press her lips to mine. Her kiss is timid but so fond it leaves an ache not in my cock but somewhere in the vicinity of my heart. I brush my fingers over her hair and kiss her back with equal ardor.

I told her last night that nothing we did in this bed would affect her fate, but maybe I was lying to both myself and her. After this intimacy, after the trust she's shown me, the thought of handing her over to the arch-lords brings a growl into my throat.

And it's not even the greatest trust she's offered. I kiss her on the forehead next, and then say, "You stayed."

"I told you, I felt safer here than in my—"

"No, I mean the night before. After Kellan attacked you. You meant to leave, did you not?"

Talia's body tenses, but she doesn't push away. "I did. I thought *that* would be the safest thing—getting back home."

"But you changed your mind."

"When—when I saw how far you'd go to protect me… I don't know if there's anyone else in this world or the one I came from who'd care that much what happens to me. My real family is gone." She lapses into a momentary silence. "I know your people need me and the cure that comes from my blood. I know you can't promise anything. But at least here, I know where I stand."

I wouldn't have thought I could admire her resilience more than I already did, but she's proven me wrong again. I pull her a little closer against me in anticipation of letting her go. "I'll endeavor to ensure that's always true."

By my life, let me always be capable of that, regardless of what may come.

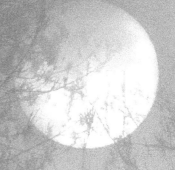

CHAPTER TWENTY-THREE

Talia

When I make it to the kitchen, changed from my nightie into jeans and a tee and with my hair combed into as neat a state as the waves will allow, at least half an hour has passed since I left Sylas's bed. Tingles still race across my skin at unexpected moments, with the graze of my shirt's fabric or the brush of my fingertips as I tuck an errant pink strand behind my ear.

Being with him was so exhilarating that I want to hole up with him in his bedroom and never leave, and that desire somehow makes the whole thing frightening at the same time. What I did with him and the affection he showed me hasn't really changed anything—about my status, anyway. My situation here is just as precarious.

But at least, if the days ahead are only one last short taste of freedom, I've experienced a lot more passion than I had before I came here. I've had more of a life.

August is already in the kitchen, grabbing baking dishes off the overhead racks. When he sees me, he shoots me one of his warmly enthusiastic grins, and an odd little wobble runs through my gut. August was the first man to help me discover the hidden pleasures of my body. I'm still not totally sure how to act around him.

He seems capable of acting as if nothing is at all different, though. He appeared downcast during Kellan's funeral, but he's back to his usual energy now. "I was thinking pancakes for breakfast," he says, pouring pale purple flour into a mixing bowl. "How does that sound to you?"

My stomach chooses that moment to gurgle its approval. August laughs. "Worked up an appetite in your dreaming, did you?"

More like after my dreaming, but I'm not going to mention that. I hop onto my usual stool. "Pancakes sound delicious."

"And you've never had them made with fallowrot flour before, I'll bet. Fluffy as clouds but full of flavor. Have a sniff."

He thrusts the bowl toward me, and I lean over it to inhale. A creamy, savory-sweet smell like hazelnuts fills my nose. My mouth starts to water. "Two thumbs up from me!"

"You can be my stirring assistant, then." He sprinkles a couple more powders over the flour and passes it to me along with a spoon. "All the dry components need to be evenly distributed to get the best effect."

"Aye, aye, chef." I grip the spoon, and he flashes me another grin. Even after the experience I just had with Sylas, and as much as I wanted Sylas from the moment he loomed over me last night, that grin manages to wake up a familiar flutter in my chest.

Is it *normal* to be this attracted to two men at the same time? Maybe it's something about them being fae.

As I get to work stirring, a sense of loss creeps through my chest. I should have had friends I grew up with, or new ones I met at high school or college, who I'd be able to talk to about this sort of thing. Maybe I'd even have felt comfortable discussing men with

Mom once I'd gotten older and out of the goofy puppy-love crush stage where I got the giggles after just locking eyes with a classmate I thought was cute.

August cracks several eggs into a different bowl and whips them into a froth with a whisk. I watch the muscles shift along his shoulders and chart the fall of his dark auburn hair against the nape of his neck.

Sylas has already had a proper mate—a fae woman. Maybe fae men only marry once and that's it. August must want to find someone he could really share *his* life with, which obviously can't be me.

Whitt strolls into the room with his usual languid nonchalance, glancing over both August and me as if the sight of us amuses him.

"Breakfast won't be for a little while yet," August tells him. "You're up early."

Whitt yawns. "I'm not really up. Just grabbing something to ease along the rest of my sleep. Pretend you never saw me."

He heads into the pantry. A clink here and a rustle there follows. August shakes his head, his mouth forming a crooked smile, and returns to his preparations. I do the same.

The flour mixture is giving off an even more powerful—and saliva-inducing—perfume now, which seems like a good sign that I'm doing my job right. August splashes a little liquid from one bottle and then another into his bowl, whisks it one last time, and leaves that to check on me.

"Let's see how you're doing, Sweetness," he says, leaning over by my shoulder.

The second I realize that's a nickname he's given me—and what a nickname it is—a deeper flutter shivers against my ribs. At the same moment, August stiffens beside me.

I glance down at the bowl, afraid I've screwed up the mix in my distraction, but he shifts closer—not to the bowl, but to me, with a sharp inhalation. A current of air tickles over my skin, and I realize he's taken a whiff of me, his nose nearly grazing my hair.

He yanks himself backward, his muscles tensed and his golden eyes fiercely bright. I stare at him, my own stance going rigid, utterly bewildered about what's going on.

"You… and Sylas…" he says, his voice hoarse. His hands flex at his sides as if he's trying to restrain himself from clenching them into fists.

Heat courses over my face. I washed myself before I got dressed, more thoroughly than I usually would, but I didn't have anything like a full bath. And the fae's wolfish noses are as keen as their ears. Sylas's scent could easily have lingered on my neck where he placed so many of those searing kisses.

"I—" I start, and don't know what to say. Should I admit it? Deny it? Why should it matter to August anyway, when he made it clear he didn't think anything should happen between him and me?

Right now, it appears to matter to him quite a lot. He paces to the counter and back, his eyes still blazing. "It's fine. You have every right—*he* has every right—"

With a choked growl, he wheels toward the parlor. "I've got to —to look after something." He barges across the room and throws open the back door. It slams behind him. Through the window, I see his form hunch and lengthen, fur rippling over his brawn. In mere seconds, he's not a man but a massive ruddy-brown wolf tearing across the field toward the forest.

The mixing bowl teeters on my lap. I grip it before it can topple onto the floor, my pulse stuttering. Does he even want this anymore? Is he abandoning breakfast completely? I don't understand.

Was he *angry* with me, because I—

The joy this morning's encounter left me with drains away, leaving only a pinch of guilt. I don't know what's going through

August's head, but he was obviously upset. I never wanted to hurt him.

"Quite the little drama you've decided to star in, mite," Whitt's voice drawls from the other end of the room.

I startle, nearly falling off my stool. This time, the bowl does slip from my grasp. It thumps on the ground, half the flour mixture jostling out of it in a purplish poof. I scramble to collect the bowl with its remaining contents and spin around. I'd forgotten the other man was in the room.

Whitt ambles by, casting a disparaging glance at the floor. "And what a mess you've made in the middle of it. Think you can manage to clean it up?"

I can tell he's not just talking about the flour. "I didn't mean— I wasn't trying to cause any trouble."

"It's starting to seem like the stuff follows you. Don't worry. I'm sure Sylas won't blame you." He turns toward the hall.

His tone has stayed light the whole time, somewhere between teasing and needling, but the impression pricks at me that he means his remarks more than he's showing. Is *he* angry with me too—because I upset August? Because of Kellan? They never appeared to like each other all that much, but what do I know from two weeks' observations?

If I'm going to keep any of the peace I've started to find in this place, I need all three of the men still ruling over it to at least accept my presence.

"Whitt," I say, setting the bowl down on the counter. "Wait."

He swivels partway around and cocks his head. "Why?"

"I—I'm sorry."

A frown curves his mouth. In that moment, he does look angry. Then it's gone again, and the breezy tone comes back. "Whatever for?"

I don't really know. I drag in a breath, searching for an answer, but I'm so uncertain of what he's bothered about in the first place that anything I say could just as easily be wrong as right. I don't want to piss him off *more*.

"Hmm," he says into my awkward hesitation, and wags a finger at me. "Work on that too." Then he's sauntering away, leaving me in the kitchen alone.

There's still no sign of August. I wait for a few minutes, my stomach knotting, and then I poke around the room until I find a dustpan and a twiggy whisk-broom. I've finally managed to sweep the last bits of flour off the floor and am dumping it into the waste bin when footsteps thunder down the spiral staircase beyond the doorway.

"Sylas?" Whitt calls, the note of urgency in his voice so unusual that my nerves jitter. I creep over to the doorway. What's going on now?

The fae lord emerges from the dining room holding a steaming goblet he must have poured himself while waiting for the breakfast that now might never be coming. He looks as surprised as I am by Whitt's tone. As Whitt hurries over to him, Sylas studies the other man's face. "Bad news?"

"I'd call it a decidedly fraught combination," Whitt says, working in a little wryness despite the apparent emergency. "I've gotten word from one of my people that Tristan and his cadre mean to pay us an unexpected visit. At least now it's no longer unexpected."

Sylas raises his eyebrows. "Other than as much as we don't know why they'd mean to. What business do they have here—and why would they want to catch us unawares?"

"I'm not sure. My man wasn't even clear on when exactly they plan to come, only that it sounded as though it'd be fairly soon. It may be they simply want to check up on us, or it's possible—"

As Whitt speaks, he glances toward the kitchen and catches sight of me. His mouth snaps shut in mid-sentence. Sylas follows his gaze, his mismatched eyes pinning me in place before I can consider ducking out of sight.

I grip the doorframe tightly and decide to pretend I was part of the conversation all along. "Who's Tristan? Why would it be bad for him to come?"

Whitt frowns again, but Sylas answers me as if I asked a totally reasonable question. "He's a second-cousin to one of the arch-lords. Which means he has plenty of prestige and influence, and he can decide to use those for good or ill. And seeing as we've already lost rather a lot of favor that we're hoping to regain…" He grimaces and returns his attention to Whitt. "We'll need to begin preparing immediately."

"Are the three of us going to take on the entire task?"

I open my mouth to offer that I'll help in any way I can, but Sylas's gaze slides to me again, so abruptly solemn my voice dries up.

"No," he says. "We'll need to incorporate the pack. Talia, I'm afraid I'm going to have to ask you to confine yourself to your room until this matter is dealt with."

CHAPTER TWENTY-FOUR

Talia

On the TV screen, a screeching woman leaps at the girl she's been berating, trips, and lands face-first in an icing-slathered cake. Not even a hint of a laugh tickles from my lungs at that or at the sight of the goopy mask of frosting covering her face when she straightens up, her eyes bulging.

I turn the movie off and flop onto my back on the sofa. I should be glad that after Sylas said I'd be confined to my room, he amended that to *two* rooms. I've spent most of the past few days in the keep's entertainment room, flipping through books I'm too distracted to really focus on and watching movies from the fae lord's collection—with headphones on, to make sure none of the pack members he's brought in to help prepare the keep catch on that I'm down here.

But now I'm bored out of my mind. I can't even remember whether this is the fourth day or the fifth, they've blurred together so much—even more than before.

I've barely seen Sylas or his cadre. They knock when they leave meals outside the door and when it's time for me to move from my bedroom to the entertainment room or back again, and a couple of times Sylas has spoken to me briefly from the doorway to confirm I'm all right, but otherwise I've been totally isolated. They don't want to take the chance that the rest of the pack will smell me on their clothes if they've spent too much time around me, he explained.

If he's that intent on keeping my presence here a secret, then that's got to mean he isn't planning on offering me up to this second-cousin of an arch-lord dude, right? Or maybe he just wants it to be a big surprise. With every hour that passes since I cuddled against him in his bed, those intimate moments feel less real, less trustworthy.

Aren't faeries supposed to be tricksters? How can I trust *anything* any of them have said to me?

My stomach grumbles despite the tension wound through it. It must be getting on toward dinner. I've got even less sense of time than usual in this windowless basement room.

The knock comes as if on cue. But when I open the door, I find not a plate of food but August standing a few feet away, empty-handed.

He smiles at me, and I'm ridiculously relieved by the genuine warmth in his expression. I haven't seen him since he took off from the kitchen the other morning. However he felt about what he guessed about Sylas and me, at the very least he doesn't appear to hate me.

"Hanging in there?" he asks.

I shrug, feeling abruptly awkward. I'm not going to mention that earlier incident if he doesn't. "It hasn't been the time of my life, but it's still way better than an actual cage."

He winces at the reminder of how they found me and beckons me out, starting down the hall a couple of paces ahead of me. "A scout reported seeing Tristan and two from his cadre on their way into our domain. They should be here in less than an hour. Sylas thinks you'll be more secure in your bedroom. I've already brought up some food so you don't go hungry."

"Thank you." My gaze skims over the hall and the stairwell we head up. Every inch of surface area has been scrubbed and polished to gleaming. New artwork—fanciful paintings and twisted gold-and-bronze sculptures—hang on the walls on the main floor. Extra lantern orbs dangle from a winding branch that stretches along the ceiling. Every time I've come up, the keep has become fancier. I can only imagine how the other rooms have transformed.

"This guy is a pretty big deal, huh?" I say, continuing up the broader spiral staircase to the second floor. "I mean, I know he's related to one of these arch-lords and all…"

"Casting us off this far into the fringes is only one step up from total banishment," August says. "They'll be watching to see how we've handled the disgrace, and you can be sure he'll report back to his cousin. The higher we can hold our heads despite our situation, the more respect we'll earn. A real lord isn't diminished by his location."

That last bit sounds as if he's quoting Sylas. I can't help thinking that anyone who puts conditions like this on their respect after casting people off is such a dick their respect shouldn't matter anyway, but I don't say that either.

August leaves me at my bedroom. It, at least, looks the same as it always has. Sylas obviously doesn't anticipate that the visitors will be examining it. I find a plate on the bedside table with a simple meal of bread, cheese, and a cold cut of meat, but since August prepared it, it's delicious in its simplicity.

I'm halfway through the sandwich I've assembled when a knock comes that I didn't expect. Are they moving me again?

"Yes?" I say from where I'm perched on the side of the bed.

The door eases open to reveal Sylas's imposing figure. He takes a couple of steps inside and then stops, studying me with both his unmarked eye and the scarred one. "All these restrictions should be over soon," he says. "It's unlikely our guests will want to spend the night, and if they do, we'll ensure they leave early in the morning."

I *am* looking forward to having full run of the keep again. I nod. "I guess I should just stay quiet up here?"

"Yes. If you can manage to sleep or at least attempt to, that would be best. Although I know how quietly you're capable of moving on your feet." He glances at my brace, which I've already taken off and set by the end of the bed. "Even if they stay over, we've set up a guest suite on the first floor. There's no reason for them to venture anywhere upstairs. You should be perfectly safe."

He doesn't intend to make a farewell gift out of me, then. More tension than I knew I was holding unspools through my chest. I inhale deeply into my loosened lungs. "I'll make sure I don't do anything that'll tip them off that I'm up here."

"Good. I apologize for the stress this will have put you under."

He pauses, and like in other moments when he's stopped by to talk to me, I have the abrupt impression that he's going to step even closer, touch my face, maybe even kiss me again. Something smolders in the depths of his unmarked eye, and an answering flame sparks in me—but whatever he might have been considering doing, he holds himself back. If I didn't simply imagine the whole thing out of wishful thinking.

"Until tomorrow," he says with a slight dip of his head, and leaves.

Whitt must have been waiting in the hall. His voice travels through the door. "If they realize what we've been hiding—"

Sylas's answer is firm. "We've discussed this. It won't be a problem."

"You know we can't pretend her out of existence forever. It's not even a week until the next full moon."

"Which I haven't forgotten."

"The whole *point* of taking the risk of stealing from Aerik was—"

"I haven't forgotten that either," Sylas replies, a growl creeping into his voice, and they move beyond my hearing.

My stomach clenches, but I manage to put Whitt's complaints out of my mind and finish my sandwich. Then I curl up on the bed, wishing I'd thought to bring one of the books from the entertainment room with me. After doing little more than lazing around on the sofa all day, I'm not remotely tired.

The thumping of hoofbeats tells me the visitors have arrived. I ease over to the window, which Sylas assured me has a "glamor" on it that makes it look from the outside as if the curtains are always drawn. To my frustration, no angle lets me see the front of the keep. Sylas's voice rings out in a greeting too muffled by the distance for me to make out the exact words.

A woman I vaguely recognize from Whitt's revels comes into view, leading three horses more elegant than any steed I ever saw in the human world: slim-legged and necked with gracefully sloping heads, hair and manes glinting with an opalescent sheen, one dusky gray, one pale bay, and one nearly white. They prance across the ground so light-footed I'd believe they were gliding above the grass.

She brings them around the other side of the keep to where the stable must be, and I see nothing more to do with the new arrivals. I sink back down on the bed and rub my foot absently. A trace of the rich smells from the extravagant dinner August will have whipped up—with help from pack members, presumably—trickles around my door. My stomach pinches even though it's full of a perfectly tasty sandwich.

I lie down and burrow my head into my pillow, but even with my eyes closed, my thoughts keep racing too quickly for me to have any hope of sleeping. I kick off the covers and then pull them back over me. What are they talking about downstairs? Why *did* this fancy-pants guy and part of his cadre come calling?

Even if they don't know I'm here, the outcome of this visit could still change how Sylas decides to deal with me.

Finally, curiosity niggles down too deep for me to ignore it. I *have* proven I can move silently through the halls. The shape of the spiral staircase means that even if someone approaches the second floor, I'll have plenty of warning before they can get a look at me. I need to know what's going on here and in the world around if *I'm* going to make the right decisions, as much as I'm able to decide anything at all about my fate.

Not bothering with my brace, I limp carefully to the door and open it only wide enough for me to slip by. With careful if uneven steps, I make my way to the bend in the hall and around it. My bare feet make no sound against the floorboards.

I don't even need to walk all the way to the top of the stairs. When I reach the lavatory door, the voices traveling up from the dining room sharpen enough for me to follow most of the conversation—at least on one side. The newcomers seem to enjoy talking in loud, sweeping voices, as if their volume makes them more impressive.

"From what I heard, the stuff didn't make it out this way very often," a deep male voice is saying.

"We managed without," Sylas replies. "After all, until recently, no one had it at all."

A female voice pipes up, throaty and strident. "True. And I suppose you can't blame Aerik for not wanting to bother sending his people right out to the fringes."

Aerik. They're talking about the tonic he made to cure the fae of the full-moon wildness—the tonic he started making once he had access to my blood. Whitt mentioned that Aerik hadn't always shared that tonic with Sylas's pack, but I didn't realize the snub was major enough that the whole community would know about it. It sounds like he pretty much *never* let them have any.

With everything I know now of Sylas's ideas about honor and

integrity, I have to think he must have been awfully desperate to have gone as far as breaking into Aerik's home.

Did this lord come all the way here himself because of the tonic —because he heard something that made him suspicious? I creep a tad closer, my ears pricked and my mouth bone dry.

It seems like the subject only came up so the visitors could needle their hosts, though. The man—Tristan?—starts rambling on about some quest he went on to slaughter an ivory boar, with occasional interjections from the woman. Then I think Whitt speaks—I can't fully make out his voice, but the laughter afterward sounds like the sort of response he'd be aiming for.

"When I last visited my cousin, he made some mention of you and your circumstances," the newcomer says eventually.

"He's welcome to call on us himself anytime he'd like to observe those circumstances firsthand," Sylas remarks, and I catch a snicker as if he's made a joke, though it didn't sound at all like one to me. I bristle on his behalf.

Whatever he did that forced him and his pack to move here, I can't imagine it was *that* horrible—only horrible by the standards of these stuck-up, pompous aristocrats who're clearly more interested in lording their power over those who have less than making anyone's lives better.

There's a span of quiet there I can't discern more than a word here and there. Kellan's name reaches my ears, and my back stiffens, but I miss whatever follows.

Then the voices get abruptly louder. The speakers are moving this way, I realize.

"Aren't you going to give us the full tour?" Tristan says, casually but with a hard edge that indicates he expects to be obliged.

Are they going to come upstairs after all? My pulse hiccups, and I scoot backward, spinning around. With one hand braced against the wall to help my balance, I scuttle back toward my bedroom as quickly as my legs will take me without betraying my steps.

I picked up on their intentions just in time. I'm barely two steps around the corner when I hear the bunch of them tramping up the steps. I limp onward, shaky with the rush of adrenaline and fear.

My bedroom door closes behind me with the softest of clicks. I stand on the other side, listening hard, but I can't even make out the visitors' voices anymore. Surely they're too far away still to have noticed that small sound? After wavering for a moment between eavesdropping and the comfort of the bed, I wobble over and clamber under the covers.

I assume the danger is past. My heartbeat evens out, and I slump deeper into the mattress, berating myself for risking leaving my room in the first place. If I'd been any less alert—

But I wasn't. I got out of the way in time. Everything's fine now.

Then Sylas's voice penetrates the wall, sounding as if he's just come around the corner. "There's not much down there other than spare rooms. We haven't bothered to do them up. I doubt they'd interest you."

He's talking a little louder than before. I shift upright, my fingers curling into the covers. Are they going to come down here—are they going to open up *my* room?

What the hell am I supposed to do if that happens?

"I'm impressed enough with what you've done with the rest of the space that I can't imagine they'll be a disappointment," Tristan says in the same demanding tone.

A chill floods my skin. He's going to insist on looking in here. Oh, hell.

Sylas laughs—again, louder than I'm used to. "Well, you'll see for yourself that there's nothing to look at other than a bit of furniture."

He *wants* me to hear him. He's warning me. The room needs to look as though no one's been living in it.

There are a few rooms between the bend and mine. I have a minute or two.

My head jerks around. The wardrobe—I can hide in there… and hope they don't smell me. It's farther from the door than the bed is. They won't walk right through the whole space, will they?

I don't have time to worry over that. I shove myself off the bed, remembering only at the last second to set my feet down gently, and tug the covers as smooth as I can make them. The dinner plate has to go too. I snatch it, set it as far under the bed as I can reach alongside my abandoned crutch, and whirl toward the wardrobe.

I'm nearly there when a jolt of horror wrenches through me. My foot brace—it's still leaning against the bedframe in easy view of the door. How could Sylas explain away *that*?

There was a pause in the voices, but they're on the move again, getting louder as they approach. I scramble back to the bed and accidentally set my bad foot down at an awkward angle that pinches the nerves. Clenching my jaw against a gasp at the sharper throbbing that forms between the misshapen bones, I bend down to grab the brace.

Every particle in me is hollering to dash to the wardrobe at top speed, but if they hear me running around, I'm toast anyway. I hobble over as nimbly as I can, cringe at the faint squeak of the hinges when I open the door, and crawl inside amid hanging quilts and folded sheets.

There's enough of a ridge on the inside of the door that I manage to pull it all the way shut. I crouch there, unable to see anything in the room beyond, unable to hear anything over the thunder of my pulse.

The bedroom door clicks open. Sylas's voice is brisk. "A simple guest room. We have more appropriate quarters prepared downstairs should you require them."

Someone chuckles. "I should certainly hope so."

There's a sniffing sound, and my throat aches with held breath. Then the woman from before says, "You've taken to keeping human servants again, I gather."

"It is difficult to do without any extra aid," Sylas says smoothly. "And easy to bring them over while we're situated here. If the scent bothers you, I can assure you your rooms were seen to solely by my pack."

She hums to herself, and then the door thumps shut again. I press my hand against my mouth to hold in a sigh of relief.

Nestling deeper into the sheets, I lay down my head. I don't know if I'm going to be able to sleep a wink until they're gone, but if I do, I think I'll do it in here.

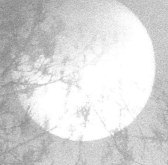

CHAPTER TWENTY-FIVE

Talia

I wake up the next morning back in my bed—and realize after a few bleary blinks that it isn't actually morning at all. The angle of the light, only an indirect glow seeping through the window, means the sun has already passed from east to west. I've slept into the afternoon.

That's not much of a surprise. I'm not sure how late it was when I finally crept out of the wardrobe and crawled into bed after hearing the visitors' horses canter away, only that it was well into the early hours of the morning and my head was aching with nervous exhaustion.

The exhaustion has diminished, but my nerves are still jumpy. The past week may have brought new pleasures into my life, but it's also driven home just how easily any security I've found here can be shaken. Sylas couldn't even ensure his own cadre wouldn't try to hurt me. He couldn't prevent this other lord's visit either, despite the dangers of letting him in.

Within the keep, Sylas rules with an authority that feels so solid it's hard to imagine anyone not bowing to his commands. But there are people outside these walls—lots of people, apparently—who have more power than he does.

What happens to me may not be entirely up to him in the end, as much as he'd like it to be.

I fumble out of the bed, still groggy-headed, with those uneasy thoughts churning in my mind. Someone must have checked on me during the day: there's a new plate heaped with purplish pancakes on the side table. Seeing it, the hazelnutty scent reaching my nose, my heart squeezes. It feels like a peace offering, no words required.

Since I haven't eaten all day, it doesn't take long for me to wolf down the whole stack. My stomach no longer aches when I eat more than a bird-like portion of a meal, which I guess is some kind of progress. The pancakes leave a creamier hazelnut aftertaste on my tongue, so delicious I don't want to rinse my mouth and wash it away. I probably should, though, since my morning breath will have evolved into a higher level of blech by now.

I don't run into any of my captors in the hall. The view from the south-facing window suggests it's later than I assumed. Whitt is out on the field, his tall form casting a long shadow, the lowering sun searing off his bright brown hair. He appears to be directing a few of the pack members in setting up for one of his parties, one laying out cushions here, another arranging goblets on a table there.

As I watch, he produces the flask from his pocket and takes a swig from it that I suspect is an early start to his reveling. Apparently last night's hosting wasn't enough festivity for him. Or maybe he needs this party to recover from that one.

When I make my way downstairs, the rooms on the first floor are all empty, the halls silent. I feel like a ghost walking through them—like maybe I'm not really here at all. After hiding for the better part of the last week, could I have faded away completely? It sounds absurd, but then, how can anything be more absurd than the fact that I'm living in a realm of faeries?

I venture down to the basement and gravitate toward the entertainment room at the lively music emanating from that direction. Peeking past the door, I find August braced at the edge of the sofa, his gaze intent on the TV as he jabs at his controller. On the screen, a digitized fighter whirls in the air with a spinning kick that knocks his opponent's head right off.

August lets out a whoop and lowers the controller with a grin. He looks so at ease that I convince myself it's perfectly fine to intrude.

"Hi," I say, slipping inside.

His grin widens at the sight of me, and there goes that damn flutter turning my insides all wobbly. When I was seeing him all the time, I must have started to get used to how handsome he is. Now it takes me a moment to catch my breath again.

He beckons me over to the sofa. "You're up! You looked pretty wiped out when I brought up your plate—I didn't want to wake you." A trace of shyness softens his expression. "How did you like the pancakes?"

"As delicious as you promised. I guess I lost most of the day."

"We all did. Tristan's bunch kept us up until it was almost dawn, and then Sylas wanted to go over everything they said before our memories had faded." He stifles a yawn. "We're all on Whitt time now. I'm not sure what's going to happen with dinner. Breakfast was already a late lunch. Sylas went out to check on something, and I don't know when he'll be back."

"Well, I won't be needing dinner anytime soon. I just stuffed myself with those pancakes." I step closer, halting by the sofa's arm. "I've had enough of my own company after the last few days. Do you mind if I watch you play?"

August waves off any concern I might have had about my welcome. "I've got some games you could even play with me."

I sink onto the sofa at the farthest end from him and grimace. "I haven't played anything in years. I don't even know what game system that is. I'm not sure I'll give you much competition."

August aims another grin at me. "I'll go easy on you. It'll still be fun for me. I can hardly ever convince Sylas to play, and Whitt only will when he's so loopy on whatever he's been drinking or eating that he spends more time shooting his mouth off than actually handling the controller."

He's so enthusiastic my hesitation melts. "All right. I can give it a try, anyway."

"Let's find something a little less violent for this…" He shuffles through his stack of games, makes a triumphant sound, and swaps out the discs. Then he hands me a second controller, pointing out the buttons. "This one's for jumping. This one for picking things up and then throwing. This one lets you run double-speed. You move around using this joystick. It's pretty simple. You'll get the hang of it fast."

I peer at the bright cartoony graphics on the screen. "What am I supposed to be doing?"

"We're competing to solve the puzzle first. The first levels are really straight-forward. It only gets complicated once you're warmed up." He gives me a playfully ominous look. "Just watch out for the beetles."

Even though it's been nearly a decade since I last faced off against my little brother on our old Playstation—which I guess is probably an antique by gaming standards at this point—my hands fall into the rhythm of button pushing and stick swiveling with just a few hitches. Apparently video games are like bikes, and once you've learned how to work them, your body remembers.

I direct my character through a maze and across a few obstacles to hit the goal at the end ahead of August—but I'm pretty sure he let me win. "Nicely done," he says, and I resolve that I'm going to win at least one level of this game fair and square.

The puzzles do get harder, but my fingers fly faster as I get used to the strategies. I can tell I'm actually putting up a decent fight when August starts aiming all of his attention at the screen rather than regularly checking in on me. He leans forward on the sofa, his golden eyes gleaming and intent. When I pull off a double jump and push a switch just in time to leap to the goal ahead of him, he rocks back with a little cheer. "You're a natural!"

I aim a teasing kick at his leg. "Don't go easy on me now."

He laughs. "Oh, I'll give you a run for your money."

He does, dashing through the next course so swiftly I'm breathless trying to keep up, even though the only part of my body that's moving is my hands. August wins that level, and we launch straight into the next.

As I sink into the flow, my mind creeps back to those long ago days when I played with Jamie—not this game, but plenty of others. He'd get so excited when he was winning that he'd hop right off the sofa in the living room and bounce up and down on his feet, as if he could propel his character faster that way.

I'm never going to see that gleeful smile again. Never going to trade joking challenges as we try to one-up each other.

The loss is nine years old, but the grief wallops me as if it's just happened. When have I really had space to grieve? I'm not sure I can even now, when I have no idea what happened to Jamie after Aerik wrenched me away, who found him, what was done with his body…

My hands shake where I'm clutching the controller, and my character collides with one of the chomping beetles. I'm sent back to the start of the course.

August glances over at me and presses pause. "Are you liking the game all right?" he asks, studying my expression.

I don't want to talk about what's really on my mind—about the carnage left in my wake, the blood spilled because of *me*. My throat has choked up, but I manage to swallow the emotions down. My stomach aches with them, but that's okay. I've had a lot of practice at tuning my discomforts out.

Instead, I focus on everything that's good about this moment I'm in right now. "Yeah, it's perfect for taking my mind off that Tristan guy and his 'surprise' visit."

August sets down his controller. "You must have been terrified last night. Sylas couldn't find a way to dissuade them from going upstairs without making them suspicious, which would have been even worse. You did a good job, hiding away as well as you did. As far as we could tell, they didn't catch on at all."

I'm glad I didn't screw anything up for them, at least. "Do you know why they came to see you? Was it really just a coincidence that they decided to after you brought me here?"

"Not exactly." August makes a face. "From the questions they asked, we got the impression Kellan must have said something that caught their attention. He handled most of our trade with the other packs when we needed anything we couldn't get or make in the domain, which is a lot more here on the fringes, and pretty much every lord has spies here and there listening for anything… interesting. I'd imagine the arch-lords have men scattered all through the domains keeping an eye on things too."

My shoulders have tensed. "He mentioned *me*?"

August shakes his head quickly. "No, nothing as specific as that, or I'm sure they'd have been asking a lot more pointed questions. Probably it was a more general discontented muttering… He might have given away that Sylas had some sort of plan in the works, one that Kellan thought he was handling badly, something along that line. And as soon as an arch-lord catches a hint that there are plots afoot, they tend to be wary of the worst. Understandably, since there are plenty of lords who'd like to add 'arch' to their title. And—"

He cuts himself off and shakes his head again, more emphatically this time. "In any case, they seemed satisfied that we weren't in the process of preparing a coup and decently impressed by the state of the keep, so that's all good. Sylas came up with a story about why Kellan wasn't here that should also have hinted at a reason he would have been irritable for reasons unconnected to treason—or any thefts we've committed." He shoots me a smile.

Even dead, Kellan has left more trouble for Sylas and the others to deal with. I nibble at my lower lip. "Everyone's going to find out that Kellan is dead eventually, aren't they?"

"Of course. But Sylas will manage how that news comes out. He'll know the best way to frame it. And honestly, if he has to admit that he was the one to make it happen… Plenty of folk have seen what Kellan was like. It won't come as a surprise that he could have pushed his lord that far."

"But Sylas took him into his cadre anyway."

"There are expectations of duty…" August sighs. "I don't think any of us was really happy about it, including Kellan. But we hoped he'd settle in and adapt. Not so much."

It takes a little of the burden off me knowing that Kellan rubbed just about everyone the wrong way, that Sylas was telling the truth when he said his death was a long time coming. But I can see that even though he didn't like the guy, even though they fought, Kellan's death doesn't sit easy with him.

I can't say the thought of my own eventual death—sooner or later—doesn't horrify me, and I've been a lot closer to it than August likely ever has. How hard must it be to grapple with the idea when you should have centuries ahead of you?

August turns to me again, and I realize I've been staring at him, taking in the details of his face, which is even more stunning with that haunted expression over the boyishly handsome features. I jerk my gaze away, and it catches on the tattoo peeking from beneath his sleeve instead.

I motion at it, grasping onto that seemingly safe topic of conversation. "Do those mean anything? Your tattoos?" As far as

I've been able to see from a distance, the regular pack members have a few here and there, but they aren't as inked up as Sylas and his cadre are—or Aerik and his. Maybe they're some sort of symbol of rulership?

August taps the one I pointed to, the arcing black lines twisting together like claws. "They're not exactly tattoos—not the way humans have them. We don't put them on ourselves. When we master a true name, the representation of it forms on our skin. The more true names you see a fae marked with, the more magic they can wield."

"True names?" I repeat. The term sounds vaguely familiar, maybe from faerie stories I read back home. With all the stealing of humans into the Mists, it makes sense that a little valid information about the fae would trickle back to our world.

"All things have true names tied into their essence. When you learn the true name of a substance or a plant or animal well enough, you can command it to your will." August gestures to the room around us. "We called up most of the keep from the trees that grew here, using their true names."

So they simply talked a bunch of trees into forming this massive building? Sounds like an awfully useful skill. "How do you learn them?"

"If you find someone willing to teach you who already knows, that gives you a huge step up. But most fae are protective of their knowledge. Otherwise, you work with whatever it is you're attempting to master in various ways until its true name reveals itself to you." He raises an eyebrow at me. "I wouldn't get any ideas, though. I've never heard of a human wielding magic."

I've wielded it, though. Once, anyway. Thinking of how I convinced the latch on my cage door to unlock, my pulse skips a beat. I'm not sure that's something I want August and the others knowing. Would it make me even more of a prize rather than a person?

"I think maybe Aerik used something like that to lock my cage," I say tentatively. The syllables are still burned into my memory. "What's 'fee-doom-ace-own'?"

August blinks at me. "You've got a good memory—your pronunciation is almost perfect. That's bronze. Your cage was made of it, wasn't it? There are other types of magic we can use, but true names are usually the most potent if you're not worried about someone else who knows them trying to counteract your spell."

And Aerik definitely wouldn't have worried that a lowly human could manage that. *Did* I really? Maybe it was only that he didn't concentrate quite hard enough that time, and the spell broke on its own. I haven't noticed any unexpected tattoos springing into being on my body.

I'll have to find an opportunity to test it. Except I have no idea how to use it when I'm not specifically undoing a spell someone else made. Well, I'll just have to see what happens.

"How many true names do you know?" I ask, setting those thoughts aside.

"Fifty-four," August says with obvious pride. "Whitt has close to eighty, but he's had a lot longer than I have to learn. I think Sylas has over a hundred… He's always developed his spellwork whenever he can. That's a lot even for a lord. It gets harder once you've covered the simple ones and the areas you have the most affinity for."

Right. August said before that he had a knack for bodily magic like healing. Does he have symbols on him for skin and muscle and bones?

As I remember how he checked my foot, another possibility occurs to me, bringing a chill through my nerves. "Do *people* have true names?" Could the fae command me by knowing mine? Would "Talia" be enough or would they need middle and last name as well?

August nods. "Fae do. August is the name my father gave me,

but we're all born knowing a deeper one that's bound to our soul. From what I understand, it's not the same with humans." He pauses. "But then, we have so many other kinds of magic that humans can't defend against, it wouldn't be necessary to go to the trouble of finding out."

Not exactly a comforting statement. "I guess you must keep your true names hidden most of the time," I say. Why would anyone want to give others that much power over them?

"All of the time is more like it," August says with a chuckle. "I've never shared mine. There are some lords who demand it of their cadre... I trust Sylas enough that I'd give him mine if he wanted it, but the reason I trust him that much is because he's *not* the kind of lord who'd rule that way, so it hasn't been an issue."

His admiration for Sylas reverberates through his voice. I think of the way he reacted when he smelled the fae lord's scent on my skin. My gut tightens, but August has been speaking freely and warmly enough that I find the courage to form the words.

"Were you... angry because Sylas and me—because we—" I can't figure out how to finish the question, both out of embarrassment and uncertainty about how to even describe what happened between the fae lord and me. We didn't have sex. Could you call what we did "making out"? That doesn't feel like the right phrase either—like something teenagers do in the back of a car, nowhere near the intensity of the energy created between the two of us in his bed.

Thankfully, what I have said is enough for August to catch my meaning. He drops his gaze, his shoulders tensing, but he looks more awkward than upset.

"I'm sorry about my reaction," he says. "I had no claim—it just took me by surprise. But it isn't as if I could compete with him."

It takes a few seconds for that comment to sink in. I knit my brow. "I didn't think it was a competition. I didn't think— You said we shouldn't do anything together."

His laugh comes out hoarse. "Not because I don't want to. Skies above, Talia, you have no idea— But I've seen what happens to humans who're taken in with the fae that way. It doesn't often end well. I'm not sure, even if I *mean* well… It matters more to me to protect you than to take you as a lover. But Sylas can protect you better than I can, so he can probably manage both. I can't resent him—or you—for that."

A jumble of emotion fills my chest, confusion and longing and frustration and more that I can't easily label. "It's not as if I've married him or something. It was just one night." So far. I also can't say I wouldn't want another, given the chance. But I couldn't say that about August either. Argh.

I bring my hands to my face. "I like you a lot too, okay?" I go on, my voice partly muffled by my palms. "I don't think he's… better than you, or whatever. This is all just really overwhelming. I don't know how I'm supposed to act."

August's tone softens. "You're doing just fine. I really wasn't angry with you. If I was angry with anyone, it was myself—and I've dealt with that."

He reaches out to stroke his hand over my hair, and a quiver runs across my skin that's both eager and anxious. I want to kiss him, but I'm also terrified of screwing this whole thing up.

Maybe it's better if I don't get too intimate with any of the fae men while my future is still so uncertain. But that doesn't mean I can't allow myself a little closeness, does it?

I swallow hard and lower my hands. Then, carefully and deliberately, I shift my body over on the sofa so I can lean my head against August's shoulder.

He hesitates for a moment, and then he presses a whisper of a kiss to my forehead. His arm tucks around mine. A sense of peace I haven't experienced since Whitt first announced that Tristan was coming wraps around me with the warmth emanating from his side.

In this moment, being nestled against him feels perfectly *right*. This is all I need, and I don't want to risk it by experimenting with more.

"Do you want to keep playing, or are you chickening out in the face of my immense skills?" August asks, lightly teasing.

A smile crosses my lips. "No chickens here. Bring it on."

After a couple more losses, I manage to beat him at a level, bringing our points to a near tie. "Maybe I'm the one who should be worried," August jokes, nudging me with his elbow where I'm still leaning against him, and the door swings open.

Sylas looks in at us. For the first instant, he looks weary but contented, maybe expecting to find only August in here playing alone.

At the sight of me cuddled up to the other man, the fae lord's jaw clenches and his unscarred eye blazes like it did when I told him about August guiding me in the pool. He barrels into the room with an aggressive energy so potent it seems to lift the dark waves of his hair with a rising wind. His voice is little more than a growl. "I told you—"

He's looking at August, not at me, and August is already jerking away from me as if burned. Guilt stabs through me—and then something even sharper, a blaze of my own it takes me a second to recognize.

It's anger. I've forgotten what it's like to be angry myself.

"Stop it!" I snap. My voice squeaks, but the reprimand is firm enough that Sylas actually does halt in his tracks.

I catch August's hand and twine my fingers with his before meeting the fae lord's eyes again. "He wasn't hurting me. We were just sitting together. What's wrong with that?"

Sylas's gaze is still searing, but it's dampened from a full-out inferno to a more subdued smolder. "He did more than that with you before," he says.

"So what?" My pulse is rattling through my veins, so fast I'd almost think it's going to burst free of my body, but all of a sudden I am *so* angry. I'm not sure I've ever been quite this furious in my life. About the way Sylas is acting right now, about how he ordered me shut away for so many days before. About all this time waiting to find out whether I'm even going to have any kind of life beyond the next full moon. About all the moons that passed before I came here, while I was tortured and bled by the whims of the fae.

I've been terrified and anguished and despairing and grieving, but whatever anger started to rise up before, I must have bottled it away. Now it's overflowing, swelling through my chest and spilling from my mouth.

I cling onto the rush of power that reverberates through the anger. "You can force me to stay here and take my blood if you decide to, and I can't do anything about that. But I don't *belong* to you. I don't belong to either of you. So don't treat me like I'm a toy for you to fight over."

Sylas inhales slowly. The smolder retreats, although it'd be hard to say he looks *happy* about the situation. His shoulders come down too, his arms folding loosely over his chest. He eyes me for a moment as if waiting to see if anything else is going to burst out of me.

"That's fair," he says finally. "It wasn't my intention to treat you that callously, and I apologize. Your affections are yours to do with as you see fit. If this is your choice, I—"

A growl of my own escapes me, and he's so taken aback he shuts his mouth.

"I haven't made any choice," I say, more irritated than angry now. "I don't know if I'm *going* to make a choice. Like I said, we're just sitting together. I think that's about as much as I'm interested in for the time being. I'd be happy to sit with you too. There's plenty of room on the sofa. Why does it have to be such a big deal?"

August has been sitting rigid with tension through the whole conversation, but at that question, he gives my hand a gentle squeeze that soothes some of the terror that's coursing through me beneath the anger.

Sylas blinks, apparently lost for words. His gaze slides to the younger man and back to me. Then, to my enormous relief, the corner of his mouth twitches upward.

He lowers himself onto the sofa at my other side and gives my knee a light squeeze. "I suppose it doesn't."

"There. The world didn't end." Now that my fury is fading, I'm a bit dizzy from the sudden surge of emotion. And maybe also from being tucked between the two sexiest men I've ever met, the heat of their bodies enveloping mine.

I drag in a breath, composing myself. "Is there another controller? You've got to have at least one three-player game, right?"

August's grin comes back, wary and then widening. "I can scrounge something up." He glances at Sylas. "If you're not afraid of getting your ass whooped by a human girl."

Sylas glowers at him but without any real rancor. "I don't know about her, but you can count on being thoroughly whooped yourself."

"I accept that."

He gets up to switch games and comes back with a third controller. Sylas accepts it happily enough, and the tension in the room ebbs.

As the game starts up, I snuggle deeper between the two men, resting my feet against August's thigh, leaning my head on Sylas's shoulder. I don't know what's going to come out of any of this, but I'm struck by the sense that as long as this moment lasts, I'm exactly where I want to be.

CHAPTER TWENTY-SIX

Whitt

The berries burst between my teeth, their sweet-and-sour juice trickling down my throat and vibrating through my senses. I let the dizzying rush consume me, knowing from a multitude of experience that the initial tsunami of a high will temper into a milder exhilaration if I give myself over to it.

The stars that dot the night sky sparkle brighter. The three-quarters moon glows so starkly it burns my eyes. Music and buoyant voices surround me. I turn on my heel, ingesting it all like a decadent feast.

I don't ever lose myself for very long. I'm exorbitantly familiar with my limits and how to avoid crossing certain lines. But these fleeting moments when nothing exists but the glittering sensations of the present are the only times the constant tautness wound through my chest ever dissipates completely. Without them, I might find myself stretched so far I'd break right in half.

And that wouldn't do, now would it?

The dark thought signals the dwindling of the high. I exhale in a careless huff and return my attention to the business at hand. Because these revels are as much business as they are entertainment —for me, at least.

Brigit drifts closer to me, peachy smoke wafting snake-like from her lips. A stoned haze clouds her eyes. She offers me a lopsided smile as if she can't quite remember how to curve her mouth into the right shape and then giggles at herself.

"You've outdone yourself tonight, cadre-man," she says. "Such a celebration for the pack."

"Such a pack to celebrate," I return, the play on her words slipping glibly off my tongue. "I thought you deserved every pleasure we could afford after the work you all put into preparing for our visitors."

"Stuffy lordly ones," she mutters, and I immediately perk up to a sharper alertness I don't show. The first rule of success is to never be more than half as inebriated as you appear to be. Already I'm filing away the knowledge that Brigit is definitely not someone we should be including in any revels that include visiting lords or their cadres. If her tongue can slide into disrespect around me, it could around anyone.

But I was *hoping* to hear that disrespect from a few of my pack-fellows. I'll get the most truth from those bold enough to show their true feelings.

"Well, they didn't stay all that long," I say, carefully not approving of her choice of words while tacitly encouraging them.

"I'd say they wore out their welcome." She takes another gulp of smoke from the spindly pipe she's holding and lets it stream from her arched nostrils. "Coming back around to poke at us."

I study her from the corner of my eye. No one else mentioned Tristan lingering, but after the show Sylas made of how important it was to give the intruders a spectacular welcome, it's no wonder they'd feel hesitant voicing any criticism. They may respect Sylas as their leader, but they have a healthy dose of apprehension mixed in as well, as it should be with any lord.

"All three of them?" I ask.

"Just that woman. Bad enough. Stares at everyone like she's considering how their heads would look mounted on pikes." Brigit's voice starts to slur. "I was just getting up to pick thistledew—you know it's best if you catch it just before dawn—and spotted her lurking by the outer homes, writing something on paper like she was making a report."

Perhaps that was exactly what Jax, the female cadre member Tristan brought with him, had been doing. It would have been beneath any lord, let alone one of Tristan's stature, to admit to an interest in the lives of the faded folk of our pack. Apparently he took one anyway and sent one of his cadre back to indulge it.

They were sly enough to escape the notice of our official sentries. If this ordinary pack woman hadn't been headed out for some pre-dawn dew-gathering, we would never have known that their concerns weren't fully resolved.

A prickle condenses in my gut through my light-headedness. What would Tristan have wanted Jax to look for? What did that bastard Kellan say that made them so concerned?

It wouldn't have mattered a month ago. A month ago we had nothing to hide. Now, we've just spent days covering up the presence of a girl who could solve the arch-lords' greatest problem. The longer Sylas lets this insanity go on, the worse it'll be for us if some small misstep reveals our secret.

Brigit's chosen mate weaves through the revelers to her side and plants a sloppy kiss on her cheek. From the dilation of his pupils, he's indulged at least as much as she has in the recreational substances on offer.

He casts his bleary gaze toward me. "I hope our lord will rest easy now that the visit is over."

I keep my voice light, even though that remark turns the prickle inside me into a deeper jab. "Lord Sylas wanted the best for our honored guests, but I'm sure he wasn't overly troubled."

The man hums. "So it should be. He did seem rather—" He cuts himself off, focusing more clearly on me for an instant and remembering I'm more than a fellow reveler.

Brigit sways in his arms. "Our lord has a lot on his mind these days."

They drift away, leaving me with a hole in the pit of my stomach that seems to drain away the lingering effects of the berries and the wine I drank before.

The folk of the pack have picked up on Sylas's distraction. He would never want to present anything to them but total assurance and attentiveness. The problem of the girl is affecting him more than he must realize.

We're lucky even this many have stuck with us so long—and none of us can pretend it's entirely out of loyalty. If the risks of staying under Sylas's rule began to appear greater than the risks of searching out a place in another pack, one better situated as well... We wouldn't have a mass exodus on our hands, but our numbers would dwindle more than they already have. And the fewer are left, the less secure our position becomes, as well as our chances of bettering it.

I laugh and eat and dance with a couple of the women, but all the while that knowledge stews inside me. When the revel peters out, some of the folk sprawling under the stars to sleep and others ambling away to their homes, I head back to the keep far more sober than anyone—least of all me—should ever have to be.

I need to speak to Sylas. When I make it clear how precarious our position may have gotten, he'll *have* to see he can't keep delaying the inevitable. Lovely as the mite is to look at, damaged though she may be through no fault of her own, at the same time she's a ticking bomb that could explode at any moment, taking all of us down with her.

I won't pretend not to see why he might hesitate. That moment after he felled Kellan when she crept to his side and offered her regrets, even after the way the bastard meant to savage her... The way she apologized to *me* after August stormed off on her...

A soft twinge passes through my chest, but I dismiss it as quickly as it rose up. She puts on a good show of honor and compassion, as if any being could really be that benevolent—and Sylas buys into it just like that. This despite the fact that her presence has caused more turmoil in and around this keep than we've faced since we were exiled here. Despite the fact that she has far less reason to consider our welfare than Kellan ever did.

It's hard to believe those gestures weren't actually strategic. How could she possibly truly care that much about any of us? Even Isleen—

I cut off that line of thinking with a jerk of my head and stalk onward. I don't have to convince our lord that the mite is playing to his sympathies. I only need him to see the bigger picture. Nothing and no one could make him shirk from his duty.

Sylas isn't in his study or his bed chamber—he isn't one to ignore an insistent knock. Frowning, I prowl through the main floor and then down to the basement.

A murmur of voices and the jangle of modern human music carries from the entertainment room. He must be watching one of those absurd movies.

The door stands a few inches ajar, so I can see into the room before I reach it. I jerk to a halt within arm's reach, my body stiffening.

I've approached quietly out of habit with the stealth it's my nature to fall into when I'm alert enough. None of the figures in the room have noted my arrival. They *are* watching a movie, the shifting lights of the screen playing across their faces in the semi-darkness: Sylas, August, and the human girl tucked between them.

Her eyes have closed, her features even more delicate in sleep.

Her head is tipped against Sylas's shoulder, and his hand rests on her leg. By her other thigh, her fingers lie interlaced with August's. As I watch, he glances at her with unmistakeable tenderness.

When he shifts his attention to Sylas, his expression tightens. Our lord glowers in return, his thumb tracing a gentle line across the girl's knee.

What's left of my stomach balls into a knot. Before I'm aware of the motion, my jaw has clenched. I have to tense my legs against the urge to storm in there and demand to know whether they're out of their minds.

She's wormed her way even further into their affections than I suspected. *Both* of their affections. And whatever truce they've come to tonight, that look exchanged tells me it's far from settled. There will be a reckoning—there will be *several* reckonings, between them and within themselves.

August, I can understand. He's got a soft heart under all that muscle, especially for vulnerable things. But Sylas—by all that is dust, I thought he was wiser than this.

Neither of those facts justifies the rage boiling up inside me, the grating of my teeth against each other. Of course she would turn to both of them and not to me. The one who's buttered her up with his chumminess and his cooking, and the one who's protected her at the risk of everything else he holds dear. What have I done other than offer her a few wry remarks and a spectacular high? Oh, and a panic attack, let's not forget that.

That shouldn't be a problem. It *can't* be. I want nothing to do with her, this treasure of Sylas's. I learned my lesson far too well for that.

Yet against my will, my mind slips back to fragments of a dream a few nights back—of a slip of a girl dancing naked in starlight, her pink hair flying wild and her arms stretched out with the uninhibited joy she took to so easily when I gave her the cavaral syrup. Of her bright eyes gleaming with abandon… and then glowing with a more wanton vitality as she reached for me.

My fingers twitch. Would her skin feel as smooth, her body move as lithely against mine as it did in that delusion? Or would I rather have her crouched in my bedroom like the other morning, shaking and then unexpectedly shrewd—

Whirling, I yank my eyes away from the actual scene before me. I stalk back to the staircase, groping for my flask as I go. The first gulp—duskapple wine tonight—burns the edge off my frustration. The second clouds over the images I wanted to banish. The third brings me back to that glimmering plateau where my wits fly free of any hindrance of emotion but I haven't quite tipped over into unsteadiness. I stop there.

It's no good talking to Sylas. I can see that much. If he's already allowed himself to stake that much of a claim over the girl, there's nothing this situation can end in but an absolute mess, no matter how well I master my… curiosity, no matter that Kellan's no longer spurring the tensions onward. As long as she's with us, the fissures that were already forming will only widen.

As long as she's with us.

I pause in the hallway outside the kitchen, the fermented spirits fizzing through my veins. My gaze lifts to the door at the far end of the parlor.

Wouldn't our lives be so much simpler if she'd made her escape as she intended to a week ago?

What of it if we lose our "cure"? She could never have been a permanent solution anyway, as Sylas himself admitted. We're only delaying the inevitable. We are wolves—we're meant to be wild. Why shouldn't the rest of my folk accept that?

There are other ways we can win back the arch-lords' favor. Ways that won't mean fracturing the bonds between lord and cadre even more. Ways that won't require me to watch my brothers—

I shove off that thought and the memory of her striking, pink-haired head tucked between them. It *isn't* about me. I was weak once and nearly destroyed us myself. This time...

This time I can save us.

And to do that, the girl must go.

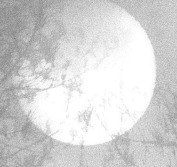

CHAPTER TWENTY-SEVEN

Talia

While I bathe in the pool, August keeps up a steady stream of seemingly aimless conversation, chatting about everything from human sports—it seems he's a football fan; big surprise—to what exercises I might try to strengthen the muscles around the warped part of my foot. I don't think his rambling straight from one subject to another really is so aimless, though. The aim is to avoid any mention of what happened between us here several days ago.

I'm okay with that. For a little while last night, everything seemed so simple and right. But it's been impossible not to notice throughout the day how the energy between August and Sylas has changed.

They haven't argued—they haven't said anything directly about their interest in me or mine in them at all—but there are pauses where there didn't used to be before, glances that give me the impression of sizing up rather than comradery.

I'd rather not fuel whatever tensions are lurking unspoken any more than I already have inadvertently. In the pool, I stay away from the jets, and when I get out, I dry off and pull my clothes back on quickly. August smiles at me as he emerges from behind the folding screen, but he leaves a few feet between us as we walk down the hall to the stairs.

In less than a week's time, I might have much bigger problems. I thought getting closer to the fae lord would make it harder for him to give me up, but with the way things are going, maybe he'll decide it's better for his cadre if he hands me over to the arch-lords and lets them work out how to best make use of my blood's inexplicable power. I'm sure he'll try to arrange things so that they'll treat me kindly, but he won't really have any say once I'm in their keeping, will he?

Every step I take here, every decision *I* make, feels so precarious. I can't even predict all the consequences that might ripple out from a single word or act.

I shrug off those worries as well as I can—nothing's happened *yet*, and I don't know what I could do right now that would definitely make my situation better rather than worse anyway—but it's hard to ignore them when we reach the top of the stairs to find Sylas waiting for us. Or rather, for me. He gives August a nod of acknowledgment with another of those brooding looks and waves the younger man off before turning to me.

"I'm still attempting to work out what's causing the effect you have over our 'curse'," he says. "Would you allow me to take a few of your hairs to test?"

The request eases my nerves a little. My wellbeing matters enough to him that he's asking even when he could probably have snatched a few without my noticing. And he hasn't given up his search to find a way to free me from his people's needs.

"Of course." I swivel to offer him the full array of my hair, damp but not outright wet after the recent toweling. "I hope the dye won't interfere with testing it."

"I'll take that into account. Close to the root, there'll be an unaffected section. It's better that I waited until it had time to grow."

He plucks the hairs so deftly that I only feel the faintest twinge in my scalp, careful not to touch me otherwise. The nape of my neck still tingles with the awareness of him standing so close, his hands mere inches from my skin.

We walk up to the second floor together, my foot brace tap-tap-tapping against the floor since I can't keep up with him even at his slowed-down pace if I aim for silence. At the branch in the hall, Sylas brushes his fingers over my shoulder in the lightest of caresses and heads in the opposite direction, presumably to his study.

Even that brief touch sends a wash of heat through me. It's like I've been starved after all this time without the slightest affection, and now my body is ravenous for whatever contact I can get.

I'll just have to keep a close eye on myself until I have a better idea where I stand now—and how Sylas and August are going to work out their uneasiness.

In my bedroom, I curl up in the armchair August recently brought up and open a book I borrowed from the entertainment room in recollection of how much I wished I had reading material up here the evening of Tristan's visit. The sky beyond the window is darkening, but the amber orb mounted over the chair wakes up with its wavering glow. This is some kind of life, at least. It could be so much worse.

I've sunk deeper into the chair, my legs slung over one of its arms and my mind sucked well into the story, when my bedroom door swings open. My head snaps up with a flinch, my pulse skittering in alarm. Sylas and August always knock—unless maybe it's an emergency…

But it isn't either of the fae men who've come to my bedroom before. Whitt stalks inside, shutting the door behind him and coming to a halt halfway to my chair. His sun-kissed hair looks even more wildly ruffled than usual, his blue eyes stormy, his jaw firmly set. He's so fiercely stunning that my heart stutters again in both awe and fear.

I scramble to straighten myself, clutching the book tightly as if it'll defend me from whatever he's come to demand. "Is everything all right?"

He cocks his head and considers me. "You've proven yourself decently observant, mite, even when you shouldn't be observing. Do *you* really think everything is 'all right'?"

I blink at him, my stomach twisting even in my confusion. "I don't know what you're talking about."

"Oh, no? So it's truly escaped your notice that your two paramours aren't quite as at ease with each other as they used to be —as they're meant to be?"

My face flushes at the clear insinuation of the word "paramours" before I've even processed the rest. How does he know—did Sylas or August tell him what's happened between us? Has it been obvious without anyone needing to mention it?

How *much* does he know?

Enough to realize the tensions he's picked up on are my fault. I tuck my legs up, hugging my knees with the urge to shrink in on myself. "I didn't mean for anything like this to happen."

Whitt waves an erratic hand through the air. "Of course you didn't. Why would it even occur to you to consider it?"

"Have they been fighting about it when I'm not around?" How bad have things gotten?

"From the looks of them, it's only a matter of time. And believe me, you won't want to find yourself in the middle of *that* squabble."

I grip my knees harder. "I don't know what to do. I tried to tell them— I haven't let anything happen since I realized— Me being here has already caused so much trouble with all of you. The last thing I want is for them to be at each other's throats."

Whitt pauses, studying me with his scowl shifting into a frown that's more puzzled than foreboding. What reaction was he expecting?

Whatever threw him off, he recovers quickly. "There's an easy solution," he says, brusquer than before. "They're riled up over you, so we take you out of the equation."

My body stiffens. I knew this might happen, and still— "Sylas is going to send me to the arch-lords now?" I ask, my voice thinning.

"No. I think you'll like this solution much better. You can head right back home."

This time I'm so startled I outright gape at him. "*Home?*"

He smiles, but it has none of August's warmth. "Yes, exactly. That's what you've wanted all along, isn't it?"

It is, but I didn't expect to have the opportunity handed to me like this by one of the cadre. I never anticipated getting an offer like this at all. It's a second before I can wrangle my words into order again. "You're saying Sylas would let me—"

"No," Whitt interrupts. "Sylas doesn't know about this. *I'm* arranging it. It'll be better for him and August—for all of us. Obviously it's better for you too. But you'll need to get on with it. Sylas is holed up in his study now, and August's taking out his frustrations on that long-suffering punching bag of his, but the window when they'll both be distracted is relatively short."

He wants me to go *right now*. My mouth opens and closes again. I ease my legs down, scanning his face for any hint that this is a trick or a trap. I wouldn't have thought Whitt would mess with my head like that—he's never seemed outright cruel—but I don't really know him.

"What—what about my blood? The cure? It's not much longer until the full moon."

"That won't be your problem anymore. This is your ticket out of the whole mess."

"But—" The twisting in my gut spreads through the rest of my body. "It'll still be *your* problem. All of yours. If I'm gone, you won't have any way of making the tonic."

Whitt pauses again, the frenetic energy that appeared to have gripped him faltering. "Why should that matter to *you*?" he asks abruptly.

I guess that's a reasonable question. I give the best answer I can. "You rescued me from Aerik. Sylas has protected me—you've all been... kind." Well, maybe that's not the best word for Whitt's behavior. "You've been counting on me to help you in return."

And honestly, I want to. I wouldn't hesitate for an instant if there was a way I could help that didn't require me to remain a prisoner for the rest of my life.

What will Sylas think when he realizes I'm gone—that I've run off on him after all?

Whitt seems to be rolling over my explanation in his head. His fingers flex at his sides as if he's grasping for a response. He takes a slow breath, and then says, "Your freedom matters more than that, doesn't it? We'll make do. We always have before. We *won't* make do if having you around tears our cadre apart."

Maybe he's right. I don't know Sylas or August all that well either—I don't know how fae in general act when they're vying over a potential lover. Whitt would have a much better idea about the potential for disaster than I do, wouldn't he?

And he's offering me a way out that will help me too. How *can* I say no to my freedom?

I push myself to my feet, tensing my thighs so my legs don't wobble. A lump has risen in my throat, but I force my voice past it. "Okay. I can see that. But the magic on the doors—and I don't know where to go even once I'm out..."

Whitt nods, his expression relaxing. "Go now. I've left the parlor door unlocked for you. Walk straight ahead from there across the fields and through the woods. You'll know you've reached the very edge of the Mists when the actual mist thickens. Watch for a thicker patch—by twilight, it'll look like a puddle turned sideways, deeper and darker, almost liquid. Walk through that, and you'll be back where you belong."

This is happening so fast, my head is spinning. I don't like running out on Sylas or August, but would *they* let me go like this? I can't imagine it.

But if I exist, then there have to be other cures out there somewhere, right? They'll find another way, and I won't stir up any more animosity between the two of them.

"Okay," I say, psyching myself up. "Okay." I raise my head to meet Whitt's gaze as directly as I can, letting all the gratitude in me color my voice. "I'm sorry for—for all the trouble I've already brought down on you. Thank you for this. And thank Sylas and August for me too, when they realize—tell them I know they tried to do right by me, and I really was happy here some of the time."

Whitt stares at me for a long moment. Has his face paled? Maybe he's thinking forward to when the others discover my disappearance and how they'll react. I can't imagine they'll be pleased, even if it's for the best.

"Yes," he says. The word comes out strained. He clears his throat and goes on. "Yes, I'll do that. Go on now. If we're lucky, they won't notice you're missing until morning when you'll be well away from here."

I nod. He steps into the hall ahead of me, checking that the coast is clear, and motions me out.

"It's for the best," he mutters, so low I'm not sure whether he's talking to me or to himself. "It's all for the best."

And that's why I have to do this. I hustle down the hall, setting down my foot in its brace as lightly as I can manage without sacrificing too much speed. Whitt meanders off toward his room.

Down the stairs, through the kitchen, my heart thumps faster. I'm still half-expecting to find out this is some hugely elaborate joke.

It isn't. The handle on the parlor door turns smoothly in my hand. I push the door open.

A light wind tickles over me. The long sprawl of the field lies ahead, the forest thick with shadow beyond it. My legs momentarily lock. Then I propel myself forward with a sharper skip of my pulse.

For the first time in more than nine years, I emerge into the outside world. The scents of hay and wildflowers that lace the warm evening air are familiar from the breezes that've carried through my bedroom window. They fill my lungs more swiftly out here, though, wrapping around me, teasing through my clothes and hair.

It's overwhelming to the point of dizzying me, but I can't let myself linger. As long as I'm in view of the keep and the pack's houses, someone could spot me and raise an alarm. Training my gaze on the dark stretch of the forest, I hurry toward it as fast as my limp allows, worrying less about stealth on the soft grass that muffles most of the sound of the brace.

I'm going home. I'm really going *home*. Whatever that might look like after all these years. A giddy tremor shoots through me. I can't tell whether I'm excited or petrified.

Once I've slipped between the trees, the tension in my chest loosens a little. The air licks cooler over my skin but stays warm enough that I don't regret my tee's short sleeves. I pick my way across the uneven terrain more carefully now, squinting through the dimness as I watch for rocks and jutting roots on the forest floor.

How far is it until I reach the edge of the Mists? Will I find it in the forest or somewhere on the other side?

I should have asked Whitt more questions. But he sent me off so urgently… He must have been concerned I wouldn't get another chance—or that even one more night with me around would push Sylas and August into a fight they couldn't come back from.

I won't think about how disappointed or worried or—being realistic—*angry* Sylas will be when he notices my empty room. I won't think about all the uncertainties that await in the world I was stolen from. Better not to think at all.

Just keep walking. Just keep going forward, and somehow this insane scenario will sort itself out. It has to.

An ache starts to creep through my warped foot despite the brace. It wasn't meant to support me on a hike through the wilderness. But ahead of me, through the twilight, I can see the trees are thinning. Strands of mist trail around them, glowing in the moonlight.

My spirits leap. I'm almost there.

I take several hasty steps and stub my toe on a fallen branch. As I catch myself against a tree trunk, hissing at the pain, a rustling sound from somewhere to my right makes me freeze. I hold totally still, listening, straining to see through the thickening darkness.

Nothing moves in my view. It must have been a deer or a squirrel or some faerie equivalent.

I move to keep walking, and a figure materializes out of the shadows just a few yards away.

A long hooded cloak covers her from head to knee, but I can make out enough of her face to know she's a stranger. Heavy-lidded eyes skim over me as an amused smile curves full lips.

"Well, well," she says, and with a jolt, I realize she's not a *complete* stranger. It's the female voice I heard carrying from the dining room two nights ago—the woman from Tristan's cadre.

She stalks a few steps closer with predatory grace, her lips pulling back to reveal her gleaming teeth. "Where do you think you're going so far from your master, little human runaway?"

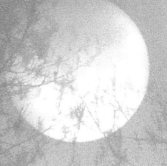

CHAPTER TWENTY-EIGHT

Sylas

The tincture I drip onto the root end of Talia's hair shows no reaction whatsoever—not a hiss or a gleam or even a wobble. I lean back in my chair with a growl of frustration.

There's magic in her somewhere—there has to be. So why does the source and nature of it elude every attempt I make to understand it?

Humans aren't meant to possess magic at all, and I've seen no indication that she's anything other than human besides the effect of her blood during the full moon. Whatever causes it, it must be with her at all other times as well. If Aerik discovered some spell that would bring out that power in any human's blood on command, he wouldn't have needed this particular human so badly.

My sense of the waxing moon beyond the keep weighs on me. It's merely days now before the full moon is on us again. I may find a few other tactics to use, but those will be last-ditch efforts rather than anything I believe has a solid chance of unraveling this mystery.

At some point, sooner rather than later, I'm going to have to accept that I *won't* unravel this mystery before the wildness takes us again. I've let myself hold off on making any broader decisions while hoping my tests would reveal answers that would guide me, but that hardly seems likely now.

None of my possible solutions will let my conscience rest easy. If I offer Talia to the arch-lords as the solution to our curse, I betray a woman I've come to care about more deeply than I'd willingly admit even to my cadre—a woman who's earned that affection with the strength and generosity she shows at every turn. By handing her over, I might fracture my cadre as well, knowing how August feels about her.

Even forcing her to give up her blood to myself and my pack would be betraying the trust she's put in me, and I doubt word could fail to reach Aerik that somehow only my pack resisted the wildness during the first full moon after his treasure was stolen. As soon as he's aware we stole her, we'll have a battle on our hands, one that could ravage those who've stood by me and depend on me.

And if I require nothing of Talia at all, I betray all those folk—I fail the pack I've sworn to serve and shield in every way I can. They deserve my loyalty above all others.

Will I run more of my tests and grasp at straws for weeks longer until some misstep gives us away after all, and instead of being celebrated, we're reviled for withholding the "cure" from the rest of our Seelie brethren?

No, there are no good answers at all. And I have seen the consequences that can come when I fail to tackle an uncomfortable situation head on. My pack has paid for my reluctance once before in spades.

That acknowledgment provokes a resolve that stabs through me as brutal as a blunt dagger, but I can't avoid the realization as much as it pains me. I must bring Talia to the arch-lords. For my pack, for my people, I cannot let my selfish desires undermine my responsibilities to those I rule over.

There's no more time for dallying. If I'm going to make proper arrangements to ensure the transition will be as safe as possible, to fulfill my promises to her as well as I can, I need to begin now. I can still do *some* right by her, even if not as much as I'd wish to.

With a heavy heart, I stand up and head into the hall.

She deserves to know my decision. She deserves to be heard, to be given a chance to speak, even if I can't imagine what she could say that would sway the balance. She's surprised me more than once before, after all. I'll tell her she has a few days to prepare to leave and that I'll see to it she finds herself in the care of the arch-lord most benevolent to humankind. With the strength and tenacity she's shown, who's to say she won't carve out a *better* place for herself there?

And I'll back off on any attempt to claim her. If she and August should wish to seek each other out in those remaining days, they can proceed without fear of reprisal.

By the Heart, let that be enough.

As I walk to Talia's bedroom, the burning sensation in my chest doesn't fade. Even my final act of charity digs into me like a wound. Last night, I meant to claim her for myself for as long as I could have her with me. And she refused to be claimed at all—by myself or by August.

I want her. She wanted me. I'm not used to contending with the possibility that a potential lover might want another man as well, let alone one of my cadre-chosen. But I doubt she'll have much affection left for me after our conversation tonight. She'll be better off with him in what time they have, if she wishes it. Even if the thought stirs a denial in me so furious it sears through my ribs.

How ridiculous is it to be worrying over that when I'll be quite literally casting her to the wolves in a few days' time?

I steel myself and knock on her door.

No answer comes, not even the sound of movement from the other side. I knock again, listening closely. Even if she has fallen deeply enough asleep that she wouldn't rouse at the rapping on the door, my sharp ears will make out her breathing.

They don't. There's no indication of any living being in the room beyond.

Frowning, I ease the door open. It's as empty as it sounded. The only sign of Talia's presence is the book lying haphazardly on the seat of the armchair by the window.

The moment my gaze catches on it, an afterimage floats through my vision from my dead eye: Talia sitting up with a jolt of her spine, her mouth tensing, her eyes startled and… sad? The book falls from her hand to the cushion—and then I'm seeing only the chair before me again, that fragment of what I have to assume was the recent past vanishing.

My hand tightens on the side of the door. Why would she have looked upset just now? What drew her from her reading and her room?

There could be a perfectly simple explanation. It might be as innocuous as that the book reminded her of some uncomfortable event in her own life, and she went to find another activity to distract herself. But as I stride down the hall, a thread of uneasiness weaves through my gut.

Both the shared lavatory and the privy are vacant. Talia isn't in the kitchen, the dining room, or the entrance room, but those weren't likely possibilities at this time of night anyway.

I barrel down the stairs to the basement, checking the entertainment room, the sauna, and then heading toward the gym. She could have gone to August before I even gave my blessings—

No. August emerges before I've reached the room, rubbing his dampened hair with a towel, his face flushed from the exertion he's just put his body through. The wary look he gives me sets my teeth on edge, as annoyed with myself as with him. He is my brother-by-father, my cadre-chosen—it isn't right that he should mistrust me.

But that is a hurdle we'll need to overcome another day.

"Has Talia been down here?" I ask.

His wariness falls away behind a flash of concern. "I haven't seen her, not since she went upstairs with you."

By all that is dust, that's not the answer I wished to hear. "She headed to her room, but she isn't there now. Nor any of the other places I might have expected. I haven't checked *every* room in the building yet, though."

Perhaps she's gone to one of our bed chambers. I've already covered the lower two floors thoroughly.

We lope to the upper floor together, veering in separate directions at the split in the hall without needing to consult one another. All of the bed chambers are empty other than Whitt's. As I come up on his door, his voice carries through it in a dull mumble. "…the best."

Is he talking to Talia? The idea that she's in his chamber with him—for what purpose?—sparks a clash of relief and possessiveness. I shove the door open.

She isn't with him, though. Whitt sits slumped against the footboard of his bed alone, his head tipped back as he drains the dregs from a goblet. A large bottle of absinthe sits beside him, only a thin ring left in the bottom. Its heady, sour scent fills the room.

Has he gone through that entire thing tonight? It's not like my older half-brother to get drunk to the point of stinking, especially on his own.

As he glances up at me, the swaying of his torso while he repositions himself not giving me much confidence that he'll be any help at all, I rein in my annoyance. He couldn't have known we might need him.

"Looking awfully serious, li'l brother," he slurs. "Have some of this to ease your spirits." He waggles the bottle in my direction and then focuses blearily on it, his face falling as he must realize there's none left to share.

Skies above, I can't remember the last time I saw him so inebriated he couldn't even talk straight. He hasn't been far gone enough to call me "little brother" rather than "my lord" or at least "Sylas" since I took Hearthshire. What's gotten into him?

I don't have time to try to shake him out of it. "Have you seen Talia?" I ask.

His gaze sharpens then, the haze clearing for an instant. His mouth forms a grimace, and he sets the bottle down with a thump. "Why would I have?"

August comes up beside me, his unusually grim expression giving away the bad news before he speaks. "There's no sign of her anywhere."

I exhale slowly, willing the turmoil inside me to settle. She couldn't have left the keep. I set the spells on the doors myself before I came upstairs with her. I didn't even think I *needed* them after she decided to stay rather than go through with her first escape attempt.

"Maybe we've just missed her," I say. "Let's go through the keep from top to bottom together. Call her name as well as looking into each room. She'll be here somewhere. You take the rooms to the left, and I'll take the right."

August nods without a moment's hesitation. Whatever tensions had risen between us, they've fallen away now that we face a shared concern. I can't forget that he earned his spot as a trusted member of my cadre.

As I turn from the doorway, Whitt lurches to his feet. From his bedroom doorway, he watches us begin our sweep. The ruddiness of intoxication still colors his face and neck, and his gaze veers at odd moments, but he's holding himself up steadily enough.

He wouldn't be a trusted member of my cadre if I didn't know he's rarely as soused as he lets himself appear to be.

"You lost the mite?" he says, and chuckles hoarsely. "One slip of a human girl giving two big bad fae quite the run-around."

I don't need his snarky remarks. "Help us look, or keep quiet," I bark at him.

We head downstairs, and he shuffles after us, seemingly more out of curiosity than with any intention of assisting.

"Did you check the pantry?" August asks. When I shake my head, hope lights his face. I head into the kitchen after him, scanning the space between the counters and the islands, the chairs in the parlor—

My deadened eye prickles. A ghostly figure swims into my vision. The specter of Talia grasps the back door, her expression so miserable it makes my throat constrict. She tugs, and it opens.

I stop in my tracks, staring, but the image is gone. It can't be from her first escape attempt—she was at the front door then. And how can I imagine it's from some future moment when she's missing right now?

My voice comes out rough. "She isn't in the pantry, is she?"

August emerges, the hope that kindled in him faded but not gone. "No. There's still a lot more—"

I cut him off. "She's gone. Out that door." I stride up to it and can sense before I even reach it that the magic in the lock has dispersed.

Nothing moves on the starlit field beyond the windows. How long ago did she take flight?

August sucks in a startled breath. "How? I swear she didn't have salt this time."

"I know." He gave me his word when I laid into him over that indiscretion before, and I have enough faith in him that I wouldn't have asked. "She must have discovered some other trick. Maybe her blood gave her the ability to crack the spell." Who can say when I can't discern the slightest thing about how that power of hers works?

"But—*why?*"

The same question twisting through my thoughts. The immediate impression may be gone, but the memory of the filmy image of her, of the misery on her face, has etched itself in my memory.

She didn't even look as if she wanted to leave. Why now? She couldn't have known what I was going to say to her tonight. What changed since she told me she felt safest by my side?

That question has barely crossed my mind before the obvious answer strikes me. I felt her gaze on me every time August and I interacted over the past day. I know she was taking in the friction between us. And she made it quite clear how she felt about any show of animosity to stake a claim over her.

"Perhaps she no longer felt secure while there was tension between us over her affections," I say. "She'll have picked up on it, as much as we held it back. She's a sensitive one."

August pales. "That would be just like her, wouldn't it? To leave because she didn't want to cause problems for *us?*"

My hands clench at my sides. I resist the urge to drive one of them into the wretched door that released her. "I should have heeded what she said last night more. She couldn't have been clearer that any aggression to compete for her favor made her uncomfortable."

Whitt coughs where he's leaning against one of the islands. I'd almost forgotten he'd trailed in behind us. His forehead has furrowed. "She told you *not* to fight over her?"

August lets out a laugh, short and humorless. "She put us right in our places. But I didn't think— We've kept the peace, even if we can't completely control our feelings. What could have pushed her to this point so quickly?"

Whitt glances from one of us to the other, looking rather green all of a sudden. I'm about to shove a bowl in front of him in case he's about to vomit all that absinthe up when he appears to shake the queasiness off. "It's better for her in the long run if she's rid of us, isn't it? Puts us in a bit of a bind to be sure, but we've managed in the past well enough. She wanted to get home."

My gaze travels back to the window. Another memory hits me —an observation that unsettled me at the time and now chills me straight through to the bones.

"*If* she makes it out of the Mists. If she's not caught by folk worse than us. I saw evidence of trespass in the woods during my evening run. Someone's been lurking in our domain." I march forward, jerking my hand for my cadre to follow. "We have to go after her and hope we find her before our enemies do."

In Whitt's current state, I'm not sure he'll come, but he hustles out alongside August, his eyes clearing with a gleam that looks almost frantic. "They wouldn't dare—to attack what could be one of our servants in our domain…"

"Are you sure enough of that to gamble on it? We went right into another lord's *home* to steal her in the first place, didn't we?"

He doesn't speak again—and then none of us can, because we've released our wolves. We all know we'll cover ground much faster in lupine form.

We sprint toward the forest at the fastest pace we're capable of on all fours, knowing we'll have to slow as soon as we reach the trees. I drag the cooling summer air into my lungs, tasting every breath for a trace of her scent, training my ears to pick up whatever sounds they can over the thump of our paws. As we pass between the trees, we slow to a trot that won't throw us headlong into a stump or boulder, but I keep going as quickly as I dare.

There—a scuff in the dirt with her smell and the imprint of the bottom of her brace. She made it this far unhindered. I run onward.

I could lose her—I could lose all the hopes I had for my pack. If this goes wrong, I will have failed everyone, and I'll have no one to blame but myself. I delayed too long in my selfishness when I should have taken decisive action.

If we find her, I can't let this incident become another excuse. I have to do what's right, as hard as it may be. I have to be the lord my pack put their faith in.

I push myself faster still, the brush scraping at my shoulders and haunches. And then a sound reaches my ears that makes my blood run cold: a cry of fear, so faint in the distance I don't know if we can possibly reach its source in time.

CHAPTER TWENTY-NINE

Talia

The woman from Tristan's cadre draws a dagger from a sheath at her hip. She stays where she is, braced to spring, her dark eyes fixed on me. "I asked you, where are you going?"

My whole body has frozen, including my vocal cords. I'm not remotely prepared for a fight. I have no weapons, nowhere to take shelter. There's no sign of any of those thicker patches Whitt mentioned that should lead me to the human world—and even if I found one, I wouldn't be surprised if this fae woman followed me through to continue her interrogation.

My gaze focuses in on the gleam of the moonlight catching on her dagger. Bronze. One of my last conversations with August wavers up from my memories—true names and the magic that comes with them.

I don't know if there's a hope of working magic, but it might have happened once before, and I haven't got anything better. *Fee-*

doom-ace-own, I repeat in my head. *Fee-doom-ace-own.* Like a mantra, like a shield.

"I'm taking a walk," I say aloud. For once, despite my fear, my voice comes out clearly—not booming by any means, but more than a whisper. My heart is thudding, panic twisting through my veins, but holding me steady against the terror is that new emotion I've discovered. I'm scared, but I'm also *angry*.

Every faerie in this realm seems to think they have the right to demand things from me and order me around, if not outright torment me, even this woman I've never met face-to-face before. If I don't belong to Sylas, I sure as hell don't belong to her.

"A walk so far from home?" the woman says, spinning the dagger between her fingers. "Does your master know you've come all this way?"

"Of course he does. He told me to come." There are other stories I could spin, lies I could tell, but I stop there. I don't know what magic *she* might cast on me, what secrets she might force me to reveal, but I suspect the less I say, the better. What I have told her could even be presented as true if I count Whitt as one of my "masters."

"Somehow, having watched you for a while, I doubt that." Her eyes narrow. "And what have they done with your hair? That can't be its true shade."

"They thought I looked nicer this way."

"And for all they care about prettying you up, they didn't allow you to make any appearance during our recent visit to your keep." She cocks her head, her grip on the dagger tightening. "I think there's more to this than you're saying, but that's easily fixed. I think you'll find that if you don't volunteer the truth, I can cut it out of you quickly enough."

A deeper shiver runs through me. Panic is gaining ground over the solid foundation of my anger. It's a struggle to get my next sentence out. "I don't think Sylas would appreciate that."

"Oh, he'll have to understand when I explain how uncooperative you were."

Without any more warning than that, she launches herself at me, snatching at my wrist and yanking me toward her and her blade. The painful jolt through my arm shocks a yelp from my throat.

I kick out instinctively, and the foot brace gives me one small advantage. The wooden slats smack into her shin harder than my foot could have on its own, throwing her off balance. As I try to wrench away from her, I stumble, and we both topple over.

The fae woman throws herself onto me a second later, pinning my arms, her knife flashing toward my neck. A snarl reverberates from her chest. At the same moment, the syllables spill from my lips in a ragged gasp. "*Fee-doom-ace-own.*"

The dagger slams down toward me and droops as if melting. When it hits my shoulder—she wasn't trying to kill me after all, only wound me into submission—the sharp tip has folded in on itself into a blunt end that jabs me hard enough to bruise but doesn't slice into my flesh.

The fae woman spits out a curse and yanks her dagger back to stare at the collapsed blade. I stare at it too, my pulse skittering, hardly able to wrap my head around the fact that *I* did that.

I don't think even my attacker realizes that. Why would she even imagine I could have when it's supposedly impossible for a human to use fae magic? I said the true name so raggedly she might not have heard it at all over her snarl.

She mutters a few more curses aimed specifically at Sylas and tosses the apparently useless weapon away before glowering at me. "What protective charms has he put on you? Why is he so concerned about one feeble human girl?"

"I—I don't know," I stammer. Squashed beneath her, I can't fend off the panic anymore. It floods my mind and stiffens my body. If I could just grab the ruined dagger myself—or a stick—something— But I can hardly breathe, my lungs closing in on themselves.

"One more answer I'll have to discover for myself," she snaps, and flicks her wolfish claws free from her fingertips.

The immediate surge of fear sends a sharp enough spike of adrenaline through me to break me from the vise of panic. I flail out with another cry, so abruptly and wildly I must take her by surprise. My knee slams into her gut. She reels backward with a wince, and I shove myself out from under her. Where's the dagger? I have nothing, nothing but a word that can't do a thing against her claws or fangs, or her magic if she turns to that instead—

Recovering in an instant, the fae woman hurls herself at me again—and a massive, furred shape charges out of the shadows with a roar.

The wolf rams into my attacker, sending her rolling across the forest floor. She shifts as she spins and leaps onto her feet in her own wolfish form. My rescuer is already leaping at her, fangs bared, eyes glinting with fury—one dark, one scarred through and ghostly white.

My pulse stutters, grateful for Sylas's arrival but also terrified of how he'll react once he turns his attention on me. I fled; I abandoned him and his pack. He might be furious with me too.

Watching the immense beasts tussle and growl in the darkness sends me spiraling back to the night Aerik and his cadre found me —to the slashing of claws and the splatter of blood…

Another wolfish form bursts from the depths of the forest to join the fight. The pale wolf of the fae woman wheels, bringing her dangerously close to where I'm sprawled.

A sound like a whine seeps from my clenched throat. I try to scramble backward, my fingers fumbling against the dry earth, and strong arms grasp me from behind.

I've lost so much of my breath that what would have been a scream comes out as only a squeak. But then the hands that have grabbed me tug me partway around, and I catch a glimpse of Whitt's face, his ocean-blue eyes focused on the skirmish beyond me.

He pulls me with him a few feet back through the trees, putting the broad trunk of an oak between us and the fighting. Then he tucks me close against his chest. I gulp for air, feeling like a fish tossed into the open air of a beach.

It should be fine. Sylas could probably have overpowered that woman on his own, and now it's two against one. But all I can see now, flooding my mind and drowning me in terror, is Jamie's body the way it lay mangled on the grass the last time I saw him under trees like these, the vicious paw cracking open his skull, the teeth flecked with scarlet—

My fault. And Mom and Dad and— They came after me. It was all my fault.

Whitt's voice penetrates the icy fog in my head, his breath coursing over my forehead. "I've got you. Sylas and August can take her. You're safe now."

My cheek is pressed against his shoulder. His scent washes over me, warmer than I would have expected, like sun-baked sand tossed by the summer wind. Between that and his melodic voice, the suffocating sensation begins to ease.

I manage to drag in a breath, catching a strong alcoholic tang as I do. Either he was drinking quite a lot before he showed up here, or he spilled a sizeable portion on his shirt.

As the muddle in my head clears, confusion creeps in. This doesn't make any sense. I thought he wanted me gone. He could be hauling me off to one of those passages to the human world right now while Sylas is distracted.

Instead, he's hugging me to him so tightly you'd think he's afraid to let me go.

"There," he says. "That's better."

Is it? I twist my head to see as much of his face as I can. "Why are you protecting me?" I say, my voice still wobbly. "Shouldn't you be telling me to get going?"

He gazes down at me as if it's taking him a moment to remember who I am. Then he makes a sound somewhere between a laugh and a huff. "It's become clear I owe better to my brothers."

He's looking after me for their benefit? That makes even less sense. "You said they'd be better off if I left."

His head lists to one side. He's definitely not totally sober. "They refused to accept as much. And perhaps, having now experienced your absence, I've drawn new conclusions."

"I kind of wish you'd figured that out before I nearly got mauled," I can't help saying.

Whitt snorts. "My apologies," he says, in a tone that's not apologetic at all. He pauses, and his arms adjust around me, his nose grazing the top of my head. When he speaks again, his voice has softened. "I *am* sorry for the way I talked to you. And not just because of the distress it caused those two. I was… I was mistaken. We all gain something from your presence. Please, stay."

As if I could go anywhere right now while I'm gathered in his embrace. But there's an actual pleading note to those last two words, like he really means them, for himself as well as his brothers. I don't know what to make of that, and before I need to, he's straightening up, helping me stand with him.

Sylas and August are tramping over to join us, back in human-esque form. Blood seeps along Sylas's jaw from a thin scratch mark, and teeth marks stand out against August's forearm, but those appear to be their worst injuries.

"Are you all right?" Sylas asks the moment our eyes meet.

"Just shaken up," I say. "She hadn't managed to actually hurt me yet, just scare me."

He glances over my head to Whitt as if needing secondary

confirmation, and his shoulders relax incrementally. "That's one relief. She can't know what you are—what powers you hold—if she hasn't drawn your blood to smell or taste it."

"Are you saying you let her *get away*?" Whitt says, so incredulous it's as much a compliment to their skill as a complaint.

August grimaces. "She was fast, I'll give her that. Tristan wouldn't have picked wimps for cadre, would he?"

"We had to moderate ourselves so as not to damage *her* more than could be seen as warranted in trying to force a yield," Sylas adds. "She could obviously tell the odds weren't in her favor. The first chance she got, she was off like a shot."

"Does it matter if she didn't yield as long as she's gone?" I ask.

Sylas swipes his hand across his jaw and eyes the streak of blood on his palm as if it's no more concerning than a smear of paint. "If she'd yielded, I could have required that she not speak of you or what went on here again. I could have formally banned her from our domain. As it is, she's faced no consequences, and she can tell her lord whatever she likes." His eyes fix on me again. "Did she say anything to you before she attacked?"

I grope to remember what happened before the real chaos began. "She wanted to know where I was going—whether you'd sent me out here." My muscles tense up again at the thought of just how far I've gone *against* what Sylas would have wanted, and I hurry onward. "And she thought it was strange that my hair was dyed and that she hadn't seen me when they visited. I didn't say much to her. I don't think I mentioned anything that would have given the truth away. That was why she attacked me—because I wasn't cooperating as much as she wanted."

"Then she's only left with whatever suspicions she and Tristan must already have had for him to have tasked her with patrolling our domain." Sylas frowns. "I still don't like that she was here at all or that she encountered you." He peers down at me, his gaze abruptly twice as intent. "Why *are* you out here? How did you even get out of the keep?"

Behind me, his hand still resting against my back, Whitt stiffens. I hesitate. I could say he told me to go and opened the way, but that'll only stir up even more conflict between Sylas and his cadre, won't it? Whitt didn't force me to leave. I made that decision on my own, and I can take responsibility for it.

"I—I was worried about how upset the two of you seemed to be with each other because of me," I say, tucking my arms around my chest to hug myself. "It seemed like I was making things worse for you, not better. I found the door unlocked—I realized I could just leave—it seemed like the right thing at the time."

I can't see Whitt's reaction to my partial lie, but Sylas's makes my heart ache. He lowers his gaze, his mouth twisting. "I'd like to think my cadre and I are made of stronger stuff than could be broken that easily," he says. "And it shames me that it would have appeared otherwise to you. Whatever tensions arise between us, those are our duty to manage, not yours."

"Okay." The breeze licks over my shoulders, cooler with the deepening night. "I'm sorry. I should have talked to you first. I didn't know that woman would be out here."

"I can't blame you for taking the opportunity that presented itself." Sylas squares his shoulders. "Are you ready to return to the keep?"

Not "Do you want to" or "Are you willing to"? Just a given that I will go back. Because their rescue was never just about defending me as a person but protecting the power my blood represents as well.

August makes a soft sound of consternation, but the thought of him arguing on my behalf sends a different sort of ache through me. Even if I was sure I'd be better off in the human world, which I'm not, I can't fight or outrun Sylas. If I was leaving to avoid drawing them into an even greater conflict, then I can return for the same reason.

"Yes," I say, raising my head as if it was completely my decision. "Let's go."

CHAPTER THIRTY

August

When Talia doesn't join me in the kitchen at the typical breakfast-making time, I take a detour upstairs to stand outside her door. I don't knock, not wanting to wake her, but the whisper of her breath reassures me that she *is* still here.

But is this really where she should be?

Normally I get so wrapped up in the bustle of meal preparation that just about everything else falls away. Today, that question keeps nagging at me. I crack an egg too hard and have to fish bits of turquoise shell out of the bowl. I fold the pastry dough so vigorously it turns stiff in my hands and I have to start over again. Before I can ruin anything else, I go off in search of Sylas.

We'll all survive a slightly late breakfast. I'd like to be sure Talia's going to survive the next week, and in a state I can sit easy with.

A quick prowl and traces of scent lead me to the orchard. The summer heat is already expanding over the fields, the potent rays of the rising sun baking the leaves on the fruit trees. As I venture between them, their dry, green smell fills my nose.

Sylas is standing under a duskapple tree, his hand on the trunk, his gaze scanning the branches. This one and a couple of its neighbors developed patches of sickliness over the past few months. Baking with their fruits might be my area of expertise, but the magic of all types of plants comes most naturally to our lord. They've started to thrive again with his coaxing.

He turns at the sound of my footsteps, regarding me with typical composure. It's easy for him to criticize me for getting riled up when keeping a rein on his fiercer emotions seems to come naturally to him too. Does that pale eye of his tell him what I'm here to talk about before I've even opened my mouth?

Or maybe he knows me well enough not to need any Mistborne awareness to figure it out. My half-brother has been a constant presence from the moment of my birth. He remembers more of my life than *I* do.

"Come to harvest some fruit?" he asks in a tone that suggests he does already know the answer.

Might as well get straight to the point. I sniff the air to confirm there's no one else nearby and then meet his gaze head on even though the deferential part of me wants to dip my head in recognition of his authority. I pitch my voice low. "I want to talk about Talia."

Sylas's jaw tenses. He steps away from the tree, letting his hand fall to his side. With one word, the breeze ripples around us, and I know he's persuaded the air to muffle our conversation as an extra precaution.

He returns his attention to me. "What's there to talk about?"

He thinks he can still sidestep the issue, does he? A prickle of frustration wears at my sense of respect. This kind of evasion isn't like the brother who guided so much of my upbringing or the lord

I swore to serve—at least, I don't want to believe it's like him. The loss of our former domain and the shattering of his mate-bond and his pack have taken their toll, possibly to a greater extent than I've seen.

I keep my stance firm. "We brought her back last night. You didn't even give her the option of continuing on to make her way home. It's almost the full moon. What are we going to do with her?"

Sylas sighs. My heart starts to sink, preparing for him to dodge the subject even more blatantly, but instead he says, "What do you think, August? It isn't really a choice even for us, especially now that we have Tristan's cadre sniffing around more than they should. We must turn her over to the arch-lords."

I wanted a straight answer, but now that I have it, everything in me resists. "We *can't*. They might throw her into a cage no better than the one Aerik shut her away in. They won't care about anything but keeping her alive enough so they can harvest her blood."

"Skies above, don't let yourself ever talk about them so carelessly in anyone else's company." Sylas frowns. He isn't happy with the decision, but that doesn't change the fact that he's made it. "You think too little of our overlords. Celia isn't known for unnecessary violence, and Donovan has some kindness for humans—his servants have always been well-treated when I've visited his domain. I intend to approach him, to see that she goes into his care."

"But none of them will see her as worthy of having an actual *life*, not when she's the answer to this unsolvable problem all our kin are facing. And if they let Ambrose take the lead regardless…"

Tristan's second-cousin has never made a secret of his disdain for all things mortal. He might lack Kellan's concentrated hostility, but I saw plenty of casual cruelty when we were held in high enough esteem to call on the arch courts.

He'll probably *insist* on taking lead when he finds out it's us offering up this gift. He was the one who spoke the most harshly against Sylas when the judgment was laid down. *Not surprising,* Whitt said at the time. *Those who usurp their way to a throne are always the most offended by any whiff of treason from anyone else.*

"Do you think I wouldn't send her off to live in peace in her own world if I could?" Sylas demands. "She lost that chance the moment Aerik tasted her blood. Even if we returned her and gave up what she offers us, how long would it take before he tracked her down again and she was even worse off than before? He found her once without even meaning to. You know he'll never give up."

I do, and the knowledge angers me more than the pronouncement Sylas made. But Sylas is the one in front of me— Sylas is the only one I can argue with.

"Then we keep her here where she's protected and we figure out the rest from there."

"I can't see any way to protect our *pack* and keep word from getting back to the arch-lords—and she'll be treated much more harshly if she's taken through force."

"Then we don't use her at all. Whatever caused this curse, it's ours to bear, not hers. She deserves better."

"We can't *offer* any better." Sylas motions for me to head back toward the keep. "Enough, August. You've said your piece. I've made my decision, and believe me, I wasn't hasty in it."

I should stand down. The instincts honed through decades of service wrench at me. But this once, something stronger holds me in place: the memory of Talia's mouth against mine, her taste on my lips, her body both delicate and unimaginably strong pressed to mine.

I swore to myself that I wouldn't let her down.

When I don't budge, Sylas moves to walk past me. I step into his path, blocking my way. "I'm not done."

A hint of a growl creeps into Sylas's voice. "*We* are done, because I've said we are. Move aside, son-of-my-father."

His tone dredges up another memory—of his expression when he came to the entertainment-room doorway and found me with Talia. So sure he had a right to claim her. The possessive heat that rushed through me when I smelled him on her skin surges up again.

I clench my jaw, my fangs itching to emerge. "What kind of man are you to take her into your bed and then cast her aside so callously? I never thought I'd see you model yourself after our father."

Sylas can't quite suppress his wince. He bares his teeth. "If you can't see the difference between—"

I push on before he can continue, driven by that roiling anger. He might know me better than anyone, but I know him pretty well too. I'm aware of exactly how to best wound him. "You treated *Isleen* with more leniency, after everything she—"

"Do *not* bring her into this." Sylas takes a step toward me, drawing himself even straighter to emphasize the few inches of height he has over me. His unmarked eye burns. "This is nothing like that."

"No, it's not. Because Talia has done nothing at all to prompt this outcome, and you're punishing her anyway."

Sylas advances farther, nearly close enough to shove me. "I'll say it one more time, August. We're done talking about this. Get out of my way."

He starts to shoulder by me, and the fury that's been swelling inside me boils over. Adrenaline and the horror of defying him hitting me at the same time, I push him backward.

Sylas snarls and tries to cuff me in the head. I dodge the blow and sock him in the jaw. He lunges at me then, looking as shocked as he does enraged, and I release my wolf without any conscious thought, all my senses shifting into combat mode.

As I whip around on all fours, my claws digging into the rich soil of the orchard, Sylas transforms in mid-leap. He's larger than me in wolf form just as he is as a man. I manage to roll under him, raking my claws across his foreleg and spinning around to face him again.

He doesn't give me a chance to go on the offensive. I've barely found my footing when he's slamming into me, sending me toppling onto my side. I slash out with all four legs, gnashing my teeth, watching for an opportunity to bite, to gouge, anything to get the upper hand.

The instant I began this battle, it became a matter of who could overpower who the fastest. I might not have much of a chance, but I can't surrender.

Sylas snaps at my neck, but I yank my body to the side at the last second. With all my strength, I heave him off me and spring at him. He smacks my muzzle hard enough to make my head reel.

I throw myself to the side, bound off the trunk of a tree, and hurtle toward my lord. He swivels, just barely escaping the lash of my claws, and clamps his jaws around my leg.

One hard jerk sends me tumbling. Before I can scramble up again, he's on me, his full weight jamming me into the ground. His paw presses against my throat, claws digging in only enough to prick my skin. His hindlegs are braced against the most vulnerable part of my belly.

Even knowing it's pointless, I struggle, forcing him to jab his claws deeper in warning. He presses me into the dirt until I start to choke. Then he swipes his paw across the underside of my chin, opening four stinging welts through my fur, and pushes himself off me. Not even bothering to demand a full yield. Just enforcing his power and rebuking me with a superficial wound, like a parent chastening a pup.

Shame ripples through me, stinging sharper than the scratches of his mark. He shifts back into his usual form, standing over me, his scarred brown face intense with an emotion I can't read.

I rein in my wolf and sit up with the transformation. Without meeting Sylas's eyes, I lean back against a tree trunk, grappling with my own frayed emotions. The air is so warm I only faintly feel the blood trickling down my neck.

"She means that much to you?" Sylas says. I can't read his tone either.

"I've trusted you in so many things, but you're wrong about this one," I reply. "I'll fight for her again if I have to."

"It shouldn't come to that. It shouldn't have come to *this*." Sylas makes a rough, wordless sound and lowers himself to the ground across from me.

We sit there for several minutes in silence. When I dare to look at him, he's staring into the distance, his expression gone pensive.

"I will not rule like our father," he says finally. "I made that decision so long ago that maybe I didn't remember it well enough. It's no kind of lord to be, staying on top by browbeating everyone less powerful than you. I intend to be worthy of every bit of loyalty shown to me. That's why the pack has stayed with us, as many of them as could—because they knew I *wouldn't* compromise my convictions and stoop to baser methods to get ahead."

I'm not completely sure where he's going with this. "You never have," I venture.

His gaze comes back to me. "But I almost did. Those convictions should apply to this girl as much as they do any other being. The moment we found her and saw what Aerik had done to her, she came into our care. It should be beneath me to turn my back on her or look the other way knowing how others might treat her."

Hope flickers into being within my ribs. This—this is why I would lay down my life for this man, why seeking another lord has never occurred to me. "What will you do, then?"

The muscles in his jaw flex. "We've survived the curse this long. We'll continue to survive it until we find our own way to overcome it, permanently. What kind of fae would we be if we find ourselves dependent on a single human girl to save the whole of the Seelie race?" He considers me. "Would you also fight to see her returned to her own world?"

I hesitate, uncertain of how much my answer will sway his judgment regardless of what it is, wanting to be certain of my answer in case he does take it into account. Some of the impulses that jolt through me at that question are selfish, but I think I get the same result even when I separate those out.

"You were right before when you said Aerik will keep hunting her. She's safest with us, as long as no one else discovers the power her blood holds."

"I'm glad to hear I won't have to grapple with you over that point as well." Sylas's tone is dry enough to be a gesture of forgiveness. "It will be… complicated. But following what is right often is. I'm sure we can work out a strategy that minimizes the potential damage."

"You'll talk to her?" I ask. "It's been weighing on her—the uncertainty. I can tell. She should know as soon as—"

"I'll talk to her this morning," Sylas says, gruffly amused. "Give me a moment or two to get my thoughts together first, whelp."

The wolfish part of me wants to lay down in the dirt belly-up in prostration, to say I recognize his authority and that I'm sorry for challenging it. But the marks on my chin are enough of a chiding—and maybe if I hadn't fought, he wouldn't have recognized his miscalculation in time. I won't regret it.

I might regret what I'm about to say next, but the words tumble out anyway. They've been jostling around in my head too forcefully since the other night.

"Many other cadres have shared lovers between them. Maybe

the lord wasn't generally involved in those cases… but it could happen."

The corner of Sylas's mouth twitches upward. "I'm aware of that. But perhaps you should enjoy your first victory before chomping after the next."

He brushes his hands on his slacks and stands. As he strides toward the keep, I can't help noting that while that wasn't a *Yes*, it definitely wasn't a *No* either.

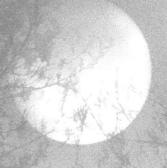

CHAPTER THIRTY-ONE

Talia

The next time I wake up in my bedroom in the keep, it feels almost like the first morning. I don't remember reaching the building or getting into bed. But the dissonance of finding myself there unexpectedly doesn't come with anywhere near as many fears this time.

Somewhere along the hike back here, fatigue and the ache in my foot caught up with me, and Sylas scooped me into his arms. I must have fallen asleep there. He carried me the whole rest of the way and tucked me in afterward. A tender warmth unfurls in my chest at the thought.

When I kick off the covers, my foot still throbs dully from all the walking. I massage it, careful of the malformed ridge of bone where the broken bits fused wrong, and other memories from the rest of the evening begin to surface. The tension between Sylas and August. Whitt's insistence that I leave. The woman from Tristan's cadre, so suspicious of me and determined to get answers.

I shiver. Are we all in even more danger now? This world scares me, but at the same time, I hate that so much is happening that I can't play a part in. I'm here now. I wish I had more say in my future. I wish I could be more of a participant in the conflicts going on around me instead of an object to be fought over.

I wish my life in the realm of the fae could be as simple as resting nestled against Sylas's chest, but fat chance of that. Even cuddling against him doesn't seem all that simple when I think of how August must have felt, watching us.

The sun is bright beyond my window. I've slept in after that late night, but from the smells seeping under my door, I don't think I've completely missed breakfast. There's definitely a whiff of bacon in that mix. While I'm filling my stomach with deliciousness, it'll be easier not to worry about all the things I can't control.

I've pulled on my clothes and am just fitting the brace around my ankle when there's a knock on the door. Sylas's voice filters through. "Talia?"

"Come in." I pull the last strap tight and straighten up where I'm perched on the seat of the armchair.

As the fae lord steps into the room, my pulse stutters. He didn't chastise me for running away last night, but maybe he didn't want to lay into me while I was exhausted and recently attacked. The full reprisal might be coming now.

Sylas doesn't look angry, though. His unscarred eye gleams bright with an energy I haven't seen in him before, his expression both determined and I want to think a little hopeful. He holds his head high, his massive frame as imposing as ever, but there's something oddly hesitant in the way he stops partway between the doorway and the chair.

I don't know what to make of it. A quiver of anticipation tickles over my skin.

"I've made a decision about your place here," he says, and my heart outright stops.

I curl my fingers around the edge of the seat cushion to steady myself. "Okay."

The corner of his mouth curves upward into a hint of a bittersweet smile. "Don't look like that, little scrap. It isn't bad news —at least, I'd like to believe it isn't. We won't be turning you over to the arch-lords or anyone else."

The shock of the reprieve hits me so hard it's a second before I can breathe again. "What?"

He doesn't wait for me to produce more than that single started word. "You can stay here with us. And I won't demand blood from you either. We *do* believe you're safest if you stay in our domain rather than returning to your own world while Aerik is still searching for you."

I grope for words, still stunned. "Won't you get in trouble for hiding me here?"

"I don't intend for anyone to discover what we're hiding. While you're with us, we can shield you from anyone who might prowl by. And if they should put the pieces together regardless, we can protect you in ways no one in the human world could."

"But—you don't even want a cure for your own pack—?"

His smile widens and tightens at the same time. "I do, but not like this. Whatever has afflicted us these past decades, you aren't a real solution, only a stop-gap that might very well lull us into a false sense of security when we should be seeking out a full cure. We've weathered the wildness plenty of times already, and we can weather it again."

I can stay here, and I won't have to bleed to earn that kindness. A smile of my own splits my face so suddenly my cheeks ache with it.

"We can't keep you cooped up in the keep for all eternity," Sylas goes on. "And now at least one fae beyond these walls knows there's a pink-haired human in our midst. August's bit of frivolity works in our favor, though, since Aerik isn't looking for a girl so brightly colored. Your face and your figure have filled out some since you started getting regular meals, too. We can put a glamour on you to make your limp slip others' notice, and there'll be nothing at all to identify you as his stolen captive. You could go out into the lands around the keep with us, even meet the rest of the pack."

That thought sends a jitter through my nerves. I haven't done a regular "getting to know you" with anyone since I was a kid. What will the regular fae think of me? "Won't they wonder why I'm here?" I ask. "You don't have any other human servants."

He studies me, probably reading my anxiety in my stance. "We don't need to rush that part of things. You might be best off waiting until after the full moon, as everyone gets more tense in the last few days leading up to it. But after... I thought we'd simply tell them that a human girl caught August's fancy keenly enough that he insisted on bringing her home."

Like I'm a kitten the fae man spotted in a pet shop window. The picture that forms in my mind brings back my smile, but it's a little shier than before. "Only *August's* fancy?"

Those three words are all it takes to spark the smolder in Sylas's eyes, hot enough to warm my skin even from a few feet away. His voice drops. "I suppose what happens in that tale next depends on who you bestow *your* fancy on, if anyone."

The heat trickles into my chest with a giddy flutter that's tempered by just one question. "Having me here—it's not going to cause problems between you two, is it?"

"I think we've worked that out," he says, and pauses. "Cadres frequently enjoy the affections of the same woman—or man, as the case may be. When their first loyalty is to their lord, they can't fully devote themselves the way a regular mate would, and sharing a lover can be a way of... offsetting the potential deficiencies in their attentions. If that can be so, then there's nothing to say a lord and his cadre-chosen couldn't have the same arrangement, even if it isn't typically done."

"So, no more fighting?"

The smolder in his unmarked eye darkens, and the memory of his touch the other morning teases over my skin. "You've shown qualities I've found to be rare in fae and humans alike, Talia, so perhaps it's not startling that you've affected both August and me as much as you have. I won't pretend it would be easy for me to share you. Every instinct in me wants to possess you for myself alone. But you *don't* belong to any of us, and if you want us both... I'm willing to suppress those instincts and see what we can make of it."

The giddiness spreads through my whole body. "Okay. That's fair."

Sylas steps closer, his gaze never leaving my face. "Can you accept the life I'm offering you? All I ask for is honesty. If you still feel caged, and you'll try to run off again—"

I shake my head vehemently, willing the relief that's flooded me to color my voice. "I won't. I'm sorry about yesterday—I... I didn't really want to leave, as crazy as that might sound. I don't have *anything* back in my world. It hardly feels real at this point. My family is gone; my friends will have moved on. And to live with the constant fear that Aerik or some other fae might stumble on me and realize what my blood can do... I think I can be happy here. For now, at least."

Maybe in the future, if the fae find some other cure and I'm no longer such a commodity, I'll want to see what kind of a life I could make back there. The keep already feels more like a home than the house that's faded into fragments of memories, though. And that house wouldn't still be mine anyway.

Sylas's voice drops even lower, washing over me like a caress. "I'm glad to hear that." He touches my face in an actual caress, his fingers brushing over my hair and down across my cheek, and all the heat in me seems to pool deep in my belly.

I do want him—I want so much more with him than we've already done, more than I know how to put into words. But I find there's also something I need to know before I can totally come to terms with that desire.

"You had a mate," I say. "Before. Kellan's half-sister?"

Sylas inclines his head, his smile falling away. "I did. She died before we came here."

I wet my lips, measuring out the question carefully. "Will you tell me what happened to her?"

With a slow exhalation, he sinks onto the edge of the bed across from the chair. His eyes focus on the distance beyond the window. "She was always very… ambitious. And not always in ways I agreed with. Some aspects of temperament ran in her family that you'll have seen in Kellan—stubbornness and a certain ruthlessness." He lets out a rough laugh. "She attempted an incredibly risky move that brought the wrath of the arch-lords down on her. In the ensuing battle, she was cut down. She fought until her death was inevitable, like he did."

The wrath of the arch-lords. A lump rises in my throat. "Is that why you lost your original domain—why you had to come all the way out to the fringes? They punished you too?"

"And also why we have arch-lord's second-cousins concerned enough at the slightest whiff of malcontent to come investigating and leave sentries skulking about."

"But—you've been here for *decades*, haven't you? And if it was all her fault to begin with—"

Sylas makes a dismissive gesture, bringing his gaze back to me. "Her faults were mine. Soul-twined mates are essentially considered one being, reasonably so. You're simply born with something about the essence of your being that resonates with that one other person, and once you complete the bond, your souls *are* literally intertwined. You're aware of each other's thoughts and emotions… I knew what she meant to do. I tried to persuade her otherwise, but I didn't manage to stop her. In that, I share responsibility for her actions."

That still doesn't seem fair to me, but obviously the fae have different ideas of justice. And this whole "soul-twined" thing sounds pretty intense. Maybe I don't understand well enough.

I look at his hand, resting next to his thigh on the bed— wanting to reach for it, not sure if the gesture would be welcome while we're discussing this subject. "It must have been hard, losing her."

"It was. But it was a long time ago. And in some ways it was hard *having* her too. There's a reason only true-blooded fae can make a soul-twined match, and only once in a lifetime. Even the most powerful of us can't always find a way to a happy equilibrium."

True-blooded—I've heard August use that term. Fae who don't have all that much human heritage, the only ones who are considered "pure" enough to rule as lords. I glance up at Sylas's face. "Then August and Whitt—they won't ever have a mate like that?"

Sylas shakes his head. "They could form a mate bond if they and a partner decided to, but it would be voluntary and not so all-consuming. But Whitt has generally preferred not to tie himself down in any area of his life other than his role in the cadre, and August hasn't had a great deal of opportunity… None of us are considered ideal prospects in our current situation."

His tone has become wry. I don't get the impression he's all that bothered about a lack of consistent female company. And I can't say I'm exactly *sad* to hear that fae women aren't lining up at the keep's doorstep to offer themselves as mates. Maybe August mourns that lost opportunity, though.

As I study Sylas's face, a swell of emotion that's much more than just desire reverberates through me. He's giving me as much freedom as he believes he can without risking someone stealing it away, he's shown more patience and passion than I ever could have hoped for, and it's all been while carrying more responsibilities and regrets than I can imagine. Responsibilities and regrets he shoulders without complaint or letting them weigh his spirits down.

If all those fae women think someone like *Aerik* is a better "prospect," they should have their heads checked.

In my silence, he pushes himself off the bed and moves to go, his demeanor business-like now. "Well then, everything is settled for the time being. I'll determine the best way to construct the glamor around your foot and gait, and there'll be measures to take to ensure your safety during the full moon, but we have a few days for that." He takes a sniff of the air and aims one more smile at me. "There's no rush, as August had a bit of a… delay in getting started on his cooking, but I expect you'll be welcome down for breakfast in a half hour or so."

"Okay. And—wait."

Driven by that rush of emotion, I scramble to follow him, but when I reach his side I find I don't know what to say. The only way I know how to express everything I want to is to grip his shirt and rise up on my toes, seeking out his lips.

Thankfully, Sylas recognizes what I'm attempting, because there's no way I'd reach high enough on my own. He bends to meet my kiss with a fervent rumble that carries from his chest into mine.

For a few seconds, as our mouths meld together and his arms wrap around me, I can't think about anything but the hot, heady thrill of being caught in his embrace. The earthy, smoky smell of him, rich and wild, overwhelms all my senses. I kiss him harder, feeling as if, as long as we're locked together like this, nothing could harm either of us.

Sadly, we can't kiss forever. Sylas lifts his head, and I ease down on my feet reluctantly, still clutching his shirt.

"Thank you," I say.

He leans in again, just long enough for his forehead to graze mine. "And here I feel as if I should be the one thanking you. If I didn't have other matters to attend to…" He makes a frustrated growl. "Well, there is plenty of time ahead of us."

I wait a minute after he's left the room to catch my breath and let the flush fade from my cheeks. Then I limp down the hall to the lavatory for a quick wash and to dampen down the twisted bits of my slept-on hair. A stronger smell of breakfast cooking wafts up the stairs. With a gurgle of my stomach, I emerge, only to find Whitt standing in the hall outside.

Not just standing—waiting for me. As I step past the door, his pose shifts from an aimlessly nonchalant stance to sharper attention. A glint dances in his blue eyes over unfathomable depths that could rival the ocean they stole their color from.

I halt where I am, uncertain. Yesterday, he went from coldly accusing to protective and repentant in the course of a few hours. How much of either of those states can be blamed on wine or drugged syrups or whatever else he's ingested?

Which side of him am I going to get today?

His gaze is clear enough, his posture steady as he tips his head to me. The suspicion prickles over me that he's sizing *me* up as much as I am him.

"You didn't rat me out to our glorious leader about my role in last night's escapades," he says, his dryly melodic voice quieter than usual. Because he doesn't want Sylas overhearing, presumably.

I can't tell whether that's a statement of gratitude or accusation. Does he think I should have?

I will my posture to stay as straight as his. I'm so tired of being scared. And after last night, after the way Whitt held me… I don't think I need to be. "You said it was a mistake. Unless you've changed your mind about that?"

"Not at all. May you remain our honored guest." The glint in his eye is more a twinkle now. "I still wouldn't have expected you to shoulder the blame."

I shrug. "I made the decision. And I can't see that anything good would have come out of bringing the rest of it up."

Whitt's lips quirk upward into a slanted grin. "Too true, too true." He runs his hand along his broad jaw. "It would have been an awful shame if this beautiful fae face of mine had ended up getting bashed about."

A renewed flush creeps over my face. He's teasing me about the comments I made after drinking that faerie syrup of his and nearly losing my head. The joke doesn't entirely sit right with me, though. "Would Sylas really have attacked you?"

Whitt gives me a shrug of his own, so purposefully casual that I don't believe his indifference. "Probably not. My lord brother has always been more generous than I truly deserve."

A little too much truth carries through in his tone and the momentary flick of his gaze away from me. Did he seek me out not because he wanted to make sure that I wasn't planning on tattling on him later but because he feels guilty... about this? Or more than that?

Without thinking, I step toward him, drawn by the urge to meet that trace of vulnerability with some fraction of the gentleness he showed me pulling me from the fray last night. But the moment I move, something in the fae man's expression shutters. He dips into a mocking little bow and sweeps his arm toward the staircase. "I believe our breakfast awaits. Ladies first?"

I can't see anything good coming out of pushing him either. I turn toward the staircase and drag in a breath, ready to begin my first day here as an actual guest rather than a prisoner.

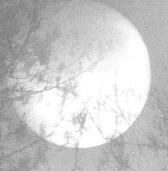

CHAPTER THIRTY-TWO

Talia

Sylas tests the uppermost sliding bolt on the door for what must be the hundredth time, giving it a tug with the full heft of his massive shoulders. It doesn't budge, but he still doesn't look entirely satisfied, even though there are three of those bolts now ready to lock my bedroom door from the inside. Watching the fae lord, August frowns, unusually serious himself.

I shift on my feet as if I can squirm away from my anxiety. "Is this necessary? You wouldn't really…" I can't bring myself to finish that question.

Sylas glances from me to the open window. Light glows through it, but it's turned an orange-gold hue as the sun sinks to the west. Soon the day will dwindle into evening. And then most of the light that shines over the keep will be that of the full moon.

"I wish I could say no," he says gravely. "But when the wildness takes over, it clouds our minds completely. We won't remember in the morning, won't have any idea where it took us other than what we can piece together from the evidence around us and on us.

Often there's blood. We have a solid enough strategy here that no one's been gravely injured so far, but you are a new factor."

A vulnerable human factor. I restrain a shudder. "But if you taste my blood, that should snap you out of it."

"Any of us could do an awful lot of damage on the way to that tasting." Sylas's gaze falls to my shoulder, the ragged ends of the scars peeking from beneath the short sleeve of my shirt where Aerik or one of his cadre mauled me.

"But if you took it before the moon—"

He cuts me off with a sharp shake of his head. "I will not ask that of you," he says emphatically. "This affliction is our responsibility to deal with, not yours. You've already given up far more for my Seelie brethren than you should ever have had to."

I can tell there's no point in trying to argue. Since the other morning when he told me he wouldn't require me to offer up my blood to the pack, he's stubbornly avoided the subject of my cure and what it could mean for him, as if allowing me to make that offering would injure me in some way far greater than a few drops pricked from my finger.

Still, I can't let it go completely. "Will *you* be all right?"

"As I've said, we have a solid strategy. The one saving grace of the wildness is that we can't work magic or useful things like doorknobs while we're in that form. We lock ourselves in separate areas of the keep so there's no chance we'll injure anyone. The pack members who are most vulnerable stay shut in their homes while the others roam far before the moon has fully risen so there's less chance of them meeting up and savaging one another."

"We've had to patch up wounds here and there the morning after," August puts in. "But nothing serious so far. The furniture and the lesser beasts in the forests are in much more danger than any of us."

Sylas pats my door, grim but apparently satisfied. "This should hold. You'll be fine as long as you stay inside with the bolts drawn.

So do that." He glowers at me as if he can force me to follow his command with a stare.

I'm not in any hurry to seek out the company of the fae in murderous wolf form. Just the thought stirs up too many memories, ones that send a chill over my skin. When I've seen Sylas and the others as wolves before, they were always still in control, even when they were fighting. In the grips of the uncontrollable rage the full moon brings out in them, they might be just as vicious as Aerik and his cadre all those years ago.

Whitt's voice steals in from the hallway. "Let's hope all the packs who've had the benefit of Aerik's tonic these past years manage to prepare at least half as well as we do after all this time resting on their laurels." He appears in the doorway, eyebrows arched. "Or, on the other hand, perhaps let's not."

"We shouldn't wish the wildness on anyone," Sylas mutters at him, but it's a mild rebuke.

August motions to the plate he brought up with him, now sitting on my bedside table covered with a silver lid to keep in the heat. "You have your dinner whenever you want it. Did you grab a new book so you don't get bored?"

I motion to the armchair. "I picked out a couple." Though I suspect I won't be able to concentrate on either of them.

Sylas comes over to give my arm a gentle squeeze. "We should check with the pack and then get ourselves situated. As soon as we leave this room, engage the bolts and don't open them until after sunrise, no matter what you hear from the keep or outside. Even if one of us throws ourselves at the door, you should be safe in here." He's checked over the hinges too.

I square my shoulders, trying to sound much calmer than I feel. "I understand. I'll be fine. You just… look after yourselves, as well as you can."

August shoots me a soft smile, Whitt a thinner one, and the three of them tramp back out, Sylas shutting the door behind them.

His footsteps stop in the hall, waiting for the sound of the bolts. I hurry over and shove them into place.

For a while, as the glow deepens from gold to amber and then fades into a mere haze, nothing disturbs my sort-of vigil. I spend an hour or so trying to read one of the books, finding myself gazing at the page unsure of what I've just read and having to backtrack more often than not. Then I bring the dinner plate over to the armchair and eat with it balanced on my lap as I peer out the window at the darkening sky.

I can't see the moon from here, but I can feel it coming in the apprehensive tingling that creeps through my body.

The natural light dwindles completely, my orb-like lamp gleaming on beside the chair. The last of the blue in the sky vanishes into blackness speckled with stars. A warm breeze drifts through the window, wildflower-sweet, but with it comes a distant snarl. The hairs on my arms stand on end.

As if that sound has set off a chain reaction, there's a sudden thumping from somewhere below me. A rattle as if the windows in one of the lower rooms are shaking. A howl erupts through the night, followed by the scrabbling of claws and gnashing of teeth from the direction of the pack village. Then a wooden groaning reaches my ears—a door straining with the weight of a heavy wolfish body attempting to thrust it open?

I curl up in the chair, my pulse skittering. More bangs and scuffling sounds carry through the floor. I don't know exactly where Sylas and the others have shut themselves away, only that Sylas intended to keep them all out of this section of hallway. The fact that he put those bolts on my door despite those other precautions shows how wary he feels he needs to be of their potential for violence. Have they broken down barriers they set up before?

How can he be completely sure *my* door will hold?

The creaking groan starts up again outside—or maybe it's a different beast in a different building attempting the same escape.

Something crashes through the brush near the edge of the forest. A roar of rage splits the air from some distant spot, followed by a vicious snarl, and I suspect two of the pack members didn't manage to steer totally clear of each other.

The thought of them tearing into each other makes me cringe. I get up and yank the window shut to block out most of the sound.

The sound from *outside*, anyway. Without that distraction, the noises within the keep come into sharper focus. The smack of a body ramming into a wooden surface reverberates through the walls. Claws scrape against the boards. A strangled growl reaches my ears, angry but also… anguished.

I know how much Sylas and his cadre hate falling into this state, and it doesn't sound as if the wolves they've become are enjoying the wildness either.

I get to my feet, a twisting sensation in my gut driving me to pace the floor in my hobbled way, worrying my lip under my teeth.

How can I sit here when the men who've sheltered me, cared for me, and fought to the death for me struggle in the grips of this curse? I don't know what caused it or who might be responsible, but they don't deserve it. No one deserves to be forced into becoming the thing they hate most.

Thunk. Thunk. One of them is hurling himself into a door or perhaps a wall over and over again. Oh, God. How bruised will his body be when he comes back to himself? Will they tear into themselves when they can't find anyone else to take out their rage on?

I can't let it come to that. I wanted to have more say in everything going on around me; I wanted to be a participant rather than an object. Well, this is the one time I definitely can intervene in a way that'll make a real difference, isn't it?

The second that thought crosses through my head, a strange stillness fills my chest. I stop by the door, the tension in my gut easing. My heart is thudding faster, but not with fear—or at least, not only fear. There's resolve in there too. Resolve and hope and a sense of power like the moment I let myself become furious for the first time. Except this calm certainty is more potent than the chaotic surge of anger.

Sylas wouldn't let himself ask me. He wouldn't take my blood even when I offered. He probably didn't trust that I was doing it freely and not because I felt I owed him.

The wolf he's turned into won't refuse me, though. If I can bring him and August and Whitt out of this wild state, no one will find out. It won't hurt any of us, and it'll release them from this horror.

I can make this one small offering of help after everything they've done for me. I'm the *only* one who can help them through this.

The resolve spreads through my limbs, bolstering my courage. It isn't a question of whether I'll do it. It's only a matter of how.

If I'm not careful, if I end up getting hurt, they'll come out of the wild state only to be wracked with guilt. There's got to be a way to avoid their jaws. All they need is a tiny bit of blood. Aerik never took more than would leave me a little light-headed, and that was enough to make tonics for dozens, maybe hundreds of fae.

I lean close to the door. A savage bark reaches my ears, then a sound like glass smashing, but it's definitely not *close*. There's at least one more door between my room and wherever the fae men have shut themselves away.

I have to go out and see what I'm working with before I can come up with a plan.

My throat tightening, I push the bolts aside and ease open the bedroom door. I keep my hand clamped on the knob as I peek outside, but the hall is empty as I expected, nothing but the dim glow of the single lantern orb halfway down its length.

Creeping out, I can discern the violent noises more clearly. As far as I can tell, they're all coming from below—I don't think any of my protectors are on this floor. They'll have wanted to keep themselves as far from me as possible.

Sylas is going to be pissed off about how I risked myself even if I *don't* get injured in the process. Oh well. I raise my chin and limp onward. I belong to me, and this is my life to risk or not. He'll just have to get over it.

I've reached the top of the staircase when a roar loud enough to make the floor tremble tears through the keep. My legs lock, my pulse lurching.

An icy wave of panic races through me. The images flicker up: blood and grass and twilight shadows, cries and snarls, pain searing through my shoulder—

I close my eyes and grit my teeth, my hands clenched so tight my fingernails dig into my palms. That night was horrible and brutal, and maybe I'll never make up for the devastation I caused, but it's been nearly ten years now. I'll definitely never make up for it if I let the horror overwhelm me every time I'm faced with a vivid reminder.

If that moment stops me from doing what I think is right, what I *want* to do, then I don't belong to myself after all. I'm letting the fear and the vicious fae who triggered it own me.

The fae in this keep aren't vicious, not like Aerik and his men. They might be lost in their wildness right now, but I know they're different. I know that even if they do hurt me, they'll make it right.

The terror doesn't leave. It stays tangled through my ribs and stomach. But with a few gulps of air, I manage to master it enough to move my feet. One and then the other, the soft padding of my bare sole and the tapping of the brace forming an uneven tempo, I slip down the steps slowly but surely.

CHAPTER THIRTY-THREE

Talia

The first stretch of the main-floor hallway looks as normal as the hall upstairs, but when I reach the bottom, I'm met by even more unnerving sounds. Thuds echo up from the basement along with ragged grunts and then an inhuman moan. At least one of the fae men has locked himself away down there.

But the clearest noises carry from up ahead. I propel myself onward to where the hall splits.

A solid wooden barrier stands toward the end of the passage to my right, where the entrance room should begin. Now I know exactly where one of these crazed wolves is. As I approach the barrier, racing animal footsteps pound across the floor on the other side. With a harsher *thump*, the wooden surface shudders. The beast on the other side must have thrown himself against it.

It's holding—but I can't do anything for the man it's holding back while it's in place. My breath coming shakily, I walk down the hall until I'm only a few feet from the barrier. At the snarls and snapping of teeth on the other side, my whole body shivers with the urge to flee as fast as I can. I tense my muscles, willing myself still so I can examine this new door.

It fills the entire width and height of the hall, which is substantial. As far as I can tell, it's constructed so that it slides out from behind a panel in the wall, which must be why I never noticed it before. The thick bronze hinges barely quiver when the body in the room beyond slams into the barrier again. The thumbturns for five deadbolts form a line up the other edge, securing it in place.

Did one of the others lock him in from here? Or maybe it's safer having access to the locks from both sides of the door in case whoever's trapped beyond injures himself in his wildness and can't release them himself the next morning. Either way, I can get to him. The question is how I do that without being halfway devoured.

While I stand there, gathering my nerve and grasping at my options, the savage noises from the front hall travel farther away. A few distant thumps, rattles, and scrapes suggest the beast is grappling with the front door now. Then there's the sound of tearing fabric and a feral growl.

Fabric—maybe I could work with that. I hurry back through the halls to the kitchen and jerk open the drawers until I find the rags August uses to wipe the counters. Gripping one against my palm, I scan the glinting metal handles of the knives in their sharpening block. As I pull the smallest one free, my mouth goes dry.

No big deal. Just make a little cut, dab a bit of blood on the cloth, and make sure the wolf gets it in his mouth. Aerik cut me open enough times. I should be able to handle it when I'm the one holding the blade.

Sitting on my regular stool, I brace myself against the island behind me and bring the cutting edge to my thumb. My hands shake. The knife glides through my flesh like I'm made of butter, slicing deeper than I meant to with a lance of pain that shoots right through the joints to my wrist.

Hissing through my teeth, I press the rag to the wound. A crimson splotch blooms across the cream-colored fabric faster than I was prepared for. As I stare at it, my head swims. I close my eyes, clamping my pressure around my thumb and breathing in slow, soothing breaths, imaging sparkling ponds and serene forests.

I can't stay in the peaceful images conjured in my head, though. Not if I want to see this task through.

The pain eases but doesn't disappear. As I fumble for another rag to tie around my thumb as a bandage, stinging jolts keep radiating through my hand. The rag I'll use to offer the wolf his cure is streaked with plenty of blood now, so at least I've got that part of the plan thoroughly covered. I can't imagine it won't be enough.

I just have to get the cloth into the creature's mouth. A raging, ravenous creature that sounds ready to slaughter the walls themselves if it could. No big deal.

A slightly hysterical laugh spills from my lips. It's either that or give in to the urge to sob.

My pulse races faster with each step I take toward the front hall. Halfway there, I have to stop and catch my breath, fighting the terror constricting my lungs.

I can do this. Just one taste of the blood on this rag, and the beast on the other side of the door will be himself again.

I stop at the sliding barrier and listen. A low growl reverberates through the room beyond. The grating sound of claws against wood paints a picture of the massive wolf stalking back and forth, pacing with frustration.

If I simply toss the rag in there, will he even bother with it? One little scrap of cloth isn't likely to interest or enrage him. In this wild state, he's seeking out a real fight.

A sense of understanding settles over me. I have to make sure he sees me. That he comes this way with enough aggression that he'll snap up the cloth when I throw it. Once it's in his mouth, I'll be safe again. There's no reason that tactic shouldn't work.

But there's no reason to assume I'll pull it off exactly as I'm picturing it either.

At the thought of the ferocious monster in the hall charging at me, another wave of panic smacks into me, leaving me dizzy. My fingers curl around the bloody rag. I brace myself against the door, gulping for air and willing back the images flooding my mind, the shivers wracking my limbs.

It would be so easy to scurry back up to my bedroom, throw the bolts, and curl up in bed until morning. No one expects anything more than that from me; no one would blame me for it.

No, that's not true. *I* expect more. I would blame me.

I'm here. I've done everything I need to except face the beast. How many battles have these men already fought for me?

If they're going to keep me safe, nurture me, and stand up for me, then I've got to find a way to stand *with* them.

As the seconds slip by, I drag breath after breath into my lungs. When the images from my attack flash through my mind, I train all my awareness not on landscapes I've never visited outside of my imagination but on the very real times when the men I mean to help kept me safe. August offering me the pouch of salt. Sylas nestling me against his chest. Whitt hugging me to him, murmuring soothing words to drown out the snarls of a fight.

Gradually, my chest loosens. Each breath courses deeper than the last. The violent images of the past dwindle, and then it's just me in the hall, one hand flat against the wooden barrier and the other clutched around a bloody rag.

Despite everything my former captors put me through, I haven't been broken. I'm still alive. I'm still living. Nothing they did can stop me now.

My heart continues pounding against my ribs, but I focus on

the movement of my free hand: raising it to twist the highest lock open, and then dropping it to the next, and the next, and the next. As I reach the last one at the bottom, my arm trembles. I inhale once more, long and steady, and turn the tumbler over.

There's no sound on the other side of the barrier. Has the wolf heard the click of the locks? What's it doing now?

Only one way to find out.

Before my fear can paralyze me again, I give the sliding door a forceful yank. It's heavy enough that even that effort opens a gap of mere inches. But inches is enough.

Orbs glow amber in the hall on the other side—except for one that lies shattered on the floorboards. Floorboards mottled with gouges from brutal claws. And the source of those claws, the hulking wolf whose dark fur glints with that hazy light, whirls to face me at the rasp of the door.

That instant is all it takes for me to recognize it as Sylas—the scarred white eye reveals him at once. An instant is all I really have, because the next second his wolf has pitched toward me, barreling across the hall like a speeding Mack truck, a snarl tearing up his throat.

My spine stiffens, and panic blanks my mind. My hand gropes to heave the door shut again, but I've readied myself for this act well enough that the rest of me moves automatically. I resist the terrified impulse and tense my other hand. Sylas's wolf hurtles toward me, faster with every stride, jaws yawning open—and I whip my arm forward.

The bloody rag flies through the air. The wolf lunges at it, close enough that the momentum of his charge ripples through the air and over my skin. His fangs snatch the cloth out of the air, the bloody folds falling into his open mouth.

He skids to a halt, claws scrabbling against the floor, so close that if I stretched, I could touch his thick fur from where I'm standing. I don't, because I'm gasping and shaking, renewed tremors shooting through my limbs just at being this close to the beastly form.

The wolf shakes his huge head. He spits out the rag and looks up at me. And those eyes…

Those eyes are Sylas in every way, not just by the color and the scar. For the first time, I'm close enough to see *him* in the wolf. To realize that the other times I panicked, the other skirmishes I witnessed—it was always my men fighting for me. Not monsters, not even really animals. Except for this night with the full moon's curse, they've always been themselves, just in a different skin.

Sylas hunches, and then all of him transforms into the man I'm used to, kneeling there on the floor. He's wearing a simple short-sleeved shirt and loose slacks for tonight, barefoot, with the waves of his hair falling riotously around his face. Still, he looks every inch a lord.

"Talia," he says, his voice so hoarse I suspect even saying my name took some effort. "You—what are you *doing*? I told you—"

I grip the side of the sliding door and stare right back at him with a flare of defiance that cuts through my dwindling fear. "You told me to stay in my room. I know. But *I* decided it mattered more to me to snap you out of the curse." My throat closes up all over again, but this time it's not out of terror. "You broke me out of a prison I never deserved to be in. Why can't I do the same for you?"

That wildness trapped him in his wolfish body and the feral rage even more soundly than the bars of my cage had trapped me.

His mouth slants as if he wants to argue but can't quite bring himself to. "We talked about this."

"We talked about why it wouldn't be safe for me to help the whole pack and why you didn't want to ask me to help just you. You didn't ask. This was totally my decision, made freely. And no one will know you came out of the wildness early, will they? Right now, every other fae in this realm is mad with it."

He glances down at the crimson-splotched rag by his knee and then at the cloth wrapped around my thumb. "I could have hurt you."

"But you didn't. So there's nothing to complain about."

His lips twitch. I think that time he might have suppressed a smile. "I suppose this is what I get for stealing away a little scrap of a woman who's got more mettle than anyone would give her credit for."

The corners of my own mouth curl upward, and the last lingering traces of panic melt away. I set my hands on my hips. "Yes, it is. Now come on. You can help make sure I take care of August and Whitt without getting torn to bits."

"Taking orders from a human," Sylas mutters to himself, but he gets up, grabbing the rag as he does. He eyes the damp fabric. "I think this should do the trick, no more bloodletting on your part required. I doubt you needed half this much."

"Well, I didn't want to take any chances. And also, the knife slipped." At the darkening of his eye, I wave off his impending objections. "I'm *fine*. But August and Whitt aren't. Are they both in the basement?"

"Yes." Despite my insistence about my wellbeing, he slips his hand around my wrist and mutters a magically-charged word. My skin prickles beneath my makeshift bandage, the ache in my thumb fading as his power must seal the wound. Then he pulls ahead of me, stalking toward the basement stairs as if either of the other wolves might come barging up right this minute to attack me. If taking the lead makes him happier about the situation, he's welcome to it.

The basement hall has been barricaded at both ends with sliding barriers like the one upstairs, the first by the gym and the second just beyond the entertainment room. Having seen the smashed lantern orb in the front hall, I have to guess the TV and game systems wouldn't survive a full moon night intact if one of the beasts got at it.

The wolf behind the barrier at that end is clawing at it, letting out a sharp howl when I pause.

"That's Whitt," Sylas says. "As much as it actually is him in this state."

I turn toward the other end. "Let's start with August." I'd rather save whatever snarky remarks Whitt is going to make for after I'm finished with this ordeal.

It's less of an ordeal with the fae lord by my side, though. I insist on standing by the door, but he unlocks it and shoves it aside, braced to shield me if the gambit doesn't work. August's ruddy-furred wolf wheels from where he was wrestling with the high, narrow window frame and springs toward us. I barely have time for my stomach to flip over before Sylas has tossed the rag and my blood has touched the wolf's tongue.

When August shifts back into his usual form, he scrambles to his feet at once, blinking at us. "What— I thought—"

"So did I," Sylas says, a trace of amusement lightening his baritone. "Our lady had other ideas." He grazes his hand over the top of my head, rumpling my hair.

Our lady. Not "the girl" or even "our guest." As if I'm an actual part of this household now. I beam at August, afloat on the pleasure of those words and of seeing him freed, and he grins right back at me. "You're a marvel," he says.

"I'm not done yet. Let's get Whitt."

I've got even less to worry about with two immense fae warriors flanking me, but somehow the sight of Whitt's wolfish form still sends a jolt of panic through me. Tawny furred and as muscular as his half-brothers, he tears toward us with fangs gleaming. His own blood darkens one side of his muzzle where he must have scraped his flesh raw in his attempts to break free.

When he snatches the tossed rag out of the air and falters, the ocean-blue eyes gleaming in his wolfish face look dazed. He seems to gather himself as a wolf, dipping his head and rubbing his wounded muzzle against his foreleg, before he transforms with a dog-like shake of his frame.

He cocks an eyebrow as he pushes himself upright, ignoring the abrasion still seeping blood over the edge of his jaw. "Change of plans?" His gaze lingers on me.

I smile at him, a little nervously. "We're all in this together."

August steps toward him, and after a half-hearted protest, Whitt lets him speak a few words that transform the shallow wound into a patch of solid if pinkish skin. Afterward, the younger man glances in the direction of the outside houses, the muscles in his arms flexing with restless energy. "What about the rest of the pack? They'll be so scattered by now—and it'd still raise all kinds of questions if we bring them out of the wildness."

"We'll have to let them ride out the moon," Sylas says, and touches my head again. "But don't think you haven't given them a gift as well. Now that we have our heads, we can go out and keep some kind of order between them. Fewer injuries to treat in the morning."

Whitt rolls his shoulders. "Good. I could use a run after being cooped up down here."

Sylas nudges me around so I'm fully facing the fae lord. "*You* will remain inside behind locked doors—and actually *stay* this time. We won't be able to protect you out there with so many fae roaming around. Understood?"

I nod emphatically. I don't have a death wish. "I'll stay inside. I swear it."

"And I accept your oath." His fingers skim down my arm and back up again, and a tingle travels over my skin at his touch. "I can only imagine how difficult coming to us in this state must have been for you, Talia. You will never owe it to us to do so. And I won't forget your bravery on our behalf."

"It was the least I could do after everything you've given me." I glance at the other two men standing around me. "All of you."

Sylas hums low in his throat. When I turn back to him, his hand glides up to my jaw. He tips my head back and claims my mouth with the hot brand of his lips. The earlier tingle blazes with a rush of heat.

A rough sound like a choked-down growl emanates from August's chest. When Sylas releases me, I don't let myself hesitate. I reach for the other man who's made my heart and body sing and rise up to kiss him too, ignoring the very definite growl that escapes Sylas before he bites it back.

August meets my kiss tenderly but determinedly, unleashing a torrent of passion with the press of his mouth. I could get drunk on this. I *feel* a little drunk as I sink back down, which must be why when my gaze reaches Whitt, I bob up without thinking and kiss him on the cheek.

It's only a peck, and I barely even reach his cheek, my mouth skimming the uninjured side of his jaw, but Whitt stiffens. I swivel toward Sylas, my face flushed. I don't want to witness the other man's rejection of even that small gesture of affection.

The fae lord's gaze smolders down at me, but he keeps any possessive emotions he's grappling with under wraps. "We'll likely be out until dawn. Don't wait up for us."

Even with Whitt's reaction, the sense of being part of this household hasn't left me. I balk at the thought of losing it, even for a moment. "What if I want to?"

Sylas chuckles softly. "Then I suppose that's up to you, as you've well proven." He nods to the others. "We'd best get moving."

CHAPTER THIRTY-FOUR

Talia

True to my word, I don't venture outside the keep. Instead, I settle into one of the parlor armchairs and watch from the windows as Sylas and his cadre shepherd their pack.

They've shifted back into their wolfish forms to do it, as makes sense when they're contending with beasts in the grips of the full-moon ferocity. Sylas, the most massive creature of them all, lopes across the field emanating feral power and shoulders apart two wolves who've started snapping at each other. August clamps his jaws on one's neck, just tightly enough to hold and not wound, and tugs it in one direction while Whitt shoves the second wolf in another.

I've heard them refer to the pack so many times, but I've never grasped just what that means until now, witnessing them working together as leaders over their people, watching the other wolfish fae respond even in their wild state. Seeing it, the glimpses of fangs and claws no longer spark the fear they used to.

Those aren't the marks of monsters. They're tools to be used as their owners see fit. And Sylas and his cadre bring them to bear with care and conviction.

When the first rays of the sun peek over the horizon, my head is muggy but my eyes still open, if starting to ache. The three wolves of the keep come trotting around the side of the building as one being. I push myself out of the chair and head to the entrance room to meet them.

The gouges from Sylas's raging claws still scar the floorboards. I guess he must use his magic to fix them once he's recovered from the night's horrors. Now, the fae lord bobs his head to me and sprawls on the floor with a wolfish yawn as if too tired to move any farther, to even shift into his typical body.

I hesitate and then, my heart beating only a little faster than usual, walk up to him. As I sink down on the rug next to him, I stroke a tentative hand over his fur.

It's a mix of coarse and silky, so thick I could bury my fingers in it and barely make out my knuckles. The wolf lets out a pleased thrum and nuzzles me closer to his side. As I rest my head on his body, his chest rising and falling with slowing breaths beneath me, August and Whitt join us.

The other two wolves recline on the floor, forming a circle around me. I stretch my arm to rub the spot between August's ears, and he gives me an eager pant with a flash of his tongue before tucking his muzzle over my knee and closing his eyes.

My eyelids slip shut too. It's been a long night, and the rhythm of Sylas's breaths within that ring of warmth lulls me right to sleep.

I wake up late enough that the sun shines brightly through the skylights, and find not fur beneath my head but the fabric of Sylas's shirt. Sometime as they slept, the fae lord and his cadre have transformed back into men.

Sylas's arm rests protectively against my back. Fingers are stroking over my ankle. Glancing down, I'm surprised to see they belong to Whitt. His head is cushioned on his arm just inches from my heel, his other hand drifting idly as it rests against my calf, maybe caught up in some dream. From their relaxed expressions and the slackness of their bodies, all three appear to still be asleep.

I suppose they tired themselves out a lot more than I did last night. My part of the work was over pretty quickly. And maybe they're more used to sleeping on floors. When I ease myself into a sitting position, my back protests, an ache running from my shoulder blade to my hip.

A yawn stretches my jaw, but my bladder pinches at the same time, demanding release before I try to get any more rest myself. August stirs but doesn't wake as I step carefully over his legs. I slip down the hall, setting my foot brace down as quietly as I can given the stiffness of my joints. Once I reach the staircase, I let myself move a little faster.

When I emerge from the second-floor privy, the brilliant gleam of the sunlight catches my eye. I meander over to the big window where weeks ago I watched Whitt host a revel and realized there was more to him than wry remarks and artful carelessness.

A few of the pack members have gone to sleep in the field, finally at peace after that long, horrible night. No one is moving around the houses that I can see. My eyes travel beyond them, over the wider plains and the distant forest, and then across to the rolling hills at the southeast end of Sylas's domain.

My gaze stalls on a lupine form poised at the top of one of those hills. A fae still embracing his wolf.

There's nothing so odd about that. It could have been that one of the pack members woke up early and went for a run to shake off uneasiness leftover from last night. But what's frozen me in place isn't the fact that there's a wolf at all, but the color of its fur catching in the sunlight.

It's a blueish white like a thick layer of ice over open water. Like icicles reflecting a clear winter sky.

Like the hair of the sharp-edged man from Aerik's cadre.

The wolf is watching the keep just as I'm watching the wolf. It tilts its head at a devious angle so like my most vicious former captor that the bottom drops out of my stomach, taking any doubt I'd held onto with it.

Then the creature whips around and vanishes down the back of the hill, leaving me clutching the window frame and wondering how long I have before the home I just won is wrenched from me.

CAPTIVE OF WOLVES - BONUS SCENE

W *ondered what was going through Whitt's mind while he went from convincing Talia to leave the keep to protecting her in the woods? Enjoy this bonus scene from his point of view!*

Whitt

Setting the plan in motion is unnervingly simple. The magic Sylas uses to lock the keep's outer doors was never meant to foil his cadre —*we* still need to come and go, after all. I wait until August descends to the basement for a workout and Sylas ensconces himself in his study, and then I dismiss the spell sealing the parlor door with a moment's concentration and a few carefully picked words. The energy prickles over my skin and drifts away.

The way is clear. Now I simply need to send the girl along it, and everything here can return to how it was before—humbled, yes, but not balancing precariously on the edge of catastrophe.

No one will know I've saved the pack, but I lost my right to that glory the moment I nearly destroyed it all those decades ago. *I'll* know. The relief will be its own reward.

The next part should be even easier. She's already sought her freedom once. The fact that she stayed is hardly so miraculous when she'd already been caught and wounded before making it out the front door. She'll charm my half-brothers while her security depends on them, but given the opportunity to leave us all behind, what will any of us matter to the mite? Soon her stay in Fairyland can transform into nothing more than a bad dream.

I can smell her before I reach her bedroom, traces of the woodsy sweet scent that's become far too familiar over the last few weeks seeping into the hall. Can hear the soft intake of her breath and the whisper of a turned page—she must be reading. Funny that the human would prefer literature while our lord indulges in their mindless moving pictures…

I stamp out the flicker of affection that thought provokes and push straight past the door.

Talia startles in her chair, her fingers clenching around her book. In that first glimpse, the momentary daze in her eyes tells me how deeply she was wrapped up in the story she was reading. She's sprawled in the chair in a pose both comfortable and careless, her slim legs dangling over one of the padded arms, her shoulders nestled against the other. At the sight of me, though, she tenses even more.

Well, she should. I'm here to bring her to task for the potential disaster she's instigated and to give her a welcome avenue out. She'll thank me when I'm done—or at least, she should.

She shoves herself around into a proper sitting position, gripping the book in front of her, her eyes wide. "Is everything all right?"

What a question. I restrain myself from rolling my eyes. "You've proven yourself decently observant, mite, even when you shouldn't be observing. Do *you* really think everything is 'all right'?"

She knits her brow, blinking at me. "I don't know what you're talking about."

So innocent when it serves her. I've seen enough sharpness to her mind to find it hard to believe she can't connect the dots. "Oh, no? So it's truly escaped your notice that your two paramours aren't quite as at ease with each other as they used to be—as they're meant to be?"

Oh, she's noticed, all right. A blush blooms across her cheeks before I've even finished speaking. But she keeps playing into her fragility, setting her book aside and drawing her legs up to her chest, her shoulders hunching as she wraps her arms around her knees. "I didn't mean for anything like this to happen."

No, obviously not; it's merely a totally natural consequence of her actions. I sweep my hand dismissively, unable to prevent a trace of acid from creeping into my tone. "Of course you didn't. Why would it even occur to you to consider it?"

"Have they been fighting about it when I'm not around?" she asks, no doubt attempting to determine how I know what she's been up to with them at all. She won't have realized I discovered last night's little interlude in the entertainment room.

I shrug, willing the rancor in me to simmer down. If I seem outright hostile, she won't listen to my offer.

Lay the groundwork. Make it clear it's so much better for her if she heeds my advice.

"From the looks of them, it's only a matter of time. And believe me, you won't want to find yourself in the middle of *that* squabble."

She hugs her knees tighter. "I don't know what to do. I tried to tell them— I haven't let anything happen since I realized— Me being here has already caused so much trouble with all of you. The last thing I want is for them to be at each other's throats."

Her voice wavers with a note of something like... anguish. A shadow of what I'd swear is pain has crossed her face, as if it truly does agonize her that she's inflicted this trouble on us.

I pause, frowning. I've just indicated that her status here may be under threat—how can she be focused on worrying about us?

A ploy to win *my* good favor, I have to assume. She doesn't know yet where I'm going with this topic. Why would I respond to a plea for her own wellbeing over that of my lord and cadre?

I shake off the uneasiness that's crawled over my skin. "There's an easy solution. They're riled up over you, so we take you out of the equation."

She goes rigid at that statement, the color that rose in her cheeks draining away until she's as sallow as the evening we found her. Seeing it sends a pang through me I can't suppress. Her voice comes out reedy. "Sylas is going to send me to the arch-lords now?"

There's the self-concern I was expecting. I leap straight to the boon that should wipe that panic from her eyes.

"No. I think you'll like this solution much better. You can head right back home."

I hadn't thought it'd be possible for her eyes to widen more than they already had, but it is. Her jaw slackens. "Home?" she repeats, little more than a longing whisper.

A smile stretches across my face. That's right. Follow this gilded carrot right out of our lives. "Yes, exactly. That's what you've wanted all along, isn't it?"

She's so stunned that for a second she can't speak. Hope lights in her eyes, but at the same time she looks almost… sad. How by the Heart can she be *sad* about this opportunity? Doesn't she know what I'm risking to hand it to her?

She gapes for another second before managing words. "You're saying Sylas would let me—"

Yes, why not give Sylas credit for the gesture like she's apparently given him so much else? Why is she dawdling talking about this at all instead of getting her pretty little ass into gear?

I cut her off. "No. Sylas doesn't know about this. *I'm* arranging it. It'll be better for him and August—for all of us. Obviously it's better for you too. But you'll need to get on with it. Sylas is holed up in his study now, and August's taking out his frustrations on that long-suffering punching bag of his, but the window when they'll both be distracted is relatively short."

She finally unfolds herself, setting her feet on the ground, but she doesn't shift her weight onto them. She's eyeing me with the shrewdness I've seen in her before, that she cloaks so deftly behind her more obvious vulnerabilities. Is she really going to look this gift horse in the mouth?

"What—what about my blood?" she asks. "The cure? It's not much longer until the full moon."

I suppose after the fuss every fae she's met has made over her vital fluids, that question is understandable. "That won't be your problem anymore," I say briskly. "This is your ticket out of the whole mess." *So take it already, by all that is dust.*

The wretched girl is still hesitating. "But— It'll still be *your* problem. All of yours. If I'm gone, you won't have any way of making the tonic."

She's hesitating… because she *won't* be required to bleed for us? The question crackles up my throat before I can think better of it. "Why should that matter to *you*?"

Her hands shift over her lap as if helping to assemble her answer. "You rescued me from Aerik. Sylas has protected me— you've all been… kind." Her pause needles me—would she really say that of my behavior?—but she barrels onward. "You've been counting on me to help you in return."

I still don't know why she would care about any of that. Does she really, or does she simply think she should, that this is some sort of test of her loyalty? I haven't exactly presented myself as the most straight-forward of allies before now.

"Your freedom matters more than that, doesn't it?" I say, and then tell her the same thing I've been telling myself since last night when the flame of inspiration flared in my mind. "We'll make do. We always have before. We *won't* make do if having you around tears our cadre apart."

She winces, as if the thought of harm coming to us genuinely hurts her. But before the sinking sensation in my stomach can fully grip me, she's getting to her feet, her hands balling at her sides. "Okay. I can see that. But the magic on the doors—and I don't know where to go even once I'm out…"

These questions make sense. Logistics and self-preservation. All she needed was a nudge.

I nod in a vague attempt to reassure her that I've considered all potential obstacles. "Go now. I've left the parlor door unlocked for you. Walk straight ahead from there across the fields and through the woods. You'll know you've reached the very edge of the Mists when the actual mist thickens. Watch for a thicker patch—by twilight, it'll look like a puddle turned sideways, deeper and darker, almost liquid. Walk through that, and you'll be back where you belong."

"Okay. Okay." She squares her shoulders, her chin coming up, preparing to brave the fae woods to make her way home—and then she meets my gaze with so much emotion swimming in her striking green eyes that I couldn't have torn my attention away if I'd wanted to. "I'm sorry for—for all the trouble I've already brought down on you. Thank you for this. And thank Sylas and August for me too, when they realize—tell them I know they tried to do right by me, and I really was happy here some of the time."

With those words, with that expression on her face, it's not just the bottom of my stomach that drops then but the entire blasted thing, with a sickening lurch. I can't deny what I'm seeing, what I'm hearing, not when the truth of it is staring at me so fervently.

Genuine affection for my brothers and the sense of loss at leaving them rings through her voice. She doesn't want to go. She'd rather stay and throw in her lot with us than return to all the familiar mortal things Aerik tore her away from. The core of my job is distinguishing truth from lies, authentic threats from ephemeral ones, and not a single shred of me can still believe Talia is following my orders for her own good.

No, she's doing it for Sylas and August. I hammered home my case about the damage she's doing to the cadre because I thought she'd need a clear reason for why I was helping her before she'd trust me enough to go along with it, but if I hadn't told her she was hurting them, if I'd simply led her to the edge of the Mists and invited her to leap… I don't think she would have.

When has *anyone*, even our closest fae brethren, ever shown as much devotion to us as that?

But even as the queasiness of that realization rolls through me, I can recognize that it changes very little. She might feel guilty about the trouble now that I've pointed it out to her, but did she do anything to stop it in the moment? She encouraged both of my brothers' affections, flitted from one to the other and then nestled there between them—it'd be more of the same if she stayed. No matter how good her intentions are in the face of my accusations, her presence here *will* continue fracturing our hard-won harmony.

I can't back down now.

"Yes," I say, itching for a drink from the flask in my pocket to dull the jab of my own emotions, and clear my throat to shed the roughness that's colored my tone. "Yes, I'll do that." It's the least I *can* do for her after the proclamation she just made. "Go on now. If we're lucky, they won't notice you're missing until morning when you'll be well away from here."

Grateful for the excuse to break from her impassioned gaze, I turn and ease back into the hall. No sign or sound of either of my brothers. I beckon her out without looking at her.

"It's all for the best," I say, to keep her going—and maybe to remind myself as well. "It's all for the best."

She darts by me toward the stairs with the soft tapping of her foot brace. I haven't yet recovered my stomach. Perhaps if I fill it with some provocative beverage, one that'll numb and uplift my spirits at the same time, it'll settle.

Her leaving *is* for the best. Sylas and August can fall back into their usual comradery. Our glorious leader can stop agonizing over how to treat our acquisition. Neither Aerik nor the arch-lords will be able to stumble on her presence and accuse us of any crime.

It doesn't matter if she wanted to stay. She'll find her place back in her own world quickly enough. I haven't actually *taken* anything from her—I've given her what no one else would.

A swig from my flask isn't quite convincing enough. I prowl to my bedroom, to the near-full bottle of absinthe I left by the chair. I'd sampled just enough to decide it'd be fitting for the pack's next revel, but I have greater need of it now.

I snatch up it and a goblet. Only a drunkard imbibes straight from the bottle. Then I sink down, propping myself against the foot of my bed, wondering if Talia has already made it out the door.

How long will it take her to cross the field? To trek through the forest?

It should be safe—we've had no reports of hostile beasts venturing into our domain recently. Of course, what our sentries would consider a threat and what would actually pose a danger to one limping human girl are very different things.

The first searing gulp of the absinthe knocks that niggling thought to the back of my mind. The second, more of a chug, drowns it out completely.

Think of the cadre, think of the tension that's been simmering between Sylas and August—that I've diffused.

Don't think about the fondness on either of their faces when they looked at *her*. The fondness I'm now sure she returned in full.

Better yet, don't think at all. The absinthe slides down my throat more smoothly with each tip of the goblet. Finding it empty,

I pour more of the bottle in. The usual fizzing sensation expands into a cloud that fills my head. But somehow a twinge of loss manages to pierce through it.

What's there for me to miss? *I* never won her fondness. Even if —so many things I could have shown her—if she'd embraced them with all the delight the cavaral syrup brought out in her—and what more might she have had to say for herself as she grew confident enough to let her shrewdness show?

I drown that question too. My stomach burns, but it's definitely back where it belongs now. My head has become more top-heavy than I'd prefer, listing to the side every time I try to straighten it. I can't stop, though. The doubt has dwindled to a pinch, but it isn't gone yet. I have to wash it away completely.

"For the best," I murmur to myself. "It was for the best." The more times I say it, surely the truer it becomes.

The haze stretches out a long, long ways into the passing minutes—almost as far as crossing the fields to the woods. Then my bedroom door swings open. I lower the goblet from my lips and peer across the room.

Sylas has come in. My lord, my brother I've known since he was but a whelp. That scarred face of his is frighteningly grim tonight. I fixed everything for him. Doesn't he realize?

Words slip through the cloud fogging my mind and off my tongue. "Looking awfully serious, li'l brother. Have some of this to ease your spirits." I grasp the bottle by the neck to offer it, but it's lighter than I expected. Where has it all gone?

It's a good thing my brother doesn't appear inclined to drink. "Have you seen Talia?" he demands.

An image parts the clouds: pale face framed by deep pink hair, green eyes fixed on me, a quaver of a voice. Vanishing down the stairwell. The pang shoots up through my chest, not drowned but merely temporarily muffled.

Dust and doom on us all. I bang the bottle on the floor. "Why would I have?"

A question can't be a lie, no matter what it implies. So very clever am I. Poetic too, it seems. I almost laugh, but the arrival of my second brother stops me.

When has *that* whelp ever looked so somber? August takes to smiling like a wolf to the moon.

"There's no sign of her anywhere," he says to Sylas.

Of course not. There wouldn't be. But he can't know—they can't realize—soon enough they'll see that it truly is for the best.

Sylas doesn't appear to have considered the possibility that she's left the building yet. Our lord turns back to the hall looking even grimmer than before. "Maybe we've just missed her. Let's go through the keep from top to bottom together. Call her name as well as looking into each room. She'll be here somewhere. You take the rooms to the left, and I'll take the right."

Ha. A wild goose chase. A wild mite chase.

I shove myself upright. The floor seems to have tilted in various directions since I last walked on it, but I make it to the doorway with my feet still under me, which I'll count as a victory.

My brothers sweep the hall, checking every room with intent precision. As if they could simply have misplaced her. They work together in perfect unison, as I would have expected before—before she came between them. How ironic that somehow she's brought them back into sync without even being here.

It's almost as if her influence didn't have to be destructive but actually—

I shake that uncertainty off with a ragged chuckle before it can fully form. "You lost the mite?" I can't help saying. "One slip of a human girl giving two big bad fae quite the run-around."

Sylas shoots a glower over his shoulder. "Help us look, or keep quiet."

August shakes his head at the final door. They tramp toward the staircase, checking the rooms along that hall too, and head downstairs. My steps grow steadier with each passing moment, my mind focusing on the singular goal of witnessing their reaction when they determine she's gone for good.

For good. Yes, for good.

August pauses at the bottom of the stairs. "Did you check the pantry?" he asks, and my heart skips a beat in anticipation.

Sylas stalks after him into the kitchen. I trail behind. As August disappears into the pantry, our lord halts, staring at the parlor door with both his whole eye and the ghostly one.

"She isn't in the pantry, is she?" he says in a tone that barely passes for a question.

August returns, his face fallen even more than before. The pang inside me spears sharper between my ribs. But this is only now. They can't yet see how much simpler our lives will be in her absence.

"No," he says. "There's still a lot more—"

"She's gone. Out that door." Sylas marches up to it, his entire stance radiating foreboding.

"How?" August asks. "I swear she didn't have salt this time."

"I know." Sylas frowns at the door, and I brace myself in case he picks up some detail that points to my involvement, the jitter through my nerves dispelling more of the absinthe-induced haze. I mustn't have left a trace, though, because all he adds is, "She must have discovered some other trick. Maybe her blood gave her the ability to crack the spell."

Even more distress darkens August's expression. "But—*why*?"

"Perhaps she no longer felt secure while there was tension between us over her affections. She'll have picked up on it, as much as we held it back. She's a sensitive one."

August blanches. "That would be just like her, wouldn't it? To leave because she didn't want to cause problems for *us*?"

It would. It so very would—exactly as she expressed it to me before I cast her off. I lean against one of the kitchen islands, willing the hard edge of the countertop to ground me against my discomfort.

Sylas's hands have curled into fists. "I should have heeded what she said last night more. She couldn't have been clearer that any aggression to compete for her favor made her uncomfortable."

The statement slams right through the center of my skull, sobering me at the same time as it knocks a startled cough from my throat. Last night—the way they were cuddled up together—I must have misheard him. "She told you *not* to fight over her?"

August barks a laugh, too flat to hold any humor. "She put us right in our places. But I didn't think— We've kept the peace, even if we can't completely control our feelings. What could have pushed her to this point so quickly?"

Not what—who. All that absinthe I poured down my gullet curdles in my gut.

Talia didn't only feel guilty in the moment when I accused her of inciting the conflict between my brothers—she'd already been actively addressing that conflict. And it'd worked, at least enough that they'd been willing to share her attention last night. Enough that they're working together to find her now without a hint of animosity.

A light has gone out in August with her departure. Even Sylas the ever-stoic looks haunted. And I can't deny the inexplicable sense of mourning that's been eating at me since the moment she vanished down the stairs on my command.

Is it possible that for all the trouble she brought with her, she enriched our existence enough to make it worth the bargain? Just what have I thrown away?

My stomach lists, and I grip the edge of the island, clutching at my one remaining justification. "It's better for her in the long run if she's rid of us, isn't it? Puts us in a bit of a bind to be sure, but we've managed in the past well enough. She wanted to get home."

Sylas glances toward the landscape beyond the window, his frown deepening. "*If* she makes it out of the Mists. If she's not caught by folk worse than us. I saw evidence of trespass in the woods during my evening run. Someone's been lurking in our domain." He yanks the door open, making a brusque gesture for us to follow him. "We have to go after her and hope we find her before our enemies do."

One of our enemies is lurking in the forest I just propelled her into? I hurry after him and August, my gut lurching all over again. "They wouldn't dare—to attack what could be one of our servants in our domain…"

Sylas gives me a dark look. "Are you sure enough of that to gamble on it? We went right into another lord's *home* to steal her in the first place, didn't we?"

He's springing forward into his wolf form before I can answer. What could I answer anyway? It's true. Fae will bend and even break our own laws when we can get away with it, when we think it'll benefit us.

I broke Sylas's trust in me, thinking I knew so much better when I barely understood what I was seeing at all. Heart help me if I've sent our mite off to be further broken as well.

I release my wolf, letting the rush of the transformation sweep away the worst of the ache inside me. But as I race across the fields with my brothers, the pang rises up again, as wrenching in my wolfish chest as when I was a man.

I didn't ask. I didn't try to talk to either of them about what I'd witnessed. I barely talked to *her*, assuming I knew what the situation called for before I even stepped into her room.

There were a lot of truths I missed. A lot of signs I misread, perhaps understandably, perhaps colored by old resentments more than I'd like to admit.

In the face of Sylas's revelations, there is one thing I can admit with all my being, if only to myself: I don't want to lose her. Not the soft smiles that brighten her whole face nor the incisive remarks she summons at unexpected moments, not her giddy laughter nor the way she looked at me the morning when August ran off on her, apologizing as if she cared so much about my opinion of her.

She didn't want to go. She wanted to stay, with them—with *us* —and I chased her off like she really was some kind of vermin.

With their battle-trained bodies, Sylas and August pull ahead, melding with the shadows of the forest first. But I'm hardly a slouch, charging through the brush at their heels. We all slow to maneuver between the trees, but Sylas doesn't pause his forward momentum for an instant. His ears swivel, his breath hisses between his fangs, and he inches up our pace again from a trot to a lope.

I've just scented her on a stray pink hair snagged on a bramble when a cry peals out in the distance. The fur all down my back rises in horror.

It's Talia. She's terrified. And still ever so distant.

No communication is required between the three of us: we all hurtle toward the sound as one being. My paws batter the ground, heedless of the jabs of sharp-edged stones and splintered twigs, the scrape of brambles and bark I can't quite dodge. Faster, faster, every muscle bunching and stretching, my strides lengthening until I'm hardly aware of the ground at all.

The cry has fallen away. What's happening to her? Is she even still—

Another yelp splits the air, spurring us faster still. My heart races in time with the pounding of my feet. There's a thump and a scuffling sound nearby—

Ahead of me, Sylas lets out a snarl and launches himself at an attacker I can't yet see. Teeth gnash and flesh rasps under claws. August springs after him with a growl of his own.

I veer to the left, instinctively circling the spot to confirm we've identified every lurking menace. No scent reaches my nose but

Talia's and that of the woman from Tristan's cadre—the pale wolf now snapping at August as she whips around to avoid Sylas's claws.

My lips curl back, but there's no room for me in that fight, not with the two of them already in the mix. Where *is* Talia? Is she—

There. She's sprawled in the dirt, staring at the dueling wolves with a glaze of panic in her eyes. Her hands grope against the ground, a whimper squeezing from her throat even though she's rescued now.

She can't see that. I recognize the terror etched across her features. All she can see is the snapping of jaws from wolves like the ones that savaged her all those years ago.

I don't think, just leap toward her, shifting from wolf to man in the same instant. The moment I've caught her in my arms, I tug her backward, out of the clearing, out of reach of the fray. The heady sweetness of her fills my lungs, dizzying me almost as much as the lingering alcohol, and I hug her tighter, willing my body to be the shelter she needs.

I made a mistake, an epic one, but this time I still have the chance to make it right.

She isn't mine. She may very well be theirs already, in mind and heart. But I will defend her now in every way I'm able to, accepting the hand I've been dealt. In whatever small way is allotted to me, I have this compassionate, canny, joyful soul back in my life, and I won't let her go again.

She's still shaking, gulping vainly for air like she did in my room days ago. I tip my head close to hers and speak in the most soothing voice I have in me. "I've got you. Sylas and August can take her. You're safe now."

Another shudder runs through her, but then her muscles begin to unclench. She inhales raggedly, her lips grazing my chest. A quiver runs through me from the point of contact straight to my groin, as if this is any kind of time for that sort of desire.

I adjust her against me, tucking her closer while angling that lovely mouth just an inch farther away. It takes all my self-restraint not to nuzzle her hair.

"There," I breathe. "That's better."

She peers up at me, her eyes clearer now and her forehead furrowed. Her voice wobbles. "Why are you protecting me? Shouldn't you be telling me to get going?"

That intention feels so foreign now that it takes me a moment to decipher her confusion, especially with the fuzziness of the absinthe still clinging to the edges of my mind. Yes. Indeed. Why aren't I, in simple enough terms to explain my change of heart away in a sentence or two? And succinct enough to leave out the ache that's constricting my chest. There's no need to burden her with more fondness than she's likely to welcome.

I force a laugh that comes out short and rough. "It's become clear I owe better to my brothers." Focus on them. That's the sensible route.

"You said they'd be better off if I left."

The impertinent mite. I cock my head as I grasp at a more thorough answer. "They refused to accept as much. And perhaps, having now experienced your absence, I've drawn new conclusions."

Do her eyebrows manage to arch just slightly? There's definitely a bit of bite to her voice as the last of her panic falls away. "I kind of wish you'd figured that out before I nearly got mauled."

A snort jolts out of me of its own accord. This, this is the woman I ran myself ragged to save. The woman I missed the second she left the keep. Battered and fragile but with a core so steely she can put me in my place a mere minute after that near-mauling.

"My apologies." The words come out drier than she deserves. I swallow hard and search out the pieces of truth it seems safe to offer up. "I *am* sorry for the way I talked to you. And not just because of the distress it caused those two. I was… I was mistaken. We all gain something from your presence. Please, stay."

FERAL BLOOD

BOUND TO THE FAE #2

CHAPTER ONE

Talia

Three men lie sleeping on the red-and-gold rug that stretches the length of the grand entrance room. Their bodies form a loose circle around the spot I recently left. They look totally relaxed now, but vicious claw marks gouge the polished floorboards on either side of them.

I suspect that the floor has seen worse on previous occasions, and that fae magic will heal the wood easily enough. In spite of those signs of violence, the warm midday light beams cheerily down from the windows high above and no sound reaches my ears but the soft, rhythmic rasp of the men's breaths. The scene should give me a sense of peace.

I braved my deepest fears for these men-who-aren't-really-men, the three who freed me from years of cruel captivity and offered me a real home. With a taste of my blood, I brought them out of the curse that turns their wolf forms mindlessly violent under the full moon. I watched them bring the chaos of their wild pack into some kind of order, and then I nestled in the middle of the ring of their bodies to sleep in perfect safety.

But that safety was an illusion. They can't protect me from everything in this strange, savage faerie realm—and I've just seen one of the gravest threats this realm poses lurking in sight of the keep.

I hesitate in the doorway, regret twisting through my chest. I don't want to wake them up to bad news. I'd give anything for a few more hours by their sides, basking in the joy *I* woke up with. But that joy has vanished. However serious this threat turns out to be, Sylas will want to know about it right away.

It turns out I don't even have to wake them. With my first uneven steps, the wooden slats of the brace around my warped foot tap against the floor, and Sylas stirs. He pushes himself into a sitting position and rolls his shoulders, his head turning so he can watch me approach.

The fae lord who rules over this keep and the pack that lives alongside it looks every inch the stalwart commander even in the simple shirt and slacks he wore for last night's transformation. He studies me with one darkly penetrating eye and one gone white with the scar that bisects his tawny skin from eyebrow to cheekbone. The purple-brown waves of his shoulder-length hair part around the high points of the ears that mark him as one of the few "true-blooded" fae, a status that gives him his authority over his cadre and his pack.

Even sitting, his tall, well-muscled frame exudes authority. So do the multitude of arcing black lines supernaturally tattooed on his body, everywhere from his temples to his neck to his forearms and, I know from past experience, the sculpted planes of his chest beneath that shirt. Each one of those marks represents the true name of some plant or animal or material he's learned, that he can bend to his will through his powers.

As recently as a few days ago, I found him intimidating. Now, the warm welcome I can recognize in his gaze and the reserved smile that curves the corners of his lips offset his imposing aura. Sylas was a little frustrated that I ignored his instructions to stay locked in my room to release them out of their wild state, but he also appreciated the dedication I showed with the gesture. The greatest thank you he gave me wasn't those words themselves but when he referred to me to the others as "our lady."

I don't belong to these men, but I belong *with* them, standing beside them. I proved it last night, to all of us.

And now I might be bringing a new threat down on their heads, after everything they've already risked for me.

That last thought must show on my face, because Sylas's smile fades. As I reach the edge of the rug, he stands, looming more than a foot taller than my slim—not long ago half-starved—figure. The movement rouses his cadre. Whitt rolls onto his back with a muffled groan and a stretch of his brawny arms; August swipes his hand over his broad, boyish face and aims a bright if slightly groggy grin at me.

Sylas's attention stays focused on me. "What is it?" No "Good morning" or inquiries about how I slept. How does he see so much with only the one working eye? Sometimes I feel like he looks straight into my head.

I come to a stop a few feet away from him, the news I have to deliver forming a lump in my throat. I force it out. "I think I saw one of the men from Aerik's cadre on the hills past the houses, watching the keep."

Sylas's lips pull back from his gleaming teeth with a restrained snarl. I thought of him as a grizzly when I first met him, and he's never fit that impression better than right now. August leaps to his feet with surprising nimbleness given his strong but stocky frame, his gaze darting to the door, his posture tensed as if ready to lunge straight into a fight. Whitt draws himself up at his typical languid pace, as if he's not particularly concerned despite the others' reactions, but his ocean-blue eyes have turned stormy.

"He left," I add quickly. "A few seconds after I saw him, he took off. He was in his wolf form—I'm not completely sure it was him. But the color of his fur was just like his hair, this blueish white, and the way he moved…"

Just remembering the cock of the wolf's head so like the cruelest of my former captors, I find myself wrapping my arms around my chest. Sylas takes a step toward me and sets a firm hand on my shoulder. Ferocity still smolders in his unscarred eye, but it's *for* me, not at me.

"He will not touch one hair on your body," he says, so emphatically I can hear the vow in the words. "Not him nor his cadre-fellows nor that pissant Aerik." He looks at his cadre. "From her description, it'd be Cole."

Whitt nods, his mouth slanting at a displeased angle. August runs his fingers through the short strands of his dark auburn hair, his golden eyes more unearthly than ever with a protective fury burning in them. His voice, normally buoyant with its enthusiasm, contains the edge of a growl. "He was trespassing on our territory."

Sylas looks at me. "Did he see you?"

I think back to my frozen moment by the upstairs window just minutes ago. "I'm not sure. But he was far enough away that even if he noticed me at the window, I don't think he could have made out much other than the shape of me and the color of my hair."

One of my hands rises to finger the strands that trail over my shoulders. In an offering of kindness when I first arrived here, August used magic and faerie fruit pulp to dye my natural dusky brown a deep pink that wouldn't be *un*natural on a fae woman.

At the time, the change seemed frivolous, a superficial way of moving beyond the abused captive I'd been for the past nine years and reclaiming something of my real self. Now, it's also a line of defense—my former jailors aren't searching for a pink-haired woman.

Cole. I have a real name for the man with the blue-white hair and sharply jointed limbs who took such pleasure in using the pointed edges of his body to draw pain from mine. A memory flickers up of my cheek being mashed into the hard metal floor of my cage, a harsh chuckle in my ears. Fingers digging into my cheek and an elbow ramming against my ribs as Aerik's other cadre-chosen sliced my wrist to steal my blood…

I don't realize I'm shaking until Sylas's grip on my shoulder tightens and I feel myself shudder against his hand. My lungs have clenched up, my throat straining to draw breath into them. I hug myself again, tighter, fighting to get a hold of myself.

It's over now. It's over, and I'm not going back to that filthy cage or the horrible monsters that look like men.

"Not one hair," Sylas repeats, his deep baritone managing to be both fierce and soothing. "I'll tear their throats out if they so much as try."

August steps toward me as if he can shield me from the horrors inside my head, his teeth bared. "If I don't get to them first."

I take gulps of air, focusing on the solid warmth of Sylas's hand, the determined blaze in August's eyes. The tremors subside. My chest still aches, but the panicked tension releases enough that I can inhale fully.

Whitt has stayed where he was, a little apart from our cluster of three. In the past, he's defended me—but he's also accused me of threatening the cohesion between the cadre and their lord. I'm still not totally sure where I stand with him.

As long as Sylas wants me here, Whitt will follow his lord's orders—I'm sure of that. But will this new development change his mind about whether my presence here does them more good than harm?

Even if it does, I wouldn't expect him to show it. Whitt rarely lets much obvious emotion slip from behind his nonchalant front. He rubs his jaw, the storminess in his eyes retreating but not vanishing as his expression turns pensive.

"Whatever he was doing here and however unwelcome his visit, Cole can't have observed anything damning," he says in his dryly melodic voice. "Without the benefit of our mite here, Aerik and his pack will have lost themselves to the wildness of the curse last night as much as every other Seelie. He wouldn't have been in any state to observe that the three of us appeared to have kept our heads."

An idea that chills me rises up in my head. "What if they saved some of their 'tonic' and didn't go wild at all?"

Sylas shakes his head. "It wouldn't have worked. We tried that once, on the rare occasion when Aerik deigned to share portions of the tonic with us. Only some of the pack took it, so they could shepherd the others, and we set aside the rest in anticipation of being skipped over later. The next month, they didn't bother with us, so we took some of the remainder—and it had no effect at all. It appears it's not only necessary to get a taste of your blood but for it to be fresh as well."

I guess that's a small comfort.

Whitt makes a vague motion with his hand. "It is a concern that Cole was snooping on our lands at all. I've gathered that they've been traveling around asking questions all over the realm, but for them to have been here specifically on the night of the full moon doesn't bode well."

August frowns. "Yes. Why us? You don't think Kellan let more slip than we realized…?"

He glances at Sylas in question. Kellan was the third member of Sylas's cadre, but he wasn't satisfied with that honor. From what the others have said, he'd been challenging Sylas's authority and generally making trouble for a long time before I came into their midst. He particularly hated humans, and when he took that animosity to the point of attacking me, Sylas was forced to kill him to save me.

I didn't like the man any more than he liked me, but the thought of him still sends a pang of guilt through my gut, knowing how it wrenched at Sylas to have to go to such extreme measures against one of his own.

Kellan made his unhappiness known to at least a few fae from other packs, but it'd sounded as if he'd been vague about the latest developments in the situation here. If it turns out he mentioned that Sylas had brought a human girl into the keep, one with some sort of special power—it wouldn't take long for Aerik to put the pieces together.

Sylas stays silent for a moment, his thumb running up and down my shoulder in a steadying caress. "It seems unlikely that he could have said enough to alert Aerik without our recent guests also having some idea. Tristan didn't raise any questions that had anything to do with Talia. But we were in and around Aerik's fortress for some time. It's possible we didn't cover our tracks quite as thoroughly as we would have hoped."

"If he had definite proof, he'd challenge you about it," August says. "If they're just skulking around, they might suspect, but they don't know for sure."

"That would be my conclusion as well." Whitt swivels toward me. "What exactly did you see? Every detail from when you first spotted him."

I drag in a breath, letting myself lean into Sylas's touch as I dredge up the images. "Less than half an hour ago, I went to the window upstairs that faces south, wondering how the rest of the pack was doing. Cole—his wolf—was at the top of one of the nearest hills to the east of the forest. I couldn't see *him* all that well either, that far away, but the color of his fur was obvious. When I noticed him, he was just standing there, staring at the keep. It couldn't have been more than a minute. He didn't move except tipping his head like—like I've seen him do as a man. Then he ran off down the far side of the hill, out of view."

Whitt taps his lips, his face still solemn but a glint lighting in his eyes. "I'll speak to the sentries and send a few to make discreet inquiries farther abroad. He was acting boldly, showing himself like that—they may be preparing for some kind of overt move. I'll find out whatever I can so we can be ready for that."

Sylas nods to him. "Good. Let me know as soon as you discover anything at all." He turns me to face him with a gentle squeeze of my shoulder, his gaze catching mine with all that lordly intensity. In spite of my anxiety, my heart skips a beat with the memory of that dark eye smoldering as he touched me in his bed several days ago, of his mouth claiming mine just last night.

Both he and August have become something more than protectors to me. I'm not sure what, or where it'll lead, but the thought makes my pulse thump faster all the same.

"I'm afraid we'll have to delay your introduction to the rest of the pack by at least a couple more days," he says with obvious regret. "We should wait until we have a better idea of what Aerik's next move will be—and it'd be best if no one associated your arrival too closely with the full moon. It's not my wish to keep you trapped in the keep. As soon as we can—"

I set my hand over his much larger one, giving him the bravest smile I have in me. "It's all right. I don't *want* to leave the keep if it might mean Aerik finds me. And I don't want to put you at risk either."

The affection that darkens his gaze sends another flutter of heat through my chest. "Our lady indeed." He raises his hand to stroke it over my hair. "I swore you'd be safe here, Talia, and I mean to make good on that promise—come what may."

CHAPTER TWO

August

The day after a full moon, I'm always ravenous. Even though I was only in the feral state of the curse for a short part of last night, today's no different. So, when my older half-brothers set off to deal with the potential threat of Aerik, a business that Sylas doesn't seem to have any use for me in yet, it's only natural that my first impulse is to head to the kitchen, which is my favorite room in the keep anyway.

No matter what my lord and my cadre-fellow are doing that I can't fully contribute to, they'll always need to eat.

Talia drifts with me toward the hall, her arms crossed loosely over her chest. At least she's not still hugging herself as if that's the only thing keeping her from shaking to bits. Still, the shadow of worry that lingers on her pale, pretty face makes my body itch to let loose fangs and fur and go racing across the realm until I can maul Aerik and his cadre beyond recovery.

It was horrifying enough seeing the state she was in when we came across her in that cage. Imagining her having to endure that treatment for nearly a decade, from when she was little more than a *child…*

I catch my growl before it creeps from my throat. My temper is rising on her behalf, but letting it out in front of her will only make her more anxious. We can't deal with Aerik yet. The best thing I can do for her is offer a way to keep her mind off those worries.

I give her hair a playful rumple, reveling in the softness of it, in the way she brightens at my touch. "We could all use some breakfast—or I suppose lunch at this point. Can I get the help of my favorite kitchen assistant?"

She beams up at me. "Of course. I'm starving. What are we making?"

"I haven't decided yet. Let me take a look in the pantry and see what that inspires."

Before I do that, I spread some butter on a thick slice of bread to address the worst of her hunger—it's no good creating an elaborate meal if she's too famished to enjoy it while she's shoveling it into her mouth. And the last thing I want is to give her any further reminders of her time in captivity. I gulp down a hunk for myself as I peruse our current stash of ingredients.

The lake quails in the cold room won't take too long to bake. I gather several of those, the makings for fresh rolls, and duskapples to poach for dessert.

When I emerge with my haul, Talia's eyes widen where she's perched on her usual stool. "How many people are you expecting to feed?"

I laugh, the sound startling me but instantly lifting my mood. "We worked hard last night. Now we have the appetites to match."

I toss together the ingredients as quickly as I can and get Talia started kneading the dough for the rolls while I stuff, season, and truss the quails. For several minutes, we work in companionable silence. When I sneak glances at her, she's intent on the movement of her hands in the dimpling mass of dough, a small but definite smile curving her lips.

She likes having something useful to do with herself just as I do. And I was able to give her that when she must have needed it more than ever.

The pride that tickles through me comes with a memory of last night, of the fog clearing from my head when the taste of her blood reached my wolfish maw, of gazing up at her resolute form and understanding what she'd done. Sylas was with her then, but she must have approached him in his slathering beastly state alone. This wisp of a girl, filled out some now that she's getting proper meals but still slim and delicate—yet not remotely fragile.

Somehow the torments Aerik subjected her to forged a soul that's so resilient without hammering the kindness out of her.

She looks up and catches me watching her, and the corners of her mouth lift a little more even as a flush colors her cheeks. A hint of longing seeps into the sap-sweet scent her skin gives off. Suddenly I want to set so much more than my gaze on her.

The serious cast that crosses her face a moment later snuffs out my flare of desire. Her hands pause over the dough. "Most of the summer fae, like you," she says. "The 'Seelie.' They think about humans more like Aerik does than like Sylas, don't they?"

I grapple with my answer, buying myself a little time as I arrange the quails in their roasting dishes. I won't deceive her, but I'd rather not terrify her any more than she already is either. After I've washed the grease and herbs from my fingers, I take the dough from her and begin forming it into balls.

"I think it'd be most accurate to say they're somewhere in between," I said finally. "And it's not simply about attitudes toward humans. Pretty much all fae see mortality as a weakness. They look down on those of us with a lot of human heritage too." I motion toward my ears, their rounded shells resembling my human mother's so much more than my true-blooded father's. "I can't say even the three of us are immune to that kind of thinking completely."

"Kellan definitely wasn't." Talia gives a little shudder.

"Exactly. And he also, like Aerik… Many fae use that sense of superiority as an excuse to become cruel. They enjoy crushing whoever they can with their powers; they deal with boredom by squabbling over lands and possessions. They'll just as happily ruin a fellow true-blooded fae as a human. It's just easier to exert their will over beings with no magical protections."

"You aren't like that at all. Or Sylas and Whitt, from what I've seen. It was only Kellan."

"That was the largest point of conflict between him and Sylas." I set the last of the shaped rolls on a baking tray and turn to face her. "Sylas's main ambition is to provide for the pack as well as he possibly can—to see everyone have everything they could want, including peace. Any glory beyond that would cost our pack-kin pain and possibly even their lives. He'll fight to protect the pack and the Seelie in general, but not out of selfishness. And there are other lords who prefer peace over conquest too."

Talia runs her hands down her thighs to her knees, her shoulders hunching slightly. A ruddy, raised scar caused by tearing fangs pokes from the neckline of her shirt above her collarbone: a stark reminder of just how cruel the lords who *aren't* like Sylas can be. "So, if it comes out that I'm here and what my blood can do, pretty much every fae will think they have more rights than I do, but some of them won't want to outright torture me?"

Those words sum the situation up far more accurately than I like. I can't leave her bearing the burden of that understanding alone.

I move to her, touching her arm, bowing my head over hers. My voice drops low. "It doesn't matter what anyone outside these walls thinks. You're with us now. Sylas meant what he said—we're not letting Aerik—or anyone else—hurt you. If they try, I won't hesitate to make them regret it."

My voice turns fierce with that last promise, my own fangs tingling in my gums, but Talia doesn't flinch at my vehemence. If anything, it appears to restore some of her own confidence. Her shoulders straighten again, her mouth firming but her eyes staying soft as she gazes up at me.

"I know he meant it. I know *you* mean it. That's why I wanted to do everything I could for you last night."

She reaches up to rest her fingers against my jaw, and all my awareness narrows down to the heat stirred by that tentative caress and the memory of what else she did for me last night—of the moment when she turned from Sylas after he kissed her and immediately drew me to her, marking her own sort of claim. Showing that she wanted me just as much as she did him, that she wasn't going to leave me on the sidelines.

I don't know how I got so lucky to have earned that devotion from her when she could have offered it all to my lord, but I don't have it in me to refuse it. I can't even refuse the hunger that surges through me now with her body so close to mine, her scent in my nose, and those tender words in my ears.

I lean in, and she tips her chin up so she can meet my kiss. That simple gesture nearly undoes me. My wolf rears its head, and what I intended as a gentle peck transforms into a scorching melding of our lips.

As I capture Talia's mouth, a needy, breathless sound escapes her, sending a bolt of lust straight to my groin. Her hand slips to my chest, her lips part to welcome me, and it's all I can do not to outright plunder the tart heat within.

It's hard to believe this is only the third time we'd ever kissed. As I tug her closer, every inch of her body feels familiar; every breathy noise falls into harmony with the pounding of my pulse. I've watched her; I've longed for her; I *know* her. And she embraces that yearning with all she is.

I want to hoist her onto the island and bury myself completely in the arousal that's already lacing the air, want to bring her gasping to a climax ten times as ecstatic as the one she found with my guidance in the basement sauna pool. Want to feel her come apart around me, clutching me and arching against me, every fear and worry forgotten.

Skies above, how I want it.

But as I let my tongue delve between her lips, as hers flicks out to tease over it, a tremor runs through her frame. Her fingers grasp at my shirt as if she needs to hold onto something or she'll be swept away. The eagerness doesn't fade from her kiss, but my lust recedes at the reminder of how new this sort of encounter is for her. Two weeks ago, she hardly knew what pleasure she could bring to her body on her own.

If I follow my hunger to its intended end, she might go along with it, caught up in the sensations I'm provoking within her—but will she be happy afterward? How can she know how much *she* wants if she's too overwhelmed to consider that question?

I will not be like— I will not use her. I won't let my wants trample over hers, human as she is. Until she's had more space to decide—until she's sure of what this all means—until *I'm* sure I can be everything she needs—

I brace my hand against the edge of the island behind her and ease back just a few inches. Talia's pale green eyes glow with desire, her cheeks flushed, her lips darkened by the kiss. I swallow hard, having to master myself all over again.

"I'd love to keep doing this all day, Sweetness," I murmur, brushing the lightest of pecks to her forehead. "But I did promise you a meal."

From her smile, I've managed not to make my retreat feel like a rejection. "Better not to find myself among three starving wolves?"

she teases, and glances past me to the counter. "How long will the quails take in the oven?"

"Twenty minutes or so."

"I should probably take the opportunity to get some clean clothes on, then. If I'm going to be 'lady' of the keep, I'd better at least kind of look the part." She tugs at her shirt, which is rumpled from being slept in but doesn't at all detract from her charm. I force myself to step farther back so she can slide off the stool. A very large piece of me is gnashing its teeth in self-reproach for not having taken the opportunity to strip her of those clothes myself.

I watch her slip out of the room, so nimble now despite the faint limp the foot brace Sylas made for her can't quite correct, and then turn to my baking. As I set the trays in the oven, my mind is still on Talia, the heat of our encounter thrumming on through my veins, a more ardent warmth wrapping around my heart.

I've never felt this all-consuming adoration for anyone before. There hasn't been anyone in our diminished pack who roused enough attraction for me to think it was worth courting them and risking the tensions that might follow if my interest dwindled. When I've passed the fringes of the Mists into the human world to blow off more carnal sorts of steam, I've always gone to women who make a job of it, who I can compensate with money with no chance of misunderstandings about the encounter leading to more.

What am I supposed to do with so much feeling? If I offer it all up to Talia in a deluge of emotion, will she welcome *that* or shy away from the implicit hope of receiving just as much in return?

Those questions leave me restless, but I don't know where to find the answers. All I do know is I have to show her she's so much more to me than an object to lust and fight over. There's got to be more I can do than cook for her, kiss her, and unleash my rage when an immediate threat appears.

A vague but forceful sense of resolve grips me. As the scent of roasting quail wafts into the air, I head upstairs to Sylas's study.

"Come in, August," he answers at my knock. Does his deadened eye give him a glimpse of who lies on the other side, or does he know us well enough to differentiate the sound of our knuckles? That seems like an impertinent question to ask.

When I step inside, shutting the door behind me, my lord is at his desk, frowning at a map and a page of notes set across it. He rests his elbows on the corners of the map and looks up at me expectantly. "I assume you're not here simply to summon me to lunch."

His unshakeable aura of measured authority always sends me back to the days when I hadn't yet come of age to join his cadre at all and he oversaw much of my education. Probably because nearly a century later, that level of studied control still eludes me. But I have plenty of other skills to compensate—at least, I'd like to think so.

I square my shoulders to better look the part of cadre-chosen. "I know my main duty has been defending the pack from physical threats as they come up, but I'd like to become more involved—in the planning and strategizing. It might not be my greatest strength, but I'm sure I have enough experience by now to contribute something, and you and Whitt have so much more on your plates now with Kellan gone."

Sylas considers me with a contemplative expression. I suspect he can guess that this proposal has been driven at least partly by my desire to protect Talia in every way I can. I did brawl with him the other day to secure a better fate for her. He seemed to respect the show of commitment even as he rebuked me for the insubordination, though. It might work in my favor more than against it.

"Did you have anything particular in mind?" he asks.

I came up here in such a rush I hadn't taken the time to think that through. "Well, I—I'm not sure what you and Whitt have already discussed or how you'd want to approach the situation with

Aerik. But I'm at your disposal. And if I could be included in discussions of those strategies from now on, I'd happily share my views."

"Fair enough. Perhaps I should have brought you into them sooner." Sylas rubs his temple, the subtlest sign of the burden he's carrying as lord. I might have gotten frustrated with him over his plans for Talia before, but I can only imagine how difficult he's found this balancing act, weighing the needs of the pack against her safety. He saw a way through, as difficult as it might make our lives going forward, and that's why I'd throw myself into any fray in front of him.

After another moment's thought, he motions to the wall in the direction of the pack houses. "You *are* my general of sorts. There's a chance this dispute could escalate into a battle. With most of our warriors at the border, we need *every* pack member as prepared to defend what's ours as they can be, regardless of age or physical prowess. Let them know that tomorrow you'll begin training them."

The thought of a battle sends an uneasy prickle through me— most of the pack *isn't* in any state to go to war. But that's exactly why he's giving me this responsibility.

I nod sharply. "I can do that. Thank you for trusting me with the task."

"Of course. I'd have had you do it sooner if I hadn't wanted to spare our people the stress of wondering *why* we're preparing them. But as things look now…" He exhales with a grimace and pauses. "Talia should learn whatever you can teach her too. Work with her here in the keep for the time being, and with the others once she's revealed herself to the pack. She's had to fend off claws and fangs too many times already without the means to give her a fighting chance."

Yes. The image of a wolf lunging at her swims up from my memory, and my muscles tense instinctively. Anything I can to do to teach her how to protect *herself* is twice as good as the protection I can offer.

I dip my head to my lord again, drawing myself up even straighter. "I'll see to both. If it comes to blows, we'll be ready for them."

Whether we'll be ready enough to *win*... That'll come down to how well I do this new job I've demanded.

CHAPTER THREE

Talia

A hand slams my head down, fingers digging into my scalp in five bruising points of pain. The weight of the man's body squashes me into the cold floor so forcefully I can't breathe. My legs flail instinctively—no, *no*—and all at once he wrenches backward.

He snatches my foot, fingernails sharpening into claws. With a violent twist, the bones snap. Pain floods my leg. I shriek, and the stale air clogs my throat with the stench of urine and blood, choking me, suffocating me as the agony blares on and on—

"Talia."

A steady but determined whisper. A hand, much gentler, stroking down my arm. I jerk awake, barely processing those sensations, my heartbeat booming with panic for the few seconds before the bleariness clears from my gaze and I make out Sylas looming over me, sitting on the edge of my bed.

A nightmare. I've had another nightmare about my time in captivity. I've thrashed the covers off down to my waist; the thin fabric of my nightgown sticks to my back with sweat now turning clammy. A sour, acidic flavor laces my mouth. I swallow hard, trying to rein in my racing pulse.

The fae lord's hand stills by my wrist. He peers down at me with his mismatched eyes, and not for the first time I wonder which sees more. "You cried out," he says evenly. "More than once."

Crap. As my terror retreats, embarrassment prickles in to take its place. "I'm sorry I woke you up."

He shakes his head dismissively. "I was still working, but even if you had woken me, it wouldn't be your fault." He pauses, his thumb grazing my forearm in an arcing caress. "You haven't had one that bad in some time."

That's true. During the month I've stayed here, the nightmares never went away, but in the past week or so, they'd lost some of their potency. The sense of Aerik and his cadre stalking me must have riled up those fears all over again.

I'm sure Sylas can connect those dots himself, so I simply say, "I know I don't have to really worry. Here you are saving me from them even when they're only in my head. Thank you for breaking me out of the dream."

It isn't the first time he's called me out of one of those nightmares, and I doubt it'll be the last.

His mouth twists. "I wish defeating our foes in reality were half as simple. But we *will* shield you. Are you all right now?"

My heartbeat has nearly evened out, and the suffocating sensation has faded from my lungs, but I hesitate at the thought of being alone again. Sylas takes that momentary silence as an answer in itself. Without another word, he stands and scoops me out of the bed, the covers falling away from my legs. His arms tuck me close to his broad chest, the rich earthy, smoky scent of him washing over me with his warmth.

"I'm okay," I feel the need to clarify, even though it's hard to want to be anywhere but nestled in his embrace now that I'm there.

The fae lord gives a low rumble that sounds amused. "But you could be better. You told me before you felt safer in my room than yours."

As he strides out of the room and down the hall, carrying me as if I weigh nothing at all, the warmth condenses into a deeper heat at the thought of the things we did in his room the last time I slept there. The heat pools between my thighs, but I'm too groggy still to sort out whether I'd want to make some kind of move now and if so, what.

Is Sylas expecting something? Other than that night when he caressed me while encouraging me to take myself to a bodily release, we haven't shared more than a few kisses.

When we enter his bedroom, I glance up at him, searching out his expression in the dim moonlight that drifts through his window. He meets my gaze.

"I do want you to sleep," he says, setting to rest those anxious questions. "Sleep here where you know any enemy, real or imagined, will have to get through me to reach you."

"And after I sleep?" I ask tentatively.

The curl of his lips brings out an ache low in my belly, the rumble of his low baritone only intensifying it. "We'll see what tomorrow brings." He brushes those lips to my forehead and lowers me onto the far side of the bed. "I'll make no demands. When you're sure of what you want, I'll be more than happy to oblige."

The heat flares in my cheeks, but as my head settles into the down pillow, sleep is already creeping back over me. Sylas lies down a couple of feet away from me and tugs the covers up over us. I scoot a little closer, not quite touching him but basking in his smoky warmth.

The last thing I'm aware of before exhaustion pulls me back under is the stroke of his fingers easing a few stray locks of my hair back from my face.

ᨠ

I wake up to bright sunlight and the impression of body heat fading from the mattress by my arm. As I rub my eyes, Sylas emerges from his private lavatory, his dark hair falling damp across his shoulders from a shower. He finishes securing the ties that close the sharp V neckline of his shirt and lifts his gaze to meet mine, that now-familiar smolder kindling in his unmarked eye.

"Back to work already?" I say, hoping I don't sound too disappointed. I'm not sure if I was hoping for a repeat of the last morning I slept in his bed or even more, but I definitely wouldn't have minded cuddling up to his brawny form while I was alert enough to fully appreciate it.

Sylas's mouth twitches into a smile that holds a hint of apology. "One of the sentries reported evidence of intrusion near the borders. I want to take a look at it myself as soon as possible. Stay here and sleep as long as you like."

He bends over the bed in a motion that's almost a prowl and steals a kiss that's quick but impassioned enough to leave me flushed all over. With the passion it rouses in me, I'm tempted to grab hold of his shirt and pull him right back into the bed, but he's already drawing away with a purposeful air. Nothing will keep the fae lord from an urgent duty—and those duties are partly aimed at protecting me, so I can't really complain.

For several minutes longer, I sprawl in the bed, soaking in Sylas's scent and the last tingles of warmth. But after years of having no more than a cage less than half the size of this bed to roam around in, I'm not one to squander my new freedom by lolling around. I get up and limp to the door, intent on retrieving some clothes and my foot brace from my bedroom and then discovering what August has planned for breakfast.

When I slip out, another strapping figure is just stepping out of his own room on the other side of the hall. Whitt pauses and cocks his head, the tufts of his sunkissed-brown hair typically mussed and his bright blue eyes sparkling, as inscrutably gorgeous as ever. He's left his high-collared shirt unbuttoned partway down his chest, giving a glimpse of the true-name tattoos winding across the tan skin over his sternum. August told me Whitt has nearly as many as Sylas.

"Good morning, mite," he says in that tone that always seems to skirt the line between teasing and outright mockery. "I'm guessing it was a good night as well."

A fresh blush burns my cheeks. I'm abruptly aware of the thinness of my nightgown and the fact that I have nothing at all on underneath it, although Whitt is keeping his gaze rather studiously on my face. I cross my arms over my chest. "I had a nightmare."

He arches his eyebrows. "Hmm, don't let Sylas hear you talking about your trysts with him that way."

"I wasn't—" I cut myself off at Whitt's smirk and settle for glowering at him. I could tell him that all I did in there was sleep, but he might not believe me anyway—and I *wanted* to do at least a little more than that, so what does it matter if he thinks I accomplished it?

Whitt chuckles, and something in his expression softens just slightly. "I like this new ferocity you've been cultivating. One of these days I may have to promote you from 'mite' to 'mighty'."

"You could call me Talia. That *is* my name."

"But where would be the fun in that?"

He starts down the hall—in the same direction I need to head in, naturally. I could hang back and let the conversation die, but that feels awfully wimpy after he just complimented me on being fierce.

Whitt told me not that long ago that he's glad I'm here, that he wants me to stay. I shouldn't need to be nervous of him, even if something about his temperament always seems to put me off-balance.

"Does having fun matter a lot to you?" I ask, summoning a little more boldness as I follow him. "Is that why you hold all those revels for the pack?"

"I arrange our revels for many reasons, but enjoyment is certainly a significant part of them." He glances at me, the teasing glint in his eyes sparking brighter. "I suspect you'd enjoy them too. You'll have to attend one and find out what all the fuss is about."

"I *can't* attend one right now," I remind him. "I'm not supposed to let the rest of the pack see me still."

"True, true. Just something to keep in mind for future plans. I'll have you know—"

I don't get to find out what he thinks I need to know, because right then he halts in his tracks, his head cocking again as if he's listening intently to something with those lightly pointed fae ears, though my human ones haven't picked up anything unusual. His smile tightens into a more determined shape. "As enjoyable as *this* talk has been, you'll have to excuse me."

He stalks off and vanishes into the room where I've gathered he carries out whatever work exactly it is that he does for Sylas. The room where I overheard him talking to a pack member once—a pack member who somehow vanished from the room without leaving through the door. They were discussing a conflict with the fae from the winter realm, the ones the men of the keep call the Unseelie. Has more news come about that?

What if Sylas ends up having two wars to fight?

That question twines uneasily through my gut. I grab a change of clothes from the assortment the fae men have gathered for me over the month I've stayed here—they must travel into the human world now and then and… steal them? *Could* they even buy them properly if they wanted to play fair?—and duck into the lavatory so I can wash myself as well as get dressed.

Even though Sylas and I *didn't* do anything all that intimate, my skin probably picked up plenty of his scent from sleeping in his bed. August might have agreed to the idea of both he and Sylas pursuing some sort of relationship with me, but smelling the other man on me one time before upset him enough to send him charging off in wolf form. I'd rather not risk provoking any possessive inclinations if I can help it.

I don't really care what Whitt thinks of my nighttime activities, but I don't want August thinking I've devoted myself much more to Sylas than to him after all.

When I've finished, less exposed in my daytime clothes and skin tingling from the scrubbing, I nearly run into Whitt striding down the hall outside with a more purposeful attitude than I'm used to from him.

"Is everything all right?" I ask.

He stops long enough to say, "Yes. Better than we expected, I think, though I'll have to see what Sylas makes of it."

Before he can hurry onward, I make a vague motion toward the stairs. "He's gone out. He said a sentry reported something and he wanted to take a look."

Whitt lets out a faint huff. "Well, then. I suppose this matter is hardly earth-shattering enough to require his immediate attention. No reason I should go chasing after him when I could wait here while indulging in a leisurely breakfast with prettier company." He winks at me.

Even though I know he's teasing, my lips can't help twitching into a smile. I toss my nightgown into my bedroom and have just tapped my way down the stairs when the front door at the other end of the keep thumps. The fae lord comes around the bend looking as collected as always, so whatever he checked out couldn't have been too much of a problem.

Whitt appears at the dining-room doorway in an instant. "A word, my liege?" he says in a sardonic voice.

Sylas comes to a halt by the doorway. "What is it?"

Whitt casts his gaze toward me where I'm approaching them

and hesitates. I brace myself for him to draw his lord aside to speak with more privacy, but then he gives a curt nod. "You may as well hear this too."

I wanted to know what was going on, but now that he's implied that his news affects me somehow, my pulse stutters. I join them, shoving my hands in the pockets of my jeans to stop them from clenching into nervous fists.

Whitt focuses back on Sylas. "One of the people I sent to check up on Aerik reported in. From what he gathered and overheard, Aerik's cadre and some others from his pack have been making comments rather publicly about how we've seemed pleased that no one has the tonic now. Trying to raise suspicions about our motivations or what have you."

"That's all?" Sylas says. "Nothing more damning than assumptions about our attitudes?"

"That was it. It might be simply an attempt to displace attention from themselves when the packs who relied on their regular deliveries of the tonic must be upset, but in combination with their interest in our territory… Aerik probably does see us as among the likely culprits in this one's disappearance." He gives my shoulder a swift pat. "But not the only ones—there's no certainty to it. He's trying to lay the groundwork for a larger case against us in case he needs to make one, yes, but he hasn't got anywhere near enough ammunition to do a thorough job of it. We do make easy scapegoats."

Sylas hums to himself, considering Whitt and then me. "We'll wait until the others give their reports," he said. "But if the rest of the word aligns with that… We can't hide her forever, and it seems to me that showing we have nothing to hide may be a better tactic for dealing with such unsubstantiated concerns."

"What does that mean?" I ask.

"If all's still well tomorrow, we'll introduce you to the pack and get you settled in as a regular fixture in their lives. Once that's done, perhaps it's time we invite Aerik and his cadre for a dinner to show there are no ill-feelings over their frequent neglect of our 'friendship'."

Wait, what?

Whitt grins. "Give him a chance to investigate up close and find nothing, and he won't be able to justify continuing to suspect us. I like it." He aims that grin at me. "With a few careful glamours, you'll slip by right under his nose as a totally different woman."

Sylas regards me with a solemn expression. "If you feel you're ready for that, Talia. We won't rush the matter—and I wouldn't ask you to be around them at all if I didn't think it's our best hope of getting them to back off for a long while afterward."

Face my former captors again. See them here in the keep that's become my sanctuary. An icy shiver ripples over my skin.

It's not just for myself. How much more danger will the men of this keep have to face because of my presence here? Aerik's already being so hostile toward them. They shouldn't have to deal with him at all, let alone invite him into their home where he can attack them up close—an attack that might involve not just words but teeth and claws if the truth comes out.

I'm drawing them here, just like before—just like—

Images of blood splattering grass and leaves in the darkness flash through my head. Snarls and cries, the strained rattle of a last breath. I flinch, holding in my shudder as well as I can. *No!*

But even as panic clangs through my chest, I understand why Sylas is suggesting this strategy. Stealing me away has already set him and his cadre on this path. It doesn't seem like we can avoid Aerik forever. Wouldn't it be better to get the confrontation over with and have him gone from my life than to be constantly on edge waiting for them to spring at us?

At least this way, Sylas can control the circumstances, completely on guard rather than taken by surprise.

I take one breath and then another, thinking of curling up

between the three fae men last night, about the warm shelter of their wolfish bodies. When I manage to speak, my voice comes out quiet and a little hoarse but steady. "Are you sure you could disguise me enough that they wouldn't recognize me?"

"You barely look like the little scrap we stole away anymore, even without magic," Sylas says. "The main identifying factors will be your shoulder scars, your wounded foot, and your scent. The first can be covered easily enough with clothing, and we won't reach out to them until I'm sure beyond any doubt that we can mask the other two."

My body balks again all the same, but I force myself to nod. "All right. If this is the best way to make sure they don't keep sneaking around here, we should do it."

"Then tomorrow you make your debut." Whitt claps his hands. "It looks as though you may get to attend one of my revels before much longer after all, mite."

CHAPTER FOUR

Talia

I've only left the keep once before, and that was several evenings ago, in such a hurried mission that I didn't dare look back. I've seen most of the scenery from the windows before, but it's different taking it in at my leisure with the fresh outside air all around me and warmth of the ever-summer breeze licking over my skin. And I haven't gotten a really good look at the keep itself before.

I turn on my heel where I've stopped on the soft grass that tickles my bare feet. Beyond the nearby fields, patches of forest darken the horizon in almost every direction except the low, rolling hills to my left. To my right, spires of pinkish stone jut up from the distant treetops in spindly towers, dotted with lime-green vegetation. And behind me…

Getting a good eyeful of the place I've lived in for the past month, my breath catches. Inside the keep, it's easy to imagine that while the structure is a bit odd—every wall and ceiling made of the same polished wood as the floors, lighting fixtures that look like branches—it's still simply a very grand house. Outside, it's both one of the most beautiful and the most alien buildings I've ever seen.

It looks as though several immense trees sprouted up and fused into one being, only the curves of one bending into the next showing where they might have begun and ended. Nothing sprouts from the smoothed bark of the outer walls, but above the second floor, branches weave together into an intricate pattern like the finest sort of lace. Delicate rings spiral out around the arched windows as if they used to be knots in the wood.

"It doesn't quite live up to Hearthshire, but we built it under direr circumstances," Sylas says beside me, as if he thinks I'm underwhelmed rather than overwhelmed by the sight. He tips his head toward the pack village. "Are you ready?"

Right. We did come out here for a reason. One I haven't really forgotten, nervousness making my stomach jump. I might have been using the view as an excuse to dawdle. I square my shoulders. "As I'll ever be."

Heading over to meet the larger pack feels weirdly like showing up in a new classroom halfway through the school year. The people Sylas is about to introduce me to have their own friendships and probably rivalries, histories that stretch back farther than I've even been alive. How am I going to fit in with all that?

Actually, it's a gazillion times worse than a classroom, because these "people" aren't even people. They're fae, and I'm human, and August has already told me that pretty much every fae views humans as something lesser than themselves.

I limp along beside Sylas, his pace slowed in consideration of my own, sucking the wildflower-scented air into my lungs and willing my heart not to hammer straight through my ribs. Several fae are already moving around their houses, which look like much smaller versions of the keep's construction: enormous tree stumps that've been twisted off to form a pointed roof a few feet above their heads.

A woman is tending to a garden full of bright leaves and berries in a cacophony of colors. A couple of men are working together to bend several pieces of wood into some kind of contraption, it appears with magic, while small pearl-gray hens peck at the grass by their feet. A small group is just tramping back into the middle of the village with weapons over their shoulders or at their hips and a large doe carried on a harness between them.

At the sight of their lord, all activity ceases. Sylas's pack leaves off their work to approach us, more emerging from the houses as if his presence alone sets off some sort of signal to alert them.

Sylas and I come to a stop at the edge of the patchier grass on the foot-worn paths between the houses, his hand rising to my shoulder. It's a gesture mainly for their benefit, I suspect—to emphasize that I'm under his protection? That they should treat me with all the respect he'd require?—but his firm grasp helps me stand straight and steady before all these strangers.

And there are a lot. Not compared to most packs, from what the men of the keep have indicated, but to me, when I haven't been around more than four other people at a time in nearly a decade… My gaze darts across them too nervously for me to do a proper count, but I'd guess there are about thirty. And this isn't the full pack. There are others off on sentry duty or fighting in that conflict with the Unseelie too.

I couldn't say all of them are exactly *attractive*, but there's an eye-catching, unearthly quality to their faces and forms, as difficult to look away from as Sylas and his cadre's stunning features. They range from twig-thin to barrel-chested, dressed in simple shirts and slacks or dresses of a thin but tightly woven flowy material. Most of them have favored the earthy tones Sylas and August generally wear, but some, a few of which I recognize as regulars at Whitt's revels, are decked out in vibrant jewel tones closer to his preferences.

They're eyeing me with open curiosity, but that makes sense. Sylas told me he hasn't taken human servants since Kellan joined his cadre because of the other man's intense hostility toward mortal beings, so these fae haven't seen someone like me in their domain in quite a while. Whether they've *ever* seen a human with starkly pink hair is debatable. I'm just glad that I don't pick up any obvious animosity or disdain in their expressions.

"It's good to see you all looking well," Sylas says in his authoritative tone. "I'd like you to meet a newcomer to our pack. This is Talia. She's come from beyond the Mists. My cadre-chosen August has brought her here as a companion—*not* a servant—and she's still becoming accustomed to our ways. I expect you all to help ease that transition and to offer every reasonable kindness."

Heads bob in acknowledgment all through the crowd. I smile at them, hoping my mouth doesn't look as stiff as it feels. How much kindness will the fae consider "reasonable"?

Sylas scans his pack with a smile of his own. "Excellent. Why don't you take leave of your work for a short while and tell me how you find yourself these days? And if you wish to get to know Talia a little better, I'm sure she'd be more than happy to make your acquaintance."

No pressure at all. I shift my weight on my feet, a faint tingle reminding me of the illusion that's hiding my brace and any unevenness to my gait from our spectators. Since bodily magic is one of August's specialities, he contributed to the glamour, instructing me to focus on steadiness over speed. If I lurch around too much, the glamour won't be enough to disguise my old injury.

Sylas glances at me, probably appraising how well I'm coping. Even if my nerves are jittering all through me, I have to show him I can handle this. He's taking on my enemies for me; I'd better at least be able to take care of myself among my allies.

I raise my chin a little higher and take a step forward to meet the fae heading our way. Apparently reassured, Sylas ambles on into the crowd, pausing here and there to speak with his people.

Many of the pack-kin gather around him to wait for his

attention, but several drift closer to me. They look me up and down tentatively as if I might prove unexpectedly dangerous, but one woman who doesn't appear to be much older than I am plants herself right in front of me.

Her long, smooth hair gleams such a pale but warm blond you could believe it was made out of sunbeams. She peers at me with close-set blue-grey eyes that are just a tad overlarge, giving her an unsettling insect-like appearance. But her grin is broad and as far as I can tell genuine when she thrusts out her arm at an awkward angle, as if she's been told shaking hands is how humans greet each other but has never actually done so to know what it should look like.

I clasp her hand in return, finding her grip warm and firm, and give it a quick shake, even though I feel a bit silly. "Talia," she says in a silvery voice, lingering over each syllable as if tasting it. "You've come a long way. I'm Harper of Oakmeet—I mean, obviously. I hope you like it here."

"I like what I've seen so far," I say, which is true if we don't count anything outside this domain or Kellan or the fae from other packs who've intruded here.

More fae have drawn up around her. "What part of the human world are you from?" a burly young man asks, his voice gruff but his eyes gleaming with curiosity.

"Um, America." I'm not sure if I should get more specific than that when I can't answer any specific questions about what's been happening there recently.

He hums as if that's good enough anyway, and a knobby middle-aged woman pushes between him and Harper to inspect me. "You're taken with our August, are you?" she asks in a possessive tone, as if evaluating whether I'm worthy.

I guess it's not much surprise that August with his cheerful, kind demeanor and innate protectiveness would have a lot of fans in the pack. A blush tingles across my cheeks at the thought of what they might already assume about our relationship, but with luck that only makes my answer sound more honest. "It's hard not to be."

"You wanted to come, then?" Harper says eagerly. "Did you know where he was bringing you?"

"I—I knew a little, but it's hard to be prepared before you've actually seen the place."

She hums to herself, her gaze going distant. "It must be so exciting."

A pleased exclamation pulls the attention away from me for a moment. Sylas is brushing his hand to the forehead of a willowy woman in what looks like a gesture of benediction, his face glowing with happiness.

"A new member of the pack," he booms with such blatant delight a smile catches my lips that I don't have to force at all. "What a blessing. We'll make his or her arrival a safe and joyful one."

My gaze skims down the woman's body and catches on the slight swell of her belly. Fae are nearly immortal, but the trade-off is that they struggle to have children. How long has it been since this pack last had a child in its midst?

The woman and the man at her side who I assume is her husband—mate?—duck their heads with pleased smiles of their own, but all at once something clenches in my chest. Sylas has so much to defend here, so many people who are depending on him, who couldn't easily fight for themselves if Aerik or some other lord launched an attack. It isn't just the men of the keep I'm putting in danger but all of the pack as well.

He's risked their security for me. He's put it all on the line to give me some kind of freedom. I don't know how I'm ever going to repay him for that.

I don't know how I'll live with myself if Aerik hurts any one of them.

Before those gnawing worries can grip too much of my mind, one of the fae women near me leans in and twists a lock of my hair around her finger. "How is your hair this shade? It can't be natural."

"August dyed it," I say quickly. "He thought it looked nice like that."

She makes a slightly disgruntled sound. From what I understand, only the truest of true-blooded fae with barely any human heritage in the mix would generally have coloring this unusual. Even Sylas only has a purple-ish tint to his coffee-brown hair. Maybe she thinks I'm attempting to rise above my proper place.

A stout man at my other side jabs at my thigh. "What are these pants? It's an unusual material."

I manage not to flinch away from him, but it's a near thing. My pulse skitters at how tightly they're closing in around me now. "They're called jeans. They're very popular in America these days."

More fae nose in on our gathering, volleying another question and another. "Have you been out to the pastures yet?"

"Are you going to stay here forever?"

"Do you know any crafts?"

"Will you be hunting with us?"

"What of your human family?"

I have no time to come up with answers under that bombardment, and the last question gouges straight through my heart. The smack of pain constricts my throat. Before I can manage to regather my smile and my voice, a wiry figure elbows her way through the throng to my side.

The woman who reaches me is the first faerie I've seen who actually looks *old*, so she could have a couple of millennia on me. Her serene forest-green eyes study me from a pale, wizened face framed by tight coils of slate-gray hair. She stands half a head shorter than me but not at all stooped, her posture straight and bearing commanding enough that I doubt she bows to anyone other than Sylas. There's a kindness in her expression, though, that lessens the ache of my loss like a balm.

She spins to frown at the others, who've already backed up a step, whether out of respect for her seniority or her general presence, I can't tell. "Let's not badger the poor thing," she says in a spirited if raspy voice. "I'd imagine she was overwhelmed plenty already before you lot started hailing questions on her head."

"It's all right," I say, not wanting any of the pack members to think I've taken offense, as grateful as I am for her intervention.

She glances at me with a twinkle in her eyes and a wry tone that makes me like her even more. "Very polite of you to say so. Speaks well of your upbringing. Still…" She turns back to the other fae. "Give her some space. August isn't the fickle sort. I expect she'll be here more than long enough for you all to indulge your curiosity bit by bit rather than in a deluge."

The others start to drift away with a few offers that I should seek them out if I'd like to see this one's garden or that one's weaving, leaving only the wizened woman and Harper, who's stayed with an air of impenetrable confidence as if it never occurred to her that the woman's orders might apply to her too. I don't mind. Two is a much easier number to cope with than a dozen.

I lower my voice in the hopes that the other fae won't overhear. "Thank you."

The newcomer pats my arm. "Think nothing of it, my dear. Our days around here tend to be much the same, so it's not surprising they get overeager with the appearance of someone new, but that's no reason you should have to weather a storm of interrogation." She steps away herself. "I'm often out on sentry duty, but if I'm around and you need a helping hand, you can always ask for Astrid."

"Thank you," I say again as she heads off.

Harper tucks the silky fall of her hair behind her ears, as if she's anxious about making a good impression herself. "If there's anything in our territory you might like to see—I don't know what sorts of things you enjoy—I'd be happy to show you around. Without *too* much badgering." Her shy grin suggests she has at least a few more questions she'd like to ask.

Explore the domain—experience more of this world I've spent the past nine years in but have seen so little of. My spirits lift at the idea, but a twinge of fear deflates some of that elation. How safe is it for me to roam farther beyond the keep, especially without Sylas or his cadre ready if the wrong fae crosses paths with us?

"I—I'm not sure," I say, stumbling. I don't want to dismiss her friendliness. If I'm going to be living here for a while—maybe even forever—I'll probably be happier the more I integrate with the pack. And Harper seems like one of the friendliest of them, with no sign that she's put off by my mortality. "I should talk to August before I make any plans. I think he'd be worried if he came looking for me and found I'd wandered off without telling him."

He probably would be, and Harper doesn't appear to take offense to the excuse. "Well, whenever you want to." She pauses and sidles closer, her voice dropping to a stealthy undertone. "What Astrid meant to say is that living here can be unspeakably *boring*. But I think you just might change that."

She looks like she might say more, but at Sylas's return, she settles for flashing me another grin and meandering off toward the forest. The fae lord sets his hand on my shoulder again, watching her and then glancing down at me with a trace of amusement. "Already making friends, are you, little scrap?"

I'm comfortable enough with him now to wrinkle my nose at his old nickname for me, even though I kind of like it—or at least the tenderness with which he says it. "Maybe. She seemed as if she'd like to be friends."

He nudges me toward the keep, and we stroll across the grass to the main door. In the entrance room, he stops and turns to face me. "It might do both you and Harper good to spend some time together. She's one of the few of the pack who was born in Oakmeet and hasn't had the opportunity to venture beyond this domain... She's dedicated enough to have remained with us when she could have struck out on her own, but I can tell she's restless. As I suppose you must be too after staying cooped up so long."

"I can't complain about the treatment I've gotten here." My gaze travels back to the door. "But it was really nice getting outside. Do you think—she suggested that she could show me more of your territory—would it be safe?" And there's also the matter of my foot. Disguised or not, with the misshapen bones and their perpetual ache, I'm not up to any extended hikes.

Sylas pauses, considering. "Until the most immediate concern of Aerik is dealt with, I'd prefer that you remain within hearing—in the fields around the keep, on this side of the hills, or no more than a few steps into the woods. One of us can reach you quickly at a single shout, and it's unlikely anyone would harass you that close by anyway. Perhaps we could arrange a venture farther afield with appropriate transportation and August accompanying you when the timing seems right."

"Okay," I say. "That makes sense."

He gazes down at me and strokes his fingers over my hair, trailing heat in their wake. "I want you to have as normal a life as I'm capable of offering you here, Talia. I know what it's like to lose a home you loved and to be unable to safely return... Whatever is in my power to make up for that loss, you'll have it."

The intensity of his tone strikes a chord deep inside me. A home he loved—the Hearthshire he still uses in his title, even though he and his pack haven't lived there in ages. That they were driven from after his soul-twined mate was killed over the crimes she committed.

I swallow hard. "You still miss your old domain a lot, don't you?"

He shrugs, but with a weight to his shoulders that stops the gesture from looking remotely casual. "It was the first territory that was truly my own, and we built our home there from the ground up by our own power, with every feature I could have wished for. The thought of it falling, neglected, into disrepair..." A growl creeps into his voice. He dismisses it with a shake of his head. "We will have it again. As many centuries as it takes, I will earn it back for us."

And it may take centuries longer now that he's decided not to use me as a bargaining chip. Emotion swells in my chest for the sacrifices he's made, this powerful and devoted man who's barely known me a month and yet saw something in me worth shielding. I grasp his wrist. "Thank you."

When he meets my gaze again, I bob up on my toes, and he lowers his head to accept my kiss. The ardent press of his lips leaves no doubt that he's satisfied with his decision. When I drop back on my heels, giddiness is tingling through me.

"I didn't mean to pull you away from your new friends for long," he says, his voice a touch rougher after the kiss. "Don't venture far, but explore all you like within those boundaries. This place is yours as much as it is the rest of ours now."

I squeeze his arm and let him go, stepping toward the door. But as I slip out into the sunlight, a question I'm afraid to voice sinks heavy in my stomach.

What *will* become of Sylas and his people if Aerik does discover their theft of me? Will they lose even this backwater fringe domain they've made their own?

How many more lives will be ruined because of my blood and the monsters who crave it—because I'm too weak to stand against them alone?

CHAPTER FIVE

Sylas

"You wouldn't know it at first glance, but she's got grit to her." Astrid gazes toward the waning moon from where we're standing at the edge of the northern woods before shifting her attention to me. "I suppose she needs it if she's going to carve out a real place for herself here. You're expecting her to be around for quite some time, my lord."

It isn't a question. Astrid has been with me long enough to recognize these things without asking.

"August has already become quite fond of her—and she of him," I say, measuring my words. "She has little to return to." Not after Aerik and his cadre slaughtered her family. It's pained her too much to share the details, but from what she has said and her reactions when the subject comes up, I can picture the scene far too vividly. The image brings a snarl to the back of my throat.

Perhaps Astrid notices that defensiveness, or perhaps something in my demeanor when I introduced Talia this morning gave it away. Either way, the smile she offers me holds a grandmotherly amusement along with due respect. "I'm guessing the fondness extends beyond August."

I'll accept that prodding—she is as old as my actual grandmother, after all, and she's been a presence in my life since I was born. I count it as an honor that she left my family's domain to follow me to Hearthshire and then here. That doesn't mean I have to confirm her suspicions, though.

"She is pleasing enough to have around," I say in the same even tone. "But somewhat unsure of herself in such unfamiliar surroundings. I'd prefer that her transition to this life didn't involve any trauma." Any more than the immense amounts it already has. "The rest of the pack has accepted her well enough? There hasn't been any muttering or disparaging?" I kept my ears pricked after Talia returned to the village, but without standing over her shoulder monitoring every interaction, I can't be sure of what might have been muttered or conveyed in a hostile glance.

Astrid shakes her head. "Not that I witnessed. You laid out your expectations clearly—and she hardly made it difficult to follow them. It didn't take half an hour before Brigid had her gamely mixing paints for some new mural her lot has going up in their house, and after that a bunch of them had her going from garden to garden so they could show off their coming harvest. She never gave any sign she was anything but pleased to compliment their work."

Relief sweeps through me, more intense than I'd expected. She's already fitting in here, establishing bonds—it's not the life she'd have had if Aerik had never rampaged into her childhood, but it's the closest to a normal one I can offer her.

I tip my head to Astrid in thanks for her report. "I'm glad to hear it. If any trouble does come up, even a murmur of it—"

"I'll make sure you're aware of it, my lord. Though I will say, if you'll allow it, that I think the girl could hold her own all right against a sharp remark or two. She'll garner more approval if anyone with doubts sees her stand up for herself rather than having you intervene."

No doubt she's right. I can't help that picturing Talia receiving even a hint of cruelty from my pack makes my hackles rise, though. Bad enough that she had to tolerate Kellan's viciousness behind my back. If he hadn't been kin-of-my-mate...

Well, that is dealt with now, even if I wish it could have happened in a better way, and the fae of my pack are much more of my choosing.

"Your service and your wisdom are as appreciated as always," I tell Astrid.

She sketches some semblance of a bow and slips into the deepening shadows of the evening to take up her sentry duty. I head back to the keep. As my gaze skims over the horizon, my deadened eye conjures a brief wisp of a vision: three hazy figures on horseback cantering toward us, there for a blink and then vanished back into the aether the image arose from.

A hint of our future or a glimpse from our past? It could be either. With no news that suggests Aerik has any real reason to suspect us of wrongdoing, Whitt has sent out an invitation to him and his cadre. I might have gotten a backwards echo of their arrival.

My spymaster has also slunk into Copperweld to spy on their reaction firsthand as well as he can, not trusting anyone else with that job. There's no telling whether Whitt will return later tonight or perhaps not for another day or two, if he becomes concerned and stays to monitor the situation further.

As such, the keep is even quieter than usual. I have to walk the whole length of the hall before my ears pick up the thump and the grunt of activity from the basement gym.

Apparently ingratiating herself with the pack didn't wear Talia out too much. I come to the gym doorway to find her and August circling each other on the mats, the sweat shining on her forehead a testament to how long they've already been sparring. Her slim body is tensed in the T-shirt and sweats my younger brother obtained for her training, her balance impressively steady despite her damaged foot in its brace.

I stay to the side in the shadows, but August picks up on my presence as I'd expect him to. He acknowledges me with a flicker of a glance but otherwise stays focused on his pupil, his teeth gleaming in his eager grin. Talia doesn't appear to notice me at all, her concentration entirely on her opponent.

"Ready?" he says.

The second she nods, he springs, snatching at her waist. Talia ducks and tries to dodge to the side, but he catches her, swinging her back in front of him with a force that sends a ripple of protectiveness through me even though I know he'll be careful with her.

Her sputtered curse makes August chuckle. "You can't always get away. How would you make an attacker let go?"

They must have gone over some of the strategies before, because that's all the prompting Talia needs to ram her elbow toward his nose. When he jerks his head out of the way, she slams her good foot into his knee. Releasing her, August falls back with an *oof* that's only partly feigned, and Talia scrambles around, crouched animal-like on the mats but beaming at her success.

A strange cordial of emotions floods my chest. Fondness, yes— Astrid wasn't wrong about that. But a surge of admiration twines through it, for the strength this scrap of a woman manages to summon from somewhere within that delicate mortal body. It can't be easy for her, practicing these moves against an opponent twice her size while she has a permanent injury holding her back as well, but she's throwing herself into the training whole-heartedly.

Isleen would have laughed at a human imagining they might brawl with fae and come out anything other than beaten to a pulp, but Isleen would never herself have tackled a challenge this great to begin with. My departed mate, Heart keep her soul, bristled with frustration when any task became difficult for her. She had many talents, to be sure, but that led to her expecting *everything* to come easily and to finding fault in anything that didn't rather than seeking to improve her own skills.

I hadn't expected to encounter a disposition that so puts that aspect of hers to shame in a human.

And through the fondness and the awe winds a sensation too clawed to be called protectiveness now. No, that's pure possessive instinct, the drive in me to shove August away from this ever-surprising woman and gather her up where he can't set a single finger on her.

Not because I have any fear he'd hurt her—oh, quite the opposite. There was no mistaking the way his eyes flared as he held her in his arms, no mistaking that the flush in Talia's cheeks now is more than just exertion. A trace of arousal laces the tang of sweat in the air.

I will the barbed urge to claim her down with a tightening of my jaw. She isn't mine. If I tried to force the issue, I've no doubt she wouldn't have a single thing to do with me from that moment onward.

Why *shouldn't* she have August to turn to as well? It isn't as if I can offer her all the attention a devout lover should. I have too many responsibilities pulling me in too many directions… I should be glad she trusts me enough to allow me any intimacy in the times when I can be at her side.

If I truly mean to give her the best possible life here, then sharing her affections is part of that.

Talia straightens up, and I catch August's gaze with the slightest twitch of my eyes for him to stand down. We should find out how our lady reacts when she hasn't been given a chance to prepare for an assault.

In the swiftest of strides, I sweep into the room to whip my arms around Talia's shoulders from behind. Her flinch tells me she clearly hadn't registered my arrival at all in the midst of their tussling.

She yelps, but rather than crumpling, her limbs strike out, her elbow jabbing my ribs, her heel smacking my shin in the instant before she realizes who holds her and how gently. The blows land hard enough to sting.

"Sylas!" she gasps, jerking in on herself with a deeper flush blooming across her face. "I'm sorry—I didn't—"

I can't pass up the opportunity to nuzzle her hair. "You did well, Talia. Your defensive reflexes are already becoming honed." I give August an approving smile over her shoulder, aware that he may now be experiencing the same jealousy I felt a moment ago and hoping to assuage it. "A credit to both yourself and your teacher."

August's grin comes back easily enough. "She's an avid student."

As I release her, Talia's head dips humbly. She glances from me to August, a hint of pride coming into her expression but worry clouding her light green eyes. "How likely do you think it is that I'll need to use these lessons for real?"

"You've already had a couple of aggressive confrontations," August says. "I think it's better for us to assume the worst, and if you never find yourself under attack again, we'll all celebrate that fact."

Her lips twitch with another smile that doesn't reach her anxious eyes. "But no matter how much you train me, I'm never going to be able to fight off someone who's fae, am I?"

If only I had a better answer to give her. "That's not your fault. No human would have an easy time of it. But every extra second you can buy for yourself, fending off severe wounds or capture, allows us another second to reach you and finish the battle on your behalf."

"It isn't even physical strength, really," August adds. "We can bring magic to bear. Without that, you can't help being at a disadvantage." He chuckles roughly. "If I could teach you *that* part of battle…"

Something in Talia's hesitation after that statement puts me on the alert. She looks down at her hands and swipes one of them across her mouth, her body tensing all over again even though the sparring is over. I'm about to ask her what's wrong when she raises her head, her expression determined.

"I—I think there's something I should tell you. About me and magic."

CHAPTER SIX

Talia

When I finish my account of how I unlocked my cage door using the magical true word for "bronze" and later warped an attacker's dagger the same way, Sylas and August stare at me in stunned silence. A nervous itch runs up my arms.

I've been afraid to tell them about this additional strangeness, adding to the qualities that a typical human who's been dragged into the fae realm wouldn't possess. Will my seeming ability to use magic make me even more a target than when the only inexplicable specialness about me was my curse-curing blood?

But these men have saved my life more than once—Sylas has *killed* for me, a member of his own cadre no less. Keeping the secret from them when the subject has been brought up directly felt too close to lying for comfort. I should be able to trust them with this. I want to show them I trust them.

Not to mention that it sounds like my unexpected talent could be a deciding factor in my surviving another attack.

Sylas recovers first, peering down at me intently. "You're

absolutely sure that you produced those effects yourself and using magic? Aerik might have failed to secure the cage properly…" He trails off, obviously unable to think of a reasonable explanation for how the fae woman's blade could have gotten bent out of shape.

"I tried the lock that day," I say. "Several times before I got it right. And I *felt* the word work, like there was some kind of power to it when I said it right."

August gives his lord a perplexed look. "Have you ever heard of a human who could call on true names—not from the legends but in our lifetime?"

Sylas shakes his head. "Not one. Even in the legends—which may have some truth to them—it's always been men and women with at least a little fae heritage in the mix." He frowns as he examines me even more thoroughly, leaning close and inhaling—testing my scent. "In all the tests I conducted before, I've noticed no signs that you're anything but human through and through. But if it were a small enough element, with the other power of your blood as a distracting factor, it might be nearly imperceivable."

I might be a tiny bit fae? A shiver runs through me that's as much anxiety as it is excitement. I don't know if that makes my situation better or worse. "Is it all that common for people in the human world to have a fae ancestor?"

"No. Given our issues with conception and inheritance, we're particularly careful with potential and actual children. But very occasionally one slips by and is a weak enough half-breed to go unnoticed during their mortal lives, continuing to spread that heritage to their children. You would have to be several generations removed from the source to show no physical signs of it, though." Sylas's brow is still furrowed. "I find it hard to believe that with so weak a link, you could have managed to teach yourself not just a little trickery but an entire true name without any outside guidance."

"What else could it be?" August asks.

"Who can say? We don't understand the effect Talia's blood has on our curse either. Perhaps the two factors are intertwined somehow—arising from a common feature we haven't yet discovered." Sylas rubs his jaw. "I don't know of any other way to investigate the cause that we could easily pursue in our current situation. There are resources that might help elsewhere in our world, but that would risk exposing Talia's secrets to our brethren."

I hug myself, the idea of the impenetrable mystery lurking inside me overshadowing any satisfaction I felt in sharing this secret even with these two men. "But even if we're not sure how it happened, it's a good thing, right? You were just saying that the reason I'll never be able to defend myself against fae on my own is magic. If I can learn more true names or other spells…"

Sylas appears to shake himself out of his pensive state. "I don't like dealing with dynamics I'm uncertain of, but it can't be helped. You're right—this should work to your benefit, so long as you continue to keep it secret from everyone other than my cadre and me. If word got out that we'd gotten our hands on a magic-wielding human, we'd face nearly as much scrutiny as if they knew what benefits your blood offers."

A chill ripples down my spine. "Of course." I'm getting more practice at keeping secrets than anything else these men are training me in.

August moves toward the door, his usual cheerful energy coming back. "You'll have to show us what you can do already, and then we can build from there. I have some bronze utensils in the kitchen that it wouldn't be any great loss to see mangled."

As I follow him, my stomach knots. What if I can't manage it? What if I *am* somehow wrong even with the two instances of proof?

It won't matter. I don't actually think Sylas or August will judge me for a lapse like that. I just don't want to let them down now that I've raised their expectations.

Sylas comes with us, his demeanor more reserved. Not because he doubts me, I don't think, but because of his qualms about the consequences this revelation might lead to. But I already had a huge bullseye on me for my blood, so I can't really regret the possibility that a second oddity about me might allow me to fend off the people who'd want to use me for the first.

The smells from our dinner—roast fish in a wine sauce and a bake of mixed berries and leaf vegetables that made a startlingly delicious combination—linger in the kitchen. August goes straight to the drawers beneath the counters and digs around until he produces a slightly battered bronze ladle. He sets it on the larger of the two islands and motions me over. "Give it your best shot."

What exactly am I supposed to do with it? I step up to the countertop and eye the lone spoon, picturing it bending in the middle like the fae woman's dagger did. It's hard to summon much determination over an act that seems so random. I nibble at my lower lip and mentally sound out the syllables I spent so much time committing to memory. *Fee-doom-ace-own.*

I reach out my hand to grasp the spoon's handle like I clutched the latch on my cage. The cool metal warms against my palm. Focusing all my attention on it, I propel the true name from my throat. "*Fee-doom-ace-own.*"

The two fae men watch, tensed in anticipation, but the spoon just sits there in my grasp looking as spoony as it did before. My heart sinks. I try to gather all the energy inside me and declare the word again. "*Fee-doom-ace-own!*"

Nothing. No tingle on my tongue, no change in the utensil I'm holding. I swallow hard, a ridiculous burning forming behind my eyes.

I know I did it before. It must have taken a thousand tries, but I got there eventually with the lock on the cage. And the woman who attacked me, her dagger—I warped it on my first try.

With panic and anger surging through my nerves. When I finally managed to unlock the cage, it was after that man from

Aerik's cadre—icy Cole—suggested they break my other foot and have me crawl around their fortress cleaning the rooms like a slave.

"Talia," Sylas starts, so kindly the tears threaten again, but I shake my head before he can finish whatever he means to say.

"Let me keep trying. I think—I think I need to get back in the same mindset as when I did it before. Maybe some of the power came from my emotions."

He falls silent, giving me the space I need without any sense of impatience. I reach back through my memories to the terror of the fae woman's attack, but that was a sharp jolt in the face of a sudden threat, hard to stir again when I'm here in one of the few places I feel safe.

My years under Aerik's control—those have stuck with me much more deeply, the horror twined through my spirit to the point that it seeps into my dreams, grips me at just the mention of my family. I hate the gut-wrenching chill that fills me when I think back to my imprisonment, but if I can use it, if it can give me power after everything he stole from me…

My heart thumps faster, the sickly chill expanding through my abdomen, but I force my thoughts to return to the filthy, starved existence of my captivity. To the endless hours where I had nothing but a few harsh words spat at me, a little food and water shoved between the bars, and my imagination offering a far too ephemeral escape. To the days when Aerik and his cadre would come to cut my wrist and drain a vial full of my blood, Cole pinning me beneath his body as painfully as possible, all of them laughing and sneering. To the splintering of pain and the crack of bones fracturing in my foot the one time I dared fight back.

To the wolfish beasts that lunged out of the shadows that night I teased Jamie into chasing me through the woods. Fangs and blood and guttural shrieks.

My legs tremble under me. My lungs have clenched, but I manage to produce the syllables, imagining myself facing those beasts again, preparing to do everything I can to defend myself and my family. I can't save them now, but maybe I can save Sylas and his pack from more violence.

My fingers tighten around the spoon. "*Fee-doom-ace-own. Fee-doom-ace-own!*"

With that second utterance, an almost electric energy quivers over my tongue. The spoon shudders and hitches farther forward, the rounded end jutting and narrowing into a point vicious enough to stab.

August sucks in a startled breath. Sylas traces his fingers over the back of my hand, and I jerk my arm back from the makeshift weapon I shaped using a magic I barely understand. The fae lord picks up the spoon-turned-spike and turns it over, studying it from all angles.

"You really did it," August says, awe glowing in his eyes. A grin leaps to his face. "You called its true name, and it answered. Do you have the mark?"

I glance down at myself as if one of those curving black tattoos might have appeared on my body just now. "I haven't seen it. I checked everywhere I could see on my own and with a mirror after you told me what those are."

Sylas lowers the spoon. "The magic might not leave its stamp on humans the same way it does on fae. Impossible to know when we have no other examples. And regardless, you haven't fully mastered the word. Once you're completely in tune with it, it shouldn't take that much out of you."

"If she was fae," August puts in. "Maybe that's different for humans working magic too."

The thump of footsteps at the doorway draws all our attention away from my handiwork. Whitt stops just over the threshold, his hair windblown and his eyebrows arching. "Humans working what now?"

August points at the spoon-spike. "Talia knows the true word for bronze—she called on it, and it followed her will. That used to be a ladle."

Whitt blinks, some of his usual nonchalance fading behind a flicker of shock. "*What?* You're sure it was her and not—"

"We both watched her do it," Sylas interrupts firmly. "I was certainly skeptical of the idea, but there was no mistaking what I saw. It was a struggle for her, though."

"But she'll improve with practice." August looks as though he's barely holding himself back from jumping with joy. "We can start trying to teach you more words—I guess we should start with the simplest ones—"

"Those that are relatively simple but also useful for self-defense," Sylas says. "No more than one or two to begin with. We don't want to strain her budding abilities."

Will I have to take myself back to the awful moments from my past *every* time I want the magic to work? A shiver shoots through my gut, but there's elation in it too.

I've proven it. There's something magical in me. Whatever I have to do to use that power, it'll be worth it to have a chance of standing up for myself against our enemies.

Whitt stares at me for a second longer before his face snaps back into a more typical unconcerned expression. He clears his throat. "We have another, more pressing matter to discuss. Aerik accepted your invitation, my lord. We can expect him and his cadre for dinner in three days' time."

CHAPTER SEVEN

Whitt

I never enjoy Ralyn's visits from the Unseelie border. They've rarely brought any news worth celebrating—generally the opposite. But this report promises to be even more troubling, when rather than meeting me in my office via the concealed outer entrance, he instead sent a leaf gliding through a window to me on a conjured lick of breeze. Its message asked only that I meet him at the edge of the southwest woods.

Does he have some reason to fear being seen approaching the keep? He could have waited until nightfall when he'd have blended into the darkness. Instead the leaf's urgent patter against my face got me out of bed much earlier than I'd have preferred, especially after spending most of yesterday prowling around Aerik's domain. The mid-morning sunlight glares straight into my weary eyes.

As I reach the forest, my nostrils flare. Amid the pungent scents of pine and cedar, I pick up a trace of the man's scent from just a little farther south—mingled with the metallic tang of fresh blood.

My pulse quickens, all my senses going on alert. I stalk into the cooler shadows between the trees, and Ralyn's lean form rises from where he was crouched in the underbrush some twenty feet away.

Rises and then sways. I hurry forward and catch his elbow just before he collapses. When I squint, I make out a dark, damp patch that stands out against the deep green fabric of his tunic by his waist.

"What are you doing here?" I demand, checking him over for other wounds and taking in the scrapes on his wrists and knuckles, the splotch of a bruise at the corner of his jaw, the talon-shaped scratches across his temple that look inexpertly sealed. "You should be in one of the healers' tents, not roaming around here. And you'd better not tell me the arch-lords have done away with healers along the front."

Ralyn manages a hoarse chuckle at my disparaging tone. "Saw a healer. He didn't do a good enough job, apparently. Rushing when there were so many— I tried to give it a chance to heal on its own, came when I thought I was good enough to travel, but the cut opened up again while I was heading here. I thought… it wouldn't be good for morale if the pack saw me staggering up to the keep like this."

He's lucky I was there to receive his message. So wretchedly loyal he'd have rather bled out here in the woods than come straight for help. I inhale with an irritated hiss that's mainly directed at whichever Unseelie bastards inflicted his wounds. "Better if we get August to look at it. Patching people up is much more his specialty than mine, especially if the battlefield healers weren't quite up to the job."

The last bits of color drain from Ralyn's already sallow face. "I'm not sure I can even make the walk at this point."

I wave off his concern before he can protest more. "If I can make the trip across the fields, my cadre-fellow can join us here too." I pluck a leaf off an oak—possibly the same tree Ralyn made use of—and murmur my intention to it. It flits toward the keep, where no doubt the whelp is puttering around in the kitchen as he so enjoys.

"What are you doing back here at all?" I ask, guiding Ralyn down until he's sitting. "A regular report could have waited until you'd given yourself more of a chance to recover. Has the tide turned? Do the others need more supplies?"

Ralyn grimaces. "The blasted ravens hit us twice as hard a few days ago—the morning after the full moon. We were still disorganized after the wildness. None of the squadrons were fully prepared. We—we lost Filip and Ashim. The pricks tore them to pieces. A couple of the others took bad blows, worse than mine." His voice has become even more ragged. "Reinforcements from farther south came in time to push the feather-brains back, but I don't think there are more than three or four of us from Oakmeet out there who can give our all going forward, and that's hardly enough to hold our own. None of the other squadrons will have our backs."

My jaw works. Of course not. They can't forget about maintaining appearances in the hierarchy of the packs even when our mutual enemies are slaughtering us wholesale. Maggots eat all those mangy bastards.

"They attacked *after*, not during the full moon?" I have to clarify. If the stinking ravens have discovered that weakness—

But to my relief, Ralyn nods. "I'd hate to think what would have happened if they'd been bold enough to strike during the night and found us in the grips of the curse. The usual glamours and the rest must have convinced them we were standing strong then." He pauses. "I thought you should know as soon as possible. The moment this wound is sealed again—"

I cut him off again. "You're not going back until *you* can give it your all. Stay and rest at least a few more days once August has patched you up. And consider that an order."

The man doesn't look happy about it, but he holds his tongue on that subject. "I don't know how we can gain an advantage if they keep at us that fiercely. There always seem to be more of the ravens, and they're only ramping up their efforts. When we're barely holding our own..."

"Don't fret over it. That's for me to think on."

With a pounding of paws, August dashes over to us as a wolf. He straightens up into his regular form, his expression already worried. "What's happened?"

I explain Ralyn's situation in as few words as necessary. My younger half-brother is already kneeling next to him before I've gotten out the second sentence. He grunts disapprovingly at the sight of the re-opened wound.

"See that his innards will stay securely in his belly and that he makes it to his house for some much-needed recuperation," I instruct August when I'm done, and glance at Ralyn. "I'll come check on you tonight."

As I cross the fields to return to the keep, my gaze slides over the cluster of houses our pack-kin call home, instinctively taking a tally of who remains and how fit they might be to join the battle against the Unseelie. My gut twists at how sparse the pickings are.

We have a few good fighters left and a handful of decent ones among those who keep up the sentry duty, but they're barely a large enough force to hope to push back someone like Aerik if he decides to storm our domain. I've already allowed our resources to be stretched so much thinner than I'd like. If I send even more of them to the border, we'll be nearly defenseless.

But without a cure for the curse to get us back in the arch-lords' good graces, bringing about any kind of noticeable triumph on the battlefield is our best chance at re-earning their favor and leaving this fringe backwater behind. I might not have the same sense of ownership that Sylas does when it comes to Hearthshire, but I miss the stronger pulse of the Heart's energies, the greater ease with which any act of magic came when we lived so much closer to its light.

And if we regain Hearthshire, perhaps we can find real peace there, at least for a time. After several decades, this constant holding pattern while living in disgrace starts to wear at the nerves.

I can't offer Sylas that gift yet. I may never be able to offer it if we continue to falter in the conflict with the Unseelie. I'm the brains of his cadre, the schemer—I should be able to deliver this one thing to him.

And now we're several steps farther from achieving that goal. Two pack members lost to dust, others badly injured—I can already picture how the news will pain him.

Before I deliver *that* dire admission, I want to conjure some inspiration that'll give at least a little more cause for optimism to go alongside it. A revised strategy for our presence at the border. Some other approach to proving ourselves to the arch-lords. There could be scraps of information in all my notes and records that I haven't quite connected before.

Inside the keep, I head to my office rather than seeking out Sylas. I'll give myself an hour to unearth that inspiration, and then there'll be nothing for it. If he realizes I've delayed reporting to him, he won't be pleased.

I stride around the corner in the upstairs hall—and find our human interloper poised outside my office door. She's a few feet away but eyeing it with obvious interest, her head cocked and a few waves of that absurdly pink hair drifting across her cheek.

At my arrival, Talia startles, drawing back a step with a guilty expression. A few weeks ago, I might have taken that to mean she'd been up to no good. Now, with everything I've seen of and heard from her… I have to admit the most likely reason for her anxiety is that she *does* still feel like an intruder despite the official welcome into the pack she's gotten, as if she has no right to so much as look at the entrance to a room she hasn't been granted access to.

I did come down on her harshly enough to give her a panic attack the last time I caught her out here, eavesdropping.

The pinch of guilt that comes with the memory dispels any rancor I'd feel now. How can I blame her for being curious? Most of the secrets we fae have kept from her have been to her detriment. If anything, I've got to admire her tenacity.

"Even Sylas couldn't unlock a door simply by staring at it," I say with a playful lilt. "Getting awfully ambitious with those unexpected powers of yours."

The mite blushes, but she squares her shoulders at the same time, no longer half as intimidated by my light-hearted heckling as she used to be. Maybe she shouldn't be, given that we've now discovered her specialness extends to supernatural talents I'd believed only fae could possess. *That* memory, of walking in on Sylas, August, and her in the midst of their little experiment last night, sends a renewed twinge of uneasiness through my chest, but I ignore the sensation.

Sylas has decided she's staying with us, and while that's the case, the more ways she can defend herself, the better off we'll all be. Even if it's yet another inexplicable variable surrounding her that I can't account for in my plans.

"I wasn't trying to break in," she says. "I only stopped for a moment. I just… wondered what you do in there."

She overheard me talking with Ralyn in the office before. I suppose Sylas hasn't spelled out to her what my responsibilities to him and the pack are.

I tip my head toward the other end of the hall. "Our glorious leader has a workspace. Why shouldn't I have one too?"

"August doesn't have a study, or whatever." She pauses. "At least, he's never mentioned it."

I can't help smirking at that. "You could say August's office is that gym downstairs where he's been beating your fighting skills into shape. Preparing to lead the charge should we need to do battle doesn't require much paperwork."

"*You* were talking about some kind of war the other day with… one of the pack members?"

"My area is more logistics than dealing out the blows, although I'll bring out the claws should I need to. Believe me, August would be more than pleased to be out there tackling the Unseelie if Sylas didn't want him here in case the rest of the pack comes under threat."

As I reach for the doorknob, the spell on it keyed to my touch, Talia adjusts her weight on her feet. "Why is *anyone* having to fight the Unseelie? What are they attacking you for… or are the Seelie attacking them?"

"So many questions," I tease, but the truth is that her desire to understand everything she can about this place strikes a chord in me. She's found herself here through no will of her own, been mistreated or outright savaged at nearly every turn, and nevertheless she's determined to learn enough to hold her own. I've met plenty of fae with less drive than that.

I roll the question around in my mind before releasing it. "Do you want to come in?"

Her eyes widen slightly, but with an eager glint that lights up those grass-green irises to something as brilliant as polished jade. It's enough to elevate her from fairly pleasing to dazzling, enough that a different sort of sensation reverberates through me: a twang of desire that settles low in my gut.

For a second, I regret my offer, but it's already out there. I'll have to make the best of it.

I push the door open wide and stalk inside, assuming Talia will follow without further invitation. She eases over the threshold. Her momentary return to timidity subsides as she takes in the desks and the bookshelf, the drawer units built into—or perhaps more

accurately, grown from—the wooden walls, and the map of the
Mists stretched out above them.

Not surprisingly, it's the last of those that draws her first close
inspection. She walks up to it, her hand rising as if to trace the lines
of our world with its erratic borders.

She points to the mark like a sunburst in the center of the uneven
circle. "That's the Heart of the Mists. This is all Summer realm on the
west side? And the Unseelie live on the east… Is it always winter there?"

"Milder or harsher depending on their proximity to the Heart,
but yes. I'm told they like it that way. But given our present
conflict, I may have been misled."

She glances back at me. "They're trying to steal parts of the
Summer realm?"

I nod. "As far as we can tell. They haven't made any actual
demands. They simply began storming domains along the edges of
the border and attempting to claim those lands for themselves. They
took the first couple of domains they tried, but once our arch-lords
caught wind of what was going on, they summoned enough of a
force to push them back. But it's been a constant clash since then,
them vying for more ground and us aiming to hold ours."

"How long has that been going on?"

My gaze drops to my desk, to the stack of leather-bound
notebooks at one side, the sheaves of old reports at the other. I'll
have the exact date of the first incursion written down somewhere,
but it's not something I've spent much time mulling over recently.

"Not quite three decades," I say. "Longer than you've been alive.
There've been lulls now and then, but in the past few years they've
started to press particularly viciously."

"Has anyone tried *asking* them why?"

I give her a baleful look. "I'm sure our arch-lords have reached
out to their Unseelie equivalents to some extent. The content and
outcomes of those attempts wouldn't be shared with a fringe-

banished pack like us. But there've often been tensions between the two realms—it's in our natures to clash—and I wouldn't be surprised if they haven't been inclined to share much. They'd rather simply take what they want than negotiate."

"Even if it means thirty years of fighting?"

"Thirty years is barely a blink for fae, mite."

Talia makes a face at the indirect reference to her human mortality and turns to face me where I'm standing behind my desk, my arms resting on the top of my chair. "And there are people from this pack out there helping fight the Unseelie. I wouldn't have thought Sylas would want to risk *anyone* when he's said the pack is already a lot smaller than it was before… before you ended up here."

"Ah, well, we're hoping that with a little well-placed assistance, we might win over the arch-lords again and reverse that whole 'ending up here' situation. That's where I come in." I motion to the mess on the desk. "I work out how we can best contribute with the warriors we can spare—and how many of them we *can* reasonably spare, given the likelihood of other trouble coming our way. I have other contacts stationed in or making the rounds through various other domains, passing on information to help me judge those odds."

I can't deny that it's a delight seeing comprehension dawn on her face as she puts more of the pieces together. "That's how you found out how Aerik's been talking about Oakmeet—those contacts."

I offer a modest shrug. "Any lord worth his while wants to keep tabs on what his brethren are doing. Even among the Seelie, we squabble plenty over territory and whatever else we take a mind to wanting."

Now that she's been in the room for a short while without that bringing any catastrophe down on us, I feel comfortable enough to sink into my chair. Leaning back in it, I rest my hands on the arm rests and give her an appraising once-over. "Do you think you're ready for Aerik's visit? I know you must have… reservations about seeing him and his cadre again."

I'm being polite with my phrasing. What I really mean is she's undoubtedly terrified—a terror that stiffens her posture and tightens her lips the moment I say his name. Spirited as this woman is proving herself to be, I've seen her spiral into panic at even a reminder of her former captors. Confronting them in the flesh won't be easier on her nerves.

"If seeing them in a couple of days means I won't ever have to be around them or worry about them coming for me again, I'll make it through," she says, managing an air of defiance even though her breathing has gone shallow. She swallows audibly and adds, "I'm getting better at coping. I faced the three of you as wolves in the full moon wildness, didn't I?"

She did. I wouldn't have expected that—couldn't have been more startled to emerge from the brutal haze to find her standing with my half-brothers, the flavor of her blood in my mouth. She deserves full credit for that.

As I continue to size her up, a kernel of a possible scheme sparks in the back of my mind and tickles its way to the fore of my thoughts. The moment I've latched onto it, I know it's perfect, but part of me balks.

I'm going to be asking her to endure so much more anguish than I'd imagine she's been preparing herself for. How does she deserve *that*?

But she wants to be a full member of this pack, and I should at least give her the choice. It'll benefit her in the long run too. This is my job, and right now I can do it well, however the proposal might sound to her.

"What if you had to see them for longer than a quick passing-by?" I ask.

Talia frowns. "Why? Do you think they'd insist—"

"No, not at all. But I'm thinking the best way to remove any suspicion from their minds about a human in our midst is for us to show off that human rather than giving any hint of trying to hide you. You're supposed to be August's recently acquired lover. Him insisting on you joining us for the dinner would support that story."

Her arms come up, stopping just shy of hugging herself. The fear that flashes across her face provokes a sharper pang of guilt. But she draws herself up straighter. "I'd have to sit with them through the whole meal?"

"Yes. At the same table. We can tell them you're shy to give you an excuse not to talk or even look at them much. And you'd be with *us*—we could seat you between Sylas and August. You'd have both of them right beside you through the whole thing."

I'm not going to delude myself that she'd take any comfort from my presence, even if my fangs itch in my gums both at the fact that she wouldn't and the fact that she'd take so much reassurance from my brothers'.

That isn't my part to play. Why should it be? I can keep my paws off what isn't mine.

Talia worries at her lower lip, which tugs my attention to that lovely rose-pink mouth of hers. She appears to gather herself. "All right. I'll practice coping with the panic—I think I'll be ready. I'll just focus on August. And if—if I feel like I won't be able to handle it after all, we'll stick to the original plan?"

"Absolutely." And there definitely isn't an ache closing around my heart with the knowledge of just how much I'm asking this gentle soul to handle.

"Okay. Okay." She drags in a breath and gives me a tense smile. "I'm sorry—I should let you get on with your work. I didn't mean to badger you with questions."

"Badger whenever you like," I say breezily, half-hoping despite myself that she'll take me up on the offer right now. Any conversation with her sounds exceedingly more enjoyable than the one I need to have with Sylas.

But the mite slips away, leaving me alone in the office with all the scribblings and reports that, if I'm honest with myself, I already know won't give me any brilliant solutions to offer to my lord. I sit there staring at the piles on my desk for a few minutes longer, and then I heave myself out of my chair with a sigh to go in search of him. No point in putting off the inevitable any longer.

CHAPTER EIGHT

Talia

The basement gym feels larger in the darkness, as if the walls might have fallen back with the thickening of the shadows. I crouch on the moss mat, its surface spongy beneath my feet, and fix my gaze on my hand, which is little more than a silhouette even though it's only inches from my face.

"*Sole-un-straw*," I murmur at my fingers, attempting to propel some kind of power into my voice. "*Sole-un-straw*."

Behind me, August shifts his weight with a rustle of his clothes. "A little more emphasis on the last syllable."

I try again. "*Sole-un-STRAW!*"

Nothing sparks. From August's tone when he speaks next, he's swallowing amusement. "Not *quite* that emphatic."

I grimace in his general direction and exhale raggedly. It took me years to get bronze right. Maybe there isn't any point in attempting to master more true names. By the time I get this one, all our battles might be over with—in victory or in failure.

But I said I'd learn—I *want* to learn—so I have to give it a proper shot. Anything that'll make me feel a little more powerful before I have to face Aerik and his cadre again is a good thing.

At least this time I have a teacher instead of going it alone.

"*Sole-un-straw*," I say, with just a little extra force at the end. The air around my hand stays dark.

August steps closer and grazes his fingers over my hair. "That sounded pretty much perfect to me. You'll get there. Have you tried using your emotions like you needed to before?"

I think back to Aerik's fortress, to the cage, but the distress that quivers through me doesn't quite fit my intentions. I'm attempting to produce light, and that terrible room was always already lit up when he and his cadre visited me. If anything, I'd have wished for more darkness during those times to escape their disdainful gazes.

How can I magic up some light if I'm picturing a place that's already bright?

My grimace softening into a frown, I give it a go anyway. If I could have summoned a full-out blaze, cast it right into Aerik's or Cole's face…

The idea stirs a little satisfaction, but no light sparks with my next few recitations. Sighing, I sit back on my ass, resting my hands on the mat. "Didn't you say this is one of the easy spells?"

With a gesture from August I feel more than see, the globes that normally illuminate the room flicker on. "It's one of the first most fae children learn," he says. "But it still usually takes them weeks or even months to master."

"When they're kids."

"When they're *fae* and it comes naturally to them. Don't forget it's practically a miracle that you can work any magic at all." He hunkers down next to me, cupping his hand over mine. "You're not going to get there in a couple of days—none of us would expect you to."

But the longer it takes before I can pick this up, the more time we'll all sit with the uncertainty of whether I'm just a one-hit-wonder. I press my fingertips into the mat as if I can dig the power I need out of the thick layer of moss.

"We should take a break from that now," August says. "Getting frustrated only makes it harder to connect to your goal. What do you say to burning off some of that frustration with a little more physical training?"

I raise my eyebrows at him. "That's what you'd rather be doing anyway, isn't it?"

His grin is sheepish. "Hey, I've never denied that hand-to-hand combat is my area of expertise. If you think you'd do better practicing the magic side with Sylas or Whitt—"

"No," I say quickly. "You're good at teaching that too." The tattoos etched across his arms and neck—and more beneath his clothes—prove that he's mastered plenty of magic even if it isn't his go-to solution. The last thing I want is to put another responsibility on Sylas's shoulders, and Whitt...

Would that unpredictable man even agree to teach me? Maybe if Sylas ordered him to, but having a reluctant teacher, especially one known for snarky remarks, doesn't sound like much fun.

I push myself to my feet and stretch out my arms and shoulders in preparation for the sparring. My gaze travels to the far wall, picturing the landscape outside, the houses of the village. "When do you think I'll be able to start joining the rest of the pack while you're training them? It'd save you time not having to give me separate lessons for the actual fighting techniques."

"Time spent with you is never a waste, Sweetness," August says, his grin turning cheekier. He tugs on a lock of my hair, his golden eyes so brightly eager that a giddy flutter passes through my chest. "Unless you're getting sick of having so much of my attention."

"No, not at all." The words spill out so quickly that a blush flares in my cheeks, but the way August beams at my enthusiasm takes the edge off my embarrassment. "But if I'm going to be a real part of the pack—if they're going to get used to me and accept me even though I'm human… I thought it might be good for them to see I'm working at this stuff too."

"They will see," August promises. "I just—I want to be sure *they're* ready to train with you. None of them have any recent experience working around humans… They have to know what they're doing well enough to adjust to your differences."

"My weaknesses, you mean." I say it matter-of-factly—I know the fae are naturally stronger. I don't really want any of them coming at me as if I'm one of their own either. Although I guess that's the end goal: fending off the supernatural beings despite my frailer human body.

August winces. "It might turn out you have an advantage or two. I want to be careful about it; that's all."

"I do appreciate that," I say honestly. But I'd still feel better knowing I stand some kind of a chance if Aerik turns on us during his visit. Of course, I can do plenty of work toward that goal with just August.

I roll my neck and raise my hands the way he's shown me, poised to block a strike or deliver one depending on my opponent's moves. "What should we start with?"

August cocks his head, considering. "We've gone over a lot of the strategies for when you have room to punch or kick. Why don't we cover grappling today?"

"Grappling?"

His grin returns. Before I have a chance to react, he's sprung at me. In one swift movement, he knocks me off my feet and tackles me to the floor, his arms braced against me to make sure I don't hit the mat too hard. He's so gentle about it that only the faintest flicker of panic darts through me, extinguished with one glance into his fond eyes.

"When you end up tussling wolf-style on the ground," he says, close enough that his warm breath tickles my face. "You don't have to worry about balance, so your injured foot won't hold you back, but you've got much less room to maneuver. How do you think you could get me to back off, at least long enough so you'd have a chance to get free?"

An actual attacker wouldn't be this polite about the whole thing, body held a respectful distance above my own. I know that from prior experience. Thinking about more likely scenarios if I were knocked to the ground…

"Claw at your eyes?" I suggested. That was a technique we'd already gone over for being grabbed while upright, but my assailant's face might be even easier to reach in a situation like this. "And a knee to the, er, groin if I can manage that."

August laughs. "Right for the tender spots. Good. Another option that's surprisingly effective: if someone goes for *your* face, grab their fingers and twist as hard as you can. Those joints are easy to dislocate, and put your attacker in a lot of pain while making it harder to grab you. A fist to the nose can be awfully distracting too if you can't quite get at their eyes. Try all that out to get a feel for the motions."

I rake my curled fingers in the vicinity of his eyes, aim my knuckles at his nose, and raise my knee—*very* careful to not actually land that particular blow. When August makes a mock swipe at my hair, I catch his index finger and give it a light jerk to the side, evaluating how much more strength I'd have to put into the move to really break something.

Having him looming over me while I'm lying here like this brings an uncomfortable possibility to mind. "What if my attacker pounces on me as a wolf?"

August pauses, a trace of his own discomfort with the idea showing in his expression. "It's not likely anyone who simply wanted to capture or subdue you would use that tactic against a human who can't match them. We can control ourselves in wolf form, of course, but it's harder to moderate a bite or a slash of claws than it is to pull a punch, and a wolf can't pick you up and cart you off… If a fae comes at you like that, they're probably aiming to kill you."

My throat tightens. "Good to know. How do I make sure they *don't*?"

"The eyes and the nose will still be vulnerable areas. And the throat, if you can get in a solid strike." He eases back on his knees, rubbing his jaw. "We'll get you a small dagger to carry with you too —I'll teach you the best spots to hit with that."

I can read what he's not saying from his hesitation. No matter what he teaches me, he doesn't believe I'd survive an attack if a fae came at me in full wolf mode, not unless I got extraordinarily lucky. But then, is that really so surprising? I'm not sure there's any way I could fend off a regular wolf that was determined to savage me, let alone a fae one capable of complex strategy.

"Okay," I say, suppressing a shiver. No need to dwell on that right now. "Let's focus on the human-shaped attacker tactics for now."

His stance relaxes. "Get ready then."

August gives me a few seconds and then lunges at me. He deflects my first jab at his face with a smack of his hand against my forearm, but I manage to bump a fist just below his nose. He pulls back with a nod. "That's a good start. See if you can manage to land that first strike."

We run through that scenario several more times until I'm anticipating his movements well enough to have a decent shot at his eyes. Then we try more intensive setups where I have to start defending myself while he's tackling me.

By the twentieth or so run-through, sweat has broken over my skin and my breath is coming short. After I've lashed out with my hands and knees in the ways we've been practicing, I sink into the mat with a huff of exhalation.

August chuckles. "You're doing great. Go ahead and take a breather."

He leans in to nuzzle my cheek. The affectionate gesture wakes up a whole lot more of my body. The exhilaration of the exercise deepens into a headier sort of thrill, desire tingling low in my belly. Down by where I'm abruptly twice as aware of his leg poised between mine, of his arm braced next to my chest, his wrist brushing the side of my breast.

August inhales with a rough sound, and I can tell before he speaks that he's picked up on my reaction. "Talia," he murmurs, and then, as if drawn by a magnet, lowers his head to press his lips to the side of my neck.

My breath catches, a sharper wave of heat rushing through me. Longing twists through my torso from my sternum down to that now-blazing spot between my legs. August's tongue darts out to lick the sheen of sweat along the crook of my jaw, and an eager whimper tumbles from my mouth.

There's so much I've wanted to do with this man, to discover about how his body can feel against mine, from even before I totally understood what I was longing for. I have a better idea now. The clear indications that he's longing for it just as much only electrify me more.

My hands rise of their own accord to grip his close-cropped hair. August lets out a pleased rumble. He teases his kisses along my jaw with nips that send shivers of giddiness over my skin. My hips lift toward him instinctively, the most sensitive part of me grazing his thigh, and I can't restrain a gasp at the flare of pleasure.

With a groan, August's mouth crashes into mine. I melt into him, lost in his musky scent, floating on the swell of passion that feels as though it might carry me all the way to the bright sky above the keep. Our breath mingles, hot and shaky with need, and all I want in that moment is to give myself over completely, to finally satisfy the ache for bodily connection that's never quite been answered by him or Sylas.

There isn't anything to stop us here and now, is there? No

responsibilities August needs to attend to, no breakfast at risk of burning or likely interruptions, no worries that he's somehow betraying his lord by following his desire.

A trace of nervousness flickers through my chest. What if it hurts? What if I can't please him in the same way as the women he's been with before, women who must have known what they were doing at least a little better than I do?

Then August shifts his weight on his arms so he can stroke one hand over my breast, and the fresh wave of heated giddiness, the possessive growl that works from his throat as he kisses me even more deeply, wash my worries away. This man who isn't exactly a man won't let any harm come to me, not while he's in charge, and he's showing nothing but delight in what I have to offer.

August tugs up my shirt so he can caress me skin to skin, his fingertips circling the tip of my breast. They flick over my nipple and massage it to a stiffer peak until I'm whimpering for release.

My body squirms beneath his, not entirely sure how to move. For a moment, he pauses his teasing exploration of my chest to run that hand down the side of my body to my hips, urging my core more solidly against his thigh. My sex pushes against his leg, setting off a flood of bliss. My fingers trail down his back to cling on to the flexing muscles there.

When August pulls away from my mouth, I almost cry out in protest, but the next second his lips have closed around my pebbled nipple. A very different cry escapes me. My back arches up, and he sucks harder with a lap of his tongue that leaves me quivering like a stretched bowstring. I want, I want, I *want*—so much it's almost frightening.

My hand slides up under his shirt, tracing the scorching planes of his back. August drops his head lower, slicking his tongue down the center of my chest toward my stomach—and stops just above my belly button. His whole body stills where he's poised over me.

His voice comes out strained. "We can't—we can't do this."

He may as well have dumped a bucket of icy water over me. My back stiffens against the mat.

"Why?" I ask, the question coming out in the timid whisper I thought I was done with among these men. Is there something wrong with me—did he realize he doesn't actually want to be that intimate with someone so—?

Before the worries can even finish forming in my whirling mind, August looks up to meet my gaze, his expression fraught but the warmth unmistakeable in his golden eyes. "It isn't anything you've done, Talia. By the Heart, I want to take you in every way. But I can tell—there's a difference in scent—you're fertile right now. Children don't come easily even between a faded fae and a human, but there's still a chance. I don't want to risk it."

The chill recedes, and I relax enough to tug at him so he eases back up alongside my body. The thought of getting pregnant—with *August's* child—sends a weird, wobbly sensation through my stomach. There's a tiny thrill to it, but mostly the awareness of how unprepared I feel for even the idea of motherhood.

"So fae don't have some magical kind of birth control?" A ridiculous image of a glowing condom pops into my head—not that I've ever seen a regular one used other than on a banana in health class.

"No. It's so difficult for us to conceive at all that attempting to prevent that while enjoying the act is considered basically sacrilegious. In defiance of the Heart."

Okay, then. I reconsider his refusal along with the fact that he didn't ask me for my thoughts on kids and can't help asking, "Do you not want children at all?"

August brushes a kiss to my temple with a tenderness that rouses my desire all over again. "Someday, I'm sure. But not—it would bind you completely to this place. To me and the rest of the pack. We've just given you back a small bit of choice over your fate; I'm not going to steal that away."

An emotion that's much more than longing rises up so swiftly that it takes my breath away. It winds around my heart until my whole chest aches with it.

I care about this man so much. Admire him so much. I might be bound to him already in ways that he can't control. I think—I think this must be what love feels like.

My pulse hiccups with the thought. Would I be willing to leave August now even if staying here put my whole life in danger? Even if what I'd face by his side would be so much more torment than otherwise? I'm really not sure. A significant portion of me already balks at the idea of being apart from him even for a day.

I don't know what to do with all that feeling. Saying it aloud, making it that much more real, unnerves me even more. So I swallow the ache down and trail my fingers over his dark auburn hair. *He* still looks unsettled, even though I haven't argued with his decision.

"Some humans end up wanting to stay, to have kids and—" I hesitate, realizing I don't actually know whether fae ever take humans officially as mates. August's mother obviously had a relationship with his father, but that father is also Sylas's and Whitt's, by two other women. Only Sylas was the child of his soul-twined mate.

"It's generally not quite a choice." August sinks down on his back beside me, our shoulders touching. "If they want to, it's because the glamours have convinced them to—or the fae who keep them never bother to check whether they do or not. That's not the fate I'd want for you."

That was why he hesitated to get involved with me at all. He told me weeks ago that he'd seen how badly things often turn out for humans who became lovers of the fae. The fervour in his voice stirs a suspicion I can't shake—the best reason I can think of that would explain how vehemently he's defended me from the moment I came into this keep.

"Is that how it was for your mother?"

He's silent for long enough that I start to worry I've overstepped somehow, pried more than I should. "I'm sorry," I say. "I—"

August takes my hand and tucks it close to his cheek. "No, don't apologize. It's a good question. I'm just deciding the best way to answer. It's not something I've ever really talked about. Even Sylas doesn't know all the details."

The ache around my heart sharpens at the anguish already bleeding into his voice. "You don't have to talk to me about it either."

"Maybe I should, though, so you can understand. I just—I'm so ashamed I didn't stop it…"

He closes his eyes and then opens them again, gazing up at the ceiling. "When I was not quite old enough to be considered out of childhood, my mother made some comment or minor mistake with her chores—no one ever bothered to tell me what it was, it mattered so little. But my father was in a particularly dark mood, and he decided he'd had enough of her hanging around the palace. I was with her when he stormed in with three of his warriors. He ordered me to sit and watch while they—while they transformed into wolves and tore her to pieces."

My stomach lurches. August's hand has clenched tight around mine, and I squeeze it back with all the sympathy I have in me. "That's horrible. Why would he be so cruel—and not just to her but you too?"

August shrugs, his shoulders as rigid as his jaw. "He didn't go out of his way to torment the human staff, but he didn't see their lives as meaning much more than a mouse's either. He never had any real affection for her. She was a convenient vessel to satisfy his carnal urges with when he no longer had his mate, and then she was a convenient vessel for him to act out violent urges as well.

"As for me—he thought it would help harden me up. That I needed to understand how expendable every life, but particularly mortal lives, could be. He believed that the best way to rule was to have all your subjects aware that at any moment, if they made the slightest misstep, you wouldn't hesitate to dispatch them."

I shudder. "That's awful."

"And I just sat there…"

"If you were just a kid, against the four of them—you *couldn't* have stopped it."

"I don't know. I did jump up when they first attacked her, and my father enchanted the chair to hold me in place. But maybe if I'd tried harder, I could have broken that spell, I could have done *something*…" His voice has gone so ragged it's painful to hear. "I was frightened of him, of going against him, of what he'd do to *me* if I provoked too much of his anger."

I let go of his hand to wrap my arm right across his chest, nestling my head against his shoulder. "That sounds totally understandable to me. *He* was the one who gave the orders—you can't blame anyone but him."

August lets out a breath that's equally ragged. "He treated me well more often than not, you know. Even though I wasn't his true-blooded son. He paid for good tutors and had me sit with him at official meals like a real part of the family—in his good moods sometimes he'd come around and invite me on a hunt or coach me in my training himself. It'd be easier to look back and simply hate him if he'd been equally horrible all the time. Sometimes I think I have so much trouble restraining my anger because I used up all my self-control not aiming it at him the whole time I lived under his rule."

"*I've* only seen your anger come out when it was deserved." I push myself up on my elbow so I can look him in the eyes. The love I thought I felt a few minutes ago has somehow grown even larger with his confession. "And I know you'd never treat me *anything* like he treated your mother. I'm not the tiniest bit afraid that you'd ever hurt me. So you shouldn't be afraid of that either. Okay?"

August stares at me for a long moment, anguish still plain on his face but retreating behind a light that looks more like hope. All at once, he lets out a strangled sound and rolls toward me, hugging me to him as his lips seek out mine.

Somehow these kisses are more tender but also more urgent than the ones before, as if he'll die if he can't show me just how much he cherishes me. The flames of passion that had dwindled during our talk blaze up. I kiss him back as hard as I can, over and over, until every part of my body is clanging with need.

"August," I murmur against his cheek in a brief space for breath. "I—I don't want to be getting pregnant right now anyway—but there are other things we could do that would feel almost as good without taking that chance, aren't there? Together?" Not just me finding my pleasure alone, as he and Sylas have guided me through before. I want to do this *with* him.

"Yes," he mutters around a shaky exhalation. "By the Heart, yes."

He eases his hand down my body and cups it between my legs, where he taught me to touch myself to such blissful effect. Feeling his fingers there now, rocking against me, lights me up twice as bright. A moan slips from my lips.

It's not enough, though. This can't be all about me. I reach for the bulge pressed against my hip through his pants, reveling at the shockingly hard length of it as my hand curls around it.

August groans and kisses me fiercely. As our mouths collide again and again, I buck with the motion of his fingers and stroke him as skillfully as I can manage. When I'm starting to tremble, August tugs my workout pants down and tucks his fingers right inside my panties. They skim over the slickness of my arousal in a caress that has us both groaning.

"You feel so good," August says, his voice low but so heated I practically catch fire. "Both touching you and the way you touch me. You're perfect, Talia."

The words send a giddy quiver through my chest. I pull myself tighter against him, hooking one of my legs over his instinctively.

As our bodies lock together, August plunges a finger right inside me. Oh, God. I hadn't thought anything could feel better than when I got myself off this way, but knowing it's him, that he's filling me the way he wishes he could with the erection I'm still fondling, sends me spiraling up on a wave of sensation like nothing I've ever experienced.

My hips sway to meet his careful thrusts, matching him and urging him on until he adds another finger, faster. His breath spills hot and shaky against my lips. His thumb swivels over the sensitive nub just above my opening.

It's so much, so good. Before I can catch myself, try to bring him all the way with me, I've already careened over the edge, my vision whiting out with the surge of bliss. My hand clamps around his hardness, and August presses into my touch as he nuzzles me in my return to earth.

My limbs sag, wanting to slump boneless into the mat, but the ecstasy he just brought me to only makes me more determined to offer the same to him. I fumble with the waist of his pants and work my hand beneath the fabric until I encounter the surprisingly soft skin that encompasses his rigid length.

"Talia," August whispers as I close my fingers around him. I'm afraid he'll try to tell me I don't need to, even stop me, but after a moment's pause he tugs me to him instead. His mouth scorches mine with kiss after fervid kiss as his hips drive into my grasp. Moisture beads on the tip of his erection and slides with my fingers down his length.

I don't know what I'm doing, not really, but my unpracticed attempt has him twitching against my palm, grunting when I stroke him firmly from base to the thickness of the head. There's no mistaking how genuine his responses are. With the simple grip of my hand, I'm conjuring the deepest of pleasure in this powerful man.

The man I love.

Maybe I'm not ready to say those words out loud, but I can show how much I adore him with connection between our bodies. Following his reactions, I clutch him harder, jerk my hand faster. His chest heaves, his muscles clench, and then he's shuddering against me with a spurt of wet heat over my wrist.

"Oh, my Sweetness," he says, gathering me in his arms. He hugs me so close I feel I could meld right into him.

Joy blooms through the ache of love around my heart, shining and fluttery. It comes with a tingle that sends a sudden jolt of certainty through me.

I draw back just enough to speak clearly and lift my hand between our chests. "*Sole-un-straw.*"

The tingle dances over my tongue, and a spark shimmers between my fingers. Only a faint one, and only for a second before it snuffs out, but clear enough that August goes still, watching. Then he beams at me, his expression so full of pride and adoration that any fear inside over the depth of my feelings for him is swept away.

CHAPTER NINE

Talia

I t's strange seeing people other than August working in the kitchen. A few of the pack members have taken over the space, bustling to and fro with their final preparations for tonight's dinner, because it wouldn't do for someone from Sylas's cadre to be cooking for or serving the guests. Even with my stomach twisted into a tight little ball at the thought of those guests, the savory scents of roasted boar and seared root vegetables make my mouth water.

August comes up behind me, tucking his hand around my waist and pressing a kiss to the top of my head. He peers past me into the room, his muscles flexing as if he's holding himself back from striding in there and taking over. His scent, like fresh-baked cookies with a musky undertone, is delectable in itself.

I let myself lean into his chest, taking comfort in that smell and his arm wrapped around me. Since getting so intimate in the gym the other day, I've found it even easier to relax around him, knowing how much of my affection he returns, how much he treasures the connection between us. If anyone can get me through this confrontation, it's him.

August hugs me tighter as if to shield me from what he's about to say. "We've gotten word from a sentry that Aerik's people should be here in the next ten minutes." He glances down at me, a worry line forming on his brow. "Are you sure you want to go through with this? We can still—"

I set my hand over his. "I'm sure. It's better to do it now when I'm ready for it than some surprise attack if they decide that's justified."

I will get through this dinner without falling apart. I just *will*.

Turning in August's embrace, I tip my head back and hold out my arms. "Am I ready for my role?"

He eases back to look me over with unusually pensive consideration. He and Sylas worked together to weave the subtle glamours that should make my eyes appear more brown than green and that adjust the planes of my nose and cheeks, as well as the one disguising the misshapen ridge of bone on the top of my right foot.

They adjusted the notes of my natural scent as well, although how much Aerik will remember of that after leaving me in filth most of the time I'm not sure. As long as I'm not openly bleeding, he won't be able to smell the aspect of me that mattered most to him.

Whitt confirmed that he couldn't sense the magic clinging to me unless he came within a few inches of those spots, which Sylas has no intention of letting Aerik or his men do. They'd be insulting their hosts if they nosed in on a woman August has claimed like that. By all expectations, I should be safe from discovery.

I'm dressed much more for the part of a lover tonight. This afternoon, August brought me a calf-length dress of the same thin, flowy material most of the pack members wear, narrow enough in the neckline and with enough of a sleeve to completely cover the scars on my shoulder. It's a sky blue that looks striking with my deep pink hair, and the fabric must be made out of some substance we don't have in the human world, because I've never felt anything so soft and airy. I spent the first several minutes after I put it on swiveling this way and that just to feel it lick across my calves.

I wish the men of the keep were the only ones who'd get to appreciate it on me, the way I can tell August is from the heat that's tinted his golden eyes. I feel more like a lady in it compared to my usual jeans and T-shirts, but also more exposed, even though technically the dress covers nearly as much skin. My legs are bare beneath it all the way to my feet, where I'm not even wearing my brace. It was easier to shape the illusion closely over just the limb rather than adding the wooden frame to the mix. We're planning on avoiding having me do any real walking in front of our guests.

"You're spectacular," August says, his eyes glowing as they meet mine again. "Any man, fae or otherwise, would be honored to have you at his side. And the glamours appear to be holding steady."

His flattery sends a flush from my collarbone up my neck. August strokes a finger along that path as if charting it, and the heat of it deepens. He's dressed more formally too—in a finely woven V-neck tunic like those Sylas often wears and fitted slacks that show off the muscles beneath. The outfit definitely suits him.

I grope for my words. "Good. Then everything's in place. Except me. I'm supposed to wait in the dining room, right?"

August nods and walks with me down the hall. "I'll have to be with Sylas and Whitt greeting the visitors as they come in, but we'll be back here quickly. I'll make sure I come into the room before they do, so you'll have me with you the whole time. If you start to get overwhelmed, just give my hand a few quick squeezes in a row, and I'll find a way to get you out of there."

"Right." I inhale and exhale, willing myself to become as steady as the magic disguising me.

The dining room is decked out more elegantly than I'm used to. A sapphire-blue cloth drapes the table, embroidered with silver thread that shimmers as if it's made of stardust. The usual amber globes that dangle from branch-like fixtures on the ceiling are tinted a matching moonlight shade. Silver plates, goblets, and utensils with intricate floral patterning already sit at each seat we expect to be filled.

Behind me, August chuckles at my awed hesitation. "It was even fancier for Tristan's visit. After what Sylas pulled out for an arch-lord's cousin, I have trouble imagining how we'd top it for an actual arch-lord. Aerik doesn't command half as much respect."

I slip into the room, walking slowly to offset my limp. "But you all still want to impress him."

"Not so much impress as show him the respect *he* believes he's due so he can believe we have no bones to pick with him." August's smile turns grim. "He can keep believing that until we have a chance to cut the bunch of them down like the curs they've proven themselves to be."

Whitt sweeps by, tapping August's shoulder as he does. "They're arriving. Time to look sharp, Auggie." He spares me a quick glance and a lip-twitch of acknowledgment.

"We'll get through this," August tells me, and steps away.

I haven't even heard the sound of the front door, but my pulse stutters. As I circle the table, my heart keeps on beating at a nervous tempo.

The plan is that I'll wait here standing by the corner of the table, next to my chair. Aerik and his cadre will get to see me standing solidly and then taking my seat without my having to do much actual walking before their eyes.

Of course, that depends on me keeping my head through my growing panic. I thought I was prepared for this moment, but now that it's actually happening, my skin has turned clammy and the knot of my stomach is churning with queasiness.

Voices carry from the other end of the keep. The front door

thuds shut. My spine goes rigid, and I have to take several breaths to relax it.

Why did I agree to do this? Why did I let myself believe I could handle seeing my former tormenters again? What if they take one look at me and see right through the magical disguise?

I close my eyes, willing down my bubbling panic. Sylas wouldn't have agreed to this plan if he wasn't sure he could keep me safe. As long as I don't collapse in a trembling mess at the sight of them, it'll all go smoothly.

If only that didn't feel like such a tall order right now.

The voices travel down the hall, getting louder with their approach. I try to concentrate on Sylas's measured baritone and Whitt's jaunty interjections, but I can't tune out the flat rasp that belongs to the man I now know as Aerik, the one who watched his cadre torment me with constant disdain, or the sharply nasal tenor of the equally sharp-limbed one with the blue-white hair.

Cole. Just the thought of his name turns my stomach all over again.

A bead of sweat trickles down the back of my neck. My fingers curl around the edge of the table until I force them to release it. August promised he'd come in before them. I'll see August—I can focus on him and pretend the others aren't even here.

Yeah, right.

It's actually Sylas who strides into the dining room first, looking downright regal in his embroidered vest over a stiff-collared dress shirt. He stops just inside the doorway to conduct the others in, the confidence in his bearing reinforcing my own. Then August hustles past him. He flashes me a smile and comes around to stand beside me just as the visitors enter.

I can't stop my gaze from jerking straight to Aerik's face, topped with that daffodil yellow hair. A hint of a sneer is already playing with his lips, and it hardens at the sight of me.

My heart thumps even faster, a wave of dizziness surging

through me from gut to forehead. Everything blanks from my mind but the memory of him looming over me while I crouched, aching and grimy, in his horrible cage—

Strong fingers close around my hand where it's fisted beneath the level of the table, holding me tight. August's arm rests against mine from wrist to shoulder. My thoughts tilt and scramble, and I grip his hand just as tightly, yanking my awareness back to the present. Back to the men who've sworn to defend me, who I know would enjoy nothing more than to rip the throats from the villains they've admitted into their home if they could get away with that retribution now.

Sylas's voice reaches my ears as if from much farther away than the other side of the room. "This is Talia, a recent... acquisition of August's. He's rather attached to her at the moment. I assure you she won't disturb our conversation."

My former captors never asked my name or used it, so as far as we know they can't connect it to the girl they stole. I stare at August's muscular chest in its fine shirt for long enough to get a grip on my nerves and then dare another glance toward our enemies.

All three of them have entered now. Cole and the portly fae man who always did the cutting and collecting when they took my blood flank their lord. I manage to keep all of my attention on Aerik, to avoid the even more vicious jolts of terror I suspect the others' faces would provoke. His nose has wrinkled, his sneer still in place, as if I'm a dog turd someone has left on the dining table.

For all his apparent disgust, I catch no sign of recognition in his expression. With a shiver of relief, I force my mouth into the briefest of smiles and then look to August again.

My lover slings his arm around my shoulders just for a second, with a broad grin I know is as forced as my smile was. "She's a shy thing. Wouldn't speak to anyone but me for the first week. I don't like to leave her alone for very long."

Aerik lets out a huff as if this kind of deviance is only to be expected from a cadre like Sylas's and moves at the other lord's gesture to his spot across from August. "I'm sure we'll find her of no significance."

From the corner of my eye, I think I see Cole's piercing gaze trained on me. Thankfully, Sylas directs him around the table to sit beside August, where he can't study me very easily. He still gets in a snarky remark: "Doing her hair up like that won't make her any closer to fae."

August gives a laugh that only sounds a little stiff, still gripping my hand. "Oh, I wasn't the one who chose this color. She had her own ideas of fashion well before I found her."

The fae avoid lying as much as they can—Sylas explained to me that it damages their connection to the Heart of the Mists, which gives them their magical power—but August is purposefully making it sound as if I'd already dyed my hair when he met me without saying anything untrue. If Aerik believes August really did grab me from the human world just a little while ago, he'll be even less inclined to connect me to his missing blood dispenser.

August tugs me gently to sit down as he does, and it's only as I sink into my chair that I recognize how wobbly my legs are, how rigidly I've been tensing the muscles in my calves to keep myself from visibly swaying. The second my ass hits the wooden seat, those muscles turn to jelly. I stare down at my blurred reflection in the silver plate, wondering how I'm going to manage to swallow any of the lovely food the pack has prepared.

Even as I think that, the kitchen helpers glide into the room carrying platters with the first course of appetizers. Aerik views them with only slightly less disdain than he showed me, and some small part of me that isn't frozen with fear bristles on behalf of Sylas's—of *my*—pack-kin.

"I haven't scented any other humans around," he says to Sylas. "I heard you preferred to keep your domain clear of them."

"Not due to any aversion," Sylas says. "My other cadre-chosen, Kellan, has a particular animosity toward them that it's been best for all of us not to provoke."

"But you're changing your tune for the young one? Where *is* Kellan?"

Another treacherous subject the men of the keep will need to tread lightly around. Sylas can't easily explain why he had to end Kellan's life. I stare at the fried dumpling and fresh-picked salad that August sets to my plate rather than risk watching the conversation play out. My heart is pounding so loudly it's a wonder it isn't deafening me.

Sylas spears a few sprigs of greens with casual ease. "He departed a few weeks ago by my decision. He had many concerns about how we've been handling our affairs and wanted to investigate other options. I don't expect to see him back any time soon, and on such a return, if the girl is still with us, at least she'll have had a chance to settle in."

If we count his death as a metaphorical departure, it's all true. Kellan did have concerns; if he did somehow return, I'm quite settled in now. The smoothness with which the fae lord disarms his enemy's curiosity soothes my nerves enough that I bring the dumpling to my mouth. If I don't eat at all, they'll wonder why.

The other lord appears to buy the story, but he isn't done prodding. "She's still the only human you're keeping here, then?"

At least he doesn't seem to think *I'm* the specific human he's searching for.

Sylas nods. "For the time being. I promised August a trial run after he made his case. If that goes well, we could consider bringing over a few servants to help with the running of the keep."

Cutter grunts. "It does seem as though your pack is stretched thin enough, sparse as it's become."

Sylas doesn't let the mild jab affect his poise—or even acknowledge the words. He keeps his gaze on Aerik. "Are you looking for more humans to add to your own staff?" he asks in a slightly wry tone that implies he finds it odd that the other lord is so fixated on his dealings with mortals.

Aerik's shrug doesn't look remotely casual. "I have no issue with quantity of manpower," he says, which feels to me like another subtle sneer at Oakmeet's pack. But then, to my immense relief, he drops the subject of humankind completely, as if he's already convinced he was barking up the wrong tree by suspecting Sylas.

"The Unseelie bastards have stooped to new lows, haven't they?" he says in a tone that suggests the outcome of those battles affect him very little anyway, and the men all fall into a discussion of the ongoing conflict.

I want to pay attention to the threads of that discussion, to better understand the tensions Whitt sketched out for me, but it's hard to keep my thoughts in order. Every minute or two, one of my former captives snaps out a comment, makes some gesture, or rasps out a laugh that yanks me back weeks ago to the bone-white room where they set up my cage. The spurts of panic hit without warning, blanking my mind and clamping around my lungs, over and over.

So I look at my plate or at August, still gripping his fingers without any complaint from him even though he wouldn't normally eat left-handed, and pick at my dinner bit by bit. By the time the kitchen staff takes away our plates in preparation for dessert, not even the honeyed notes drifting through the air can soothe my frayed spirits. I'm so exhausted I'd lay my head down on the table if these guests weren't here.

August brushes a reassuring caress over my knuckles. All I had to do to claim victory was survive this meal, and I've just about managed that. To achieve anything else was probably asking too much of my shaken nerves, stripped raw all over again in the presence of these monstrous men.

Aerik leans his elbows onto the table and considers Sylas with a more penetrating expression than before. "I've appreciated the food and the talk, but let's not beat around the bush any longer. You must have had some particular reason for inviting me to enjoy your pack's hospitality."

My pulse hiccups, but Sylas offers a reserved smile, as if he expected that question. Well, he probably did.

"Tensions have been high throughout the summer lands in recent weeks," he says. "I'd rather mend bridges than burn them down. It was important to me to show you that we hold no animosity over past… oversights."

Snubbing them when distributing the tonic, he means, as Aerik can obviously tell from the distasteful curling of his lips. "We had to make our choices as we saw fit," he says, as if they couldn't have stolen a tiny bit more of my blood each full moon to produce a slightly larger batch of tonic. "And I did have to consider how any favoritism toward your domain might look to the arch-lords, after they consigned you to this distant spot."

Whitt leans back in his chair. "After all these years, I'd imagine the arch-lords have seen they have no reason for concern when it comes to our loyalties."

Cole lets out a harsh guffaw that raises the hairs on the back of my neck. "Arch-Lord Ambrose and Lord Tristan don't exactly speak highly of the bunch of you still."

Aerik's gaze flicks to Whitt for only a moment before returning to Sylas. "When you make a misstep that grave, it's a wonder anyone bothers to remember you're here at all, unless they happened to take a mind to wipe the realm of your pack completely."

He speaks with an odd lightness, as if he means the cruel words as some kind of joke, but I can taste the acid underneath. His disparaging tone takes me from cringing to bristling on Sylas's behalf.

"If the arch-lords felt our crimes were severe enough to warrant that level of sanction, I'm sure they would have carried it out in the beginning," Sylas says evenly, with just a hint of a growl as the softest of warnings.

"No doubt it's convenient to view circumstances as you do when one is out to scrape up whatever favor they can from crumbs dropped for them," Whitt adds.

Aerik glowers at him for longer than his previous glance before cutting his gaze to Sylas once more. "I trust no one in your pack resents our making use of what resources we had at our disposal to raise our standing. It would have been ridiculous not to share that boon and reap the benefits."

The boon of my blood. "Reap the benefits," he says—how much prestige did these monsters gain from *using* me, tormenting me, while Sylas's pack languishes so far from their real home? And this jerk thinks that's something to be proud of, something he *earned*, when it was nothing more than a bit of horrible luck that he stumbled on me?

Real anger stirs somewhere in between the tightness in my chest and the knot of my stomach. The thought that any part of me helped these awful fae win glory makes me want to vomit—and to punch that smug expression right off Aerik's face.

He's nowhere near the leader Sylas is. If anyone should have been banished, it's him and his people. But no, here they are expecting some kind of red carpet to be rolled out for them while they mock my pack's hardships.

My free hand balls into a fist where it's resting by my thigh. I bite my tongue. There's nothing I could say even if I dared to open my mouth that wouldn't make things worse for the men I care about.

"Certainly I wouldn't have expected anything different of you," Sylas says to Aerik in an inscrutable voice, and then the kitchen workers arrive with glistening pastries topped with dollops of peach-colored cream, and the men all have something other than talking to do with their mouths for a little while.

As I pick at the dessert, my anger simmers inside me, gaining vigor by the second. By the time I've choked down as much as I'm capable of, delicious as the treat is, the furious energy thrums through me so strongly that I almost believe I could walk without a single hitch the whole length of the keep if I needed to.

And maybe I will need to, because the careful way Aerik is eyeing the kitchen helpers suggests his suspicions aren't entirely put to rest. He licks the last of the cream off his fork and says offhandedly, "You built this place from the ground up, didn't you? I wouldn't mind having a look around."

Not even asking for a tour, just expecting Sylas to leap to offer one. More indignation sparks inside me—and then Cole leans his knobby elbows on the table, his slim form tipping unavoidably into my view. His mouth curves into the vicious smirk that always came before he'd ram me into the cage floor.

"Yes, let's see what you've made of *your* crumbs," he says, and thumps one elbow on the table hard enough to rattle his plate.

Like the rattle of the bars as he'd clamber into the cage after me. The smack of his elbow as he'd pin me down. The sound reverberates through my back with an ache between my ribs as if he's bruised me there all over again, and a silent wail of horror snuffs out the power of my anger in an instant.

A tremor runs through my limbs before I can stiffen against it. August's hand clamps firmly around mine. I drag air through thinly parted lips, grappling desperately to fill my terror-clenched lungs without outright hyperventilating so the visitors won't notice my reaction, but the dinner has worn me out so much, the control I've been holding onto has unraveled—

August stands, offering a respectful bob of his head to the guests even as he scoops me out of my chair. My body settles against his solid chest, his warmth washes over me, and his scent floods my lungs. With my face tipped out of sight against his shirt, I gulp just enough breath to keep from suffocating.

"I'll join you for that tour once I've tucked this one away where she belongs," he says, putting on a cheerful front. "It'll be easier without her underfoot."

He must give a convincing enough performance, because the only response I hear is Aerik's chuckle followed by, "Yes, and I'm sure you'll want her well-rested for later."

"Don't be long," Sylas tells him with an impression of exasperation, as if to say this is all youthful folly, and then August is marching out of the room with me in his arms, leaving my former tormenters behind.

He ducks his head close to mine the moment we reach the hall, and the tension gripping my muscles starts to unwind. I'm abruptly aware of my bare feet dangling beyond his arm—they'd have been in plain view of all three of those monstrous fae men—but maybe that's a good thing. They didn't spring up with accusations of theft, so the glamour must have fooled them. August provided them with one more reason to believe I'm just a regular, random human girl.

We're halfway up the stairs before he risks speaking, in the quietest of undertones. "You were amazing, Sweetness. I can't imagine how hard that must have been. Be proud of yourself."

Unexpected tears prickle my eyes, driven by a swell of affection that chokes me up. I curl my fingers into his shirt and nestle even more closely into his embrace, utterly protected. But at the same time, the jeering words of our enemies flit back through my head. The anger they stoked flares again, spreading with a steady burning through my abdomen.

No one will ever use me like Aerik did again. I get to decide who I'm a "boon" to from here on. And I'll do everything in my power to see that Sylas, his cadre, and the rest of the pack return to the home they deserve with their reputations restored so well the fae like Aerik won't dare insult them ever again.

CHAPTER TEN

Sylas

*A*s I walk into the kitchen, I'm struck again by the shift in energy between August and our shared lover. There's a synchronicity to their stances, their expressions, as they exchange smiles and remarks over the lunch preparations. When I first noticed it a few days ago, I caught a whiff of their mingled scents as well, undeniably intertwined. Something happened between them that day other than training and sparring.

They pause in their conversation at the sight of me, and an image swims up from my deadened eye: hands tangled in each other's hair, mouths locked passionately together. It's a mere flicker, but my wolf stirs in an instant.

I come to a stop and smile at them, hoping I've summoned enough genuine warmth to hide the itching of my fangs in my gums behind that smile. I meant to launch into my purpose here immediately, but it takes me a moment to yank back the wolfish possessiveness lunging up inside me.

I will not claim her. She'll slip away from me completely if I go back on my word and start picking fights over who's gotten how close to her when.

But skies above, the urge is nearly overwhelming—to sweep her up now like August did at the dinner table yesterday and carry her straight to my bedroom so I can demonstrate every intimate pleasure *I* could inspire in her.

There'll be time for that later. And I'm more lord than animal, thank the Heart. I clamp down on the defiant howl within and turn to the business at hand.

"You wanted to be included on more of our strategy discussions," I say to August. "I'd like to consult with you on a few matters. But if you're already occupied, it can wait until after we eat." It's early for lunch yet, but my cadre-chosen does sometimes get rather ambitious in his meal-planning.

August's eyes gleam eagerly at the opportunity, even without any idea what I'm looking for from him. He really has been craving this kind of recognition far beyond what I realized, hasn't he? Maybe it was Kellan's presence, that constant thorn in all our sides, that stopped me from noticing before how capable the youngest member of my cadre has become. All I can do to make up for that oversight is honor his loyalty and determination in every way I can now.

He brushes flour from his hands and glances at the loaf he was shaping. "It's nothing too elaborate. Just needed to get started now to leave time for the baking. Give me five minutes, and we can talk while the oven's doing the rest of the work."

"Excellent. I'll be waiting in my study." I tip my head in greeting to Talia, about to turn on my heel and leave, but she slides off her stool onto her feet with a flash of her own determination.

"Can I—would it be all right if I came too?" She hesitates, her shoulders drawing up in a hint of the defensive pose I saw so often during her early days here and wish I never needed to see again. She's still a little uncertain of her place here, still nervous about asking for anything beyond what she's already been offered. "I mean, I'd like to know about what's going on. Even if there's nothing I can do to help, it's scarier not knowing what problems you're dealing with."

How could I deny the request framed like that, even if I wanted to? I'd rather she didn't need to worry about the conflicts we face beyond this domain, that she could simply roam the village and relax among the pack, but she's seen too much of our world to believe in the appearance of peace whole-heartedly. If being included in our discussions will give her more of that peace, then I won't stand in her way.

I give her a deeper nod of acknowledgment. "Fair enough. I have no plans I intended to keep secret from you. I'll only ask that you hold any questions until we've worked out what we need to."

"Of course. I won't get in the way." She beams at me, the fearfulness melting away, and it's hard to imagine *not* wanting her at my side, wherever I am and whatever I happen to be doing. I can't resist giving her cheek a brief caress before I depart.

This little scrap of a human woman has worked her way so much deeper into my regard than I would have thought possible a month ago.

As I head to my study, I knock on Whitt's bedroom door to let him know the meeting I already warned him about is proceeding. He came to me around dawn with a report from one of our few warriors remaining at the border, and as far as I can tell he promptly went back to bed—if he'd even gone to bed before that in the first place.

Despite the late hours he's kept, he saunters into the study just a few steps ahead of August and Talia, his eyes perhaps a little weary but his stance alert enough. Knowing he's mainly there to witness my conversation with August and offer his opinions if need be, he drops into the armchair in the corner and steeples his hands over his chest. His eyebrows arch at Talia's entrance, but he makes no remark.

August comes to a stop right in front of my desk, his head high and his shoulders rigid as if he's doing his best to give every impression of dedication to whatever purpose I might have for him. Talia lingers near the doorway, her head swiveling as she takes in the room she's never seen before. After a moment, she relaxes enough to lean against a nearby cabinet, her slim arms folding loosely over her chest.

I focus on August. "You know our contributions in the conflict with the Unseelie have… not been proceeding well."

He grimaces. "Yes. It's looked like Ralyn is recovering from his injuries fairly quickly, at least. This morning he even joined part of the training exercises I organized for the pack—moving at his own pace, of course."

"I've been glad to see him pulling through. He's given a lot for the pack—he deserves a chance to get some rest." I inhale deeply. "But between that and the losses we suffered in that last battle, we have barely enough people in our already small squadron to have an impact in the conflict. There's no point in leaving *any* of our people in harm's way if what they're doing won't help us win back our home."

August rubs his mouth, clearly thinking over the problem. His gaze is uncertain but steady when he meets my eyes again. "Where do you think I can help? Did you just want to know if I had any ideas for proving our worth against the Unseelie?"

"I'm definitely open to ideas in general," I say. "But in particular, since you've been working with our pack-kin here, I wondered if you've noticed any of them showing particular aptitude and enthusiasm for combat that they might not have previously—if we might have enough between them and our existing sentries and other warriors to send a few more to the border."

I don't ask with a great deal of hope. Plenty of fae aren't cut out for battle, especially the sort of sustained conflict we've faced with the Unseelie. We'd already sent every capable pack member Whitt and I felt we could spare. But attitudes and proficiencies can shift and develop—and it's possible August has seen things from his differing perspective that we haven't.

August rocks on his heels with a more pensive expression than he usually shows, but the eagerness in his eyes hasn't faded. "I could answer that more easily with a better understanding of what our warriors are facing out there. What sort of tactics have the Unseelie been using lately?"

A reasonable question. I glance at Whitt, who's been getting most of the direct reports. He leans forward in the chair, his expression intent but his voice in its typical dry drawl.

"The stinking ravens like to keep us on our toes. From what I've gathered, there's been no clear pattern to when they strike. The forces assembled along the border might have to defend the lands there every night for a week or spend a month or two simply waiting, on guard. Anytime they *have* let down their guard, thinking maybe the bastards had given up, they've regretted it. The bastards have tried both swarming and picking us off one-by-one at a distance, flying overhead to avoid the patrols completely, taking hostages of vulnerable pack members…" His lips curl with distaste. "There's little they won't stoop to. As best as anyone can determine, they'll do whatever they can, whatever looks like a reasonable approach in the moment."

"Then we'd want people with a good amount of experience, who can adapt quickly to changing offenses." August frowns. "I don't think any of the pack members not already part of our defensive force would be prepared for that. We'd be sending them to be slaughtered. I'm sorry."

The regret in his voice, as if he's letting me down somehow by saying what he knows to be true, sends a sharp twinge through my chest. "I appreciate your candor, August. Then, if you were making the decision… Would you withdraw the few warriors we're already contributing?"

"They haven't been able to count on any of the other squadrons cooperating with them," Whitt adds, his tone darkening. "With their numbers diminished, they're easy pickings for a slaughter themselves."

Talia has been so quiet I'd stopped paying her any mind, but now she lets out a disgruntled sound that's almost a wolf-worthy growl. "The other fae would really leave your people to *die* rather than work with them so they can fight off the Unseelie together?"

Her vehemence provokes a tight smile. "Our politics are… complex. But at the core of it, the other packs don't wish to be tainted by our misfortune—to risk any victories they win being dismissed because of our warriors' involvement or any losses to be blamed on their associating with us. Until we can prove on our own that we have just as much honor as we always did, any action we're a part of will be seen as suspect."

"It isn't fair," she mutters, but softly enough that it's obvious she realizes fairness hardly comes into it. She's experienced plenty of evidence that many of the fae value their own interests far above anyone else's wellbeing.

While the rest of us have talked, August has been mulling over my last question. He shifts his weight from one foot to the other. Then he exhales in a rush. "There is someone you can send who might be able to turn our part in the battle into something good."

Whitt's eyebrows shoot up higher than before. I can barely prevent my own surprise from showing. "Who?" I ask.

"Me." August holds up his hand before I can even think about responding. "I know you haven't wanted me to leave the domain— but if it's that or give up on this chance completely, I think we have to take the risk. Kellan isn't around anymore to stir up trouble. Aerik seems to have backed off. We don't face any immediate threats, other than the threat of losing the chance to win back the respect we deserve."

My instinctive reaction is to deny him, but I can't refute the points he's made. I bite back the arguments I'd like to make and motion to him. "I'm not convinced yet, but you can continue making your case."

"I have plenty of training—you know I had the best possible teachers—and I've made it through enough skirmishes over the years to know my way around a battle. I'll just go out and speak with our squadron myself, plan out the best approach when I can see exactly what we're dealing with—or tell them to come back with me if that seems like the best we can do. If there's an attack while I'm out there, so much the better. Maybe I'll win us a few allies by showing that our cadre is willing to join the fight."

He might be able to spin the situation around from a total disaster into something closer to victory. And as long as no one launches a full-out assault on us while August is gone, we should manage without him.

The older brother in me doesn't want to say yes, but the lord knows I should. I catch Whitt's gaze again, and while he doesn't look any more pleased than I feel, he inclines his head in the slightest of nods.

I return my gaze to August, forcing myself to see the man, the proven warrior and cadre-chosen, not the boy whose progress I guided so many decades ago.

He can handle this. The fact that he kept his cool around Aerik despite all the animosity he holds over Talia's torment is all the proof I could ask for of the control he's gained over his fiery temper. And a little fire might be just what they need out there on the endless front.

"All right," I say. "You'll take a short time longer to increase the defensive skills of the rest of the pack, and when Ralyn is ready to return, you'll join him. I'll give you ten days, but if you feel you may as well bring them all back, of course you may return sooner. I want you back with us well before the full moon."

August gives me a brief bow, looking both proud and relieved that I saw him as worthy, and I hope with all my heart that I'm not making a mistake.

CHAPTER ELEVEN

Talia

In theory, I've already said my goodbyes. Then August turns before stepping onto the conjured carriage that's going to whisk him away to the battlefield and gives the assembled pack one last wave. I can't help dashing to him as quickly as my foot allows to wrap him in one last hug.

Everyone knows we're lovers. It shouldn't look strange. But still my face heats a little at the public show of affection even as his arms come around me in return.

"It's only ten days," he murmurs close by my ear. "I promise I'll come back to you, and in one piece, Sweetness."

I know it's not that long. I waited almost ten *years* to get out of Aerik's prison—ten days is nothing.

At the same time, it feels like forever. I've seen this man every day since our lives collided. I'll have no idea what's happening to him out there at the border where other members of the pack have already died at Unseelie hands.

I understand why he's doing this, though, and if he finds a way to impress the arch-lords, it'll be more than worth it. The last thing I want is to make him feel guilty about going. So I force myself to step back with the best smile I can summon for him. "I'll hold you to that promise," I say, relieved that my voice doesn't waver.

As he gets into the floating wooden carriage next to the man named Ralyn, Sylas comes up behind me with a steadying hand at the small of my back. I exhale, letting him take just a little of my weight. He must be worried for August too, and he's managed not to show anything but confidence in his younger half-brother. If both he and Whitt think this was a reasonable plan, August can't be in *too* much danger, right?

I'm not sure I actually want the answer to that question.

The carriage glides off, and the pack members drift toward their houses, other than the couple of fae who are taking over cooking duty in the keep while our usual chef is away. My relationship with Sylas *isn't* public knowledge, so he ruffles my hair where otherwise he might have offered a kiss. His voice comes out low and gentle. "Do you have enough to occupy yourself with, Talia?"

I don't, but I know I need to find something to do, or the anxious questions will take over my brain. "I'll get my exercises in —August gave me some moves that I can practice on my own." Maybe imagining I'm kicking our enemies' butts will take me from feeling helpless to formidable.

Working out in the basement gym does distract me for a little while, but when I sink down on the mat, sweaty and panting, after putting myself through the paces, memories of my interlude with August here rise up in my head. A lump forms in my throat. I shove myself to my feet and limp to my bedroom to change out of my damp clothes.

The sun shines warmly through my bedroom window. I bask in its glow for a minute before reminding myself that I can go right out into it for as long as I'd like now. I still feel a little shy intruding on the pack's village, even though everyone has been uninterested at worst and friendly at best, but Harper did encourage me to drop in on her whenever I wanted to. Maybe her cheerful curiosity will give me a longer diversion.

Harper pointed her family's house out to me when I last spent time with the larger pack. Though they all look very similar in their immense twisted-off tree-trunk forms, the smaller details make them easy to distinguish. She shares her home with her parents and one set of grandparents, and true to her name, there's clearly a musical inclination in the family. Someone has carved an elegant image of a flute embraced by a fiddle on the door.

Her father is crouched outside the house tending to the garden. As I approach, I'm embarrassed to realize I've forgotten his name. "Hi," I say tentatively. "Is—is Harper around?"

He bobs his head with a soft smile and motions me toward the house. "Deep in her work, but I expect she won't mind you interrupting."

Because she doesn't mind interruptions in general or because she wouldn't want to turn me away? I haven't quite figured out what Harper finds so fascinating about me, other than from what I've gathered she's never gotten to talk to any human at all before. I guess that's a reasonable explanation right there. Maybe it's also that I look like a newcomer who's about the same age, even though I know her youthful appearance is deceptive. She might be just out of adolescence, but in fae terms that means she's still several decades old.

I venture into the house cautiously, met with an odd hissing sound from behind the door to my left and a disgruntled muttering. I hesitate and then knock. "Harper? It's Talia."

"Oh! Come in."

I nudge open the door to find her grappling with a sheet of satiny lavender-purple fabric draped across a table. She gives it one last tug, snatches up her scissors, and shoots me a bright smile. "Sorry. Sometimes spider-weave just won't behave."

A wooden dummy stands on the other side of the table, a few pieces of fabric already pinned around it to form a bodice and the start of a waistline. It's a more elaborate construction than the simple dress Harper's wearing right now—the kind most of our pack-kin appear to prefer. Maybe there's a celebration of some type approaching.

"You're making a special outfit?" I ask. "What's the occasion?"

"Oh, no occasion." She pops the head of a pin into her mouth, snips a chunk of fabric off—that hissing sound I heard from outside was the scissors, I realize—and fixes it against the dummy with a shallow fold. "This is just… practice. I figure the more proof I have of my skills—and the more I can improve them—the better off I'll be when I really want to use them. I've already got a pretty good collection."

She waves me farther into the room so I can see the rack by the far wall. The rack holds at least a dozen dresses in every color from bright ruby red to deep earthy brown, all in a formal evening-gown style with long skirts and fitted bodices adorned with sashes, gauzy panels, or delicate flowers and leaves sculpted out of fabric. Stepping closer, I run my fingers over a vine that looks almost like an actual plant winding around a skirt and find it silky soft.

"These are amazing," I say.

Harper sets down her scissors and breezes over to join me. "You should try one on! I don't get many willing models around here—the only ones who think dressing up is fun would probably end up spilling wine all over them. Here, I think this would fit you."

After giving me a glance up and down, she plucks a gown with panels of alternating grass- and spruce-green that make it look like a landscape of distant treetops, caught here and there by golden glints of embroidery like sunlight. "And it'll go perfectly with your eyes."

My heart stutters at the thought of putting on something this beautiful—and valuable. But it's not as if I have anything around that I could spill on it, and Harper only looks eager at the prospect.

"Are you sure?" I ask anyway.

She gives me a little shove toward a curtained area in the corner that can serve as a changing room. "Go on, go on. It'll help me see if there are any little flaws I missed. It's hard to tell for sure on the dummy or myself."

Well, if it'll *help* her … I bundle the delicate fabric in my arms and duck behind the curtain. I'm so careful ensuring I don't rip it that it takes me a few minutes to ease the dress onto me and adjust it against my chest and hips, especially wary of the fluttery sleeves against the ridges of scar on my shoulder. The glamour stops Harper from seeing them, but it won't stop the fabric from catching on them.

"Are you planning on making a business selling these or something like that?" I ask as I settle the fabric against my skin.

"That's the gist of it." Harper pauses, and for a moment there's nothing but the hiss of her shears through the spider-weave. Her next words tumble out in a rush. "I don't want to sound ungrateful to Sylas and everything he's done for us here. I know how hard he's worked to keep the pack safe and give us a good home in spite of everything. But—I never got to live anywhere other than here. And here is kind of… boring. None of the other packs want to visit us. Heart knows they never invite *us* to visit them. I want to see more, do more."

The longing in her voice resonates with something deep inside me. My position in the world of the fae is too precarious right now for me to want any more excitement than I've already got, but I remember the pangs I felt as a kid before, thinking of all the incredible cities and landscapes I hadn't gotten a chance to experience, pasting printed-out photographs into my travel scrapbook as if having a concrete representation of those dreams would help make them real.

At that time, I was way too young to travel on my own anyway. I might have made those dreams come true if Aerik hadn't torn my life apart. Harper has been stuck in the same place for ages longer than I've even been alive. I don't think Sylas would blame her for her restlessness.

"And the dresses will help you get out more?" I say.

"I hope so. The ladies of the more prestigious domains—they're all having balls and banquets and things like that. Wanting to show off that they've got clothes nicer than anyone else. At least, that's what I've heard from how the older folks tell it." She gives a little laugh. "If they're right, then I figure the offer of a dress could be my ticket into getting a warm welcome other places, if it's spectacular enough."

"They are pretty spectacular." I edge out from behind the curtain, still checking that I'm not about to snag one of the panels anywhere. The fabric shifts with my steps like the softest of breaths rippling over my limbs. I can't tell how it looks on me, but when I glance up at Harper, she has her hands clasped over her chest, her eyes shining.

"It's even better than I pictured. Oh, so lovely. Hmm, but I think a couple of the bits here need a few extra stitches."

She dives in with needle and gold thread at the ready, sewing a portion by my waist. I keep my arms raised so I don't bump her head. "It feels nice—wearing it," I say. "I wouldn't have expected clothes this pretty to be comfortable."

"That's the best thing about spider-weave. It holds its shape so well but stays so soft at the same time." She leans back, cocks her head, and pinches another spot closer to the back. "Almost perfect. Do you think…" She glances up at me. "Do you think humans would like this sort of thing too? I mean, most of them. I'm glad that you do."

I don't have much sense of adult fashion tastes, especially in the current decade, but I can't tell her that. What I do know: "I'm sure there'd be some people who'd *adore* dresses like these just because they're so unique. We don't have spider-weave or whatever back in my world. And anyone would be able to tell these are gorgeous."

"Oh, good." She giggles again, a hint of a blush coloring her cheeks. "I've thought about forgetting all the snobby Seelie who live closer to the Heart and going in the other direction, to see the mortal world… But I know a lot less about how to impress them. Maybe, if you ever take a trip back there, I could come with you and you could teach me a few things?"

She says that last bit so bashfully that any lingering shyness in me falls away. That's why she's been so friendly—because she's honestly intrigued by all the things I've experienced that she hasn't, as mundane as my former home feels to me compared to this place.

The thought of returning, of having to navigate everything that's changed alone, unnerved me before. It might not be so bad with an enthusiastic tourist along for the ride, turning it into an adventure.

"I don't know when I'd be going there or if I will at all," I say. "But if I do, I don't see why I couldn't show you around. The place I lived wasn't all that amazing, though."

"It'll all be new to me! And very different from here. But, no pressure, no pressure. You just got here. You should enjoy yourself. I'm sure it's much more interesting when you're not used to it."

Interesting is definitely a word for it. My mouth twitches with a bittersweet smile—and then I freeze as an unexpected but familiar figure ambles through the doorway.

Whitt's stride is casual, but I've been around him enough by now to see the tension in his jaw. He halts at the sight of me, blinking with a slight widening of his eyes that makes my cheeks heat. That startled—and maybe even appreciative?—expression vanishes a second later, his gaze snapping down not to check out any provocative part of me but to my feet, just barely visible beneath the hem of the dress.

Is he worried that Harper might have noticed the brace beneath the illusion while she's been standing so close? Should *I* have been worried about it? She hasn't touched my feet or ankles. At Whitt's entrance, she's leapt to her feet and dipped her head.

Before I can panic over the possibility that I've blown my cover, Whitt flicks his hand toward us. "Talia, we have need of you in the keep. Finish up whatever exactly you're doing here, and come speak to Sylas as soon as you're able."

He strides out as quickly as he arrived. Harper stares after him and then glances at me. "What do you think that was about?"

"I don't know." That's true, but I have more of an inkling of the various possibilities than she would, since she has no idea that I'm anything more than August's lover. I grip the skirt of the dress. "I guess I'd better get this off and go find out as quickly as possible."

When I emerge from behind the curtain in my regular clothes and offer the green gown to Harper, she shakes her head. "You should keep it," she says with a sly little smile. "I've got plenty. Surprise August with it. I'll think of it as a gift to both of you."

My face outright burns then. I stumble over my words. "Are you sure? It's so lovely—I wouldn't have asked—"

"You didn't ask. I probably owe you at this point for all my questions. Go on, before our lord or his cadre come to round you up again."

I hustle back to the keep with the dress clutched to my chest. The thought of welcoming August home in this treasure of a gown is giddying enough to push back my apprehension until I've tucked the garment into my bedroom wardrobe and am heading down the hall to Sylas's study. What could have made not just him but also Whitt concerned enough to call me back from my visit with Harper?

Probably hearing my footsteps approaching, Sylas opens the study door before I've quite reached it and ushers me in. Whitt is standing to one side of the desk, his posture unusually tense. Knowing that whatever this is about is enough to rattle even his careless air, my skin prickles with twice as much uneasiness as before.

"What's going on?" I ask, glancing between them as Sylas crouches down by my legs. He inspects my foot and its brace like Whitt did.

"I agree, the glamour appears to be holding well," the fae lord says to Whitt, and moves to his chair, focusing his attention on me. "Whitt has made a small but disconcerting observation this afternoon."

The other man's mouth twists. "That's one way of putting it. I've personally been conducting an extra patrol since Aerik's visit. It hasn't turned up anything before, but today I caught a whiff of magic along the southeast border of our domain that had a distinctive scent to it. I'd be willing to place a sizeable bet that Cole cast whatever spell left that trace—and within the past day."

A shiver I can't suppress runs through my body. "He's still sneaking around here?"

"It appears that way," Sylas says. "It could be that Aerik simply sent him to quickly check up on us once the dust of the visit had settled, and since there wouldn't have been anything shocking for him to notice then either, that's the last we'll hear of them."

Whitt makes an even sourer face. "Or he could be making a continuing habit out of it."

"None of which matters as long as he sees nothing to raise the suspicions we hoped we'd put to rest." Sylas offers me a small, tight smile. "They *can't* know you're their missing prisoner."

I rub my arms, chilled despite the summer warmth in the air. "But you expected them to leave us alone after that dinner. They mustn't be convinced after all." What is it going to take for those monsters to give me some peace?

"Unfortunately, that's the only conclusion I can draw, although we can still hope it was only a brief and temporary re-flaring of their interest."

"I'll increase my patrols even more," Whitt says. "And tell the sentries to attack any unknown fae in our grounds matching Aerik or his cadre-chosen's descriptions without hesitation. If we can catch them intruding, we'll have the high ground."

"Or perhaps you'll find that there are no further intrusions." Sylas sighs. "But if there are—it's poor timing with August having just left."

A jolt I didn't anticipate rattles my nerves. "You're not going to call him back, are you? He'll have only just gotten to the border!"

Sylas's eyebrows rise at my vehemence. "Wouldn't *you* rather he was here? If Aerik escalated to an actual attack, we'd do everything possible to defend you, but our pack against his... As much as I hate to admit it, it'd be a difficult victory even with August alongside us."

Which means if I asked Sylas to call him back... I could simply be summoning him to be slaughtered.

Flashes of memory waver up—the searing pain in my shoulder, the branches seeming to wheel over my head, my brother's choked off wail. My voice tearing up my throat with a sob. *Mom! Dad! Help!* The thudding of their footsteps, snarls and rustling of monstrous furry bodies spinning around—

My stomach lurches. I hug myself, shoving those fragments of the past away with all the force I can manage. Focusing on the solid wood of the floor beneath my feet. On my arms pressed tight to my chest. The images recede, but the nausea that came with them remains.

"Talia?" Sylas says gently.

I shake myself and look up at him. The resolve that prompted my protest only grips me harder, for so many reasons, at least some of which I can find it in me to say out loud. "No. He went to oversee the war against the Unseelie for good reasons. I—I don't want you jeopardizing that over some small risk to me. It *is* a small risk, right? That Aerik would launch some kind of assault on your domain out of the blue?"

I've already inadvertently contributed to the villain's increase in prestige. No way am I going to be the reason Sylas and his pack lose their chance at restoring their proper place in their society.

Whitt eyes me, a bemused expression playing across his face. I can't tell how much of that emotion is aimed at me.

"I'd say it's quite small," he says. "But not impossible. Less so if I manage to restrain myself from doing what I'd like to if I get my claws into that mangy prick from his cadre." He bares his teeth in the fiercest of grins.

Sylas rests his elbows on his desk. "You're the one most threatened by his interest in our pack, Talia. I swore you'd be safe here. Regardless of the circumstances, if you'd feel more secure—"

I shake my head emphatically, ignoring the ache of my heart at the knowledge that I'm giving up the chance to see August again so much sooner than planned—and safe from the Unseelie's weapons and talons. The only reason I'd really need him here is if I'd be dragging him into even more danger.

"I'll be fine. Do whatever you'd do if I wasn't here and you didn't have to take me into account. That's what would make me happiest."

And if I come to regret that decision later, the only one who'll be suffering for it is me.

CHAPTER TWELVE

Talia

I thought playing August's video games might be soothing, giving me the impression of him being here with me, but really it's the opposite. How can I get absorbed in the game when something as simple as the digitized music makes me sharply aware of the empty space beside me? He would have given me a teasing nudge with his elbow, bantered about who was winning, and then nuzzled my hair in consolation any time he took the lead.

After just a few minutes, I turn off the game and flop down on the recreation room sofa. I've already watched a movie. After dinner, Sylas and Whitt went off to discuss some new plans with their sentries. They haven't found any more signs of Cole lurking around in the past few days, but he could just have gotten sneakier. I'm glad they're not taking any chances, even though my stomach knots at the idea of what might happen to the pack if Aerik figures out who I am after all.

An amused baritone carries from the doorway. "Becoming a lay-about, are you?"

I push myself upright to see Sylas standing on the threshold, his expression weary but a small smile curving his lips. He's tired from staying on top of all the steps he's taking to protect *me*. The knots in my stomach pull tighter.

"If there's something I can do to help the pack—"

He makes a dismissive sound and walks over to give my head a fond caress. "You do plenty already. Ivy's told me how much you're contributing in the kitchen. I'll remind you again that you're not a servant here."

"I know. I kind of got to like it after helping August so much. And it keeps me busy." But working in the kitchen doesn't feel like enough, not when I know Ivy and the fae man who pitches in too could handle the meals on their own easily enough. "You've been working on training some of the pack like August was. He was thinking I might be able to join in with them soon."

Sylas shakes his head. "If Aerik is still keeping an eye on our activities here, having my cadre-chosen's supposed lover learning combat skills would raise concerns even if he has no idea who you really are." When I start to make a face, he taps my chin. "But I was thinking we shouldn't neglect another area of your training. How have you been coming along with your magic?"

"I think I'm getting better at quickly bringing up the emotions I need to command bronze." I've been practicing several times a day, and picturing enemies charging at August on the battlefield stirs up my fear and anger in an instant. "I just keep making that spoon twist into different shapes, since I don't think August would appreciate me going through all the bronze equipment in the kitchen."

Sylas chuckles. "No, I expect not. He was attempting to teach you the true word for light as well, wasn't he?"

"Yes." I look down at my hands, remembering the brief spark I conjured while filled with joy and love in August's arms. While he's been gone, I haven't been able to summon *that* feeling again, not strongly enough to bring another flash of light with it. Every happy memory of him is tainted by the knowledge that he's beyond my reach where those enemies could stop him from ever returning. "I haven't had as much success with that. But he did say it usually takes even fae a while to learn new true names, especially when they're just getting started learning magic."

"It does." Sylas lowers himself onto the sofa next to me, stretching out his impressive legs. "Why don't you give it a try now, and I'll see if I notice any areas you could work on?"

Doubt fills my gut, but he asked me to try, so I will. He's the most adept magic user out of the men of the keep, from what August has said. Maybe there is something I've missed that would make the process come easier to me, without needing quite so much, er, inspiration.

I sound out the syllables in my mind before rolling them off my tongue with all the energy I can channel into them. "*Sole-un-straw.*"

I can tell even as I speak that no magic is reverberating through me. I pause to gather myself and think back to the one moment it worked before, to the afterglow of pleasure shimmering through my body and the adoration in August's voice as I brought him to his own peak. Will we get to be that close again—or closer?

A flutter runs through my chest, but it's joined by a pang of worry. "*Sole-un-straw,*" I say, willing the word to call light out of the air, but nothing flickers around my splayed fingers.

Sylas rubs his jaw, studying my hands and then my face. "You've gotten the sound of it right to my ears. I'm surprised you're not seeing at least a small effect. I assume you're drawing on your emotions as works when it comes to bronze. Have you managed to produce any light at all during previous practice, or is this how it typically goes?"

Heat creeps up my neck. "Well, I—I managed to conjure a tiny bit once. It seems like the light might rely on different emotions from bronze."

"Interesting. What sort of emotions?"

"Well, happier ones. I don't know if it would *have* to be exactly like this, but—" The heat tickles across my face. "When I managed it before, it was after August and I had—we'd been making out." That would be the right word for it, wouldn't it? Even if what we did together felt nearly as intimate as I imagine actual sex would.

An answering heat glows in Sylas's unscarred eye. For a second, I'm afraid he'll let some hint of aggression slip out at the thought of August and me together, but to my relief, all that crosses his face is a broader, knowing smile. He rests his arm against the back of the sofa and strokes his thumb down the side of my cheek, taking the skin there from hot to searing. "I see. And you've tried drawing on *those* memories to no effect?"

"It hasn't worked so far. I mean, it's hard to know when any time I think about him, I can't help remembering where he's gone and getting anxious…" I duck my head. "And obviously it won't be very useful if I can only speak to light if I've just been intimate with someone."

"No, but you've progressed in how you can work with bronze, getting better at calling on the power you need even if you're not in literal danger. I'd imagine you could do the same with light." Sylas pauses. "Would you be open to seeing if you could stir up some of that power with me?"

His voice has dropped so low it sends an eager quiver right through my body. I glance up again, meeting his intense, mismatched gaze, recalling so vividly how good his capable hands felt traveling over my curves, his mouth branding my skin. The breathless answer slips up my throat without a second's hesitation. "Yes."

The fae lord gives an approving rumble and traces his fingers along my jaw to draw me into a kiss.

The way his mouth meets mine is every bit as thrilling as when I'm with August, but at the same time as different as the two men's dispositions. Sylas's kiss is all controlled power, capturing my lips with the giddying impression that he's moderating the full force of his passion, keeping fiercer impulses that might crush or bruise in check. As my mouth moves against his, parting with the commanding probe of his tongue, he makes a hungry sound that's almost a growl. But I don't for one instant fear he'd mark me in any form I haven't made clear I want.

His other arm comes around me, tucking me closer—trailing over my hip to shift my legs across his lap, then circling my knee. I never thought of my lower legs as being all that sensitive, but they wake up with a tingling rush that shoots straight between my thighs.

My fingers curl into his shirt, grazing the taut muscles of his chest. Sylas pulls back just an inch, his breath still mingling with mine.

"You deserve better than a hasty tryst on a worn sofa," he says roughly. "Come with me?"

The moment I nod, he scoops me up in his arms, much like August did taking me from our dinner with Aerik what feels like years ago. I lean against Sylas's even brawnier frame, his smoky, earthy smell filling my lungs, and am struck by the urge to melt right into him, as if I could.

The lights in the first-floor hall have dimmed. The kitchen staff have returned to their homes for the night. As Sylas strides on up the staircase to the bedrooms, a warm ache forms in my chest amid the heat blazing between our bodies.

This man has offered so much to and given so much for me. He's valued my safety above the security of his pack; he's awarded me with every ounce of freedom he can at the expense of recovering the honor he lost so unfairly and has spent decades striving to recover. I've seen how deeply he cares about the pack—I know it hasn't been easy for him. I know he'd fight to the death for any of us.

I told him I didn't belong to him, but nevertheless he's made me his own.

I don't know how I could possibly deserve all the compassion and generosity he's shown me, but I can't help reveling in it, beaming from the inside out with the awareness of it. And burning at the same time to give just as much back to him, as if there's any way I could.

How can I feel this much for him when I only just recognized that I'd fallen in love with August? But the pang can't be denied. It isn't just desire coursing through my veins but that bone-deep affection that brings a nervous shiver with it.

I told *both* of them I didn't belong to them, and yet my heart already does. Where will that leave me in the long run? For all they care about and desire *me*, I'm still only a human girl, and a damaged one at that.

How long can this last? How much could they possibly feel for me beyond the affection they've already shown?

What a horrible irony it would be if it isn't Aerik's torments but my saviors' kindness that breaks me in the end.

As Sylas shoulders past his bedroom door, I try to push all those worries aside. He lays me out on the bed, both his eyes gleaming with their disparate lights, and so much wanting swells between my legs and behind my sternum that I practically yank him to me, raising my head to meet his kiss. For a short while, between his dizzying kisses and the scorching caresses that remove my blouse, I lose myself in the bliss of the moment just as I did before.

But when Sylas's mouth closes over my nipple, stoking the pleasure that's already inflamed me, my head arches back into the pillow with a gasp. The fresh woodsy scent of the linens hits my nose more sharply than before—and I remember cuddling next to him here, sheltering from my nightmares.

I tangle my fingers in the thick waves of his hair, but I can't shake the conflicting emotions—the sense of careening toward uncertainty contrasting with the comfort I took from him here before, the fire of my hunger for him and the ache of my love for him, and the fear that wrenches through it all.

I could lose myself with this man, and then what will become of me?

I must tense up without realizing it. Sylas stops, raising his head to gaze down into my eyes. My mouth is tender, my breath shaky with need, but he sees more than that, maybe with that ghostly eye of his.

"Is it too much?" he asks. "You only ever have to say the word, Talia. I'll never force anything on you."

Out of nowhere, a lump rises in my throat. How can I feel like crying just like that? "I know," I say, fighting to keep the rasp from my voice. "I *want* this. I just—It doesn't make sense."

He hums. "It's my experience that 'making sense' is rarely a quality that can be ascribed to one's feelings." Lowering his head, he brushes a softer kiss to my cheek. "If you're willing to try to tell me about it, I'll listen."

How can I deny him when he asks so sweetly? The words clamor to spill out, but there's too much—I can't say it all. How ridiculous would he think I am if I start making proclamations of love out of the blue when he clearly isn't offering any kind of forever?

I focus on the parts that don't make me want to outright squirm away inside my skin. "It's—it's a little scary, feeling like I depend on you so much. You keep me safe and take care of me, and I also want so much more with you than I've ever had with anyone." I find myself staring at the dark scruff along his jaw instead of meeting his gaze, worried that I might inadvertently offend him with the admission. "It's not your fault. So much of this is new to me."

"Little scrap." Sylas says the old nickname with nothing but affection, tipping my chin up. "I told you before that your situation here doesn't depend on what you do with me in this bed—or anywhere else in the keep, for that matter. That will hold true as long as you're with us. I won't inflict my desire on you like another sort of cage. You spent too long in the last one as it is. Heart knows I want you, but only as long as it truly is making you happy, in every way."

I inhale shakily, relief smoothing some if not all of the jitters from my nerves. "Okay. It will. I'm not sure—I just have to get my head on straight."

He nods. "Take all the time you need. You decide how far we go, what you're ready for. And if there are things you're never ready for…" His mouth curves into an uncharacteristically teasing grin. "I can't say I won't feel at all disappointed, but I'll be glad you drew whatever lines you needed to."

And just like that, I love him even more. I smile through the ache that's squeezing my heart. "Thank you. For everything."

"Believe me, I enjoy every bit of it—protecting you… and the rest." He gives me another tender kiss on the lips and sinks down on his side next to me, apparently having decided it's time to put a stop to our intimate activities today. As much as the hungry part of me still throbs low in my belly, I can't say he's wrong to hold off for now. My emotions are still too churned up.

I can't imagine asking him if he thinks he could ever love me or if it would even be possible for us to have any sort of official relationship. But I can't help wondering about the one woman he did have a bond with already. His soul-twined mate, fated for him, their entire spirits aligned. Just how far out of my reach is that kind of connection?

"What did it feel like, having a soul-twined mate?" I ask tentatively. "How do fae—the true-blooded ones who get one—know when they've met theirs?"

Sylas slides his muscular arm around my waist, collecting me closer against him. It takes a while before he answers.

"The connection doesn't solidify until you've both reached adulthood," he says. "You might meet them before then and never know. But the first time you see each other once the bond is fully formed—the first time your eyes meet or your bodies touch—it hits you like a lightning bolt straight down the center of you. Like being suddenly burned through by a blast of energy, and that hollow is immediately filled with impressions and thoughts that belong to your mate. From that moment on, you're not only yourself anymore. They're part of you, and you're part of them."

Having a stranger blast their way right into the core of your being sounds more unsettling than romantic to me, but I guess it wouldn't be so horrifying to someone who hadn't spent years stripped of every bit of privacy and freedom except what went on inside their head. Still… "It must be hard to adjust."

"Well, we anticipate it. All true-blooded fae know it's bound to happen eventually—and earlier is better so you can build your lives together."

"So, you just always know what the other person is thinking and feeling? There's no separation at all?"

"There is some. Unless you're purposefully sending thoughts to one another, what you pick up is fairly vague sensations and flashes of ideas. And you can tune even those out to some extent if you need to."

Sylas pauses, his thumb stroking up and down my naked side, but the rest of him has gone so still that the caress doesn't reignite my desire. When he speaks again, it's in a tone so measured I can tell he's being extremely careful with his words.

"That's one of the reasons I can't fault the arch-lords for placing some of the responsibility—and the penalty—for my mate's actions on me. I *should* have picked up on the fact that she was planning something that treasonous before she had a chance to try to carry it out, but we'd been arguing for some time and she acted in a way she knew would wound me in retaliation for my refusal to support her. It did wound me, enough that I withdrew so that I didn't need to have any more knowledge of it than I'd already been forced into. But that meant I missed other knowledge too."

I frown, tucking my arm over Sylas's with a sudden flare of protectiveness—as if *I* could defend *him* from any threat. "What did she do?"

Another long silence. I'm about to take back the question when Sylas drags in a breath. "It's often expected that fae lords will dally outside their marriages. When children are so rare in a true-blooded coupling, it's the typical way of ensuring any heirs will have close blood to choose for their cadre, although we can draw from outside the family if we need to."

"That's how you have Whitt and August." I restrain a shudder at the memory of the story August told me about their shared father.

"Well, not exactly. Our father has more than his share of faults, but he was utterly devoted to my mother while he had her. Whitt came about before they found each other, and August… after she left. I subscribed to the same attitude, especially because true-blooded *ladies* are expected to remain completely faithful to their mates, since any outside pregnancy could obstruct the one that should be most wanted. When I married Isleen, I swore to her that she would have all my affections as I would have hers."

That matches the just and devoted lord I've gotten to know. But he still hasn't answered my question. "That seems fair," I venture.

"Yes, we agreed it was. She knew how seriously I took my vow and how much our loyalty to each other meant to me as a foundation to hold our relationship steady even when we disagreed. And then she shattered it all in the course of an hour." His arm tenses against me. "She sought out another lover. I felt her pleasure at their coupling—and her *glee* at knowing I would feel it—and I was afraid if I let in any more of it, if I caught wind of who she'd broken her vows with, I'd ruin our partnership even more than she had." A ragged laugh escapes him. "Of course, in the grand scheme of things, it turned out I couldn't possibly cause more ruin than she'd planned."

My arm tightens around his. To think of someone hurting this noble, passionate man so horribly—not just anyone, but the person in all the world who should have had his back the *most*—makes me want to punch someone. Preferably her, if she wasn't long dead.

Then a jolt of cold shoots through my chest. My voice quavers. "Is that why—you were upset that I'd done something with August, before—"

"Hey, no, *you* didn't do anything wrong." Sylas hugs me close and kisses my temple. "I had no claim over you. You'd made no promises to me. Sharing doesn't come naturally to me, but under these circumstances, I'm satisfied with the choice I've made."

"Okay." I nestle my head against his shoulder. "Why would you *want* to stay with her after all the arguing and then her betraying you like that? Is it impossible to leave a soul-twined mate?"

"No. It happens from time to time. But the bond withers with distance and often it turns into something rotten. I told you my mother left my father. He was devoted to her but cruel in so many other ways that after a time she couldn't bear to continue supporting him. So she left to join another pack in a distant domain—and that's when he became truly cold-hearted."

"She left you behind?"

"Oh, I was fully grown by then. I could take care of myself. And she needed to take care of herself, so I can't blame her for going. But after seeing how it broke something in my father... I was afraid of what would happen to Isleen if I abandoned her." He grimaces. "In essence, I took the coward's way, and it's for that my pack and I were punished."

With everything I've heard about soul-twined mates so far, I'm starting to think it's a good thing that "faded" fae like Whitt and

August won't have to deal with one. I press a kiss of my own to Sylas's shoulder. "I don't think you were a coward. It was an awful position to be in. Anyone would have had trouble finding the right thing to do."

"But most wouldn't have had so many who paid the price with them. I appreciate your affirmation, though."

Fae live such a long time. If looks are anything to go by, I don't think Sylas is even middle-aged yet. I'd have put him in his late thirties at most. "Could you ever take another mate? Not soul-twined, I know, but a regular one, like you said Whitt or August could? Or are fae only allowed to marry once?"

"There are no limitations in that regard," Sylas says. "Of course, I haven't exactly been in a hurry to fill the position that was vacated so violently."

Why would he? As I soak in his warmth and his powerfully gentle embrace, it occurs to me that in a weird way I should be grateful to Isleen. If she hadn't been a traitor, she might still be around, and they'd still be living in Hearthshire. Sylas would never have come looking for Aerik's cure and found me. And if she hadn't been so vindictive in her resentment, he might have already offered his affections to another fae woman, and there'd have been none left for a damaged human girl like me.

What I get might not come close to the wrenching bond he shared with her, but I'll take every bit of it without complaint.

CHAPTER THIRTEEN

Talia

Everything is dark. Metal groans.

The cage—the cage is collapsing in on me.

A bar slams across my belly. I can barely see it, only feel the battering of metal against my body, the pain welling in my gut.

I flail and twist, trying to shield myself, but my arms are leaden, my back glued to the hard ground—

And then I wake up. It's still dark, the room lit with the faintest of starlight from beyond the window, but I've got a mattress beneath me rather than the rigid floor of my former cage. Only soft sheets are wrapped around me—tangled after my nightmare-induced squirming, damp from my sweat.

Everything is safe. Everything is as it should be… except a prickling pain that sears through my belly again.

I tense beneath the covers. The sharp ache digs in for a moment and then fades to a duller twinge, but it doesn't go away.

My hand slips down under the covers to touch my stomach, but the skin there is smooth and uninjured. The pain radiates from somewhere deeper inside.

Is it just my anxiety? Has so much of the horror seeped out of my nightmare into reality that I can't completely shake it?

I shift my weight on the bed and freeze, my posture stiffening even more than before. The linens beneath me aren't just sweat-damp. They're *wet*, with a slickness that creeps across my legs. And even as I notice that, a sour scent reaches my nose, far too close to the raw, sickly scent of the animal carcasses that I've watched August carve into roasts.

Panic bubbles at the base of my throat. I shove myself toward the headboard and jerk my hand at the lantern orb fixed to the wall over my reading chair. After a few desperate waves, the amber light washes the room. I wrench back the sheets, and a strangled cry escapes my throat.

Blood. There's blood streaked all across my thighs, blood soaking through the pale fabric of the sheets.

The smell of it thickens, and my stomach lurches. So much blood—I must be *dying*—oh God—

The bedroom door flies open, Whitt barging past it. His face is flushed, his eyes gleaming with an odd erratic light as he takes in me hunched on the bed. He stops just over the threshold, abruptly uncertain.

"Are you all right?" he asks. "I was coming up the stairs—I heard a yelp."

He can't see the blood from where he's standing. I have the absurd impulse to shoo him away, to claim everything's fine, to not have to admit that I've somehow mortally wounded myself while *sleeping* as if the embarrassment of it is worse than bleeding out.

Even if I would have attempted that tactic, Whitt has his wolfish senses. Before I can form any words at all, he inhales sharply and strides straight to the side of the bed. But when he comes up next to me, the concern that tensed his features relaxes. He looks at the mess and then at me.

"I—I don't know how—" I stammer, and it occurs to me that I feel reasonably okay for someone on the verge of bleeding to death, no pain anywhere except that dull knot in my gut.

Whitt blinks and then chuckles softly, stroking his hand over my hair to rest on my shoulder. "It's your monthly bleed. Have you never had it before? I had the impression it was common knowledge in the human world."

Oh. A rush of embarrassment twice as scorching washes away the chill of my fear. Of course. Of course. The cramps, the blood in that specific spot…

I drop my flaming face into my hands. "It's been so long since I had one—I forgot." And waking up to it out of a nightmare, I guess I wasn't thinking all that clearly. I had a few periods back home before Aerik took me. But never one after he tossed me into that cage. I'd remember the shame of trying to deal with it if there'd been even one.

Whitt makes a rough sound that's almost a growl. "It doesn't come to a body that's been starved or put through too much trauma. All those years…" His hand drops back to his side, his teeth baring as if he'd rip Aerik to pieces out right now if the man were standing in front of him. With visible effort, he reins in his anger. "Having it come now is a good sign—that you're healing. Everything's working as it's meant to."

That is a relief in some way, but still, my stomach flips when I look at the sheets again. "I made such a mess."

"Easily dealt with," Whitt says briskly, back to his usual blasé self. "I believe human servants—well, the females—are given cloths with approximately the same enchantment we use on bandages to absorb the blood. I should be able to manage that. And magic will clean your sheets just fine as well. Hold on a moment."

He sweeps out of the room and returns a minute later with a

folded cloth he must have grabbed from the kitchen, apparently already enchanted, because he hands it straight to me. "I assume you can determine where to put this."

I scramble out of the bed, wobbling when I put too much weight on my warped foot. "I—yes." I glance toward the wardrobe, unsure about fiddling with my undergarments right in front of him.

He motions to the door. "I'd imagine you'll want to get cleaned up. You can bring your things to the lavatory while I handle the bed."

He's going to—? But then, would I rather he woke up the others or called in someone from the pack to clean up after me? It isn't as if I've got any magic that could take care of it myself. Whitt must have a fair amount of experience with other sorts of blood, so maybe it's not that uncomfortable for him.

I've limped to the wardrobe and retrieved a new nightgown and a pair of panties when a strange sort of inspiration strikes. I spin around.

"Could the blood from this—if I'm going to bleed every month *anyway*—"

Whitt can clearly follow my thinking even though I'm having trouble getting the full idea out. He cocks his head and leans closer to the bed. His mouth twists. "I'm afraid the answer isn't likely to be that simple, mite. Even if we could line up the timing, this sort of bleeding isn't pure blood like from the vein. The scent is altered. I suspect we'd see the same result as when we tried to hoard some of the tonic to use after it'd gotten old."

A pang of disappointment hits me, but I hadn't had time to get all that hopeful about it anyway. It's not as if I even mind the thought of letting these men take my blood from my arm as long as I'm treated like I have the right to decide whether I do. Getting it this way might have sat easier on Sylas's conscience, though.

I scurry down the hall to the lavatory and wipe myself off as well as I can, cringing at the reddish streaks flowing from the sponge down the tub's drain. The folded cloth fits into my panties without any trouble. I pull them on and my fresh nightgown, then rinse the ruddy streaks from the nightie I was wearing as well as I can.

When I return to my bedroom, Whitt appears to have finished whatever magic he worked. The sour tang has left the air. My sheets lie neatly on the bed without a hint of a stain. When I set my hand in the area it was worst, they're not even slightly damp.

"Hurray for magic," I say with a laugh that comes out a bit shaky.

Whitt grins, taking his striking face from handsome to breathtaking. "It does make a great many things a great deal easier."

"Thank you." I tear my eyes away from him and climb back into the bed. Sitting there, I tug the sheet to my waist, feeling abruptly shy. The fae man might be hard to read at the best of times, but he's been patient with me, *kind* even, in between his wry remarks. Not just now but throughout the past couple of weeks, even when I intruded on his work—answering my questions, taking my ignorance and uncertainties in stride.

I wish I could express how much I appreciate that, but I'm not sure how, at least not in any way that wouldn't come across as awkward. I settle for focusing on the moment at hand. "Thank you —for checking on me and everything else. I didn't mean to interrupt whatever you were doing. I should have realized what was going on instead of panicking."

Whitt dismisses my attempt at an apology with a flick of his hand. "I was merely turning in for the night after our revel. It'd probably have taken me at least this long to clear my head for sleep anyway. This way I was able to use that time productively." He pauses, and his expression gentles again. "Will *you* be able to get back to sleep now?"

The image darts into my mind of him sweeping me out of the bed and carting me off to his own like Sylas has after other nightmares. A weird thrill shoots through me, as much unnerved as excited by the thought. Maybe some small part of me wonders what it'd feel like to be caught in this inscrutable man's embrace, but that's definitely a bit of curiosity I'm not looking to indulge.

I exhale slowly, releasing as much of my lingering tension as I can. "I think so." And yet I don't feel quite ready to return to the darkness and the dreams that might emerge from it. I fidget with the edge of the sheet. I could at least show a little more friendliness. "Was it a good revel?"

"I'd say it was. Much love made and very little war. Spirits were high; complaints were few."

His tone is so carefree that the final prickles of uneasiness leave me. How could anything be all that wrong when he's that at ease? I find myself unexpectedly smiling back at him.

A sly twinkle lights in Whitt's eyes. "A few of my pack-kin inquired about you. I told them you were busy pining for August."

I glower half-heartedly at him, and he chuckles. "Don't worry. I'm sure the whelp will be home where he belongs soon." Whitt turns to go, with a final remark tossed over his shoulder. "There's no shame in leaving a lantern on. Sometimes the best way to fend off darkness is to keep it at bay in the most literal sense."

He steps out with a light click of the door, leaving me wondering what darkness *he's* had to fend off that he could say that so confidently.

CHAPTER FOURTEEN

August

$\mathcal{A}$ damp breeze greets me when I clamber out of the carriage, the grass dewy beneath my boots. I drag in the cool air of the dawn, tasting daisies and clover, and let it settle against my skin for a moment before I head toward the keep.

Oh, how glad I am to be home. And oh, how I wish I was bringing better news with me.

Unsurprisingly, no one in the keep is up yet. I hesitate at the base of the staircase, debating whether to wake Sylas to deliver my report immediately, but the bad news isn't *urgent*, at least. I'd rather pass it on to him when he's fully rested.

I haven't gotten a whole lot of sleep myself over the past week and only managed a couple of hours during the carriage journey. Tired as that's left me, there's too much uneasy energy thrumming through me for me to think I'll be able to doze off any time soon. I head into the kitchen to reacquaint myself with the part of the keep that falls the most under my domain.

The pack members who took over cooking duty have left it

clean and tidy—almost too much so. A little mess would have given me something to focus on, would have made me feel missed. Well, I'll just have to remind my family how good the cooking is when I *am* here. A decadent breakfast might help my report go down smoother. I can always hope so, anyway.

I fall into the familiar rhythm of measuring flour and cracking eggs, the motions grounding me. Out by the border, even without any attacks, the meal situation was pretty dire. We generally ended up eating whatever the warriors could hunt down or scavenge in their brief treks away from the line of defense, charred over an open fire. When I had the chance, I managed to scrounge up a few savory herbs to add some flavor. With all the sacrifices my pack-kin out there are making for us, the least I could do was ensure they got a few good dinners into them.

I'm just shoving the first batch of pancakes into the warmer to keep them hot when Sylas appears in the doorway. "I thought I heard something unusual going on down here. Although given that it's you, I suppose this isn't unusual behavior. Welcome home, August."

His smile is typically reserved, but there's no mistaking the happiness—and maybe a little relief—in his tone. "Glad to be back," I say. "I take it no one starved without me around."

He chuckles. "We managed, but that's not to say we won't appreciate your culinary talents now that you've returned. Have you been up to see Talia yet?"

My heart leaps and pangs at the same time, picturing my lover's sweet face, how she'll feel in my arms when I get to embrace her again. "I didn't want to wake her."

"She worried about you. Somehow I don't think she'd mind the intrusion."

I imagine walking upstairs and climbing right into her bed next to her, tucking her into my arms and inhaling her sweet scent. Yes,

I'll do that—but I have my duty to my lord to fulfill first. I can't let my desires distract from that.

"I assume you'll want my report too," I say.

He walks in and leans against the island across from me. "Naturally. Although it'd appear the situation isn't incredibly dire, since you returned alone rather than escorting the rest of our warriors with you."

I take a moment to flip the next batch of pancakes, gathering myself and taking comfort in the ease with which the spatula moves to my will. Then I look at Sylas again. "It wasn't bad enough to call the whole effort off, but—it wasn't good either. All around, not just for our pack."

Sylas's smile fades. "Go on."

"What Whitt has heard about our situation is true. The nine warriors we have out there are essentially shunned by the packs stationed nearby. I saw no Unseelie attacks while I was with them, but it's clear they're on their own when one occurs, and that if the enemy broke through the area they're protecting, they'd be blamed for failing, not the others for refusing to support them."

"Unfortunate but unsurprising. Was there something else?"

I think he already knows there is. I balk instinctively. My nature demands loyalty to the arch-lords—the fae who rule over *all* the packs, above even my own lord. But I don't obscure the truth for them, not to the man I directly serve.

I turn to check the frying pan. "The arch-lords came out to check on the squadrons along the northern stretch while I was there. Their leadership… was not as I'd have hoped."

Sylas hums to himself. "In what way?"

In every way? I restrain a grimace. "They seemed very tense, to the point that they couldn't hide it, which made the squadron leaders restless too. I didn't speak to them directly—none of them were particularly interested in our small group—but I followed the proceedings as well as I could, to try to find out more, and I overheard a few squabbles between them over the best way to proceed, within hearing of many others as well. I would have expected them to present a united front at least in public."

When I glance over my shoulder at Sylas, he's outright frowning. "As would I. That doesn't bode well. What did they argue about?"

"It wasn't totally clear. They didn't give any details, and parts of the conversations they kept hushed. All I gathered was that they feel some urgency about coming up with a new strategy soon. Maybe they've gotten wind of some new development they don't want to share widely yet. In any case, after they finished their inspection, they each left one of their cadre-chosen to continue patrolling that whole stretch at the far north, overseeing the squadrons' operations."

Sylas's eyebrows rise. "They spared cadre-chosen on a permanent post away from their domains? Whitt hasn't mentioned hearing of that sort of presence before."

"It hasn't happened before. Our warriors said this was the first time in years that the arch-lords themselves have come so far along the border, and the first time they've *ever* left anyone that high ranking posted there." I toss the pancakes onto a new tray and reach for the bowl with the remaining batter. "I didn't like it."

"No, I can't blame you. It definitely sounds as though they're anticipating some new, larger offensive. Did you leave our squadron as they were, then, or did you come up with some advice to improve their situation?"

The hiss of the batter hitting the hot pan gives me a moment's reprieve before I have to answer. "I made a pretty major adjustment to their approach, one you may not be completely pleased with… I didn't think we were likely to make much of an impact or, honestly, become anything other than corpses and scapegoats by acting as though we could hold an entire section of the border. So I had our warriors pull back behind some of the other squadrons where they can take a supportive role. The other packs may not want to come to *our* aid, but they're unlikely to shun help from us in the middle of an attack."

I shoot Sylas a quick grin. "I did tell them to be especially alert to any opportunities to shield one of the arch-lords' cadre-chosen. That could win us some points."

He rumbles in apparent agreement, but his expression stays gloomy. As I get started on the next batch of pancakes, my stomach clenches. "If you don't think that was the right call—"

"No, it sounds like a wise decision. Possibly even wiser than I'd have expected of you, so clearly I haven't been giving you enough credit." Sylas's smile comes back, but only for a moment. "I'm just considering how we proceed from here... and I'm not liking any of the options."

The portent in his voice casts a shadow over the pride I took in his compliment. "Do you think we *need* to do something else right away?"

"Soon, in any case. If the arch-lords are becoming that invested, we may be on the cusp of a major shift in this war—it might be coming up on the point where we have to throw ourselves all in not only to regain our good names but to protect the entire summer realm."

Uneasiness ripples through me at his words. Could the Unseelie really take over enough of our lands to make a difference? What would they do with us—slaughter us? Enslave us?

It's difficult to wrap my head around the idea. I've barely even seen any of the raven-shifting winter fae across my lifetime. For them to suddenly become an unavoidable part of our lives seems impossible, but Sylas clearly believes there's a chance they could take things that far.

Before I can ask him what he means by throwing ourselves all in, a faint tapping on the stairs reaches my ears. My head snaps around with a joyful skip of my heart. I'd know the patter of Talia's feet anywhere.

I drop the bowl on the counter and hurry past Sylas into the hall. My sweet woman is just reaching the bottom of the stairs. The moment she sees me, her face lights up so bright it's almost magic.

"You're back!" she says, and anything she might have added is lost when I sweep her up into my arms. She hugs me back with a strength in those slim arms that still surprises me, her face burrowing into my shoulder, and lets out a quavering sigh that tells me everything I need to know about how relieved she is. A strangely delighted ache fills my chest, pained at the thought of how she must have worried but undeniably pleased that she cared so much about my safe return.

How can it be that less than two months ago I didn't even know this woman existed, and now I can't imagine my life without her?

"And I'm perfectly fine, as promised," I tell her. "I didn't even see an Unseelie warrior the whole time I was out there."

Her arms tighten around me, and then she loosens her grasp so I can return her to her feet. As she gazes up at me, her mouth slants downward. "All the pack members still out there will have to fight them again, though. How much longer is this war going to go on? I still don't understand why the Unseelie won't just *talk* to all of you about what they want."

Whitt's lazy voice carries from behind her. "Probably because whatever they've gotten their feathers in a twist over, they realize we'd never give it to them willingly." My oldest brother comes to a stop on the lowest step and props himself against the railing. "It seems you all decided to have a party down here without inviting me. I'm very offended."

"We know how much you value sleeping in," I reply, rolling my eyes at him. "Good to see you too."

Whitt smirks at me. "Oh, don't worry, you were very missed, Auggie." He sniffs the air. "And so were your epic breakfasts. There are a *few* things I'm occasionally willing to peel myself out of bed at this hour for, and fallowroot pancakes is one of them."

I'm home, surrounded by the three people I care about most in the world, and just for a moment, that knowledge melts away any apprehension inside me. I grin back at him. "I guess I'd better start serving, then."

Talia's already heading to the kitchen. "I'll get the plates!"

"How has your practice been going?" I ask her as I follow her in. "The physical exercises and the magical ones?"

She hops onto her knees on a stool to reach the plates stacked on a shelf over the counter. "I think I'm pretty solid with most of the moves you wanted me to focus on. You'll have to try me with some sparring to make sure my form is good enough for you." She aims a sly glance at me that heats me up far more than the stove I've just leaned over. "And the magic—I still haven't made much progress with light, but I can bend bronze pretty easily now."

"I'd like to see that." I rummage in one of the drawers, searching for another bronze utensil old enough that I don't make much use of it anymore, and hand her a slightly singed skewer. "You made a spoon into a spike. Think you can make that into a spoon?"

I'm mostly joking about the spoon part, but Talia turns her gaze on the skewer in full seriousness without protest. Last time I watched her work her inexplicable magic, it took her a few minutes to gather the power inside her. Now, it can't have been more than ten seconds, her jaw clenching and her eyes narrowing in a way that takes her from pretty to fiercely gorgeous, before she spits out the true name like a command. "*Fee-doom-ace-own!*"

The upper half of the skewer shudders and flattens into a wider, circular shape. It's not *exactly* a spoon, really more like a narrow trowel, but I'm not sure I could have fashioned a much better spoon out of the thing myself. Talia looks up at me, hesitant in her pride, and I can't resist leaning in for a kiss.

"That was wonderful. You've really gotten control over it."

"Not enough," she says, though my kiss has left her flushed and smiling. "If I needed to work something bronze quickly and I wasn't already scared or angry, I might not manage it in time. But I'm definitely getting better!"

"So you are," Whitt says, watching from the doorway with his arms crossed loosely over his chest. "You know, with all that skill, you might even be ready to hold your own at the next revel I host. You can be reasonably sure you won't need to skewer anyone there."

Talia smiles at him too, more shyly. "I'd like that."

A sharper sensation prickles up from my gut at the look they exchange, familiar and almost fond. But then, why shouldn't they be becoming fonder of each other the longer they've been living together? I should want them to be.

And I do. I just can't completely tune out the murmur inside me that wonders how much room there'll be for me if she has both of my older brothers' affections to enjoy as well.

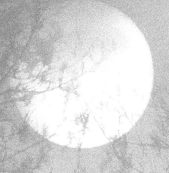

CHAPTER FIFTEEN

Talia

The sunset stains the distant clouds purple and gold. The colors ripple down over the spires of pale stone that rise above the western forest. It's a beautiful image, like the world has turned into a watercolor painting, but I can't help thinking about all the uncertainties that lie beyond this scene. I came outside after dinner to breathe in the fresh air, but the soft warble of the breeze isn't settling my nerves the way I'd hoped.

Astrid wanders over from the village and comes to a stop beside me, following my gaze. When I turn to her, I think I see sadness in her wizened face.

"The battles are a long way off," she says. "Unlikely they'll touch any of us while we're here. If that's what's making you look so serious now that your man is back."

August is back, but whatever he saw at the border still haunts him. A shadow has been hanging over his normally cheerful demeanor all day. But then, he hasn't faced a conflict like this before, has he?

How many wars before this one has Astrid seen in all the centuries she's been alive? Is this one really the worst so far?

I can't quite bring myself to ask that, so I let a simpler question slip out instead. "Have you ever needed to fight against the Unseelie?"

Her thin lips draw back with the slightest baring of her teeth. "Once or twice, when a few of them needed to be put in their place. But they *used* to generally know well enough to stick to their own territory and leave us to ours. It's the Murk that's caused most of the trouble if we don't stamp their little insurgencies out quickly enough."

"The Murk?" I repeat, trying to remember if the men of the keep have mentioned that.

Astrid takes on a creaky singsong tone.

"Wolves of summer, winter ravens

Where they dwell find no safe haven.

But most beware the rats of Murk

Sowing spite wherever they lurk."

A shiver runs through me at the lilting words. When she's finished, Astrid glances at me. "I suppose the young ones don't sing that rhyme in the human world anymore. When *I* was young, enough of them knew what to watch out for. But anything tied to the Mists fades from mortal minds quickly."

I shake my head. "I've never heard it. Where's the Murk? Is it part of the Mists?"

She makes a rough sound in her throat. "The fae of the Murk live nowhere and everywhere. They gather in the grimy shadows of the human world and along the fringes of ours, wherever they can steal a little space and spread their rot. They're rats, after all." She shows her teeth again, this time in a thin grin. "No match for a wolf's jaws, much to their dismay. They mostly trouble humans, not us."

"So, they don't have their own realm like you have summer and the Unseelie have winter."

"No. They've always been the dregs, the fae that didn't quite fit anyplace. And they resent that we do." Astrid lets out a huff. "But don't worry yourself about them. This once, it is the ravens causing the strife. I expect we'll sort them out soon enough."

I hold myself back from pointing out that the war has already been going on for decades. From Astrid's aged perspective, a century would probably be "soon."

The elderly but sprightly fae gives me a light pat on the arm. "Really, you shouldn't worry yourself about *any* of this. I can tell you with the wisdom of much experience that nothing ever truly ends; it only changes."

With that declaration, she walks off again, across the field toward the hills. She must have sentry duty tonight.

Her remark isn't exactly comforting—there are plenty of things I'd rather not see even change—but I slip back into the keep more at peace than when I stepped out, which was my goal, after all.

Sylas and his cadre are standing in the hall outside the dining room in intense discussion. As I approach, Sylas sighs and makes a gesture as if waving the subject away. "I have more thinking to do. But I value both of your perspectives."

He turns toward me, his somberness falling away with a quiet smile. "Talia, there you are. There's something I wanted to show you. And you should come as well, August."

As the fae lord ushers the two of us toward the staircase, Whitt eases back. When I glance his way, he's disappearing into the basement, already too deep in the shadows for me to make out his expression. It feels strange, splitting their group up with the three of us together and him on his own.

I've tried so hard not to come between Sylas and August. Have I severed the cadre in a totally different way instead?

But then, Whitt has always seemed to enjoy his independence, and he definitely hasn't shown any interest in becoming part of our carefully negotiated arrangement. If he took issue with where he stands with his half-brothers, I'm sure he wouldn't hesitate to tell them.

"What's this about?" I ask Sylas, curiosity nibbling at me.

"Patience, lady of the keep," he says lightly. "I've conducted a minor... renovation, you could say. It's best explained when you can see it."

August gives me a shrug that seems to say he has no idea what Sylas has in mind either. At the top of the stairs, the fae lord leads us down the hall to the area where the men's bedrooms are. He stops at a door I don't remember noticing before, just beyond his and August's rooms, and rests his hand on the knob as he turns to me.

"I was thinking about the things you said the other day, Talia, and about how entwined you've already become in our lives... How difficult it might be for you to draw boundaries when you're relying on us for so much. So I think this might help make those boundaries easier for us all to navigate."

He nudges the door open to reveal a small but cozy room. A large skylight in the high ceiling shows the stars starting to twinkle in the darkening heavens. Amber orbs at the edges of the ceiling flood the space with a broader, warmer light, glowing over the four-poster bed that takes up most of the floor. The silver and blue duvet draped over the bed looks so fluffy just looking at it makes me want to dive right into it. A small vanity and a dressing screen stand in one corner.

"I tried to think of an appropriate name for this spot, and the best I came up with was 'the tryst room'," Sylas says, one side of his mouth quirking up into a crooked smile. "Your bedroom can remain your own place of refuge, and if you need to come to either of us in our own bedrooms for security in the night, you shouldn't have to worry about whether there'll be expectations beyond that. I think we can manage to keep our paws to ourselves unless you invite us in here."

He glances at August with a mildly questioning expression, and the younger man laughs. "I can agree to that. Anything that makes it easier for Talia to fend for herself amongst us beasts is good with me."

"You're not *beasts*," I protest automatically, still staring into the room. The sight of it and Sylas's explanation fill me with a glow as warm and bright as the lanterns beaming over the bed.

This is exactly what I needed, this clarifying of expectations and knowing I wasn't offering more than I realized or disappointing anyone by not making the offer. Sylas figured it out without my even being able to fully express it to myself.

I bring my gaze back to him, reaching for his hand. "Thank you. It's perfect. I didn't expect—you've already given me one whole room—"

"Well, this one is for all three of us, after all." He squeezes my hand gently and then moves as if to drop it.

Something inside me pangs in sharp objection. I grip his fingers before they can completely release mine. The words stick in my throat for a second before I can propel them out, my cheeks flaring at the same time. "Maybe… we should give it a trial run?"

Between the looming threat of the Unseelie and the uncertain truce with Aerik, I don't know what's going to become of us in the days ahead. But right now, standing between these two men with this show of devotion… I can't imagine feeling safer or more cherished.

What does it matter if they'll never see me as quite as valid a mate as someone of their own kind? I can still love them with all my heart and make the most of what they're offering me—which is already more than I would have dreamed. They've made me a part of their world in so many ways, and I—I want to experience everything that can come with that. Before one or both of them has to leave again and might never come back.

Heat sparks in Sylas's dark eye. He runs his thumb over the back of my hand in a tingling caress. "I suppose you can make whatever invitations you'd like as you'd like to, Talia. I have nothing urgent to otherwise occupy me."

At my other side, August starts to pull back with a dip of his head. No. That's not—I want something more, something that doesn't exclude either of them.

I don't know if they'll accept that, I don't know what it will even look like, but my gaze jerks to the other man and the question tumbles out with only a slight stammer. "What if—what if I want to invite both of you? At the same time?"

The moment I've said it, my entire body flushes, embarrassment at my awkwardness burning beneath my skin. But neither of them laughs or scoffs. Sylas hesitates for a second and meets August's eyes. There's a subtle flexing of muscles and shifting of stances between them, as if in some silent conversation. Maybe even a debate.

With each other? With themselves? Have I asked for more than I should have?

August drops his gaze first to look at me instead. Something fierce and hungry shimmers in his golden irises. "If it would please you, I'd happily see what we could do for you together."

Sylas chuckles, and some of the tension I'd barely noticed building in his posture relaxes. "Yes. A collaboration for our lady. Perhaps that would be good for all of us." He sweeps his arm toward the bed. "Lead the way."

My momentary elation at my victory falters in my limping trek to the bed. The tapping of my foot brace sounds so loud in the stillness of the room. Wanting to do away with that reminder of my human fragility, I sit on the edge of the mattress—where the duvet really is soft and puffy as a cloud—and reach to remove the contraption.

The men follow, Sylas shutting the door and uttering a quiet word I assume will lock it so we're not interrupted. My pulse kicks up a notch in anticipation. My mouth has gone a little dry. I set down the brace against the side of the bed and look up at my lovers, abruptly shy despite the bold request I just made.

"I'm not really sure what to do now," I admit.

August sinks down on the bed next to me and kisses my cheek. "Why don't we take it slow and just see how it goes?" He glances at Sylas, and again I get the impression of a silent negotiation, although this one only lasts a moment.

Sylas nods, sitting at my right. "Show us when you want us to continue—or tell us if we should stop. We'll only go as far as you enjoy."

Nestled between their bodies, my nerves settle. "Okay. That sounds good."

August eases across the bed to the far side, giving me a gentle tug to follow. He sprawls out with his head by the pillows, and as I lie back next to him, Sylas follows suit at my other side.

When I look toward August, he teases his fingers up my jaw and brings his mouth to mine. At the same time, Sylas kisses the top of my head, his hand coming to rest on my waist. I'm contained between them, heat sparking everywhere they touch.

It's a good thing we're taking this slow, because these first sensations are already overwhelming me with giddiness.

As August's lips brand mine, Sylas's thumb traces an arcing line just below my ribs. Then August drops his head to kiss my neck and my shoulder, and I turn my head, instinctively seeking out the other man. Sylas is right there, his head ducking so he can meet my lips. The brush of his mouth sears right through me. I grasp his hair, pulling him deeper into the kiss.

Just this is so good. I thought it was some kind of paradise being cherished by just one of these men's hands and mouth, but both of them—I don't have the words for it. However seriously they take this arrangement, I mean enough to them that their desire to please me matters more than the instinctive possessiveness I've seen in them before. What's happening between us no longer feels like two separate relationships but something we're building together.

For several blissful minutes, we lie like that, the two men restrained in their caresses, one claiming my lips and then the other. As I adjust to the rush of stimulation, a growing need thrums through my veins. When August strokes his hand right over my breast for the first time, I'm so ready for his touch that my back arches up in encouragement.

"Hmm," Sylas murmurs by my ear, his breath deliciously hot as it spills down my neck. "I think our lady needs more attention than we've been offering."

His hand rises to cup my other breast, the flick of his thumb over the peak sending a jolt of pleasure through my chest. I gasp and make an encouraging sound in my throat, in case there's any doubt at all that I'm *very* much enjoying how this "tryst" is proceeding.

August claims my mouth again, the slide of his tongue over mine echoing the movement of his fingers over my curves. I kiss him back hard, and then turn to Sylas again, more and more heat flooding me with every skillful touch. With each swivel of their fingers over the tips of my breasts, my nipples stiffen with headier tingles.

The pleasure quivers down through my belly to pool between my legs. I'm unspeakably grateful that my first period after my long starvation only lasted a few days, and I was able to do away with the enchanted cloth Whitt gave me this morning. No need to worry about bloodying *these* sheets, whether my lovers would actually mind or not.

Sylas slips his hand up under my shirt, and I break our kiss to push myself farther upright. He takes my cue to ease the loose blouse right off me, August helping from his side. The room is warm enough that no chill touches my bared skin, but looking at the two men still fully dressed doesn't feel quite right.

"You too," I say with a tentative tug at Sylas's shirt. I glance at August to make it clear my request also applies to him. With a grin, he sheds his typical T-shirt, revealing all the muscular, tattooed planes of his chest. As I trace my fingers over the curving lines of the true names etched on his pale skin, Sylas undoes the lacing at the V-neck of his more formal shirt and sheds it.

His brawn is equally impressive, with even more of the interlaced lines dappling his darker skin. Taking it in, I have the sudden urge to taste those solid ridges of muscle.

When I lean closer, the fae lord's rich earthy scent with its hint of woodsmoke fills my nose. A low, hungry growl escapes him at the cautious graze of my lips. He tastes even smokier than he smells, like a midnight campfire in the depths of a dense forest.

I test Sylas's skin with the tip of my tongue, and a rumble sounds from lower in his chest. His fingers tangle in my hair, trailing across my scalp in a way that makes my own skin shiver eagerly. August kisses a scorching line from the nape of my neck to partway down my spine, fondling my breast with his warm, broad hand, and certainty swells through the twist of longing inside me.

This is where I'm meant to be. This is who I'm meant to be with. It may have taken the most horrific of paths to get me here, but I can't imagine feeling any happier than I am right now, doused in affection from these two different but equally awe-inspiring men.

I raise my head so I can kiss Sylas on the mouth, melting into him skin to naked skin. The throbbing between my legs intensifies. I roll over, their hands tracing lines of pleasure across my body with the movement, and reach for August. His mouth collides with mine just as passionately, drawing a needy whimper out of me.

Our breaths mingle and part, back and forth. I drink in both of them until my head spins. Every inch of my skin that brushes theirs lights up with a sharper flame of pleasure.

August ducks down to suck the peak of my breast into his mouth, and when my head arches back with a breathless moan, Sylas is there to meet me, his mouth blazing against my jaw, my neck. I slip my arm back in a partial embrace, hugging him to me, and stroke my other hand down August's bulging arm. My hips sway between them, driven by more desire than I can hold in.

I don't want slow anymore. I've waited weeks to see all this desire through to its natural finale, and my body is so ready my blood sings with it.

But first I want them to know just how much this means to me.

August swipes his tongue over my nipple once more and releases me. I slide my fingers along his jaw so he raises his gaze to catch mine. All the emotion in me bubbles over.

"I love you," I say, quiet but steady, and twist so I can meet Sylas's mismatched eyes. "And I love you. Both of you. So much."

August's voice comes out hoarse, maybe even shocked. "Talia…"

Sylas cups my face, his dark eye as intent as I've ever seen it. "You are a treasure, and I will treasure you as you deserve."

It isn't exactly the same sentiment I expressed, but it's more than I expected. I lean into him as he captures my mouth, grasping August's hand when he wraps his arm around my waist, not so much lost between the two of them as so very deeply *found*.

August rains kisses across my shoulder blades. His hand glides down my belly to the fly of my jeans. My breath spills shaky against Sylas's mouth, and I squeeze August's forearm to urge him on.

As he tugs the zipper open and peels the jeans off me, I flip over and kiss him hard. Sylas's hands smooth over my hips and join August's in freeing my legs. I reach for August's trousers with a jerk of the waist, and he growls against my lips as he kicks out of them. Then he turns me back toward Sylas, his mouth burning where he nips my earlobe, his hardness unmistakeable against my thigh.

I keep one hand on August's shoulder, clutching tightly, and run the other down Sylas's chest, watching his expression. The smolder in his unscarred eye deepens as he rids himself of his own slacks. He grazes my lips with a teasing kiss that travels down my throat to my collarbone and then devours the tip of my breast.

August dips his fingers between my legs over my panties, sparking a bolt of electricity. I buck into his touch, the pressure of his fingers showing me just how wet I already am.

More pleasure pulses from his caress, tingling through my limbs and lungs. He keeps stroking me there as Sylas works over my breasts with devout attention, until I'm squirming between them, caught in the currents of heated desire.

"Please," I mumble. "I want—I want everything." The core of me aches with emptiness. Every particle in me demands to know how it feels to be truly filled.

August exhales in a shudder against my back. He yanks my panties down and tucks his fingers right against my slick folds. His touch inflames me.

At my whimper, he groans. Then he raises his head to look over my shoulder as he slides his hand along my leg to open my thighs.

"I believe she's ready for you, my lord," he says. He doesn't sound disappointed at the thought of offering me up to Sylas—not with that rasp of eagerness in his voice.

Sylas releases my breast, taking in August's expression and then mine. His fingers trace a gentle line down my cheek. "Do you agree, Talia?"

"Yes," I gasp out. I let my hand drop to the fae lord's silky boxers, almost gasping again at the corded length pressing so solidly against the fabric. I want all of him.

Sylas kisses me fiercely, stroking my belly and then my sex as I trail my fingers up and down his rigid erection. August teases my inner thigh a little longer before taking over fondling my breasts. Somewhere in the midst of that whirlwind of sensation, Sylas tugs his boxers off. I wrap my fingers around his length, shivering with delight at his groan, guiding him toward me.

He clasps my hip and rubs the head of his erection from my most sensitive spot to my opening and back until I'm throbbing twice as urgently as before. Easing my leg over his thigh, he pushes ever so carefully inside me.

That first moment of penetration comes with a burn that's both pain and pleasure. A sigh stutters out of me, and Sylas stops completely. He stays there, no more than an inch inside me, circling his thumb over the sensitive nub above, kissing me gently. August squeezes my nipple and nibbles along my shoulder with little flicks of his tongue.

The burning eases back into a headier heat. I flex my hips just slightly, and Sylas groans. He presses a little farther in, and a little more, until the stretch is nothing but a blissful ache. I clutch at him. "It's good. It's good."

I can feel the control wound through the fae lord's muscles as he pulls back and plunges in, again and again, each time a little deeper than before. The bursts of pleasure make me cry out. I rock into him, our careful pace gathering momentum.

Some distant, wild part of me calls out for him to unleash every bit of his passion, but I'm not sure I'm ready for that yet. This is so much on its own.

He's treasuring me with every movement of his body, just as he promised he would. The expanding fullness inside is like nothing I've ever experienced before, as if he's splitting me in two but in a way that's inexplicably satisfying, like I've been waiting all my life to be cleaved apart.

Sylas's mouth melds with mine and pulls away again, his breath erratic. August keeps up his dizzying caresses of my chest. He lifts his head to kiss my jaw, and I manage to turn enough to meet his lips. His tongue twines with mine as his lord drives into me.

We're all one being, one act, moving and burning together. The glow I felt looking into this room sears through me to light up my skin.

Somehow my need is growing again, even though I couldn't be more filled. I push into Sylas's thrusts, trying to find that final horizon. He rocks harder to meet me, but it's not quite—not quite—

Just as the pressure inside me skirts the edge of painful again, Sylas's voice tumbles out hoarsely. "Let's both bring our lady to the finish she deserves."

"Yes, my lord." Without hesitation, August drops his hand from my breasts to my sex, to the spot that throbs the most just above where Sylas and I are joined. He teases over that spot and presses harder, and something in me crackles right apart.

I shudder and moan, my fingernails digging so deep into August's arm and Sylas's shoulder that I must leave marks. The surge of my release crashes through me from the deepest part of my being to my curling toes and my quaking scalp.

Sylas pulls me even tighter against him with a few last bucks of his hips. His muscles go taut beneath my fingers, and his head bows next to mine with a searing exhalation.

After a few moments, he eases out of me as gently as he first entered, running his fingers along the side of my face, over my arm, and then stealing a peck from my lips. His eye searches mine, brightening when I beam at him. I'm spent and riding on a ripple of the pleasure still echoing through me. Not just thanks to him.

I shift over to tug August into a proper kiss. He returns it so enthusiastically that it steals my breath all over again. After, still nestled against Sylas's chest, I peek up at him. "You—I should do something for you."

I can't offer him everything I just did with Sylas. A faint burn lingers inside me, like muscles on the verge of strain after an intense workout—unused to this intimate act, for now. But I could still—

August shakes his head and brushes his lips to my temple. "You've given me plenty. All I want is this."

He tilts my head on the pillow so it's tucked against his chin. Sylas ducks his own face close enough that his warm, slowing breath ruffles my hair, his arm hooking around my waist. My adoration of these two men swells inside me and tingles onto my tongue. I can give them one more thing.

I hold up my hand toward the starry sprawl beyond the skylight and murmur with all the joy inside me, "*Sole-un-straw.*"

It's more than a spark this time. A flicker like a flame wavers from my palm, a visible manifestation of my love. It's there and then gone, but clear enough to bring delight into the faces on either side of me.

"Beautiful," Sylas says, kissing my temple. August hums in agreement and nestles even closer to me.

As I relax into the bed, I wonder why anyone has to be so cruel as to try to tear a happiness like this apart.

CHAPTER SIXTEEN

Talia

Brilliant sunlight streams over my closed eyelids, but not from the angle I'm used to. I yawn and blink at the odd glow—coming from above me rather than beside my bed.

Because I'm not in my bed in the bedroom that's only mine. The sunlight is beaming from a skylight overhead in the room Sylas made—through magic?—for those times when I want to do something in a bed *other* than sleep. Apparently I was content and cozy enough after last night's tryst that I drifted off accidentally.

The fluffy duvet has been drawn up over me to my shoulders, but I'm not the only one warming the space beneath. My arm rests against August's bare chest. As I stir in my waking, he wraps his arm around me and nuzzles my hair. "Good morning, Sweetness."

It is good. I've never slept next to August before, and he's definitely an excellent morning companion. I snuggle closer to him before registering that it's just the two of us in the bed.

As I glance toward the other end of the mattress, my pulse stutters. It isn't totally unexpected that Sylas might have gone—he seems to be an early riser, based on the times I've slept in *his* bed— but after the intimacy we shared last night…

Before my doubts can fully form into words, August rolls me toward him so his golden eyes can seek out mine. "Sylas wanted me to apologize to you for him. It was urgent that he check with the night sentries as soon as they came in from their shift." A smile crosses his lips, lit with unmistakeable pride. "He said he's glad our arrangement means you nonetheless have someone worthy you can wake up to."

I can almost hear Sylas's voice saying those words, and they send a thrill through me as bright as August's face. So far, the two men— especially Sylas—have treated my refusal to let one or the other of them claim me solely for himself as a challenging situation they're only tentatively accepting. For him to suggest that sharing my affections might be a *better* situation is a big deal, and he included a compliment that obviously pleased August as well.

I can't resist meeting August's smile with a quick peck. "He said that's why cadres sometimes share mates—isn't it? Because you're all so busy with your duties you can't devote as much time to a partner as a regular fae could?"

August chuckles. "Yes, but lords generally aren't expected to be so generous with their lovers. The honor of being chosen is supposed to make up for the limited attention, I guess. You get the best of both worlds." A sparkle dances in his eyes.

"Yes, I do," I say, meaning it with every particle of my being, and cuddle up to him again.

August tucks his arm right around me and rests his chin against my forehead. "You're still feeling good about everything that happened last night, then?"

"No regrets," I assure him, remembering the worries about fae-human relations he admitted to before.

"It must have been different from how you'd have imagined your first time would be."

I shrug and breathe in his musky sweet scent, like manly fresh-baked cookies. Yum. "I didn't have much of a chance to imagine it before. It felt exactly right for what my life is and who I'm with right now."

"Good."

We lie there for a bit just enjoying each other's warmth. I skim my fingers over August's shoulder and chest, tracing the lines of his true-word tattoos. The one that circles the right edge of his collarbone looks like a teardrop that's grown claws. Curiosity nibbles at me. "What's this one for?"

August cranes his neck to see which one I'm touching. "Slink salmon. Makes an excellent dinner. There were a lot of them in the main river that cuts through Hearthshire, so it made sense to pick up that one at the time."

Of course he'd focus at least some of his magic on meal preparation. I tap one partway down his sternum next, an angular spindly shape. "And this one?"

"Skin. Which helped me fix this lovely color to your hair, since it's nearly the same material." He teases his fingers over the pink waves and then points to the other marks in a column down his chest from neck to belly. "All the bodily ones formed in a line. Bone, eyes, blood, skin, muscle, heart, stomach, teeth, liver, lungs. I've been working on brain for nearly a decade now, haven't quite mastered it to get the mark. That's the most difficult one. Many never fully conquer it."

"I bet you will. I guess no one is teaching you like you're teaching me light."

He nods. "The simple ones—air, light, water, earth, and fire, basic metals, common plants and animals—get passed on in our early training. Anything more specialized, those who've mastered them guard the knowledge more closely. When I have time to spare, I meditate with the idea, I speak to the tissue in the animals I've hunted, that sort of thing. It's hard to explain. The sound of the word slowly forms in your mind as you get closer to it."

I'm pretty sure I'm never going to meditate my way into that kind of magic, considering how much trouble I have with total guidance. I'm about to ask what the mark for light looks like when my stomach gurgles loud enough that August laughs. "Sounds like I'd better magic up some breakfast."

He presses one last kiss to my forehead and moves to get up. I push out from under the duvet after him. "I'll help. Um, I just need to get some clean clothes."

Since I'd rather not streak down the hall, I grab yesterday's blouse and jeans from where they've fallen onto the floor and shimmy into them, not bothering with my foot brace when I'd just have to take it off again while I change. August tugs on only his shirt, but then, everyone else living in this building are his siblings, and he only has to walk one door down. He waits for me to finish and holds the door open for me all gentlemanly.

As he crosses the hall to his room, I set off for mine, buoyed by a vaguely floaty feeling, as if my happiness has grown wings. I've only made it to the branch that leads to the staircase when unexpected footsteps thump across the floor behind me.

Before I can turn more than halfway, August has caught me in his arms. He hugs me close and then kisses me with an urgency that leaves me giddy, as if he thought he might have lost me just by letting me out of his sight for a few seconds. His voice spills out low and rough, his head still bowed next to mine.

"I love you too. I should have said it last night when you did, but I hadn't thought about it quite so—I didn't realize—and then I thought I'd wait until it was the perfect time. But I want you to know now. I love you. You are the sweetest, kindest, bravest woman that I've ever met, fae or human, and you *should* know that."

An odd trembling spreads through my body. In that moment, I have the impression I'd float right up to the ceiling if he wasn't holding me. I hug him back so tightly my shoulders ache, but not as much as the ache of joy that's condensed around my heart.

"Thank you," I say, not knowing how else to answer. That he could feel so much for me, that I could matter that much to him… It leaves me speechless.

But the sweetest and kindest man *I've* ever met doesn't appear to need more than that answer. He kisses me again, more lingeringly, and forces himself to draw back to smile down at me. "I do still need to get some breakfast into you. I'll meet you in the kitchen?"

Sudden inspiration sparks in my head. I squeeze his arm. "Meet me outside my bedroom after you've changed. I want to show you something first."

As I hustle to my bedroom, even my warped foot barely seems to touch the ground. I throw open my wardrobe and grab the dress Harper gave me. She said I should show it off to August—and what better time could there be?

I slip it on, a little less nervous now that I've worn it before without doing any damage to it. The delicate material hugs my slender frame just as smoothly as I remember. Looking down at it, I feel as if I've become one with the forest outside. As if I could be almost as fae as the beings around me.

At the sound of steps beyond my door, I limp over and peek out. August comes to a stop just outside, his head tipped to the side, an eager gleam in his eyes. "What's the secret, Talia?"

"I think I've made a friend in the pack. And she gave this to me." I pull the door farther open and step into view.

I'm not sure any sight has ever been quite as gratifying as the widening of August's eyes as he takes me in. When he meets my gaze again, so much fondness shines through his expression that I couldn't possibly doubt what he told me earlier.

"I forgot gorgeous," he says. "Definitely the most gorgeous woman I've ever met too."

My face flushes, both pleased and embarrassed. I doubt *that's* true, having seen just what kinds of otherworldly beauty the fae can possess, but I'll take the compliment anyway. I turn a little from side to side, letting the intricate skirt rustle around my legs like so many leaves. "I just thought you'd like to see it. I should save it for some kind of special occasion. If I wear it to breakfast, I might end up making a mess of it."

"Oh, I can ensure that doesn't happen. You've seen how enthusiastically the fae can party from watching Whitt, haven't you? I'd bet a spell to protect clothes from stains was one of the first pieces of fae magic ever invented." He grins at me and then pauses. "If you'd like me to work that on your dress, that is."

I beam back at him. "Please." It feels like a day for a dress like this. A day to look the part of lady of the keep.

My happiness keeps tickling up inside me like fizz in champagne while August casts the spell with a couple of syllables and a gesture of his hands, while I wash berries next to him in the kitchen, and while we lay out the table for breakfast together. It's spread so deeply through me that I can hardly believe I could ever be unsettled again—until Sylas walks into the dining room with an expression so serious it stops my heart.

Whatever's weighing on him, it can't have anything to do with me. The moment his whole eye catches on me, the shadows retreat for an instant, an approving smile curving his lips. He makes a detour on his way to the head of the table to steal a quick kiss. "Looking every bit the lady," he says, his hand lingering by my cheek. "You slept well?"

I get the impression he's asking not just about my sleep but how I felt when I woke up. "Very," I say, and wrap my arms around his torso in a hug that I hope says everything else I'd want to.

Sylas returns the embrace with a pleased rumble. But after I let him go and he's settled into his seat, his somberness has returned.

Watching him, I debate whether it's my place to ask what's

wrong. Before I come to a decision, August does it for me. "Did you get concerning news from the sentries?"

Sylas shakes his head. "I have something important to discuss with all of you—but that includes Whitt. I did indicate to him that he should make an appearance in a reasonably timely fashion…"

Whitt's jaunty voice carries from down the hall. "And your wish is my command, oh glorious leader." He ambles into the room, his high-collared shirt as rumpled as his hair as if he's just rolled out of bed with both, and drops into his usual chair, already reaching for the egg-glazed pastries. "What announcement is so important that it couldn't wait until a more respectable hour of the morning?"

Sylas gives his strategist a baleful look. "It's closer to noon than dawn. And I expect we'll want the rest of the day for preparations."

As I watch him, my fingers tighten around my fork. "Preparations for what?"

The fae lord's solemn gaze lingers on me long enough for my stomach to plummet all the way to my feet. Then he glances around at the others. "I believe we should travel to the front. The three of us."

Whitt's jaw halts in mid-chew, his eyebrows leaping up. He swallows. "All of us? A couple of weeks ago, you were hesitant to send even August."

"That was before I heard his report. With the observations he made on top of what we've heard from our warriors previously, I'm convinced that the arch-lords are aware of some imminent escalation in the attacks. Something they feel is a large enough threat that they needed to become directly involved. Something that could change the entire course of our world's future."

August is studying him. "And if we're there to play a decisive role in that battle, it could be all we need to redeem ourselves to the arch-lords."

"Exactly." Sylas nods to him and turns back to Whitt. "I don't make the decision lightly—and as always I'll consult with you on our best approach. But if we're going to make a major show of loyalty and strength, we have to do so decisively, and this may be the only chance we get. I don't want to risk the opportunity slipping through our fingers or our pack being slaughtered in the fray. I have to be there, and I want my cadre with me."

"Fair enough," Whitt says. "As long as you two do most of the battling and I get to call out advice from afar." He smirks, but the humor fades from his expression as his gaze slides to me. August's follows it.

I swallow thickly. "What about me?"

Sylas meets my eyes steadily. "What I've heard from our sentries is that there's been no sign at all of intrusion—from Aerik's people or anyone else—since that first trace Whitt encountered many days ago. By all appearances, they've given up their suspicion of us. We would lay down magic around the keep before we leave, and I'd assign Astrid—whom you seem to have gotten along with—to stay here with you for direct protection, as well as others from the pack if you wished. What warriors we still have in our domain would watch over the keep from the outside. I think it's highly unlikely you'd face any trouble, or I wouldn't be considering this at all, but if you did, they could hold off most until we got word and could return."

His evaluation of the risks is probably correct—he knows so much more about this world than I do—but my body balks all the same. "How long would you be gone?"

"Unfortunately, I can't know for certain. Once we're out there, we'd gather whatever information we can on the expected threat. If it appears to be less pressing than we assumed, we'll return straight away. Otherwise, we'll wait it out. The first stretch will only be a matter of days. It's only a week until the next full moon, and we won't leave you to fend for yourself during that, obviously."

Then I'd be going nearly a week without seeing *any* of them— and after that, for who knows how long, they'd only return for brief visits? The rest of the time, they'll be out at the border fighting enemies who've *killed* other Seelie, all so that they can reclaim their honor that way rather than risking my safety.

And meanwhile, what am I going to be doing? Puttering around the keep uselessly? Watching movies and reading books and worrying three times as much as when it was just August in the line of fire?

Every part of me resists that imagined future. My throat constricts, but I force out the question. "What if I want to come with you?"

Sylas blinks in a rare show of confusion. "It would hardly be safe for you by the border, Talia. The sort of fighting we'd be engaging in—I wouldn't put you in danger like that."

I gather more determination into my voice. "I don't mean I want to fight. I—I know I'm not in a position to take on a bunch of fae warriors. But you'll have some kind of camp set up while you're waiting for the next battle, won't you? A place to live. I could stay there—I could get food ready for you and the other pack members, maybe help with whatever equipment you need. *I'll* feel safer if I know you're close by… and then none of you would have to worry about what's happening to me back here." I spare a glance at August, hoping he might argue on my behalf.

Whitt chuckles, staring at me in bemusement. "So eager to leap straight into the fire after everything the fae have already put you through, mite?"

A shiver runs through me, but it doesn't shake my resolve. That glimmer of fear only reminds me of why this matters so much.

"It doesn't feel that way to me," I tell Whitt, and focus on Sylas again, since the decision will be his. "I spent more than nine years shut away from everything important that was going on around me, knowing barely anything about the world beyond that room… I don't want this keep to feel like that too. I promise I won't get in the way and I'll help every way I can. I'll follow whatever rules you give me. I just… I want to be a part of this, not the kind of treasure that gets locked away for safe-keeping."

Have I gone too far, throwing his term of affection from last night back at him? I can't read the fae lord's expression. He considers me for a long moment. August reaches for my hand beneath the table and twines his fingers with mine. He draws in a breath as if to speak up for me, but Sylas lifts his voice first.

"I suppose you are in fact in more danger from Aerik than from any Unseelie. We could construct our living quarters well away from where any fighting should reach. And I did promise you as much freedom as I could give you. If this is what you really want, Talia, I can give it."

Relief swells inside me, shot through with another quiver of nerves. "Yes. I want to go."

I'll brave whatever waits out there a thousand times before I'd ever consign myself to another kind of cage.

CHAPTER SEVENTEEN

Talia

"*A*re you sure you won't come with me?" I ask August with a playful tug on his arm.

He laughs and gives me a quick kiss by the keep's front door. The glowing orbs lining the entrance room reflect off his golden eyes, making them shine even brighter. "It's better for the pack if we all keep to our areas of expertise. They don't want to *think* about their lord or the cadre-chosen who's supposed to be prepared to defend them at the drop of a hat getting high on faerie wine, let alone see it. You don't have to worry. No one ever gets *too* wild, and Whitt will look after you."

The other man did promise as much when he extended the invitation, pointing out that it might be my last chance to enjoy one of his revels in a while—and that I was already dressed for one. I think he's holding this one specifically to raise the pack's spirits before their leaders depart for some unknown length of time. Still, an anxious quiver runs through my stomach as I step toward the door.

"You don't have to join in if you're uncomfortable," August reminds me.

I shake off my nerves as well as I can. "No, I'll be fine. I've been curious about these parties for a while."

That's true, but it's not just curiosity compelling me out into the thickening dusk. Sylas may have accepted my arguments for why I should come with him and his cadre, and August seems happy that he'll be nearby to defend me if need be, but I got the impression that Whitt was still skeptical. How can I expect him to believe I can handle being on the fringes of a war zone if I won't even brave a revel with the pack I now call mine?

When I step outside, my gaze flits first over the shadowy fields to the southeast, the direction we'll be traveling tomorrow morning to head to the border camps. Our fate there feels as murky and uncertain as the darkness before me. I turn away from it, toward the rollicking music drifting from around the other side of the keep.

As I circle the towering wooden building, the warm summer breeze licks at the hem of my dress. In the nearby field just beyond the village houses, bordered by the orchard on one side, several lantern orbs float in midair. Their orangey glow lights up the blankets and pillows laid out here and there, the fae men and women sprawled on those and others wandering between them, and the two musicians perched on seats that look like bent saplings, one with an instrument like a clarinet and the other with a fiddle.

With each swipe of her bow across the strings, the woman with the fiddle sways, the smooth fall of her flaxen hair slipping across her shoulder. Even with her eyes narrowed in concentration, I can tell they're just a little too large and close-set to look totally human. Harper's mother passed a lot of her looks on to her daughter.

But not her interest in music, apparently, as deft as Harper's fingers are with a needle and thread. The younger woman isn't joining her now.

I spot Harper lounging on a velvet cushion at the other end of the revel area, watching her pack-kin alone. The other fae are dressed up more than the pack typically is during the day, the magical glow catching off silver embroidery and tiny gems woven into their clothes, but Harper's dress outshines them all. It must be one of her own creations, the filmy gold fabric billowing around the skirt and bodice like dawn clouds drifting over a turquoise sky.

When she sees me, she scrambles up and skips over to me with a warm, wide grin that offsets the alienness of her features. "I heard you were joining us tonight, so I had to come," she says, and glances around. "I don't usually bother."

I smile back at her. "You'd rather be making your dresses?"

"Most of the time." She drops her voice, as if anyone is paying all that much attention to us. "The revels are for people who want to *pretend* they're somewhere else for a little while. I'd rather be getting to work making it really happen. If I can."

"Well, I'm glad you do that work, because I love this dress even more now that I've gotten to wear it for more than a few minutes." I skim my hands down the intricately patterned sides. "August likes it too, by the way."

Harper gives a pleased little clap. "Perfect, perfect. Maybe someday he'll take you to one of those balls or banquets in some other domain, and if the other ladies like it, if they ask where you got it—"

I laugh at her eagerness. "I'll tell them all about you, I promise."

"It's a good thing we fae live so long, because you may have to wait a while yet on August attending any festivities abroad, Harper," Whitt remarks from behind me, resting his folded arms lightly on the back of my shoulders and tipping his head past mine. His bare forearms conjure more warmth in my skin, and I'm abruptly aware of all of him just inches behind me, of the corner of his jaw grazing my hair. "I'll add 'procure ball invites' to my to-do list, but I'm not sure anyone we'll meet where we're going will have dancing on the mind."

Harper ducks her head bashfully. "I wouldn't expect—I mean, I'm sure you have more important things to do anyway. I wasn't trying to imply I'm not happy with everything we're provided with here."

I feel more than see Whitt's smirk. "Don't worry, I'm not going to report you to Sylas for treason. You're allowed to get restless." He straightens up, giving a lock of my hair a playful tug. "Have you introduced our first-timer to the refreshments yet?"

"Oh! No—I should have—" Harper beckons to me, hurrying off between the blankets. "There's lots to eat and drink, whatever you'd like."

As we follow her over to a low wooden table set up beneath a couple of the glowing orbs, I glance over my shoulder at Whitt. "Are you trying to give her a heart attack, thinking she's not being hospitable enough?"

He's still smirking. "Oh, if I *wanted* to give someone a heart attack, I could do a much more efficient job of it. I enjoy giving the pack their entertainments, but I can't have them getting too complacent either. A little anxiety is for her own good."

I jab my elbow at his chest, but he dodges the half-hearted blow with a chuckle. "Clearly I need to make sure I don't get too complacent around *you* after all these combat lessons with August."

"Don't harass my friends, and we're good," I tell him.

I think his grin softens a little around the edges. "I'm glad you're settling in with the pack enough to consider some of them friends."

I'm not sure it's so much "some" as "one"—or maybe two, if I can count Astrid, although I don't know that she enjoys my company particularly rather than simply watching out for me on behalf of her lord. The other fae of the pack have been welcoming enough if they've bothered to pay attention to me, but they treat me like more of a novelty than any sort of equal. Like right now, watching me cross the revel area with apparent interest but only speaking to each other.

Well, I guess seeing me as a full member of the pack will take time. Hopefully joining in their revel will help with that too.

Harper gestures toward the table, where silver platters are heaped with jewel-like fruits, brownie-like squares, and more fae delicacies, as well as several tall bottles next to a few remaining empty goblets. "You can eat whatever you'd like—the mirrornuts are particularly good at this time of year. Some of the wine is my father's brew."

I hesitate, my fingers curling into my palm. A nearby woman draped across her partner's lap is breathing out a stream of glittering smoke from a spindly cigarette. Beyond her, a cluster of fae are giggling madly between sips from their goblets.

I've experienced what effects some of Whitt's preferred "refreshments" can have on a person's mind as well as their stomach before. I can't imagine he'd have anything here that would muddle my head and twist my gut quite as horribly as the pulp Cole forced down my throat more than once when Aerik wanted me incoherent, but the memory rises up anyway with a shiver through my belly.

It's probably better to keep as much of my good sense as I can during this party anyway. If I turn all goofy again, won't he be even more convinced that I *shouldn't* be coming to the border?

Then again, I also don't want to look like a coward.

I glance at him where he's come up beside me, his hands slung casually in the pockets of his elegant slacks. "What's normal food, and what has… special effects?"

He quirks an eyebrow at me. "Not looking for the full revel experience? You seemed to enjoy letting loose before."

Before I hadn't realized what I was getting into—and I made some embarrassing remarks, like about how beautiful that admittedly stunning face of his is. I wrinkle my nose at him. "Maybe another time."

He hums to himself as if disappointed but points to the nuts Harper mentioned, little spheres so bright and polished they reflect the shapes around them as if they really are mirrors, and a bright blue fruit that looks jellied within its brittle husk. "You'll be safe with those. The tumblemeld will give you a slight lift to your spirits but nothing that'll addle your thoughts. You may need to avoid the beverages entirely."

"Thank you." I pick up a handful of the mirrornuts and pop one into my mouth. It crackles apart with a delicate flavor that reminds me of the tea my mother used to make for me when I wanted to join her in her morning ritual on the back porch—mine always decaf and mixed with a large helping of sugar.

A mix of fond nostalgia and homesickness squeezes my throat. I chew the next one more slowly and nod to Harper. "Those are really good."

She snatches up a few for herself and then sighs when her father calls her name. "Enjoy yourself," she tells me, and marches off to see what he wants.

Whitt is still watching me. Wondering whether I trust him enough to take both of his recommendations? Maybe I should show that I do if I want *him* to trust me.

I pick up one of the husked fruits he called tumblemeld and nibble at the jelly-like lump. The flesh dissolves on my tongue with the consistency of caramel, but tart almost to the point of sourness rather than sweet. When I swallow, a flicker of warmth kindles in my chest in its wake. Okay, that's not so bad.

"You appear to have survived," Whitt teases.

A fae couple drifts by, their dreamy smiles suggesting they've been consuming more potent stuff than I have. "Aren't you going to dance, human girl?" the woman asks. "I thought mortals loved to frolic with the faeries."

"I'll take her for a spin-around," the man offers, dipping in a bow and extending an arm in a sweep so extravagant he nearly loses his balance in the process. The woman titters.

I'm not sure how to answer, but Whitt saves me from figuring it out. He grasps my hand and tugs me away from the table. "She's already promised me all tonight's dances, I'm afraid."

Drawing me into the center of the gathering, he raises my arm to turn me in a circle slow enough that it doesn't challenge my brace-bound foot. When I'm facing him again, he sets his other hand on my shoulder. We sway and swivel together with the music like the other fae around us, although many of them are more tightly intertwined.

"This doesn't seem to be a very complicated dance," I say. "I don't think I'm going to need your guidance the whole night."

"Perhaps not, but I think it's best you stick with me for anything handsy."

"They know I'm with August. What do you think they're going to do?"

Whitt shrugs, his voice dipping secretively. "Intoxicated fae don't always make the wisest decisions. And you do look awfully charming in that dress."

I make a face at him. "Are you sure I don't need to worry about *you* then?" I haven't seen him drinking yet, but he never seems to go anywhere without his flask, and his breath carries a faint tang of alcohol.

"Definitely not. For one thing, I'm never half as drunk as I seem."

"I guess that's reassuring."

"It should be." He turns me again but only halfway, stopping me when my back is to him with a clasp of my waist and lowering my arm so it falls across my torso. "What do you think of your first revel, then, mite?"

I look at our fellow dancers and the fae sprawled around us, taking in their laughter and the lilt of the music, the sweet and tart flavors still mingling in my throat. More tension than I realized I was holding in unravels with my next inhalation. Seeing everyone enjoying themselves so free of concern makes it easier to shed my own worries. "It's nice. I'd like to do it again. Although it'd be nic*er* if the pack wouldn't think it was strange for August and Sylas to join in."

"Am I not enough protection for you?"

"That's not what I meant." I twist my neck to glance up at Whitt. "And is that what you're doing—protecting me?"

He leans in close enough that his lips graze my ear, his voice so low now that no one other than me could possibly hear it. "Every expression, every comment, is useful information. Just by having you out here with us for a short while, I know much more than I did before about who looks the most benevolently on you and who I wouldn't count on to dose you in water if you were on fire, who I should be sure to *never* let dance with you and who would probably be safe as long as they've gone easy on the absinthe. If you're going to stay with us as long as it appears, I may need to bring every bit of that information to bear."

I hadn't realized he was paying that much attention to everyone around us—or that so much of his attention was centered on their reactions to me and what that could mean for my safety or simply my comfort. I hadn't realized my safety and comfort mattered enough to Whitt that he'd focus that much thought on it. Of course, he's probably doing it for his brothers' benefit more than mine.

I turn myself in his grasp, trying to suppress the tingle that races over my skin at the slide of his fingers along my waist, so I can look at him without straining my neck. "Is that what these parties are about for you? Just gathering information?" When I watched him from the keep's windows before, I thought he was basking in the festive energy.

His blue eyes glitter. "I get plenty of fun out of them too, and it's always a pleasure to bring some delight into my pack-kin's lives. Although nothing I pull together out here compares to the grand revels I could put on back at Hearthshire, closer to the Heart's power and with so many more to join in. Oh, we did have a time or two then…"

A hint of melancholy crosses his face, suggesting he misses their old home just as Sylas does. It vanishes quickly, though, leaving him with the same sly expression. "But a spymaster's work is never truly put aside for the night. I wouldn't be much of one otherwise."

He says those words flippantly, but something about that breeziness, maybe because of the commitment he just made to my protection, sends a pang through my gut.

"You must be able to relax *sometimes.* You don't have to be on guard like that when it's just Sylas and August around."

He guffaws. "I'd argue that being aware of my lord's and my cadre-fellow's concerns is even more vital than any other's."

Is that really how he feels about them? Like they're part of his job more than family? "But—you need someone in your life you can just *be* with, without having to think about all that."

"Do I? I seem to be getting by just fine as I am."

Getting by, sure, but what about being happy? What about having the space to just be *himself,* not a spymaster or whatever?

I know what it's like to stay constantly wary, evaluating everyone around you for warning signs, never having a chance to fully relax. It wore me down even when I was living here in the keep with proper food and shelter. To just accept that as a permanent state of being…

I'm probably reading too much into it and Whitt doesn't mean it the way I'm taking it. Still, I can't help wondering what that handsome face of his would look like lit with the kind of open, unfettered joy I saw on August's this morning when he told me he loved me. I think I'd like to see that.

An odd flutter passes through my chest, and I yank my gaze away, abruptly aware that I've been staring. "I guess you've been gathering information on me too? Making sure I'm up to tomorrow's trip?"

Whitt adjusts his hand against my side, his fingers barely touching me now. "As far as I can tell, your participation in our 'trip' has already been decided."

"But you're not convinced it's a good idea."

"Did I say that?"

I can't help raising my eyes again. "You didn't have to."

He tsks at me with a slanted smile. "You made a perfectly convincing argument. As many distractions as you might create at the border, I'd imagine certain parties would find it even more distracting contemplating what might be happening to you back here beyond their reach."

"So you think I'm going to distract them if I'm with you. I said I'd stay out of the way—"

"Talia," Whitt says firmly, cutting me off. He bows his head next to mine again. "You don't have to prove anything to me. I made my decision that night in the woods, and I'll defend your right to be with us—wherever we go—with claws and teeth if it comes to that. Of all the things you have to worry about, you can rest easy when it comes to my good will."

He sounds serious when he so rarely ever does. The night he must mean is the one when he practically ordered me to flee to the human world so my presence wouldn't provoke any more conflict between Sylas and August. When they caught up with me, fighting off another fae who'd attacked me, Whitt told me he'd changed his mind, that I was good for them. He asked me to stay.

I didn't know how much I could trust that unexpected flip, but apparently he meant it even more than I'd have imagined.

A lump rises in my throat. I want to reach out to him somehow, which doesn't make any sense because I'm already less than a foot away from him, one hand enclosed in his.

Whitt turns us with a lift in the music and falls back into his usual breezy tone. "We've been talking far too much about my predilections. This obviously isn't where you could have pictured you'd be at this point in your life, back before Aerik rampaged into it. If you'd never left the human world, what do you suppose you'd have been up to by now?"

My earlier homesickness hits me with a fresh twinge. "I guess I'd have gone to college. I was going to study something like environmental science—ecosystems and climate patterns and all that." If I'd even stuck with that by the time I had to choose. I hadn't researched it a whole lot, only snagged onto an idea that might give me the chance to explore the world and get paid for it at the same time.

"Hmm, so practical. What would you have been doing for *fun*?"

My mind drifts back to my scrapbook, to the hours spend reading up on exotic locales across the continents. "If I'd gotten together enough money, traveling. There were all kinds of places I wanted to visit. It seemed like there was so much out there that was so much more interesting than our little town, so many *different* things…"

Whitt laughs, with a note that sounds almost sad. "You couldn't have come much farther than you have now, could you, my mighty mite?"

I manage to smile, even though my throat is outright aching now. "I guess not." I pause. "You know, I wouldn't have complained about coming to this place if I'd had more choice in how I came. To the Mists in general, I mean. It's not exactly the kind of adventure I imagined going on, but now that I have more say in how I live here… there are definitely a lot of good things along with the bad."

Whitt is silent for a long moment as we sway together and the music winds around us. Then he inhales sharply and raises his hand to my cheek in the briefest of caresses. "And tomorrow we'll manage to take you even farther."

"Yes." Another shiver travels through my body, but this one is almost giddy, and not just because of the heat his touch woke in my skin.

"And you're not a fraction as frightened as you probably should be." He tsks at me teasingly again.

I meet his eyes steadily. "I don't think it can be worse than what I've already been through."

"No, perhaps not. I'll give you that."

Whitt rotates me in one more slow spin, my misshapen foot only just starting to twinge at how long I've been putting my weight on it, and then lets me go. "Have a little more tumbleweld, mite. We won't have treats like that out at the border."

Harper has returned from her chat with her father, and I settle onto a cushion next to her with another husked fruit to nibble on. The ache inside me fades with the blooming warmth the stuff sends through me. We trade more stories, my memories of human life in exchange for her limited but still fantastical rambles around this part of the fae realm, and then lie back to peer up at the stars, Harper pointing out the constellations the fae have legends about.

Every now and then I peek Whitt's way, watching him circulate through the other revelers, bringing a smile to each face with his passing remarks. This might be work for him, but I think he does like it too.

When my eyelids are starting to droop and the cushion is feeling so comfortable I'm not sure I want to bother getting up, the music dwindles. A few pack members sprawl out on the blankets to sleep beneath the stars. Others gather the now-empty dishes from the table. As Harper sits up with a stretch of her arms, Whitt comes for me.

"Up you go," he says, lightly but briskly. "I have something else to end off your night."

I peel myself off the cushion drowsily but with an itch of curiosity and follow him to the keep. The lantern orbs waver on to meet us.

Whitt leads me up to his office and simply points to a silver box about the size of a textbook on his desk. He stays standing off to the side as if he doesn't want to come too close to it.

Opening the box, I find a velvet bag that sags across my entire hand with a shifting weight. As I tug it open, a mineral smell reaches my nose.

It's full of salt crystals—maybe ten times the small portion August secreted to me weeks ago so I had some small protection against Kellan. The salt I used to break the magic locking the keep's doors. The salt Sylas chided August for giving to me.

When I stare at Whitt, his smirk comes back, though it looks a bit tired now. "August's job might not be cleverness, but that doesn't mean he never has any good ideas. Salt will work just as well against the winter fae as those of summer—and I can't promise every Seelie you might run into by the border will be friendly besides. We couldn't have you coming completely unarmed, could we?"

I do also have the small dagger Sylas presented me with this afternoon that August taught me a few basic techniques with, but that would only make for a last-ditch defense. Salt is one rare thing I can wield that none of the fae can match.

Whitt managed to get this from the human realm, however much discomfort being near it would have caused him. He must have gotten it *today*, since they didn't know I'd be coming with them until then.

Just how much is going on behind those ocean-blue eyes, feelings and intentions that he hides with his smirks and mockery?

My fingers curl into the thick fabric of the bag. "Thank you. Does—does Sylas know?"

"You don't need to hide it from him. He seemed pleased enough when I suggested it. I wouldn't go flashing it at any fae beyond the three of us unless you mean to use it right then, though."

"Of course not." I have the urge to hug him or to figure out some other gesture to show I recognize how much he's offering, but I'm not sure how he'd react. He seems to want to treat it as if it's no big deal.

I'll never scoff at the idea that he intends to protect me again, I can say that much.

Whitt gives me a gentle nudge toward the door. "You'd better get your rest. We have a long trip ahead of us tomorrow."

CHAPTER EIGHTEEN

Whitt

I always forget how much I hate dealing with arch-lords and their cadres until I'm faced with the pompous bastards again. Of course, given the way the three cadre-chosen representatives are eyeing me, I'm lucky they agreed to meet with me at all.

"What's so urgent that Sylas of Oakmeet felt the need to come all the way out here himself?" asks Cashel—the one who belongs to Ambrose, so naturally the most obnoxious—folding his arms over his chest. We're meeting in one of the temporary war camp buildings near his post, and the sunlight seeping through the massive woven blades of grass that make up the walls turn his ruddy skin sickly greenish. "If he had a matter to bring before the arch-lords, I'd imagine he hasn't forgotten how to make a standard petition."

Sylas would be here himself standing up to these pricks if it wouldn't have been an act of humiliation for a lord to negotiate with another lord's cadre, as if he didn't trust his own cadre to do the job. I doubt they'd offer him much more respect than they're giving me regardless.

"My lord isn't here to *ask* for help," I say, smoothing as much of the edge out of my voice as I can manage. "We're here to offer it, as I believe I already mentioned."

Maeve, the hawk-nosed woman from Celia's cadre, snorts. "And why would any of the arch-lords require 'help' from Oakmeet? Your pack hasn't exactly contributed any stunning victories so far, and I'm not sure I want to hear any ridiculous schemes you've come up with, 'Wild' Whitt."

My reputation, carefully cultivated as it is, does occasionally have its downsides. Never mind that I'm truly ridiculous even less often than I'm fully drunk. Never mind that the warriors we can spare are no more than half what any other pack would be able to send out—or that not even the arch-lords have won any truly decisive victories with their far greater numbers. If they had, we wouldn't be standing around in a stuffy hut having this damned conversation.

"They've contributed enough that we're aware of shifts in the tide," I say, glancing from her to Donovan's man, Hollis, and back to Cashel. "You're anticipating a strike beyond anything the Unseelie have pulled off yet, aren't you? How many of the other lords have put together the pieces—and bothered to make an appearance to show their support?"

None of them bothers to answer that. Hollis adjusts his weight on his feet, his narrow face tight with apparent discomfort. Out of the three arch-lords, his tends to be the most lenient. But even Donovan didn't argue all that hard against our banishment to the fringes, so I can't expect much cooperation from that quarter.

Like any fae, they're not inclined to lie, but that doesn't stop them from talking around the truth. Cashel raises his head at a haughty angle. "We have no news to report. Perhaps you've come here on a misguided errand."

Perhaps, not *definitely*. And they have no news they want to report to *me*. If the fact that they reacted with defiance rather than confusion hadn't already convinced me that Sylas's theory was correct, that response would have done the trick.

I restrain myself from rolling my eyes. "All three of you know that our pack's current standing can be blamed on the unfortunate ambitions of my lord's deceased mate—which he did not share or act in favor of—not any deficiencies in strength or wits. Whatever's coming, we'll push it back however we can, but we'll be a much more effective tool in the arch-lords' arsenal if you share what you've learned about the Unseelie's plans."

Maeve tosses back her tawny hair. "Even if we did have some foreknowledge, anyone with *wits* would be able to figure out it'd hardly be sensible to share it with a pack that's been associated with treachery against our arch-lords once before."

Cashel nods in agreement. "Yes. Tell Lord Sylas that he may as well go home. We have no scraps to offer you poor beggars."

The two of them stride out without another word. Hollis shoots me a grimace that might be slightly apologetic and follows, equally silent. I glower at their retreating backs and draw in a breath to settle my temper.

I hadn't really expected them to say much. Getting confirmation that some scheme is afoot was enough. Judging by their attitudes, I feel confident in telling Sylas that they don't know exactly what to expect from the Unseelie themselves. They know *something* bad is coming, but not enough to want to toss some sort of "scrap" our way to let us take the brunt of the attack.

Stepping out into the thin early-morning sunlight, I roll my shoulders and then stretch out into my wolfish form to lope back to our own camp.

The meeting tent of sorts stands about a mile back from the border, near enough that I can see no raven warriors are piercing the haze there at this particular moment. Beyond the scattered buildings constructed based on their inhabitants' magical affinities for plant-life or stone or metal, the ephemeral wall that separates the summer half of our world from winter rises all the way up to tint the stark blue sky gray. Minor eddies whirl through the haze's glinting surface, which combines the shimmer of heat rising off a scorched earth with the clotted fog of a cold damp night.

If I were to lope *that* way, within a few steps of heading through the haze I'd find myself treading on icy ground in frigid air—for however few seconds it'd take before the Unseelie warriors descended on me and bashed my brains out.

The Seelie camp buildings stand in clusters for each squadron, spaced apart across the flat terrain here. Most of the tall, hissing grasses that cover the fields have baked beneath the sun so long the blades now shine like brass. Here and there, one squadron or another have cut the grass down to make room for scruffy gardens.

Warriors don't enjoy playing farmer, but they must also tire of hunting and foraging. Some of them, like many of our own, have been stationed out here for years on end.

A few distant wolfish figures prowl along the base of the hazy border, reassuring me that our fellow packs are at least organized enough to be keeping up their patrols even though there hasn't been a full-out attack since the one that sent Ralyn back to us weeks ago. I turn away from them and speed up my strides, weaving through the grass and skirting the beehive-like hillocks that rise from it farther afield.

I'm just coming around one of those pocked protrusions when an unpleasantly familiar form stalks into view—the skinny, pale-haired man from Aerik's cadre: Cole. The one who's been spying on our domain for reasons still not entirely clear. And now he's lurking near our current settlement?

I veer toward him, and he stops at the sight of me, cocking his head. I can't tell whether he recognizes my wolf, but the moment I shift to stand upright in front of him, my skin prickling with the abrupt transformation, his lips curl with an equally familiar sneer. He must have learned it from his lord.

"What brings you all the way out here?" I ask in a conversational tone that may be slightly undermined by the fact that I haven't bothered with so much as a greeting.

Cole's eyes narrow, but he makes a careless gesture as if unperturbed by the question. "The same thing as you, I'd imagine. Hard to keep the squadron's spirits up if they start to feel abandoned by their leaders. Especially so in your case, given the history, I'd imagine."

I ignore the barely concealed barb in that remark and glance around. "And where exactly is this squadron of yours? Awfully far from home all the way out here, aren't they?" Sylas would never have picked this spot if he'd thought we'd be near neighbors with Aerik's warriors. Last I'd gathered, they were farther south along the border, closer to the Heart and to Aerik's domain.

"We decided a change in scenery was in order. As it seems your lord has too." Cole's grin is so sharp it can barely be called a smile. "Has Sylas nothing better to do than dawdle around waiting for a battle to come to him? Or perhaps he doesn't trust his cadre to handle things without his direct supervision."

I bristle inwardly but keep my expression mild. He's given away more than he might realize. Aerik isn't here, only Cole. And I have a strong suspicion this interest in seeing another portion of the border was driven by curiosity after hearing that Sylas had arrived here himself. Cole is chasing glory and guessing there's no reason Sylas would have come if an opportunity wasn't imminent.

"You'll have to ask him yourself, if you're so concerned," I say, baring a few teeth of my own, and spring forward as a wolf again.

I glance back once to check which direction Cole heads in, and then set off at a full run. Within a few minutes, I reach the stream where the current sings like harp strings, bound across the swaying reed bridge, and skirt the edges of the village built on its far bank.

No one likes to live both this far from the Heart and this close to the winter lands, especially now that the Unseelie have made themselves a continuing, concrete threat. The fortress that rises beyond the cluster of houses is a lopsided affair grown of brambles, looking like little more than a massive thicket. I hate to think what the walls and floors within must offer.

I may be biased, but I have to say that the building August and I helped Sylas call up yesterday evening, about a half a mile farther west, looks a damn sight more appealing for all its flimsiness. We're a little closer to the Heart here than right out on the fringes in Oakmeet, but not enough to change the fact that we were attempting to conjure an entire multi-bedroom home in the space of a few hours. It's certainly not as elegant as the Oakmeet keep, let alone the castle in Hearthshire, and a bad windstorm could knock down those thin oak walls, but it'll do for the few weeks we're staying here.

Heart help us, let it be no more than a few weeks.

My own heart is thudding in my chest at a pace I can't entirely blame on my swift journey. It hitches faster when I spot a head of deep pink hair off to the side of our new building, which looks like the polished stump of a mountainous tree. Talia is crouched in the hasty garden Sylas and August coaxed into growing, pulling berries off of the plants there.

If Cole slunk by here recently, he'll have seen her.

It shouldn't worry me so much when I know Sylas bolstered the glamours around her just before we arrived yesterday and no doubt checked on them again this morning. I shouldn't worry about her at all when she has her two paramours doting on her at every turn.

It *definitely* shouldn't send an icy twinge through my chest when her eyes widen with terror at the first sight of my wolfish form—or warm me quite so dizzyingly when that fear flees in the wake of one of her shy but brilliant smiles as she recognizes me.

She isn't mine, I remind myself as I have so often in the past few weeks. She isn't mine, and she won't be. But the way she gazed at me the other night during the revel, so concerned about my happiness of all things—the way she looked when she talked about finding her own happiness in our world—

I shake those thoughts away and shed my fur at the edge of the garden.

As she takes in my expression, Talia's smile falters. "Is everything okay? Did they get angry with you?"

More concerned for me than for herself yet again. I jerk my head toward the arched door of our new abode. "The people I went to speak to were exactly as much pricks as I expected. But I had a less expected conversation we should discuss."

She grabs her basket and heads inside without argument—trusting me. In the open-concept space of the first floor, a couple of our warriors are sprawled asleep on the cushions in the living area, having come from the main camp area to wait on their lord. Talia sets the berries on the short span of kitchen counter, and I motion her up the stairs to the four cramped bedrooms.

Hers is the farthest back from the narrow staircase, I suspect because Sylas wanted any intruder to have to get by all of us before reaching her. No sign of Sylas or August—August mentioned meaning to hunt, and Sylas wanted to speak to a few of the other squadrons, as much as they might tell him.

Talia limps straight to her roughly-hewn bed and stops there, waiting until I've closed the door behind us. We need the privacy, but I'm abruptly aware with a quiver over my skin of how little space lies between us.

"Is it safe to talk now?" the mite asks, canny enough to understand why I'd have brought her away from everyone.

"We set down all the magical protections we could around these rooms," I say. "It'd better be." Then I hesitate, because I don't actually want to tell her what I need to. But I do need to. "I don't think you should be pitching in outside the fortress anymore."

Talia blinks at me. "Why not? If I did something wrong—"

I wave off any question of that. "It's not you. Aerik's squadron has moved nearby. Cole is already sneaking around. I'd imagine he's wondering what brought Sylas and the rest of us out here just now. That bunch are always looking to improve their advantages any way they can. I think it's best if we give them as little opportunity to study you as possible."

She has already tensed up, her back stiffening. "With the glamour—he shouldn't have been able to recognize anything about me, right? He didn't come close enough that I saw him."

"You should be fine for now. We simply don't want to push our luck. Let me check the glamours, just in case."

I can see already that the one across her shoulder, to hide any trace of her scars that might peek past her shirt, is solid as ever. I motion for Talia to sit. She sinks down on the edge of the bed, and I kneel to examine her malformed foot.

Close up, I can squint through the illusion and make out the awkward jut of the bones, the curves of the wooden slats that form her brace. But when I set my fingers against her ankle, the glamour obscures even them. Cole would have to be mere inches away to see through Sylas's magic.

That doesn't mean he couldn't notice something odd about her gait if he watches her walking around outside, though. I hate telling her she should stay confined—but she doesn't want another encounter with that bastard any more than the rest of us do. Less so, presumably.

"Is it okay?" Talia asks, and I realize I'm still crouched there before her, holding her ankle. Stroking my thumb across her skin to tease out its warmth, without even thinking about it.

I drop my hand as gracefully as haste allows and look up at her. Her vivid green eyes pin me in place.

"Yes," I say. "Nothing to worry about."

"For now."

"Exactly." I pause, considering. Her words from the other morning, when she said she didn't want to stay locked away, ring through my memory. "If you didn't venture far from the building, and you kept particular care with how you walked when outside—you shouldn't have to stay completely cooped up in here."

Her bittersweet smile could slay me. "This was the risk I took when I insisted on coming out to the border. I'll manage. The house is still a lot bigger than Aerik's cage. I'll just focus on the cooking and other tasks I can do indoors."

"So stoic, oh mighty one," I can't resist teasing.

As my reward, her smile brightens for a moment. She gives my arm a playful kick. "It isn't easy for you either, is it?"

I raise my eyebrows. "What do you mean?"

"Well, you must have to be even more on your guard all the time out here. The other packs' warriors are all over the place. None of this territory is actually ours. Even if you're always on alert around other people back home, you at least have the space to get away from everyone if you need to."

I'm not sure what makes my heart twinge harder—the fact that she just referred to Oakmeet as "home" as easily as if she's always lived there, or how clearly and matter-of-factly she's extrapolated about my wellbeing from the few admissions I made the other night. Maybe it's neither but the fact that she cares enough about my wellbeing to consider it that far.

I give her calf one last gentle pat through her jeans. "Save your worries for yourself, mite. I have plenty of practice at tolerating discomfort as need be."

She shrugs. "So do I."

Who could deny that?

I don't know how long I'd have stayed there, kneeling at her feet and basking in her attention if Sylas's voice didn't carry from downstairs just then. "You've returned, Whitt?"

I stand, torn between gratitude and regret at the interruption. I might have enjoyed lingering longer, but that doesn't mean it'd have been good for me.

"I'll explain the situation to Sylas," I tell Talia. "And maybe we'll all get lucky and the wretched Unseelie will peck Cole's head off before we have to deal with him again."

CHAPTER NINETEEN

Talia

It doesn't make sense, not really. We just came to the border, and now I'm standing in the field outside the keep with the lights and music of a revel all around me.

The initial burst of doubt slips away with the whirling of the dancing figures surrounding me. I turn, the lanterns seeming to spin above me, and Whitt is there. He takes my hand to spin me around like he did at my first revel, and his eyes hold mine with a heat that washes through me from head to toe. His mouth curves into a sly grin.

He looks fierce and somehow free as I've never seen him, as if there isn't a single thought in his mind except me and what he'd like to do with me. A thrill races after the rush of heat.

I twirl before him as if my feet are steady. The dancers around us fade away. The music keeps playing from some distant source. When I come to a stop facing Whitt again, he's dropped to his knees in front of me like he did when checking my foot this morning.

His fingers glide over my bare skin, skimming my ankle and up my calf, raising the hem of my dress until it reaches my knees. As my pulse thumps, he leans in and kisses the inner side of that knee. Then a little higher, and a little higher, his hands easing the dress farther up with each movement of his lips.

A sharper tingling shoots to the meeting of my thighs with every kiss. He's teasing me and worshipping me at the same time. His fingers slide upward until they're nearly grazing the place now throbbing with need, his mouth rising after them, and I want—I want—

A creak shatters the spell. I snap awake amid the coarser sheets of the bed in my temporary new room, my body flushed and my heart still pounding, though in a much more eager way than past moments when I've jolted out of sleep.

In the darkness, I just barely make out the silhouette of a brawny figure in the doorway, lit by the faintest of glows from the hall. The fall of wavy hair and the gleam of one pale eye reveal him as Sylas, not the man I was dreaming about.

The memory of that dream sends a renewed flush over my skin just as Sylas steps inside. He tips his head questioningly. As I sit up, my eyes adjusting to the dimness, I catch the quirk of the corner of his mouth.

"I heard you gasp and thought you were caught in a nightmare," he says, the rumble of his voice low but warm with amusement. "Now I'm thinking it wasn't a bad dream after all."

How well can his wolfish senses pick up my bodily reactions? I wet my lips, willing away the thrum of arousal still coursing through my veins. "It wasn't. I'm all right. I'm sorry if I disturbed you."

He makes a dismissive sound. "I was turning in for the night. There was nothing to interrupt." His voice dips even lower, with no less amusement. "Although now I'm curious exactly where that dream of yours was taking you."

My drowsy mind slips back to the moments before I woke, to the gleam of Whitt's sun-kissed hair below me and his lips hot against my inner thigh. More heat spikes from low in my belly, but at the same time my stomach twists uncomfortably.

Why would I dream that? Whitt and I *haven't* done anything. Even if I've felt flickers of attraction now and then, I already have not one but two men I've promised my heart to. How can I even *think* of anyone other than them?

How would Sylas react if I told him? My tongue turns leaden, my mouth going dry, remembering the flares of possessive aggression when he first found out about me and August. And that was before I'd made any sort of commitment to him. After what his former mate did to him... The thought of him thinking I've betrayed him, that I lied when I told him I loved him, makes something deep inside me shrivel in dismay.

"Talia." When I glance up at Sylas again, his expression has turned so serious that I can see the concern in it even in the faint light. Whatever he's seen in me—with his good eye or the ghostly scarred one—it brings him to the side of my bed. He perches with surprising deftness on the very edge of the thin mattress so he isn't crowding me and takes my hand where it's clenched on top of the covers.

"You don't have to tell me anything," he says, his voice somber as well as quiet now. "Your dreams are your own. I would never make a demand like that—and if it was a dream of August that stirred your body that way, I wouldn't be angry with you. How I reacted in the past was not a reflection on you, only my own urges to deal with."

His determined reassurances loosen the tension in my stomach. I still balk at revealing exactly what my mind conjured up.

But maybe he *should* know. What if my body gives away some hint of desire at a time when I'm awake, when he can see who's provoked it?

"What if it wasn't August?" I say tentatively.

Sylas lets go of my hand to stroke his fingers over my cheek. "I'm certainly not going to take issue with you dreaming about *me*."

My head ducks at his touch. "What if it wasn't either of you?"

He pauses. "Then I'd remind both myself and you that we don't choose our dreams, and be glad this one brought you pleasure rather than terror."

That's true. How could anyone blame me for something I only dreamed of doing? It isn't as if I want to find myself back in Aerik's cage, but how many times has my mind conjured *that* scene up?

I relax enough to lean toward the fae lord, and he tucks one arm around me, nestling me against him. My initial fear seems absurd now. This man has been nothing but patient with me, despite his natural inclinations. That's part of *why* I love him. So maybe that's why the confession tumbles out in the faintest of whispers. "I dreamed about Whitt."

Sylas lets out a soft chuckle. "Well, I suppose you wouldn't be the first lady to do so. Does it bother you to have imagined him that way?"

I consider that question. Now that Sylas has reacted so calmly, my uneasiness has fled completely. "Only if it bothered you. It's never happened before—nothing like that has happened with him in real life. I wasn't expecting it."

"Sometimes dreams reveal desires we hadn't known we were harboring, just as they can reveal buried fears. There's no shame in it. Especially with him. If I didn't think he was among the best of our kind, he wouldn't be in my cadre." He's silent for a moment, his fingers grazing my shoulder with a light caress. "Do you care for him, then?"

"Not—not like you and August. I don't really know him all that well." My mind drifts back to the waking moments I've shared with Whitt—the way he rushed to keep me safe from Cole this morning, the way he spoke about protecting me during the revel, the bag of salt he gave me that's hidden beneath my pillow right now, just in case.

The warmth of his embrace while he apologized for sending me away, weeks ago. The playful remarks that can startle a smile out of me or banish my anxieties when I need it most. The devotion to his brothers I've seen in every move he makes on their behalf, despite how much he heckles them.

"I like him," I add as I sort through those impressions and the emotions they stir up. "I think I'd like to know him better. And I—there's definitely some attraction there. For me. But it doesn't really matter. I'm already happy having you and August. And it's not as if Whitt would be interested in anything… romantic, or whatever, with me anyway."

"Has he said that?"

I frown. "No, but—he's never said he *would*. He's never acted as if he wants something like that to happen. It always feels like there's at least a little distance he's keeping when we're talking." Like he's holding himself slightly apart from me, even when he's literally holding me. All the times when I've seen something like fondness light in his eyes and then fade away as if he's shuttered them, shutting me out.

Sylas hums to himself. "Whitt is capable in many ways, but close relationships of any sort aren't exactly his forte. I'm not sure there's anyone in his life he'd even call a true friend other than myself and August, and even there, he tends to act as a colleague first. If he's doing more than tolerating someone's presence, that's a high mark of approval in itself."

Having seen Whitt in action, I can believe that. But… "It doesn't make any difference, does it? However he feels, I'm with you and August. I know it was already difficult for both of you to share even that much. I'm not going to pursue anyone else."

"Not even if you had our blessing?"

My gaze jerks up so I can stare at Sylas. "What do you mean?"

His face doesn't show any sign of jealousy. "You know that the precedent for an arrangement like ours comes from cadres sharing a lover. Typically in those cases, the lover in question is involved with all of the members of that cadre, not just so that their needs are being met amid the cadre's responsibilities, but also to avoid tensions rising if one or another isn't so favored. It's a difficult balance—one that's already been on my mind as we navigate this unforeseen territory."

I remember the moment back at the keep when the three of us left Whitt behind, the pang I felt at excluding him. "That does make sense. But this isn't a typical situation, is it?"

"No. Typically Whitt would have more claim to join in than I do." Sylas presses a kiss to the crook of my jaw. "I have no intention of giving you up. But I've made my peace with what we have... and in some ways I'm coming to enjoy knowing how well you're taken care of, even though it can't always be by me. If you wanted to explore whatever you do feel for Whitt, and he's developed some affection for you as well, it might serve us all to see how that plays out."

My pulse flutters as I consider it. "I don't know—How would I even start?"

"Hmm. Maybe leave that to me. Perhaps when we have returned to the keep, an ideal opportunity will arise to put the matter to him. Although if you see an opening before then—you do have my blessing."

The love that's a constant pulse behind my ribs swells to the base of my throat. I twine my fingers in Sylas's hair and pull his mouth to mine. The force of his kiss leaves no doubt that this conversation hasn't cooled his desire for me one bit.

"Thank you," I murmur against his lips.

He smiles. "It's the least the lady of our keep deserves. And now that lady had better get some sleep, before I get too tempted to turn this into the new tryst room."

"You forgot to make one of those," I point out as I lie back down.

He stands, a light laugh spilling out of him. "If we find ourselves here for very long, you can be sure I'll rectify that oversight."

The late-night conversation leaves me settled enough to drift back to sleep, but when I limp downstairs in the morning, the sight of August already puttering around in the kitchen area reawakens a twinge of anxiety.

Sylas has given me his blessing to indulge my tentative feelings for Whitt. August doesn't even know I've considered it. Even though I haven't done anything yet, a sense of betrayal pinches at my gut.

This wonderful fae man loves me. By some miracle, he loves *me*. How can I even suggest that what we have isn't enough?

But then, maybe he'd feel better including Whitt in whatever exactly this strange relationship is rather than leaving him out. If even Sylas could see it that way, it isn't hard to believe August might.

Either way, I can't keep it from him.

This isn't the time to bring up the subject, though. Two of the pack warriors, including the one who came back to Oakmeet injured a couple of weeks ago—Ralyn—are hunkered down in the living area. Ralyn is fletching arrows and his companion sharpening a dagger. From the number of balls of dough August is tossing onto his baking sheet, he's preparing a breakfast for the entire squadron I know is stationed a short distance nearby.

"What can I do to help?" I ask, glancing from him to the warriors. Yesterday, along with cooking, I learned the art of sword sharpening and mended a couple of armored vests. If anyone regrets my coming out to the border, it won't be because I failed to carry my weight in every way possible.

August motions me over. Since we arrived here, he's been wearing more formal clothes like the ones he put on for Aerik's visit, not his usual human-style tees. Today's V-neck tunic is a rich pine-green that brings out both the ruddy tones in his dark auburn hair and the golden gleam of his eyes.

I slip past him into the warmth that wavers through the kitchen area from the stove, which is little more than a clay box around a smoldering fire. No time for the complex magics that went into his kitchen equipment back at the keep.

"Slice up the rest of the cheese," he suggests, motioning to the crumbly orange block on the counter. "It won't last much longer."

"You're going to make us all homesick for the foods we can't usually get here," Ralyn remarks. "The cheese they make in this domain isn't any match for Elliot's. All they've got is goats."

"I'll be sure to tell Elliot how much you miss him and his sheep," August replies with a grin.

By the time I've chopped all of the block of cheese into fairly equal portions, August has fried a few panfuls of thinly sliced meat that gives off an appealingly buttery scent and is starting on another. Together, we assemble a couple of large baskets with cheese, apples from the bushel someone picked yesterday, fresh-baked rolls, and most of the fried meat. As the warriors heft the baskets and see us off with a wave, August lays out the rest of the meal on plates for the four of us living here.

Neither Sylas nor Whitt have made an appearance downstairs yet. I nibble on a stray chunk of cheese and debate whether I should try talking to August now. It's not as if there's any rush while we're here in a battle zone… but the subject is going to nag at me as long as I'm keeping it secret.

I open my mouth—and chicken out. "So far, there haven't been any signs of another attack coming, have there?" I ask instead.

"None at all. The ravens are lying low for the time being. Most of the activity around here has been building up our usual magical defenses to scare them off if they try to attack during the full moon. So far we've been able to stop them from realizing how vulnerable our forces are then."

I glance down at my arm. My blood could mean none of the warriors here need to succumb to the wildness… but giving it to them would automatically expose me to Aerik. Even without knowing where I am, he's stopping me from having full freedom.

"Will our squadron be okay when we head back to Oakmeet?" I ask.

"They have been for many moons before. We always make it look as if the border is particularly heavily guarded then, with glamours and the rest. Although with the spats the arch-lords' cadre-chosen keep having about where the squadrons should be directing their energies, it's lucky we're getting that much done." August lets out an exasperated huff.

I grimace in sympathy. "I wish they'd tell you what they think is going to happen."

"So do I. But we're here, so eventually we should see for ourselves. I'm staying ready for just about anything." He slings his arm around me and tugs me closer to give me a peck on my head. "Are you worrying about that, Sweetness? You look like something's on your mind."

I guess I don't have much of a poker face. I swipe at my mouth and decide I might as well just spit it out.

"It's—it's not about the war or anything like that."

"That's fine. I could use a break from patrols and battle plans."

I draw up the courage to push onward, measuring out my words. "You've been okay with me also being with Sylas. What if— what if it was Whitt too?"

August's arm tenses against my shoulders, and my pulse stutters. "Nothing's happened," I blurt out quickly. "I don't even know if he'd want it to. Nothing *will* happen if you aren't okay with it. I'm happy with the way things are. I just—I wondered—and Sylas said it might even be better if we weren't leaving him out—*if* he'd even want to—"

August cuts off my babbling by pulling me right into a hug. "It's all right. It's a reasonable question." He gives a short bark of a laugh. "If *Sylas* is already on board, who am I to argue?"

I peek up at him. "I don't want you to go along with it just because I mentioned it." My arms slip around his broad chest, hugging him back. "I love you. I wouldn't do anything I knew would hurt you."

"You're the last person I'd ever be afraid of coming to harm from, Talia," August says gently. He tips my face up so he can kiss me, long and tender, until I'm tingling all the way to my toes. Then he stays there with his head bent close to mine, his nose grazing my forehead. "And because *I* love *you*, I want you to have all the happiness you can. I'm guessing you wouldn't be asking if you didn't think getting closer with Whitt would make you even happier."

"If he even would want to," I say again.

August makes a dismissive sound. "I don't think that's much of a question. It has felt a little odd the past few weeks, having something so separate from our connection through the cadre." He runs his hand over my hair. "And this way we can hope that at any given time, there'd always be someone there for you, no matter what we face."

I hug him tighter, and he matches my embrace. When I ease back, he's smiling so easily that the nervous pinch in my stomach melts away. "You're sure it doesn't bother you?"

"I promise it's fine. No more worrying. Now sit and let's get some breakfast into you."

Despite his order, I insist on grabbing a couple of plates and carrying them over to the small wooden table between the kitchen and the living area, then coming back for the goblets to go with the sparkling juice August brought from home. As I duck back into the kitchen on one final trip to scoop up a few apples, the stairs creak.

Sylas emerges from upstairs, running his fingers through his dark hair before rubbing his hands together in anticipation of the meal. "Even with as little as you have to work with out here, you manage to impress, August. If the Unseelie knew you're as good with a sword as you are with a carving knife, they'd never cross that border again."

August beams at the praise. "I could skewer plenty of ravens with a carving knife too. We have to make the best of what we've got here, don't we?" He veers toward the kitchen. "Here, I have one more portion of—"

The front door bangs open. Without a word, several armed fae march into the house, weapons drawn.

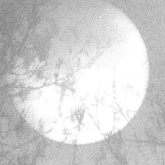

CHAPTER TWENTY

Talia

At the intruders' entrance, Sylas stiffens and strides toward them. August steps forward too, placing himself closer to his lord—and between me and the unfamiliar fae with their armor and weaponry.

Are these Unseelie? I tense up, but my men aren't acting as if they see these warriors as an immediate threat. And as I peer past August, standing rigid with an armful of apples braced against my chest, I realize the fae who've barged into our house aren't all strangers to me. The five of them standing most closely together I've never seen before, but off to the side, in a bronze vest a little more dinged up than what most of the others are wearing, stands Cole, the icy-sharp spikes of his hair unmistakable. He elbows the woman next to him, who appears to be a colleague of his rather than of the others.

My heart lurches. I curl my fingers around one of the apples as if I can use it as some kind of weapon of my own. Somehow I don't think throwing it at these fae would accomplish anything other than making them very pissed off at me. Maybe I should reach for the little dagger in its sheath at my left hip or the bag of salt I've been tying to a belt-loop at my right, but I suspect a show of overt aggression from a human wouldn't improve their moods either.

I set the apples down on the counter just in case I need to anyway.

"What's the meaning of this?" Sylas demands, planting himself in front of the fae man at the front of the main bunch. "I'd have thought Ambrose's pack was civilized enough to understand the concept of knocking."

Ambrose's pack? Ambrose is one of the arch-lords—the one who blames Sylas for how his former mate and her family attempted some kind of rebellion.

Why have the warriors of his squadron come in here so forcefully? You'd think *we* were the Unseelie they're meant to be fighting, the way they're posturing.

"If you have nothing to hide, you shouldn't mind us paying you a visit, Lord Sylas," the leader says with only the slightest tip of his head in recognition of Sylas's title. His gaze roves through the airy room.

Sylas folds his arms over his chest. "And why would we have come all the way out here in order to hide something?"

"Why have you come all the way out here at all is the real question. We thought we'd best make a real stab at answering it."

"I believe one of my cadre-chosen spoke with one of your lord's yesterday about that very matter. We haven't made any secret of our intentions."

The other man takes a step to the side to get a better view of the living area. "Forgive us for not being willing to take you entirely at your word. We serve only Ambrose, and we'll ensure no treachery comes from our side of the border."

Do they really think Sylas would have traveled to the border to carry out some scheme against the arch-lords? The idea seems ridiculous to me, but the solemn expressions on all of the warriors' faces suggest they find it totally plausible, the jerks. I have the urge to pelt them with the apples after all.

Cole, of course, is simply smirking, like this is all great entertainment. Sylas shifts his weight, the muscles in his arms flexing, obviously wanting to chuck the lot of them out of the building but wary of the repercussions. These aren't lords, but they're an arch-lord's pack-kin. My stomach knots, watching.

"If there is anything else you want to know, you need simply have asked," Sylas says tautly. "But I'm sure you can see there's nothing startling within these walls. I've only ever wanted what's best for all Seelie kind, as plenty of our brethren can attest to."

"Hmm. And yet *one* of your cadre-chosen isn't among you. What could Kellan be up to?"

"You wouldn't expect me to leave my domain completely undefended, would you?" Sylas asks, as if it's Kellan back there doing the defending, not a handful of sentries.

The leader of Ambrose's squadron—or whatever part of his squadron this is, since I'm sure the arch-lord has more than five warriors at the border—makes a skeptical sound, but he doesn't push that line of questioning any further. He marches through the living area and parks himself behind one of the chairs at the dining table, his narrowed gaze sweeping into the kitchen. When it comes to an abrupt halt on me, my stance stiffens twice as much.

The fae man's nostrils flare. His eyes flash, a sheen of magic taking them from a deep indigo to crystalline sapphire in an instant. "You've brought a *human* with you. What could have possessed you to haul a wretched dung-body all this way? Are your pack-kin so inept you don't trust them to wait on you?"

Sylas's lips curl back over his teeth, his sharp canines glinting where they've protruded just a fraction into fangs. "She isn't a servant. She's my cadre-chosen's companion."

The squadron leader glances at August, whose shoulders twitch, the muscles coiled all through his body. I can tell it's taking all his self-control to hold himself in place.

The other man's eyes flick back to Sylas. "You brought a dust-destined *whore* then. Somehow I question whether you truly are taking this fight as seriously as you claim."

August starts forward with a growl low in his throat, but he only makes it one step before the jerk of Sylas's hand stops him. Sylas's mismatched gaze stays fixed on the squadron leader. Somehow he manages to draw his already substantial frame even taller. He's got to have at least fifty pounds of brawn on the other man.

There are five of them—seven if we count Cole and his lackey—and only three fae in this house on our side, one of whom is upstairs still sleeping. And how quickly will they call Sylas a traitor if he lays so much as a hand on them?

"If we didn't take it seriously, we wouldn't be here," he says, a growl laced through his own steady voice. "You've had a good look. *I've* had enough of your insults and insinuations. Let me show you out."

"You're not in your own domain, you forget, Lord Sylas," the squadron leader replies. He ambles around the table toward the kitchen. "And technically all domains fall under our arch-lords' rule. I say this runt is an unnecessary distraction. How much can one frail human girl be worth? Consider how easily she could be removed."

A chill washes over my skin. The threat is barely implicit—he's talking about how easily he could kill me. My hand drops to the pouch of salt, fingers looping through the string so I can jerk it open in an instant. He's only pointing out my fragility, but that doesn't mean he won't decide to act on the threat.

"You keep your paws off her," August snaps.

Sylas moves to form a barricade with him. "We're well aware of the mortal nature of humans. I'm sure you wouldn't make an unnecessary demonstration that destroys a being under my care."

The squadron leader lets out a cold laugh. "If I wanted to, would you challenge the authority of—"

He's cut off by a cheerily melodic voice that carries from the stairs with the thumping of careless feet. "Why, look at this! A whole horde of guests. My lord, you should have told me we'd have company."

Whitt saunters into the room with a feral grin and a wild glint in his eyes. My pulse hiccups at the thought of how one of his insults might take this from a standoff into a full-out brawl. But Sylas's spymaster takes in the crowded room and the plates on the table with a chuckle, as if we're all in on some joke together.

"Heard about my cadre-fellow's excellent cooking, did you, lads?" he says, clapping August on the back. "It looks like we don't have quite enough for you. Next time you'll have to make an advance order."

The squadron leader blinks at him, completely diverted from his previous goal, whatever exactly that was. With his eyes off me, I shrink back against the counter, my hand lingering on the pouch of salt.

"What are you talking about?" the intruder asks.

Whitt tsks at him. "I suppose if you're so desperate for breakfast, we might make an exception. But it would come at a price. We wouldn't ask you to sing for your supper, but perhaps a little dance would allow you to dine."

The squadron leader simply stares, all of his followers wearing matching expressions of confusion. Cole's mouth has twisted at a sour angle, apparently disappointed that the potential for violence has faded.

Whitt sighs in mild exasperation. "I'm sure you must know how to dance, with all the balls the arch-lords host. Just give it a little whirl, and we'll see what we can do to fill your bellies." As if he thinks they need an illustration, he makes a few graceful steps to some internal rhythm, with a flourish of his arm and a spin to finish.

As he turns, his gaze catches mine, and he shoots me a swift wink. Despite the fear churning inside me, a giggle tickles up my throat. All these fearsome warriors with their blades and their posturing, and he's disarmed them with a few wry remarks.

Whitt looks at the squadron leader expectantly, his eyes gleaming with restrained amusement, utterly in his element. I can't tear my gaze away from him. A different sensation is fizzing through my chest now, one as heady as faerie wine.

That dream last night didn't come out of nowhere. I'm falling for him too. I don't know how long I have been or how far I'll fall, but I recognize this feeling.

How could anyone *not* find themselves overwhelmed with affection, watching him turn this hostile situation around so brilliantly?

The woman with Cole lets out a rough laugh, and that sound shatters whatever remains of the tension. The squadron leader shakes his head, looking a touch embarrassed but not aggressive anymore.

"Have your breakfast," he says, waving his hand toward the table. "We've got plenty of our own. Just make sure your attention is on defending our people, not the dung-body, when the next attack comes."

His ego apparently satisfied, he turns on his heel and stalks out, the other warriors hustling after him. Cole slinks out behind them with one more disdainful glance our way.

As soon as the door has closed behind them, Sylas gives Whitt a baleful look, but his lips have twitched into a smile. "You do choose your moments, don't you?"

"It seemed like the right time to make an entrance," Whitt says breezily, so unconcerned that most of the anxiety melts out of me.

He drops into his chair at the table. "I just hope those pissants haven't soured the food."

"I'm sure it's still edible," August replies, his shoulders coming down. He gives himself a little shake as if shedding the defensive energy the intruders provoked and gives me a onceover to confirm I'm okay. When I manage a smile, he returns it and holds out his hands for the apples I'd gathered. I offer them up, gratified to see my arms don't even tremble.

Ambrose's warriors were only throwing their weight around, but I'm awfully glad it didn't have to come to a fight after all, with whatever fallout would have resulted.

Sylas touches my arm, studying me for a longer span than August did. He's relaxed some too, but his face is grim. "I'm sorry. I hadn't thought—clearly I overestimated how well we could shelter you from that kind of aggression here. I don't believe he intended to truly harm you, but you shouldn't have had to hear any of that."

"It's okay," I say. "I mean—it's not okay that they came and talked like that, but I know it's not your fault." I hesitate. "Do you think they'll keep badgering us?"

"I wouldn't expect so now that they've had their look around and come up with no reason to accuse us of anything, but we can't be sure. I'll create an enchantment you can use to signal me if you need help while I'm away—I should have done that to begin with."

I exhale slowly. "Thank you. I'd appreciate that." My gaze slides past him to where Whitt is tossing the apple August passed him in the air with a flick of his wrist, and my smile comes back. "At least this time it ended without any disasters."

"It did." Sylas follows my glance, and his expression lightens just a little. His voice drops. "Perhaps I could see about giving you something that might make your day more pleasant sooner than we discussed... if you'd like?"

A current of warmth ripples over my skin, merging with the pang that echoes through my chest. There's nothing I want more right now than to feel secure in the embrace of my protectors—all three of them, if the third will have me too. Especially when that third is the one who did the most to protect me just now, if not in a traditional way.

My answer slips out in barely a whisper. "I would."

Sylas considers the scene for a moment and then ushers me over to the table by August's chair. "I think our lady might enjoy some special attention after that unsettling encounter," he says to the younger man, lightly and steadily. "Remind her how devoted we are to her wellbeing… among other things."

August looks at both of us, his gaze uncertain and then sparking with interest. He glances across the table at Whitt, who's paused with his fork in midair, and then back at me. At my nod, he eases his chair back and opens his arms to welcome me onto his lap.

I sink onto his thighs, instinctively tucking myself against his chest and soaking up his warmth. My heart thumps faster, but this time with eager anticipation rather than nerves.

Yes, I did need this. To wipe away the awful things the other fae said. To ground myself in August's love.

And to discover whether the man on the other side of the table takes any interest in me like this at all.

"What would you like, Sweetness?" August murmurs into my hair.

I tip my head against his shoulder, offering him my neck. With a pleased hum, he lowers his mouth to kiss me there. Heat floods my skin with the press of his lips and the stroke of his fingers across my torso, just below my breasts.

Right now, I want that heat everywhere. I want to burn so fiercely I can believe I'd sear right through any enemies who ever threaten me again.

Chair legs rasp against the floor, and my eyelids flutter open. Whitt stands up, holding his plate. His voice comes out as flippant as always but with a note of strain. "Well, *I'm* clearly not needed here. I suppose I'll dine upstairs."

My chest hitches at the thought that I've made him feel even more an outsider from his family than before, but Sylas must have observed more than I can. He rests his hand on the table and tilts his head toward August and me. "Or you could take part. That's what you'd like to do, isn't it?"

Whitt goes completely still, looking as taken aback as the squadron leader did faced with his antics not that long ago. His jaw tightens. "I'm perfectly capable of controlling my—"

"But we're not asking you to rein in your desires," Sylas interrupts in the same measured tone. "It was never our intention to exclude you. We simply didn't realize—but I should have been more aware, and I apologize for that. I think August and I have already shown we're capable of sharing."

Whitt looks at me then, for the first time since he got up. There's a wildness in his eyes again, but much stormier than his earlier playfulness. It's desire, yes, but anger and confusion too, and a starker yearning that shines through all the rest, so raw it makes my heart ache.

"Shouldn't Talia be the one who makes that decision?" he says tartly, but his voice has thickened. I don't know where the anger and confusion are coming from or who they're aimed at, but in that moment, I can feel that yearning for me all the way down to my bones.

Even as a flush creeps over my cheeks, I hold his gaze. My words come out soft but clear. "I have."

Whitt doesn't look relieved by the admission. If anything, his stance goes more rigid, the muscles of his face twitching in shock.

Sylas teases his fingers over my hair with a fond smile. "Talia's been the one calling the shots in this arrangement from the start. If cadres of four or five can form a balanced relationship around one lover, I'm sure we'll—"

Whitt smacks his plate down on the table with a clatter of the silverware. "Did you ever think that maybe *I* wouldn't want to share with *you*?" he snaps, and spins on his heel. He stalks across the room and out of the front door so quickly and resolutely it leaves no doubt that he means to be gone for quite a while.

I stare after him, my throat constricting. How did this go so wrong?

Sylas frowns, but he gives my shoulder a gentle squeeze. "I don't know what's gotten into him, but given space, he'll sort himself out. At least now you have your answer about his interest, whether he decides he's going to act on it or not."

I do. Whitt wants me, with a greater force of feeling than I'd ever have guessed. Only he doesn't seem at all happy about that fact.

I thought reaching out to him would be a chance to bring the three men who've watched over me back into harmony, but what if I've wrenched them apart instead?

CHAPTER TWENTY-ONE

Talia

"*Fee-doom-ace-own*," I murmur, channeling all the protective energy that rises in me at the thought of Sylas or August meeting a bunch of attackers' blades. As I center all my concentration on it, the bronze chink in the battered chainmail vest closes in a loop to connect it to the one above.

For once, I'm using my smidgeon of magical power to defend someone other than myself. Better that I use my copious amounts of spare time to mend armor damaged in past battles than any of the actual fae waste their own when they have so many other responsibilities outside this house.

A rustle carries through the open window next to me. I pause where I'm perched on one of the living room cushions, a slightly lumpy construction that seems to be made out of overgrown leaves melded together and stuffed with I'm not sure what. When I'm alone in the house, I can't help freezing at every sound from outside.

Three days after we arrived, the Unseelie still haven't launched an attack, but that only means that with each passing hour it feels more imminent. I can't even see the border from here other than a vague shimmering haze August pointed out to me far in the distance, but even if *I'm* safe here, Sylas and his cadre won't be.

For a few seconds, all I hear is the whisper of the breeze passing through the tall grass, its crisp, hay-like scent drifting in to me. I've just resumed my work when more rustling reaches my ears. It solidifies into the more definite sound of footsteps.

The steps could simply be someone from Oakmeet returning or dropping in. Of course, if it's anyone other than Sylas or August, I won't feel that much more at ease. I've exchanged a little conversation with the warriors stationed here, but they don't linger for very long unless it's to sleep. They're still essentially strangers to me. I definitely can't continue this work in front of them. And Whitt...

Whitt hasn't said more than the briefest of polite greetings to me since that awkward breakfast yesterday morning. He's barely been around to. Somehow he's always coming or going when we end up in the common areas together, and most of the time he manages to avoid that altogether.

He hasn't been cold or cruel about it, but every time I sit down to a meal without him or watch his retreating back vanish through a doorway, my stomach knots tighter.

Maybe he really is busy—but he wasn't quite that busy before we pushed him to admit he felt some attraction toward me. For whatever reason, Sylas's suggestion about joining our arrangement upset him, even with my clear approval. I don't know how to mend the bridge between us, especially while so many other tensions are running high by the border.

I have to figure out something. Even if he doesn't want anything more with me than we already have, I miss his smirks and his wry remarks and the cheerful gleam in his fathomless eyes.

I set my hands in my lap, my ears pricked to the sounds from outside. The rustling footsteps become louder, moving toward and then past the window—away from the front door rather than toward it. Just someone passing by?

Then a voice that sends a spear of ice down my spine breaks the quiet. "I told you they were all occupied elsewhere."

It's Cole—I'd know that sharply sneering tone anywhere.

The voice that answers I don't recognize at all, but it might be the woman I saw with him the other morning. "What are we trying to accomplish here?"

A third voice, gruff and male but equally unfamiliar, speaks up. "The mutts of the Oakmeet pack are a bunch of treacherous bastards. Now Sylas comes out here and acts like he's better than every other lord because he turned up personally? He deserves to be put in his place."

Cole chuckles. "Exactly. I'm glad *someone* understands. Now are we going to get on with this, or are you disobeying orders from cadre?"

"No, no, I'm on board," the woman mutters.

I don't like the sound of their conversation at all. Skin prickling, I set down the vest as quietly as I can and ease toward the kitchen. After the intrusion yesterday, Sylas shaped a little wooden bird for me and showed me how to work the markings he etched in it to activate its magic. It's sitting on the counter.

No other sound except the occasional murmuring travels through the window as I cross the room. Reaching the sculpted bird, I hesitate.

Sylas looked so somber when he left after our hasty lunch a couple of hours ago. He said he was going to demand an audience with the arch-lords' cadres and make whatever case he could appealing to them directly. There was some specific strategy he planned to propose. That meeting might already be over, but if it isn't—if I interrupt him at a moment that could make a difference in them finally accepting his offer of help…

A harsh snicker filters through the wall. My pulse stutters. I hold still and silent. Cole's command is just loud enough to carry to me. "Shatter it all, every bit of it."

If he breaks something important to our cause, that could be worse than any interruption. I balk for a second longer, wishing I could drive away the monsters outside myself, but my little dagger and my salt will only get me so far against three fae. From what I understand, the salt's toxic effect will only ward off the fae for a minute or two, and I have no idea when any of the pack-kin will return. These weapons are meant as a last line of defense, not for me to start a fight.

Steeling myself, I grasp the sculpted bird and run my thumb over its belly. Sylas's instructions run through my mind. Trace the deepest groove here, press the bump there, swipe back and forth over the shallower line in between—

The sculpture's wooden wings flutter against my hands. I pull back my fingers, and the enchanted bird flits away, veering out the nearest window.

Sylas said its magic should send it straight to him. The moment he sees it, he'll know there's trouble here, that he needs to come back. Now I just have to hope he's close enough to make it back before Cole carries out whatever damage he's attempting to cause.

Listening carefully, I dart back to the living room. The hushed voices outside are intoning words I don't recognize. True names? Some other sort of magic? My skin crawls all over again.

I reach to the pouch of salt and loosen the opening, just in case. With careful steps, I slip up the stairs to the second floor and go to my bedroom window. I can peek outside from there without worrying that Cole will spot me right away.

I can't see him from this angle anyway, but the woman from before wanders into view, her eyes fixed on the house and her hands weaving through the air in time with her indecipherable mumbling. When her gaze flicks upward, I jerk to the side with a lurch of my pulse. She doesn't give any indication that she saw me.

Maybe they wouldn't care even if they knew I was inside. Cole must have been monitoring Sylas and his cadre and maybe the rest of the warriors, so he'd have to at least suspect August's human companion is still in the building. Given the way he treated me even when he thought I was valuable and his amusement at the thought of Ambrose's squadron leader "removing" me, I don't think he's sparing much thought to how his plans will affect me. In his mind, hurting me—possibly killing me—might even be a bonus.

I still have no idea what exactly the three of them are up to. I lurk upstairs for a few minutes longer, watching in quick peeks and straining my ears, but the tight space of the small room starts to niggle at me. At least downstairs I have more room to maneuver if they decide to break in.

I hurry down the narrow hall. Just as I'm reaching the top of the stairs, a shudder runs through the floor beneath my feet.

"Almost," Cole says in a tone so triumphant it chills me straight through. "Let's get those final protections down…"

A quavering rush of magical energy flows around me in a wave. My nerves scatter. As I clutch the banister, the entire house shudders again.

Fighting the impression that I'm about to be tossed from the stairs, I scramble down them before the house shakes so hard that I actually will be. The tremors rippling through it grow with every lurching step. I stumble at the bottom, one of the slats of my foot brace catching on a rough spot in the floor and throwing me forward. As I hit the floor with a painful smack of my palms and knees, the walls fracture around me.

I spin around so I'm sitting with my hands steadying me from behind. In every direction, the wooden growths Sylas and his cadre summoned into the house are cracking and crumbling. I jerk my arms up over my head an instant before the floor above crashes on me in a shower of splinters. As the bits rain down, both those shards and the floor beneath me disintegrate into dusty mulch.

When I dare to lower my hands, crumbs of destroyed wood tumble off my arms and trickle through my hair. I'm crouched in the midst of a total ruin. Nothing remains of the house except scattered heaps of that pale mulch, sprinkled with scraps of leaves, wisps of seed fluff that must have filled the pillows and mattresses, and lumps of metal and stone.

My stomach heaves in horror. After all the magic my men put into constructing this house and its contents, Cole and his lackeys smashed it to pieces in a matter of minutes. I'm lucky they didn't smash through me too.

Of course, I'm not safe from that yet. Cole steps forward from where he was standing at the edge of the destruction, the sunlight glancing off his blue-white hair and his teeth bared in a vicious grin. "Look what we have here. Just think of all the fun we can have with you now."

The sight of his cruel face and the familiar menacing pose right in front of me are enough to make my chest clench up. My ribs seem to close around my lungs, squeezing away my breath while my heart hammers against them in vain. As I gasp for air, my head spins.

No. *No.* I can't let the panic take over, can't let myself become helpless the way I was before. I'm not in a cage. I have ways of fighting back.

How *dare* he think he's going to torment another girl the way he did with me.

The flare of anger steadies me. I draw in enough oxygen to clear my head, one hand dropping back to the ground for balance and the other leaping to my pouch of salt.

My pulse is pounding so hard my body shakes with it, but I've practiced with August enough to move into a low fighting stance without needing to think. My fingers close around a handful of salt crystals. I shift my weight forward.

All I have to do is fend him off for long enough for Sylas to get here. I can't focus on anything but making it to that moment.

Cole strolls closer, his lackeys hanging back to watch. His fitted boots crunch through the dry shreds of wood. His gaze skims over me. "Look at you. Just what do you think you're going to—"

He comes to a halt with a jerk, staring at the ground. No, staring at my *feet*—at the foot I've just slid forward in my defensive pose.

The foot he broke nearly nine years ago, now encased in Sylas's brace.

Oh, God. He can see it. He can see *me*.

Panic hits me in a frigid blast. Whatever spells Cole and his pack-kin cast to crumble the magic that built this house, they crumbled the glamours on me too.

Cole's attention snaps back to my face. To my eyes, which must now be the same color they always were, my features more fleshed out but otherwise a match for his former prisoner. What little color was left in his face drains away. Then his eyes spark with a light that's twice as brutal as before.

"Oh," he growls, "Lord Sylas is in so much more trouble than I even thought."

The last word has barely left his mouth when he springs at me. A yelp breaks from my throat, but my horror hasn't knocked those weeks of training from my mind. My hand yanks back automatically and flings toward Cole, hurling all the salt I could hold straight into his face.

As they strike his skin, the crystals burst apart. With a pained snarl, Cole reels backward, swiping at his eyes, his mouth.

My flicker of triumph snuffs out as quickly as it appeared. His lackeys who were standing by bewildered a moment ago leap to their boss's aid.

"I'm fine," Cole barks, jabbing a finger toward me. "Get the wretched girl."

I shove my hand into the pouch, every muscle tensing. Panicked dizziness sweeps through me again. The crystals pinch my skin. I can only throw at one of my attackers at once. Who do I have a better chance against: the man or the woman? They both look ready to tear my throat out.

I ready myself, fighting the trembling of my body, and a roar echoes across the fields. Three massive wolves race into view—wolves I know so well a sob of relief jolts out of me.

The one in the lead with the white scarred eye slams into the fae man who's just about to lunge at me. From right behind him, the ruddy-furred one springs at the woman, knocking the sword she's drawn from her hand and sinking his fangs into her forearm. And the sandy-colored one whose ocean-blue gaze stands out starkly in his wolfish face charges straight at Cole.

The lackeys are no match for a lord and his cadre. The man starts to shift, and Sylas clamps his jaws around his neck, halting him. The woman doesn't even try, glowering up at August with lips pressed tight against the pain of her gouged arm.

Cole might be stronger, but he's still distracted by my salt attack. Before he can do much more than swing a couple of fists at Whitt, the wolf has him pinned, claws poised against the underside of his chin.

"I yield," the male lackey cries out.

Sylas shifts into his usual form, gripping the man's throat with his hand instead. "You will leave here and do us and the human woman no more harm."

"Agreed!"

As Sylas frees him, the woman makes a similar promise to August. The two lackeys scramble to the sidelines, the woman clutching her arm to her side. Whitt stays in wolf form, glaring down at Cole, who has recovered from the salt enough to glower back at him.

Sylas strides over to them. "Are you going to yield, Aerik's cadre-chosen, or shall I bury you in the ruin you made of my camp?"

Somehow, even on the brink of death, Cole finds it in him to sneer at the fae lord. "I invoke the right to seek justice served."

Sylas hesitates. Even Whitt's muscles tense up where he's restraining Cole against the ground. The fae lord's head jerks around, his mismatched gaze finding me—hunched, shivering, and glamourless.

August growls out a curse.

"You've stolen my lord's property, Lord Sylas," Cole says with a vicious grin, looking far too satisfied for a man with a wolf's claws only a smidge from dealing a fatal wound. "Such a crime cannot go unaddressed."

Sylas's lips curl back from his teeth, his fangs out, but he slices his hand through the air in a gesture to Whitt. The wolf recoils, launching himself off Cole but staying in animal form, his snarl daring Cole to give him an excuse to lash out again.

The gangly fae picks himself off the ground and makes a show of brushing off his tunic and slacks. He backs up a few steps to where his lackeys are standing, but his head stays high.

"Lord Sylas of Oakmeet, you have twenty-four hours to make right how you've wronged Lord Aerik of Copperweld," he announces with a ring of power in the words. Then he lowers his voice. "I'll tell my lord he can expect his property returned to him by this time tomorrow, or the whole Seelie realm will know that you're just as much a criminal as your departed mate."

The threat wrenches at me. I wish desperately for Sylas to tell him off, to tear him down after all, but I can already tell my saviors are bound by some tenet of fae law.

My fingers dig into the crumbling wood. Everything they'd

spent so long working for could be ruined. Their chances of ever returning to Hearthshire, their standing with the other lords— shattered as completely as this wrecked house. All because of me.

"Let us not see you or your pack-kin before then," Sylas says. As Cole motions to his lackeys to shift and they lope off toward the river, all he and his cadre can do is stand there.

CHAPTER TWENTY-TWO

Sylas

The carriage hitches with a gust of the breeze, swaying beneath our feet. Normally I'd have constructed a steadier vehicle, but in my haste and fury, I may not have given this conjuring the focus it deserved.

It doesn't help that I've urged it to the fastest pace I feel is safe. The landscape of clustered trees and rough knobs of beige stone seems to whip past us beneath the glare of the mid-day sun. At least moving this swiftly, we should make it back to Oakmeet within a few hours.

I'd hoped to spend most of those hours determining our plan of action, but I think we all needed time to settle ourselves in the aftermath of Cole's threat and our leaving. My memory of the events after he dashed off blur together—checking over Talia for injuries, fragmented discussions with my cadre about what to do, my hurried cajoling of the juniper tree into our enchanted ride while Whitt sped off to inform our squadron of our unexpected departure.

My older brother has stationed himself at the prow where it juts out from beneath the arched beams shading most of the carriage. The jostling of the ride must be getting to him, because in the full sunlight his face looks slightly green, his knuckles pale where he's gripping the low wall beside him. He peers out at the passing landscape intently, as if searching for an antidote to a churning stomach.

I can't help noting that he picked that position after Talia tucked herself into the small, padded seat at the stern, where a few sunbeams streak across her vibrant hair. As far away from her as he can get. He didn't hesitate to spring to her defense when it mattered, so I can't chide him for failing her. All my observation leaves me with is a dull ache in my own stomach at the sense that I've stepped wrong with him in a way I don't fully comprehend.

He cares for the woman—I know him well enough to pick out the indications, the remarks and gestures that wouldn't mean a great deal from someone as open as August but from my spymaster are tantamount to doting. His desire for her was clear on his face when he watched her in August's arms. He's never been particularly finicky about monogamy in the past—certainly he's never offered it of himself to any woman I'm aware of, let alone required it from his lovers—but it isn't as if I've demanded a full accounting of his personal affairs.

I've missed something, something that seems to have outright wounded him. It might simply be a misunderstanding, phrasing I used that gave the wrong impression of my meaning, but I can't clarify that without broaching the subject again, and I can tell he wouldn't let me get very far if I tried.

I may be his lord, but I'm not going to command him to share his personal concerns with me. There will be a time; I will make it right.

But first I have to rearrange this much more urgent catastrophe into a shape that's at least vaguely acceptable.

The carriage shudders again, and I decide I'm best off sitting rather than standing. I sink onto the bench along the left side, across from the matching seat August took after Talia asked for space while she gathered herself. My younger brother is leaning forward with his elbows braced on his thighs and his hands fisted together in front of his chin, his golden eyes darkened to a muddy hue. I'm not sure I've ever seen him so troubled, even when he challenged me on Talia's behalf weeks ago.

I tip my head to him. "I don't suppose all that deep thinking has produced any brilliant stratagems?"

August shakes himself and straightens up with a grimace. "I've been wracking my brain for a way I could have prevented us from getting into this situation at all—but that's a waste of time when there's no way to undo it now."

Talia eases her legs down from her huddled pose and glances from me to August and back. Her shoulders remain rigid, as if braced for the worst. "What will happen if you don't give me back to Aerik in twenty-four hours?"

I drag the crisply warm air into my lungs. "Cole couldn't speak for his lord with full authority, but his terms were standard for a claim for justice. I'd expect if we resist they'll either attack our pack at Oakmeet or turn the matter over to the arch-lords." Neither of which would have an outcome in our favor.

"Whichever Aerik thinks will undermine *his* position the least," Whitt says from the front of the carriage, still staring out over the passing landscape. "Cole could have said they'd be taking the matter to the arch-lords immediately. That would have been the simplest solution with their cadre-chosen already stationed right there. But I don't think Aerik and his cadre want to bring the arch-lords into it if they can help it."

Watching him, Talia hesitates for a second before venturing, "Why wouldn't they? The arch-lords could force Sylas to hand me over, couldn't they?"

Whitt shrugs. "Aerik knows that as soon as it becomes clear that the source of his cure is so easily moved around, the arch-lords are likely to insist on taking over the process of making it. He'd lose his bargaining chip and the glory that came with it." He allows himself to glance toward Talia for the first time since we climbed onto the carriage. "But he'd rather the arch-lords end up with you than see us keep you—you can be sure of that."

I wish I could argue against any point he's made, but I agree with his assessment entirely. "It does buy us a short amount of time to come up with a solution."

Whitt's gaze returns to me, alert despite his apparent queasiness. "Do you think the arch-lords' cadre-chosen will be suspicious of our abrupt departure so soon after you spoke to them?"

I grimace. "More likely they'll see it as running off with our tails between our legs, considering they tossed my proposal aside so easily."

Not that I could blame them for their reasoning, which was sound enough. I offered to send a small foray of two or three warriors into the Unseelie realm to pounce on however many ravens it took to uncover more information about their plans. They rightly pointed out that if they approved such a foray and the Unseelie discovered it, the ravens would use that violation to justify further attacks. The arch-lords prefer to keep the high ground of merely defending what's already ours.

But they dismissed the offer so brusquely—showed so little appreciation for the fact that I'd made it—it rankles me that I lowered myself to appealing to them when at least two of them extended no respect at all to me in turn.

"I don't think it should affect how we approach the situation with Aerik," I add.

Talia looks down at her hands, clasped on her lap. "What *can* you do? They know who I am now and that I'm with you. They're going to keep trying one thing or another until they've gotten me back or at least ripped me away from you, aren't they?"

My hands ball at the hopelessness in her voice. If I could wallop Aerik out of existence and all our problems with him, I'd do it in an instant, just to bring the light back into her.

"The only way we could get them to back down is if we forced a yield," August says into our momentary, dire silence. "From everything we know, it doesn't seem Aerik has told anyone other than his cadre about Talia. Too much chance of word getting back to the arch-lords, probably. So if we could get the three of them in a position where their lives hang on the balance and insist they swear to leave her alone…"

He trails off, swiping his hand over his face, no doubt as aware as I am of how unlikely we are to orchestrate that kind of coup, especially within the next not-quite-a-day.

Talia knits her brow. "You tried to get Cole to yield, but he used that 'right to justice' thing to get out of it. Wouldn't they just do that again anyway?"

I shake my head. "The right to justice served can only be invoked once for any given crime. Cole claimed it for anyone concerned with your 'ownership' and had his chance to set the terms. But I can't see any of them putting themselves in a position where we could get the upper hand, let alone all three of them."

"If they don't want to involve the rest of their pack, it'll be just the three of them at any hand-off we arrange." Whitt rubs his jaw, the sickly pallor fading from his skin as he focuses on the conundrum. "That would be our best chance."

"They'll ask for an accord against hostilities," I point out.

"Hmph. We can negotiate that down to first strike. They can hardly expect us to agree to show up utterly incapable of defending ourselves if *they* launch an attack."

August lets out an irritable sigh. "So, your plan is that we provoke them into attacking us and then somehow turn the tables on them? While also keeping Talia out of danger that whole time? They won't engage with us in the first place if we're not at least acting as if we're handing her over."

Whitt throws his hands in the air. "At least I'm *trying* to think of some way out of this disaster. If you've got a better idea, feel free to contribute."

The two of them glower at each other for a moment until Talia breaks in. "What's first strike?"

I turn to her. "We'd give our magical bond that we wouldn't initiate an attack. Essentially it guarantees their safety as long as they don't lash out at us. It's a typical request for a scenario like this."

She nods slowly, sucking her lower lip under her teeth to worry at it. Her gaze goes briefly distant. Then she aims her attention at me again. "Would you specifically say that you'd only fight if *they* start it, or only that the three of you won't start anything?"

"Usually the wording would be more along the lines of the latter, but I expect they'll also request that we come alone. The most we could hope to agree on is the three of us to match the three of them."

"But… I'll be there too. They won't ask you to swear anything about *me* fighting them, will they?"

Oh, my precious lady. It's hard to imagine I once thought of her as a little scrap, slight though she is, when she lets that inner fierceness show.

A pang runs through my heart that I have to say, "You wouldn't stand a chance against them, Talia. Even if we could arm you for the hand-off, which we can't. The instant you showed them any aggression, they'd hurt you worse than they already have."

Her gaze holding mine doesn't waver. "But there are things I can do that they won't expect. They don't know I have any magic. That's a kind of weapon. And I wouldn't have to beat them—I'd only have to get in the 'first strike' so that you'll have fulfilled your end of the deal, right?"

In the startled silence that follows, Whitt lets out a rough laugh. "She isn't wrong. That's our loophole right there. Find a way to position her so that once she makes her move, we'll have the advantage, and they'll never see it coming."

Everything in me balks at the idea. I promised to keep this woman safe. How can I now toss her to the front lines—to face off against the villains who tormented her for so long, who still feature in nightmares that wake her in a trembling panic?

"She'd be too vulnerable. They're not going to allow us to surround them or be poised right over them. By the time we get to them—"

"They kept her in a cage, didn't they?" Whitt interrupts. "Bars can keep a creature out as well as in. If she's using magic, she doesn't even need to be touching them."

Shove her back into a *cage*? My fangs itch at my gums just thinking of it. I swore to *myself* I'd give her some semblance of a normal life here, a chance at happiness.

But Talia is nodding. "The only true word I can really get to work is bronze, so maybe there could be something about the cage I could use… I don't know if I'd manage to injure them much, but if I could restrain them even for a few seconds, that should help you overpower them."

A grin has stretched across Whitt's face. I can practically see the schemes spinning behind those bright eyes. Even August has perked up, as if this plan is totally reasonable.

And perhaps it is.

Even as I recoil from the possibility, I can't deny it. The strategy isn't solid yet, but it holds up to every challenge I've made.

Every challenge except the one resounding from deep in my soul.

I hold out my arm to Talia, and she comes to me, lowering

herself onto the bench next to me. I bring my hand to her cheek, studying her expression. "Are you sure about this? We have more time to discuss—there might be another way. I would never ask you—"

"I know," she says quietly. "I don't expect it to be fun. But given the alternatives… I'm not going to give up without some kind of fight. And I'm not going to let them tear apart your pack to get to me. No one else should have to get hurt when it's me they want."

A tremor runs through her voice with those last few words, but she keeps her chin defiantly high. A rush of affection courses through me. This beautiful human woman, more concerned about the fate my pack might meet than the danger she's throwing herself into.

It's an honor to have earned her love. Right now, I wish I could offer her my own. This deep, unwavering desire to bring her every possible joy doesn't have much in common with the whirlwind of emotions I felt for Isleen, even the positive ones, and I loved my soul-twined mate for all her flaws. I'm not sure I want to place Talia in the same category as her—and not because it would diminish Isleen any.

But exactly what to call my ever-growing fondness doesn't matter. What matters is that the woman who's given me her heart and her trust is asking me to trust her now, to believe that she's capable in taking part in this battle in her own way. To accept that taking on those risks might even be what's best for her.

If I made my old promises for her benefit and not my own, it shouldn't matter how much giving her this opportunity pains me. How can I deny her?

"All right," I say. "Then you will be the bait and the trap in one. Let us work out as many of the details as we can before we reach Oakmeet. I want every particle of this idea so solid there's no chance of it ruining us instead."

CHAPTER TWENTY-THREE

Talia

$\mathcal{I}$ pause in the keep's upper hallway, torn between knocking on the door in front of me or simply easing it open and slipping inside. It's past dawn, thin light just starting to streak through the window at the far end of the hall, the birds outside picking up their twittering. The faint clink of dishes that carries from downstairs tells me August is already up preparing breakfast.

We all turned in for the night fairly early after our long hours of planning—Sylas insisted on it so we'd be fresh and alert for our final preparations this morning—but I suspect the man on the other side of this door is still asleep. These aren't the sort of hours he normally keeps.

Would it be better to startle him awake with a rap on the door or to take a gentler approach?

In a few hours, I'm going to be confronting my most vicious enemies. I shouldn't be this afraid of facing one of my allies.

My gut twists. I dawdle a moment longer and then turn the knob.

The door glides open without a sound, none of the creaks and rasps of our house by the border. I didn't appreciate how finely crafted this building is until I had a much less polished construction to compare it to. How long did Sylas and his cadre spend coaxing the wood from the ground into the massive form around me?

Stepping into the room, I nudge the door shut. At the click of the latch, the figure in the bed stirs beneath the thick covers. That damned wolf hearing. I freeze, my pulse stuttering.

Whitt rolls over with a swipe of his eyes and peers toward me, his gaze still bleary. At the sight of me, he sits up with a start. The covers fall across his well-muscled frame to his lap, revealing the full expanse of his tattooed chest. With a tingle that ripples straight to my core, I wonder if he sleeps totally naked.

"Mite," he says, his voice airy but his hands clenching on top of the rumpled fabric. "Clearly I need to start locking that door. If you've come to seduce me, let me save you the trouble and pre-emptively decline."

His wry tone melts most of the nerves that had been prickling inside my stomach. Whatever's happened in the past few days, he's still *Whitt*. I've heard how he speaks to and about people he dislikes. There's no acid in the words he just directed at me. I might even have heard a little genuine amusement.

That realization generates enough confidence for me to roll my eyes. I limp over to the side of the bed, glancing down at my T-shirt and jeans before meeting his wary gaze again. "If I was trying to seduce you, I'd have come in the middle of the night in my nightgown, not first thing in the morning fully dressed."

He chuckles. "Spoken like one who's done it before." When my cheeks flush, he raises his eyebrows. "Ah. Well. You have gotten up to all sorts of adventures since you've arrived here, haven't you."

"I'm not here to talk about that either," I insist, willing the heat from my face.

"Do tell what you've come sneaking into my bedroom for at this wretchedly early hour, then." He folds his arms over his chest, but he draws his legs up under the covers at the same time as if giving me more room. I perch carefully on the edge of the bed by the footboard.

Now that I'm here and he's listening, the words I rehearsed in my head jumble together, every arrangement sounding cringingly awkward. I drag in a breath and force myself to look at him again. "You've been avoiding me since that morning when—when Sylas suggested… I've barely seen you. It's okay if you'd rather not have anything to do with me *that* way. I won't bring it up again. I still liked what we already had—being friendly, or whatever you'd call it."

A lump fills in my throat, and I have to lower my gaze and gather myself before I can go on. "I just wanted to see if we could talk it out."

Whitt is quiet for a moment. Then he says, in a voice gone rough despite its light tone, "And you thought now was an ideal time for that?"

I swallow hard. "I think now's the *only* time for that if I want to be sure we actually get to talk about it. We don't know what's going to happen with Aerik today."

"Talia." He says my name like a command, and when I glance up at him, his eyes are so fierce my pulse hiccups in the second before he speaks again, just as vehemently. "We are *not* going to let that mangy bastard or his stinking cadre get one claw into you. However things work out with our plans, they won't walk away with you."

I wish I could believe the situation was that simple or sure. "Still, I'd feel better going to the meeting knowing everything's okay —or as okay as it can be—between us."

This time it's Whitt who looks away. His arms loosen, but his jaw stays tense, his eyes stormy. His chest rises and falls with a sigh. Then he turns back to me.

"You haven't done anything wrong. It isn't even exactly about you. And it's not that I'm not interested. It's a complicated situation."

With Sylas and August being involved too, he means? I duck my head, the lump in my throat expanding. "If I've ended up messing up your bonds in the cadre after all—"

Whitt is shaking his head before I can finish the sentence. "No. There are factors that developed well before you were ever in the picture. I promise you, you're not to blame for any of this."

"And because of those factors, you're not comfortable with anything happening between us."

"That's the gist of it." He rubs his hand over his face. "I didn't mean to make you feel shut out. I assumed it would be easier for everyone if we all had some space, but maybe I was mainly thinking of myself."

I make a vague gesture, not sure what to say. "That's all right. And if you still need space, you shouldn't have to—I mean, just because I—"

Whitt cuts off my fumbling by leaning forward and slipping his hand around mine where I'd rested it on the covers. At his touch, I fall silent, waiting. Trying not to let the feel of his warm, strong fingers provoke too much giddiness. He contemplates our joined hands and lets out a sigh with a hint of bittersweet laughter to it. "Oh, mite. I don't know whether I'm more afraid I'll ruin you or you'll ruin me."

I blink at him, my spine stiffening. "I wouldn't hurt any of you. Not purposefully."

He meets my eyes, his a clearer blue now but no less vast. "I know that. But sometimes events spiral beyond our intentions, faster than we can catch them."

The remark cuts straight through me in a way he couldn't have intended, slicing through blood and bone down to the hollow that formed in the pit of my stomach the moment Cole threatened Sylas. The anxious tension coiled there swells into a vicious ache.

I open my mouth to take a breath, and a sob slips out instead. Tears flood my eyes so abruptly the salt stings them.

I fight to draw them back, to get a hold of myself, but my body starts trembling despite my best efforts. Dropping Whitt's hand, I pull my knees up to my chest and hug them tightly. "I don't want to hurt *anyone* else."

"Of course you don't. I wasn't implying—" The bedspread rustles, and Whitt's arm comes around me tentatively, his fingers stroking over my hair. "It's all right. I can look after myself, and Sylas and August aren't any slouches either."

Somehow his reassurance makes the tears spill out faster. The ache spreads all through my abdomen. "It's not all right," I mumble against my jeans. "It's never going to be all right." Blood splashed red across patches of shadowed green. The shriek, the gurgles, the sounds of tearing flesh. I squeeze my eyes shut, but they overflow anyway.

I'm never going to be able to undo what's already happened.

Whitt hesitates, and then he's tugging me closer, leaning me against his solid frame. His summery, sun-baked smell trickles into my lungs. That and the circle of warmth of his arms around me should comfort me, but I can't seem to tamp down on the searing inside. I've been stopping up this feeling, this *guilt*, for so long, and now the seal has cracked too wide for me to stuff it all back in.

Whitt's voice manages to be wry and gentle at the same time. "I'm guessing you're upset about a little more than anything that's happened just now. You can tell me about it if you'd like. Or you can simply drench me in snot and tears. Your choice."

In spite of everything, a laugh hitches out of me. I tuck my face against my raised arm so that I'm not actually getting either of those substances on him, but he's broken the worst of the emotional onslaught. I inhale raggedly and exhale in a rush, sniffling and dabbing at my eyes.

Part of me wants to brush it off, to laugh and pretend my lapse was nothing, like Whitt himself might do. But I still ache from sternum to gut, and tears keep burning behind my eyes, ready to tumble free at the slightest provocation.

And maybe someone *should* know—what I did, how I failed.

"I already ruined my whole family," I say in a rasp.

"As much as I loathe giving Aerik credit for anything, I believe he deserves it in that particular case."

"You don't know. I—" I close my eyes again when they prickle hotter. "We wouldn't have been in the woods where he found us at all if I hadn't been teasing Jamie. My little brother. I dared him to chase me away from the road—I knew he was scared of the dark, that if I called him a couple of names, he'd try to prove he wasn't. If I'd just left him alone— If I'd kept quiet when they had me instead of screaming for my parents—" I press my face tighter against my sleeve. "They came running to help us, but there was nothing they could do." And then the wolves ripped them apart too.

Whitt lets out a dismissive huff. "Skies above, Talia, how old were you? Twelve? How in the world could you have known what might be lurking in the woods right then? You had no idea monsters like us even existed. And I've yet to see a child who wouldn't cry for their parents when they were frightened out of their wits. It would have been ridiculous for you to act any differently."

"I still could have. I was—I was selfish, and I got them all killed."

"Aerik and his mangy cadre got them killed. Unless you sprouted fangs and claws, you can't possibly be anywhere near as responsible as they are."

I suck in another breath and raise my head. Whitt eases back, giving me room but staying close. I stare at the wall, my eyes stinging when I blink. "I still wish I'd done things differently."

Whitt chuckles low and raw. "Then you're in fine and extensive company, mite. But I can at least assure you that my own worries have nothing to do with failings on your part. And it is possible I'm being overly cautious even so. We lost an awful lot over a woman before, but she had nothing to do with you, and you're certainly not a speck like her."

I peek over my shoulder at him. "You mean Isleen."

His mouth flattens. "The less of anyone's attention she claims now that she's gone, the better."

"I *could* ruin you all, though. Even get you killed. If I can't pull off the magic I need to today—"

"No one could have expected you to pull off any magic at all. I certainly won't blame you if it goes sideways on you."

"I know. But I'm scared. I was too weak when Aerik caught me, and it took me nine years to find the strength to unlock that cage, and now I'm going back into one like I'm giving up all over again. Even if I'm not *really* giving up, I could freeze up or start stammering—and it'll be the pack who pays for it if you can't overpower Aerik right away." More blood, splattered across the fields outside. My stomach lurches at the thought.

There *is* one way I could make sure that doesn't happen: I could give myself up to Aerik. But every time my mind strays in that direction, every inch of me recoils in horror.

Sylas would probably start a war to get me back if I tried to turn myself over, but that's not the main reason I balk. As selfish as it might be… I'd rather die than end up back in Aerik's prison. And killing myself won't help anyone—even if I was willing to go that far, he'd blame Sylas for the lost "property" anyway.

So what can I do except fight as well as I can?

Watching me, Whitt moves as if to get up. "If you want to talk to Sylas and August about adjusting the plan—"

I rub my forehead. "No. It's not actually a bad plan, is it? You're the strategist."

The corner of his mouth quirks upward. "It's a good enough plan that I'm ashamed I didn't come up with it entirely by myself. I think it's the best possible plan we could have pulled together given the time we had."

"Then we should still do it. If I tell Sylas and August I'm scared, they might decide we can't go through with it no matter what else I say."

"And who's to say I won't make the same call?"

"You won't," I say simply, with total confidence in that one fact. "Because when I say I think we should do it even though I'm scared, you trust me to make that call. Even when you didn't like me, even when you wanted me to leave, you've never *forced* me to do anything. You always let me decide."

Whitt considers me for a long moment, as if he's not sure what to say. Then a hint of his usual smirk crosses his face. "I'm not sure that's entirely true. To begin with, I always liked you, even when I didn't want to. But no, I won't go tattling to Sylas about your qualms."

He pauses before continuing, more quietly than before. "You know, there's a lot of power in pretending to be powerless. Playing into your vulnerability. Most of the time, I learn more when the folk around me believe I'm stumbling drunk than when I try to pry information out of them directly. I don't always love the reputation that comes with it, but—you learn to appreciate the benefits enough not to care. As long as *you* know you're not really that fragile, that's all that matters."

His take sends a quiver of rightness through me. I lift my head, trying out the words. "I'm *not* fragile." That feels right too.

Whitt's subtle smirk stretches into a full grin. "No, you're not, my mighty one. Not in the slightest. And I think Aerik is going to regret ever asking for you back."

I find myself smiling back at him with the same fierceness he showed when he spoke about Aerik earlier. "I hope he gives you all the excuse you need to tear out his throat instead of taking a yield."

An appreciative gleam has come into Whitt's eyes. "Oh, so do I —so very much."

The heat in his gaze washes through me. Not letting myself think, just following instinct, I shift onto my knees.

"Thank you," I say, meaning the whole conversation, and tip forward to brush a kiss to his cheek like I did that last full-moon night.

Like before, Whitt tenses, but I know better than to think it's with revulsion now. As I draw back a few inches, he swallows audibly. His hand moves to my side, only resting there, not pushing me away or pulling me to him.

My heart thumping, I risk leaning in again. My lips graze closer to his jaw.

Whitt closes his eyes. His voice comes out strained. "Talia, it's best that you go now."

Right then, I sense that if I ignored that remark, if I crossed the last short distance to bring my mouth to his, that's all it would take. Whatever dam he's built against his emotions would fracture, and he'd unleash all the passion simmering beneath his artfully composed exterior.

But I don't want him like that if he's going to regret it afterward. Even thinking about it brings the ache back into my gut.

Ignoring the desire clanging through my veins, I shove myself farther backward and then off the bed entirely.

When I reach the doorway, I let myself glance back. To my surprise, Whitt's expression looks startled for an instant before he recovers his typical unruffled self. "I'll come down to breakfast in a bit, mite. Since you've apparently missed my beautiful face so much."

A smile springs to my lips, the teasing rousing only a tiny shred of embarrassment now. "Good. I have missed it."

I head downstairs feeling if not exactly secure in today's plan, then absolutely determined to give it everything I have. For myself, and for these men who've taken me in as their own.

CHAPTER TWENTY-FOUR

Talia

The cage isn't completely the same as the one Aerik held me in for all those years. It's a little bigger, because Sylas wanted me to have enough room to dodge if anyone slashes at me through the bars, and the door has a latch I can easily flip open if I feel it'll be safer for me to make a run for it once the fighting starts than to rely on this structure for protection.

Aerik's cage never had several thin chains dangling from the base either.

But despite the differences, the looming bronze bars and the hard metal surface beneath me bring back all sorts of memories I'd rather leave behind. As Sylas and his cadre lower the cage in the middle of the large, grassy clearing where they've arranged to meet Aerik and his men, my pulse rattles through my limbs. My ribs seem to be digging right into my lungs.

I close my eyes and focus as well as I can on the parts of this scenario that remind me that I'm loved and cared for, and that the fae men around me are nothing like the ones who tormented me.

The soft fabric of my blouse and jeans hugs my skin, a far cry from the rough texture of the filthy blanket that was all the covering I had before. My stomach might be knotted with nerves, but no pangs of hunger resonate from my belly. Muscles flex through my arms where they're braced against the cage floor, toned from the training I've been given.

And a word that shimmers with magic hovers in the back of my throat, ready to be launched like a weapon.

The clearing itself is a far cry from the chilly, windowless room with its bone-white walls where Aerik kept my former cage. Sunlight beams down from the blue sky dotted with a few puffy wisps of cloud. Summer heat drifts through the bars to kiss my skin, bringing a sweet clover scent with it. A squirrel is chattering from the branches of one of the nearby trees. It would be a lovely spot for a picnic if I wasn't shut up behind these bars.

With the cage now set on solid ground, I adjust my pose, trying to find the most comfortable stance to wait in. I might be sitting in here for a while yet. I don't want my muscles cramping up if I need to move quickly later.

We've come early—early enough to hope that Aerik won't have anyone watching this spot yet—although we're taking precautions just in case to make sure he won't become too suspicious. Like having me in the cage for the whole trek from the carriage that's parked about a ten-minute walk back in the forest.

Now, Sylas and August move around the cage as if checking it over, surreptitiously stretching the bronze chains across the ground to nestle hidden in the long grass. Whitt steps back, scanning the clearing and the stretch of forest on the other side. The more normal-looking trees are interspersed with narrow cone-shaped ones that jut with their fluttering blue streamers of leaves several feet above the others.

The spymaster inhales deeply, speaks a few quiet words that I assume hold magic, and then offers a grim smile. "No sign of their arrival yet."

"Nothing to do but wait then." August hunkers down on the grass near the cage and glances at me. Seeing me trapped like that, even knowing our plan, turns his expression pained.

I want to reach through the bars to clasp his hand, both for my comfort and his, but we agreed we wouldn't act or speak as if we're anything but captors and prisoner once we arrived at the clearing.

While Whitt paces the edge of the glade, Sylas stays on his feet too, still and watchful. When he rests his hand on the roof of the cage, I look up at him. Our gazes meet for just a second; I see an echo of the question he asked me during the carriage ride in his.

Are you sure you're up to this?

Yes, I said then, and I'd say it again now if he could voice his concern. Of course, now that we're here, there isn't any turning back. I'm committed.

My heart keeps thudding on at twice its usual pace. I lean against the frame of the door, which is behind me when I'm facing the way Aerik should approach from. My escape route. The thought of flinging open that door and dashing toward the trees only makes my pulse race faster.

I close my eyes again and let my thoughts drift into the escape I took so often when I was truly locked up—the only sort of escape I had, into the landscapes from my scrapbook of travel dreams. My imagination works just as well as it always did. I picture myself floating in a warm pool of turquoise water, gazing up at craggy white rock forming a ring around the sky above. Scrambling up those rocky walls to gaze out over lush jungle surging toward the expanse of the ocean.

There's so much more of *this* world, with all its mystery and magic, that I haven't gotten to experience yet. Maybe if this plan works, if we no longer have to worry about Aerik tracking me down, I'll be able to discover all the epic sights the faerie world has to offer. I should at least be able to trek around Sylas's domain more freely. Harper will be happy about that.

Despite the situation, my lips twitch with a smile at the thought of the fae woman's likely response if I tell her she can play tour guide. I might even be able to show her some of the human world. That could be enough adventure to cure her restlessness for a while.

As long as we have the freedom to roam around like that, that is. Aerik isn't even the largest threat Sylas and his pack face, as frightening as he is to me.

What if the Unseelie break through the defenses at the border and start a real invasion? What if the arch-lords come up with some new reason to accuse Sylas of treason and punish him even more? The way Ambrose's squadron leader spoke to us the other day…

As I shudder at the memory, the rasp of footsteps over the forest floor jerks me back to the present. The men around me have gone still.

Whitt cocks his head and nods to Sylas, moving into position by the cage. August stands up. I push myself into a crouch, my weight on my feet now, balanced so I won't strain the injured one too much. I'm going without my brace, since that kindness would look extravagant for a prisoner.

Aerik and his two cadre-chosen slink out of the forest. At the sight of all three of the men who orchestrated my years of torture, viewing them through bars the way I did back then and knowing they're here to reclaim me, I have to clench my teeth against the urge to vomit. My heartbeat stutters in its now-frantic rhythm. I press my hands against the solid floor and will back the dizziness sweeping through me.

"You arrived early," Aerik says without any greeting. He, Cole, and the stout man I think of as Cutter come to a stop about ten feet from where my men are poised around the cage.

"So have you," Sylas points out, his low baritone impeccably calm. He motions to me. "As you can see, we've brought her, already restrained. I assume you have a vehicle nearby. We can carry her to it."

He and the others move as if to heft up the cage—immediately, but slowly enough to give Aerik time to protest. That's part of the plan, to make him think they're eager to get access to his carriage.

Exactly as we hoped, Aerik steps forward with a jerk of his arm. "Leave it. We can manage. Just consider yourselves lucky I'm not dragging you before the arch-lords for the theft. If you breathe one word of *my* prize to them, I'll see they get a full accounting of how you and your cadre violated my domain."

Sylas raises his hands and eases back. He and his cadre have to take several paces backward before Aerik and his approach. I tense, unable to shake the sensation of being abandoned.

They haven't left me, not really, but now there's nothing between me and my former tormenters except these awful bars. And in this final move in our scheme, I truly am on my own. The three men behind me gave their vows. They can't harm Aerik unless someone else makes the first attack.

It all relies on me.

As Aerik, Cole, and Cutter inspect me and the cage, still from a short distance, the fae lord's mouth curls into a typical sneer. Watching him, the churning inside me starts to burn into something hotter and fiercer. Currents of anger sear through my fear.

These men—these *monsters*—savaged me for nearly half my life. They slaughtered my family, starved and broke my body, stole my literal life's blood from my wrist over and over, and laughed at my distress.

Why shouldn't this moment come down to me? They deserve every bit of fury I can aim at them. Let them know that when they fall here, it's because of *me*, the 'dung-body' they dismissed as helpless and weak so many times.

I roll the syllables silently over my tongue. Having found no reason for complaint, my former jailors step right up to the bars. The cage is big enough that it'll take all three of them to lift it. They bend down to grasp it from the bottom.

Now's the time. *Now*—but my voice catches at the back of my mouth.

My throat constricts, the fear that I'll mess up the one chance I have nearly stealing the chance from me altogether. Then Cole shoots me a vicious, triumphant smile, and all the rage in me rushes back to the surface.

My lungs unlock. I hurl the word at them like a spear, calling the chains disguised in the grass to do my bidding. "*Fee-doom-ace-own!*"

My voice rings out, so powerful and clear I can hardly believe it's mine. Magic surges through it, and three of the chains whip up and around the men's wrists, melting into place like a larger version of the chinks I wove into that chainmail vest, so tight I can almost taste how they bite the skin.

All three of them jerk back, but the chains stop them from going far. Aerik sputters in surprise, Cole rasps a curse, and before any of them can process what's going on well enough to free themselves, my allies have pounced in full wolf form.

August tackles Cutter, knocking him onto his back on the ground. Whitt launches himself at Cole, his fangs bared in an expression that looks downright eager for a rematch. With a roar, Sylas springs right over his cadre-chosen to land on Aerik, sending the other lord sprawling just as Aerik spits out the true name to loosen the bronze bond.

I've scrambled against the back of the cage, my hand by the latch on the door, my veins thrumming now with a mix of terror and excitement. I did it—but this isn't over yet.

As they struggle, our enemies shift into their own wolfish forms, snarling and snapping. Whitt and Cole roll across the grass, scrabbling at each other with their claws until Whitt manages to shove the white-furred wolf down more firmly with his jaws at the beast's throat. Cole keeps flailing against him.

Across the clearing, Cutter slams a massive paw into the side of August's head. My hands clench with a jolt of horror, but the ruddy wolf just shakes himself and rams his opponent harder into the grass. He slashes Cutter's jaw and rakes his claws down the underside of his chin, just shy of gouging straight through.

Between them, Sylas's dark wolf and Aerik's beige one grapple with each other, Sylas still braced over the other creature but battered by swinging limbs. Snarling, he snatches one of those vicious paws between his teeth and yanks so hard the crack of bone echoes through my ears. Blood spurts across the grass, but this time I don't mind the sight.

Heaving himself into a better position, Sylas swats Aerik's muzzle hard enough that the other wolf lets out a pained huff. My rescuer jams his claws against the most vulnerable part of his enemy's throat. Planting the rest of his body to pin down Aerik's legs at the thighs, he clamps his other front paw against the other lord's unbroken wrist. Then he barks in a sound not quite a word but that even I can understand. *Yield.*

Aerik squirms against him in vain. His eyes roll in their sockets, searching out his cadre—and finding them equally subdued. A wrathful noise hisses out of him, but he must be able to see he's beaten. He sags against the ground, falling into the shape of a man at the same time.

Sylas transforms too, keeping his claws out, jutting from his broad fingers. He glares down at Aerik. "Do you yield?"

Aerik scowls back at him, his daffodil-yellow hair strewn like straw amid the grass, his right arm lying limp at an unnatural angle. "Are you really going to kill me if I don't? There'll be an awful lot of questions about how exactly this confrontation went down."

A harsh grin curls Sylas's lips. "We followed every letter of our agreement. My cadre and I swore not to make the first strike, and we didn't. Ours was the second."

"You can't really expect me to believe that the *dung-body* worked that true name herself."

"I do, because that's what happened. We *couldn't* have gone against a vow so sworn—do you really doubt your ability to judge what magic has been cast? But if you're willing to risk it all on the idea that I somehow deceived you with our oath, I'll be happy to rip your head from your body and show anyone who asks that your soulstone shines true."

Aerik's gaze slides to me where I'm still crouched in the cage. At his cold stare, a shiver runs through me, but I manage to give him a tight little smile. "I don't belong to anyone but *me*."

To emphasize the declaration, I reach back and unlatch the cage door. A sense of lightness rushes through me as I clamber out into the open air.

"But—"

Sylas grasps Aerik's jaw and yanks his face away from me. "Don't you worry about her. In fact, that's the main condition of your yield. I will let you leave here with your miserable life, and you will make no further attempt to gain control over that human woman, nor will you so much as *hint* through word or action that anyone else should take any particular notice of her. You won't mention any special qualities she possesses or of this skirmish here today. And you'll spare me and my pack any further hostilities as well. Considering the years of torment you put her through, I'd say you're getting off incredibly easy. So please, give me an excuse to drench this glade with your blood instead."

The fae lord's voice is even as ever but brutal in its force. As Aerik meets his stare, the color leaches from his face. From this angle, I can't see what rage Sylas's expression holds, but I doubt I'd want it directed my way. He means every word of that threat.

"If you really think this is going to be enough to buy your way back to prominence," Aerik begins, but his voice is too thready for the disdain in it to have any impact. He can't even manage a real sneer now.

"I tire of waiting for your answer," Sylas rumbles. "How many more seconds do you suppose it is before I can reasonably count your delay as a direct refusal? You won't have any prominence at all in your family's mausoleum."

"Fine," Aerik snarls. A magical thrum enters his voice. "I accept your conditions and yield. I'll leave the girl, you, and your pack alone. Now get your mangy paws off me."

Sylas retracts his claws but keeps his hand braced against the other man's collarbone, holding him down. "Hmm. Not quite yet. Tell your cadre they'd better take the same bargain, or you'll find yourself a little short on supporters."

Aerik tips his head to call to the others. "You heard him. Yield. We did plenty well without that cringing thing; we don't need her."

My hands ball into fists at the way he's describing me, but he doesn't so much as glance my way. It's better for all of us if they yield and Sylas doesn't find his actions under the scrutiny outright killing them would provoke. All the same, in that moment, I wish he would make one wrong move to ensure his murder.

The other men have shifted while Sylas and Aerik debated. Cole grimaces and offers his yield in a sharply snarky tone. Cutter gives his dully, his nose dribbling blood. Then my three men shove off my former captors, drawing back to surround me.

He may not be dead, but it's still incredibly gratifying to watch Aerik stagger to his feet, favoring a knee that seems to have been knocked off-kilter during the skirmish, holding his broken arm carefully against his abdomen. Dirt smudges his lordly face; his yellow hair doesn't gleam quite so bright. He raises his chin, but he can't quite overcome the doleful slump of his shoulders.

"Come on," he snaps at his cadre. "We have no more business with these cast-offs."

They turn their backs on us and shuffle away into the forest. As their forms disappear amid the shadows, sweet relief wells up inside me. For the second time today, tears prickle at my eyes, but these ones barely sting.

It's over. I'm free of them. They might haunt my dreams for who knows how much longer to come, but they can't do one more bit of real harm to me.

Sylas squeezes my shoulder. "You were perfect, Talia. I know how hard that must have been for you, but you showed them what you're really made of. Let's get you home."

Yes. Home. The home Aerik can now never steal me from.

Sylas speaks the true name to melt the cage's materials back into the earth, since we have no more need for it. As we turn toward our own vehicle, I slip my hand around his on one side and August's on the other.

An ache of determination rises up through my joy. These men showed just how far *they're* willing to go on my behalf. I won't really deserve to share their home until I find some way to fight just as hard for them.

CHAPTER TWENTY-FIVE

August

The carriage is just passing into our domain when Talia raises her head. She's spent most of the journey nestled between Sylas and me in grateful silence. Holding her close, reminding myself and her that we made it through the confrontation with Aerik with all our skins intact, felt much more important than anything I could have said.

But there are other important matters we haven't dealt with yet, and somehow Talia is already thinking beyond the freedom she just won for herself.

"Are we going back to the border now?" she asks, glancing up at Sylas. "I guess you'd have to rebuild the house, but at least we wouldn't need to worry about having the glamour on me or what Aerik might do."

Sylas frowns, and my spirits sink. Both of us know we accomplished a lot less than we were hoping for out there.

"I'll have to think on that," my lord says. "The other lords—and arch-lords' representatives—weren't exactly open to our offers of assistance. I'm not sure we were achieving anything more than looking incompetent because we *couldn't* make ourselves more useful."

Whitt swivels on the bench where he's been poised watching the forestlands fly by. "The full moon is only three nights from now. We shouldn't plan to be on the move in the midst of that."

Sylas nods. "We can't leave the pack in Oakmeet completely unguided, but we do have more flexibility with less to hide."

Talia straightens up. "We can give them my blood. The pack-kin in Oakmeet, our squadron at the border—*all* the packs. Make some kind of tonic like Aerik did so we can spread it out without having to take too much from me. No one should have to keep suffering from the curse, not while I can prevent that."

She makes the offer so easily my heart lights up like it does so often in her presence. Of course that would be her first thought at the reminder of the full moon. Of course she'd want to solve this problem as only she can, giving of her own body. That generosity and compassion is what makes her Talia.

The softening of Sylas's expression tells me he's touched too, but he shakes his head. "I don't think we're in a position to make that leap yet. I'm not even sure it's the right leap to make."

"But if Aerik can't come after me again, then we don't have to keep it a secret, do we?" she says. "That was why we couldn't risk helping even our pack before."

"Yes, but— We also have to consider the same possibilities that led Aerik to keep you secret. If I suddenly present myself as the provider of the tonic, there'll be a lot of questions. The arch-lords will demand an explanation, and when they find out where it comes from, it's likely they'll want to take you for themselves. We can't fend them off as easily as we could Aerik."

I let out a rough laugh. "I'm not sure I'd call what we just did exactly *easy*."

Sylas smiles wryly. "Indeed. And on top of that, I meant what I said before about us needing to find a more permanent solution to the curse. Relying on Aerik's tonic gave too many of the Seelie a false sense of security."

Talia clasps her hands in front of her. "But if I can at least spare everyone from the violence and the loss of control while you're looking for a real solution…"

Sylas touches her cheek with a stroke of the backs of his fingers. "I appreciate the devotion you're showing to my people, Talia. Perhaps if we can regain the arch-lords' favor, I could count on them trusting me to preserve such a… resource." He grimaces at the phrasing. "I won't put you in their sights until then."

She sinks back against the seat with a resigned sigh. "Eventually."

"Eventually."

I give her hand a quick squeeze. "You still have so much more freedom now than you did before. No more glamours—we can tell the pack that we hid your injury until you'd gotten to know them a bit because you were self-conscious. No more needing to stay so close to the keep all of the time."

Talia brightens up as I hoped she would. "I know. I'm looking forward to being able to just… *be* without all those worries hanging over me."

Whitt hums to himself and stretches his legs toward the opposite bench. "You know, even the arch-lords aren't half so intimidating when you've found yourself in a position to learn their odd little quirks. A bunch of kooks they all are, I'd say."

Sylas snorts. "Thankfully I know *you* know better than to say that in anyone else's hearing."

As Whitt smirks in response, Talia looks across the carriage at him. Her own smile falters. Abruptly, I'm aware of the separation between us, my oldest brother set apart from the three of us—and based on his reaction the other morning, it's not by our design this time but by his own. I don't like the unexpected division that's formed within our original unit, but if that's what he wants, what can I do about it?

My love appears to have her own ideas. After a moment's hesitation, she eases to her feet and limps over to sit on the bench next to Whitt, gingerly but deliberately. She leaves a foot of space between them, hardly cuddling like she was with Sylas and me, and her stance is cautious, but a twinge of possessiveness quivers through my chest anyway.

I told her it was fine if she wanted him too, that I wished for her to have every happiness—but it turns out that confronted with the reality, a part of me would rather scoop her up and hide her away someplace only for myself.

It's a selfish urge, especially after witnessing the bliss Sylas and I were able to bring her to together. And it feels even more selfish watching the startled expression that crosses Whitt's face now, flickering into something like delight before he recovers to his usual nonchalance.

"I want to hear *all* the crazy arch-lord stories you've got," Talia informs him, leaning back against the side of the carriage. "Laughing at them sounds a lot better than being scared of them."

Whitt relaxes, setting his arm on the edge just an inch from her shoulder so carefully that this time I'm hit with a twinge of brotherly affection rather than jealousy. Whitt and I don't always agree, and I often don't understand his moods, but I've never doubted his loyalty to our family and to the pack. And I can see that same devotion gleaming in his eyes as he prepares to launch into a tale for Talia's benefit.

He fought for her as hard as any of us. If he can offer her things I can't, why shouldn't she have those too?

After everything that's been stolen from her and all the abuse she's had to endure, she deserves every bit of love she'll welcome.

"It's my opinion that Ambrose goes around like he has a stick up his ass," Whitt says in his typical wry tone, "and that might be due to all the cartilage he ingests. I've had it from a member of his household staff that he likes to gnaw on the old bones from the roasts and stews when he's working, as though he's some kind of woe begotten mongrel rather than a regal wolf. Leaves the chewed-up bits all over the floor for the servants to clean up too." He makes a tossing gesture as if flicking a bone across the carriage.

Talia makes a face. "He's the one Tristan is related to, right?"

"Yes. Pricks, the whole lot in that family. Oh, and Celia, our lady arch-lord? I hear she's so terrified of smelly feet that she has her chamber maidens paint her soles with rose petal paste each night before she goes to sleep. Frankly, she'd do better slathering it on that sour face of hers."

Even Sylas guffaws at that. Talia scoots a little closer, so her shoulder rests against Whitt's elbow. "What about the third one?"

Whitt rattles off a story about Donovan's insecurities with being the youngest of the arch-lords, and Talia watches him with rapt attention while I watch the two of them.

No, clever tales aren't my forte. But I have other strengths. If I want to be sure I stay worthy of her, I have to play to them.

My gaze travels past them to the distant horizon now appearing where the trees have fallen away. A kernel of an idea tumbles through my mind. We weren't done out at the border, not by a longshot. I can work on proving myself to Sylas at the same time.

When the carriage comes to a stop at the edge of the forest closest to the keep, we climb off, and Sylas dismisses the materials that made it, a juniper tree springing up in its place. Whitt rolls his shoulders.

"I'll make the rounds, check in with the sentries," he says.

Sylas tips his head in acknowledgment and heads toward the keep with Talia. I hang back a moment, raising my hand to signal to Whitt to hold on.

He raises an enquiring eyebrow at me. "What's on your mind, Auggie?"

There's enough fondness in the teasing nickname that I can let it roll off me. "I just wanted to say, in case it wasn't clear—what Sylas said the other day about Talia and sharing—he was speaking for me too. If you want to pursue something with her, at any point, I won't resent it. I just want her to be happy."

Whitt considers me for a long moment—long enough that the back of my neck starts to prickle with the sense that I might not have been entirely coherent, or at least not to his standards. Then a small smile crosses his lips, more subdued than his usual smirk. "I appreciate the vote in support, little brother."

Without another word, he leaps away, shifting into his wolfish form in mid-spring. As he trots off to survey our domain, I turn toward the keep.

Sylas has stopped on the way there to speak with a couple of our pack-kin, Talia already vanished into the keep. I pause and catch my lord's eye, and when he's finished, he strides over to join me. I wait until we've reached the privacy of the entrance room before I speak.

"I have an idea about how I might be able to advance our cause with the arch-lords at the border."

My lord folds his arms over his chest. "Let's hear it then."

A jab of nerves makes me hesitate, but only for an instant. He's trusted me with major tasks before, if nothing *quite* this significant.

"I can go back to the border now, alone, and carry out the mission the arch-lords denied. They didn't want to approve of anyone sneaking into winter territory to try to pick off a warrior who could betray their plans, so we won't ask their approval again. If it goes wrong, they can blame our defiance. But if it goes right, I may come up with the information we need to fend off whatever attack they're anticipating."

Sylas studies me with more intensity than Whitt aimed at me. He's watched me train—he's carried out some of that training himself. He knows I'm as capable as any fae warrior out there. *I* know I am. What has all that training been for if I don't put it to use in the field when it matters most?

"You'll keep your distance, only press in if you can catch one alone?" he says. "I don't want you risking yourself against more than one of them, even if I'm sure you could give two or even three a good fight."

I nod adamantly. "Only one, only when I can do it out of sight of any others. I may have to prowl along the border for a while—that's why I think it's best I head out now so I can start tonight."

Sylas's jaw clenches and then releases. "All right. You know your way around those lands now, and you've always known your way around a battle. Do me proud, and make sure you come back hale and whole—for both my and our lady's sake, hmm?"

A grin springs to my lips despite my attempt to remain cool and professional. "You can count on it."

Several hours later, as I stalk through the haze that marks the border between the summer and winter realms, I'm starting to think that while I may return to Oakmeet whole, it could be a whole man who's frozen solid.

On the winter side, the wind howls loud enough that I could hear it before I even stepped into the heat haze that's the summery part of the border. Snow whirls through the air, some of it wisping into the narrow strip of the border, bringing currents of frigid air with it. My wolf fur can fend off the worst of it, but the cold is starting to seep through to my skin.

I don't like it. Cold is for leaping into a chilly pond to escape from a heatwave. This constant, icy bluster is pure torture. How can any fae stand to live in it?

I guess that might explain why they're trying to move on our lands, though not why they're doing that *now* after putting up with their wintery weather for so long before.

Thankfully, while I don't know the true name for snow, water was one of my first, and the crisp flakes are nothing but frozen water. With a little coaxing, I've gathered a barrier of snow around my body that both deflects the worst of the wind and hides me from the view of anyone patrolling the edge of Unseelie territory.

I need the camouflage. Even though it's the middle of the night, the light of the near-full moon reflects off all that icy ground starkly enough that my dark fur would be unmissable against it.

I had a close call in the evening when I first slunk out here. I emerged into view of the winter realm just as a squad of five Unseelie warriors were marching past. If my well-honed instincts hadn't sent me recoiling at the first glimpse of them, they'd have charged after me in a matter of seconds and called a whole bunch of their brethren to join the patrol even if they hadn't caught me. I'd have lost my chance and possibly my life before I'd really gotten started, not to mention the disgrace to the pack if the arch-lords found out we defied their orders and failed.

I've passed another, smaller group since then, and spotted a few lone sentries at a distance across the glinting plain, too far for me to risk stalking after them. My paws are starting to ache with the splinters of ice that have collected in the fur around my toes.

I can't stop until I've fulfilled my goal. I didn't say good-bye to Talia for the second time this month for nothing.

Finally, a spindly shape of a sentry ventures closer to the border up ahead. Like all of the Unseelie warriors I've seen, he wears a silvery helm and a similarly pale chest plate with looser plating hanging to his thighs for ease of movement, his padded jacket and trousers an even paler gray to blend into the landscape. He peers into the border haze and then turns to amble toward me.

Perfect.

I prowl a little closer, lacking the patience to simply sit and wait. Anticipation coils through my muscles. This bastard is one of the wretched winter fae who've killed my pack-kin and so many others over the past three decades. For all I know, he slaughtered some of them personally.

I spent too long hanging back waiting for something to happen when we were staked out here before. It's time to bring a little of the attack back to the ravens.

When he's mere feet away, I pause, letting my form meld into the haze and the gusting snow. The sentry meanders a few steps farther. I gather myself—and pounce.

I'll give him credit: he reacts quickly, squirming to the side the second he's hit the ground, dagger already in hand. But that only gives me the chance to let out more of my bottled aggression. I smack the dagger from his fingers with a swift paw, raking my claws across his palm and wrist as I do, and pummel him harder into the frigid earth. With another swipe, I've sent his helmet spinning into the haze.

His body twitches as if to transform. *Oh no, you don't.* I clamp my jaws tight around his neck, a trickle of his Unseelie blood dribbling over my tongue. A warning that if he tries to shrink into his raven form, I can snap that birdish head from his shoulders before he can so much as squawk in protest.

As the sentry aims an ineffective blow at my chest, I haul him right into the haze where his colleagues won't spot us. Then I shift so quickly I've got a sword at his throat in place of my jaws before he can do more than shudder.

"Why don't you just kill me and get it over with, cur?" the sentry sputters. "Or do wolves like to play with their food now?"

I bare my teeth at him, letting my still-protruding fangs show. "I'd hardly make a meal out of a scrawny feather-brain like you. And you might get to keep your life if you talk quickly. Tell me about the next strike your people are planning against us."

The man manages a choked guffaw. "You think I'd betray my people to save my hide? Go ahead and kill me. I'm not talking."

I should have anticipated he'd reject the opportunity to yield, but I've never taken a prisoner for interrogation before, never battled in circumstances where the future of an entire people could be at stake. I press my blade a tad harder, watching blood well up along the gleaming edge, my mind scrambling for my next move.

If he'd rather die than speak, I can't beat the information out of him. I'm going to have to rely on my wits rather than my brawn. Heart take me if I don't wish Whitt was here to advise me right now.

Well, what would my oldest brother do if faced with a problem like this? I've watched him work his own strategies plenty of times.

He might weave a sort of glamour with his words. Create an illusion that would draw out the answers he needs. Pretend he doesn't need it all that much, so his target has that much less to fight against.

What do I already think I know, that I can simply get this wretch to confirm—and maybe even add a little more as a bonus?

I pick my words carefully, only lying in implication. "You're too loyal for your own good—more loyal than others I've toppled who valued their lives more." Those others were Seelie fae I fought for very different reasons, but he doesn't need to know that. "If you won't tell me anything about the coming assault along this section of the border, you'll lose your life, and I'll simply lose another hour or two finding someone else who will. And then we'll see how many more of your raven necks we get to wring."

"You won't wring any, from what I've heard," the sentry retorts. "When the full moon rises, you're as likely to savage each other as any of us, aren't you?"

The question hits me like a lance of ice straight to my gut. I harden my expression before too much of my shock can show on my face. "That's when your people will attack, is it?" I snarl.

The sentry's flinch as he realizes what he gave away is answer enough. He hasn't denied that they're going to attack *here* either, accepting what I said rather than taunting me about being mistaken. Maybe I can batter a little more out of him while I have the chance…

But he doesn't give me that chance. With a jerk of his body, he starts to contract, his arms slipping from my hold as they fling into wings, his armor rippling away into ebony feathers.

No. If he makes it back to his kind, he'll warn them of what I've discovered, and they'll adjust their plans.

I slam my sword down, and a shrunken head—half-feathered, half-human—rolls to the side, blood gushing from the severed neck.

I push away from the ruined body and wipe my blade on the frosted grass right in the center of the border. His brethren may not find him for days—or if they do, all they'll see is that he ventured too close to our territory and met an expected fate. But that fact gives me no comfort.

Our enemies know. After all this time, the ravens have discovered our curse. And they mean to use it against us at the first opportunity.

If the Unseelie attack while the border squadrons have lost their minds to the wildness, the blood that drenches the fields next will be all our own.

CHAPTER TWENTY-SIX

Talia

The keep's front door thumps loud enough to startle me out of sleep. I flinch beneath the covers and then go still. It takes a few seconds of straining to listen over the thunder of my pulse before my mind emerges from its dreamy muddle enough for the obvious explanation to occur to me.

August is back.

I throw off the covers and scramble out of the bed so quickly my warped foot jars against the floorboards at an awkward angle. Wincing, I fumble for my brace, not bothering with day clothes or the hairbrush on the bedside table, or anything other than getting to him as quickly as possible.

If he's back, then he's okay. Well, he's okay enough to have made it back. Ralyn made it from the border to the keep so injured he had to spend days recuperating.

By the time I reach the stairs, two hushed voices are already traveling up from the hall below. Sylas was already awake, maybe even waiting for August. The other man might have sent him some kind of magic-born message to let him know he'd be coming.

I hurry down the stairs, not bothering to try to disguise the tapping of the foot brace's wooden slats, the hem of my nightgown brushing against my knees. When I reach the bottom, August and Sylas have gone silent, watching my arrival.

In that first moment, both their expressions are so grim that my heart plummets. Then a smile breaks across August's face. He strides over and sweeps me up, claiming a kiss I'm happy to return.

After, he nuzzles my hair. "Couldn't wait to see me, huh, Sweetness?"

He definitely doesn't appear to be bleeding profusely or missing any limbs. I beam back at him. "Had to make sure you got here all right. And to find out the news. If you're back so soon, does that mean you managed to question one of the Unseelie warriors?"

August's smile fades. He sets me down gently on my feet and glances at Sylas, who looks as solemn as before.

"What?" I say as the silence begins to stretch uncomfortably. "You can't just *not* tell me."

Sylas's mouth twists as if he'd prefer it if he could take that tactic, but he motions to August.

"Fill her in on the part you've already told me, and then get into the rest."

When August looks at me, his face has fallen so much that I want to kiss him again just to see if that would bring the light back into his golden eyes. My hands clench at my sides, bracing for the obviously bad news.

"I caught one of the ravens' sentries," he says. "And I found out enough to know why the arch-lords are so concerned, if they know even half of it. The Unseelie have learned of our curse. They know that on the night of the full moon, the warriors at the border will be too crazed to properly defend our lands, and they mean to launch an attack then, presumably a large one."

He turns to Sylas. "The sentry essentially confirmed that they'll be targeting that northern section of the borderlands. I'd guess they're still wary of assuming the battle will go easily, so they figure they're better off focusing all the resources they're comfortable assembling into one spot rather than attacking all across the realm."

Sylas nods. "That's what we would do if our situations were reversed. I wonder how they found out after all this time—and how much the arch-lords know. As far as I heard, they hadn't warned anyone specifically about the full moon."

"No, nothing beyond the standard preparations. They didn't say the additional protections they were arguing about were for any specific time or reason." August lets out a huff of breath. "The Unseelie could get enough of a foothold that we'll have trouble kicking them back to their side of the border even once we have our heads again. And that's without considering how many Seelie will fall while we're unable to properly defend ourselves. What can we do? Shoving more forces at the problem will only make the chaos worse."

A chill has collected in the bottom of my stomach. The Unseelie know the summer fae's greatest weakness, and they're already looking to exploit it. Tomorrow night could become an outright bloodbath. But my horror comes with a twinge of confusion.

I step toward Sylas to catch his attention. "There doesn't have to be any chaos. You've got the cure right here. We make the tonic after all, make sure all the warriors at the border get it—and whoever else the lords can spare. The full moon isn't until tomorrow. There's plenty of time."

I hadn't thought it was possible for Sylas's expression to turn any graver, but I was wrong. He grazes his fingers over my head in a careful caress. "As much as I appreciate your selflessness, Talia, we can't jump straight to that solution. We'd still face all the same problems of keeping you with us and safe once your powers are exposed. If there's any other way—"

"How can there be any other way? You've been trying to figure out other cures for decades. What are the chances you'll come up with something in the next twenty-four hours?"

His whole face tightens, etched with anguish. "We didn't go through all this strife only to throw you to the wolves as some kind of sacrifice now."

The tension radiates off him. I can only imagine how torn he feels. He grappled enough when I first came into his care over keeping me safe despite the benefits he might earn for his pack by offering me to the arch-lords, and that was before he'd made me so many promises. Before not just his pack but his entire society had come under an immediate, dire threat.

He'll have trouble living with himself no matter what he decides.

Fine. Let it be my decision then. *I* can't live with myself if I hide away like a coward when so many lives hang in the balance that I could save so easily.

I raise my chin. "Then don't throw me to them. Put all your thinking toward figuring out your best shot at keeping me safe while offering my blood. It is *mine*, and I don't want anyone dying so that I can hold on to all of it."

Sylas sweeps his arm through the air. "It shouldn't be your problem to solve. We aren't even your people. You were never meant to be here in the first place."

"But I am here. And it *is* my problem, because wherever I came from, you all are my family now. I'm part of this pack. You saved me—let me save you too."

Resistance still shows all through Sylas's stance. Next to him, August looks from his lord to me and back again, clearly hesitant to override Sylas but unwilling to argue in favor of abandoning the border either.

As if there's any real choice here. We could debate all day, and in the end, the only real answer would still be to use me. They just don't want to admit it yet.

I glance toward the wall in the direction of the pack village. Inspiration hits me with a rush of determination. I can end this argument right now, claim the decision so utterly there's no way Sylas will be able to deny it.

I spin away from them toward the kitchen and march to the door at the opposite end, my foot brace clacking in time with my uneven steps. "Talia?" August says, startled. At the sound of him and Sylas following, I pick up my pace as fast as I can without outright running.

They haven't been locking the exits against me anymore. I push past the door and hurry out into the yard by the herb garden and the orchards. At a limping jog, a throbbing pang forming in my foot, I hustle around the side of the keep toward the twisted-off-stump houses where the rest of the pack live.

My lovers' footsteps sound behind me, but they don't know what I'm up to yet, so they're not putting in enough speed to stop me. Soon, they won't be able to.

A few of the fae are up and about in the pale early morning light, puttering around their homes. Not enough to make this tactic really work. As I cross the last short distance around the edge of the keep, I pitch my voice to carry. "Hey! Everyone in the pack! Get up, come out—there's something you need to hear."

Behind me, Sylas's breath hisses between his teeth in dismay. But I've already hurtled onto the field into full view of the houses, the pack-kin who were outside staring my way and others emerging from their doorways or peering from their windows to see what the fuss is about. I plant myself before their puzzled eyes, my heart hammering in my chest, counting on Sylas not wanting to bewilder them even more by charging in and hauling me away but prepared to keep shouting anyway if he does.

I launch straight into the most important part of the matter. "*I* am the main ingredient in the tonic that can cure the full-moon curse. My blood is, I mean. I didn't only just arrive in the faerie world. Another lord was keeping me captive and using my blood for the tonic. Sylas—" I trip over my tongue for a second, realizing I probably shouldn't admit to his crime even to his own people. "When I got away, Sylas and his cadre helped me. And now I want to help all of you. As long as I'm around, I don't want any of you to have to go through the full-moon wildness again."

While I've made my announcement, Sylas and August have come to a halt behind me. Sylas clasps my shoulder, but he doesn't haul me away. Too many gazes are fixed on us now, too many gaping fae taking in my proclamation. More slip from their houses —I see Harper outside hers with her parents, her startled eyes even larger than usual.

As the buzz of adrenaline fades, it occurs to me that I must look pretty ridiculous standing here in nothing but my nightgown with my bedhead hair. A blush warms my cheeks, but not enough to stop me from standing tall and taking their scrutiny.

One of the older men starts laughing. "That's absurd. A human's blood, curing our curse?"

"It's true," I say, keeping my voice loud enough for everyone to hear. "If you need proof—someone give me a knife. All I have to do is cut my finger, and you'll be able to smell the—"

As I hold out my arm, Sylas's grip on my shoulder tightens. He steps past me, authority radiating off his pose. "That won't be necessary."

I brace myself for him to try to cover up my story somehow, but I must have played my cards well enough. Too many people heard what I said—too many people who might repeat the story, even if they don't believe it, to fae beyond this pack, who could pass it on to the arch-lords in turn.

"I can confirm that Talia speaks the truth," Sylas says. "And thanks to her compassion for our pack, we will escape the curse beneath tomorrow's full moon. With that in mind, I expect you to treat her with twice as much kindness and respect as you already have." He glances down at me, his mismatched gaze just shy of a glower. "For now, we have much to prepare."

A pinch of guilt jabs my stomach at the way I've forced his hand, but it was going to be forced one way or another anyway. I think from the way he phrased his confirmation that he's accepted my right to make this call.

Aerik used my blood over and over for his own selfish gain. This time, I can claim it for a cause that matters to me.

Whatever consequences come from that decision, at least they'll be the ones I brought down on myself.

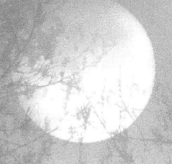

CHAPTER TWENTY-SEVEN

Whitt

"You know," I say, stretching my hands out over the earth, "if we'd really been thinking ahead, we'd have gotten Aerik to throw in his stash of vials when he yielded. He must have a rather large supply he no longer has any use for."

Sylas lets out a low guffaw from where he's standing in the shadows of the parlor doorway, checking on my progress. "Perhaps I'll offer to take them off his hands next month. Your magic appears up to the task today. We should only need a few dozen more."

"On it, oh glorious leader." I shift my concentration away from him to the ground beneath me, sensing with my mind rather than seeing with my eyes in the darkness of the much-too-early morning, and roll the true name for sand off my tongue.

With absolute focus, I will the particles that shiver up through the soil to meld together into the tiny glass flasks that will each hold one dose of our tonic. The true name's mark, just beneath my left shoulder blade, itches with the amount of power I'm directing through it.

I've certainly summoned *larger* constructs into being, but not quite so many items in a row. The kitchen counters are already packed with vials. Sylas is lucky I even bothered to commune with sand enough to command it. None of the domains we've occupied are exactly beachy, but my fondness for weather magic led me to mastering some of its more obscure forms. I can conjure a mean sandstorm if need be.

Hmm, maybe that would be just the thing to send toward Aerik's domain one day. I'm sure I could manage it without leaving any trace of who guided it there. Let him and his lot find themselves shaking sand out of their drawers and picking it from their teeth for weeks to come.

The minor trauma we got to inflict on them for their yield was definitely not enough.

Sylas wouldn't approve of that plan, though, and I have more urgent concerns at the moment. It's only a couple of hours before dawn, with the full moon approaching at next sundown. Sylas wants to be on his way to bargain with the arch-lords before any sane person has taken breakfast.

As I shape the last few vials, the itch in the mark deepens into a piercing sensation. I restrain a grimace. The vials may be small, but they require quite a bit of precision. With the amount I've created, I've nearly drained my stores of magic, which aren't as bountiful living so far from the Heart of the Mists as they used to be. If we require even more, I may have to sacrifice a bit of my flesh to the process.

Well, it'd be worth it if this gambit takes us back to Hearthshire where I can bask in the deeper thrum of the Heart's energy at my leisure.

I lift the woven basket I've been conjuring the vials into and carry it into the kitchen. A flurry of activity fills the lantern-lit room. Along the islands, pack-kin are sorting the existing vials into groups by squadron according to my written instructions with my best estimates of the numbers at the border. A couple of others are bustling in with supplies Sylas asked for—another bucket of fresh glist-oak sap, another jug of rock-tumbled water. A few more have joined August where he's assembling our tonic in his largest pots, him stirring his current batch and them filling trays of vials with the earlier ones.

Sylas stands off in the corner with Talia, who's perched as so often on one of the stools, although not helping with the preparations in quite the same way as she would with a meal. She's holding out her arm, which Sylas is holding gently while he murmurs over it. A larger vial gleams scarlet with her blood on the shelf beside him.

The few times that Aerik deigned to offer us his tonic in the past, we studied it closely and came up with a pretty clear idea of the main ingredients—ones we didn't realize were simply there to dilute and disguise the only element that mattered. We're replicating that formula as well as we can, since while it may not be essential, we at least know it didn't impair the effects of Talia's blood. But we're not quite sure exactly how *much* we can safely dilute the stuff. It appears my lord has just asked her to contribute a little more of her body's gift.

She doesn't look bothered about it, though. She accepted the initial blood-taking with equal calm, her posture straight and her expression determined. Why she's quite so determined to put her freedom on the line to save a whole host of fae who've mostly been horrible to her, I can't entirely fathom, but perhaps that says more about me than about her.

Our mortal lady is a lovely sight sitting there watching the results of her sacrifice come together, her striking hair cascading over shoulders still slim but no longer spindly, her eyes brightly alert. She knows what she's risking—and she insisted on it anyway.

I hadn't thought I could be more awed by her than in the moment when she summoned her inexplicable magic to bind the men who once caged her, but now the combination of admiration and longing socks me in the gut.

At that exact moment, she glances up and catches my gaze. A small, hopeful smile crosses her face, and I can't bear to do anything except smile back, even though my stomach has just twisted twice as tight.

She wants me. She wants *me*. I told myself she was out of reach, but now that she's shown that's not true, I can't shake the sense that with one touch, one taste, I could destroy everything I care about. How could having her possibly be as simple as August made it sound?

And yet a part of me can't let go of the desire either. No, from the moment she met my eyes in our house by the border and told me she returned the feeling, that hunger has only expanded at a pace too manic to rein in. One kiss on the cheek the other morning, and all I could think about was having her gasping and moaning beneath me.

I shove those memories away and hand over the new set of vials to the pack-kin sorting them. Sylas hands off the container of blood to August and surveys my contribution.

"It looks as though we'll have plenty—including extra doses if we've miscalculated," he says. "If I could get it to every fae who isn't at the border too…"

I wave to the room around us. "Considering we assembled this production line less than a day ago, I think we've accomplished an incredible feat. If anyone complains that we fell short, let them choke on their vial."

Sylas snorts and motions for me to follow him. "I'd like to speak to you for a moment."

Speak to me alone, it appears. We cross the hall to the dining room, where he shuts the door. To my irritation, a nervous prickling runs over my skin.

Given the subjects that have come up between us over the past few days, I may not like the direction this conversation takes. I can't decide whether it'd be worse to have him chide me for refusing Talia's advances or announce that he isn't so keen on allowing me to pursue her after all.

He glances in the direction of the kitchen and then fixes his gaze on me. "I don't feel it'd be safe for Talia to come with us to the Heart. It'll be harder for me to negotiate her safety with the archlords if she's right there for the taking. Since we'll be joining the fighting at the border as soon as we've made our arrangements, I'm going to have August come with me. I ask that you remain here and watch over her."

My eyebrows arch automatically. "So, I'm the babysitter?"

Sylas gives me a baleful look. "I think you know as well as I do that she doesn't need a keeper. But she may very well require protection. We'll keep the sentries watching the edges of our territory, especially to the south—at any indication that the archlords have sent forces to claim her, I trust you can ensure that the two of you are nowhere to be found."

Fair enough. I do have extensive knowledge of all the ins and outs of this domain, as loath as I was to see us banished here. I nod. "I won't let them get so much as a glimpse of her."

"Heart willing, it won't come to that in the first place. We'll see what sort of reception I get."

He sighs, and then grasps my shoulder firmly, holding my gaze with both his dark eye and the deadened one that sees more than it should. "I trust *you*, Whitt. As my brother, as my cadre-chosen. I know you will serve her well, in this and in any other ways you choose to attend to her. In case there was any doubt, when I spoke of sharing her affections, it was without reservation. I'd no sooner cage her heart than the rest of her, and I can't think of anyone more worthy of her regard than my own cadre."

I stare at him, speech stunned out of me. Sylas has never been cold —we are summer fae, after all—but I'm not sure I've ever heard him express *his* regard for me that earnestly. It was more the sort of thing taken for granted with the call to the cadre and the responsibilities he's offered me since. And there were times when I wasn't sure his full trust was a certainty at all, rather than a boon I needed to re-earn.

The declaration feels like a peace offering—or perhaps simply forgiveness for things we've never spoken of. Relief sweeps through me, sharp and sweet. Whatever I thought I'd broken here, it either never was or it's mended now.

"I appreciate that, my lord," I say, falling back into formality while I'm unexpectedly fumbling for my words.

Sylas peers at me with deeper attention. "I *am* still your brother as well as your lord. And I wouldn't want to be the sort of lord who holds himself above criticism regardless, as I hope you know. If the way I approached the subject before offended you in some way, I'd want you to tell me. That wasn't my intention."

He's worried... that *he* offended *me*. I can't hold back a sputter of a laugh, but I manage to recover quickly. I set my hand over his briefly in a firm pat. "There was no offense taken. I apologize if it appeared that way. I was taken by surprise—I had some things to sort out in my own thoughts—but my mind is clearer now. Thank you. For your trust and your concern."

Speaking that earnestly myself brings a clenching into my chest, but not enough to offset all that's good about the moment. Sylas offers me one of his subdued but warm smiles, claps my shoulder once more, and turns back toward the kitchen. And I realize there's now nothing standing in my way at all.

After all, if our glorious leader believes in me with all his lordly experience and wisdom, who in the lands am I not to?

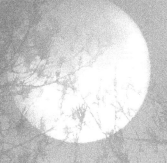

CHAPTER TWENTY-EIGHT

Talia

The dawn glow is only just seeping over the fields around the keep when Sylas and August load up their carriage. I watch from a short distance beyond the keep's front door, my arms crossed over my chest against the night coolness lingering in the breeze—and against the anxiety twining through my ribs over the mission they're setting out on.

Only the two of them are going, figuring that when—*if*—the arch-lords agree to their terms, there'll be plenty of fae on hand who can help distribute the tonic. They didn't want to leave Oakmeet completely undefended. Sylas assured me that fae law will protect them from any harm from the arch-lords, but I can't help wishing they had a few more allies with them for their own defense.

Of course, it's not just the arch-lords we have to worry about. Even if everything goes well at the Heart, the men I love still plan on joining the warriors in the battle along the border. It'll be *easier* to fight the Unseelie without the curse gripping them, but that doesn't mean it'll be *easy*. Warriors from our pack died in the last skirmish.

To hold the baskets upon baskets of vials, Sylas has summoned a carriage twice as long as the ones that conveyed us before. The magic has left a tang of juniper scent in the air. The thing looks like an immense canoe with a wooden shade arching over the middle portion, albeit an immense canoe that's floating a foot off the ground.

When the baskets are all nestled in their compartments, the two fae men walk back to me. August tugs me into a tight embrace, his heat and musky scent wrapping around me. "We'll be back tomorrow, Sweetness. I always kept my promises before."

Between the lump rising in my throat and the mugginess from lack of sleep that's filled my head, I don't know what to say in return, so I just hug him as hard as I can. He pulls back only far enough to find my mouth, capturing it with a kiss so tender and lingering that I'm tingling down to my toes when he's finished. He smiles, apparently not concerned about our audience—most of the pack has come to see them off too, gathered in a loose cluster at the edge of the village.

Sylas merely tucks a strand of my hair back from my cheek and brushes a kiss to my forehead, but I can feel the affection in that reserved gesture. "Little do the ravens know their downfall will be a single human woman. Get some rest and try not to worry yourself too much."

He glances at Whitt, who's propped in the doorway behind me, and gives his cadre-chosen a confident nod. Whatever instructions he had for the other man, he's clearly already given them. Then he turns to the assembled pack.

"Thank you all again for your assistance in preparing the tonic. Enjoy this full moon free of the wildness, and let us hope we can ensure we never face it again. I look forward to rejoining you with good news tomorrow."

An eager murmur ripples through the crowd. They bob into bows, with calls of "Thank you, my lord!" and "Safe journeys!" and from Astrid, off to the side, one, "Give those feather-brains plenty to regret!" Sylas raises his hand in farewell, and he and August climb into the carriage.

I stand there watching as it glides away toward the south-eastern horizon. The pack drifts back to their homes, but Harper hesitates. When the carriage has vanished from sight amid the trees and rocky spires, I drag my gaze away, and she wanders over to join me.

"Hey," she says. "How are you doing?" Her attention falls to my arm, where a faint mark shows just above my wrist. Sylas sealed the cut after I gave my blood, but wounds don't disappear in an instant.

Harper and I haven't talked since I made my dramatic announcement to the pack yesterday morning. In the rush of activity that followed, there hasn't really been time to. The wariness in her wide eyes sends a twinge of guilt to my stomach.

"I'm all right. They didn't need to take all that much." I look at the ground and then back at her. "I'm sorry I lied to you about how I came here. We just—we were worried the lord who brought me to the faerie world in the first place would find me, and he... wasn't anywhere near as kind as Sylas is."

Harper blinks, her lips parting with surprise. "I'm not upset, not at all! Of course you'd be careful. You must have been through a lot." She cringes. "I'm sorry I asked you so much about your home beyond the Mists and all that... If they dragged you away against your will and then kept you like a prisoner, it must be painful thinking about what you lost."

"That's not your fault. You didn't know." I take in the houses beyond her, the terrain that stretches out all around the keep, becoming more familiar with every day. "This is my home now. And you helped me feel like I could belong here. And now that Sylas has taken care of the lord who dragged me away, it's safe for me to do more adventuring. You can show me the most interesting places in the domain that are farther out from the keep."

A smile brightens Harper's face. "Perfect. And… People are saying that by giving the tonic to help with this battle, Lord Sylas might be able to reclaim *our* real home in Hearthshire. It's right in the middle of everything instead of out here on the fringes, and if we have the arch-lords' pardon then the other packs will be more friendly again." She throws her arms around me in a hug so quick I barely have time to return it before she's stepped back again, outright beaming now. "If that's true, then you've given us so much more than if you'd just talked up my dress with the lords and ladies."

I grin back at her. "I hope that all works out. But I'll still talk up that dress if anyone asks. It's the most gorgeous thing I've ever worn."

She cocks her head, considering my foot caged in its brace. "The fae who kidnapped you did that to you. No one can heal it?"

"No. August looked at it and said the bones have been set like that for too long." I shrug. "I'm used to it now, though. I can't complain about having to limp when there were years when I couldn't do anything at all. This brace Sylas made for me makes walking a lot easier, so it's not too bad anyway."

Harper taps her lips. "If you could… ask him if he'd make another one that I could examine? I have some ideas—I'd have to work with it to see if I could pull it off."

"I don't see why not." Assuming Sylas makes it back. A shiver runs through my nerves, dampening the good mood the conversation sparked.

Maybe I droop a little, because Whitt stirs in the doorway, where he must have been keeping an eye on me this whole time. "I think this mighty human should get the rest Sylas ordered," he says, ruffling my hair from behind, and yawns. "I certainly need mine."

I can't really argue. My eyelids are getting heavier, the

mugginess around my thoughts thicker. Harper bobs her head and ambles off, and I let Whitt usher me into the keep.

Despite my worries, which no lord can order away, I'm so tired that I'm out moments after my head hits the pillow. I wake up to the dazzling sun of what I'd guess is early afternoon, my mind still a bit muddy but too much restlessness winding through my chest for me to think there's any hope of getting more sleep now.

My stomach grumbles, unhappy that the only food it's had so far today is a hasty sandwich August assembled for me in the wee hours of the morning between batches of tonic. I heave myself out of bed and grimace at the clothes I've been wearing since yesterday, now wrinkled from being slept-in too.

Opening the wardrobe, I'm about to reach for another of my usual jeans and short-sleeved shirts when my eyes snag on the simpler dress hanging next to Harper's gown. The sky-blue one in the style many of the pack women wear that I put on for our dinner with Aerik and his cadre.

I wore it then to make it look as if I was integrated into the pack. Why shouldn't I wear it now that I've proven how much that pack means to me, now that I no longer need to care whether Aerik or any other fae sees me as I really am? It's not a disguise—it's just me. I should leave the trappings of my old human life behind sometime.

This *is* my home now. I already know the people here better than anyone still alive back in the human world. The faerie realm comes with all kinds of dangers, but at least I'm not facing them alone.

I give myself a quick wash in the bathroom and pull the dress over my head. The soft fabric flows over my body, hugging what little curves I have now that my ribs no longer stand out like the rungs of a ladder up my torso. Looking down at myself, I feel like the lady of this keep more solidly than I ever have before.

The kitchen is still a bit of a mess, the pots August used for mixing the tonic stacked beside one of the sinks, shreds of dried reeds from the baskets scattered on the floor. I head to the pantry and emerge with a heel of seed-laced bread that I don't think has been reserved for any upcoming meal.

As I stand there gnawing at it, Whitt saunters into the room, looking shockingly alert for someone who hasn't gotten any more sleep than I have. He takes in my scavenged food and shoots me a broad grin. "I think we can do better than that for our mighty one. Let's see what we can throw together."

He pushes the cuffs of his loose sleeves past his elbows, revealing the true-name tattoos curving all across his muscular forearms, and grabs one of the more modestly sized pots that's still clean. "Stew. Anyone can make a halfway decent stew. At least, that's what I've heard. You must have absorbed some of August's culinary wisdom. Between the two of us, we should be able to produce something absolutely fantastic."

"Aiming high?" I say, unable to hold back a smile.

Whitt clucks his tongue at me. "No other way to live." He adds water to the pot with a hiss from the faucet and thumps it onto the stove. "Let's see what the whelp left us in the cold box."

The cold box is practically a room in itself, a closet-like space full of shelves and air kept chilly through magic, about twice the size of any fridge I remember seeing in my former life. Whitt grabs a papery bundle that I think holds leftover sausage patties, a bowl full of the tiny blue quail eggs, and the few stray vegetables that didn't end up getting used during August's past cooking sessions.

"Pilfer some herbs and spices from the pantry," he tells me. "Whatever catches your fancy."

I enter the dim room cautiously, with no idea what will be a good match for the assortment of ingredients Whitt has already picked out. But then, that's sort of the point, right? Toss a bunch of stuff in, have fun with it, see what happens. Even if it's a mess, it'll keep me thinking about things other than what Sylas and August are facing right now.

I pull sprigs from a few bundles of herbs I like the scent of and snatch a couple of jars of powdered spices off the shelves. Back by the stove, Whitt has already dumped the meat and the eggs into the pot and is halfway through dicing up the vegetables with one of August's enchanted knives that slides through anything edible like cutting butter. I drag one of the stools over to the other side of the stove and scrape the leaves off the sprigs with my fingernails to sprinkle them in.

"What are you adding?" Whitt asks.

"Spindle-slip, cinnamon, and a bunch of I don't know what they're called but I like them." I sprinkle a dash of the cinnamon and some of the bright orange powder I grabbed after the herbs.

"That's the spirit." Whitt gives me another smile and pours the chopped veggies into the mix. The liquid is already bubbling. He stirs it, peering into the pot. "I feel we're missing something. A stew should be thicker. What've we got for that, mite?"

My mind trips back nearly a decade to my mom grumbling as she attempted to thicken the Thanksgiving gravy. "Flour?" I leap to my feet with a burst of inspiration. "We could try fallowroot." I've only had the stuff in pastries and pancakes before, but the thought of its rich, nutty flavor makes my mouth water.

Whitt nods gleefully. "Everything is better with fallowroot."

I retrieve the small sack of the flour from the pantry and drop spoonfuls in while Whitt keeps stirring until we agree that the base is satisfyingly gooey-looking. Then I toss in a handful of dried berries just because, to his energetic approval. He goes back to the cold box and returns with a chunk of cream—"Because everything is also better with cream"—that absorbs into the simmering mixture in a matter of seconds.

Whitt takes a sip of the broth and frowns, then snaps his fingers. "Pepper." He adds a few unfamiliar syllables that must be a true name with another flick of his hand, and a jar of gray powder flies straight out of the pantry into his grasp. Once he's sprinkled that in and stirred again, he offers me the spoon to taste.

I lick a little off, momentarily concerned, but the flavors that flood my mouth are unusual but tempting enough that I clean the whole spoon. Nutty and savory with a bite of warmth and a zestiness I think is from the egg yolks. "It's *good*."

Whitt snatches the spoon back and waves it at me. "No need to sound so surprised. I think the caulderims need a few more minutes if we don't want to be chewing them for days, and then we'll have a meal."

When he deems the stew ready, I get a couple of bowls and he slops the mixture into them with apparent abandon, although he manages not to spill any. We carry them over to the dining room.

Whitt eyes the regal chair at the head of the table in an unexpected hesitation. Making the decision for both of us, I limp to the far end where none of us usually sit so there can't be any sense of displacement. Our kitchen experiment managed to distract me from my worries about the men who aren't here. The longer I can hold back those worries, the better.

I drop into the seat right at the foot of the table. With a chuckle, Whitt follows and takes the chair kitty-corner to me. He spoons up a dollop of the stew and pops it into his mouth to chew it with a contemplative expression.

"Well, I probably wouldn't serve it to August, lest he tell me all the things we got wrong, but I'll personally give us top marks."

I laugh and dig in. It's true that the combination of flavors is odd, and maybe a few of them clash in ways that don't entirely work, but our creation is definitely more satisfying than my hunk of bread. And even more satisfying when combined with the memory of freely flinging whatever we felt like into the pot. August might not approve of a technique so haphazard, but it *was* fun.

After another mouthful, Whitt points his spoon at me. "So, mighty one, I gather you're already making plans to leave us."

My heart lurches at the thought of being anywhere but here. I sputter, almost choking on a lump of sausage before I catch the sly glint in his eyes. I make a face at him. "What are you talking about?"

"I was right there when you were discussing future travels with your dress-making faerie friend," he reminds me, smirking.

I'm feeling bold enough with him now to take the smirk as permission to kick him under the table. "I was only talking about checking out other parts of the domain, like a day trip, and I think you know that."

"Ah, but why restrict yourself? The faerie world is full of wonders beyond those you could have dreamed of discovering where you came from. I thought you were such an avid traveler?"

I hadn't really had the chance to do much more than dream about traveling, but remembering that tightens my chest in a way I'd rather avoid. "What should I make sure to see here, then?" I ask instead, raising my eyebrows to encourage one of his spiels. "With all your spying, you must know the best places, right?"

"Hmm, you know me so well already." Whitt's tone is still teasing, but his smirk has softened. He takes another bite of stew and leans back in his chair.

"Let's see... If you're simply interested in breathtaking spectacles, there's the Shimmering Falls not far from the Heart. The water tumbling over that cliff sparkles brighter than the most finely cut diamond, so lush the vegetation around the pool at its base displays foliage and flowers twice as vivid as anywhere else in the land. It's one of August's favorite picnic spots—or was, when we lived closer and the arch-lords didn't object to us passing through their domains at our leisure."

That caveat makes my heart sink, thinking of August and Sylas traveling through those domains now. "You haven't been there in a while, then."

Whitt makes a careless wave of his hand. "Don't look like that. It only means we'll enjoy it nearly as much as you do when we make it there next. Let's see, what else? If you're in the mood for more adventure, I hear the Shifting Dunes are quite thrilling, although of course you have to watch out for the sand sharks…"

Between bites, he spins pictures of a dozen other fantastical places I can barely imagine being real, answering my awed questions as they come. By the time I'm scraping the bottom of my bowl, my stomach satisfyingly full, I've created a substantial mental scrapbook dedicated to Faerieland. Whitt discusses it all so breezily that a tickling sensation of hope has risen in my chest.

If *he* believes I'll get to see all those places, that Sylas and August will succeed in making their deal with the arch-lords and I'll keep my freedom, then maybe I don't need to worry at all.

Whitt pauses to lick his spoon. "What of your world? What wonders did you plan to seek out there? I have to admit my explorations on that side have been much less extensive."

Still more extensive than mine, I'm sure. I rub my mouth. "There was the series of mountain pools above the jungle, somewhere in… Tanzania? Tunisia? I don't remember for sure. The photos looked so gorgeous. And the pyramids in Egypt—all that desert… The rainforest in Ecuador…"

My stomach tightens unexpectedly. Trying to put those dreams into words makes them feel so flimsy compared to the descriptions Whitt just gave me.

I duck my head. "I used to imagine places like that all the time when Aerik had me. Float away inside my head. Now that I've imagined them so much, I don't know if the reality would actually live up to all those hopes. But—I'm getting a chance to focus on new dreams now."

Whitt's eyes have darkened at the mention of my past imprisonment, but he taps the table with gusto. "Yes. Yes, you are."

He scoops up the last of his own stew and gulps it down. Then he motions toward my bowl. Before I can nudge it toward him, he's already spoken a true word I can recognize from past experience as *clay*. Both his bowl and mine lift from the tabletop and whisk away to the kitchen as if drawn by a homing beacon.

I stare after them and then yank my attention back to Whitt. "You do that so easily." None of the men of the keep have worked magic that casually in front of me before. From the pleased expression that brightens Whitt's face, I suspect he was purposefully showing off.

"Centuries of practice. But I'd better hold off on more than little gestures like that until I completely recover from all my vial-constructing last night." He sets his elbows on the table and leans forward to study me. "How have *your* magical studies been progressing?"

My fingers curl instinctively, recalling the feel of the bronze spoon I was holding just a minute ago. "Well, you've seen what I can do with bronze now. I still need to be upset before it seems to work. But I guess any time it's urgent that I need to use that word, chances are I'll be upset without even trying."

"August has been working on teaching you more true names, hasn't he?"

"We've just focused on light so far. I haven't made as much headway with that. It doesn't come quite the same way."

Whitt cocks his head. "What do you mean?"

I gesture vaguely. "I can only seem to get the energy right when I'm really happy. And somehow it's harder to *make* myself feel that than it is to bring back fear or anger from my memories."

"Hmm. I don't think that's so odd. There are so many things one can be afraid of or angry about, especially having been through as much as you have. True happiness is harder to find."

My voice comes out quiet. "Yeah." But as I gaze back at him, the rare but no longer unfamiliar glow of joy beams through me.

This has made me happy: goofing around with Whitt, listening to his stories, simply enjoying each other's company. The longing grips me to show him, to make him see that he hasn't ruined anything. On this day that should be agonizing, he's the one who's made it better.

Still meeting his eyes, I raise my hands above the table and channel that emotion into the word. "*Sole-un-straw.*"

Light flares between my palms, dazzling me for the few seconds before it wisps away. When my vision clears, Whitt is staring at me, his expression tensed but otherwise unreadable.

Maybe it was so brief it seemed more like an insult. My cheeks flush. "I—I don't have much control over it yet, even when I *am* feeling happy. I can't manage more than that."

When Whitt speaks, his tone is unusually gentle, with a rough note running through it. "Talia, it was lovely. There isn't another human in the world who could have conjured even a spark, you know."

A smile stretches across my face, and I find myself saying, before I can second-guess the impulse, "They mustn't have the right inspiration."

His eyes flicker, and he wets his lips. Then he scoots his chair back from the table and beckons to me. "Come here?"

My heart suddenly thumping, I get up and walk the few steps to his side. Whitt reaches out to take my hand, carefully tucking his around mine. He considers our intertwined fingers as if searching for something in the shape they make. His palm rests warmly against mine.

"The more I'm around you," he says, "the more I see how valiant and vibrant and *good* you are. I want you to know I've set aside any fear that you'll ruin anything at all, even unintentionally. But that doesn't mean *I* won't."

I swallow hard. "Whitt—"

He shakes his head against whatever he thinks I'm going to say. "I don't lie, but I'm in the habit of talking around difficult subjects rather than confronting them directly. I stay up to all hours, and I'm irritable if woken for any reason short of the apocalypse. I'm not sure I'll ever fully trust anyone, including myself. I have many stellar qualities, but you'd have trouble finding kindness, patience, or generosity among them."

He rattles those declarations off in a flippant tone, but he's speaking to our hands rather than to my face. When he looks up at me, I raise my eyebrows. "Are you trying to talk me out of wanting to be with you?"

The corner of his mouth twitches, so briefly I can't tell which direction it was headed in. "Just making sure you know what you're getting into."

Am I "getting into" it? Into *him*? My heart pounds harder. Right here, on the verge, my position feels abruptly precarious. I've already offered so much of myself to the men of this keep.

But I want more. I want everything this unexpected arrangement can bring with all three of them. Maybe it isn't romance the way I might have imagined when I had no reality to judge from, maybe I have no idea where it'll lead, but while I don't belong to them or they to me, I'm more sure than ever that we all belong together. We fit—a lord, a lord's cadre, and their lady—with this one piece that hadn't quite settled into place.

There's so much about the future that I'm frightened of, but I'm not scared of the man in front of me, not even a little. This is my choice as much as giving my blood was, and I'll accept whatever consequences might come from it too.

This is a dream I can already make real.

I squeeze Whitt's hand, grappling for the right words to erase whatever doubt he's still holding onto. "You always find a way to talk that lets me believe everything's okay, no matter how upset I was a second ago. You stay up so you can give your pack-kin something to celebrate, even though none of you really want to be here. You might not always trust me, but when you've realized you saw things wrong, you've fixed your mistake in whatever way you can. And I don't know how you define kindness, patience, or generosity, but I've seen with my own eyes how far you'll go for Sylas and August and the entire pack—and for me. I couldn't ask for more than that. I wouldn't. I want you exactly like this."

I stop, worried that I've strayed into babbling territory, but Whitt's expression washes away my own doubts. It's as if something has fallen away behind his eyes and through the planes of his stunning face—as if I'm *really* seeing him, without the sly calculation and the affected nonchalance, just a man who never expected to hear anyone speak of him so fondly. Who's disarmed by it with an elation he can't hide or isn't trying to.

Is this the open, joyful version of Whitt I imagined the night of the revel when he talked about how he's always on guard? Maybe not completely; maybe he hasn't lowered all his armor. But it's closer than I've ever gotten before.

Close enough that I can't stop myself from leaning in to kiss him.

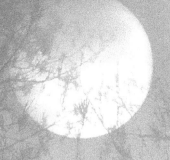

CHAPTER TWENTY-NINE

Talia

J ust before my lips brush his, Whitt raises his free hand to catch my cheek—not stopping me but urging me on. Our mouths collide with more force than I was prepared for.

But it's good—so good. His fingers slip from my cheek into my hair, teasing over my scalp. He drops my hand to loop his other arm around my waist, and his mouth slides against mine, hot and firm yet soft, with just a hint of roughness. Each movement of them sends a tingle down through my chest.

He draws out the kiss, coaxing my lips a little apart, tracing the tip of his tongue along the seam, tilting his head to deepen the embrace. It isn't like August's worshipful eagerness or Sylas's commanding passion. The sense rises up with a flutter around my heart that Whitt is *reveling* in me, drawing out every particle of enjoyment he can from our closeness, savoring me as if I'm the most exquisite dessert.

I may as well be made of spun sugar when he's touching me like this. One kiss and I'm already melting into him.

He eases a few inches back with a chuckle that grazes my cheek with the heat of his breath. His voice is raw. "I could get drunk on you."

I trail my fingers over his cheek and into his hair like he did to me. "Then why don't you?"

I'm not sure who closes the last of the distance, but an instant later we're kissing again. Whitt devours me, leaving me aching for more, for things I can't even put words to. With every press of his lips, my breath grows shakier. My knees wobble beneath me, and I find the wherewithal to brace one next to his legs on the seat of the chair and swing the other over to straddle him.

The skirt of my dress rides up on my thighs. Whitt lets out an approving murmur at the increased contact, fitting his mouth against mine even more deeply. His fingers twine in my hair, pulling to the barest edge of pain that somehow provokes an electric pulse of pleasure right down my spine. His other hand strokes up my side to cup my breast.

He seems to know exactly how to touch me to draw out the giddiest waves of bliss. His thumb finds my nipple and raises it to a peak with one swift swivel; his tongue coaxes mine to explore his mouth. All I can do is kiss him back and clutch onto his shirt, holding on for the ride.

He's been with other women before—lots of other women, from how Sylas has talked. He knows what he's doing from practice. But that thought only stirs the faintest twinge of jealousy in me, there and then washed away by the pleasure he's conjuring all through my body.

It's me he's with right now. It's me he *wants* right now. He's taking his time, relishing me, drinking in my reactions and following what makes me whimper with need.

I echo his movements, wanting to spark the same thrill of desire in him as he's lighting in me: tangling my fingers in his rumpled hair, melding my lips to his, running my hand up and down his sculpted chest over his shirt. The groan that escapes him suggests I'm doing something right.

He wrenches his mouth from mine to chart a path of kisses down the side of my neck before burying his face in the crook of my shoulder. His breath scorches my skin as his lips and tongue work over the sensitive span of skin. He skims that spot with the edges of his teeth and then, when I quiver and gasp, nips me with sharper intensity.

It isn't hard enough to break the skin, but the sensation shifts from exhilarating to unnerving so abruptly my whole body stiffens. A memory flickers up of jaws tearing into my flesh, fangs raking through that shoulder—

Whitt jerks back. He holds my face close to his until I relax again with the stroke of his thumbs across my temple.

"I'm sorry," he murmurs. He drops one hand in a caress along my neck to my scarred shoulder, gliding his fingertips over the mottled ridges in the gentlest of caresses. "You taste so good, mighty one. But I will *never* bring my teeth to bear on you where they're not wanted. The ones who savaged you like this deserve to be torn to pieces limb by limb and sent up in flames for good measure."

He follows those words with a delicate kiss to each raised line of scar, until any memory of past pain is lost under the desire trembling through me. I tip my head back instinctively, and he flicks his tongue across my throat before marking a line down to my collarbone with the softest of nibbles.

Slowly, waiting on my encouraging hum, he eases the strap of my dress down my arm. His kisses delve lower, following the fabric until the neckline grazes my nipple to spark a quiver of anticipation.

While Whitt bares more and more of my skin, his is staying

frustratingly under wraps. I swallow a needy sound that's almost a whine and focus enough to yank at his high-collared shirt.

"If my clothes are coming off, yours are too," I inform him, a command that would probably be firmer if it hadn't come out breathless.

He grins up at me. "Fair is fair. I do appreciate a woman who knows what she wants."

He loosens the fastenings below the collar and tugs the shirt off over his head, leaving his hair even more rumpled than before. I got a good look at his muscular form in his bed the other morning, but not with quite so much freedom to explore. As I gaze down at him, he merely strokes his fingers along the edge of my dress's straps, not diverting me from my inspection.

Taking him in with my eyes isn't enough. I trail my hands down from his shoulders to the packed muscle across his abdomen, pausing here and there to trace the whorls and angles of his tattoos. His smooth skin blazes beneath my fingers. I tease them along his sides, finding a spot that draws a rumble from his chest, and then give in to the impulse to taste him as he's tasted me.

I lean in, pressing my lips to a coiled mark on his neck, a jagged pinwheel on his shoulder, a clawed twig-like shape over his sternum. Whitt slides his hand into my hair again, following my progress, a hint of a rasp creeping into his breath. I flick my tongue over one of his taut nipples, delighting at the hitch of his chest, and kiss my way across the powerful expanse to the other.

As I absorb his summery, sun-baked scent, my fingers edge lower. Past his belly button, over the waist of his trousers where my dress is pooled, until the heel of my hand brushes the rigid bulge just below.

Whitt lets out a growl and pulls my mouth back to his. He brands me with a kiss so searing it leaves every nerve in my body quaking with desire.

My touch has awakened something primal in his nature. His

tongue tangles with mine with sudden urgency. His hands sweep right beneath the neckline of my dress to caress my breasts skin to skin and then yank the fabric right off them. Hefting me higher against him, he sucks one nipple into the scorching heat of his mouth with a wildness that sends a bolt of sharper pleasure through me.

A cry slips from my lips. I clutch his head, his shoulder, caught in the rush of sensation. Each lap of his tongue and graze of his teeth floods me with a hunger for more. The now-familiar ache is building between my legs. My hips start to rock against him of their own accord, seeking the friction that can bring me to release.

With another growl, Whitt lifts me from the chair and sets me on the edge of the table, standing between my splayed legs. He tugs me tight against him and recaptures my mouth, all but devouring me from his new higher ground. Then he kisses my cheek, the edge of my jaw, with greater restraint. He palms my naked breasts, massaging them until the pulses of pleasure have me gasping again.

As his hands keep fondling me with teasing strokes, he gazes down at me. His voice comes out low and ragged. "Can I ask you one thing, Talia?"

His tone and his use of my name rather than one of his playful nicknames draw me out of my eager haze. I peer up at him, willing myself to focus through the delicious movements of his fingers and palms over my chest. "Anything."

Whitt gives me a crooked smile, heat smoldering in his eyes, the blue more fiery than oceanic now. "What made you talk to Sylas about pursuing me rather than coming to me directly?"

He gives the question a casual lilt, but his gaze holds mine intently. Like when he watched to see my response to his list of his flaws. Does he think I hesitated out of distrust or fear—that something about him put me off?

I kiss him as if the tender pressure of my lips might wipe away whatever worries provoked the question, and then I tuck my head against his neck to hide my sheepishness. "I didn't mean for it to happen like that. I didn't know you were interested, and I—I hadn't even fully realized that *I* was interested that way, and then Sylas checked on me when I was having an… intense dream, and the topic came up like that."

Whitt laughs lightly, his shoulders relaxing, and nuzzles my temple. "A dream, hmm? And what happened in that dream, which I assume featured me? Do tell."

A blush flares in my cheeks, but it's not as if we haven't already gotten more intimate than anything that played out in my subconscious. "You… were kneeling in front of me like when you checked the glamour on my foot brace, and you started kissing my leg. All the way up."

"*All* the way?" Whitt asks, his voice so suggestive I practically burst into flames.

"Well, I woke up before… before it could get that far."

"Hmm. Poor thing. But such an inspired imagination. I'll just make sure not to leave you wanting here in reality."

He's only just finished speaking when he eases back from me to sink to his knees. I stare down at him from my perch on the table, my pulse skittering with a dizzying mix of anticipation and uncertainty. "I wasn't— You don't have to—"

The conspiratorial gleam in his eyes is nothing but eager. "I haven't had anywhere near my fill of you yet."

Whitt undoes the fixtures on my brace and slips it off my foot to set it aside. Then he kisses the warped ridge below my ankle where the bones are fused wrong, so reverently my heart swells with a different sort of ache.

What I said to Harper is true—I can live with a damaged foot —but it's still a handicap to be worked around, a weakness I have to make up for. The veneration in Whitt's lips makes it feel like something special rather than broken. Different but far from wrong.

His mouth travels up to my calf, his thumb gliding gently over the misshapen bump instead. Kiss by tender kiss, he works his way up to my knee, with a teasing swipe of his tongue when he reaches the joint.

As he continues his journey along my inner thigh, the press of his mouth deepens, each kiss lingering a little longer. Partway up, he pauses to slide the skirt of my dress higher and melds his lips to the sensitive skin so passionately my chest hitches. A heady tingling races over my skin to my sex.

I grip the edge of the table for balance, watching his progress, wondering a little dizzily just how far he's going to take this. The ache between my legs has intensified to a throbbing need. His breath spills hot over the tender area just below that juncture, where he has to ease my legs even farther apart to offer his next kiss. My fingers curl tighter—

And, with a sly smirk, he bends back down to nibble the opposite knee.

I hold back a groan, especially because now he's charting a matching path up the inside of my left thigh. The last thing I want to do is divert him even slightly. Hunger knots in my core, threading through my veins. Every muscle has coiled in anticipation, even though I'm not totally sure what I'm readying for. This is already so much more thrilling than my dream managed to portray.

As he edges closer with that skillful mouth, Whitt slides his hands beneath my hiked-up dress and hooks his fingers over the hem of my panties. He raises his head just long enough to tug them down my legs. Then he brushes a kiss to the skin just inches from my sex, and another, and another.

Stroking my hips, he eases me even nearer and inhales with a sound of relish. He must be able to smell the arousal I can feel gathering between my folds. A renewed flush scorches my cheeks, but before my embarrassment can really take hold, he lowers his mouth to taste me there, and all other thoughts fly out of my head with the surge of pleasure.

"Whitt," I mumble, half whimper, half moan, and he hums with delight.

"That's the only way I want to hear you say my name from now on," he murmurs, his breath alone sending all kinds of giddy tremors through me, and leans in to swipe his tongue right over my slit.

He plunders my sex with lips and tongue and here and there a gentle edge of teeth. If I was dessert before, now he's treating me like a full banquet he intends to savor every morsel of.

I sway where I'm balanced on the table and find myself clinging to his hair with one hand, unsure whether I'm urging him on or begging for a reprieve from this exquisite torture. I'm panting, trembling from head to toe. The rush of pleasure keeps swelling through me until it's as vast as the ocean in his eyes.

Whitt suckles my most sensitive spot that can spark the headiest jolt of paradise and then delves his tongue right inside me. I clench around him—sex, thighs, fingers in his sun-kissed locks. The wave of ecstasy tosses me up and over my peak, crashing through me and sweeping me away, leaving me gasping for air.

My body goes limp. Whitt's kisses soften, but he stays where he is, flicking his tongue over the sensitive nub, working his mouth against my folds, until the rush of sensation rises through me again. Then he plunders me wholeheartedly, branding me with bliss as no one else ever has. I bow over him, too overcome to do more than cling on and ride the wave as it careens toward its pinnacle once more, even faster than before.

A shattered cry breaks from my throat—and I'm freefalling over the edge in a blaze that consumes every other sensation.

As I drift down into the afterglow for the second time, Whitt dapples my inner thighs with more kisses. Gradually, my tight grip on his hair releases. I stroke my fingers through the thick strands, and he beams up at me before licking his lips so extravagantly my whole face must turn red. "A perfect meal."

He stands and collects me in his arms. Settling back in his chair, he tucks me against him. Every part of him that touches me feels as feverish as my own skin.

I squirm closer, soaking in his heat, and raise my fingers to his cheek. My other hand skims over his belly again. "I want to— You haven't gotten—"

He catches my hand before I make it to the rigid bulge against my hip and kisses my knuckles instead. His gaze is feverish too, but the embrace he wraps me in is all controlled might.

"We have so much time ahead of us," he says quietly. "This first interlude—I don't want there to be any chance of you looking back and feeling I took more than I gave."

I don't think there's any chance of that after the heights he just propelled me to, but I can tell how important the principle of it is to him from the resolve in his voice. I settle for slipping my hand along his neck and kissing the crook of his jaw before nestling my head against his shoulder.

The ache of need is gone, but the poignant sensation that wrapped around my heart shines on.

Is it possible to love *three* men at the same time? I never would have thought so, but how can I argue with the emotion unfurling inside me even as I ask the question?

There's enough feeling in my heart to encompass all of them— and I can only hope it's enough to see all three of them back in this keep, whole and happy, beneath tomorrow's sun.

CHAPTER THIRTY

Sylas

*I*t's said that all of the fae world slants upward to embrace the Heart of the Mists. In most domains, including both Oakmeet and Hearthshire, you wouldn't notice any significant slope to the plains and forests. But at the borders of the arch-lords' domains, the three of them surrounding the summer side of the Heart, the land rises sharply, emerald-green fields arching up to the vast plateau of gold-veined sandstone and winding foliage that holds their castles and our Bastion of the Heart.

No other keep or fortress in the land can hold a candle to the Bastion. It rises from ground as if it grew out of the same rock—which in a sense it did, though coaxed by magic innumerable centuries ago. The currents of gold gleam amid the warm beige of the stone. Having been here at night, I can attest that those veins keep shining even in the dark of a new moon.

Towering over the flower-dotted, grassy terrain around them, the sturdy walls rise into four craggy peaks like a miniature mountain range—three smaller summits around a taller and broader central one. Birds perch in and soar past the arched windows, while hares nibble clover on the lawn. The thrum of the Heart's energy calls even to those lesser beings.

As August and I trek the last short distance along the path between Donovan's domain and Celia's, the Heart's magic washes over my skin and peals through my body. My chest opens, my pulse singing through my veins in welcome. Despite the vital but perilous mission that brings us here, a smile crosses my lips.

Skies above, it's been far too long since I basked in the full power of our world.

That sensation speaks of the Heart more than anything we can see. Just beyond the Bastion, the shimmering mist of the border condenses into a denser, pulsing glow, one that will fade to the quality of starlight with the descending of the sun. Just a few steps beyond that border, I have to assume the Unseelie arch-lords rule from some gilded fortress of their own.

It's unsettling to imagine our enemies lurking so close at hand, but thousands of years ago, our peoples collaborated in a sort of promise, a spell that flows through the border all the way through the arch-lords' domains and into a few neighboring lands as well. No one has yet come close to shattering their magic, it's so aligned with the principles of harmony and growth that the Heart resonates with.

To cross the border within that stretch, one must swear to do no harm to the fae on the other side—an oath that binds one's will against deceit. A traveler has no such guarantee of good will from the hosts that await them. Unsurprisingly, few choose to make the journey, especially in these recent years while we've found ourselves at war.

August halts for a moment, both to soak in the Heart's energy and to wipe the sweat from his brow. "I forgot what a trek it is," he says with a sheepish smile. "I'll have to add a little more mountain-climbing to my exercise regimen."

I give him a benevolent swat to the shoulder. "If you'd taken the path any faster, I'd have had to rein you in for my own survival. Come on, then. By now, they're undoubtedly waiting for us. Let's not breed impatience and frustration before we've had any chance to make our case."

There are other rules for peace in the domains around the Heart, at least on the summer side of the border. Any fae may travel the routes between the arch-lord's domains unhindered and unquestioned to petition our rulers in the Bastion. However, we're required to make the journey on foot once we reach the steeper slope.

The publicly stated reasoning is that putting in the physical effort shows our dedication and proves us worthy of being heard. I suspect the unstated reasoning is that it gives the arch-lords and their packs plenty of time to observe those who approach and decide how to greet them.

We cross the flowery lawn to the Bastion's entrance, which contains no door, only a couple of stairs up to an immense opening in the stone wall that's arched like the windows. Stepping through it, the twittering of the birds and the rustling of leaves on the nearby trees fades away. The air settles around us still and cool, as if we've walked into a cavern.

But it's a bright cavern, sunlight streaking down across the floor from windows at all angles and the veins of gold glittering across in the inner walls just as they do outside. The flow of the Heart's energy continues pulsing over us, emitting a faint, silvery hum as it courses through the building.

Standing in this place, it isn't that hard to believe a handful of fae with grand hopes for peaceful coexistence could have erected a barrier between the realms that's lasted generations. Magic saturates the atmosphere.

No one lives in the Bastion or within about a mile of it. Linger for too many weeks at a time in this kind of power, and you might go mad with it. They say at least one of the first arch-lords became overzealous and met that fate.

We walk through the airy entrance hall into an even vaster room. The gold-laced, vaulted ceiling gleams several stories high above us. The light that spills through the rows of windows all down the walls forms a shape like a flower with petals spiraling around it on the veined floor. At the edges of that light, lit by it but not caught directly in its beams, stand three golden thrones, spaced evenly around the circular space.

As I expected, the arch-lords already occupy their respective seats. Their cadre-chosen flank their thrones—at least, those of their cadre not occupied elsewhere. They each still have at least one out at the northern end of the border.

You can tell a lot about a lord by the close company they keep and how much of it they keep. Celia, old enough to have seen some of her cadre pass on before her and growing too weary to continue adding to their number, has only one figure by her side. Ambrose, hesitant to trust but even warier of lacking in protection, boasts three. Donovan, either overeager or overcautious in his youth—or perhaps a bit of both—has brought six with him.

Even if I dislike Ambrose's attitudes, I have to admit he has the most ideal outcome. Too large a cadre, and the chances that all of them will be sufficiently dedicated when it counts dwindles. Donovan hasn't been tried enough yet to discover how tenuous some loyalties can be. But then, a smaller group makes it easy to stretch one's authority and resources too thin.

Kellan might have been a bastard, but he did get things done for me. Before our banishment, I had the benefit of Isleen's cadre alongside mine. I don't have near as much authority to extend or tasks to lord over as Celia does, but in the arch-lords' midst, I feel my lack.

Ambrose leans against the arm of his throne with an expression that suggests he's suppressing a grimace. More bulldog than wolf in his appearance as a man, he rubs the jowls of his round face. The new flecks of gray in his sparse beard stand out against his tan skin. Topping his head, his cropped bronze-brown curls with their patina-like greenish sheen hold hints of gray too. He fixes his dark, beady eyes on me.

"You come all the way from the fringes on the day of the full moon, Lord Sylas?" he says flatly. "Shouldn't you be preparing your pack? Or are you so accustomed to savagery out there that you've taken to letting them fend for themselves?"

August bristles but manages to keep his mouth shut. Good man.

I ignore Ambrose's jab, letting my gaze slide from him to Celia to Donovan, acknowledging each with a respectful but not overly deferential bob of my head. "My arch-lords, it's *because* of the full moon that I come before you. My cadre-chosen August has made a crucial discovery about the Unseelie's plans—though one you are perhaps not totally unaware of—and I have brought you the solution to that potential catastrophe as well."

Celia's eyebrows rise to her wispy bangs. A pure ivory-white with a crystalline shimmer, the rest of her hair falls starkly around her narrow, ebony face. If Ambrose could be a bulldog, then she'd be a doe with her steeply sloping nose and heavy-lidded eyes. But her tall frame, though slender, fills out her ankle-length gown with imposingly broad shoulders. No one would mistake her for prey.

"Well, I think we had better hear this, then. But first I'd want to know precisely how your man made this discovery."

August dips his head lower than I did. At my gesture, he speaks. "We were told that it would risk too much for any of you to approve a stealthy foray into Unseelie territory. So my lord gave *his* approval for me to go on my own, so that you couldn't be blamed if our plans went awry. But they didn't. No one saw me except the sentry I captured. I couldn't get much out of the raven, but he cawed enough to confirm what we suspected and to reveal something even worse."

Donovan shifts forward in his throne. Even though the sunlight doesn't hit him directly, the tufts of his hair seem to dance like flames, brilliant reds and oranges mingling together. His mother's had the same effect.

It was her he inherited the throne from, mere months before my disgrace. Her death was brutal and unexpected at the jaws of a pair of chimera she'd gone out to subdue that somehow got the upper hand on her, and the first time I stood before him here, waiting to hear my pack's fate, he was too green to get much of a word in between Ambrose's domineering bluster and Celia's crisp brusqueness. But he caught me on my way down the path to my carriage to apologize and let me know he didn't agree with the sentence, that if he could make a case for me down the line he would, and I haven't forgotten that humility.

Unfortunately, I'm not sure these past several decades have hardened him enough for him to quite hold his own yet. For all his fiery hair and brawny frame, there's a softness to his jaw and stance that shows through. He hasn't been through real fire yet. Heart only knows how he'll be tempered or savaged by the experience when it comes.

"What happened to this sentry after you questioned him?" he asks.

August smiles grimly. "I removed his head from his body right there on the border. If he was found, no one would be able to say it wasn't his own carelessness in coming too close to our side—and he won't have been able to tell anyone what he gave away to me."

Ambrose runs his hand over the plate-mail vest he likes to wear even when he's not on the battlefield, as if to indicate he views every interaction as a potential threat. The faint metallic clink is vaguely ominous. "And what exactly did he give away?"

I take over to spare my younger brother the scrutiny our news will provoke. "The Unseelie have learned of our curse—enough to know that we won't be in any state to defend the border tonight if the wildness takes hold. They mean to attack along the northern stretch where you've each stationed one of your cadre-chosen. From their presence, I assume you had some idea that area was of concern."

Ambrose's mouth tightens into a sour frown. Celia has tensed as well, but her gaze is more searching than accusing. "The sentry told you all of that?"

"I pretended I already knew the location of their next attack, and he didn't deny it," August says. "Then he mocked me for thinking we'd be able defend our lands while we're running wild. There was no mistaking his meaning."

Donovan lets out a short, rough laugh and shakes his head. "So, it was true after all."

They knew our curse had been exposed but doubted it? I turn to him. "How did you come to hear of it?"

Ambrose shoots Donovan a sharp look, but the younger arch-lord has gained at least enough confidence to make his own choice to answer. "The Unseelie last attacked the morning after the full moon. A few days later, we had a letter appear in the grass here just beyond the border, as if the one who delivered it had slipped through only long enough to set it down. It was a warning that our enemies meant to take advantage of our malady, and where."

"It *claimed* to be a warning," Ambrose breaks in. "Why would any of the stinking ravens help us? We had to treat it as a potential trap—possibly not even from their side but from some schemer among the Seelie."

Donovan's hand falls to rest on the golden broach fixed to his padded doublet, ornately carved into the shape of a wolf biting its own tail. It's an heirloom passed on from his mother, and no doubt from her predecessor to her. The tale I've heard is that supposedly the family has some secret to transferring a bit of every fallen relative's spirit into it from their soulstone, keeping all those pieces of their power alive.

I've never encountered any spell by which that effect could be achieved, but I believe the broach has some kind of magic in it. A trusted warrior from my father's pack once reported he'd seen Donovan's mother summon a hail of shooting stars by calling on it. Perhaps her son takes some comfort in the thought of having those ancestors with him. Or perhaps he's dreaming of raining bolts of flame down on his colleague's grizzled head.

As I turn over their words, the pieces of the puzzle click into place. "You sent cadre to that section of border to observe and ramp up protections where they could just in case, but you didn't spread the word—for fear of panic?"

Celia sinks back in her chair, looking weary. "You're clearly well-versed enough in warfare to understand, Lord Sylas. Even if we felt sure that the note had come from the winter side, and that therefore at least some of the ravens knew of the curse, there's little we could do about that with the loss of Lord Aerik's cure. As to where to bolster our defenses and how, without the ravens potentially catching on and adjusting their plans in response, we have found it difficult to reach a consensus."

"It's good that we know now, though," Donovan says. "For the rest of the day and evening, we can put all of our power into bolstering our magical defenses along the border even more than usual and securing the nearest towns as well as we can. It may not be enough to hold them back completely—"

Ambrose's guffaw is dark. "Those sorry whelps on the front lines will be lucky not to tear *each other* to pieces once the moon rises."

"We'll pull them back as we did last month and limit our self-destruction as well as we can," Celia says firmly. "We have to take every step—"

I clear my throat, interrupting the urgent but unnecessary negotiations so I can begin my own. "You won't need to. None of the squadrons along any part of the border need to succumb to the curse tonight. We've brought the cure."

All three of them stare at me in shocked silence. "Where?" Ambrose demands abruptly.

"In our carriage, in a spot I'll lead your pack-kin to if we reach an agreement I'm satisfied with."

He draws himself up haughtily, his eyes flashing. "You'd barter over this while the Unseelie forces gather and the full moon is nearly—"

"Let us hear all he has to say first," Celia chides. Her brow has furrowed. "How is this possible? We were given to believe that a crucial resource Lord Aerik brought to bear, the one he's now seeking to obtain more of, could only be found within his domain. We knew he'd expanded his search, but I hadn't thought he'd shared his methods so freely that his efforts could be usurped."

My mouth twists. It's here that I must reveal Talia's existence.

Every sinew in my body balks at the thought. I meant to give her as close to a normal life as I could offer, one free of the demands my kind would place on her after everything she's unwillingly sacrificed for us already. As soon as our rulers know of her existence and the power of her blood, I can't guarantee any of that.

But perhaps I never could. How can I give her anything like *normal* given who she is and how she came to be here? I can still hope to offer freedom and happiness in whatever forms they might take.

And what Talia insisted on was the freedom to make yet another sacrifice on our behalf. If I deny her that right, wouldn't I be caging her in yet another way?

I could speak around the facts of the matter as Aerik did, hold off the discovery, but once it's clear that he obscured the truth, the arch-lords won't rest until they have the full story. I'll only be wasting time better spent ensuring her protection.

I drag in a breath. "Aerik misled you. The only resource

necessary to the cure has not been used up but has… relocated itself to reside in my domain, of its own free will. As I feel is for the best, given the treatment it received in Aerik's 'care'."

August stirs beside me, his stance tensing at just that vague mention of Talia's abuse.

Ambrose jerks his hand through the air in an impatient gesture. "By all that is dust, what are you nattering about? Speak plainly, or we can cut right past the speaking part."

To taking the cure by force, he means. My hackles rise, but I keep my voice even. "The only substance necessary to stave off or reverse the wildness is the blood of a specific human woman. From what I've gathered, Aerik kept her existence secret from all but his two cadre-chosen, hiding her away in the most wretched of prisons for all of the years he produced his cure, giving her only enough sustenance to continue that existence. When she came to us, she was near-starved, battered and scarred, and permanently disfigured from the wounds they inflicted on her."

Ambrose sputters, as if the idea that he's been inadvertently drinking human blood to cure his ills disgusts him beyond speech. Celia and Donovan still look bewildered, but Celia is composed enough to speak. "A human woman? And how did you discover this? How did she end up among your pack?"

On the journey here, I thought carefully over how I could present the story within the bounds of truth but without admitting to any crime. The Heart might lash out at me visibly if I attempted to lie in its very presence.

"They must have grown careless," I say. "One day she was able to unlock her cage to make her escape. We found her not knowing at first what she was capable of, only seeing a being in distress. Once we understood how she'd fit into Aerik's plans—and having seen how he'd treated her—it seemed unwise to return her. He was abusing a valuable resource. We felt it wiser to nurture such a prize."

Speaking of Talia as a thing to be used rather than a person makes my stomach clench, but it's the language the arch-lords will expect in these circumstances. Celia nods, a thin furrow creasing her high forehead. "Have you taken any steps to determine what it is about this human that produces such a powerful effect in her blood?"

"I've made many attempts—tested her skin and hair and her blood itself by the most obvious methods and others besides. I've been unable to detect any factor in her heritage or physical makeup that would create such an effect. I would pursue additional avenues given the chance, but for the moment other matters needed my attention more urgently."

Perhaps when this is over, if we can reach an agreement that keeps Talia out of danger, I'll be able to pursue those answers farther afield with Talia's blessing. Keeping her and my brethren uninjured comes before any of that.

Ambrose clearly found even my practical phrasing in regards to Talia too lenient. He's still stewing over my earlier explanation. "A human who can cure us all—and you've been worrying about her comfort. What of the rest of us?"

It takes even more effort than before to smooth the edge from my voice. "The rest of us can partake of the tonic we've made using her blood as need be. It's only effective if consumed while the blood is relatively fresh. Surely you wouldn't suggest we neglect what we've come to rely on so much, even if it's a human?"

"I'd suggest that the human had best come into our own custody so we can monitor her and her contributions to our people as we see fit," Ambrose replies.

Exactly as I feared, without a moment's grace. My fangs itch in my gums. I've enjoyed the idea of ripping Ambrose's throat out from the moment decades ago when he chuckled as he showed me the tattered flesh that was all that remained of my soul-twined mate when his warriors were done with her. Now I'll add his ribs and his intestines to the list of body parts I'd enjoy seeing violently extracted.

"I haven't stated my conditions." I slide my gaze from him to the more moderate two of the arch-lords. "I have enough vials of the tonic for every warrior along the border and more besides so you can summon additional forces from the nearby domains. Given the dire peril we face tonight, I don't think my terms are particularly extreme.

"My pack has remained in our banishment to the fringes for several decades now while offering nothing but full loyalty to you and to the Heart. Not one of us so banished was ever found to have played a role in the treason we were sanctioned for. Despite our dwindled numbers, we have fought alongside every other pack at the border. My cadre-chosen risked his life and our honor on your behalf to confirm the Unseelie threat, and we uncovered the true nature of the tonic and have revealed it to you."

"More than we can say of Aerik, I'll admit," Donovan says with a quirk of his eyebrows that feels promising.

"Indeed. And he received many rewards for what he did offer. You didn't demand control over his operations when you believed them unmovable." I lift my jaw, my spine stretching to emphasize my height. "I request that I and my pack recover our claim over the domain of Hearthshire. That we be absolved of any continuing suspicion of treachery. And that we be allowed to continue to watch over the human woman as we have seen fit, unless it should conspire that we are no longer able to arrange the cure while she's in our care."

I can't fulfill any promise to Talia without my pack's standing restored. The arch-lords could never justify leaving a being so valuable in the hands of a lord they still officially distrust. Every piece of my demand hinges together.

Ambrose snorts, but Donovan gives a careful nod at the same

time. Between them, Celia steeples her hands on her lap, her expression impenetrable.

"You request very much, Lord Sylas," she says. "But you also offer a lot. You would risk our people in insisting on these terms?"

I focus my attention solely on her. I don't need Ambrose's agreement. I've already won Donovan over, and if I have Celia, their votes will outweigh his. But I don't think I've convinced her yet.

"I have faith that the arch-lords will see justice carried out, and I must serve the needs of my pack as well as all my brethren. What kind of lord would I be if I didn't speak for them while I can?"

"Hmm." Her gaze drifts away from me, going distant. Uneasiness winds through my gut. Have I made all the case I can?

A filmy image forms before my deadened eye: a memory of a time long past when I stood before her. The echo of her past self bolts upright from her throne, her hands fisted at her sides, and makes a declaration my mystical vision can't give voice to but that I can read from her lips. *We must respect the Heart and all its tenets!*

The image wisps away, but it leaves a solid sense of certainty in its wake. I do know how to appeal to her sensibilities.

"And if I may add," I say, low and steady, "I ask for nothing more but to see the principles of the Heart carried out. There is no balance in consigning a pack who would serve you well to the fringes. There is no harmony in wrenching a living, feeling being from the one home in years where she's been treated with compassion."

Celia's eyes flick back to me. She sits up straighter. I'm not sure I've swayed her—or that I haven't pushed too far.

"This is too great a matter to put to a vote in an instant," she says. "I say we deliberate—quickly, given the circumstances. Unless my fellow arch-lords object, I ask that you and your cadre-chosen retreat outside until you are summoned."

Neither Ambrose nor Donovan raises an objection, although

Ambrose's face has turned even sourer. I bob my head alongside August's deeper bow, and we escort ourselves out of the Bastion.

The brilliant sun beaming over us provides little comfort. August shifts his weight from foot to foot restlessly. "What will we do if they—"

I hold up my hand. "Let the decision come as it will. I'll handle it either way."

It can't be more than a quarter of an hour, but when a man of Donovan's cadre pokes his head from the doorway and calls us back in, I feel as though I've been standing there for days. My heart doesn't lift until we step into the audience room and I catch the trace of a smile lingering on Celia's lips. Ambrose is scowling, but he keeps his mouth shut.

Donovan doesn't restrain his smile at all. "It is my pleasure to speak for all three of us that we accept your terms," he says, and a current of magic ripples into his voice. "Hearthshire will be restored to Lord Sylas and his pack. You will be absolved of any wrongdoing in the treason spearheaded by the Thistlegrove pack. And we will stake no direct claim on the human woman who contributes to the cure as long as you continue to provide all who need it with the tonic."

He's barely finished speaking before Ambrose rises with a sharp clinking of his armored vest. "If you're quite satisfied, let's have that tonic already. No one should have forgotten that we have a terrible battle ahead of us tonight."

I dip my head again in agreement, but even knowing that, my spirits soar. While we have the Unseelie still to contend with, I've won the battle my people have been fighting quietly and without complaint for more decades than I like to count.

All of my pack has gained a sort of freedom today. I'll snap a thousand ravens' necks before I let them steal it away again.

Evening has fallen when August and I gather our warriors near the river. I glance from one of them to the other and then to the heads of the other squadrons nearby, who've received their orders—and the word that Lord Sylas has proven his loyalty and can demand the same from them. A few of the warriors offer grim smiles of acknowledgment.

"You've all had your tonic?" I ask my pack-kin, and take in their nods. "Good. If we stick to the strategy discussed, the ravens won't know what hit them before there are feathers strewn across these fields. Let them see easy prey until they lower their guard—and then they'll be the ones pleading for mercy."

Moving among them, I give them each a bolstering cuff to the shoulder or bump of an elbow. Then I step aside and release my wolf.

There's something so perfect about stretching into my beastly form with utter control on a night when so many times before I truly became a beast. The awareness of every muscle and limb prickles through my limber body.

I wheel to confirm that the rest of my pack-kin have transformed at my lead. At my brisk bark, the squadron scatters, August roaming to the south while I wander north.

I weave back and forth on an erratic path, shaking my head, snarling at the grass, snapping at any other wolf I cross paths with. Giving every appearance of being lost in wildness. Let the ravens come. Let them see the chaos they expected.

The sky darkens to black. The round, white face of the moon peers over us. The magical defenses along the border warble, sending increasingly violent shudders through the air. Then they shatter, and hundreds of darkly-feathered bodies swoop through the haze.

Some circle over us, observing. Others soar farther west toward the nearest towns, where other squadrons and dozens of newly gathered warriors from the nearby packs are waiting to dole out the same fate.

So many more of us await the Unseelie forces than they'll have been expecting. But that won't worry them yet, not while they're still caught up in glee over our apparent incoherence.

Anticipation thrums through my veins like the magic of the Heart. Let them come. Let them come and—

The immense birds drop, transforming into armored, winged men brandishing swords and spears as they descend on us. A few of them are *laughing*, reveling in how easily they believe they'll pick us off much as Whitt revels in fairy wine. I allow myself a wolfish grin.

As one being, the wolves of summer spring to attention and lunge at our foes.

We pick those unsuspecting feather-brains out of mid-dive and slam them to the earth, claws already gouging, fangs already chomping. Cries and groans echo across the moonlit plains, too late to give each other warning. They fell on us together thinking to slaughter us in one swift strike, and we've turned the strike back on them.

I tear through one attacker's throat just above the neck of his armor and slash another. There are yelps of wolfish pain in the night, but not as many as the gurgles of our enemies. Everywhere, furred bodies spin and leap and maul, until the grass is splattered scarlet and the earth beneath runs red with raven blood, and the stragglers flee back into the haze.

Watching them, the metallic tang laced through my mouth, I raise my head toward the moon that's haunted us for so many years and let loose a howl of victory. One after another, my pack-kin and my brethren match it, until the very wind shakes with the news of our triumph.

May the ravens hear it all the way in their icy lands and feel a chill of terror in their hearts.

CHAPTER THIRTY-ONE

Talia

As the carriage leaves Oakmeet behind, watching the familiar forestlands, hills, and knobby spires of rock fade into the distance brings a melancholy twinge into my chest.

I found peace in that place. I figured out—maybe not everything—but a whole lot about who I am now and what I want. And I don't think Sylas or his pack have any interest in returning to the domain of their disgrace ever again.

But I can't regret our departure. I might not be fae, but I can feel the shift in the atmosphere the farther we venture from our former home. A softer warmth flows through the air with every mile we travel closer to the Heart. The vegetation around us grows brighter and more fragrant, filling my lungs with floral sweetness and evergreen tang. Hope lights the faces of both my three lovers and the pack grouped on other carriages in a stream behind ours.

We're heading away from the first real home I've had in the fae world but toward the one they've all missed for so long.

I'm sitting tucked next to August on one of the moss-cushioned benches, my head resting against his shoulder as his fingers idly play with my hair. While we're in view of the rest of the pack, I'm still only involved with him. But now and then as Whitt strolls along the length of the carriage, he shoots me sly smiles with a promise of what might come behind closed doors at our destination. Sylas stands at the bow like captain of a ship, but when he returned two mornings ago and announced that the arch-lords had agreed to let him "keep" me, he gathered me in his arms so tightly afterward that the echo of the embrace still tingles through me when I think of it.

We skirt the edge of a valley where a river of lavender-purple water courses, and then weave through ruddy rocks that jut like fingers from grass fine as spider webbing. When another forest looms up ahead, Sylas steps back to sink on the bench across from August and me.

"That's the edge of our domain," he says, tipping his head toward the trees. As we speed toward them, my heart starts to swell with awe. Closer up, it's obvious that they're twice as large as the grandest ordinary trees I've ever seen: trunks as thick as turrets, leaves so broad I could lie on one without an inch of me slipping over the edge.

"Did no one take over your land while you were banished?" I ask. He hasn't mentioned us displacing another pack.

He shakes his head. "It seems neither of the two new lords who set off to form separate packs were bold enough to stake a claim, and none of those who already had their own domains were inclined to relocate to this one." He gives me a rare wide smile. "I like to think they all knew I'd be back before too long."

"If there had been any squatters, the arch-lords would simply have had to find them a new territory," Whitt says. "The summer lands are hardly choked with packs. We do enjoy plenty of room to roam around."

He looks pleased in a more relaxed sort of way than is usual for him too. I snuggle closer to August, anticipation tickling through me. "I can't wait to see it."

Sylas casts his gaze toward the bow again. "Very soon."

The carriages soar between the magnificent trees. They're gliding along too quickly for me to make out many details, but I think I see a flowery vine slithering across one trunk like a snake—or maybe it's a snake that's doing a very good imitation of a vine—and a cliffside that glints like wet copper. Then the trees part to form a sort of avenue toward two of the immense pines, spaced some twenty feet apart with their upper branches reaching out and lacing through one another overhead to form a natural gateway.

Passing through that gateway, I get my first glimpse of Hearthshire's keep. Except it isn't a keep—somehow I assumed it would be, although Sylas has referred to it as a castle at least once.

It looks quite a bit like the building we left behind in Oakmeet: a cluster of polished trunks grown so close together they merged into one being. But the structure stands at least twice as broad and tall as the keep did. A few of the trunks rise higher into actual turrets, and the leafless branches that sprout all across the roof twist into forms that echo the true-name marks tattooed on the fae's bodies.

Patches of moss cling to the smooth wood, and spindly vines crisscross the outer walls, winding in and out of the windows. Wild vegetation has similarly consumed the houses clustered around the sides and back of the castle—more of them than I can easily count. Over fifty, if I had to guess. A pang shoots through my chest at the thought of how much of his former pack Sylas has lost since they called this place home.

When I look at the fae lord, his face is practically glowing, his gaze fixed on his castle. "There it is," he murmurs.

"It's beautiful," I say, awed as much by the joy shining through him as by the building itself.

His gaze jerks to me, and his smile turns slightly sheepish, as if he's embarrassed to have shown his elation so openly. "It'll be spectacular when we've had time to get everything in order. The forest has crept in on the castle grounds. No doubt weeds have swallowed the gardens. But there is plenty of time for that."

August lets out a sigh of relief. "It's good to be home."

Sylas has talked about his family and their pack as if it was separate from his own, but for the first time full understanding sinks in. "You didn't inherit this domain. You built *everything* here from scratch on your own."

"With the help of my pack," Sylas says. "But yes. My father continues to lord over Thundervale. It's not unusual for true-blooded fae to strike out on their own rather than sticking around hoping their elders will meet an early end to give them space to carve their own mark."

I know his feelings about his family are much more complicated than his dry remark would imply. The last thing I want to do in this moment of celebration is push him to think about why he left his very first home. So I don't ask anything more, just drink in the sights and sounds and scents as the carriages come to rest at the foot of the castle.

Sylas climbs out first and swivels to face his pack. I spot Harper nearly falling over the side of her carriage, her eyes wider than ever.

"If you wish to keep your old house, consider it yours," Sylas says. "If you'd rather swap for one now abandoned, by all means. No squabbles, please. We have plenty to go around. Anyone who requires help whipping them back into shape, don't hesitate to call on me or my cadre. We'll have Hearthshire good as ever in no time."

Leaving the carriages holding our luggage behind for now, he strides toward the castle. August helps me out, Whitt right behind me, and the three of us follow the fae lord into his beloved home.

The entrance room reminds me of Oakmeet's too, only the ceiling is a little higher and the room a little longer, and no orbs remain to add light to the space. The leaves on the vines that creep across the walls quiver at Sylas's passing as if even they recognize his authority.

Beyond the entrance room, Sylas turns from the hall into a doorway at his left. We follow, and all at once I see how this domain got its name.

Faded rugs scatter the floor between plump sofas and chairs that have crumpled with the passage of time. They're all arranged to face a stone hearth so massive I could step inside it without fear of bumping my head. I think maybe even Sylas could fit in it comfortably.

Sylas speaks a low word, and flames spring up from the hearth's base. The smell of warmed wood and scorched stone fills the air. We step closer to the warbling fire, drawing together as we do.

Sylas motions me in front of him, placing one hand on my shoulder and teasing the other into my hair before kissing the back of my head. August slips his hand around mine. Whitt hangs back for just a moment before I glance toward him. When he ambles over to join us, I tuck my other hand around his elbow.

We stay there basking in the hearth's heat for several minutes in comfortable silence. I should probably tell them that they can get on with all the cleaning and organizing they obviously need to do —and help them with it—but I'm so content I can't quite bring myself to say the words. My three fae men don't appear to be in any hurry to break the spell of the moment either.

We made it here, all of us together. Standing there between them, not a single part of me doubts that this is where I'm meant to be.

Out of nowhere, a loud knocking reverberates from the entrance room. Sylas makes a vexed sound but eases away from me toward the hall.

"No rest for our glorious leader," Whitt remarks. "Let's see what trouble the pack has managed to get themselves into already."

It isn't our pack, though. Sylas opens the door to reveal an unfamiliar woman in a trim blue jacket and trousers, hemmed with gold. She dips her head, hands a piece of rolled paper to Sylas, and says, "With regards from Arch-Lord Ambrose."

Apparently she hasn't been instructed to wait for a response. She marches back across the lawn to where a graceful white horse is waiting, leaps into its saddle, and has it cantering away before Sylas has even finished unrolling the letter.

Ambrose. He's the arch-lord who's been harshest on Sylas, who blames him for what his mate did, who he was the most worried about objecting to his requests. As I wait for Sylas to read, my body stiffens. At the fae lord's snarl, I flinch.

He shreds the paper into scraps so swiftly I never even see his claws emerge and flings the bits aside. A dark cloud has rolled over the joy that shone in his face. August tenses beside me.

Whitt offers a sickly-looking smile. "I take it he wasn't simply offering happy tidings."

Sylas's hands flex by his thighs. "It may not be anything. But it's probably what I think it is. I should have known better. That mangy prick."

"What did he say?" I venture.

"He 'requests' I call on him in three days' time. Which in arch-lord terms is a demand." Sylas swivels toward us, his unscarred eye so somber the iris has turned nearly black as it settles on me. "And he insists that I bring you with me."

Whitt spits out a scathing curse. "I thought the deal was settled."

"Perhaps it is. Perhaps I should be more generous in my assumptions, and he only wants to have a look at Talia. But knowing Ambrose, he'll try to weasel around the wording of our agreement and take her into his custody." Sylas's frown deepens. He touches my cheek. "I will not let that happen."

August's arms bulge as if he's preparing to charge all the way to the arch-lord's domain and pummel him, but I can't speak or move at all. Sylas's words resonate through me, stirring up the last question I want to consider.

Ambrose is an arch-lord, the highest authority in the entire fae world. If he intends to take me… how can any of these men possibly stop him?

FERAL BLOOD - BONUS SCENE

*H*ow was August feeling after sharing Talia with Sylas in the tryst room—and what prompted his sudden "I love you"? Now you can see those events through his eyes…

&

August

I'm not used to sleeping with company, but somehow the cocoon of warmth formed in this "tryst room" Sylas created feels even more like home than my own bedroom. The sound of Talia's breaths slowing into the rhythm of sleep lulls my mind, and I drift off with my head ducked close to her shoulder.

When the tremor of the mattress jolts me awake, only the faintest trace of daylight touches the sky above the high window in the ceiling. My warrior instincts snap me from unconsciousness to full alertness in an instant.

But there's no threat here, only Sylas easing off the other side of the bed. He pulls on his clothes with a faint rustling and glances back at the two of us.

Talia gives no sign of waking, her slim body curled beneath the duvet we pulled up over her, her vibrant hair unfurled around her peaceful face. A renewed rush of affection swells in my chest. She looks so fragile at rest, soft and delicate. But I've seen how much inner fierceness that small body contains.

His gaze catching mine, Sylas speaks quietly so as not to disturb her. "I would stay, but—given recent circumstances, I feel I must consult with the night sentries as soon as they return from their patrols. Give her my apologies for not being here to welcome her to the morning?"

I dip my head. "Of course."

He pauses, and a faint uneasiness creeps through me. Last night, cherishing Talia together, I thought we found ourselves perfectly in sync. Any possessive urge that might have gripped me to steal her away just for myself faded as I watched her come alive with our combined attentions. I want her to have every pleasure this world can offer her, not be restricted to only my own capabilities.

But maybe my lord and brother isn't quite so sure about how our odd arrangement has developed.

Then he offers me a small but warm smile, and my worries vanish before he even opens his mouth. "It occurs to me that one rather valuable benefit our cooperation brings is that regardless of my duties, our lady will nonetheless have someone worthy to wake up to. I'm glad for that."

That's all he needs to say for me to know he approves of everything that went on last night—and of every part of my relationship with Talia in general. A glow of pride lights inside me, and I smile back at him. "I'm glad too."

He leaves with the softest click of the door, and I lay my head down on the pillow again. Talia stirs, rolling partly onto her side.

Her arm comes to rest against my chest. I fight down the urge to pull her even closer, to wrap my arms around her and nuzzle her hair. She'd definitely wake up then, and Heart knows she needs all the peace she can get.

I'm too alert now to even doze, though. As I drink in every detail of her lovely features, the memory rises up of her eyes shining at me so brightly last night, and not just with pleasure. *I love you*, she said, steady and sure, the emotion radiating from her with a potency that left no room for doubt.

I don't know why the declaration startled me. She's shown her affection in so many ways over the past weeks. Maybe I've simply been so focused on ensuring I didn't ask for too much or push her beyond the limits of her comfort that I didn't leave room to think about how much her feelings might grow of their own accord.

Watching her now, the joy of the words comes back to me. I've earned this amazing woman's trust and adoration. I've kindled the same joy in her that I feel right now, basking in her presence.

Because I love her too. I've never loved anyone, not in the way of mates, but I probably should have recognized the sensation growing inside me anyway. I can't imagine any other being, fae or otherwise, making me half as happy as I am just lying next to her.

I was too surprised to say it back right away before the moment had passed. I'll have to create another moment—do something special for her and then say it. Is there a meal she'd particularly enjoy that I could whip up for her, one I haven't offered her yet? Or she might appreciate a venture beyond the keep, now that she has that freedom. Oakmeet isn't anywhere near as picturesque as Hearthshire, but it has a few pretty spots with minor magics.

I want every part of the experience to show how much I mean the words.

As I sort through the possibilities, my mind starts to drift again after all. My consciousness meanders off into a dream filled with Talia's brilliant smile.

The sharpening of the sunlight streaming down on us wakes me the second time. Talia is just blinking into awareness next to me. Her back arches with a slight stretch, her gaze finding mine, and I give in to the desire to cuddle her next to me. "Good morning, Sweetness."

With a pleased hum, she scoots even closer, tucking her face against my chest for just a second before she glances over her shoulder. The contentment in her expression falters.

Oh, no, she can't think— I reach for her, guiding her face back toward me. "Sylas wanted me to apologize to you for him. It was urgent that he check with the night sentries as soon as they came in from their shift. He said he's glad our arrangement means you nonetheless have someone worthy you can wake up to." I can't hold back a smile, remembering the remark.

The repeated sentiment appears to reassure Talia too. She beams back at me and leans in to give me a quick kiss on the lips. "He said that's why cadres sometimes share mates—isn't it? Because you're all so busy with your duties you can't devote as much time to a partner as a regular fae could?"

I let out a chuckle. If only it'd been that simple between him and me to begin with. "Yes, but lords generally aren't expected to be so generous with their lovers. The honor of being chosen is supposed to make up for the limited attention, I guess. You get the best of both worlds."

Talia snuggles into my arms. "Yes, I do."

I envelop her in a hug, reveling in her obvious delight. But the niggling worries at the back of my head insist I have to ask: "You're still feeling good about everything that happened last night, then?"

"No regrets," she says without hesitation.

I can't help wondering how last night's encounter would have fit with the romances she'd have pictured for herself before she was stolen away into the Mists. "It must have been different from how you'd have imagined your first time would be."

She shrugs against me with no hint of concern. "I didn't have much of a chance to imagine it before. It felt exactly right for what my life is and who I'm with right now."

Her confident tone shuts up the last of my worries. I brush my lips to the top of her head. "Good."

I have no pressing responsibilities to get to just yet, so I linger there in the bed with her, enjoying this intimacy for as long as it'll last. Talia trails her fingers over my chest, sparking heat in their wake, but the gleam in her eyes is more curious than lustful. She traces the curves of a true-name mark along my collarbone. "What's this one for?"

The sight of the arcing lines brings back memories of silver scales flashing in a rough current and tender flesh melting butter-like on my tongue. "Slink salmon. Makes an excellent dinner. There were a lot of them in the main river that cuts through Hearthshire, so it made sense to pick up that one at the time."

She draws her hand downward, all explorer now. "And this one?"

"Skin. Which helped me fix this lovely color to your hair, since it's nearly the same material." I ruffle her pink waves and then point to the column down the middle of my chest. "All the bodily ones formed in a line. Bone, eyes, blood, skin, muscle, heart, stomach, teeth, liver, lungs. I've been working on brain for nearly a decade now, haven't quite mastered it to get the mark. That's the most difficult one. Many never fully conquer it."

I haven't had much time to dedicate to that study in recent years. If we could settle the dispute with the Unseelie instead of seeing the conflict escalate—if the curse wasn't descending on us more viciously with every passing month— Well, it is what it is.

"I bet you will," Talia says with total assurance. "I guess no one is teaching you like you're teaching me light."

I nod. "The simple ones—air, light, water, earth, and fire, basic metals, common plants and animals—get passed on in our early training. With anything more specialized, those who've mastered them guard the knowledge more closely. When I have time to spare, I meditate with the idea, I speak to the tissue in the animals I've hunted, that sort of thing. It's hard to explain. The sound of the word slowly forms in your mind as you get closer to it."

Talia is silent for a moment, her expression thoughtful. I wonder like I have many times before what it will take for a true-name mark to form on her human body. If she can wield the magic, surely at some point it'll leave proof of her skill. But her skills are tentative still.

Her lips part, and then a rumbling emanates from her belly.

I laugh. "Sounds like I'd better magic up some breakfast."

After one last kiss to her forehead, I reluctantly pull away from her. Talia slips out from under the duvet, grabbing at her discarded clothing. "I'll help. Um, I just need to get some clean clothes."

I wouldn't care whether she wore the same thing every day, but I'm not going to argue with her. I'm already looking forward to another companionable morning in the kitchen, exchanging suggestions and grins while we put together a breakfast feast.

If she left, how would I ever go back to working in that space on my own? I never minded before, but now I can't imagine how it would feel anything other than horribly empty without her by my side.

Something in my chest twists with a bittersweet tone. As Talia pulls on yesterday's clothes to make the trip to her bedroom, that sensation expands into an ache.

I open the door for her with a playful bob of my head, but I can't shake the abrupt awareness of how precarious our happiness together still is. How many threats we still face. How much it would cost me to lose her.

I cross to my bedroom automatically to find fresh clothes of my own, and she heads down the hall, away from me. The ache winds around my heart, and all at once I can barely breathe.

What do perfect moments matter? Nothing will ever be completely perfect anyway. She should know—she should know and not have to wait any longer without the promise of devotion I can offer.

I whirl around and hurry after her. With each step, a determined but eager warmth spreads through my chest, melting the ache of imagined grief away.

Talia starts to turn, but I've already swept her up in my arms. I enclose her in my embrace, careful in my strength, and kiss her with a surge of all the emotion that's swelling inside me.

But it isn't enough to only show it. She needs to hear the words as she gave them to me like the most precious of gifts.

Drawing back just a few inches, I tease my fingers into her hair and let my voice tumble from my suddenly raw throat. "I love you too."

KINGS OF MOONLIGHT

BOUND TO THE FAE #3

CHAPTER ONE

Talia

There are certain things magic can't do—or at least that faeries don't think it's worth wasting magical energy on when it's simpler to do it by hand. It turns out rearranging furniture is one of those things.

I give the wooden side table a little shove and step back to eye its position relative to the rest of the furnishings in the grand living room. When we moved into the castle two days ago, my fae companions banished the vines that had crept through the windows and whisked the dust from the floors with a few powerful words. Using the true name for the wood that makes up the entire building, which from the outside looks like several massive trees sculpted together into a towering fortress, they healed the cracks and the spots of rot that formed over decades of disuse.

The existing furniture has either been mended or replaced the same way. But now we're fitting in the bits and pieces we brought with us around them, which means I can finally actually help.

I'm the only human living with this pack of wolf-shifting fae, and while they've mostly welcomed me, it's pretty hard to forget that fact.

August comes up beside me, hefting a silver-framed mirror in his brawny arms. "That does look like a good spot for the table. And I think the table is the perfect spot for *this*." He sets the mirror on the tabletop so it leans against the wall and brushes his hands together with a satisfied air.

Interior design isn't August's typical line of work. As half-brother to Sylas, the lord of this domain, and part of Sylas's cadre, his main job is protecting the pack and leading the warriors into battle if need be. But thankfully he hasn't needed to do a lot of that in the two months since I joined them.

Of course, tomorrow that might change. And just like the few times he *has* needed to fight in the past couple of months, it'll be mostly because of me.

That knowledge hangs over all of us, but I'm trying to put on a brave face. I hate how vulnerable I feel compared to the nearly immortal, magically skilled beings around me. I hate how vulnerable caring about me makes *them*. The least I can do is act as if I believe they can get us through the conflict ahead okay, as impossible as that might seem.

"It looks great," I say to August with a smile, and turn to survey the rest of the room. Sofas and armchairs, their surfaces woven out of soft reeds and leaves, form two semi-circles facing the vast hearth that reflects the domain's name: Hearthshire. By the embedded stones that frame the hearth, a couple of pack members are just finishing arranging a set of fireplace tools—made out of bronze, since iron is toxic to the fae. At the far end of the room, a few others are arguing about the exact placement of a hanging tapestry. I'm not sure what else there is for me to do.

August is always quick to pick up on my moods. He wraps his arms around me from behind and presses a kiss to the top of my head. "You've pitched in plenty, Sweetness. You don't need to look for more work."

"Everyone else is still working," I point out, but I can't help leaning into his broad chest, letting his affectionate warmth reassure me.

Out of everyone here, August cares about me the most. Over the weeks I've spent with them, my feelings for Sylas and both members of his cadre have deepened from wary appreciation to tentative attraction to what I can only call love. I never expected any of them to offer that much devotion in return, considering they're not just fae but fae of high standing and I'm a mere human, but August has expressed his love in both words and actions so emphatically that just thinking about it makes me giddy.

"I'm sure you could find a few of our pack-kin slacking off if you looked." He nuzzles my hair with a chuckle and gives me a gentle nudge toward the doorway. "Why don't you take some time just to explore? The rest of us already know the domain pretty well. You should start settling in, get comfortable with the new surroundings."

He talks as if *he's* sure I'll be returning here after tomorrow's meeting. I drag in a breath and nod. "All right. You make a convincing argument."

He laughs and waves me off, but I feel him watching me, making sure I'm okay, until I've limped into the hall.

On the way to the entrance room with its looming front door, a rhythmic tapping marks my uneven steps. The brace Sylas built for my warped foot helps me walk more steadily, but it is a bit noisy. And my foot still starts to ache if I'm on it for very long. None of my current companions has the magic to fix the warped ridge where my former captors broke the bones and let them heal wrong—it seems like that's one of those few things magic can't do at all. I'm a lot better off than before, when I couldn't do much more than hobble, though.

I heave the arched wooden door open just wide enough for me to slip outside into the vast clearing that stretches around Hearthshire's castle. The breeze tickles over the bright grass and my skin with an ever-present warmth. These fae are Seelie, belonging to the summer realm. Even if the Unseelie of winter weren't vicious villains, I'd be glad I ended up here and not in their freezing territory.

More pack-kin are bustling around the houses scattered throughout the clearing, which look like large tree trunks that've been twisted off into a spiraled point about ten feet up—a much smaller and less ornate version of the castle. A few are already urging plants to grow in small gardens. A couple are herding a bunch of bleating sheep that just arrived onto a forest path toward a pasture that's set at a distance from the village.

We've come a long way from Oakmeet, the domain where I first joined the pack. The one they were banished to after Sylas's former mate took part in an attempt to overthrow one of the arch-lords who rule the Seelie.

It's that same arch-lord, Ambrose, who's demanded Sylas's presence tomorrow. Sylas's presence *and* mine, that is. Ambrose already campaigned to take me from Sylas once because of the unexpectedly vital role I've come to play in the lives of all the summer fae. Sylas was able to negotiate my freedom, but the arch-lord wasn't pleased about that. Most likely he's come up with some scheme to steal me after all.

The thought of having to leave Hearthshire gives me chills not only because I want to stay with the men I've come to love. The chances that *any* other fae will treat me as kindly as this pack does are small. The chances that Ambrose will, from what I've heard of him, are almost zero. He might throw me in a cage just like the fae who first tore me from the human world, the ones who broke my foot, starved me and taunted me—the ones Sylas and his cadre saved me from.

that you wanted to see more of this world. Maybe these will make it easier for us to explore together."

I grin back at her. "That would be fantastic. I should try them on. I mean, I'm sure they fit. I'll wear them all the time."

Harper beams, but as I lower myself to sit on the grass, my attention is diverted. A carriage is drifting through the gateway formed by two massive trees bowed toward each other at the far end of the clearing.

Fae carriages have more in common with human boats than the things drawn by horses in past eras. This one looks ricketier than those Sylas has formed for us. It's definitely smaller, with only a rough canopy made of fluttering leaves. It hitches a little as it glides toward us, a couple of feet above the ground. Two figures peer at the castle and the village around it from beneath the dappled shadows of the canopy.

My muscles tense, and I shift into a crouch, tucking the boots to the side and letting my hand fall to the small dagger Sylas gave me that I keep in a sheath at my hip. So far, visitors arriving from any pack other than our own has always meant bad news. I may not be able to put up much of a fight against hostile fae, but I'll do my best with the defensive lessons August has given me if I have to.

I wish I had my pouch of salt, but it unnerves my pack-kin if it bumps against them when I pass them, and I hadn't thought I'd need that much defense right now. Silly me.

Harper stands stiffly beside me, equally uncertain. Someone must have run to tell Sylas, or else he's got magic that alerts him when anyone passes through the gate. As the carriage comes to a stop several feet from the castle and lowers onto the grass, he strides out to meet the unexpected guests.

Simply seeing his authoritative stride and the commanding confidence in his expression soothes my nerves a little. My shoulders come down, but I stay where I am, watching.

As Sylas passes out of the shadow of the castle, the sunlight picks up the purple tint in the coffee-brown hair that falls to his muscular shoulders. His one dark eye fixes on the figures emerging from the carriage. I'm not sure how much his other eye sees. Split through with a scar that runs through his brown skin from forehead to cheekbone, that one gleams ghostly white.

The fae who emerge from beneath the canopy make an odd pair. First comes a rosy-cheeked man with hair that's nearly mauve, who looks young enough to pass for a teenager in the human world. He offers his hand to a wiry old man whose skin is nearly as rippled as the sparse, translucent tufts sprouting from his head.

From the patience Sylas offers them, waiting for the old man to climb out, they're at least somewhat important. The sharp points on the elder's ears suggest he might be true-blooded: the most respected of the fae, the only ones allowed to become lords because their heritage has relatively little humanity in the mix.

"Lord Garmon," Sylas says, confirming my guess. His tone is respectful but not exactly friendly. He doesn't dip his head to either of the other men, but they don't to him either. "And I don't believe we've met…?"

The old man pats the young one on the shoulder. His voice is low and hoarse. "This is my great-grandson Orym."

"Lord Sylas," the young man says in acknowledgment with a quick bob.

Sylas's mismatched gaze slides over them. "Good of him to join you. We weren't aware of your intended visit, or I'd have been more prepared. We aren't quite set up for hosting yet."

Garmon lets out a couple of raspy coughs. "I hope I won't take up much of your time. I've only come to determine what's become of my grandson Kellan."

My pulse stutters. Sylas's expression doesn't shift, but then, he must have guessed this subject would come up. He knew who the man was.

Remembering Kellan makes the hairs on the back of my neck

KINGS OF MOONLIGHT

BOUND TO THE FAE #3

Watching the fae of the pack I can now call mine grin and chatter with each other eases my worries a little. They're happy just to be back in their former home, the one they've missed for ages longer than I've been alive. Even their magic is stronger here, closer to the Heart of the Mists that's the source of their power, which even I can sense from the quiver in the air.

Regardless of what August said, I'm not sure I'm up to exploring all that far from my new home yet. The massive trees that surround the clearing loom so high I lose my breath when I crane my neck to peer up at them. I don't think I've ever seen trees even half that tall before. Vines wind around their trunks, blooming with vibrant flowers that lace the air with a faint but heady perfume. Who knows what might lurk deeper within that forest that the fae wouldn't bat an eye at but that would mean certain death for a human?

I wander toward the pack village instead. I've only made it a few steps when a figure I'm pleased to see ducks out of one of the houses.

Harper, a young fae woman I've started to consider a friend, brightens at the sight of me. She tucks a few strands of her sleek pale hair behind her pointed ear and lowers her over-large eyes a little bashfully as she heads toward me. She has a bundle of what looks vaguely like birch bark clutched in her arms. When she reaches me, she thrusts it toward me.

"I made something for you. I hope you like them."

I hadn't expected to receive any gifts. And Harper already gave me a pretty big one recently: one of the gorgeous dresses she creates out of faerie-made fabric. I accept the bundle from her and unwrap the papery bark carefully in case whatever's inside is fragile.

I find myself gazing at a pair of boots. Not clunky snow boots like I might have put on as a kid in winters back in the human world or narrow leather ones like Mom sometimes wore with casual dresses. These are as intricate and graceful as Harper's dresses, different shades of brown wrapping around them and intertwining to look like rippled water, a ribbon of the same fabric woven up the sides to allow me to meld them perfectly to my feet.

When I turn them over to examine every side, a solid frame within one settles against my fingers. They both have sturdy soles that feel as though they'll hold up to hikes in the forest—more hiking than my *foot* is likely to hold up to—but the righthand one includes additional support.

She's worked the material around a foot brace. A few days ago, she asked me to see if Sylas would make her one for some purpose she didn't totally explain. He must have given it to her soon afterward. I've gotten used to clomping around with the brace showing, not having the option of much in the way of footwear. Now I can keep my foot steady without having to show off my weakness quite so blatantly—and with a beautiful covering, too.

But we've spent all of the past few days preparing for and then carrying out the move. I glance up at Harper, both overwhelmed by her generosity and startled.

"They're gorgeous. Thank you so much. I never expected— When did you have time to make them with everything going on?"

She twists her hands where they're clasped in front of her. "Honestly, there hasn't been a whole lot anyone wants me to help with. I got my bedroom and my studio all set up in my parents' old house—I might take one of the abandoned homes just for myself later, but I don't know if it makes much sense to claim one if I might get the chance to start traveling around to the other domains—and it just seemed like... like something I could do that would be useful for someone. For you. Do you like them?"

"I *love* them." I hug the boots to me, curling my fingers around the shockingly soft fabric.

A shy smile curves her lips. "I also thought—everyone else already knows this domain, but it's new to both of us. You told me rise. The third member of Sylas's cadre—his former mate's half-brother—didn't think much of humans. After they took me in, he tormented me every way he could manage while avoiding Sylas's notice and then outright attacked me. Sylas leapt in to protect me and had to kill Kellan when he refused to back down.

The fae lord and the rest of his cadre have been keeping Kellan's death secret since then, making excuses and avoiding the subject, not wanting to disturb the pack further when they were facing so much other conflict. Will they have to own up to it now?

How is Sylas going to explain why he did what he did? When fae can live thousands of years if given the chance, killing one is a grave crime. Even though Sylas believes it was the right thing to do, I know he wishes it hadn't come to that.

He's obviously not going to spit out the truth too hastily. "What gave you the impression that there was anything to determine?" he asks in his usual measured baritone.

"A few kin from Lord Tristan's pack passed through our domain not long ago," Orym pipes up. "They asked about Kellan."

Garmon nods. "They seemed surprised he wasn't with us, since he apparently hasn't been seen with you or elsewhere in some weeks. Their reactions raised my concerns." His wispy eyebrows arch. "Was I wrong to wonder?"

Tristan? An itch creeps over my skin. That fae lord poked around Sylas's former domain before. As Ambrose's second-cousin, he seems to carry out some of the arch-lord's work for him.

It's hard to believe they ran into Kellan's relatives and dropped those hints coincidentally. I'd bet they were trying to stir up more trouble for Sylas. Maybe even to justify whatever it is that's going to happen at the meeting tomorrow.

Sylas pauses with a frown. When he speaks again, his voice is lower than before. "I'm afraid this is a serious matter, one best discussed when we're both prepared for it, not just stepping off a carriage. There are guest quarters nearby. I'll have them readied quickly, and you can make yourselves comfortable there. As soon as my hands are no longer entirely full, you'll have a full accounting."

Garmon's mouth twists, but he doesn't seem to think it worth arguing. "I'll await that accounting then."

He turns back toward the carriage, but his great-grandson's gaze has drifted to me. Orym eyes me for long enough that my back goes rigid. Sylas clears his throat and steps forward, and the young man shakes himself.

"That's her, isn't it?" he says. "The human girl you've taken. The one whose blood makes the tonic for the curse."

Those words only make my muscles tighten more. A muscle twitches in Sylas's jaw. "I suppose Tristan's kin mentioned that to you as well?"

Orym gives him a narrow look, one with enough spite in it to rattle my nerves all over again. "Yes, they made a few comments. And his cadre-chosen said that soon enough his lord will be the one taking care of her."

The bottom of my stomach drops out. Orym saunters onto the carriage after his great-grandfather without a backward glance. Sylas's face remains impassive, but there's no way he hasn't understood that remark at least as well as I have.

So that's what Ambrose will be after tomorrow. That's how he plans to get around the oath he swore not to take me into his own custody. He isn't trying to get me for himself—he means to hand me off to his equally hostile cousin.

CHAPTER TWO

Talia

"What exactly was the wording of the agreement?" Whitt says abruptly. The other member of Sylas's cadre, his spymaster and strategist, has been pacing the length of the carriage for the entire trek toward Ambrose's castle, pausing only briefly to gaze and sometimes glare at the landscape we're soaring through. His ocean-blue eyes have only gotten stormier. He stops now by the prow of the vehicle to wait for the fae lord's answer, the wind ruffling his sunkissed-brown hair.

Sylas has been less openly restless, but he hardly looks relaxed where he's sitting on one of the thinly cushioned benches beneath the canopy across from me. He rubs his square jaw, his mouth set in a frown that seems to deepen with each passing minute.

"The arch-lords swore to stake no direct claim on Talia as long as I provided the tonic to everyone who needs it. We've been over this. I didn't think they'd risk making an *in*direct claim and passing her off to a different lord outside their trio, but clearly Ambrose trusts his cousin more than he does me."

Whitt makes a scoffing sound. "More fool him. I've no doubt Tristan would stab him in the back the second he got an ideal opening and the results looked promising. Not much honor among that lot, only fangs and greed."

He glances at me, his expression turning pained, and then back at his lord. "We can make an argument that this is still a direct claim. He might be claiming her in order to pass her on to another, but he's still the one making the order. Tristan would have no authority to override the arch-lords' decision on his own."

"I'd imagine he has some sort of argument to counter that, or he wouldn't be pursuing this." Sylas sighs. "I don't like relying on anyone outside the pack to fight our battles, but if Donovan and Celia will speak up on our side…" He leans forward and rests one of his powerful hands on my knee. "If Ambrose won't agree to move the discussion to the Bastion of the Heart, where all three of the arch-lords can weigh in, we can simply leave."

I hug myself. All my efforts at staying calm have crumbled the closer we get to Ambrose. "He'll see that as an act of treason, though, won't he? If you ignore his orders as an arch-lord? It'll give him an excuse to attack Hearthshire or try to get you banished all over again."

"We can take that chance. He'd need the other arch-lords to agree before he imposed any further sanctions on us. I have to believe they'd understand my reluctance after the deal we made so recently."

But he'd still be risking it. And the fact that he's in this position at all is my fault. He didn't want to bring me to the attention of the arch-lords in the first place.

Of course, the alternative was letting the Unseelie wage war across the border while all the Seelie warriors stationed there were crazed in the grips of their curse. The summer fae can shift into wolves whenever they want, but for decades now they've been unable to control their shifts or their wild behavior under the full moon. The winter fae would have slaughtered them.

Something about my blood that no one has been able to understand cures the violent frenzy that comes with the curse. I insisted that Sylas use me to protect his people. He warned me that the arch-lords would want to take me for themselves, considering how valuable my blood makes me to them. I decided to take that risk.

I didn't realize that my decision might make things worse not just for me but for him and the rest of the pack too.

I'm not sure if Sylas sees something of my thoughts with his scarred eye, which always seems to observe more than any regular eye should be able to, or if he just knows me well enough by now to guess where my thoughts have gone. He crosses to the bench beside me and tucks me against his massive frame, stroking his hand over my hair.

"Let me worry about the consequences of my actions, Talia. You may not belong to me, but you're worth so much more to me beyond the magic of your blood."

It's impossible not to melt when he talks like that. I have trouble imagining the fae lord ever expressing as deep an affection as August has, but he's already proven that he cares about me more than I could have hoped for. With every gesture he makes like this, the love *I* feel for him grips my own heart harder.

I don't want to lose this strange but exhilarating relationship I've found myself in, adoring and adored by not just one but three remarkable men.

I tip my face up toward Sylas's, and he takes the invitation to claim a kiss, his fingers tracing the line of my jaw. The gentleness of his touch combined with the commanding firmness of his lips leaves me as giddy as always.

Whitt makes a mock coughing sound. "Before you get too

distracted, we *are* getting rather close to the prying eyes around the castle."

His tone is typically breezy, but I think I pick up a thread of tension in it. Until just a few days ago, I was only sharing my affection with *two* remarkable men. While apparently it's not unusual for the members of a cadre to take a common lover, since they only have so much attention to offer when their lord has to be their first priority, Whitt initially balked at letting anything happen between us. I'm still not totally sure what about the arrangement made him hesitate, but he seemed almost angry when Sylas first suggested it.

After the passion he showed when he finally did give his desire free rein the other day, I know it wasn't any lack of interest.

There was a time when he was concerned that I might cause problems between Sylas and August—it *is* unusual for a lord to accept shared affections—and for a little while it seemed I might fracture the bonds of the cadre in another way, leaving Whitt on the sidelines. From some of the things he's said to me, it's sounded almost as if he's worried he isn't good enough for me, as absurd as that is when he's a magical, shape-shifting immortal with possibly the most stunning face I've ever seen.

I definitely don't want him feeling left out now, when whatever bond we've formed is still so new and potentially fragile.

"I'd better get this in fast, then," I say with a grin, and spring from the bench. Whitt blinks at me, surprise flickering through his expression when I bob up as far as my toes will take me, but he dips his head so I can plant a quick but emphatic kiss on his mouth.

When I drop back on my heels, he's smiling. He gives a strand of my hair a teasing tug. "You are certainly so much more than a pissant like Ambrose could ever conceive of."

The happiness of the moment stays with me only a matter of minutes, until the signs of a fae settlement rise up in the distance. The carriage veers up a steep slope toward thick slabs of glossy black stone that jut from the jade-green grass to points several feet higher than the carriage's awning. They form an uneven wall in layers we have to weave between, none of the openings lined up for easy passage. I guess the point is to make sure passage *isn't* easy in case the arch-lord and his pack are defending themselves from intruders.

A few wolves prowl along the open stretches between the obsidian rings, but they don't show any concern at our arrival. We're expected.

As we pass between the last of the standing stones, the sight of the structure up ahead makes my heart sink even more.

Ambrose's castle looms three times as high as any of the stones, made out of the same darkly gleaming rock. Not blocks or tiles like you'd find in the human world if someone built a palace out of obsidian. No, this sleek structure appears to have been carved out of a solid mountain of the stuff—or else summoned in one mass out of the earth, which is more likely from what I've seen of fae magic.

The line of trampled grass we've been following turns into a more formal path of embedded stones several feet from the castle's peaked doorway. Sylas motions for the carriage to stop before we reach that point. The vehicle remains hovering over the grass, and Whitt moves to the side so Sylas can stand at the bow.

It takes a few minutes for our arrival to be acknowledged. None of us speak, so the only sound is the breeze warbling around the stones. Then the door yawns open in the vast doorway, and a mass of figures pours out.

I assume Ambrose is the portly but robust man who strides out at the head of the bunch. His sharply pointed ears and the greenish tint in his brown hair show his true-blooded fae heritage, and he holds himself with impervious assurance as if he can't imagine anyone ever challenging his authority. He's the first fae I've met other than Sylas who's mastered enough true names that their dark tattoos creep up his neck and across the edges of his face.

He's dressed like a warrior in a plate mail vest—does he expect this meeting to come to outright fighting?

The dozen or so men and women who've tramped out with him must be his cadre and some of his pack-kin, hanging back to flank him. Their intense gazes send a crawling sensation over my skin. And off to the side, standing almost abreast with the arch-lord, is a slightly younger-looking man I don't recognize but whose companion is uncomfortably familiar.

The last time I faced that woman whose heavy-lidded eyes are fixed on me, she was wearing a hooded cloak that hid her jet-black hair and well-muscled shoulders. I'd know those eyes and the full lips now curled in a satisfied smile anywhere, though. She's one of Tristan's cadre, the one who attacked me when she found me in the forests around Oakmeet. Which means the man she's with must be Tristan.

The arch-lord's second cousin looks oddly less satisfied than his cadre-chosen. Leaner than Ambrose, his neck is just a little longer than looks totally natural, his knobby chin adding to the giraffe-like impression. His mouth, almost dainty, forms a tight line that gives his whole olive-toned face a sour expression. He must have gotten some of his coloring from the side of the family he shares with Ambrose, because his hair is greenish too—a paler, mint-like green that stands out on the otherwise straw-like strands.

If we had any doubts about the comments Kellan's relatives made, Tristan's presence here dismisses them. That's the man Ambrose wants to turn me over to. The man who's studying me now like I'm a sack of gold he's deciding how best to spend.

"Have you become melded to your carriage, Lord Sylas?" Ambrose asks, cocking his head. "Come inside; let's get on with it."

Sylas draws himself up with the lordly air that reassures me even in a dire situation like this. "We won't be coming inside, Arch-lord Ambrose. I arrived as a courtesy to fulfill your request for my presence—here I am. Here is the human. If you want to make some sort of claim on her despite the agreement we reached in the Bastion just a few days ago, I expect it to be heard before the full trio of arch-lords, not you alone."

Ambrose's beady eyes narrow. He swipes a hand across his jaw, making his grizzled jowls sway. "I'm well within my rights to call you in. I have no intention of compromising the agreement we came to. All of this can be better discussed within my home."

Sylas folds his arms over his chest. "I've been given to believe that you intend to remove the woman from my custody. Was I misinformed?"

Ambrose's gaze flicks to the side as if evaluating who might have let that detail slip. "I will make no direct claim on her myself. That was the deal we made."

"If you insist we give her over to your cousin here, that transfer would still be happening as a direct result of your authority," Sylas says. "He can't make the claim himself."

"This is all foolish semantics," Ambrose retorts. "I won't be taking her. I'm merely ensuring that she's under stable guardianship."

Guardianship. As if the man next to him would be looking out for me rather than looking to exploit me in every possible way. My fingers curl against the bench's cushion. My nerves prickle with the longing to curl up on the floor where they can't see me, where I won't have so many fae sizing me up like I'm a roast to be carved. These lords are more polite than the ones who tormented me for most of my time in the fae world, but they're just as haughty and cruel.

A movement at the corner of my eye catches my attention. More wolves are slinking past the gaps between the standing stones behind us. As I watch, I count several that appear to be gathering around the path we took to reach the castle. My pulse stutters.

Ambrose knew we might try to leave before he could get his

way. He has his pack ready to stop us. This really might come to a battle if Sylas sticks to his guns.

I jerk my gaze away, and it collides with Whitt's. His mouth is set in a grim line. The assembling warriors would hardly have escaped his notice. From Sylas's brief glance over his shoulder, he's taken stock of this new development as well.

He stands firm, turning back to Ambrose. "I heard it in the Bastion that the arch-lords accepted *my* guardianship over this woman. I won't relinquish it until I hear from all three that they've retracted their faith in me. If you refuse to call them in to hold a fair discussion, I'll take my leave."

He moves to ease back from the bow, and Ambrose steps forward with a grimace so fierce it makes my stomach flip over. "Only restored in honor for a handful of days and already back to your treasonous inclinations, are you, Lord Sylas? All the more reason I should ensure this precious resource is in trusted hands."

Sylas's voice stays measured, but it hardens. "I'd say overturning the ruling of two arch-lords is far more treasonous than refusing to do so. You've heard my position."

"And as your arch-lord, I demand you get off that carriage with the girl and behave with the loyalty you claim to value so highly. Reject my orders, and you'll have a much larger problem on your hands, I assure you."

His pack-kin approach the carriage too, and the ones among the stones emerge. In a moment, they'll have formed a ring around us. Sylas looks at Whitt, silently but with some obvious deliberation. The two men may have their differences, but they know each other well enough that they can communicate plenty without speaking.

I can't tell what they've decided, but the tensing of both their faces makes me tense up too, my heartbeat skittering at an even faster pace. They're not going to give in, and we can't just glide on out of here. They're planning some desperate measure to break past Ambrose's pack.

How easily will he be able to claim they committed treason after that? Will my pack be thrown right back to the fringes of the Mists—will Sylas face an even worse punishment for a more overt crime?

Whitt sets a hand on my shoulder, meant to look casual but with a surreptitious squeeze that urges me downward. He wants me to crouch low—so I'll be braced for whatever they're about to attempt?

Ambrose strides toward us, his teeth bared, canines gleaming in points just shy of his full fangs. "Lord Sylas, this is the last time I'll give the order—"

For a second, my heart pounds so hard it dizzies me. It's me they want—it's all about me, just like it was with horrible Aerik and his cage.

I promised myself I wasn't going to let anyone use me again, that I'd make my own decisions about what happens to me. That I'd help Sylas and his cadre in every possible way after how they saved me. I can't let myself become their downfall.

But we have nothing to bargain with, no point of leverage here… except me.

The thought hits me with a chilling certainty, and my hand has dropped to the sheath at my hip before I've even considered exactly what I'm going to do. My fingers close around the little dagger's hilt. I jerk the blade from the leather cover and to my neck in one swift motion.

Instead of crouching, I step up on the bench so Ambrose and the others can see me better. My hand shakes, and the blade nicks my skin with a faint sting. I grit my teeth and restrain a wince when I swallow.

No one gets to take me hostage except *me*.

Ambrose and his pack-kin have already halted at my display.

The arch-lord stares at me with a mix of revulsion and bemusement. "What in the skies—"

"It's me you're talking about," I say, my voice shaking but loud enough to carry. "I'm still a person. I have a say. And I'd rather die than stay with any lord other than Sylas. You won't get any more cure for your curse if I spill all my blood today."

Sylas and Whitt are staring at me too. Whitt moves an inch, and maybe he could wrench the dagger from me before I could do any real damage if he really wanted to. I cut my gaze toward him and force my hand to press the blade closer.

The pain splinters sharper through my throat. Blood ripples over my skin. I don't want anyone thinking I'm not serious about this.

How serious *am* I? Part of me wants to lie down and just sob. But another part, the part that's keeping my spine rigidly straight and my fingers tight around the hilt while my pulse rattles through my veins, knows that I absolutely would rather die than end up in Tristan or Ambrose's clutches.

I've been just a *thing* to the fae before. Never again. I can't go back. Now that I've remembered what kind of a life I could really have, I think I'd lose my mind completely.

Whitt goes still, looking queasy but resigned. Sylas's hands have clenched where he's standing by the bow, but he holds himself still too, his dark eye smoldering fiercely.

Ambrose speaks in a cajoling voice that still holds a sliver of a sneer. "Come on now, pet. You don't really want to hurt that lovely neck of yours. Do you really expect me to believe you'd slit your own throat?"

I look straight back at him, my jaw tightening. "You don't know anything about me. You have no idea what I've been through or what I'm capable of. I stay with Sylas, or you can test just how far I'm willing to go to make sure I don't end up anywhere else."

Blood is still trickling down from the incision at the edge of the blade. It streaks over my sternum and dampens the fabric of my shirt. I must *look* pretty serious, because Ambrose's tan skin turns slightly gray. His mouth flattens, but he can't seem to find any words he thinks will fix this situation.

"Let us leave," I say. "No, promise you won't try to take me from Sylas again, for anyone, and then let us leave. *Now.*"

The arch-lord clearly doesn't want to take the chance that I'm willing to do it. I can only imagine how the other two Seelie rulers would react if they found out he caused their "precious resource" to destroy herself. But he obviously doesn't want to give in either.

He lets out an exasperated sigh, as if I'm simply an inconvenience, and says in a bored tone, "Since you're so adamant about it, perhaps I should consider Lord Sylas's qualifications more closely." His attention shifts back to the fae lord. "You have three weeks—until four days before the next full moon—to make a case that proves she's better off in your care than Lord Tristan's. We'll meet again then."

"In the Bastion, with the full trio, not here," Sylas says, his voice steady but rough.

"Fine, yes, in the Bastion." Ambrose makes a dismissive wave with his hand. "All these witnesses so mark it vowed. That's enough dramatics for today."

He turns on his heel, and with that gesture, the warriors pull back from the circle they were forming around us.

Sylas directs the carriage to withdraw. As it glides backward toward the erratic stone walls, he keeps watching the men we're leaving behind, while Whitt moves to the stern to monitor the warriors by the standing stones.

I hold the dagger to my throat, the shivers that ran through my hand now rippling through the rest of my body. The pain has expanded into an ache that stretches all across my neck and up to my jaw. But I can't stop. I can't retreat until I'm sure we're safe.

Amid the rows of immense stones, Sylas swivels the carriage

around. It picks up speed slowly. We leave the last row of obsidian monstrosities behind and cruise down the rest of the slope. No wolves or warriors patrol anywhere I can see.

A shudder wracks my arm, and I drop my hand.

The instant the blade leaves my throat, Sylas springs at me. He scoops me up so quickly I squeak in surprise, but before I can even start to be scared about how angry he might be, he's lowered his head by mine, murmuring the word I've heard him use before on other wounds to seal my skin. A tingle races over my throat, and the sting numbs. Then he snatches the dagger from my fingers and hurls it between the trees in the forest we've just glided into.

"Don't you *ever* hurt yourself like that again," he growls, his dark eye blazing, his arms wrapping tight around me. I think I feel a tremor of his own ripple through them. "I will never put you in a situation where death is your best option. I swear it by the Heart."

I tip my head against his chest, and he hugs me even closer, kissing my temple. Sudden tears well in my eyes—at what I had to do, at what I might have done if Ambrose hadn't backed down. At the anguish I've clearly caused this man I love. My voice comes out reedy. "I didn't want to. But I—I couldn't let them—what would you have done if I hadn't?"

It's Whitt who answers, his voice sounding strained. "We could have summoned enough magic to lift the carriage high enough and propel it fast enough to avoid Ambrose's pack. Almost certainly."

Almost. Not good enough. And besides— I glance up at him and then at Sylas, touching the fae lord's cheek. "He was already talking about treason. If you ran off like that, he'd have called you a traitor and come to attack Hearthshire to get me, wouldn't he?"

Sylas exhales, slow and ragged. "Most likely, yes. We could have still pleaded our case to the other arch-lords and hoped they'd be reasonable… But I won't deny your approach bought us more time and a better bargaining position. You just shouldn't have to—I never like seeing you put yourself at risk, Talia."

I tuck myself close to him again, hugging him back as if I can make up for the terror he felt watching me like that. "I know."

"Next time, we'll be more ready. I won't let it come to this again. You never need to go that far. Do you hear me?"

"I do," I say meekly, but that doesn't mean I agree.

It'd be nice to pretend that this, nestling in Sylas's strong arms with his rich earthy scent filling my lungs, could be all I do from now until forever. But I've seen enough to know beyond a doubt that this world doesn't work that way. My pack and my men are in danger, and as long as I can do something about that, I won't let them face it alone.

They've risked so much for me. Risking my death might be the only way to feel I deserve all the good I've managed to find in this life.

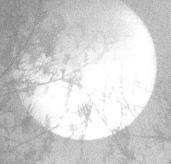

CHAPTER THREE

Whitt

Soulstones are cryptic things. They're said to be created from the essence of the fae they came from and to mimic that essence in some ways. The stone of a cheerful fae might beam brightly at all hours, while a sulkier one would show only erratic flickers of light.

Kellan's has a whirling, churning quality to its glow that suits his volatile loyalties well enough, although he was never anywhere near this quiet. If he'd been more like his stone in that respect, I'd have liked him a little better.

Sylas wraps the soulstone back in its spider-weave cloth and tucks that into the leather pouch he's kept it in. He holds the pouch out to me. "I trust Garmon will find we conducted everything according to the proper rites. Make sure you emphasize how much we regret the delay in seeing him to his proper resting place and that we'll call on them in their own territory within the next few moons."

"And what a joyful trip that will be," I can't resist remarking, even though I anticipate the exact baleful look my half-brother gives me. I grin at him. "Naturally I'll avoid expressing *that* sentiment to our guests."

"Naturally," Sylas says, sounding more amused than anything else, and an odd little quiver shoots through my chest with the recognition of the trust he's placing in me.

It's absurd, really. I wouldn't be part of his cadre if he didn't trust me. Heart knows he wouldn't put up with my snark and my more hedonistic habits if he didn't. But still. Somehow until this past full moon, I didn't recognize or had let myself stop recognizing just how much my lord values my position in the pack.

I aim to be quick-witted at all times in honor of my name, but I've clearly let past events sour my perceptions in unfair ways. It doesn't appear Sylas noticed to any concerning extent, so all's well that ends well. I'll just ensure my judgment is never so compromised again.

I give him a jaunty bob of my head, because it wouldn't do to get *too* deferential. "I'll see to this immediately. You can consider the matter dealt with."

"I expect they'll want time to sit with the news before facing the cause of Kellan's death," my lord says, "but if they do wish to speak to me right away, let me know at once."

"Of course."

Explaining Kellan's downfall to his grandfather and whatever exact relation the pipsqueak is won't be a fun conversation. Heading down the hall from Sylas's study, I allow myself a gulp from my flask, currently topped up with absinthe. Just enough to take the edge off my nerves and let my thoughts flow smoothly. While I'm never half as drunk as I may seem, I operate best with a little lubrication to grease the wheels of my mind.

A startled gasp carries from Talia's bedroom, where the door stands half open partway down the hall. A jolt runs through my veins in the instant before August's chuckle reaches me. If he's with her, she's unlikely to be in any danger.

I pass the doorway with the stealth that comes naturally after centuries as spymaster. Talia is perched on August's lap where he's sitting cross-legged on the floor, their profiles to me, her hands raised in the air and her face as bright as the space between her palms. The glow she's conjured spills through her fingers.

They're working on her magic. He's been teaching her the true name for light—and it appears it's coming easier to her now. She's finding the happiness she said she needed to fuel that magic easier, despite everything she's been through since reaching Hearthshire.

My steps slow so I can take in her joy for just a moment longer. She was a lovely creature when she first came to us, as much as I balked at admitting it then, but she's becoming absolutely radiant as she finds her footing among us.

Talia doesn't have the ears or the nose to pick up on my presence, but August's warrior instincts are ever alert. His gaze darts my way. A quick but companionable smile crosses his face before he returns his attention to his pupil.

I move on, but the sensation that gathers behind my sternum then is far more than just a quiver. It's a blooming of warmth— what I think might be happiness of my own, as unfamiliar as that emotion has become.

It's not just our home we've regained. We've recovered everything good in our partnership, as both brothers and a cadre serving our lord. I hadn't registered just how distant I was feeling from the others until that distance closed, our habits and reactions making us a cohesive unit again.

I could blame Kellan for the initial division, but I know it started before Sylas felt obliged to welcome him into the cadre. If I'm being fully honest with myself, it probably started with me.

I thought the mite would wreck us, and instead she's

strengthened our bonds. Brought us back together from wherever we were drifting off to.

And we almost lost her yesterday.

As I head down the stairs, the image flashes through my mind of Talia standing rigid on the carriage bench, her dagger pressed to her throat. The scarlet rivulet trickling down her pale skin. The desperate determination in her grass-green eyes.

The warmth inside me disappears beneath a wave of nausea. My hands curl into fists. For one white-hot moment, I'm a mere thread from unleashing my wolf and charging all the way to Ambrose's domain to tear him and Tristan to pieces.

They pushed her to that brink—they provoked that desperation—

I don't know how to convince her she'll never need to resort to a measure like that again, and I hate that I can't. The fact that Sylas is grappling with the exact same dilemma doesn't give me any comfort. She *is* precious, but for far more than the arch-lord and his crony of a cousin could conceive of. She deserves some actual peace.

But first I have to deal with our unwanted guests. Orym had better not make any more disdainful remarks about our human, or I may not be able to resist tearing *him* to pieces while he's conveniently available.

Just before I reach the front door, I allow myself another gulp of absinthe, though it's difficult to say whether it soothes my temper or inflames it more. Outside, I stretch out into wolf form and lope toward the trees. It's so short a distance to the guest houses that no one would bother with a carriage or a horse, but I have no wish to prolong this task with a leisurely stroll.

Hearthshire's accommodations for high-ranking guests include a keep only slightly smaller than the one we made do with in Oakmeet and a few smaller houses for those with a particularly large retinue. Unless Garmon has been particularly stealthy himself, he only brought his great-grandson to attend to him, so Sylas sent a few of our pack-kin over to wait on them, as is appropriate for a lord.

I wouldn't be surprised if Garmon turned up understaffed specifically to test how well Sylas would cater to him. That family has always put far too much energy into climbing the social ladder and demanding esteem from others. And look where their inclinations got them. Most of the true-blooded members of their associated packs and a great deal of the faded kin as well were slaughtered after their attempt on Ambrose's throne, those who survived were banished…

Garmon might not have been an active part of the plotting, but his children and grandchildren learned those attitudes from somewhere.

Even though the house is technically ours, I have to treat it as their residence. I rise up from my wolf and rap my knuckles against the door, tugging at my vest to ensure it's straight. Wouldn't want to look sloppy in front of a lord.

One of our own people answers the door and ushers me inside. I find Garmon and Orym in the sitting room basking in the afternoon sun. The scent of the dinner my pack-kin are making for them, roast flame-pleasant if I'm not mistaken, laces the air. But as they get to their feet, Garmon makes a point of emphasizing the stiffness of his aging limbs as if being put up here was a hassle to them.

"Whitt, isn't it?" he says, scrutinizing me. "What are you here about? When am I finally to understand what's become of my grandson?"

I force myself to bob my head as low as I did for Sylas, not because I respect this man more, but because he'd see much less as an insult. "That's exactly what I'm here for. I'm afraid, as you must already suspect, it isn't uplifting news. Perhaps you would like to sit down?"

Garmon lets out a raspy guffaw. "No, these old bones can manage to hold me up while I hear this. Go on."

It's a matter that requires a certain amount of delicacy, which is difficult because Kellan was anything but delicate himself. I weigh my words carefully. "You may have gathered over the years while we were banished to the fringes that Kellan wasn't entirely satisfied with his position there. It wasn't the life he expected to have. Lord Sylas understood his frustrations and did what he could for him, even offered to release him from service if he preferred to seek a livelihood elsewhere, but he wasn't able to find a course that suited him."

"None of this explains where he's gone."

"I'm afraid it does." I dip my head again as if the conversation pains me—which it does if not exactly for the reasons Garmon would want it to. "My cadre-fellow began to challenge Sylas's authority in increasingly disruptive ways. Lord Sylas was running out of options. And the arrival of our human guest only brought out more rancor. Despite all she can offer to the Seelie, Kellan took a dislike to her and went out of his way to harm her."

"So he went for her blood when her blood is what she had to offer," Orym tosses out, so callously my claws itch to spring from my fingertips. "That seems reasonable."

I will my gritted teeth to unclench. "Blood that *all* our brethren need. A cure that would have been destroyed if Kellan had gone unchecked. In the end, he outright attacked her, and Lord Sylas was forced to fight him to preserve her life. He asked for Kellan's yield, but Kellan chose to make another lunge at the girl. It was a choice between a boon to all Seelie kind and a single fae in an act of undeniable mutiny. My lord did not make the decision lightly all the same, and he regrets to this day that it came to that point."

As I say the last words, I pour the spider-weave cloth from the pouch and let the folds fall open in my hand to reveal Kellan's soulstone. It flares like a tiny, muted ball of sunlight in the midst of the dark cloth.

For all his bluster, I suspect Garmon knew what was coming. I don't pick up any trace of shock in his expression as he takes the stone in. Orym, though, starts to sputter.

"Lord Sylas killed our pack-kin over some cringing dung-body? What in the—"

I cut him off before he can get any farther with his insults. "Kellan was *our* pack-kin from the moment he accepted the position in Lord Sylas's cadre, and I should hope *your* kin have taught you the proper respect that's due to one's lord."

Garmon squints at the stone and then at me. "It does seem odd that this happened so abruptly. I long suspected Lord Sylas wasn't particularly enthusiastic about taking Kellan into his service."

"If you'd been there, you wouldn't have found it abrupt at all," I say, my jaw starting to tighten all over again. "You haven't seen us in decades. And you can check for yourself that the stone shines true. He was offered a fair yield and refused it. The stone can't lie."

He peers at the soulstone again and murmurs a word. The light inside it flashes pure white before dwindling again. The huff of his breath sounds more irritated than accepting.

"And Lord Sylas saw fit to send his cadre-chosen to deliver this news rather than facing us himself?"

"He felt the news would be better delivered from an uninvolved party. Why would you want to look at the man who caused your grandson's death while processing that fact?"

"So that I could take him into account as I see fit." Garmon gives another huff and collects the stone and its trappings from me. "So I can demand to know what amends he'd make."

Sylas doesn't owe these miscreants any amends for Kellan's insubordination, but I can't imagine saying as much would win us any points. I step back. "He's ready to call on you now if you wish to see him immediately. I can—"

Garmon shakes his head with a jerk. "No. We must leave at once to see this stone finally to its proper resting place. If Lord Sylas truly has the honor you'd claim, let him travel to us to pay his respects fully. I'll expect him soon."

He turns with a swish of his cloak and motions for Orym to follow him. The young man aims a scowl at me before taking after his great-grandfather.

"Wait," I say, and hustle out of the house. I dash back to the castle as a wolf, but when I shift by the entrance, Garmon's spindly carriage is already cruising through the clearing toward the gate. Even if Sylas could catch them in time, it'd hardly do for him to race after them like a chastised whelp.

I watch them go, biting back half a dozen insults I'd like to hurl after them. Do they really think they're still so important that Sylas *needs* to care what they think of him and his respects?

But Sylas will care, which is exactly what makes him an excellent lord and why I'd be a terrible one.

The only crime anyone's ever claimed we committed, we've been absolved of. Garmon is father and grandfather to a host of traitors. He should be lucky he got even a cadre-chosen attending to him. But no, in his eyes I wasn't enough. A few drops of fae blood short. If he hasn't gotten Sylas's attention, what do any of the rest of us matter?

I stride into the castle to inform Sylas of their response with a sour flavor creeping through my mouth, wishing I couldn't so vividly remember my own experience with the same resentment Garmon expressed.

I've put that behind me now. I don't give a rat's ass what they think. Let them drift off to whatever backwater domain they've slunk to. I have a precious woman to save.

CHAPTER FOUR

Talia

Every room in Hearthshire's castle is bigger—grander—than its equivalent back in Oakmeet's keep. And there are more of them: sitting rooms and a library, a third floor full of guest rooms and servant quarters, a massive ballroom in the western wing with its ceiling two floors high.

But it's laid out in pretty much the same way, with a T-shaped hallway that has the main, spiraling staircase at its base, and the atmosphere, if a little more imposing, feels familiar. I haven't lived here a week yet, and I can already call it "home." Especially when I'm sitting perched on a stool in the kitchen, kneading dough while August preps a haunch of deer for a roast.

The kitchen itself is twice the size of the one back in Oakmeet, with five islands of varying sizes and a stone oven at one end so vast you could roast an entire stag in it, but August's touch is everywhere from the organization of the utensils to the ingredients already stocked in the pantry. When I'm here working beside him, it feels impossible that I could ever be wrenched to some other castle by forces beyond these walls.

Wouldn't it be nice if that were true?

"I think it's just about ready," I tell August, judging the elasticity of the dough the way he's taught me. The purple mixture is warm and pliant against my fingers, giving off a rich nutty smell.

My lover pauses in his work to watch me stretch a section between my hands and nods with a grin that's all the praise I need. "I can take over from there."

He glances down the counter to where one of his new kitchen assistants from the pack is working. Now that he has more space and more duties to attend to, Sylas wanted to bring more of the pack-kin into the castle to help with the day-to-day chores. "How are the berries coming along?"

"Just a few more to peel!"

As the woman shoves her bowl toward August, footsteps rap against the floor outside. A call rings down the hallway. "Lord Sylas?"

Recognizing the voice as Astrid's—one of the sentries—I slip off my stool, give my hands a quick wipe on a rag, and limp over to the doorway to see what's going on. August comes up behind me, giving my shoulder a reassuring squeeze.

Astrid shoots us a quick but tight smile before turning her attention back to the staircase, where the fae lord is just coming into view. The sentry's gray hair and lined face indicate she's old even by fae standards, but her wiry frame shows no sign of weakness.

"What's the trouble?" Sylas asks, his voice as steady as always but his unscarred eye even darker than usual with concern.

"I'm not sure yet if it's trouble. There's a carriage coming this way, five passengers, faded fae. Looks like a family. No noticeable weapons or armor—they look peaceful enough. They're coming at a good clip, though. I expect they'll be here within the minute. I didn't think we were expecting anyone."

Sylas frowns. "We weren't. Thank you for alerting me. You can return to your post."

He heads in the same direction down the hall toward the front door. I hesitate and then follow, curiosity tugging at me as much as my nerves. If there *is* more trouble on the horizon, I'd like to be able to prepare as well as I can.

"Sounds like I may need to double the meal," August says after me, sounding cheerful enough that I have to think the situation can't be *that* horrible. Maybe fae dropping in on each other happens a lot more often when you're not living in disgrace banished to the fringes. Before now, I've only seen pack life at its lowest.

When I slip outside behind Sylas, he doesn't remark on my presence. The carriage is already gliding into view between the arch of the trees. I move to the side, staying in the shadow of the castle.

The five figures who come into focus as the carriage draws nearer do look like a family. There's a couple who appear to be middle-aged by fae standards and three young women who'd pass for twenty-somethings in human terms—the youngest maybe not quite out of her teens. They all have glossy brown hair ranging from chestnut on the mother and the youngest daughter to tawny on father and the eldest, and the girls all share their mother's sharply pointed nose.

Their clothes are close to the simple tunics and dresses most of our pack-kin usually wear, just a little fancier with glinting embroidery along the collars and the cuffs of the sleeves. The middle daughter's hair swirls around her head to where it's pinned in place by a gold clip that sparkles with emeralds.

As the carriage slows, Sylas steps forward to meet the newcomers. "Hello there. What brings you to Hearthshire?"

"Greeted by the lord himself," the man says with a little chuckle and a bow so casual it immediately raises my hackles. "We're honored. I don't expect you'd necessarily remember me: I'm Namior of Dusk-by-the-Heart, and this is my wife, Tesfira, and our daughters, Lili, Irabel, and Toraine. Tesfira and I attended more than one ball and banquet here when Hearthshire was at its height. When we heard it was being restored to its former glory, we couldn't resist stopping by and seeing if there was any way we could assist in exchange for your hospitality."

While he speaks, his gaze roves over the castle, the surrounding buildings, and the forest beyond. Dusk-by-the-Heart, he said his domain was called. I'm just wondering whether that's one of the arch-lord's domains in their cluster around the Heart of the Mists when Sylas says, "Ambrose felt he could spare you?"

My stance tenses even more. These are Ambrose's pack-kin, then.

Understanding clicks in my head with a chill that ripples down my spine. They can't really be here to help and admire the rebuilding efforts. The arch-lord must have sent them to look for any proof they could find that Sylas isn't fit to keep me in his pack.

Spies. That's the word for it. Where's Whitt? A spymaster should know how to deal with intruders like these.

Fae rules of hospitality must mean Sylas can't send them right off, even though from the set of his shoulders I suspect he'd like to. He makes a broad motion toward them. "I appreciate your consideration. We've been settling in quite well as it is—and I'd hardly want to put guests to work. If you'd like to join us for dinner tonight and see how the renovations are coming together, my pack would be happy to see you to the guest buildings."

Tesfira offers a coy smile. "No need to go to that much trouble, Lord Sylas. We'd be perfectly happy with the visitor quarters in the castle, and then we can be closer at hand to offer our service."

Closer at hand to lurk around and observe us, she means.

Thankfully, Sylas isn't any more inclined to accept that proposal than I would be. He shakes his head emphatically. "I certainly couldn't set you up there when the outer buildings are free, especially when it comes to esteemed kin of the arch-lord. Let me see you there myself."

He sets off without waiting for a response. The husband and wife exchange a glance, the daughters murmuring discontentedly, but they direct their carriage to glide behind the fae lord, maybe intending to argue more once they catch up with him.

Hopefully he'll be able to get rid of them completely before too long. Even watching them drifting away, uneasiness creeps over my skin. We haven't figured out a solid strategy yet for convincing the arch-lords that I *do* belong here, especially when we don't know anything about what arguments Ambrose will make other than that he isn't likely to play fair.

I could go back to helping August in the kitchen, but a restless itch tickles through my limbs. I look toward the pack village, where several of the fae had stopped to check out the visitors and have now gone back to their usual pursuits.

If I can show I really *am* a member of the pack, not just an object that Sylas keeps around for my blood, surely that would work toward convincing the other arch-lords that I should stay here? How could it be a good thing to uproot a "precious resource" from a home where I'm respected and protected by the entire pack?

I've made a few tentative forays into joining their activities— maybe it's time I do a little more.

A few of the pack-kin who were watching the newcomers have gathered closer in conversation. I recognize a couple of them by name: Elliot, whose family tends to the sheep and who supplies the pack with milk and cheese, and Brigit, a woman who always wears brightly colored dresses and who's a regular fixture at Whitt's nighttime revels. As quickly as my warped foot allows, I hurry over to them, grateful for the boots that make my feet at least look normal even if my steps are a bit uneven despite the built-in brace.

"Hey," I say as I reach the group of three, feeling abruptly awkward. "I guess the pack is a lot more popular now that we're back at Hearthshire."

Elliot smiles crookedly. "Seems that way. But maybe not the kind of 'popularity' we'd prefer." He turns to the others. "We should get on with gathering the shy-caps before they're gone."

I try to hold myself in a stance that looks capable and enthusiastic. "Is that something you could use a hand with?"

The three of them look me over, and then Brigit shrugs. "The more hands we have, the more chance we'll grab them all. Do you know shy-caps?"

"Ah, no," I admit, limping along with them as they head toward the forest, hoping shy-caps aren't anything ferocious.

"They're mushrooms," explains the other woman, whose name I haven't caught. "Elliot spotted a patch of them coming back from the pasture. They got their name because they don't show themselves for long—you get about an hour and then they fade away."

They stop to pick up reed baskets from a storage shed near the edge of the forest, and I take one too. Harper darts over to us and snatches one for herself. She taps me teasingly with her elbow. "No going off on your first adventures without me."

I smile back at her. "I don't know how much of an adventure picking mushrooms will be, but it sounds like everyone's welcome."

It turns out collecting the shy-caps isn't all that simple after all. The little mushrooms, all of them smaller than my thumb, glimmer faintly in the streaks of sunlight that trickle between the leaves in the grove where they've sprouted. But half of the time when I reach for one, it vanishes before I can close my fingers around it. From the muttered curses of the fae around me, I gather that isn't just my problem. Elliot must have spotted them close to the one-hour deadline.

I manage to fill my basket halfway and feel pretty satisfied with that. Harper has less luck, veering this way and that and then sighing in exasperation when yet another slips from her grasp. She swings her basket and ambles closer to me. "More guests—and from one of the domains of the Heart! You went out with Lord Sylas to Dusk-by-the-Heart, didn't you? I suppose it's even grander than Hearthshire?"

Even as I smile at the eagerness in her voice, my chest tightens at the memory. "The castle is very… imposing. I only saw the outside. We weren't there for very long."

My voice probably gives away my discomfort. Harper hesitates, ducking her head. She doesn't know exactly what went on during that visit, but the tensions between Sylas and Ambrose aren't a total secret. "Of course. Perhaps that's why they've come here instead. I wonder if we'll have a ball soon, now that more packs are taking an interest."

No doubt she's imagining showing off her dresses to them, hoping they'll want one and spread the word. "I don't know," I say. "I'm not sure what the guests are expecting."

Brigit snorts. "They expect to poke their noses where they don't belong. Meddlers."

The other woman, whose name I now know is Pomya, tips her head in agreement and pulls back her lips to show her wolfish fangs. "They'd better not meddle too much, or we'll show them how Hearthshire defends itself."

Elliot tsks at her. "A great look for us it'd be if we pounce on the first friendly guests we've gotten since returning."

"You call that bunch friendly?"

"No," he admits. "But they're playing at it, so we have to play along, don't we? You don't think I'd like to turn them out on their asses for Lord Sylas? But if he thought we could get away with that, he'd do it himself."

Brigit glances back toward the castle with an unusually pensive expression. "He's done a lot for us. It's a shame the best we can offer is a bunch of mushrooms when there's still so much unsettled."

Her gaze skims over me, with a prickle down my spine at the knowledge that everyone here knows I'm the main cause of the pack's currently precarious situation.

But I'm also the main reason they were able to return to Hearthshire at all. That's got to be worth something, right? Listening to them brings a pang into my chest. Their sentiments echo my own wish to contribute more, to be more than a walking blood dispenser. I can offer something very important, but it's not really something I actually *do*.

"Maybe there are ways we can help that don't go as far as tossing them out," I venture.

Pomya cocks her head. "Like what?"

"Well, they're going to poke around and spy on us, right? So we can keep an eye on *them*. Try to catch them doing something suspicious enough that it'll give Sylas an excuse to send them away —or maybe even make Ambrose look bad so he'll be less likely to keep hassling us."

She grunts. "I'd rather tear a strip off of them like they probably deserve. No one should get to threaten our pack."

Harper twists a strand of her pale hair around her finger. "But if they aren't *acting* like a threat..."

"We know they're not here because they care so much about us," Brigit says. "If I notice them putting one foot out of line, I'm not letting them get away with it. They need to see how strong we still are."

I think back to something Whitt said to me before I faced my former captors for what I hope was the last time—about how playing to your weaknesses can be a way of being strong. "I think if they're playing games, then we can too. If we pretend we're weaker than we really are, that we don't realize what they're up to, then they'll give more away. And then we can surprise them by really getting the upper hand later."

Elliot hums to himself, and Pomya looks skeptical. I'm not sure they agree with my reasoning or even think I'm making much sense. But at least I get a vaguely impressed whistle out of Brigit when she checks my basket. "You've got quick hands, girl. I'll give you that much."

Any lingering shy-caps have vanished. We tramp back along the overgrown path to the castle and find Sylas waiting by the village. He nods to his pack-kin, but his gaze focuses on me. A hint of a smile curves one side of his mouth. "I see you've been finding new ways to contribute around here. Can I have a word?"

As if I'd say no. I pass my basket to Brigit and meander with Sylas back toward the trees. My stomach knots. Have the guests already become a problem?

"Is everything all right?" I ask carefully, not sure how much I should say even with the village at a distance.

Sylas smiles wider but with a grim edge. "As right as it can be, I suppose. Just a complication at a time when my attention needs to be elsewhere. Kellan's grandfather wishes me to attend to him personally in his own domain, and I don't want to delay that responsibility for however long our visitors may decide to enjoy our hospitality. The more time he has to stew, the more chance he'll find some way to give our current enemies ammunition against us."

Ambrose is already plenty dangerous as it is. I nod in understanding. "So you're going right away, even with the guests?"

"Yes. Whitt and August can 'entertain' them well enough—but I'd like you to accompany me."

To the domain where the rest of Kellan's relatives now live? My shoulders stiffen automatically. "Why?"

"Because given the current circumstances, I'd rather not leave you *here* when I'm not nearby. And also because, as Kellan's intended victim, I hope your presence will help remind his family of how much we all might have lost if I hadn't intervened." Sylas's smile softens. "You do seem to have a way of adjusting the perspective of those around you. But—I know it won't be easy for you. They won't harm you, but they may not be kind either. I won't force you to come."

He won't force me, but he thinks me being there would help him. How can I say no to *that*?

After all the ways he's protected me, all the risks he's taken for me, I'm not sure there's anywhere in this world or mine I wouldn't follow Sylas to if he asked.

I drag in a breath. "You don't need to. I'll do whatever I can. When do we leave?"

CHAPTER FIVE

August

If you'd asked me while we were living at Oakmeet, I'd have
said I missed the chatter and companionship of visitors,
which we lost almost entirely after we were banished. But guests like this
family from Dusk-by-the-Heart? I could definitely do without *them*.

"You don't look all that different from a regular human," the
middle daughter says to Talia, sitting next to her at the dinner table.
She grabs a handful of my love's hair as if handling a doll. "Other
than this. It doesn't grow this color, does it?"

Talia's face turns nearly as pink as those locks. "No. It's just
brown naturally. August dyed it." She glances at me where I'm
seated at her other side with a hint of worry that makes my stomach
clench. So concerned that she might let us down somehow if she
says the wrong thing. I want to reach for her hand to squeeze it, but
the one nearest me is clamped around her fork.

The youngest daughter actually gets up out of her chair and
gives Talia a sniff. "Smells like a normal human too." She giggles

and flops back into her chair, glancing around at all of us like she expects us to be equally amused by her observation.

Their father waves his hand toward Sylas. "You haven't made any attempt to determine the source of her… unusual blood?"

I can tell my lord is holding himself back from a full glower. His unscarred eye shines darkly. "We've made plenty of attempts, but the answer has eluded us. It may be that it's a random natural phenomena with no specific source."

The eldest daughter pokes at the scraps remaining on her plate while eyeing Talia. "I wonder what it tastes like when it's not all mixed up in the tonic. Would you let us sample a little?"

My shoulders tense, and my gums twitch with the emerging of my fangs. I'm not sure I'd have been able to hold myself back from springing across the table at her with a chomp of my teeth to let her find out how much *she* likes offering a sample if Sylas didn't speak again, quickly and firmly. "She may contain a mystery, but she's still a person and a valued member of our pack. She bleeds enough for us when it can save us. I would not ask more from her for curiosity's sake."

He hasn't outright chided, but the rebuke in his words is obvious. The daughter—Lili, I think that one is?—ducks her head, having at least the grace to look abashed.

Talia manages to take another bite, but her nervousness shows all through her stance. Dust and doom, I can only imagine how much worse her situation will be if Ambrose pulls off his claim. She shouldn't have to put up with being treated like a curiosity, an exotic trinket we picked up in our travels, rather than a conscious living being.

But if we bite our guests' heads off—as much as I might want to in the most literal sense—we'll look undisciplined and vindictive to the arch-lords. It isn't as if they're harming her in any observable way. Ambrose won't hesitate to point to any incident that happens during this visit when making his case. So I grit my teeth and will my claws to stay within my fingertips.

At least when dinner is over, Whitt shepherds the bunch of them outside to join in his second revel at Hearthshire, leaving the rest of us in peace. Although I suspect Talia would have liked to join in the revel if these strangers hadn't been in attendance.

I slip my hand around hers like I wanted to at the table and lean in to kiss the top of her head. "Are you all right?"

She gives herself a little shake and aims a small smile at me. "It's fine. It makes sense that they're curious. As long as I have all of you, it doesn't really matter how the other fae treat me."

It does, though. It matters to me. And she shouldn't have to put up with their disrespect.

Of course, tomorrow she might be facing even worse.

After she's gone to her bedroom for the night, I track down Sylas. He's in the gym, examining the cabinet of weaponry we brought to Oakmeet when we left and restored to its proper place just a few days ago.

He takes out a short sword and turns it over in his hands, testing its weight. Apparently he doesn't have the highest hopes for how tomorrow's visit will go either.

I wouldn't normally question my lord's judgment, but the knot of worry in my belly propels the words out. "Are you sure it's a good idea for Talia to come with you?"

Sylas raises an eyebrow at me, his gaze managing to be so penetrating even though one of those eyes can't even see. At least, it can't see anything of this world. "Do you think I'd be taking her if I hadn't decided it was?"

I grimace. "It's only—it's bad enough how Kellan treated her, how Garmon and the other one insulted her when they were here. They'll be bolder on their own terrain. She shouldn't have to hear how they'll talk to her or about her."

"I don't know. Perhaps it's useful for her to see the full span of fae attitudes—to know just how wary she needs to be of everyone outside this domain, even now that we've dealt with Aerik." Sylas's voice turns grim. "I don't think this is the last challenge we're going to face on her behalf. The more steel she can find in herself, the better. You know how strong she already is."

I do. I wish she didn't have to be that strong. I wish I could slaughter everyone who so much as points a sneer in her direction.

She's been through so much pain already, and it still weighs on her.

"And our guests here?" I ask.

"Whitt will do most of the work keeping them occupied. Give them another feast for dinner tomorrow, and if all goes well, we'll be back by nightfall." He pats my arm. "I'm sure Talia would appreciate whatever breakfast you can whip up for our travels tomorrow. Will you leave something in the cold box? I want to leave at dawn."

"Of course, my lord," I say, and head back to the kitchen to see what I can pull together that might bring Talia a little joy while she anticipates her destination.

When I wake the next morning, my lord and my love are already gone. I stalk through the halls restlessly and finally whip up a small breakfast for myself, since after last night's revel Whitt isn't likely to make an appearance in the dining room until lunch. I've just polished off an omelet and brought the plate back to the kitchen when the middle daughter—Irabel?—comes slinking in.

"Oh, are you already done with breakfast?" she says with a trace of a pout, propping herself against the nearest island.

Something about her pose and her tone makes my hackles rise. I force myself to smile. "Did my pack-kin not prepare something in the guest house this morning? I'm sure Sylas intended for your meals to be seen to."

She shrugs. "They did, but I thought it'd be much more fun to have whatever you'd come up with. A cadre-chosen who's a warrior *and* a chef—there aren't many of those."

She peeks through her eyelashes at me, and the prickling discomfort solidifies into a fuller understanding. She's flirting with me. It's been decades since any fae woman thought it worth pursuing me, and I wasn't old enough to be eligible for all that long before our disgrace—I'm out of practice at recognizing the signs.

Knowing what she's up to doesn't ease my mind at all. She's aware that Talia and I have taken to each other—we didn't see any point in hiding that when the whole pack knows. But because Talia's only human, as far as this woman is concerned—because we aren't properly bonded as mates—she still considers me a perfectly reasonable target for her interest.

It takes all my self-control not to growl at her. Her assumptions are the same ones almost any of our brethren would make. That doesn't mean I have to cater to them, though.

"I'm afraid I didn't have any elaborate plans," I say, keeping my tone cool. "I have duties to attend to, but if you check with my pack-kin who are seeing to your stay, I'm sure one of them could put something together for you regardless of the timing."

"Hmm. If you're not the one making it, I'm not sure I'm all that hungry." She straightens up and saunters closer. "Could I help you with some of your duties? You must be very busy with so much to catch up on now that you're back in Hearthshire."

Another growl collects at the base of my throat. I smother it down, but my voice still comes out with a bit of an edge. "These duties are best carried out alone. And what needs I have for companionship in general are already well taken care of. Please don't trouble yourself."

My full meaning must be clear enough. Her face falls, and she gives another half-hearted shrug. "If you change your mind... I believe my father had something he wanted to discuss with you as soon as possible. Do you have a moment to call on him before you go off on your duties?"

I restrain a sigh. "I do. I'll find him as soon as I'm finished here."

She gives me one more lingering glance and then sashays off. I glare at the pots dangling over the counter for several seconds as I gather my temper.

Should I have been less brusque with her? Have I soured the situation in some way that will come back to bite us?

But the gall of her attempting to work her charms on me as if I'd cast aside Talia the second a woman with fae blood shot one coy glance at me…

No, maybe we haven't been firm enough. I trust Sylas's judgment, and he's seen fit to trust mine. I'll speak to Namior—and make it absolutely clear that we consider Talia a full member of the pack, and that disrespect shown to her is an insult to all of us.

I stride into the hall, heading toward the entrance. Yes. I'll simply… advise them so they recognize their rudeness. I can do that calmly, can't I? *They're* the ones who should be embarrassed of how they've offended us. It'll only—

A twitch in the shadows along the edge of the floor catches my eye. I pause, my head jerking around to try to track the movement.

I can't make out its source. When I inhale deeply, my entire body tenses.

Did I just catch a hint of *rat* in the air?

Another wavering shadow draws my attention to the foot of the stairs. I spin the rest of the way around and march toward it. If one of the filthy Murk has dared sneak into our home with Heart only knows what spiteful intent, I'll bite *its* head off, you can be sure of that.

I hustle up the stairs, taking another breath and another. The scent I thought I picked up downstairs has faded away. I don't catch sight of any creatures lurking on the stairwell or in the hallway upstairs either.

I prowl around for a few minutes until I'm forced to accept that my mind might have simply been playing tricks on me. I have been pretty keyed up since we first heard Ambrose had called for Talia.

As I turn back toward the stairs, a noise reaches my ears: a soft thump and a rustle of fabric. My ears prick. Someone's in the library.

I stalk toward the doorway just as the oldest of the visiting daughters emerges. She's patting the fabric of her skirt, which forms an odd lump by her thigh for a moment before she smooths it out. At the sight of me, she startles and then claps her hand to her chest. "Oh, I didn't realize anyone was up here. I was just returning a book Sylas said I could borrow yesterday."

I remember hearing her ask about that, but something about this encounter rubs me the wrong way, especially after her sister made a point of seeking out my attention downstairs. Why didn't this one say good morning on her way up? What was she doing with her skirt just now?

I can hardly demand she lift it up to show me. If I'm wrong, it'd be even worse than if I attacked her over Talia.

There isn't any chance that...? As I nod in acknowledgment, an absurd suspicion wriggles through me, and I step just close enough to catch her scent. She's a wolf—there's no doubt about that. It isn't as if we could have somehow missed the scent of five rats pretending to be Seelie after spending any time in close proximity anyway.

Still, I can't help taking on extra step to confirm that will both keep them busy and benefit the pack. "I thought I might propose a hunt, if you'd want to join in. Our pantry could still use some stocking."

There's no mistaking the predatory gleam that lights in her eyes with the stirring of her wolfish instincts. "I'm sure my whole family would be happy for the chance to stretch our legs," she says with a bob of her head.

"Excellent." I motion for her to continue on her way. "I was just getting something from my room. If your father asks, you can tell him I'll be there shortly, and then we'll see about the hunt."

When she's vanished down the stairwell, I enter the library instead. I've never spent much time in this part of the castle, never missed it when we went without a full library in Oakmeet. My gaze skims over the shelves of leather and leaf-bound books, the armchairs and their side tables, the objects on display here and there from Sylas's travels. There are a few gaps amid the books, but I can't tell whether anything we should be concerned about is missing.

Since no one's around to hear it, I let out the growl I've been holding in for so long. Sylas will know better than I do. As soon as he returns—let it be tonight—I'll tell him what I saw and let him decide what we should make of it.

It would be too much to hope that Ambrose's pack-kin didn't have any extra wickedness up their sleeves, wouldn't it?

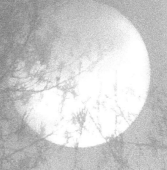

CHAPTER SIX

Talia

The wind whips my hair back from my face, bringing a trace of tears into my eyes until I avert my gaze. I think I'd enjoy this journey more if Sylas hadn't set the carriage at top speed. And also if I'd found anything to like about the place we're traveling to.

Our breakfast long eaten, there hasn't been much to do but watch the landscapes go by. Even that loses its thrill as we reach a narrow, winding valley between two steep cliffs. Sylas has to slow the carriage so it can navigate without bumping the pocked stone, and the scenery quickly merges into a seemingly endless mass of orange rock and turquoise moss.

I lean back on the bench and rub my eyes, restraining a yawn. I can't say I got the greatest night's sleep anticipating this morning's trip.

Sylas monitors the carriage's movements for a few minutes longer and then, satisfied that his magic is directing it well enough that he can trust it to pilot itself, sits down next to me. He reaches beneath the stiff fabric of his formal vest and produces a leather sheath with a matching leather-wrapped hilt protruding from it.

He hands it to me. "To replace the one I threw away. You shouldn't go unarmed."

I wrap my fingers around the leather, which is warm from lying so close to his skin. A weird mix of gratitude and trepidation coils in my chest. I hadn't been sure he'd want to trust me with another blade after his reaction to my self-hostage gambit. But... "Do you think I'm going to need it where we're going?"

His mouth twists. "Better you have it and don't than go without and do. None of those once of Thistlegrove are known for kindness toward humans. They're rarely kind to *each other* unless it serves them. Given what you offer and who you're arriving with, you needn't fear for your life, but if anyone oversteps before I can intervene, I fully support you showing how unwise that is for yourself."

And this is the family he found himself tied to through marriage—through no choice of his own, since the true-blooded fae have no control over who they connect with as their soul-twined mate.

The more I learn about how things work for the purest of the fae and their love lives, the less appealing it sounds. What good is having a soul-deep bond with someone you didn't choose and maybe never would have if you'd gotten a say in it?

I fix the strap on the sheath to the belt around my fae-styled dress. A pouch with the remaining salt from the small supply Whitt gave me dangles at my other hip.

Together, those weapons make for a small protection against the physical strength and magical power of the fae, but it's something. The salt saved me from being mauled by one of my former captors a couple of weeks ago. And my old dagger had something to do with saving me from Ambrose, at least in the moment.

With the sheath secured, I look up at Sylas, taking in his

pensive expression. "What *exactly* did Isleen and Kellan's family do? I know they committed some kind of treason against Ambrose. They tried to take over as arch-lords? How would that even work?"

The fae lord folds his hands together on his lap. "There are two ways an arch-lord can be displaced. The more civilized way is to prove them unfit for the job based on wrong-doing or incompetence, and then the two remaining arch-lords must agree on a lord they feel would make a fitting replacement and for whom they receive the Heart's blessing."

I'm taking a wild guess that's not what happened in Isleen's case. "And the less civilized way?"

"We are still wolves as well as fae in spirit. If a pack shows it's powerful enough to overcome another and take the lord's life or force their yield, they're granted the right over that domain. It's the same for an arch-lord as any other."

I shiver. "Your mate and a bunch of her family tried to *kill* Ambrose?"

"As near as we can determine," Sylas says. "They'd come up with a strategy combining their various magical specialities and a few rare true names that kin among them had managed to master. It appeared they'd been laying the groundwork to ensure their entry into his castle unhindered for months if not years, slowly and subtly. I've never heard a full report on what happened once they were inside the castle… I don't know how close they came to succeeding. But they didn't, and Ambrose, his cadre, and his guards tore every one of them they caught to shreds."

He pauses, and his voice turns even more grim. "There wasn't enough left of Isleen to form a soulstone, but I saw the remains to confirm they were hers."

My next shiver comes with a twinge of nausea. "She can't have been thinking *you'd* become arch-lord when she hadn't even told you the plan?"

Sylas shakes his head. "She was serving her mother, who would have taken the title. But it would have benefitted her and me too, having a familial connection by the Heart."

"Kellan was part of Isleen's cadre, wasn't he? Why wasn't he punished?"

"He wasn't part of the attack. I think perhaps he was meant to provide some sort of alibi if the attempt went wrong but she was able to escape unhindered. And he *was* punished—by being banished alongside me. If I hadn't taken him into my cadre, he'd have been sent off with his grandfather and the other stragglers from the family and their packs to the other end of the fringes. I thought I owed it to him to give him a chance… If I'd understood how far she meant to go with her plotting and how soon, maybe it all could have been averted."

He lapses into somber silence. He's told me before that he feels responsible for the attack and his pack's banishing even though he wasn't directly involved in the treason. Soul-twined mates share thoughts and emotions, and he'd shut Isleen's out as well as he could after she betrayed him by sleeping with another man.

"Even if you'd figured it out, you might not have been able to stop her," I have to say. "You'd already argued with her about the parts you did know, and it didn't make any difference."

"There was more I could have done if I'd known more. But it's true we can't be sure of how the past would have unfolded regardless." He lets his stance relax against the side of the carriage and brushes a strand of my hair back from my cheek with a gentle graze of his fingers. His expression softens. "I have my pack where they belong in the present, and that's what truly matters. And I'll endeavour to ensure you *never* have need of that dagger. I certainly hope you won't put it to the same use as you did the last one."

I swallow hard. "I wouldn't want to. I don't *want* to die. I just— if it comes to that or going back to the kind of torture I faced with Aerik— I've got to have some kind of control over my own life." I lean against his shoulder, soaking up more of the heat that emanates from his body. "I don't like the thought of abandoning you all to the curse. It'd only be if I didn't see any other way—and even then I'm not totally sure I'd have the guts to go through with it."

Sylas wraps his arm right around me. "I've said it before, and I'll keep saying it: what happens with our curse isn't your responsibility. You're a *person*, not just a cure. We need to find a proper solution that actually solves the problem, not this stop-gap measure that relies on your sacrifice. You shouldn't make any of your choices based on the idea that you'd be abandoning us. You've already given so much of yourself."

A sharper pang of affection fills my chest. Wanting all the comfort I can take from his embrace, I slip my legs over his and nestle myself right against his chest.

Sylas makes an encouraging rumble and hugs me to him, his chin coming to rest against my forehead. The tickle of his hot breath over my skin rouses more heat everywhere our bodies touch. Desire unfurls low in my belly.

The fae lord's keen senses have become highly attuned to my emotional state. He shifts me against him and kisses my temple with a lingering tenderness. His voice comes out even lower than usual, with a hungry note that sends a tingle straight to my core. "I wish I had more time to be with you as a man rather than as a lord. Perhaps once we've dealt with this difficulty and with Ambrose's scheme, we'll have enough peace for me to offer you the attention the lady of Hearthshire deserves."

His open expression of longing gives me the courage to look up at him with a sly boldness I hadn't known I had in me. "What would you do if you had that time?"

The corners of his mouth curl upward. He ducks his head to trail his lips down the side of my face, nipping my earlobe and then claiming the crook of my neck with a swipe of his tongue.

My head sways to the side to give him more access, every part of me lighting up at just this brief intimacy. For a moment, the carriage around us and all thought of the confrontation ahead fade away.

But *only* for a moment. Sylas lifts his head, and I realize the mossy cliffs have given way to flatter rocky terrain. He brushes one last kiss to my cheek and eases me off of his lap.

"We'll cross the borders of Garmon's new domain soon. Best that his sentries don't discover just how much you mean to me."

Even though it was short, the interlude leaves me steadier than I felt before. I can face these fae. Why should I be intimidated by them? The only person here whose opinion I care about is the lord beside me. I have to help him win them over whatever way I can so that they won't make the problems we're already grappling with even worse.

I'm not sure what message Sylas sent ahead of us, but Garmon and his pack are clearly ready for our arrival. As we come up on a sprawl of low metal buildings, several fae emerge to meet us, their expressions solemn but unsurprised. The smooth walls shine with a coppery sheen, close enough to the color of bronze to make my pulse stutter. I can't help imagining being shut up in a box with solid sides, not even the glimpses beyond that the bars of Aerik's cage allowed me.

The carriage stops, and Garmon steps out of the largest of the buildings, only one story high but stretching across the sparse grass to the width of several of any of the smaller structures. His great-grandson flanks him. Looking at his wizened face and then his companion's, it occurs to me that nearly all of the fae here are either so young they could pass for teenagers or elderly enough that their old age shows in their skin and hair.

When Isleen and her mother made their assault on Ambrose's castle, they must have taken nearly all their family's capable pack-kin with them. And none of those made it back.

"So," Garmon says in an imperious if raspy voice, "the great Lord Sylas finally graces us with his presence."

Sylas doesn't wait for him to go on. He steps out of the carriage and immediately dips into a bow so low it startles me. Orym's eyes widen; even Garmon blinks at the sight.

"Forgive me, Lord Garmon, kin-of-my-mate," Sylas says. "I wished to spare you the pain of looking on the one who caused the loss of your grandson while hearing the news of that loss, but clearly I was mistaken in my priorities. I give you my apologies and my deepest regrets for the fate Kellan met."

Garmon hesitates, his mouth twitching with uncertainty. "And yet you bring what I understand to be the true source of that fate with you." He cuts his gaze to me.

Sylas straightens up and beckons me out of the carriage. I scramble over the side as gracefully as my warped foot and his helping hand allow, which isn't much. Standing next to him, I bob my head in a poor imitation of his bow, hoping that'll curry me a little favor.

Sylas touches my back. "Talia was the greatest victim in this situation. Despite how Kellan meant to harm her, she has come to offer her condolences as well."

"I'm sorry for your loss," I say quickly, willing my voice not to squeak. "I never wanted anything like this to happen."

"And yet it did, thanks to a dung-body," Orym mutters just loud enough for me to hear.

Several of his companions murmur amongst themselves in a tone that echoes his. My stance tenses.

Sylas casts a stern look at the young fae man. "Thanks to this human woman, we were able to fend off a horrific attack by the Unseelie just days ago. Kellan deserves respect for the service he gave and the ways he supported me in my cadre, but I could not stand by while he jeopardized all our futures in a way that could have far greater consequences than we've already faced."

He turns to Garmon. "You're old enough to have seen much, to have had to make many hard decisions. I hope you can understand how a lord may need to carry out acts he wishes were otherwise."

Garmon sighs. "Well, will you pay your respects or not? We have given him his proper place in the mausoleum."

Sylas gives him another, smaller bow. "Lead the way."

We trek across the uneven terrain to a narrower cliffside that rises from the ground like the hull of a capsized ship. A copper door is embedded in its jagged face. Garmon speaks a few syllables to open it and ushers us inside. Orym and a few of the other pack members, possibly Garmon's cadre, trail behind us.

The space inside looks more like how I'd picture a bank vault than like a cave. Metal walls gleam all around us. Ridges of the same metal jut out at random intervals, each holding a nest of cloth dappled with dried leaves and flowers in a ring around a soulstone. Those stones provide the room's only light: a pulsing, wavering glow that reflects of the surfaces all around us. The copper scent in the air gives me the impression that I've bitten my tongue to the point of bleeding.

I don't think I could have picked out Kellan's stone from memory, but Sylas walks right to one of the protrusions and inclines his head. "I'm glad to see his soul finally at rest. Be at peace, my cadre-chosen. Shine a light for your kin that outlasts any darkness."

Someone gives me a swift prod. "Haven't *you* got anything to say?"

Sylas swivels, his good eye darkening, but I raise my hand slightly to hold off any complaint he'd make. These people want to see that I regret Kellan's death too. How can I show that in a way they'll believe? *I* have to believe it too.

The fae man hated me from the moment he saw me. He threatened me, pushed me around—he would have blinded me and smashed my other foot if he'd gotten the chance. Never having to see him again is a relief.

But I still meant it when I said I hadn't wanted anyone to die.

I glance at his few remaining relatives. The hostility has faded from Garmon's face. Now he only looks tired. So much of his family was destroyed, and he's watching yet another of the younger generation laid to rest here.

I know how that feels, don't I? I've lost every part of my family, some of them right in front of me in a mess of gore and screams. This fae lord must have had to identify several of the torn-up bodies like Sylas did with his mate.

A lump rises in my throat. The image of blood streaking across darkened grass flashes through my mind. So much death around me, all because of the power *my* blood holds. So many lives lost.

I'm almost getting to a place where I don't blame myself, but I never wanted *any* of it.

"I'm sorry," I say. My voice comes out quieter than I meant to, almost hoarse. Holding Garmon's gaze, unexpected tears well up behind my eyes. Before I can will them away, one spills down my cheek. I swipe at it, embarrassed, but watching me, his expression softens even more.

"You'd cry for the fae who would have savaged you?"

"I cry for everyone who's died to bring or keep me here," I say. "He meant something to you, and that means something to me. I'm sorry for your loss."

The words come out awkwardly, but I must have gotten something right. Garmon's face tightens, and then he nods, motioning us toward the door. "It was good of you to come and good of you to speak so."

During the lunch we're offered and the conversation afterward, I stay on the fringes of the discussion, watching and listening and preferring not to draw attention. The talk turns from somber remarks about the war to increasingly fond recollections of Kellan's better moments, and by the time we head back to the carriage, even

Orym has stopped frowning, though he hasn't quite managed a smile yet.

"We still have some time yet before Hearthshire is ready for balls and banquets again," Sylas says. "But once we are, we'll host you in honor of the ways our families were once joined. You have my word on that, and every respect I can offer along with my condolences."

"I would that it had been another way," Garmon says enigmatically, but he gives me the slightest dip of his head in recognition after he bows to Sylas.

It isn't just them, I think as I take my seat in the carriage. All of our enemies are still people behind the bluster, the insults, the threats, or the outright violence. Ambrose is a person. Even Aerik is, as much of a monster as he's made himself at the same time.

It'd be easier to remember that if they were all willing to see the same in me.

CHAPTER SEVEN

Talia

Night has fallen over the land like a blanket of darkness by the time we return to Hearthshire. Only a couple of orbs still glow behind the castle's windows, the pack houses mostly dark too.

I stretch my limbs in the cooling air, stiff from two long journeys in close succession, and let Sylas help me out of the carriage. When we come into the castle's entrance room, Whitt is already stalking over to meet us. August appears a moment later. No one else seems to be around—the pack-kin who've been helping around the castle have gone back to their own homes, I assume.

"Our guests didn't run you too ragged?" Sylas asks Whitt.

The spymaster smirks. "We *did* give them a pretty good run. The whelp here had them pitch in on a hunt." He gives August a playful smack to the shoulder. "They've retired to their accommodations for the night. I have a couple of my people keeping an eye on the guest buildings to alert us if they decide to sneak off on some business after hours. How was your turn as guests?" His gaze slides to me with an evaluating air, as if making sure I haven't been traumatized by the experience.

"I think that matter is settled to everyone's satisfaction." Sylas glances at me too, with a reserved but warm smile that makes my heart glow like the lanterns. "Talia played a large role in that."

Whitt clucks his tongue in amusement. "Making friends wherever you go, even among those miscreants, are you, mighty one?" He strokes his fingers down the side of my face in a brief, unexpected gesture of affection. He hasn't generally initiated any public displays in front of his brothers.

"I just told them the truth," I say. "And left out the parts that I didn't think they'd want to hear." Like what a jerk I think Kellan was.

"So wise already." Whitt seems to hesitate and then dips in to give me a kiss that's even more unexpected, so fleeting you'd think he was hoping he could get it in without the other two noticing. Even that swift brush of his lips makes my heart skip a beat.

He straights up immediately, returning his attention to Sylas with a breezy tone but a pleased glint in his ocean-blue eyes. "I should give you a full accounting of today's happenings—including an interesting observation Auggie made and our invitation to a banquet at Donovan's home. Shall we take this to your study?"

As they head off, August's gaze follows them for a moment. Then he swoops in with a near-crushing hug as if not to be outdone by his older brother's demonstration.

I snuggle close to him, a smile springing to my lips. "Missed me?"

"Always," he murmurs.

"If you need to talk to Sylas—"

He shakes his head. "I already went over it thoroughly with Whitt. You're really all right after the talk with Garmon?"

"Yeah, just tired."

He presses a kiss to the corner of my jaw, waking my whole

body out of its travel fatigue. I feel too wound up from the confrontation with Kellan's family and Ambrose's threat hanging over me to fully relax into the moment. I think my nerves need a little pampering, if that's available.

I look up at August. "Has the castle's sauna been fixed up yet? I could use a soak in the pool about now."

He beams down at me. "It's all ready. Let's get you a bath."

He scoops me up, ignoring my squeak of surprise, and carries me to the stairs that lead to the basement. "I *can* still walk," I inform him, giving him a mock-glower that the smile I can't restrain must totally undermine.

"But why should you have to?" He grins wider and bounds down the stairs.

Like most of the castle's rooms, the sauna here is like a larger, grander version of the one back in Oakmeet. There are not one but two pools, a smaller one like an oversized hot tub with heat radiating from the water and one closer in size to a real swimming pool beyond it. The marble tiles on the floor and the polished wood walls gleam from their recent cleaning.

A familiar mineral scent laces the humid air. As August sets me down, I inhale it deep into my lungs and let out a happy sigh.

A folding screen with solid wooden panels has been set up in one corner of the room, also just like in Oakmeet. August moves toward it just like he always did there, to give me privacy while I bathe but ensure my safety at the same time.

I pause where I've crouched to slip off my boots. At the thought that passes through my mind, my pulse thumps a little harder with a nervous hitch—but what do I have to be nervous about? I just held my ground in front of a whole pack that dismisses humans like me. August *loves* me. There's nothing to be ashamed of in wanting something like this or admitting to wanting it, is there?

My voice comes out quiet anyway. "August? I—I think I'm steady enough now that you don't need to worry about me drowning. You don't have to be on guard duty whenever I take a bath."

He catches himself with a chuckle that sounds mildly embarrassed. "Of course you are. I just—habit. I'll leave you to yourself then. If you do need me, I'll be down the hall in the entertainment room. I'll still be able to hear if you call."

He swivels to head for the door, which isn't what I intended at all. I force myself to blurt the words out, my face flushing. "No, I was actually thinking— If you wanted, you could join me?"

August stops in his tracks. Desire sparks in his golden eyes so hot my cheeks outright burn. "Join you... in the pool?" he asks, careful but with undisguised eagerness.

That eagerness might be the only thing stopping me from melting into a puddle of embarrassment after all. My gaze darts to the floor and then back up to meet his. "Yes. I mean—it might be... fun?"

His smile then could light up an entire galaxy. He walks over to me, his eyes molten but his expression so gentle it prompts no regrets at all about my invitation. His voice goes husky. "Yes, I think it could be."

Suddenly I have no idea what to do with myself. Well, if I'm getting in the pool, whether alone or with company, there are some pretty obvious steps to take first unless I want my clothes drenched. I busy myself with undoing the laces on my boots and the buckle on my belt.

August shucks off his own shoes and then reaches for his shirt, every movement smooth and methodical, as if he's giving me plenty of time to change my mind. But each bit of him unveiled only makes *me* more eager. I can't help watching the flex of his muscular chest as he pulls off the shirt, the way the motion ripples through his brawny shoulders and arms, how his multitude of tattoos play across his skin in response.

My own skin heats beneath my dress, reminding me that I still have work to do. I push myself back to my feet, favoring the good one, and grasp the dress's hem. Without giving myself a chance to balk, I tug the flowing fabric right over my head and drop it on the floor.

The warm air wraps around my bare breasts and legs. August makes a rough sound and peels off his trousers much faster than the rest.

We've seen each other naked before, but in the heat of the moment, not quite so deliberately. A quiver of anticipation that's still a little nervous runs through me. I strip off my panties and wobble to the steps that lead into the pool without waiting to take in August's reaction.

The heated water closing over my limbs soothes the burst of anxiety. I sink in down to my shoulders and glide around, just as August removes his last bit of clothing.

Oh. The sight of him fully naked sends a tingle straight to my core. Every part of him is taut with sculpted muscle, full of coiled strength I know can offer such tenderness as well. And the impressive shaft between his legs is half-erect already.

I jerk my attention from it to his face. At this point, it's a miracle my cheeks haven't scalded right off.

August looks anything but offended by my interest. He prowls into the water with a wolfish air and circles me before catching me in his arms from behind. His lips brush the shell of my ear. "What did you have in mind next?"

I hadn't thought that far, but with his solid arms around me and the currents in the water rippling over my skin, longing throbs down below. We've done a lot together in the past several weeks, exploring each other's bodies, but we haven't actually had sex yet. It felt so good with Sylas while August caressed me too. I want to know what it could be like with this sweet, unearthly man who loves me just as I love him.

The time we came close, he stopped things because he could tell

I was, as he put it, "fertile." I reach to trail my fingers along his neck. "Is there any reason to worry about— Can we do everything tonight?"

He tucks his head close to my shoulder and inhales, followed by a teasing flick of his tongue. "Anything you want, Sweetness."

I lean back into him, thrilled by the hard length that nudges my hip. "Then I want everything."

With a hungry growl, he whips me around. The instant I'm close enough, he cups my jaw and claims my mouth as if he was starving for me.

I cling to him, losing myself in the passionate melding of our mouths, the slide of our skin turned slick in the water. My breasts graze his chest, my nipples stiffening at the contact. I loop my arms around August's neck and kiss him back just as hard.

"My Sweetness," he murmurs in the brief breaths before our mouths collide again. "My love. My Talia."

I have no interest in arguing. He might not be the only man in this castle who's won my heart, but he does own it. And I want to be his in every possible way.

He adjusts me against him, one arm around my waist, the other easing higher. His hand glides through the water, stroking over my curves until it reaches one pebbled peak. At the swipe of his thumb, I gasp against his mouth. My fingers curl into the short, dampened strands of his hair.

My legs have splayed around August's waist. His erection, fully hardened now, presses against my inner thigh and then skims the spot where I'm most sensitive. A giddy jolt races through me.

I arch toward him instinctively, already aching with need, and August groans. His next kiss sears against my lips.

"Not yet," he mumbles. "Don't want to rush this. You deserve better than that."

Part of me wants to say I deserve him inside me *right now*, but just the thought of saying that dizzies me. And then he's kissing me again, fondling my breasts, letting the head of his shaft tease over the nub between my legs, and it's all I can do to keep my head at all.

Whimpers quiver up my throat alongside the flood of pleasure. My fingernails dig into his scalp before I realize what I'm doing, but if they hurt August at all, it only provokes an even more heated growl.

He pushes us through the water until I'm braced against the tiled side of the pool, my breasts rising just above the surface. With a fiery gleam in his eyes, August lowers his head and laps his tongue over one of my nipples. He sucks it into his mouth and swirls his tongue around it, nips it and lavishes it until I'm squirming with need at the rush of bliss coursing through my chest. Then he moves to the other, worshiping it with the same intensity.

I run my fingers over his hair and across his shoulders, hoping my touch feels at least half as good to him as his does to me. I'm still half-submerged, but I'm on fire all the same, desire flaring through every nerve.

One of his hands slips between my legs, stroking over the delicate folds there. The need swells so sharp and heady I cry out.

"I want to be in you so badly," August rasps, his lips trailing up my sternum.

A shaky noise of agreement tumbles from my mouth. He kisses me there again, deeply and passionately, and shifts me against the pool wall. The stream of one of the jets spills across my thigh, and a shiver of excitement tingles through me with the memory of how he encouraged me to put those to use in the pool back in Oakmeet.

August clearly remembers that moment well too. He pauses, testing the current with his hand, and nuzzles my cheek. "You enjoyed the jets before, didn't you?"

"Not as much as I'm enjoying you."

"But what if you could have both?"

He turns me in his hands, quick but careful, so I'm facing the wall. My arms fold over the edge of the pool instinctively. He places me right in front of the jet, and the gush of propelled water hits me right where I'm aching most.

I moan, my head drooping toward the tiles. August dapples kisses up my spine to the nape of my neck. His erection settles between my legs, teasing over my opening from behind as the jet massages the nub above.

How can my body possibly contain this much pleasure? Every time I think I've found the pinnacle of it, it turns out it can soar even higher.

August loops his arm around my waist. His lips graze my shoulder blade. "Ready, Sweetness?" he asks in a tone both so tender and blazing hot.

My voice spills out in a gasp. "Yes. Please. *Now.*"

His ragged chuckle reverberates from his chest. He slides into me, just the head, and another moan reverberates out of me.

August rumbles in answer, hugging me tight, his mouth clamped on my shoulder. My inner walls tingle and relax around him.

It's easier this second time, my muscles melting in anticipation of the ecstasy to come. He pushes deeper into me with one smooth thrust, the current of water stutters against my core, and that's all it takes.

I clench with a crackling of a release that quivers through me from my center to the top of my head and the tips of my toes. August growls encouragingly and begins to pump in and out of me, slowly at first but picking up speed and force.

Between his hardness filling me and the jet pulsing against my sex, the wave of my orgasm has barely rolled through me before I find myself racing toward a new peak. My breath shudders out of me. I feel as though I'm going to shatter apart in the most delicious way.

August buries his face in the crook of my neck, his own breath shaky, his mouth branding my skin. His hand closes over my breast and massages it in time with the rhythm of his thrusts. The water laps around us, licking our skin, the current below pulsing on against me.

I'm flung higher and higher, so much bliss rushing through me I can barely breathe at all, and then I come with another cry. The ecstasy of the moment sizzles through every inch of me even more brilliantly than before.

"Oh, Talia." August's chest hitches. He presses deeper, his muscles tensing, and the heat inside me expands as he reaches his own release.

August rocks into me gently for another few minutes, clutching me to him. His kisses on my neck and back are so tender they make my heart ache.

I push away from the wall so I can turn to face him. He holds me to him, capturing my lips with the same fierce passion as when we started. After, I let my head fall against his shoulder and press a kiss to his collarbone. "I love you. So much."

His arms tighten around you. "And I love you. No one is taking you away from us—not now, not ever. I swear it."

My throat constricts. I tuck my face against him as if I can hide from the flicker of doubt. I wish moments like this were all the future held. I wish I could believe nothing in this world existed that might force him to break that promise.

CHAPTER EIGHT

Talia

Harper bobs on her feet, clutching the edge of the immense carriage Sylas summoned for this trip and peering avidly over the side. "A banquet. My first real one—at an *arch-lord's* castle."

Next to her, Astrid offers a mild smile. "Speaking from experience, that only means more politics and less merry-making. But I'd imagine there'll be plenty of merry to make as well."

I run my hands over the soft planes of the spider-weave dress Harper gave me for the occasion, apparently unwilling to let me go out in the one she gifted me before even though most of the fae where we're going have never seen the first one. The overlapping strips of mauve, indigo, and crimson with the speckling of gold embroidery come together like the most vivid of sunsets. Possibly even more magical is the fact that somehow none of the colors clash with my dark pink hair.

"There'd better be partying when we've dressed up like this," I say, shooting a grin at Harper. I know how much this moment means to her. Born into the pack's disgrace in Oakmeet, she's been longing to see more of the world her whole life—and she's hoping her skill with fashion design will get her invites to domains all across the Summer realm.

Her own dress is a breathtaking riot of color, vibrant green with painstakingly crafted flowers of scarlet, violet, sunshine-yellow, and sky-blue swirling all across the skirt and the base of the bodice. When she moves, they create a faint rustling sound that perfectly mimics a light breeze ruffling through a forest glade.

She clasps my hand for a second, her large eyes gleaming—and not just with excitement. "What if I say the wrong thing—or dance badly—" She lets out a strangled sound. "I have no idea what I'm doing. I don't want to make a fool of myself."

I squeeze her fingers with as much reassurance as I can convey. "I don't think you have anything to worry about, but even if you make a little mistake, I bet everyone will be too busy admiring that gorgeous dress to notice. That's what I'm counting on for myself."

She flashes a smile at me. "I'm glad you're going to be there too. We'll take it on together."

At the stern of the carriage, Harper's mother watches us with a smile of her own that brings a twinkle to her eyes. Both her parents, the musicians of Sylas's pack, are coming along to add to tonight's entertainments. I'm not totally sure how Sylas decided who else would join in, other than that the two other pack-kin I'm most familiar with, Brigit and her mate Charce, are regulars at Whitt's revels, so presumably they enjoy a good party too.

Brigit doesn't look all that enthusiastic right now, though. She bounded onto the carriage with plenty of energy when we first set off, but now she's sitting on the bench opposite us with an unusually pensive set to her mouth.

As I notice that, she glances my way and catches me looking at her. She hesitates. When Harper moves a little farther away to ask one of the others a question, Brigit gets to her feet to cross the carriage.

My body tenses with the worry that I've offended her somehow. I'm still getting my footing with the rest of the pack. But there's no accusation in her expression. If anything, she looks hopeful.

She studies her hands for a second before meeting my gaze again. Her voice comes out hushed. "Elliot and I thought about what you said the other day when we were gathering the shy-caps. We've been keeping an eye on our guests when we can. Today when everyone was getting ready, I thought I overheard something that sounded… odd."

I'm instantly twice as alert. "What's that? If you think there's reason to worry, you should let Sylas know."

Her attention shifts to the fae lord and his cadre at the bow of the carriage, dressed in the most formal finery I've seen on them so far. Sylas is eyeing the landscape pensively, the breeze tickling through his dark hair. Whitt appears to be telling August a wry anecdote, which at this moment includes a quick gesture I'm pretty sure is obscene. August gives his older brother a light punch, but he's chuckling at the same time.

Brigit turns back to me. "I could be wrong. I don't want to create a problem where there isn't one. What if Lord Sylas is upset that I was nosing around the guest quarters on my own initiative?"

"I don't think he would be, but if he is, you can blame it on me," I say. Apparently too casually, because her eyes widen. "Why don't you tell me what you heard, and I'll see if it sounds like something we should bring to him?" I add quickly.

She tugs nervously at her hair and lowers her voice even more. "It was just one of the daughters talking to her mother. I couldn't hear very much because I wasn't that close—I didn't want them to notice me lurking around. But she laughed and said something about, 'When Donovan looks the thief.' Why would she think it was amusing for an arch-lord to appear to be a thief? How would she know he's going to if there isn't something strange going on?"

Exactly the questions I'm wondering now too. I pat Brigit's arm tentatively in what I hope is an encouraging way. "That definitely sounds suspicious. We should tell Sylas and the others about it before we get to Donovan's castle. I can handle most of it, since it was my idea that you keep an eye on the guests—but will you come with me so you can confirm and in case they have any questions?"

I must seem confident enough to ease her nerves. Brigit nods, even offering me a small smile that lifts my spirits despite her report. She trusted me enough to listen to me before and to reach out to me now. I'm making at least a little progress at becoming a real part of the pack.

We ease around the other passengers to reach the trio at the bow. Sylas turns, his gaze immediately intent when he marks my approach. Whitt and August fall silent, August looking concerned and Whitt curious.

I swipe my hand across my mouth, abruptly less sure of myself than I was speaking about this from a distance. Maybe Sylas won't be pleased about the suggestion I made to his pack. But it's done now, and hopefully it's uncovered information we'll be glad we have.

"What's on your mind, Talia?" he asks, mildly enough that my throat unlocks.

"I was talking with some of the pack the other day about the visitors, and I suggested that—that since they were probably in Hearthshire to spy on us and try to make a case for why it wasn't a good place for me to stay, it might be good to watch them more carefully than regular guests and see if they'd give anything away about their plans."

Whitt's eyebrows arch with amusement. "Taking over my job now, mite?"

I shoot a mock glower at him and go on. "Brigit overheard

them talking by the guest house this morning—they were saying something about how Donovan was going to look like a thief, and seemed happy about it. I thought you'd want to know."

Sylas nods, his mouth flattening into a grim line. He focuses on Brigit. "It's good that you came to us with this. I assume your presence wasn't noticed?"

"No, my lord," Brigit says with a respectful bob of her head. "I was always careful that they didn't notice I was nearby, and I had an excuse ready in case those precautions weren't enough."

"Then you've served our pack well. Would you tell me exactly what you saw and heard?"

Brigit recounts the same story she told me with a little more detail this time. The three men listen thoughtfully.

When she's finished, August glances at Sylas. "You know I thought the one daughter might have been stealing from *us*. Could that be related?"

Sylas grimaces. "I suspect so. I did discover that a couple of objects are missing from the library—items that were tucked away where I wouldn't have checked on them for some time if you hadn't raised suspicions. The sorts of things you might steal if you wanted to avoid an immediate investigation. It's possible that despite our precautions, they managed to pass those on to their pack-kin so that Ambrose can frame Donovan for the theft."

"Why would they want to do that?" I ask.

He shakes his head. "I don't know. I can't see how it would factor into Ambrose's campaign to remove you from our care, and he hasn't shown any specific animosity against Donovan. We'll simply have to stay on our guard and watch how the situation plays out." He studies Brigit again. "Thank you for your concern for our pack. Perhaps my cadre-chosen here should have you on his staff." He gives Whitt a gentle nudge.

The spymaster rubs his hands together. "We could start with that tonight." He tips his head to Brigit. "You've clearly got the instincts for stealth and subterfuge. If our possessions ended up in Donovan's home, we should be able to smell them out—but the three of us can't go searching without calling attention to ourselves. Do you think you can find an excuse to slip away and attempt to track them down?"

A quiver runs through Brigit's body, but she raises her chin at the same time, clearly bolstered by his praise. "I'll do my best. What should I do if I find them?"

"Remove them from the premises if you can," Sylas says. "Return them to this carriage. If you can't, inform me as quickly as possible. I'll handle the rest."

"Yes, my lord. I'll make sure they don't get away with this." Brigit bows lower and retreats.

I linger with the three men, worry winding through my gut. "So, Ambrose might have it out for Donovan too? He'll be there tonight, won't he?"

Sylas nods. "It wouldn't do for an arch-lord to hold a banquet without inviting his colleagues and their favored pack-kin."

Whitt rests a hand on my shoulder. "You'll be safe from Ambrose for now. He gave his word not to interfere until the time limit he gave is up."

That won't help if his scheme hurts Sylas as much as it might Donovan. We don't even know what Ambrose is aiming to achieve.

Part of me wishes I wasn't coming at all—that I was holed up in my bedroom back in Hearthshire's castle with a book and a blanket and no one else around. But I wouldn't have felt all that safe even there with Ambrose's pack-kin still "visiting" and all three of my lovers hours distant. We have to show everyone else how well I'm doing with Sylas, and attending the banquet with him is part of that.

When we come up on Donovan's domain, the sun has just dipped below the horizon, sending streaks of amber light across the darkening sky. I'd know we're near the Heart of the Mists even if I wasn't aware of where the arch-lords live. Its energy tingles over my bare arms and reverberates through my chest.

How would it turn out if I tried to use a true name now, with all that power washing over me?

I can't try, not with all these witnesses. Instead, I focus on the tall building coming into view up ahead.

It looks almost like a gigantic sandcastle, the towers and spires that rise here and there a bit haphazardly, smoothed rather than sharp around the edges as if worn by water. But the walls aren't the grainy beige I'd expect from sand but rather a rich reddish brown, gleaming with the light that spills from the windows as if glazed.

"What's it made out of?" I ask quietly as the carriage glides closer.

"Fired clay," August answers. "Donovan's family has a lot of skill with fire and anything they can put it to work on."

The palace is utterly different from the cool, rigid lines of Ambrose's obsidian home—and infinitely more welcoming, at least to my mortal eyes. When we disembark amid the carriages already parked in the fields outside, rollicking music filters out to meet us. Harper swishes her skirt around her legs eagerly, looking as though she'd like to skip right to the doorway if she didn't have enough propriety to wait for her lord to lead the way.

The hall inside gleams with the same polished, ruddy clay, the glow of the orbs spaced along it turning it more red than brown. Servants usher our party through to a room so immense I almost trip over my own feet, taking it in.

Row upon row of orbs line the high ceiling, spilling brilliant light over everyone below. Several long tables have been set up beneath them, decked out with gold-trimmed, ivory-pale table cloths, gold platters, and crystal goblets. A fantastic mixture of savory and sweet scents fills the air. My mouth is watering in an instant.

Between the tables, dozens of fae men and women in fancy

dress mill around, dipping into bows, offering cheerful greetings, and—more than anything—sizing each other up with a calculating air I don't need supernatural senses to pick up on. As we enter, quite a lot of them swivel to consider us. The intensity of their gazes prickles over my skin, and I fight the urge to shrink out of view behind my lovers.

I hadn't thought about how much of a spectacle we'd make just by being here. Sylas and his pack have been out of favor for decades, and this is their first appearance since the arch-lords pardoned them. Not to mention that most if not all of the other lords, ladies, and pack-kin must know what I represent to their people.

Despite the thumping of my heart, I square my shoulders and walk alongside August, doing my best impression of a woman who's attended dozens of fae banquets before. He grasps my hand, and Sylas catches my eye with a brief but meaningful nod. Knowing they're watching out for me sets my nerves a little more at ease.

Several musicians are already swaying with bows and reeds as they create the buoyant tune I heard from outside. Harper's parents hustle over to join them. Harper spins on her feet, taking in the tables and the glowing ceiling and the company, her grin stretching across her narrow face. "It's wonderful."

"Less wonderful if there's some underhanded business going on against the host," Brigit mutters under her breath. As we make our way down one of the aisles between the tables, she draws closer to me and speaks in the faintest of whispers. "I don't know what excuse to make to get away. Everyone's *watching*. They never looked at us like this before."

"We were never supposed traitors raised from disgrace before," Astrid says dryly. She doesn't appear to be disturbed by the attention, but then, I haven't seen anything disturb the hardy fae woman yet.

If there's a conspiracy underway to hurt Arch-Lord Donovan,

we need to figure it out quickly. Every passing second is another when Ambrose and whoever else is involved could spring a trap.

My gaze darts over the table beside us. Servants are pouring liquid from various bottles into the goblets, some fizzing, some frothy, some letting off an iridescent steam. The platters hold only appetizers. No one has taken seats for the main meal yet, so I guess we're allowed to grab whatever we want while everyone circulates.

"I could spill some wine on myself," I murmur. I doubt the fae will think anything odd of a human being clumsy. "I don't have any magic on my dress. You could take me to a lavatory to help me wash it?" That seems like the kind of scenario one of the leading ladies would come up with in the human comedy films Sylas watches when he needs some mindless entertainment.

My hands settle on the delicate fabric of the dress, and I balk at the idea even though I've already said it out loud. I glance at Harper, who's lingered nearby and turned to listen. "I don't want to wreck it, though."

Harper's mouth twitches, and then she pats my arm quickly. "It's okay! If you need to do that to help Sylas—I've made lots of them. Maybe it'll get even more people looking at it."

Brigit makes a furtive motion toward the frothy, nearly black drink in a goblet a little farther down. "No need to even worry about it. Use the crackleberry wine. I know the true name for crackleberries—I can coax it right back out."

Somehow I'm not surprised she prioritized magic around an item that probably features in a lot of revels. Grateful that I don't have to ruin my friend's work after all, I meander along the table and scoop up the goblet Brigit indicated.

The liquid doesn't stop frothing as I raise it to my lips. Its scent trickles to my nose, tart and unnervingly heady. I don't think I should let any of this make it down my throat.

Instead of drinking, I swing around abruptly as if I've just had an urgent thought. My elbow bumps Brigit's arm; I let the goblet tip toward me. The dark liquid splashes down my front with a faint hiss.

"Oh!" I shove the goblet onto the table and clap my hand to my mouth, my cheeks flaring without any subterfuge necessary. I don't *enjoy* looking like a clumsy idiot in front of this audience, even if it works in our favor.

Brigit falls into her role as if she's played it a hundred times already. Which maybe she has when it's been needed more genuinely. She grasps my arm and ushers me back toward the entrance to the banquet hall. "It's all right, come on now. I'll fix you up."

Plenty of the other guests are staring at us again. I try to focus on Brigit and swiping at my dress as if I think I can rub the stain out. Both Harper and Astrid move to follow us, but I wave them both away, focusing on Harper. "I'm sure we can handle this ourselves. You should go let everyone chat you up about *your* dress."

The younger woman blushes and steps back, but Astrid strides along behind us all the way out into the hallway outside. "I have orders not to let you out of my sight," she informs me in an amused undertone.

Because of course it'd look odd if Sylas or his cadre-chosen were running around attending to one human girl, regardless of the power my blood holds. I'm not going to argue with her about it. "Thank you."

"Lavatory… Lavatory…" Brigit scans the hallway, and a servant points to a bend up ahead. She makes a grateful gesture to him and hustles me along. "Let's see if I can fix your dress and get us 'accidentally' lost so we need to check all kinds of rooms at the same time."

As we turn the corner, she murmurs under her breath. After a couple of iterations, the dampness against my chest fades. The black stain leaches away. Brigit smiles with obvious satisfaction and picks up her pace.

Her nostrils flare with each room we pass. My stomach knots with the thought of how little time we might have to search to find any clue, how long it might take before someone comes looking for us or stumbles on us, but we've only passed four rooms before Brigit jerks to a halt at a doorway.

The space beyond appears to be a music room. A grand piano with ornately carved legs stands in the middle of a thick rug, with a silver-gilded harp positioned closer to the wall beyond it. Clay shelves holding sheaves of sheet music and assorted smaller instruments line one wall; a broad cabinet with copper-handled drawers stands against the other, framed between two chaise lounges that I assume are for listeners to enjoy a private performance.

Brigit takes another sniff and steps tentatively into the room. Astrid follows, inhaling sharply herself.

"Yes," the older woman says. "There's something of Hearthshire in here." She drags in another breath. "And if I'm not mistaken, of Dusk-by-the-Heart as well."

Ambrose's domain? I guess that would make sense—easy to obtain his own possessions to make it look as if Donovan stole them. I venture after the two fae women, not wanting to linger alone in the hall outside.

Brigit and Astrid both narrow in on the cabinet. Tugging on one of the drawers, Brigit finds it locked, but with a quick word it slides open. She holds up a small book with a crumbling leather-bound cover. "This belongs to our lord."

"And this too," Astrid says, retrieving a gem-encrusted length of wood that I'd assume was a magic wand if I'd ever seen any of the fae use such a thing. She reaches into the drawer again and takes out a glossy, thunder-cloud-gray orb. The hues inside it whirl as if it really does contain clouds that are being stirred up by a rising storm. "And this came from Arch-Lord Ambrose's home not long ago."

Brigit looks at the object and shivers, so it mustn't be just my human instincts finding it unnerving. She pulls out a few papers and an odd feathered figurine and then shuts the drawer. "That's all of it. Now to put it where it belongs."

"Can you bring Ambrose's things to his carriage?" I ask.

She nods. "I should be able to smell it out using these." She glances at Astrid with an expression of deferral to her more experienced pack-kin. "Unless you feel you should handle this."

"No, I'm sure you can carry out this duty for our lord. I have to keep an eye on our companion here." Astrid gives me a friendly nudge. "But here, let me give you a hand in disguising them. If anyone asks where you're going when you leave, say you want to check if we have any bottles to replace the wine Talia spilled."

She intones a few syllables, weaving her fingers through the air in front of the objects Brigit has clutched to her chest. A filmy impression of a shawl wraps around the other woman's shoulders, hiding all view of them. Brigit shoots Astrid a quick smile and hurries off.

Just as we step out after her, footsteps sound in the opposite direction, far too close. We don't want to get in trouble for sneaking around.

Astrid's head snaps up. She speaks a hasty word and flicks her fingers, and something rattles across the floor in the distance. Tugging me back toward the banquet hall, she gives me a wink. "That'll distract them a bit."

We slip into the banquet hall to find the festivities in full swing. Goblets clink in toasts, and laughter carries through the room. But it turns out we acted just in time. Before we can even make it back to where I spot Sylas in the midst of a cluster of other fae—true-blooded from the sharp points of their ears and the unusual hues in their hair —a young man bounds to the doorway we just came through.

"Donovan!" he calls out over the general murmur. "The

performances so far are lovely, but I hear you've got some spectacular instruments in your music room. Will you let your guests have a look?"

A fae man who doesn't appear to be that much older than the one who summoned him emerges from the crowd, his hair springing from within his gold circlet of a crown in brilliant red and orange locks as if his head is on fire. More gold is woven into every inch of his gleaming doublet, matching the thick buckle on his belt. His smile looks much kinder than Ambrose's, but I'm not inclined to trust anyone outside my pack all that much, least of all the arch-lords who banished them in the first place.

"If you're that eager, I don't see why not," Donovan says, and sweeps his arm through the air. "Anyone who's so inclined is welcome to look upon the Harp of Olervan."

Is the first man one of Ambrose's pack-kin? Whoever he is, he must be setting up their ploy. Ambrose himself comes into view, bumping up against Sylas and saying something I can't make out. Just seeing his burly frame and haughty expression makes me tense up. I'm guessing the equally haughty woman at Ambrose's elbow is his soul-twined mate. Sylas told me Donovan hasn't found his yet and the other arch-lord, Celia, had hers pass on.

Near the fae lord, Whitt glances toward the doorway and catches sight of Astrid and me. My expression must tell him everything he needs to know. In a moment, he and Sylas are moving with the trickle of guests heading to the music room.

August comes from another direction, sliding his arm around my waist as we wander back the way I just came. I resist the urge to look toward the outer entrance. Has Brigit managed to stow the stolen objects already?

The music room is large but still crowded once the twenty or so guests who've come along pour into it. The young man who initiated the trip exclaims over the harp, Ambrose runs idle fingers over the lid of the grand piano, and the others mill about somewhat aimlessly.

A woman I think I recognize from Ambrose's entourage the other day kneels down by the cabinet, setting her face into a startled expression I'm sure is put on. She can't actually smell anything now that the objects aren't there, but she clearly knew where to look for them. I give August's arm a little squeeze to get his attention.

"What's this?" the woman says, pitching her voice to carry. "I'd swear I—"

She pulls at the drawer, which slides open easily—we forgot to re-lock it. But that doesn't matter, because there's nothing in it now. As she peers inside, her voice dies. She grasps the drawer above and tugs that open too, but what she's looking for is long gone.

Donovan approaches the cabinet, his brow furrowed. "Is something the matter?"

I notice Ambrose is studiously examining the shelves on the other side of the room as if he hasn't even realized what his underling is up to. The woman fumbles for a second and then recovers, pushing the drawer closed and standing with a casual air. "No, not at all. I thought I spotted something—I must have been mistaken." She lets out a tinkling laugh.

August twines his fingers with mine. Sylas seeks out my gaze, and I incline my head just slightly. Telling them the full story will have to wait.

But we did it. We foiled whatever accusations Ambrose hoped to make against our host. Donovan ambles back to his banquet without a hint of concern, Ambrose stalks along behind him with only a trace of frustration in his bearing, and I can't completely suppress the smile that spreads across my face.

Just this once, Sylas's pack didn't need him to protect them. We uncovered this scheme and defended everything that was at stake for him.

In the banquet hall, I spot Brigit back with Charce. I give her a thumbs up, which seems like an awkwardly human gesture as soon as I've done it, but her grin in return stops that from mattering.

"Would you show me what I can drink here without any magical effects?" I ask August, and within moments I'm sipping a beverage with a cherry-sweet flavor that's cool in both its pale blue color and its temperature.

Astrid sticks close by my side when August gets drawn away again. I linger by the corner of the room, watching the activity around me and reveling in my sense of victory. Brigit and Charce are exclaiming over morsels of some food they've taken from a platter. Harper is chattering excitedly with a couple of fae women from another pack who appear to be admiring her dress, just as she hoped. Sylas looks confident and relaxed where he's deep in conversation with a couple of other lords. Whitt—

Whitt is tapping the shoulder of a pretty fae woman who giggles in response, gazing through her eyelashes at him with unmistakeable coyness.

A jolt of possessiveness and alarm races through my chest. My hand clenches around the stem of my goblet.

If I'm right that she's flirting, he isn't encouraging her. His smile stays reserved, his expression showing no more than polite indifference. She slinks closer, and he taps her again in what I realize is a gesture meant to nudge her backward. This time, she gets the message. She twitters again, but her face falls a little. She wanders off to chat up some other gentlemen.

I'd feel relieved, but the next place my gaze lands is on August, who's currently standing between *two* fae ladies, one of whom is going as far as to prod his impressive bicep. I can read the discomfort in his stance, but either they don't know him well enough to recognize it or they're hoping he'll get over it.

A woman in an extravagant dress has sashayed over to Sylas now too. She tosses her hair to show him how conjured butterflies flutter from the coiled locks.

My sense of triumph drains away. I hadn't really thought through *every* part of what the pack's return to prominence would mean.

Sylas and his cadre are eligible bachelors now—men who not just had a distinguished history before their temporary fall from grace but who're also the heroes who provided the means to save all Seelie kind. Sylas has already had and lost his soul-twined mate, so no one needs to worry they'll be usurped that way. For any pack member who isn't already attached to a lord or cadre-chosen, the three of them offer an obvious step up in status.

My three men might not be interested in those overtures at this exact moment, but how long will it take before they come across some fae woman who *does* appeal to them—in ways I'll never be able to?

Astrid touches my arm. "Are you all right there? You look as if that drink hasn't settled well."

I pull myself together, shaking off the chill of my sudden realization as well as I can. "No, I'm okay. Just got lost in thought."

Looking at her, the answer to my fears is obvious. I've already started making a place for myself in the larger pack.

I just have to keep proving myself and showing what I can contribute, and when the day comes that I can't count on my lovers doting on me quite so devotedly, Hearthshire will still feel like home.

CHAPTER NINE

Sylas

I suspected Donovan was more the sort to keep early hours than late ones, and it appears I've gambled right. Strolling from the guest wing of his castle in the thin light just before dawn breaks, I spot him down a hallway, his steps brisk but with upbeat energy. I hope the conversation I intend to have doesn't deflate his spirits too much.

On the other hand, perhaps it should. The youngest of the arch-lords won't survive much longer if he doesn't recognize a serious threat when he encounters one.

"My lord," I call out, just loud enough for him to hear me, not wanting to disturb anyone else who's stayed overnight in his castle if I can help it.

As I stride toward Donovan, he turns my way. "Up so early, Lord Sylas? I hope my accommodations weren't displeasing."

His tone is light, but his pale brown eyes have taken on a wary cast. Good. He knows I'm not likely to be approaching him like this if I didn't have an important subject to discuss.

"Not at all," I say with a respectful dip of my head. "I appreciate your saving my pack-kin the trip home in the middle of the night. But since I've happened upon you, could we speak in private? It's a rather urgent matter—of politics."

"Putting us to work already. I suppose I'll allow that you have some catching up to do on that score. Well, I haven't anything else to attend to at this hour." Donovan rolls his lean shoulders and motions for me to follow him. "My study should serve just fine."

He leads me up the stairs into the opposite wing of the castle and down a hall hung with portraits of past arch-lords from his line, all with the same fiery hair. The sound of our footsteps carries through the silence; no one else emerges.

He opens a door at the far end and ushers me into a room with a broad window placed perfectly so that the growing dawn light floods straight in. Its delicate warmth catches on a massive desk rather less orderly than my own with its scattering of papers and books. The built-in shelves show a similar state of disarray.

Donovan gives no sign of being embarrassed by the untidiness, so I suppose he sees it as normal. He drops into the high-backed chair behind the desk and waves me toward the few armchairs placed around the expansive space. I heft the nearest one around to fully face the desk and sink into it.

The young arch-lord may not be the neatest fae I've ever met, but he doesn't lack keenness. He wouldn't have survived as long as he has without that. He leans his elbows onto his desk and peers at me consideringly. "What exactly did you wish to speak about?"

I've pondered the ideal way to present the subject to him for much of the night. "No doubt you noticed some oddness about the impromptu tour of your music room at the start of yesterday's festivities."

Donovan's gaze immediately sharpens. "Indeed I did. I can't say I knew what to make of it, though. Do you have insight to offer?"

"I do, as much as I hate to be the bearer of bad news. You may or may not be aware that a family of Arch-Lord Ambrose's pack-kin came to call on us in Hearthshire some days past, not long after he made a bid to transfer my human charge to his cousin Tristan's care?"

"I heard about your rather dramatic conversation with Ambrose over the girl and the deal the two of you made. Presumably he's hoping his people will turn up evidence they can use against you to build his case."

I nod. "That's been our assumption. But it's become clear that I'm not his only target. We determined that the guests stole a couple of infrequently used but distinctive and valuable objects from my home. A conversation one of my pack-kin overheard led us to suspect Ambrose's intent was to frame *you* with the theft. And indeed, we were able to discover those objects, along with a few things that appeared to belong to Ambrose, in your music room shortly before the supposed harp enthusiast led part of the gathering there."

The arch-lord has stiffened in his seat, a little of the color fading from his normally pinkish face. "In the drawer Ambrose's cadre-chosen opened up. I wondered why she seemed confused by what she found there…"

"It was what she didn't find," I filled in. "The diversion was a set-up to reveal you as some sort of thief against both your colleague and the lords you're meant to be overseeing."

"And what became of the objects she expected to find?"

I motion toward the doorway. "My pack saw them conveyed safely to our carriage and Ambrose's. What he'll make of their return, I'm not sure, but I doubt he'll be happy about it."

Donovan pinches the bridge of his nose as if he has a headache. "Well, that is a serious accusation."

I study him, my body tensing. "I hope you believe I wouldn't have fabricated this."

"No, no, of course I wouldn't think that of you." He leans back in his chair, but his mouth stays pressed in a tight line. I ready myself to rise—chances are he'll ask me to leave and call in his cadre to consult with them—but he merely sits in silence for a span, his gaze sliding to the window.

After a few minutes, I feel I have to speak up in case he misjudges my intentions. "I understand you'd rather keep your confidences to those closest to you. I merely wanted to inform you of what I knew of the situation so you could act on it—and to let you know I'm at your disposal should you have any use of me. It does appear Ambrose's intentions toward us are somewhat intertwined."

"It does." Donovan's attention shifts back to me. He contemplates me for another long moment. "You've handled yourself honorably despite the hardships thrown at you these past several decades. Most of your pack has remained with you; you've contributed more than many along the border despite your reduced circumstances."

I'm not entirely certain where he's going with this line of thought. "I conduct myself as I believe a lord should," I say. As my father never was, not enough for me to admire *him*. "And I serve both my people and the summer realm as well as I can."

"Commendable sentiments." The arch-lord pauses again and then says, "Would you give me your word not to repeat the specifics of anything we discuss in this room beyond its walls?"

My magically-charged oath, he means. I rise a little straighter, picking up on the portent in the request. He's prepared to take *me* into his confidence—but he's shrewd enough to be cautious about it.

Just to be asked is an honor. Still, I have to consider my pack's needs as well as my ruler's.

"I'll happily give my word insofar as no information emerges that I'll need my cadre or my pack to act on for our own protection

—and should such information emerge, I won't share where I obtained it."

"That seems reasonable." Donovan exhales slowly and gestures for me to go ahead.

With the thrum of the Heart's pulse so close by, I barely need to concentrate to summon magic into my oath. "I swear I will not repeat what is said in this room elsewhere, nor share information given to me, other than as necessary to protect my pack, in which case I will not reveal its source without permission granted."

Even after I've spoken, the arch-lord hesitates. Then he tips forward, returning his elbows to their original position on his desk. "I appreciate having the opportunity to speak to you with more candor. I've always held you in high esteem, and I know my mother did as well. Skies above, all of the arch-lords did before that mess with your mate."

With the formalities between us relaxed, some of the tension leaves my body. I give him a small but wry smile. "I'm glad to hear it."

"Because of that..." Donovan looks down at his desk and then back at me. "I'd value your advice. To be honest, I'm not completely sure of my cadre, especially in a matter that involves another arch-lord, and I wouldn't feel right asking some of them to keep things from the others. It's my own fault—I swore them in quickly when the arch-lordship fell on me so abruptly, and I should have taken more time to get a true measure of their dedication and loyalty."

His assessment sounds accurate to me, but there's no need to rub in what he's already realized. "I think such an oversight is understandable given the unexpected position you found yourself in." We all would have expected his mother to live centuries longer before passing on the crown to him. He was only a few decades out of his adolescence at her untimely death. "It's a credit to you that you've handled yourself as well as you have so far."

"Yes. Well." He sighs. "It's clear I can't have any word of my plans getting back to Ambrose. He's never appeared to *like* me particularly, but I hadn't thought he had so little respect he'd try to outright undermine me. Do you have any sense of what his goal might be?"

"Unfortunately, no." I run my hand across my jaw. "It could simply be that he sees you as the largest obstacle to taking control over Talia, and he wanted to have something over you for leverage to force your decision. And to sow discord between us over your apparent theft from me. But I have trouble seeing him taking the risk of attacking you over just that."

"So do I. Which makes his actions all the more concerning."

"Since the evidence couldn't be easily tied back to him anyway, there's no way to confront him," I say. "My advice at this juncture would be to stay even more on your guard, keep a close watch on anyone who enters your domain especially if they have ties to Ambrose, and take steps to evaluate your cadre now. You can see that you make one offhand remark or another in front of only one or two of them, something that might interest Ambrose but not pressing enough that it's likely a disinterested party would mention it to anyone else. If any of those remarks appear to be passed on, you'll know who's responsible."

"I can do that." Donovan shakes his head. "I just don't like testing them when I've offered my trust in them."

"You won't lie. And if that trust is well-placed, then nothing will come of it. It's less a test than simply being aware of how you speak and who you speak to."

"That's one way of looking at it. Whatever Ambrose has in mind, I suppose he's likely to make another attempt before too long. You only have a couple of weeks before the case is meant to be brought before us for judgment."

"I expect he'll either ramp up his efforts now that this attempt has failed or back off deciding it wasn't worth it." More likely the former than the latter, knowing Ambrose. I pause and allow myself to make a more openly critical remark. "It's a shame he's pursuing the matter this way when we still have the ravens to contend with."

Donovan grimaces. "Yes. At least we can be glad the Unseelie aren't making too much trouble at the moment."

"They haven't launched any further attacks on any scale?"

"Not one. I suspect they're still licking their wounds after their routing during that last full moon." The young arch-lord allows himself a tight smile. "So for the moment, Ambrose can be our main concern. Do you have any thoughts on how *you* might evaluate his intentions?"

I've already considered that question at length. "I can allow my guests from his pack to remain with us as long as they care to and attempt to discern more about his plans from their behavior. Obviously I'll be wary in any direct dealings I have with Ambrose. And if you should uncover any further plot or need my assistance in any other way, call on me however you need to. I hope I can count on your continued support when it comes to Talia in return?"

"Naturally. Heart only knows how Tristan would handle the poor creature." Donovan frowns. "There is a way we could put that conflict behind us right now, if you see fit."

Does he think he can get Celia to make a statement with him pre-emptively denying Ambrose's request? I wouldn't have expected him to extend what would likely be perceived as blatant favoritism my way. "What do you have in mind?" I ask cautiously.

"Ambrose claims he wants the woman in Tristan's care so that she's tended to by a party closer to the arch-lord's authority. You could choose to place her in *my* care, and he could hardly argue I'm not a high enough authority."

He says those words without any hint of investment, no sign that it's more than a friendly offer of aid, and yet they wrench at me. My fingers curl over the arm of my chair, claws pinching to spring free from the tips. My jaw clenches to hold back my fangs.

In that first instant, denial blares through my mind, drowning out nearly every thought, every consideration, beyond the urge to lunge at him for so much as suggesting Talia be removed from my protection.

No. She is mine. She is *hers*. I promised her as much. How could I risk it—how could I trust—

How could I walk through the castle I worked so hard to regain, the home she won for us, without feeling her absence like a sword digging into my chest?

I manage to hold myself in place and contain my fangs and claws, but my reaction was too forceful to hide completely. Donovan blinks and makes a hasty gesture. "I'd treat her well, of course. And make sure none of Ambrose's kin or Aerik's come near her. All of my pack-kin are grateful for the cure she offers."

I will my vicious defiance to simmer down. He meant nothing by it. He meant *well*. If he still speaks of her as not much more than that cure, as more of a creature to be tended to than a being with her own hopes and dreams, I can't say that's any better than I could really have expected from any of my brethren.

He doesn't know her. He hasn't spent any time around her. He hasn't seen…

He hasn't seen what a treasure she really is, in every way.

I swallow hard, unnerved by how deeply the conversation's turn has upended my emotions. My temper feels nearly as raw as when I watched Talia bleed from a knife at her own throat.

I have to think about what's best for her. What I want, which perhaps is more than I acknowledged before now, must come second to that.

"I appreciate your offer," I force myself to say. "I think for the time being she is safest on familiar territory among those she already knows and trusts. But I'll mention the possibility to her in case she would prefer the potential security of moving here. Even if not, if the situation becomes more dire, we'll revisit the idea. For now, what matters most is that both you and Celia will continue to speak for her staying in Hearthshire."

"I will certainly do that, and I've seen no reason to believe Celia will change her mind on the subject." Donovan stands. "It seems we've covered all the ground we can with what we know. Please keep me apprised—by subtle means, as much as you can—of any new discoveries you make, and I'll do the same for you. Thank you for hearing me out and for coming to me with your suspicions, Lord Sylas."

Just like that, he's become my lord rather than an equal colleague again. Well, that's how it should be.

As I stand, a pale ghost of an image flickers before my deadened eye. For an instant, I see a second version of Donovan's face partly overlaid with the first—but without its current calm. The filmy echo is twisted with apparent distress, beads of sweat gleaming on his paled skin. I take that in, and then the image had faded from my sight.

It could be some moment from his past: when he learned of his mother's death? When some other tragedy befell him? My breath halts around the hope that it's nothing more. Because it could just as easily be a glimpse of the future—a future in which Ambrose has succeeded in some vile plan.

Nothing in what I saw gives me enough specifics to warn the man in front of me. I file that image away in my mind and bow to him. "Thank you for accepting my warning and my advice."

Then I head back to the guest quarters where my pack-kin are still sleeping, wishing I knew what to do with the deeper ache still clenching my chest.

CHAPTER TEN

Talia

"Just one more left," Elliot says, squinting through the brush. "Pesky wool-for-brains." He gives the insult an affectionate lilt, obviously fond of his animal charges even if he's frustrated that a bunch of the sheep managed to break free from their pasture.

I peer through the dappled shadows of the forest, watching for a pale tuft of fur snagged on a twig, listening for a sheepish bleat. I was chatting with Harper in the pack village when Elliot came hurrying over saying a bunch of the sheep were on the loose, and even though I know nothing about farm animals, helping the search seemed like an obvious way I could be of use to the pack. So far, I have managed to spot one of them, though I left it to Elliot to wrangle it back to the pasture.

Harper tagged along too. She cranes her neck where she's treading along next to me and swipes her hands over her dress. It's not as ornate as many of her creations, but still fancier than what most of my pack-kin wear for their daily activities, with glinting vines embroidered from shoulder to hem. She's probably worried about snagging *it* on a twig.

"Hopefully the last one won't take too long," I say. Not only for her sake. Even with the lovely boots she made for me, my warped foot is starting to throb from all the walking.

Harper shoots me a smile. "I don't think they really want to be lost in these woods. Maybe the taste of freedom will convince them to stay inside their fence from now on."

Behind us, Astrid—who I suspect joined in mainly to keep watch over me—lets out a snort. "I don't believe sheep think about much beyond what they see in front of them in that moment. If they figure they see some tasty nibbles on the other side of the fence…"

"At least they haven't gone too far." I glance at Harper. "Do you ever use wool in your dresses? I guess it's not all that practical when it's always warm here in the summer realm."

She hums to herself. "I've made a few things—shawls and cloaks for the chiller nights. It's not quite as much fun as the dresses. But maybe I should expand more. I could probably craft a good doublet with the right weave."

Her gaze slips away from me to a few of the other fae who've joined in the sheep hunt: the three daughters from our visiting family. They're picking their way through the forest gingerly, focusing more on giggling with each other than actually looking around, but I guess I can't complain about them trying to contribute. Even if I can't help suspecting it's only to bolster their claim that they came here to support Hearthshire rather than to spy on it.

It also seems a little odd that the sheep somehow broke out today even though Elliot swears he recently checked the fence for weak spots, when the daughters just happened to be taking a stroll through the village. I can't see how letting Sylas's livestock go free would further their cause, though.

Noticing Harper's glance, one of the daughters beckons her. My friend looks momentarily startled, but then she hustles over to see what they want. I'm pretty sure our guests are the reason she's been dressing up more since that banquet. She got enough compliments on her seamstress skills there that she figures she should try to impress the arch-lord pack members we have right here at home too.

They should be impressed, but I wouldn't count on it. They'd just better not gossip about Harper behind her back either. Middle-school-style cattiness is one thing I'd be glad to have left behind in the human world.

"Oh," one of the final members of our search crew says, bending low. "I think this is a hoof print. Of course, it might be from one of the others that we already caught." The woman—Shonille, I've gathered her name is—straightens up and rests a hand briefly on her belly, which is starting to show the visible swell of pregnancy.

Her mate touches her arm and points deeper into the forest. "We might as well look the way it was going."

Watching them, I remember how Sylas beamed as he congratulated her on the impending baby. I've rarely seen him show joy so openly. Having kids is a big deal to the fae… which doesn't totally fit with the stories told about them back in the world I came from.

Scanning the trees as I figure out how to ask this question, I slow my uneven steps so that Astrid draws up next to me. "Astrid, in the human world, there are lots of stories about faerie changelings—the fae stealing human kids and leaving fae babies behind. Does that ever actually happen? It doesn't seem like any fae would *want* to give up their own kids." And definitely not to swap it for what most of them would see as an inferior being.

Astrid gives a short guffaw. "No, they certainly wouldn't. But your people didn't come up with that idea out of nowhere. Proper fae know the value of family. The Murk don't have the same morals or qualms. And they have a lot more children because most of them are so mixed with humans already. I understand quite a few of their offspring come out… badly, so they might see such a trade as worthwhile."

I shiver. With every scrap I hear about the Murk, the rat-shifting fae who have no realm of their own and only lurk furtively around both the fae and human worlds, the less I want to ever meet one. Thankfully, it sounds like they're generally not bold enough to challenge any of the "proper" fae directly. If they didn't see Sylas's pack as an ideal target out on the fringes, I don't see why they'd bother us here.

Astrid studies me and adds, "If you're wondering about yourself with the nature of your blood, I can assure you that you couldn't be a changeling regardless. It doesn't take much fae heritage to leave a mark in your scent or your features, and everything about you appears human to me."

Sylas said as much before, but hearing her confirm it makes me oddly relieved. It'd be easier if we had a simple explanation like a fae ancestor to explain my powers, both my blood and my minor magical capability that Astrid doesn't even know about. But on the other hand, I'd rather not have any ties to the Murk the other fae seem to disdain even more than they do humans.

"I guess that's a good thing," I say with a little laugh, and tramp on through the underbrush, sweeping aside the creeping tendrils of a tall, softly-furred fern.

When I end up looking toward our guests again, Harper is saying something to them with a quick gesture. The other women chuckle. Then one of them glances my way, her eyes so piercing I jerk my gaze away.

The humidity of the dense forest settles more heavily on my skin. I was enjoying this hunt and acting as one of the pack when we started out, but my enthusiasm is dwindling fast.

"There it is!" Shonille cries in a victorious tone. There's a rapid rustling as her mate and Elliot converge on the final sheep. It baas defiantly when Elliot fastens a thin cord to its neck, but it trots after him at his tug toward the pasture.

"Thank you for your help!" he calls over his shoulder to us, and I recover most of my good mood.

Harper had been talking about another excursion we could go on before Elliot roped us into this quest. I wait until she meanders apart from the visiting daughters and then draw up beside her as we make our way back to the village. "Did you still want to show me the spot you found for collecting spider-silk?"

Harper opens her mouth and then closes it again without a sound. For a second, I almost think she's *upset* that I asked, which doesn't make any sense when she's the one who suggested the venture in the first place just a couple of hours ago. But then she smiles at me and makes a casual wave of her hand. "Nah, I think that's enough hiking for me today. We can do that another time. Your foot must be getting tired anyway, isn't it?"

True. I'd tuned the discomfort out, but it's getting harder to ignore the pain building in the arch and spreading up my ankle. I hope I'm not limping too badly now. What would Ambrose's pack-kin report to him about that?

Before I can contemplate that unnerving question for very long, a distant crash in the woods behind us draws me up short. As I turn, the racket of a body hurtling through the brush gets louder. Harper yelps, and Shonille lets out a shout of warning. I scramble backward with no idea of what's coming.

A beast leaps from the nearby foliage, glossy tusks jutting from its boar-like head, tail lashing against its leonine haunches. It charges straight toward me.

I throw myself to the side into a clump of ferns, but the creature veers after me. It shoves me over, one of its tusks gouging through my arm with a searing pain so deep a cry breaks from my throat.

I tumble into a tree trunk, scrambling to find my footing, my hand smacking against the wound it's far too small to cover. Blood wells up beneath my fingers.

The boar-lion beast whirls around. Its beady eyes fix on me again.

With a yell, two of our guests come running, one with a dagger raised in her hand. But before she's crossed the short distance between us, Astrid leaps into view clutching a sharp-ended branch. She plunges it like a spear into the creature's chest.

The beast slumps to the ground with a groan. Astrid hustles to my side, a breath hissing through her teeth at the sight of my wound. The searing sensation is prickling up through my arm and into my shoulder now. I squeeze my eyes shut, willing back tears.

Another crackle of broken twigs and battered leaves makes my heart lurch, but when I open my eyes, I see two much more welcome shapes racing into view: Sylas's and August's wolves. They barrel into our midst, August transforming in mid-spring to land as a man beside me. His golden eyes are wide, his teeth baring in a protective growl at the sight of me.

"I've got you," he reassures me in a softer but still taut voice, kneeling next to me.

As August murmurs the true words for muscle and skin to bind my arm back together as well as he can, the pain numbs in the wake of the magic. Sylas turns on his heel, taking in me, the beast, Astrid, and the rest of our party. When his gaze returns to my face, his mouth has twisted at an uncomfortable angle. He doesn't need to speak for me to recognize the guilt he feels—as if I'd ever expect him to follow me around making sure I'm safe every moment of every day.

This is a dangerous world, and I've accepted that. But his

expression reminds me of a few days ago when we returned from the banquet at Donovan's castle, the roughness in his voice when he told me of Donovan's offer, the fierceness of his kiss when I told him I had no interest in joining any pack that wasn't his. He tore himself away from me afterward as if concerned that even the intensity of that show of affection might have wounded me somehow.

"She'll be all right," August tells him, squeezing my shoulder. "I've stopped the bleeding." He turns back to me. "You aren't hurt anywhere else?"

I shake my head.

Sylas glowers at the beast. "Tuskcats shouldn't be roaming this close to a village. I've never seen one in this part of the forest before."

The eldest daughter of our guests steps forward with her arms crossed forebodingly over her chest, looking so indignant you'd think the beast had savaged her rather than me. "It seems some things have changed since you were last living here. I'd have thought you'd take more precautions to keep the human girl safe."

A sickly chill curdles in my gut. I'm abruptly sure that the tuskcat didn't come here by accident.

This attack is a perfect way to prove Sylas isn't taking good enough care of me, isn't it? They probably hoped they'd even get to kill the thing before any of his pack-kin could.

My suspicion is only strengthened by Astrid's gruff apology. "I'm sorry I didn't cut it off before it got to her, my lord. A vine caught around my ankle at exactly the wrong moment."

What an awful coincidence that hardly seems like a coincidence. The look Sylas gives his guests suggests he's thinking the same thing, but I guess he can't exactly accuse them outright without any evidence, not unless he wants them to spin his hostility as another strike against him.

"Back to the village," he says more tersely than usual. "My chief warrior and I will escort you the whole way in case any other monsters descend on us."

The eldest daughter gives a disdainful sniff that leaves me wanting to hurl Astrid's makeshift spear at her. I grit my teeth and let August help me onto my feet.

They've taken one shot at me. How can I stop them from getting in another?

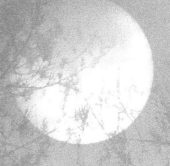

CHAPTER ELEVEN

Whitt

The grimace on Astrid's wizened face reveals just how frustrated she is. She doesn't suffer fools kindly, and she suffers our enemies with even less benevolence.

"It was those young women from Dusk-by-the-Heart," she says, directing most of her attention at Sylas. "I'm sure of it. They must have compelled the tuskcat to come this way and to target Talia using their magic—and I've no doubt they coaxed that vine into snagging my ankle just as the beast charged at us too. If I hadn't managed to free myself as quickly as I had, the elder daughter, Lili, would have played the hero."

Sylas sighs and leans back in his chair behind his desk. Like every other room in our Oakmeet keep, his study there had been trimmed down to fit the building's more modest size and the lesser magic we'd have to expend on maintaining it. I'd nearly forgotten just how homey his workspace here in Hearthshire was, with the office-like area at one end and the cluster of armchairs around a small personal hearth at the other.

A subdued fire is crackling in that hearth, adding a whiff of pine smoke to the air, but those chairs are for longer, more rambling discussions—ones not quite as urgent and fraught as this one. Today, August and I are poised at either side of the desk while Astrid gives her account from in front of it.

"I'm assuming they didn't leave any evidence we could use to prove that," I say. Ambrose's pack-kin may be treacherous bastards, but so far they've been discreet about their treachery, which is both irritating and to be expected from an arch-lord's spies.

She shakes her head. If there *had* been evidence, Astrid would have spotted it. Age hasn't dulled her senses any more than it's slowed her reflexes. "I'm sorry, my lord."

Sylas dismisses her apology with a flick of his hand. "It isn't your fault. Your quick action saved the situation from becoming even more disastrous. Thank you for that."

"Should we send the guests off?" August asks. "Now that they're actively attempting to hurt Talia, we can't give them another opportunity. Ambrose won't want her *dead*, but that doesn't mean he wouldn't be perfectly fine seeing her injured more than she already is."

That thought makes my fangs twinge in my gums. "I could certainly arrange an entirely polite excuse to boot them out of our domain."

But Sylas is frowning. "We haven't determined anything more of their larger plans. Observing them while they're here is our best chance of that. We'll just have to be even more on guard. I don't want Talia going anywhere at all outside her room without one of the four of us having her in view—and in easy reach in case something goes wrong. I've added a locking spell to her door that will respond to her touch and warn me if any outside party attempts to tamper with it."

I can imagine our mighty mite will be *so* pleased about us

ramping up our babysitting efforts. But I'd rather her irritated with us than wounded by these miscreants.

"I'll consult with Arch-Lord Donovan shortly and confer with him," our lord adds. "If he's uncovered more on his end, perhaps catering to the visitors won't be necessary any longer."

I'd be glad of that, but at the same time, an uneasy prickle runs down my back. It's for Donovan's sake at least as much as our own that Sylas is unwilling to run off the guests who've clearly overstayed their welcome. An alliance with an arch-lord is no small thing, true, but what in the Heart's name have any of those high-ranking pricks done to earn a smidgeon of our loyalty?

We've had enough trouble on our plate for the better part of the past century—and particularly the last few months—without drawing attention on that level of Seelie society. Frankly, I'd rather our lord put all his trust in his own pack and cadre.

The twinge of rancor settles uncomfortably in my gut after all the ways my half-brother has shown he *does* trust me in the past few weeks.

I focus my attention on matters I can actually control. "I'll add to our sentries on duty and have them lay down traps should any other unpleasant beasties become inclined to wander too close to the castle."

August draws himself up straighter. "I've already done a sweep personally to make sure nothing dangerous was skulking around nearby."

Of course he did. Only the need to ensure Talia's protection could have torn him from her side after he carried her back to the castle.

A different sort of twinge forms in my chest—the urge to show I can tend just as thoroughly as he can to the needs of the woman who's my lover as well. "You were able to fully heal her injury?"

My youngest brother nods. "The tuskcat gouged deep—I'm not skilled enough to completely mend all the damage—but the wound is sealed well enough that it shouldn't cause her more than mild pain over the next few weeks as her body finishes the job."

"In that case…" I turn back to Sylas. "I'll give my orders to our pack-kin, and then I'll see if Talia might appreciate a respite from all the politicking and threats that've come with our arrival here. She's expressed an interest in seeing the more exotic scenery our domain has to offer. I can make a day trip of it, give her a chance to relax where she doesn't have to worry about what Ambrose's people might be plotting next."

Sylas stiffens just slightly, a reaction he obviously attempted to hide. He doesn't like the idea of her being too far away for him to reach with a quick dash, does he? But he's committed to giving her as much freedom as he can. He inclines his head.

August bristles a bit more overtly. "If you face any kind of attack when it's just the two of you—"

Somehow I don't think he'd worry about his own abilities to protect her. I consider him, arching an eyebrow. "I know which parts of our domain should be safe from roaming monsters—and without any malicious parties around to call them down on us, there'll be no reason for them to venture where we'll go. But if it makes you feel better, I can lay out a general repelling spell once we're there to further ensure her safety."

To his credit, the whelp simmers down quickly enough. He's getting a better handle on those hotheaded emotions of his. "All right. I do think it'd be good for her to have a break from all the stress she's been under, but I promised the pack another combat training session this afternoon. The more of us are ready to defend our own, the better."

"Then I'm just the man for the job." I shoot a slanted smile at him and Sylas.

My lord's expression has turned pensive. For a second I think he's going to withdraw his approval, but then he glances toward the window as if contemplating something far beyond this room.

"The best thing for her would be to remove her from Ambrose's interest altogether," he says. "I need to take more steps in that direction. Now that we're in a more favored position, it's possible Nuldar will agree to a consultation."

August perks up. "The sage?"

"Yes. He may be able to glean something about her nature that will show us the way to creating a cure that doesn't require her blood. If we can separate the solution to our curse from Talia, then Ambrose will no longer have any reason to fixate on her."

I restrain a snort. "If he says anything much of use. But we don't lose anything by trying." Like all sages, Nuldar isn't in the habit of giving much clarity in his proclamations. Occasionally one can tease a bit of concrete information out of his ramblings, though. If we could free Talia from her obligations to the Seelie completely, that would be worth a trek all the way across every world there is.

For now, all I can offer her is a briefer escape. I sketch a sliver of a bow in parting and head out to pass on my instructions to my underlings as quickly as I can.

When I return to the castle and make my way up to Talia's bedroom, my hand rises to the flask in my pocket out of habit. I catch myself just before I pull it out.

I can handle my drink, and Talia has never shown any sign of taking issue with my habits. But... for this, I don't think I want any buzz taking the edges off my senses, smoothing out my thoughts. I want to experience this jaunt with her exactly as it is.

Assuming she agrees to the jaunt at all.

She calls out in answer to my knock immediately and meets my entrance with a narrow look that tells me someone has already delivered the news about our stricter new precautions. "Are you here to escort me to the dangerous regions of the dining room or the front yard?"

I can't help grinning at her understated defiance. "You take to sarcasm so well, mite. You should bring it out more often. But no, I thought we might take a trip farther afield. You still haven't gotten to see much of our world, and precious little of what you have seen has been a pleasant experience. How would you like to take in my favorite spot in all of Hearthshire? I promise it'll be utterly free of malicious lords and their nosy pack-kin."

A smile bright enough to make my heart skip a beat springs to her face, and she leaps just as quickly from her chair, dropping the book she was reading on the side table. "Of course! Right now?"

"No time like the present. Sylas and August have already given their blessing." However reluctantly.

Talia limps after me into the hall, one of the simple fae-styled dresses she's taken to wearing swishing across her calves with her uneven gait. As many times as I've seen the effects of Aerik's torments on her, knowing he's stolen her steadiness from her permanently still makes me grit my teeth.

I manage to shake that animosity away and turn my thoughts to exactly how we're going to reach my favorite spot. I've never made a joint excursion out of it before, and her being human does come with a few complications.

A spark of inspiration hits me, first with a jab of trepidation, then with a growing enthusiasm. At the edge of the clearing, I turn to Talia. "The route there is through some fairly dense forest, not ideal for a carriage or horses but an awfully long walk. If you think it wouldn't stir up any unpleasant memories, I could travel as I normally would, in my wolf form—I could carry you easily enough."

Talia blinks at me. "You want me to ride you?" An instant later, a blush floods her cheeks as the more provocative meaning of those words must occur to her.

A flare of similar heat shoots to my groin, but I manage a smile that's not especially lecherous. "Essentially, yes. If you hold onto the ruff at the sides of my neck, that should be enough to keep your balance. I can avoid making too bumpy a ride of it." I carried my brothers that way in play now and again when they were mere cubs. Talia has put more flesh on her bones since coming to us, but she's still not much more than a slip of a thing. I suspect I'll barely feel her weight at all.

She smiles back. "I'll be fine if you will. I know *you* won't hurt me."

She says it with such confidence that I want to kiss her. Too many pack-kin are still around—that can wait for where we're going.

I shake myself and let my wolf rise to the surface, stretching my spine and limbs, rippling fur over my four-legged frame in place of my clothes. I sink as low to the ground as I can get, my belly flat on the grass, and Talia tentatively touches my back. The gentleness with which she clambers onto me and curls her fingers into my thick fur brings a pang of warmth into my chest.

August had better believe I'd tear any creature to shreds before I'd let it lay one claw or tusk on this woman.

I stand carefully, giving her a chance to adjust her position so she's completely secure. Then I set off through the trees. At first, I stick to a restrained trot, waiting until I'm sure she's comfortable. When she's stayed in place without slipping or complaint for several minutes, I speed up by increments until we're weaving through the woods at a swift lope.

Talia's fingers dig deeper into my fur, and she leans lower on my back so her head can rest against the back of mine when she wishes to, although she keeps it raised for most of the journey. The thump of her heart echoes through her chest into my muscles, soft but even. I find myself matching the rhythm of my strides to it.

My only regret is that I can't see her expression as she takes in the changes in landscape, the innocuous but unusual flora and fauna we pass, and the experience of riding a wolf in general. But that's all right. I'll get the best view when we reach our destination.

At my faster pace, it takes little more than an hour to arrive at the spot. I slow when my ears catch the faint hiss and the patter of falling drops. Just before the trees thin, I stop and sink down again so Talia can dismount.

She slides off, bracing her hand against my haunch when she wobbles. As soon as she's straightened up, I shift into my typical form. With a few quick words of casting and a sweep of my senses around us, I lay down the deflective spell I promised August. There's no sign of creeping dangers at the moment.

Turning to Talia, I offer her my hand and a smirk. "Are you fully prepared?"

Her laugh carries through the forest. "I hope so."

I lead her forward to where the trees fall away. As she gets a clear view of what awaits us, her breath catches. And she hasn't even seen the best of it yet.

This haven in the midst of the forest is pretty striking even at first glance. Stones glinting with patches of amber form a rambling path through clusters of scarlet blossoms and then up a steep hillock that rises to three times my height. An underground spring burbles beneath the rocks, its pearlescent water catching the sunlight in small gaps here and there. A warm, honeyed scent fills the air, so heady you could believe you'd get high just breathing it in.

"Wow," Talia says. "It's—"

The rocks shift, one near the base of the hill lifting up a foot into the air and hovering there, another farther up sinking down to leave a deeper dip. A jet of water spurts from a gap between them, speckling the air with a glittering mist. Talia claps her hand over her mouth.

Several seconds later, the floating stone eases back down. Another juts higher while remaining attached to the earth. A shimmering trickle of water gushes from near the top of the hill to strike the stones with its pearly sheen all the way down.

Talia takes a cautious step closer. "Is it... alive?"

I suppose that's a reasonable question given the oddities she's seen of Faerieland so far. "No. Just animated by its own innate magic. Not enough that anyone else pays this glen much mind, but it's where I most like to come when I can step away from my work for a while."

She rests her hand on a stone. When it pushes up against her palm, a giggle spills out of her. More mist gusts into the air near her feet. "So it just keeps changing here and there however it feels like."

"Essentially. That's what I like about it. It's beautiful when you see it frozen in one place, but even more so when the unpredictability comes into play. You never know quite what you'll be looking at next, what angles it'll reveal."

Talia glances over her shoulder at me, a mischievous glint in her eyes. "Like you. No wonder you appreciate it."

I have to guffaw at that remark. "Come have a seat and relax, then, so you can enjoy both me and the scenery."

"Hmm." She peers up the precarious slope. "I think I'd like to check out the view from every available angle. I'll meet you at the top."

The image of her skidding off those stones and tumbling down flashes through my mind, and my heart stutters with a flicker of panic. I reach for her shoulder automatically. "I'm not sure— unpredictability doesn't make for the easiest climb."

"You'll just have to stick close in case I need you, then, won't you?" she says teasingly, and marches right up to the slope without another word.

I find myself remembering her comments about the dreams she had in her old life, all the travels she wished to embark on through the human world. She has an adventurer's spirit, this delicate but resilient human of ours. I bite my tongue against calling her back and letting my fears crush her joyful energy, but I stalk after her so I can be sure I *will* be there if she should slip.

Despite her wounded foot, Talia clambers up the stones along one side of the hillock with a natural agility. Perhaps I put too little stock in the physical training August has been putting her through —and her natural gumption.

I keep pace without any trouble, but I hardly have to wait around for her to navigate. She keeps her gaze trained on the rocks ahead, her muscles tensed so she can brace herself if one she's touching shifts, always balancing her weight across a few so that she has something steady to lean on regardless.

The breeze ruffles through her vibrant hair. A fresh spray tickles over us, making the pink hue glisten like a dewy rose. I watch the flexing of the lean muscles in her bare arms and calves, the deftness with which she places her hands and feet. Every time I catch a glimpse of her lovely face, it's etched with eager determination. I've given her something she's been craving, even if it wasn't quite what I intended.

I could watch her haul herself up hillsides all day.

With a triumphant sound, she grasps a stone at the top and pulls herself onto the mossy plateau. Just as she heaves her knees up over a bulging rock, that rock slides to the side with a jerk. Her cheer becomes a yelp.

I lunge forward on a surge of terrified adrenaline, but my outstretched arms aren't needed. After a brief teetering, Talia yanks herself the rest of the way up. It's a bit of a scramble, but she manages it alone.

I clamber right after her, collecting her in my arms all the same. We drop down together by the edge of the plateau, her tucked against my chest, the mossy span that stretches a good twenty feet wide and long cushioning our limbs.

Talia snorts and peers up at me. "Were you worried?"

I will my momentary distress not to show on my face or in my voice. "Perhaps a tad. You looked about ready to test my tumble-prevention skills."

She trails her fingers over my cheek with a gentle smile that holds so much affection my pulse stutters for a totally different reason. "I know I'm safe as long as you're here with me."

She tugs me closer, angling her mouth to meet mine, and there's no power in this world or hers that could stop me from claiming that kiss. Who needs absinthe when I can get drunk on this woman?

It's over far too quickly for my tastes, but Talia stays tucked next to me as she sits up. She gazes out over the glen from our new higher vantage point, her expression nothing but pleased. I remain sprawled on my side, watching her. I've enjoyed the other view plenty of times before.

She exhales in a long, slow stream and leans back on her hands. The breeze licks over us again. The sun glows off her pale face, and it occurs to me that this may be the first time I've seen her as she was really meant to be. Well, not the magically dyed hair or the fae clothes, but free and lively, making her explorations of the world, without any villains hunting her—at least not too close by for the moment.

I take it in, letting the image burn into my memory so I can hold onto it. This one thing is only mine. Sylas and August have never seen the adventurer. I've given her a gift they didn't think to.

"It's even better from up here," Talia announces, and glances down at me. "Thank you. For bringing me here. For letting me see it all. You'd normally come here alone, wouldn't you, if it's your place for getting away from responsibilities?"

A hint of concern crosses her face, tiny but perceptible enough to make my chest clench. I clasp her hand. "Don't feel you're intruding. I don't... I don't see you as a responsibility." The truth of that statement resonates through me. My next words catch in my throat before I propel them out. "You seemed to think before that it was a misfortune that I had no one I could 'just be' around, without keeping my wits ever alert. Fitting that you've made yourself that person, isn't it?"

If I thought she glowed before, it's nothing like the way she lights up now, gazing back at me. As if she truly is overjoyed that I've found some measure of peace in her presence—and that generosity of hers is exactly why I have. Somehow she sees me in a way none of my fae companions ever have, in a way I'm not certain even I could have identified before I had it.

I didn't know I'd ever meet a person who'd want to know who I am simply for the sake of knowing and understanding me, without searching for angles or pressure points to advance some personal agenda. But Talia isn't looking to gain anything from me other than whatever happiness she takes from the time we spend together. From knowing she's earned my trust.

But then, how can that be surprising when the main thing she's wanted for herself is the freedom to simply exist as *she* is?

There are parts of me I haven't shared and that possibly I never will, but when she bends down to press her lips to mine again, those seem so unimportant they may as well have never happened. I kiss her back, finding the perfect tilt of my mouth to provoke a murmur of desire.

There's something to be said for certain types of angles and pressure points.

Tangled up in her like this, it's hard to imagine how I could ever go without this unexpectedly wondrous being, so I simply don't try to imagine it. We won't lose her. Simple as that. Between my lord, my cadre-fellow, and I, by the Heart, we'd better be able to achieve that much.

This kiss doesn't end with one. Talia settles closer against me, trailing her slim fingers into my hair as she takes her fill of me and I of her. This is a far better setting for such a tryst than the dining hall back in Oakmeet, as fondly as I remember her quivers and gasps as I showed her just how much pleasure my mouth could conjure in her body. With the sun beaming above her and the breeze catching in her hair, she looks more than human, more than fae—like some kind of goddess.

I tease my knuckles down her chest to the swell of her breast. When they skim her nipple, I earn one of those gasps.

She kisses me harder, her tongue daring to flick between my lips. I coax her mouth wider to meet it. Our tongues tangle together, the sweet tang of her saturating all my senses—and she nudges me all the way onto my back, swinging her leg over to straddle me.

Apparently my mighty one has decided to try out other ways of riding me.

My cock was plenty interested before; now it leaps straight to attention, straining against my pants. As Talia kisses me even more fervently, I keep one hand tracing over the pebble of her nipple through her dress and use the other to ease up the skirt and adjust her against me.

There. With a slight shift of my hips, my erection presses against her core. The jolt of pleasure that contact sparks must flare in her as well, because her whimper matches my groan.

Her hands run down my chest. At their tug of my shirt, I know what she's after. Our mouths break apart just long enough for me to peel the thing off me. Then we collide in another kiss.

For a long spell, heady and torturous in the most enjoyable way, we stay like that, exploring each other's mouths, her touch roaming over my chest as mine incites every bit of bliss I can in hers, our hips rocking together at an unhurried tempo that starts to feel more urgent with the growing shakiness of her breath.

She tears her lips from mine, her head dipping so they graze my cheek instead. Then she lifts up so she can meet my eyes. So much hunger has darkened hers that I could practically come just looking at her. Her voice spills out, sweet as ever but with a husky note that shoots right to my groin.

"I want—I want to be as close to you as I can get. Completely connected."

Every particle in my body reverberates with a resounding *Yes*. I denied myself the bliss of being inside her last time, but if that's what she wants, what good would it do either of us to say no? Her scent holds a tang that tells me her monthly bleed is only a day or two off—there's no risk of compromising her freedom with unintended consequences.

And while we may never connect as closely as the highest of fae do, having seen one soul-twined mating crash and burn from a front-row seat, I can't regret that.

Perhaps Talia does, though. A shadow that looks like sorrow flickers through her expression, there and then gone, but enough to make me hesitate.

But then, it could be my hesitation is what's caused her concern. I *did* deny her last time. Is she worried that I don't want her that badly?

I push myself up on one elbow and draw her face close to mine, our noses brushing. "I can't imagine anything better than being inside you right now, Talia. This is your ride. You've got the reins. I'll take you wherever you want to go and revel in every second of it."

She sucks in a breath and kisses me hard, and then reaches to fumble with my trousers. With rather a lot of groping and some minor acrobatics, we divest me of enough clothing for my cock to spring free and remove her undergarment as well.

I skim my thumb over her clit and down across the slickness of her opening. Her eyes roll back at my touch, a shudder rippling through her body that's nothing but longing.

Bowing over me, she lowers herself onto me with a minimum of guidance. Her channel is so drenched with arousal that I slide up into her with only the slightest, most delicious of friction.

Her thighs clench against my hips, her inner muscles clamping around me and then relaxing, and a shudder of my own runs through me. My balls are already aching for release. But oh, this is good, letting her find her way, decide her own pace. My precious adventurer.

When she's taken me as deep as I'll go, she leans in to kiss me on the lips. I massage her thigh, her ass, staying still until she begins to rock against me again. Then I match the bob of her hips with gentle thrusts, holding back the urge to let loose my wildness and claim her with the full force of my desire. The slick heat of her is a high I never want to come down from.

I want to take her just as high. Few ladies find my general temperament all that pleasing, but this is one act where I've always been able to deliver. I can read the sounds that escape her throat, the twitches of her muscles, the flutter of her eyelids, to know which touch, which angle, which motion is most welcome.

Let her have everything she asked for and more.

Talia grinds into me, starting to pant, clutching my arm. "Whitt," she gasps, like a plea, one I'd love nothing more than to answer.

"What do you need?" I murmur, my own breath beginning to break.

"I just—I'm so close—please—"

I push myself a little higher so I can kiss the crook of her jaw. "Would you like to see stars or fireworks, my mighty one?"

A rough giggle tumbles out of her. "Everything. All of it."

"Mmm. So ambitious. Whatever the lady wishes…"

I pick up the pace of my thrusts, gripping her hip so I'm meeting her in the way that brought out the deepest shivers before and then slipping my fingers around to stroke her clit. With a moan, Talia presses into my touch. Her fingernails dig into my skin, but I welcome the tiny pricks of pain amid the rising swell of pleasure.

I like her fierce; I like her demanding. Heart knows she's owed a few demands after everything she's been through in this world.

She somehow pulls me even deeper inside her, our bodies bucking together in this exquisite harmony. I feel her come apart in the tightening of her channel around my cock. Her head falls back with a blissful cry, and there's no fighting it—my release explodes through me with a flare of the sharpest ecstasy I can ever remember feeling.

I can only hope I've brought her every bit as much in return.

Talia sags over me, boneless in her release. I raise my arms automatically to reach for her, to ease her down on the moss beside me and gather her against me.

She nestles her head against my shoulder with a dreamy smile, and I know I've come through for her in at least this one way she asked for.

CHAPTER TWELVE

Talia

When lunchtime creeps up on us as we lounge in Whitt's glen, I don't even have to say anything. Well, I guess my stomach does the talking for me. At its grumble, the corner of Whitt's mouth quirks up.

He speaks a couple of words I can tell from his tone are true names and extends his hand. A few seconds later, a broad waxy leaf laden with berries and a large nut in a wrinkled shell fly through the air from the depths of the forest to him.

He cracks the nut shell open on the rocky edge of our perch and hands it and the berries to me with a grin. "Can't have you starving now, or Sylas will take my head."

His ease with magic still awes me. I can reshape a bit of bronze when I need to, and I'm getting a little stronger at conjuring light, but it still takes plenty of concentration and effort. But then, as a human I'm not supposed to have any magical ability at all.

Rather than dwell on that uneasy thought, I bite into the nut, trusting that Whitt won't have offered me anything inebriating. He knows how I feel about faerie drugs.

The nut's flesh is chewier than I'd have expected, with an earthy toffee-like flavor. I alternate between it and the tart berries, and my belly is full before I'm even finished that offering.

"I know it's not quite up to the standards you're used to from August's kitchen," Whitt says breezily.

I wave his remark off, watching him with a rush of renewed affection for the man who's indulged so many of my whims today, most of them spontaneously. If only life in the faerie world were always this enchanting, no awful schemes of horrible villains intruding.

He's pulled his trousers back up, but he hasn't bothered to retrieve his shirt. I lick the berry juice from my fingers and allow myself the additional indulgence of trailing my fingers over his sculpted, tattooed torso.

Whitt's muscles flex beneath the sculpted planes. I trace the lines of a few of the true-name marks idly, and he simply lets me, totally at ease in his half-nakedness.

I find myself remembering things Sylas has told me about his spymaster—about the distance he's kept from just about everyone in his life, which Whitt has basically confirmed. A question itches at me. Maybe because of the tenderness with which he embraced our first full sexual encounter, I'm feeling secure enough to risk bringing up the subject.

"Sylas told me… you've never taken a mate. I mean, a regular one—I know you wouldn't have a soul-twined one. I guess August never had much of a chance before the pack was banished to the fringes, but you would have."

He raises an eyebrow at me. "Do you object to my unattached status?"

He should know very well that I don't. I wouldn't have this

closeness with him—in every possible way—if he was committed to another woman.

I give him a playful shove. "I just wondered why. It seems like most of the fae in the pack are paired off. Or is it unusual for cadre-chosen to settle down because of the whole commitment-to-the-lord thing?" That non-romantic commitment is one of the reasons sharing a lover isn't uncommon among cadres.

Whitt catches my hand before I can retract it from the shove and runs his thumb lightly over my knuckles, considering our entwined fingers. "I wouldn't say it's unusual. Plenty of cadre-chosen do take on a mate, just one who's tolerant of their divided attention. But I never met any woman I wanted that enduring an association with."

I think of the fae women who fluttered around him and his colleagues at Donovan's banquet. "You must have had lots who'd have volunteered for the spot, back before the banishment when Sylas was considered one of the more prominent lords. So, basically, you're just picky?"

He snorts. "I'd put it more as, I have enough self-respect to be sparing in who I devote my attention to."

"They were all that bad?" I tease.

I'd thought we were bantering, but his expression goes oddly serious. His fingers still against mine, and then he tugs my hand to his lips to press a kiss to its back.

He gazes off over the landscape ahead of us. "There's a reason I stay on my guard around all of my kind, mite. My fae brethren rarely do anything without at least a little calculation in the mix. When it came to ladies aiming to tempt me as a suitor, I always had to consider whether they were more interested in me or my proximity to a prominent lord."

Oh. My gut twists at the thought. "And a lot of them only cared about the status?"

Do I even need to ask that? I've seen how the other summer fae treated my pack while they lived on the fringes. No one from any other domain cared enough about Whitt to seek out his company there.

He shrugs. "Ah, I'm sure at least a few of them liked me somewhat. But I have no interest in being a stepping stone to social eminence on any scale. By the time I was old enough to be considered eligible, Sylas had been born, and it was known I'd be serving him when he was of age. There was never a time when it wouldn't have been a consideration."

He speaks casually enough, but his grasp tightens a little where he's still holding my hand. The tension in my gut turns into a pang that echoes up through my chest.

I never thought before about what it'd have been like for him. His entire adult life, he's had his role decided for him. His wants and hopes were superseded from the moment of Sylas's birth.

"Did you have any choice?" I ask. "If you didn't like the idea of dedicating yourself to service in Sylas's cadre, could you have said no?"

"Of course. No lord wants an unwilling cadre. But it was that or spend my entire life idle. There wasn't any *other* lord I'd have cared to pledge myself to."

He pauses, running his other fingers over his ear with its pointed tip—not as sharp as Sylas's but obvious all the same. "I was just shy of being true-blooded myself, you know. There's a spell to test it that's conducted at birth. A few percentage more in the right direction, and I'd have a domain of my own."

I squeeze his hand. "That seems so unfair."

"It is what it is," he says, but the darkening of his eyes suggests he's not so unaffected. He shakes himself and offers me a wry smile, the first time he's really looked at me since this conversation started. "It's ridiculous, really. I have no interest at all in ruling over a pack. I'd have to behave myself and shoulder ten times as many responsibilities, and I'd find the job an excruciating bore. I doubt

I'd be any good at it either. So it shouldn't bother me in the slightest that no one would ever have considered offering me the position."

The pang rises to my throat. My voice comes out quiet. "But it does."

His smile falters. His gaze slips away from me again, toward the distant trees. His silence is enough of an answer. After a moment, he grimaces. "It's just a faint niggling every now and then. I ignore it easily enough. I'd rather you never mention it to him."

Sylas, he means. I scoot closer to him, wanting to offer him whatever I can of myself, even if it wouldn't come close to making up for how much he's been denied over a tiny difference in his blood.

"Do you think he doesn't already know?" I ask. The fae lord has struck me as awfully perceptive.

Whitt lets out a dry chuckle that holds little humor. "It's become apparent to me that there are a few things that've managed to escape even our glorious leader's notice."

I grope for the right words. My thoughts trip back over the past couple of months, over the way Whitt has held me at a distance even though I know now it wasn't for lack of interest, of the way he balked when I first made it clear *I* was attracted to him. I grip his hand with enough strength that he glances at me.

"You know, it wasn't on purpose that I got close to Sylas and August first," I say. "That was just how it happened. It doesn't mean I love or want you any less than I do them. Because I don't. Less. Er..."

Whitt is staring at me with such a startled expression that I lose track of my words completely. His lips part, but it takes a second before any sound passes from them. "*What?*" he says.

My cheeks heat. Did I phrase my attempt at reassuring him badly and now I've made him feel worse? "I was just saying—even though out of the three of you I came to you last, I—"

Wait. I halt, realizing which part he probably wasn't expecting.

What I haven't actually said to him before, even though the emotion has been as obvious to me as one of the castle orbs, glowing inside me whenever I'm near him. "I love you. Just as much."

Maybe even more. When he looks at me like that, like I've chiseled open a crack right through the center of his being, something inside me rises up with more determination and devotion than I know what to do with. Something that longs to flood out and fill every place hollowed with loss or loneliness behind his cocky exterior.

The sense of how much I'd give to seal the wounds he tries to hide knocks the breath out of me. It *scares* me. But only a little, because I know he'd never ask me to try.

"Talia," he says with a rasp in his voice, and I lie back down, tucking my head against his shoulder.

"I don't expect you to say it back. That's just how I feel. You don't have to do anything about it. I love you, and I'm glad that I do." For as long as I get to love him before the expectations of this world intervene.

He makes a rough sound and tips my face up so he can kiss me. The sear of his mouth makes me tingle right down to my toes.

As his lips move against mine, his hands travel over my body, kindling more heat. I'm abruptly also glad that I hadn't bothered to put my panties back on yet, because I'm not sure I want to wait even those few extra seconds before I get to feel him filling me again.

But none of it compares to the deepest, giddying burn around my heart. *I love you*, I think into every kiss, every caress. *I love you. I love you.* As if, if I can pour enough of that emotion into him now, I might extend the time before I'll have to give it up and say good-bye.

CHAPTER THIRTEEN

Talia

I shift restlessly in my carriage seat, peering over the side toward the other vehicles tagging along behind us across a plain dappled with cottony flowers. "I wish we didn't have to bring this much of an audience."

Sylas follows my gaze with an apologetic slanting of his mouth. "I would have prevented it if I could have. But it may be to our benefit in the long run. Ambrose won't be able to deny or misconstrue anything that happens when all three of the arch-lords are here to witness it."

The arch-lord who wants to claim me for his own purposes insisted that the rulers of the summer realm come along for this audience with the great sage. From the way Sylas told it, Ambrose made it sound as if he didn't trust us to give an accurate account of what happens. I hope the other arch-lords noticed how petty that sounds when Sylas has been nothing but candid with them.

"Do you really think this fae will be able to figure out why I am… the way I am?" I ask.

Whitt leans back on the bench where he's sitting across from me. "They say Nuldar knows all things. He's been around long enough to, if he really is the oldest fae still living, which I have no reason to doubt. He may even be fully true-blooded, which adds to his magical prowess. The trouble is getting him to say anything in a way you can decipher into something useful. There's a reason he wasn't our first stop in untangling this riddle. The arch-lords have consulted with him before about the curse and gotten nowhere."

He's stretched out his legs, his crossed ankles resting next to mine—closer than he'd get if many of our pack-kin were around to observe, not quite as close as he might if Astrid weren't joining the four of us on this excursion. Sylas may think having the arch-lords around could be a good thing, but he's clearly prepared for something to go wrong if he thought we needed another warrior along.

The fae woman, the oldest by far in my present company, inclines her head with a wry smile. "I've heard it said that Nuldar is as likely to muddle matters more as to shed light on them."

"But we haven't figured out anything at all about why your blood has this effect on our curse," August points out, dropping onto the bench beside me. "*Any* information should be better than none, even if we have to puzzle over what he means."

"My thoughts exactly." Sylas turns toward the bow to gaze out over the landscape ahead. "And the moment we have a source for the cure that doesn't rely on you, Ambrose will have no grounds at all to demand Tristan take custody of you."

A shiver of hope tickles through my chest. Wouldn't that be lovely? To just *be* with these three men and their pack, however that plays out across the years ahead—to no longer exist as a bargaining chip or a tool but simply a human woman making a life for myself among the fae.

If only it could happen that easily.

The fae lord points to what looks like a silvery haze up ahead. "We're almost there."

I limp up to the bow and lean my hands against the polished wood with its tangy juniper scent. The wind teases through my hair.

As we glide closer, the mist sharpens into the more solid shapes of trees, all of them tall and elegant with gracefully drooping branches like weeping willows in the human world. Except the leaves on our willows never sparkled like this. There's a whole forest of them, stretching out maybe half a mile in front of us before darker treetops take over on either side.

"They're beautiful," I say, staring. After everything I've seen in the faerie world already, it can still amaze me.

"Starfall willows," Whitt says from behind me. "So named for the twinkling leaves and also the fact that they heat up like they've got little suns inside them by night. Much safer to visit now during daylight hours when we won't get burned."

That's something else I've learned more than once about the faerie world. There are as many deadly things here as beautiful things, and quite a few are both.

Our carriage eases to a halt at the edge of the forest. A whispering sound drifts out to meet us. Sylas springs out first and offers his hand to help me leap the side. "Stick close to us. The trees won't hurt you during the day, but they can be somewhat... unnerving."

Wonderful. I resist the urge to shrink inside my skin and force myself to limp alongside him with my head high, ignoring the arch-lords and the few kin they've had join them disembarking around us. August stays at my other side, Whitt venturing just a couple of steps ahead, Astrid bringing up the rear.

I see what Sylas means as soon as we enter the forest. The drooping branches with their long, thin leaves had been swaying slightly with what I took to be the movements of a breeze. The moment we walk between them, it's as if they come to life.

One branch lifts to trail its tendril-like leaves over August's shoulder. Another taps the top of Sylas's head. The ones ahead of Whitt twist and rise as if peering at him. I hear a rustle behind me and a muttered objection from Astrid. "Nosy things."

"Patience," Sylas says evenly. He glances down at me. "As Nuldar has aged, he's become more and more immersed in his magical affinities. He has strong ties to trees and other plant life, as I do, although on an even deeper scale. Though he's a lord, he lives alone here now… and he's merged somewhat with the forest. The trees act through his will."

"He's making them all move like that?" I peer around us, restraining a shudder as a branch winds snake-like past August to lick its leaves down my arm.

Whitt chuckles. "We should consider ourselves lucky he doesn't insist on an even more thorough inspection."

I expect us to reach a castle or at least a house not so different from the ones Sylas has created, grown out of trees, with this Nuldar living inside it. When Whitt stops in his tracks and dips into a low bow, I realize that the "merging" is much more thorough than that.

What stands before us isn't a building but another tree—but not *just* another tree. Its sloping branches splay to either side to give a clear view within. Protruding from the trunk is the form of a man: bone-thin and wizened to the point that it's hard to tell where his wrinkled skin stops and the crinkles of tree bark begin.

One of his hands, the impressions of the fingertips just barely visible, lifts toward the upper branches. The other stretches toward the roots. The bit of cloth around the figure's hips and the crinkled hair sprouting from his head and chin are a light gray the same shade as the bark.

The man's skin holds only a trace more color than that, a faint peachy hue mostly absorbed into the trunk's pale silver. Then his eyes blink and open fully, and I'm struck by the vivid midnight-blue of the irises, so stark amid the rest of him and the tree he's become at one with.

All the fae around me—my lovers and Astrid and the arch-lord delegates who've caught up—bow just as low as Whitt did, including the arch-lords themselves. Apparently even Ambrose can recognize this sage as a higher power than his own.

I bend at the waist as low as I can while keeping my balance, not wanting to offend the being we're hoping to get answers from. When I straighten back up, it takes my best efforts not to outright stare.

"Great Nuldar," Sylas says, his deep voice resonating through the woods, "we come before you to seek your wisdom. Are you still willing to speak with us today?"

The sage's answer rasps like leaves rubbing together, his beard twitching just a smidge with the movement of his lips. "Ask what you will and I will tell what I see, Lord Sylas."

Sylas puts his arm around my shoulders and guides me forward so that I'm fully in Nuldar's view. I stand there awkwardly, not sure what to do with my hands or if I should even smile.

"There is a quality in this human woman's blood that dispels the curse we Seelie have suffered under the full moon," the fae lord says. "We wish to understand how that quality came to be and anything you can inform us of its nature."

The sage's gaze fixes on me. I find I can't tear my eyes away from his. Neither of us moves, but I feel as if I'm falling toward those dark eyes, farther and farther, into a void with no end.

My thoughts slip away; my sense of the world around me fades. All I know is the deep dark blue and a quivering sensation racing through my head and down through my chest.

When Nuldar looks away, I sway, catching my breath with a gasp. Sylas's hold on me tightens. Without him, I think I might have stumbled. My whole body is quivering on the inside now, my thoughts spinning.

But the sage is starting to speak. I focus on his words as well as I can.

"She started in darkness," Nuldar intones in a tone that's as distant as the space I tumbled into within his eyes. "Then she came out into the light. The mother of her mother of her mother met one of the Mists who planted the seed. The seed came into bloom alongside our curse, entwined from that point forward, growing more so with the passing of generations. That is what I see." His eyes close again.

"Great Nuldar," Sylas starts, but the sage gives no response, no sign that he's even heard. I guess his abrupt withdrawal isn't that unusual, because Sylas doesn't push for more. He turns, his expression pensive, and motions for the small crowd gathered around us to go back the way we came.

I hurry along with him and August, relieved that we're not going to stick around among these creepy trees while hashing out Nuldar's proclamation. As Whitt suggested, the sage wasn't exactly clear in his statements, but I can see the obvious metaphors. The first bit especially—don't all people start in darkness and then come into the light? That's a fancy way of saying I was born. I'm not sure how helpful the rest will be if that's what he started with.

The trees prod and tug at us with their branches, but they don't stop us from leaving the forest. We all come to a stop on the flowery plain where we left the carriages.

"Well?" Ambrose demands before any of us can do more than take a breath. "You've spoken with the girl the most. What do *you* make of that?"

He has two regal-looking fae with him who I believe are from his cadre, as well as a woman in plainer though still fine clothes who's hanging back—can he not go anywhere without a servant along?

But then, it looks like Donovan has brought a couple of servants himself. They trail behind the arch-lord as he steps closer to hear Sylas's answer. Celia, who appears to have brought only a single cadre member as her companion, eyes them with a disdainful curl of her lip I don't totally understand.

Sylas folds his arms over his chest. "I'd say for Nuldar, that was an impressively straightforward answer, given what we all already know about Talia and our curse. The mother of her mother of her mother would be her great-grandmother. Planting the seed presumably refers to a pregnancy. Her great-grandmother's mate was a man with at least a little fae blood—one of the Mists."

Whitt nods. "It must have been only a very small heritage, increasingly diluted before it reached Talia, because she shows no physical signs of that ancestry. It sounds as though there was an intersection in the timing. Coming into bloom—perhaps her grandmother was born just as the curse took hold, and that synchronicity connected the two despite the weakness of the fae element in her."

He's frowning, though. Could all that also explain why I have a little magical ability? And would a curse really latch onto a random baby that was essentially human, just because it happened to be born at the same time? I don't have enough idea of how fae magic works to know how plausible those assumptions are.

In front of the arch-lords, I hesitate to ask anything that'll make me sound ignorant—or throw doubt onto Sylas's and Whitt's explanations—though, so I keep my mouth shut. Another, more discomforting thought strikes me.

If the specialness in me that allows my blood to cure the curse is something I inherited because of an unintentional coincidence... then there may be nothing else in either world that could have the same effect. Rather than giving us a way out of our problem, this trip may have made it even clearer how valuable I am to all the Seelie.

Ambrose rubs his mouth. "What of her other relatives, then? Is this grandmother still above the dust? Perhaps a human closer to the source would provide stronger results."

My heart lurches, and August gives the arch-lord a fierce look. "We're not dragging her family here to be bled."

"There wouldn't be any point," Whitt puts in before Ambrose can argue. "The sage said the connection between the family line and the curse *strengthened* across the generations. Unless this is opposite day, that means the generations before Talia's would have a weaker effect."

Would they have had any effect at all? Aerik and his cadre didn't seem to notice anything special about Jamie's blood when they— when they tore my brother apart. The memory makes me cringe inwardly, my pulse skittering faster. I reach for August's hand, and he squeezes mine in return.

Maybe it was something only passed on to the women? I'm not sure why that would be the case. Or something only to the oldest child?

Not that it matters. Both Jamie and my mother died almost a decade ago.

"I suppose this venture was somewhat informative," Celia says in a cool voice. "But it seems to change the situation very little. Some miniscule trace of fae influence over her line doesn't make this girl anything more than a human, and the cure remains tied to her blood."

It's true—nothing's different except that I have even more questions and uncertainties. I glance back toward the forest, wondering if Nuldar would say anything else if I marched up to him and demanded answers. Somehow I doubt it.

Ambrose has turned away from the rest of us. Another carriage has come into view in the distance. He shoots the others a narrow smile. "I had a brief bit of business to carry out, and this was a convenient mid-point. Allow me a moment, and then we can discuss whatever else we need to."

Celia huffs as if she doesn't think there *is* anything else to discuss. She walks over to her carriage with her cadre-chosen, and Sylas moves to confer with Donovan. Ambrose strolls a little away from our cluster but then stops, rocking on his heels as he waits for the newcomers to arrive.

August turns to Whitt. "If all that was needed is fae influence and timing, surely there could be other beings affected. If we could find plants or animals of the Mists that came into being at that same moment…"

Whitt grimaces. "Perhaps it needs to be actual fae ancestry, not simply of this realm. You know there are barely enough Seelie offspring to count on one being born across the whole realm in any given year, let alone on a specific day."

Something Astrid mentioned to me tickles up through my thoughts. "Maybe—" I begin, and then my voice withers in my throat, because I've just seen who's stepping out of the newly arrived carriage to meet Ambrose.

The sunlight glares off Aerik's daffodil-yellow hair—and off the icy blue-white of the sharp-edged man emerging behind him. I freeze.

For a second, I think I've conjured my former captors out of my imagination after remembering their attack on my family, but no, they're really here. Aerik strides over to Ambrose, Cole sauntering behind him. He cuts a quick look my way, and his expression is all ice too.

If my pulse was skittering before, it's outright rattling through my limbs now. I suck in a breath and find my lungs have constricted. I wrench my gaze away, blinking hard, fighting to control my emotions while so many powerful fae are here to witness it if I break down.

I shouldn't be affected by those monsters anymore. We defeated them—all four of us together. Sylas forced their yield. They *can't* hurt me now.

But I wasn't prepared, and I have nine years of torment lodged in my brain that isn't erased that easily. Slivers of memories stab up through my mind: the slam of an elbow into my ribs, the cold sheen of bronze bars around me. A sound like a wheeze escapes my throat. I squeeze my hands into fists, focusing on the pressure of my fingernails against my palms, on the solidness of the ground beneath my feet.

"Talia," August says, hushed but urgent. He tucks his arm around me, sheltering me.

I can feel the tension in his stance. He won't want to draw attention to my weakness either. Ambrose will find some way to spin it against my pack.

The arch-lord must have known I'd have some kind of reaction to seeing Aerik. Sylas said he didn't give the trio any details of my treatment, but they know that Aerik and his cadre are the ones who dragged me into this realm from my home, who broke my foot, who brought me to such a sorry state that Sylas would never have agreed to handing me back to them.

I'm not hiding my panic as well as I wish I could. Whitt steps closer with a flash of his teeth and a remark under his breath. "They won't get anywhere near you. I'd like to see them try." Astrid plants herself nearby between me and the new arrivals so I can't see them even if I look that way.

And—oh, no—Sylas and Donovan are approaching too. "Is she all right?" I hear the fiery-haired man say, and while he seems to be a much kinder ruler than his colleague, we still need him on our side. We need him to believe that I'm safe and well in Sylas's care.

"This is all a little overwhelming," I manage to say, hating the way my voice wobbles. "I'll just…" I sink down in demonstration rather than trying to force out more words, sitting on the grass and pulling my knees up in front of my chest.

There. It'll look as if I just needed a little rest. August crouches with me, rubbing my back, and with his touch and the stronger sense of being grounded, my inner turmoil starts to retreat.

They're all watching me. I can't exactly tell them to go away. I find myself staring through the gap between Sylas and Donovan where they're standing over me. At first my focus is hazy, but then a movement catches my attention.

One of the servants Donovan brought with him is shaking his head. He doesn't seem to be talking to anyone, though. He's standing there on his own, closing his eyes and opening them again with another jerk of his head from side to side. His mouth twists as if in distress.

As I'm distracted by him, my own anxiety fades even more. Is something wrong with him?

He touches his hip, adjusting something in his pocket—I catch a glint of a metal edge—and then he walks out of my view in the direction of Celia's carriage.

An uneasy tremor races through me that has nothing to do with Aerik. Something's wrong.

The last time Ambrose struck at us in a gathering of the fae, it wasn't just at me and Sylas. He had other plans, bigger plans. Why would this time be any different? He hasn't just shaken my nerves— he's ensured nearly everyone else's attention is on me instead of… wherever he doesn't want it to be.

I open my mouth, but my throat has gone so dry I only croak. My men draw closer with looks of concern.

It's not me they need to worry about right now, I don't think. My eyes dart and lock with Astrid's.

I make a frantic gesture in the direction the servant appeared to go. A furrow digs into her brow, but she looks around despite her confusion.

"Arch-Lord Donovan," she says quickly. "Does your servant have some business with your colleagues?"

"What?" The arch-lord swivels and swears softly. As he hustles away, I relax into August's embrace.

There's a thump and a yelp. Everyone around me turns to look, and so does Ambrose. "Whatever is going on over there, Donovan?" he asks sneeringly.

Donovan is standing over the servant, one hand pressed to the man's forehead, the other gripping his wrists, just a few steps from Celia's carriage. She's watching too, knitting her brow.

Donovan speaks a few low words, and the man stops struggling. He shakes his head, but in a looser motion than I saw before. "I— I'm sorry, my lord. I don't know—"

"It's all right," the arch-lord interrupts, and nudges him back towards his own carriage. Donovan casts a wary glance Ambrose's way. "Something about this place appears to have affected my servant badly. I've dealt with it."

"Humans are never quite as resilient as we'd hope, are they?" Ambrose says, and returns his attention to Aerik.

The servant was human? I guess there wasn't any way for me to tell when he was dressed in fae clothes. The fae can clearly pick up on some difference, but there's no visible sign that I can pick up on between the fae with a smaller portion of true blood and a human.

As I manage to get back to my feet, Sylas looks me over. "All right, little scrap?" he says, warmly enough for the old nickname to sound affectionate rather than belittling. When I nod, he hurries over to Donovan, no doubt wanting a more detailed account of what went on there.

Whatever Ambrose had planned, he doesn't let any disappointment show. After a few minutes, he waves off Aerik and Cole, his supposed business with them concluded, and the arch-lords gather with Sylas and his cadre again. It doesn't take long to determine that there really isn't anything more they can glean from the sage's metaphors.

"If anything else occurs to you or it leads you to a new

revelation, I expect you to report on that to us immediately," Ambrose declares, and marches off. The other two arch-lords follow suit, but not before Donovan exchanges a meaningful look with Sylas.

We hang back while the others set off. When they're far enough that my men must be sure they won't be overheard, Whitt turns to Sylas. "What was that about?"

Sylas lets out a ragged sigh. "It seems one of Donovan's human servants got himself under an enchantment. One that appeared to be propelling him toward Celia with a knife. And Donovan only brought those servants along because he got an anonymous warning that they'd be under threat in the castle today. He was manipulated into having them here."

I can fill in at least one of the blanks. "Ambrose must have enchanted him. I guess it's a lot easier to do that to a human than a fae servant?"

"Unfortunately, yes. And whether it was Ambrose himself or one of his underlings, we strongly suspect he was involved." He turns to Astrid. "Thank you for your vigilance. If you hadn't noticed the servant's odd behavior, he might have carried out his attack."

The warrior woman tips her head toward me. "It was Talia who spotted him. She managed to convey enough to alert me even in her distress."

"Really." Sylas's gaze comes back to me, impressed but still grim. "Protecting us when we're meant to be protecting you."

"You protected me plenty," I say.

August growls. "First the thefts and now this—on top of throwing Talia into a panic. What's Ambrose's end-game?"

Whitt arches an eyebrow. I don't think the edge in his voice is really directed at his brother. "Can't you guess? As we explained to Talia not long ago, there are two ways to displace an arch-lord. Ambrose doesn't expect he could get away with killing Donovan in cold blood."

The conversation comes back to me. "The other way is to show the arch-lord isn't good enough—because of wrong-doings? Would Donovan get kicked out over stealing a few artefacts?"

"Probably not that alone," Sylas says. "But I doubt that was meant to be the only blow. And while his servant wouldn't have had a hope of dealing much real damage to Celia, instigating the attempted murder of a fellow arch-lord would certainly be grounds for dismissal. I believe we can now say with reasonable certainty that Ambrose is looking to not just put you in his cousin's grasp but to set Tristan on a throne as well."

Whitt winces. "And if that happens, good-bye to balance in the Bastion. Ambrose and Tristan will carry the vote. Whatever the two of them want from all Seelie kind, they'll get."

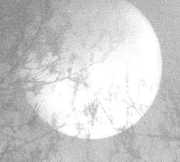

CHAPTER FOURTEEN

August

I've only just started to doze when the faint click of my bedroom door brings me back to full alertness. I jerk upright, but before my defensive instincts have kicked in any more than that, I've already recognized the whiff of scent that's reached me.

Talia peeks inside. She'd look like a wraith with her pale skin and her white nightgown if it wasn't for the rich pink of her hair, unmistakeable even in the dim moonlight that seeps through my window. She hesitates on the threshold. "I hope I didn't wake you up? It sounded like you just came to bed."

I've known this woman too long now to be surprised that she's canny enough to pick up on our movements around the castle. It wasn't *that* long ago she must have felt her survival and potential escape depended on knowing when we'd turned in for the night.

I don't have the words to express how glad I am that she's using that awareness to come to me rather than running away now, so I settle for smiling and holding out my hand. "It wouldn't matter if you had, but you didn't. Come in. Is something wrong?"

As she limps across the floor to me, she shakes her head and then seems to amend that gesture. "Not exactly. I—After seeing Aerik and Cole today, I think the nightmares might come again. If I'm sleeping on my own, anyway. I don't seem to have them when I know I'm with someone who could protect me."

A faint blush colors her cheeks, as if there's anything embarrassing in that admission. The joy I already took in having her here spreads through my chest with a headier warmth.

I know Sylas has comforted her through her night terrors before, but this is the first time she's sought me out. I don't mind that she appreciates my brothers' attentions as well as my own, but I can't help reveling in the fact that she wanted me rather than either of them tonight.

Although I wish she didn't have to worry about nightmares at all.

I scoot over on the bed and lift the covers to make room for her. "You're always welcome here, Sweetness. I'll do my best to scare off those mangy villains even if they're only in your head."

With a relieved smile in return, she crawls under the sheets and cuddles up next to me, so easily it makes my heart sing. I wrap my arm around her torso and nuzzle her hair.

A more heated hunger stirs in my chest and lower, my wolfish instincts rising to the surface with the urge to taste and take her, but she didn't come to me for that. The whole reason Sylas set up a separate room for those sorts of encounters was so that Talia could seek us out at night without any expectations of greater intimacy.

We'll have plenty of other occasions for that. And it's not as if getting to hold her against me like this, guarding over her while she sleeps, doesn't feel plenty intimate in itself.

After the trip to the sage and all the surprises and stress that came with it, it's no wonder Talia is exhausted. Her breaths slow after only a few minutes in my embrace, her muscles slackening. I press a light kiss to the top of her head and rest my own against the pillow, but sleep doesn't come to me as quickly.

I love this woman so much. So much that seeing her in pain is like a dagger through my heart. So much that the emotion pulses through me with each beat of that heart as she lies here with me. Every moment she's near me, my body balks at the thought of letting her go.

If she were fae—fae enough that any of my brethren would count her as one—I'd ask her to be my mate. But regardless of Nuldar's comments, she's so human I'm not sure such an official bond would sit right even with our own pack-kin.

By my life, I'm not sure I'd even care about that if the tiny fae influence on her blood didn't make so much difference. For me to claim her as a mate when she's the only known cure for our curse would have political ramifications I can't even begin to imagine.

And that's without even getting into what my lord and my cadre-fellow would have to say on the subject. Would they accept a shared relationship where Talia had a more official tie to me than to them? Would *Talia* accept a mate bond knowing it would skew the tentative balance we've only just achieved between the three of us?

More questions I don't know the answer to. As much as I want her to feel cherished in every way, suggesting that step could cause more problems than happiness. I'm content with what I have for now.

Maybe I shouldn't be thinking about keeping her closer to me at all. Ambrose and his pack-kin have already managed to traumatize her, wound her... We haven't been enough to keep her safe. How can I say I'd do anything to protect her when I haven't actually managed to keep her out of his clutches?

That uneasy question leaves my thoughts spinning for a while longer before I finally drift off. When I wake up to Talia snuggling closer in the dawn light, I try to put the conclusions I've drawn out of my head. I hold her while she dozes a little longer, and then whip up a quick breakfast with her help in the kitchen. Every pleased glance she sends my way, every brilliant smile, I treasure and commit to my memory.

After we've all eaten, Sylas leaves to speak with Whitt about something, and Talia gives me a quick kiss before heading off with Astrid to find something to occupy herself with among the pack. I start cleaning the kitchen out of habit until the pack-kin who've been assisting me since we returned to Hearthshire shoo me—respectfully—out of the way. If I hadn't honed my cooking skills as much as I have, they'd probably tell me it isn't for a cadre-chosen to bother with anything in the kitchen at all.

I go up to Sylas's study expecting to join his conversation with Whitt, but when my lord calls me in, the spymaster is already gone. As I enter, Sylas stands.

"I was just about to summon you," he says. "I've arranged an audience with Ambrose. I'd like you to join me."

I blink, momentarily thrown off my purpose. "Me? Last time you took Whitt." Political negotiations are definitely not my area of expertise.

Sylas smiles and motions for me to follow him. "I wouldn't want the arch-lords to get the impression that I favor either of my cadre-chosen over the other. And Whitt will be there too, just more surreptitiously. I don't expect Ambrose to react well to this conversation. Our brother will be watching to see how he responds in the orders he gives his pack."

I walk with Sylas out of the castle, glancing toward our pack village. "Then none of us will be here with Talia—"

"Astrid has proven herself more than up to that task. I don't anticipate any major moves from our guests, but she has my orders just in case." He considers me for a second before beckoning the carriage he never bothered to revert to its natural form after yesterday's trip. Had he already known then that he'd need one again so soon? "What we do today may protect her better than anything we could accomplish here by her side."

We set off at a faster pace than he'd take if Talia were with us. I don't think he wants to leave her without our protection for any longer than he has to despite the confidence in Astrid he expressed. The wind warbles over the canopy and ruffles my hair. Sylas has tied his back in a short ponytail, but a few stray strands whip across his temples.

When we reach a stretch where he doesn't need to navigate closely, he comes to sit on the bench across from me, angling his body as I have so the wind doesn't buffet his face. I push myself to say what I've been thinking about since last night. If I don't speak up about it now, I might lose my nerve.

"I think there's something more we can do for Talia, at least until things are settled with the arch-lords and we're sure Ambrose has backed off on his intent to have Tristan take her."

Sylas raises a curious eyebrow. "Well, you know I'll want to hear your thoughts on that. Go ahead."

I open my mouth and hesitate. I don't think he's going to like this plan, not at first anyway. A large part of *me* doesn't like it. But it's a selfish part, and Talia deserves better. She deserves so much more security and certainty than we've been able to give her.

"No matter where we've been—our own domain, Donovan's, Nuldar's—Ambrose has found ways to reach her, to hurt her. But now that we have more information from the sage, and the arch-lords have even suggested we should look deeper into her heritage if we can… we could reasonably do this."

"Do *what*?" Sylas prods, his tone mild.

I inhale sharply. "We could arrange to send her back to the human world. Aerik and his cadre can't chase her there because of their yield vow. Ambrose would have trouble searching the entire place for her. We can send Astrid with her for protection, say it's to investigate her family, but really Astrid can just take her wherever they're least likely to be disturbed and give her as comfortable a time of it as possible until things are safer here."

Sylas contemplates the proposal for quite a while. I can't read his expression, but my gut knots with the sense that his evaluation might not be completely positive. Finally, he says, "You're suggesting that we send her so far away we'd have no hope of intervening if grave danger came upon her?"

"I think she's a lot more likely to face grave danger in this world than that one, and we have a responsibility to do whatever's best for her."

Sylas frowns, his gaze moving to the blurred landscape we're racing past. After another long silence, he returns his attention to me. "I'll keep that strategy under advisement should our situation become worse. I'd rather not take such extreme measures unnecessarily. For now... Ambrose may be conniving, but he isn't dim-witted. We can hope he'll see some sort of reason."

He doesn't sound all that hopeful. I grimace. "What exactly are we going to be talking to him about?"

Sylas's lips curve into a grim smile. "I think he should know that his treachery hasn't gone unnoticed. Ousting Donovan from his position will only work if Ambrose can't be charged with a crime as well—and it's unlikely to work at all if he feels he'll be watched too closely from here on out."

"We don't have definite proof, though."

"We won't be able to accuse him outright, no. But by the end of the discussion, I expect we'll all at least know where we stand better than before."

He obviously doesn't believe Ambrose will necessarily back down completely, or he wouldn't have asked Whitt to keep watch from farther afield. I resist the urge to pace the carriage, knowing the wind will make the movement more uncomfortable than nerve-settling.

Going up against other lords was one thing. Facing off against an arch-lord… I don't like it. I don't like any of this.

Our return to Hearthshire was meant to be a triumph, and Ambrose's duplicity is ruining it more with every day.

No one comes out to greet us when we approach the gleaming obsidian palace of Dusk-by-the-Heart today. Though Ambrose knows we're coming, either he hasn't notified his staff, or he's instructed them to wait for us to knock before admitting us. The fae servant who opens the door for us ushers us a short distance down a hall so dark it gives the sensation of swallowing us whole. The room she points us to isn't much better, but at least the pale upholstered furniture offers some break from the dark rock.

Sylas motions for me to sit but stays standing himself. Ambrose leaves us waiting there for several minutes before he deigns to make an appearance.

He enters briskly, his ever-present plated vest clinking with his movements, his eyes already narrowed. No doubt he can guess that this is far from being a friendly call. He shuts the door to the room with a wave of his hand and folds his arms over his chest.

"Well? Have you uncovered some urgent new development in regards to your dust-destined charge?"

I bristle automatically at the insult but hold myself in place. He isn't bothering with politeness when it comes to his opinions about humans when the other arch-lords aren't around to overhear.

"Not yet," Sylas says evenly. "I wished to speak to you about a matter even more urgent—and one best not conveyed by distant correspondence."

"And what would that be, Lord Sylas? Do enlighten me."

His disdainful tone raises my hackles even more. I can force myself to stay seated, but there's no preventing my fangs from prickling out of my gums. He's lucky I'm holding my claws in check well enough not to gouge the fine fabric covering this chair.

Sylas lays the situation out with more care than I could have managed. "It's caught our attention that certain attempts have been made to undermine one of your fellow arch-lords. As if someone were seeking to have him removed from his position."

Ambrose lets out a huff, not allowing any hint show that the accusation affects him. "Then my colleague should certainly bring that to us, not you."

"Perhaps he will as well. But as one who serves the trio of arch-lords, I feel it is my duty to express my own concerns as well."

"And what would you have *me* do about it, Lord Sylas?"

Sylas regards him with the impenetrable calm I've always admired. "Perhaps you could take steps to ensure no such treachery occurs when you or your pack-kin are in the vicinity. Since I'm sure you would never risk your own position by aiding such efforts."

A smirk crosses Ambrose's face, so thin and cool it sets my teeth on edge. "Naturally. I'll certainly take your claims into account." He studies Sylas until all my nerves are prickling. "I wonder if you've fully considered all the factors involved, though."

"What do you mean?"

Ambrose gives a seemingly careless shrug and trails his thick fingers over the back of the nearest chair. "It doesn't appear you have any proof of this treachery, or I assume you'd have presented it."

"Many are aware," Sylas says. "It'll only be a matter of time."

"For sure. Only, it is such a shame that my colleague has garnered such hostile feelings, don't you think? You can't have imagined these efforts came out of the blue. I don't condone the behavior, of course, but when a ruler refuses to budge for the good of his people, it's unsurprising that this sort of thing occurs."

"On what matter has Donovan 'refused to budge'?"

Ambrose tsks to himself. "He wants to make friends with our true enemies, do you know? To extend a branch to the Unseelie, to offer that *we* will take the oath of peace and put ourselves at their mercy to speak to them. My other colleague, at least, sees the folly in that, but she hesitates to do what we truly need to. We will never be free of their heckling until they're utterly crushed."

Sylas watches him, his stance tense. "You want to initiate a full-out war against the Unseelie."

Take the battle to the ravens. Attack them on their own ground. I shift in my seat, my wolf stirring at the thought. But I have enough instincts beyond the animal to tamp down on that eagerness.

We've struggled enough with the winter fae on our own ground. How many more Seelie will die if we press on into their own realm where they're so much more comfortable than us? How much more fiercely will they strike at us if they feel directly threatened?

I wouldn't want to speak to the Unseelie arch-lords myself, but surely *someone* should before we take the conflict to greater and bloodier heights.

"I didn't say that," Ambrose said. "Only that it seems to be the clearest avenue to the peace we'd surely all welcome. Quash them and be done with it. But that can only be achieved with a united front."

That's why he wants Tristan to replace Donovan. That's why he's so set on getting control over the rulership now. I bite back a snarl at the depths of his treason. Unity, my ass. He means to tear apart the institution he's supposed to champion.

"You know," the arch-lord goes on casually, "it might even turn out to be in your benefit if such a turn were to occur. Without the conflict with the ravens, we'd have less to lose in the grips of the curse. Securing your pet wouldn't seem quite so pressing. I'm sure in such a scenario, it wouldn't seem questionable at all to allow her to remain in your keeping."

Sylas's voice remains steady, but it comes out flat enough that I'd be wincing if the words were aimed at me. "An interesting point to raise. At the moment, I'm afraid I'm more concerned about the security of the Heart and its foremost guardians."

"Ah, as well you should be." Ambrose sweeps his arm toward the door. "You appear to have said your piece. Don't let me delay your departure."

Emotions roil in my stomach as Sylas and I return to our carriage. I have enough self-control to contain myself until we've passed beyond Ambrose's domain into an open stretch of land with no fae in sight. Then the words burst out of me.

"He tried to bargain with you to support his mutiny! He truly thought you'd turn against Arch-Lord Donovan just for a suggestion that Talia would be spared. As if a word from that mangy rat of a wolf is worth anything."

Sylas growls low in his throat. "My sentiments exactly. He certainly didn't appear to be at all put off by the fact that his intentions are no longer secret."

"You don't think he'll back down."

"No. We'll have to see what Whitt observes, but after hearing from Ambrose himself, I doubt it'll change my impressions." Sylas stares into the distance, his expression so grave it pains me. Then he meets my gaze again. "I suspect there's no way to stop *his* war than to go to war with him. See his traitorous acts exposed and his power stripped before he can topple Donovan."

I swallow hard. "And he has to know that too. He'll be twice as eager to crush *us*."

"Yes." Sylas pauses. "I believe I need to reconsider your proposal for Talia."

CHAPTER FIFTEEN

Talia

"If they bounce back when you push them, then they're ripe?" I ask to confirm, glancing up at the fae woman whose garden I've volunteered to tend.

She nods with a slanted little smile as if she finds it amusing to watch a human fumbling with fae crops, but there's nothing cruel in her expression. I just have to keep at my campaign to contribute to the pack every way I can until I graduate from amusement to real appreciation.

I only manage to identify a couple of ripe gourds before August comes ambling into the village. His pace and his stance are casual enough, but there's something serious in his golden eyes that makes me sit up straighter before he's even spoken.

"Always so eager to put yourself to work," he says, his smile all warm fondness, and then motions me up. "I'm sorry to interrupt. Come back to the castle with me?"

Whatever this is about, he doesn't want to explain the details in front of our pack-kin. I stand up, brushing the stray bits of dirt from my hands, and dip my head to the fae woman. "I'll pitch in some more when I can."

"No need to trouble yourself," she says. "But there are always new ones coming ready if you happen to stop by."

August keeps up his relaxed pace as we walk back to the castle. I'd assume that's because he doesn't want to hurry me on my wounded foot if he wasn't so quiet as well. After we've stepped into the entrance hall, he turns me to him and cups my face. He kisses me for long enough that my knees start to wobble with the rush of heat.

I reach for him, my fingers curling around the back of his neck, as if I could pull him even closer, but he pulls back with a hint of a growl as if releasing me takes some effort. His expression has gone even more serious than before.

"Sylas wants to speak with you," he says. "He's in his study."

Is that all? Although with our treacherous guests roaming around still, maybe it makes sense that the fae lord wouldn't want them knowing he had something urgent to discuss with me, whether they realize what it was or not. I definitely have no idea.

Have the things Nuldar said changed Sylas's opinion about how to handle my presence here? About how involved I should be with his pack? No one's treated me any differently since we returned, but I know how close the fae prefer to hold their cards.

I find the door to Sylas's study open. He's sitting in his usual spot behind his desk, but he gets up at my entrance. He closes the door behind me with a quick word of magic that must be to ensure our privacy and motions me to the armchairs by the room's small hearth.

The fire crackling there is more for superficial appeal than necessary heat. The summer warmth spills through the open window along with a mix of clover sweetness and piney tang.

Sylas sinks into a chair across from the one I pick. There's a deeper somberness to his movements, beyond his typical gravity, that makes my chest clench. After August's attitude downstairs, I can't help suspecting he's about to deliver bad news.

"Talia," he says, his voice gentle. "I've given this a lot of thought, and I believe it would be best for you to travel—escorted for your safety, of course—back to the human world to investigate your family connections to the fae, ideally right away."

Oh. That doesn't seem all that surprising or ominous. Maybe he was worried that I'd balk because of what happened to my most immediate family? I lift my chin, pushing back those horrific memories. "Of course. I don't think my grandmother has any idea about… any of this. I mean, I don't even know for sure if she's still alive, and she must think I'm dead, so it might be a bit complicated."

My chest tightens all over again at the thought of navigating that fraught territory. It won't be any real homecoming. Since my mother's parents lived overseas in Greece and were hesitant to travel, I only ever met them twice—they're practically strangers to me.

If they are still alive, what questions will they have about how I've returned, about what happened to my parents? How will they react if I start badgering my grandmother about *her* parents and anything special she might have noticed about her father? I'm not sure how that information would make any difference to our situation anyway.

I swallow hard and focus on more immediate considerations. "I assume *you* wouldn't want to leave the pack to go that far, considering everything that's going on. Will Whitt or August be coming with me?" I'd have figured August would have volunteered without hesitation, but he didn't act as if we were about to go on an expedition together.

Sylas folds his hands together in his lap. "Actually, I'd have Astrid join you. As eagerly as I'm sure either of my cadre-chosen would offer their protection beyond the Mists and as much as I understand you'd take reassurance from their company, I'm afraid I can't spare them for that long either."

That long? I was picturing something like a day trip. How much could there be to uncover about a fae heritage even my great-grandfather might not have known he had? *He's* definitely not around to ask at this point anyway.

"How long are you thinking the investigation would take?" I venture.

"I think it would be best if you focused on that until the full moon arrives."

My pulse hiccups. "But that's—that's two weeks away. I don't know if I'll be able to find anything at all." I don't *want* to be away from my new home and the men who've won my heart for so much time, especially not in a place that now feels way more unfamiliar than anything here. I'm not sure I remember how to act, how to talk with people like a normal human being, let alone all the practical concerns... I've never navigated that world as an adult.

Sylas's tone has stayed so even, not letting a trace of emotion show. As if it doesn't bother *him* at all that I'd be gone for all that time. As if he's already moved on in his mind to plans that require I not be here.

Is this even really about digging into my history, or is it just an excuse to send me away? Has Sylas decided that having me around is more of a liability than a benefit? Does he feel like I'm getting in the way—or that Ambrose's interest in me is drawing too much conflict down on the rest of his pack?

I was preparing myself to lose these men eventually, but I never imagined they might begin disentangling me from their lives so soon and so suddenly.

"The more time you have, the more likely you'll uncover something," Sylas says as calmly as before.

Something in me refuses to give in just like that. "It doesn't seem as if we're going to find *anything* that would stop Ambrose from trying to take me. Wouldn't it be better for your case if I stay here to show how well I'm adapting?"

I catch a hint of a smolder in his dark eye. Because I'm arguing? "Do you have so little faith in my judgment?" he asks.

"No, I just—" Tears that only seem to prove my weakness prickle behind my eyes. I look down at my hands, gathering myself.

No matter what happens with my lovers, the pack will still need me—all the Seelie do. What kind of life would it be, drifting back and forth between the worlds, not really belonging to either?

I've been working so hard to be a full member of the pack, to belong as more than just a curiosity and a burden—and a lover for however long as that part will last. I hate to think what the faded fae of the pack will think if I vanish for two weeks, leaving them to deal with the trouble my presence here has already caused.

"I want to stay," I manage to say despite the constricting sensation now winding up my throat and down to my gut. I push myself out of my chair toward Sylas, as if I can present myself to him in some way that will show how much I mean this. "I want to support the pack. I want to support *you*." I grasp his arm. "If I've made some mistake, if I've screwed something up, tell me and I'll do better. I only—"

"Talia." Sylas's voice comes out so strained it's almost a growl, the muscles in his forearm flexing beneath my fingers, and then he's tugging me the rest of the way to him, leaning forward to complete the embrace.

His hand tangles in my hair. He presses his face close to mine, the movement of his jaw brushing my cheek. "You haven't don't anything wrong, I swear it. By the Heart, if I could keep you this close to me every moment of every day, I would. But I wouldn't be any kind of lord if I refused to do what's best for you."

What's best for me. Wrapped in his arms and his earthy, smoky scent, understanding washes over me in turn.

This isn't about what I'm doing but what our enemies might do *to* me. Ambrose has tried all kinds of tactics in the last several days. Sylas is trying to protect me, like he does so often.

And I can even understand why he didn't say that to begin with, because my first reaction after I realize that is to balk even more than before. I tuck myself tighter into his embrace, forcing myself to take a moment to consider my response and whether my resistance even makes sense.

But there's one piece of the puzzle I don't have. Sylas didn't give any indication he was thinking like this after our last clash with Ambrose. Last night everything seemed normal.

Easing back just enough to see his face, I seek out his mismatched gaze. His dark eye smolders on, but I can recognize the heat as possessive passion now.

"Why are you suggesting this now?" I ask. "Did something happen that I don't know about?"

He lets out a rough sigh and frowns at the fire. "I spoke to Ambrose this morning. He made it clear enough that he has no intention of backing down until he's replaced Donovan with Tristan as arch-lord—and then launched a full-scale war against the Unseelie. I can't stand by while that happens, and *I* made that much clear. The conflict between us is only going to worsen until it's resolved. I don't want you to be wounded in the middle of it."

"I've survived plenty of wounds already."

"I know. I know you've done much for the pack and that you can handle yourself better than I'd ever have expected from one who's been through as much as you have. But this... it might be too much even for you, mighty as Whitt rightly says you are."

He strokes his thumb across my cheek, and there's no mistaking the affection in his gaze. "We have the benefit of a reasonable excuse for you to leave this world completely. How can I not take that opportunity to remove you from the dangers ahead?"

I suck my lower lip under my teeth to worry at it for a moment.

"Do you actually think anything useful could come of me looking into my family history?"

"Truthfully, no. Even if you have relatives with the same benefit in their blood, bringing more humans into this mess won't really solve our problems. I doubt there'll be any records that would shed additional light on what Nuldar already told us. As far as I'm concerned, you're welcome to see it as a vacation. Get Astrid to whisk you off to some tropical beach where you can lounge for two weeks and relax."

I waver. It obviously means a lot to Sylas to offer me this, enough that he's putting aside his own instinct to keep me close. If there's no pressure and no quest to follow, it might be nice to see the world I was born in again, to refamiliarize myself. To exist for a little while without my fears dogging me quite so closely and without the constant reminders of my weaknesses.

The fae lord offers me a quiet smile and caresses my cheek again. "Take this opportunity to relinquish the pressures of being lady of the castle for a little while. You can pretend none of the horrors of this world ever existed."

Those words make the decision for me. A pang that's all defiance reverberates through my chest.

The horrors of the fae world are real, and there is no pretending them away, especially not while people I love are still facing them. And there's so much more to this place than horrors, so many wonderful things I've found.

I may be weak in many ways, but it's here that I've also discovered just how strong I can be. I won't abandon my pack or my lovers. *Sylas* doesn't get to step away from his post, no matter how much he must hate this conflict.

"No," I say softly. "I appreciate what you're trying to do, but no. I've been able to help before. Sometimes in ways the fae pack-kin couldn't have because of the way the other fae underestimate me and the things they don't know about me. If there's any chance that

I could make a difference, I want to be here. I can take whatever pain might come with that. I knew what I was risking when I revealed what my blood can do."

Sylas bares his teeth with a hint of a snarl, but it fades into a sigh of resignation. "I won't have Astrid kidnap you and carry you off against your will. Are you *sure*? No one here would think any less of you, Talia."

I drop my gaze for a second before meeting his eyes again. "I would."

He tugs me close again, and I tip my head against his shoulder. "Wretchedly stubborn woman," he murmurs, but the remark sounds more adoring than annoyed.

"I wouldn't have made it this far if I wasn't," I have to point out. The gears in my head are already whirring away. I said I wanted to stay so I could make a difference. I'd better ensure I'm as prepared as I can be to accomplish that.

I slip my hand around Sylas's elbow. "Ambrose thinks I'm weak, just like Aerik and his cadre did, doesn't he? That gives me a bit of an advantage. Maybe there's some small magic I could learn that would help us uncover more of his plans. And if there is, I want to start learning it today."

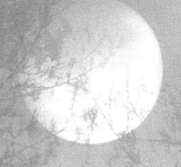

CHAPTER SIXTEEN

Sylas

The pond doesn't look at all like the sort of place where fae of importance should meet, least of all an arch-lord. The trees surrounding it cloak the spot in even thicker darkness. With the dusk, the croaking carp have risen to the surface of the water, sending ripples out from where their gaping mouths let loose the hoarse sounds they're named for.

But I suppose its lack of grandeur is exactly why Donovan suggested this spot. No one else is likely to be visiting the pond to stumble on our clandestine meeting.

I hear the rasp of his steed's hooves through the brush before I see him. He dismounts the black gelding, murmurs a word, and walks to meet me at the pond's bank. The carp are already quieting as evening deepens into night.

"I gather you spoke with Ambrose this morning," he says, without preamble but genially enough.

I doubt the other arch-lord mentioned that himself. Donovan wouldn't stand much of a chance if he didn't have sentries keeping an eye not just on his domain but all those that surround the Heart.

I incline my head. "Yes. I thought perhaps with a warning that his traitorous intentions had been observed, he might back down. Unfortunately, he left me with no doubt that he intends to see you removed from your throne, and as quickly as he can make that happen—though of course he didn't express that in any way that he could be sanctioned for. I know we expected as much already, but I didn't want to leave you unaware of the confirmation."

Donovan gazes toward the pond with a frown, clearly unhappy but not startled. He knows his colleagues' temperaments even better than I do. My attempt at dissuading Ambrose from his goal was always a long shot.

"It's good that you told me," he says after a minute. "I'm not sure exactly how I'll respond yet, but you can be sure that if it comes down to me or Ambrose, I'll see that Ambrose falls. I just wish it didn't have to end up like this." He rubs his hand over his face, and in that moment with the weight now resting on his shoulders, he looks far older than his actual age, older than his mother ever did.

"He indicated that he's particularly keen to ramp up our efforts against the Unseelie," I say. "Have they made any further moves since we last spoke?"

Donovan shakes his head. "We've heard nothing. No attacks. I'd like to think they may be completely beaten already, but I'm not that optimistic. It does worry me that we won't know what they're up to next until they enact those plans—but the alternative of taking the fight to them will see so much blood spilled on our side as well—" He cuts himself off with another shake. "But that isn't for you to worry about. Not yet, in any case."

"If there *is* any way I can be of service…"

"Yes. I appreciate the guidance and intelligence you've offered so far." He sucks in a breath. "I have no desire to see blood shed around the Heart either. It seems to me the best way to handle this is to set some sort of trap that will entice Ambrose into acting against me and then prove his treachery, and let him be sanctioned for that."

"That sounds reasonable," I say.

The young arch-lord offers me a flicker of a smile. "The exact approach will require more thought. I'll reach out to you when my plans are more solid. If anything else urgent arises, notify me at once. We can meet here again for any matters too sensitive to be conveyed in ways that might be intercepted."

I dip my head again. "As you bid, my lord. I wish I had more hope for a peaceful resolution."

I turn to go, but Donovan clears his throat meaningfully. I glance back at him.

"I can't promise anything, and if Ambrose sees reason after all there is the chance it may not come to this," he says. "But that chance seems small enough that I feel I should encourage you to prepare yourself and your pack. If we see Ambrose stripped of his title, I'll be pushing for you to take his place."

My heart stops. I knew the removal of one arch-lord would require the promoting of another lord to the throne, and obviously Donovan wouldn't advance Tristan in his cousin's stead, but somehow it had never occurred to me that I might be in the running.

It takes me a moment to recover myself and respond with appropriate gratitude. "You honor me beyond any expectation, my lord. I wouldn't have thought—when we're so recently restored to Hearthshire—"

Donovan waves off my subdued attempt at a protest. "You've proven yourself amply, both in the dignity with which you handled your banishment and your conduct in regards to Ambrose's schemes since then. The fact that you *wouldn't* have expected it, no matter how you've helped me, is exactly why I think you're the best man for the job. I have no doubt that if it comes to pass, you'll have earned it."

I can't let the nausea winding through my stomach show. I offer an even lower bow and an emphatic murmur of thanks, and watch the arch-lord leave with only a trace of relief. His departure does nothing to change the declaration he just made.

As I return to my horse, my stomach keeps roiling. The stallion stomps uneasily when I've settled onto his back, picking up on my emotions. I turn him toward Hearthshire and set him at a canter with a press of my heels, but I barely notice the landscape falling away with each magic-charged stride.

I've hardly had a chance to truly settle back in at Hearthshire. How can I wrap my head around the idea of taking over an arch-lord's domain?

In the first moment when I ride through my home's arched-tree gate, my breath hitches and my hands jerk at the reins unbidden. A horde of ghostly carriages shows before my deadened eye, spread out across the fields. I blink, and they're gone.

My pulse keeps hammering against my ribs as I ride on toward the stable. Like so often, there's no telling what that glimpse could mean. It could be a future in which we're casting off toward another new home—or when a fleet of Ambrose's soldiers have arrived here. It could have simply been an echo of a couple of weeks past when we arrived, or decades ago when we packed up to depart for the fringes. Most of those possibilities leave me unsettled.

Music carries across the fields. The glow seeping from behind the castle tells me Whitt is hosting one of his revels tonight. He hoped he might get enough intoxicating delights into our guests to loosen their tongues.

If he hadn't been so occupied, I'd have shared Donovan's revelation and the tangled reaction it's stirred up in me with my spymaster. As it is, I leave my steed with the stable-master and enter the castle alone.

The vast entrance room looms around me, my steps echoing through it in a way that feels abruptly ominous. August is likely around if I wanted to seek him out, perhaps in the basement enjoying the larger gym or entertainment room this building has to offer. But I find myself heading upstairs instead. I haven't quite admitted to myself what—or rather who—I'm pursuing before she steps out of the lavatory into the hall ahead of me.

Talia has changed into her nightgown, her feet bare beneath. Her face glows faintly ruddy from the recent washing, a few stray hairs damp along her temple. As soon as she sees me, she smiles, so easily I know the warmth is all genuine.

"That didn't take very long," she remarks.

"No, not long at all." And yet so much has changed with that brief conversation. I hesitate, uncomfortably uncertain of what I want, what I *need*—what's even reasonable to ask for. She shoulders enough burdens as it is.

Simply seeing her smile has melted a small portion of the tension inside me. Perhaps her presence is all I require to set the turmoil inside me in better order. I walk up to her. "May I sit with you for a short while?"

She blinks at me as if puzzled that I'd even ask. As if I should know she'd give up sleep and privacy and anything else I requested the moment I say the word. "Of course."

I wish I felt more certain I'd earned that level of devotion.

It feels strange, coming into her bedroom like this, sinking onto the mattress next to her as she props a pillow against the headboard for her to lean on. How many times have I arrived here much later in the night to comfort her, waking her from nightmares and soothing her in their aftermath?

The role of protector came naturally to me. To now be the one searching for comfort doesn't sit right at all.

But I'm here, and she's slipped her hand around mine and

rested her head against my shoulder as if she couldn't be happier to have me. Skies above, I can't claim that's *wrong* either.

"Was he upset?" she asks.

She means Donovan, naturally. Who else would she think has reason to be upset, when she doesn't know what news he imparted to me?

"Perhaps a little, but he wasn't surprised. The evidence has been accumulating for some time. And presumably Ambrose has made his dissatisfaction known during the meetings of the Bastion." I pause, breathing in her sap-sweet scent, absorbing the soft warmth of her body against mine. I've nearly convinced myself that this is enough, that I shouldn't interrupt her rest any longer, when she speaks, quiet but clear.

"It must be hard. For you, working with Donovan to stop Ambrose. The pack was banished because people blamed you for the attack on him—you worked so hard to prove you weren't like that, and now you might really have to fight him."

I stare down at her. I didn't say a thing to her about how I was feeling—but she's heard me talk about the past enough times. How can I be startled that she'd put the pieces together?

She knows me better than I've given her credit for.

There is one thing she doesn't know, but with her gentle words of compassion echoing through my mind, that spills out too. "It is. But more than that—Donovan has said that if Ambrose must be replaced, he wants me to become arch-lord."

Talia raises her head to meet my eyes. Her fingers tighten where they're twined with mine. "And you're not sure you'd want the responsibility?"

"I'd gladly serve my Seelie brethren however I can. And the position would come with benefits for the rest of the pack beyond anything they enjoy here. But..." I can't stop my gaze from sliding away toward the wall across from us. "Everything you said is true. I've spent decades rallying against the perception that my pack and

I are tainted by association with Isleen's actions. It *horrified* me that she and her family would turn against our rulers and attempt to displace one—and now I find myself doing the same thing."

Talia makes a rough sound in her throat. "It's *not* the same thing. Had Ambrose made any move against you or their family— or anyone else—back then?"

"Not that I have any knowledge of. From what Isleen did say and show me when she was still trying to convince me to support her lesser efforts, they chose Ambrose only because one of his family's former pack-kin had joined her mother's pack and shared inside information that gave them an edge." A bitter chuckle fills my throat. "I know when Donovan's mother fell so suddenly, they were tempted to start over focusing on *him* as a potentially weaker opponent."

"Then they attacked Ambrose's pack unprovoked, because they were greedy and wanted more power for themselves. You're trying to defend another arch-lord that Ambrose is betraying. It's not as if you stepped in so that you'd win the arch-lord spot."

"No. But to others, it might appear that way, especially if Donovan is able to follow through on his promise." My deadened eye brings up no images of that possible future as I speak, but I can imagine well enough without it the wary looks and scathing remarks that would follow in my tracks.

"Well, anyone who'd think that would need to get their head checked," Talia says firmly. "What else can you do? They're both arch-lords, and you can't support both of them. Either you help Donovan and do your best to stop Ambrose from hurting him, or you refuse to help and you're making it easier for the real traitor to attack a different arch-lord. Wouldn't that be worse? It's not your fault that protecting one arch-lord means you have to go up against another."

No, the only person whose fault it is would be Ambrose, for starting this traitorous campaign to begin with. What Donovan offered doesn't change that.

It's my duty to protect the rulership of the Heart from all threats I become aware of, even if those threats come from within. I've never doubted that. Donovan's unexpected declaration simply set me so off-balance I lost track of what led me to this point.

"There isn't any choice," I agree. "I have to step up for Donovan, or I'd be going against everything I stand for."

"Exactly." Talia raises her hand to trace the line of my jaw. "You always do everything you can to make things better for your pack, for the rest of the Seelie—for everyone *except* yourself. If a pitiful human who's only known you for a few months can see that, then there shouldn't be a single fae who can't."

Her tone is light, but the insult in her words rankles me anyway. A growl creeps into my voice unbidden. "You're not pitiful. You're anything but pitiful."

If those who disdain her could see how she stood up to me this afternoon, insisting on standing by my pack—no, *our* pack, because it's hers now too. Looking for every way she could help without bowing one bit to the fear she must feel.

And now, making sense of the turmoil inside me so deftly, cutting straight through to the heart of the matter without the preconceptions and condemnations that clouded my own thoughts. She hasn't been tainted by the twisted politics of this world, even as she's taken it in and formed such a coherent understanding.

The strength in her cuts straight through to *my* heart. It nearly tore me apart just thinking of sending her off beyond the boundaries of the Mist with Astrid. My wolf wanted to thrash Donovan for suggesting with the kindest of intentions that he take her from me. She's asked for so little in her time with me, yet she's claimed so much of my respect and devotion.

And my love.

I can admit that to myself now, can't I? This burning desire to have her with me every moment, the awe that fills my chest with every bit of might she shows, the fierceness that sears through me at the merest thought of anyone harming her… I can give it its proper name. What kind of man would I be if I denied it?

I love her. This precious, astonishing, irrepressible human woman. The truth of that fact blooms inside me with the acknowledgment of it, and a fresh twinge of uneasiness follows in its wake.

I lift Talia's chin to kiss her softly, reverently, and leave my head bowed close to hers. "Thank you. You reminded me of everything I needed to remember. Sleep well, lady of the castle."

The title brings a bright smile to her lips. As she scoots lower on the bed, pulling the covers over her, I force myself to walk away. When I've shut the door behind me, my breath courses out of me in a harsh rush. I close my eyes, willing back the new tangle of conflicting emotions.

The last time I loved a woman, I let the anguish that came with it consume me and saw everything I care about nearly destroyed. Isleen's betrayal of our vows with that unknown man wounded me so deeply I walled off my connection to her—and failed in my duty to my pack and my rulers. If I hadn't let my heart override my sense of responsibility, I'd have known how far she meant to go. Even if I couldn't have stopped her, I might have protected my pack from decades of banishment.

Will the love I feel now for Talia do either of us any good?

If it doesn't, that's my failing, not hers. I push myself forward, away from the painful memories of the past.

Whether it somehow conspires to become my downfall or not, I'll move the stars before I let it ruin the woman it's an honor to call our lady.

CHAPTER SEVENTEEN

Talia

When August asks the pack members assisting in the kitchen to fetch some more duskapples for the breakfast pastries, I can't help thinking the situation can't be quite that urgent. We haven't even started making the dough.

He waits a few beats after they've headed out the door and then says in a low voice, "Sylas told me you're wanting to learn a new true name."

Ah. I nod, grinding the cloves he gave me with a pestle. As they crumble into a fine brown powder, their crisply pungent scent tickles my nose.

August continues shelling the eggs he boiled, but I get the sense his shoulders have tensed just slightly. "Did you have anything in particular in mind?"

I hope he doesn't think my suggestion to Sylas was a complaint about the lessons he *has* been giving me. "I know I still don't have the best handle on light," I say quickly, keeping my voice similarly quiet. "It makes sense that we haven't moved on from that yet. I just thought, with everything happening—if there's something I can work on that I'm more likely to be able to use to help figure out Ambrose's plans and how to stop them, I should switch focus to that for now."

There's definitely something a little awkward about August's stance even as he smiles down at me. I can't quite put my finger on what, though, so I don't know how to ask if something's the matter without making things even more awkward. Maybe it has nothing to do with me at all; maybe he's just stressed out about the situation with Ambrose too. Why wouldn't he be?

He flicks the last egg onto the platter and cocks his head in consideration. "I'm not sure which of the simple ones would be best for that in a way it'd make sense for you to use. Why don't you give some thought to the exact strategies you think you'd want to try, and then we'll see what might enhance those?"

"Okay." My spirits deflate. I wanted to get started as soon as possible. But it *was* a bit much for me to expect him to know precisely how to teach a human with limited magic how to go up against an arch-lord effectively.

What would it have been useful for me to do when we were at Donovan's banquet, or in the forest when the tuskcat attacked, that I could have done if I'd had the right magic?

I mull that question over through the rest of the breakfast preparations, but none of the ideas that occur to me fit the two necessary criteria of being something I have any hope of actually pulling off with just a short span of training and being subtle enough that I won't give away my secret magical ability to our enemies. I'm still stewing on the subject as I sit down at the vast dining table with Sylas and August.

I don't think any of us are expecting Whitt to show up after last night's extended revel, but just after Sylas thanks the kitchen assistants for their work and they head out, the spymaster saunters into the dining room. Or maybe "sways" would be more accurate. He's not staggering, but there's a waver to his steps that gives the impression his balance isn't what it should be. He flops down into the chair across from August and rubs his weary-looking eyes.

The music from the revel was still filtering through the castle walls when I got up to use the lavatory in the early hours of the morning. He can't have had more than a couple of hours of sleep. Although, knowing Whitt, it's difficult to say how much his current state might be fatigue and how much that he hasn't yet slept off whatever drinks and drugs he enjoyed overnight.

Sylas gives him a baleful glance. "This breakfast isn't so vital that I required you crawl out of bed to attend it."

Whitt appears to restrain a yawn and plucks a duskapple pastry from its platter. "Perhaps I'm practicing better self-discipline for when I may be serving a higher authority."

A soft growl escapes Sylas, though his tone stays mild. "That's hardly enough of a certainty for us to be discussing it so casually."

The other man snorts. "I assume everyone in the room already knows about your prospective surge in prestige. I promise not to sing it from the rooftop before it's finalized."

Whitt's speaking in his usual jaunty tone, a glint dancing in his eyes, but there's a sharpness to that tone and the glint that prickles at me. Obviously Sylas told him about Donovan's offer. Is Whitt bothered that Sylas might be made arch-lord? It'd mean a major increase in prestige not just for Sylas but the whole pack, including his cadre.

But it still might have rubbed Whitt the wrong way somehow. I remember the rawness in his voice when he admitted that it bothered him sometimes that Sylas is automatically granted so many more benefits than he is. I can't blame him for that. It isn't his fault his parents didn't pass on slightly more of their fae heritage to him, that his mother didn't have as much fae blood as Sylas's did in the first place.

I've just never seen him express anything close to those feelings in front of Sylas before.

The fae lord eyes his spymaster for a moment longer, but when Whitt switches to swooning over his pastry, Sylas appears to decide there's nothing worth prodding him about, at least not right now.

I shift in my chair, the quail egg I've just swallowed dropping uncomfortably into my stomach. Is *everyone* in the castle out of sorts today? If there's something in the air, I hope a swift wind takes care of it soon.

Whitt is halfway through his third pastry when a leaf flutters in to him on a much smaller breeze than I was imagining. He plucks it out of the air, glances at whatever message it holds, and gets up while popping the rest of his breakfast into his mouth.

"Matters to attend to," he says to Sylas, the words only slightly muddled by his mouthful. "I'll report back to you as I'm able, oh extra-glorious leader."

"I look forward to it," Sylas replies dryly, but his gaze follows Whitt as the other man heads out the door. He turns back to me, taking in the plate in front of me which I haven't added any more food to for the better part of five minutes now. The subtle tensions around me dulled my appetite.

"And what will our lady be occupying herself with today?" he asks.

Brainstorming spell ideas? I'm not sure lying around on my bed or the entertainment-room sofa is going to be all that inspiring, though. I nibble at my lower lip. "I guess I'll go see what needs to be done in the village today." I can't forget my other goals. The pack still needs to see me as a real member. I might get some ideas while I'm working with them.

Sylas nods. "I'll see that Astrid is ready to accompany you."

Shadow me, he means. But considering her shadowing prevented me from taking a worse injury when the tuskcat attacked the other day, I can't really complain.

When the dishes are cleared, I give August a quick kiss—which he returns enthusiastically enough to dissolve a little of my uneasiness—and walk with Sylas to the front door, because apparently he thinks I need an escort even to cross the entrance hall.

Astrid is waiting just outside. She beckons me over, looking vaguely amused with her current duty. At least I don't get the impression *she* thinks I'm in dire need of babysitting.

"No escaped sheep or rare mushrooms to gather today," she says. "I think most of our pack-kin are taking a break."

"Well, there are always the basic daily tasks, if anyone could use a hand." I look toward the gardens around the stump-like houses. Some of them might need watering.

Water—that's one of the basic true words, isn't it? August mentioned the elements and common metals, plants, and animals as the simplest ones. Although I don't know what all is common here. And somehow I don't think drenching Ambrose with water is going to be a very useful information-gathering skill, as much as I might enjoy doing it.

As I mull that over, a patch of bright color slipping by the farthest houses catches my eye. It's one of Harper's vivid dresses. She darts across the field, passing out of my view behind the castle.

She looked like she had some business she was eager to get to. Maybe I can offer to lend a hand with that. It feels like I haven't seen her around quite as much since the day we tracked down the escaped sheep.

I limp over as quickly as I can, thankful all over again for the boots she made for me that give me the extra stability of Sylas's brace without making me stick out any more than I already do. Astrid follows a few steps behind. I come around the side of the castle just as Harper has reached the edge of the forest beyond Whitt's revel area.

She's stopped there, but I stop too, because she isn't alone now.

One of the daughters from Ambrose's pack—the middle one—is standing amid the trees. They're talking, their heads bent close, but they're too far away for me to make out even a hint of their voices, let alone what they're saying.

I stay by the edge of the castle, hidden by the wall beside me and its shadow, watching. The uneasiness inside me rises up again, though I still can't explain exactly why.

Harper hands the other woman a bundle of fabric large enough that it could contain two or three of her dresses. The middle daughter smiles thinly and makes some remark that brings Harper's shoulders up, though only for a second. Then our guest swivels on her heel and strides off toward the guest quarters.

Astrid hums to herself. "What do you make of that?"

There's a perfectly obvious explanation. "Harper must have offered them dresses as a gift. She'd be hoping they'll appreciate the gesture enough to talk up her skills to other high-ranking fae." But I don't like the way the other woman smiled or how drawn Harper's face looks as she turns away from the trees.

She doesn't look hopeful but concerned. Ambrose's pack-kin better not have said anything insulting to her.

I'm about to hurry over to make sure she's okay when a much larger commotion emerges from the far forest. A carriage drifts into view, moving sluggishly between the trees. Our guests' carriage, with the whole family on board. The middle daughter must have hurried straight to it. I hadn't realized they were leaving.

Neither had my men, I suspect, because Whitt is walking alongside the carriage, talking with the husband and wife. He looks more animated than he did at breakfast, all traces of exhaustion gone, but I think I can read a certain amount of agitation in his supposedly careless gestures.

Astrid draws closer behind me. "Hmm. Interesting timing after our lord went to see theirs yesterday."

It is. Did Ambrose decide that he doesn't trust Sylas to treat his pack-kin well after Sylas showed he's aware of the arch-lord's treachery? Or is this some new phase in his plot? Even though the summer air is warm around me, I find myself rubbing my arms.

We aren't the only ones who've noticed the family's sudden departure. Brigit and Elliot wander over, hesitating near us as if they're not sure they want to draw the guests' attention.

Brigit's mouth twists. She glances at me and then at Elliot. "We never managed to dig up any other useful info, and now they're taking off."

"We helped Lord Sylas as much as we could," Elliot says, but he's frowning too.

"What you did find out was really important," I point out. Donovan might already be on the outs if we hadn't uncovered the false thefts. "And maybe there'll be other opportunities for us to help. We just have to... to wait and see what Ambrose does next."

As I speak, my stomach coils into a knot. I don't know how *I'm* going to help if there are no leads here in our domain to follow. It's not as if I can go sneaking all the way out to Ambrose's domain on my own.

Harper has lingered by the spot where she spoke to the middle daughter. When she looks our way, Brigit waves. My friend seems to balk for a moment before heading over. She glances back to where the carriage is drifting away past the castle. I can faintly hear Sylas's low baritone where he must have come out the front to see the guests off.

"I've got to get back to work," Harper says quickly, only slowing when she reaches us, not halting. "My—my mother needs another set of hands." She hurries onward, her gaze catching mine for only an instant with a brief flash of a smile.

I wish I knew what Ambrose's pack-kin said to her. If I had fae senses, would I have been able to pick up their voices?

Is there a spell that would let me?

The thought sparks in my head with an eager jolt. As all four of us meander back around the castle to watch the carriage glide through the gate, the sense of possibility expands, lighting up my mind more and more.

Yes, that just might be it. For a start, anyway.

August is standing with Sylas and Whitt just outside the castle's main door. "Well, I may as well put the pack through their paces," he says to his brothers, and starts toward the village.

I hustle ahead of the others as quickly as I can, catching him before he's called out to his trainees. "Can I talk to you just for a second?"

His head jerks up, his gaze flicking past me and then softening when he confirms that Astrid hasn't slackened off in her guard duties. "Sure. What is it, Sweetness?"

I tug him back toward the castle, waiting until we're within its walls to speak. "Sound waves travel through the air. You said air is one of the basic true words. If I could master that, would I be able to amplify sounds—so I could overhear conversations and things like that?"

August's eyes widen. I hold myself back from fidgeting as he considers. His lips curve upward, not with quite as excited a response as I might have hoped for, but with definite approval.

He rests his hand on the top of my head with an affectionate sweep of his thumb. "I think that just might be possible. Let me give our pack-kin a good work out, and then we'll see what we can do."

CHAPTER EIGHTEEN

August

"It helps if you imagine a rushing sensation, like the wind moving over you, while you're saying the word," I remind Talia. "But don't get frustrated if it takes some time. You know you'll get there eventually."

Talia nods where she's sitting on the gym's mat of moss across from me, her legs crossed and her eyes closed as she feels out the true word I gave her during our training session yesterday. A guilty sort of hope twists in my chest.

I hope it takes a *long* time for her to get any grip on this word. At least long enough that there'll no longer be a need for any of us to be working against an arch-lord.

She wants so badly to contribute, though. How could I refuse to teach her?

I can't help watching the rise of her breasts beneath her dress as she inhales slow and deep, but the instinct that rises up inside me isn't lust but protectiveness. Her collarbone juts so delicately against her pale skin. The strap of the dress doesn't cover all of the scars left by Aerik's fangs.

What kind of lover would I be to see that and even think of letting her step into harm's way again?

"*Briss-gow-aft*," she murmurs with her exhale, keeping the syllables soft and sibilant the way I modeled for her. Another twinge of guilt joins my reluctance. I taught her right, but for more than a moment there, I was tempted to say it just a little wrong so there'd be no hope of her mastering it at all.

That kind of deception would have been beneath me too. There has to be something I can do, though. Sylas said she refused to return to her world with Astrid... Is there some way *I* could leave with her without jeopardizing the pack, for long enough that she might feel comfortable staying even after I returned? Would she be willing to venture back into the realm of humans if she had me by her side instead?

Even if she would for her own sake, I know she'd ask about my duties to the pack. We're on the verge of war. I'd need a convincing argument for why I could shirk my other responsibilities. I'd need to be sure I *wasn't* shirking them.

She lets out another breath. "*Briss-gow-aft*." The true name for air slips from her lips—and the hem of her dress stirs just slightly where it's pooled over her legs.

I flinch inwardly. *No.* Not already. But Talia's eyes have popped open. She's staring down at her dress with a smile stretching her lips.

"I think I did it," she says, offering me a brilliant smile I'm not sure I deserve right now, her lovely eyes aglow with awe. "I felt the air move, just a little."

I make myself smile back. "It's a start. Getting to the point where you can shape the air enough to propel sound waves will take a little more work."

"I know. But at least I'm getting somewhere. Yesterday nothing happened at all." She runs her hands over her knees, her gaze drifting away, her eyes going distant in thought. "Of course, I still have to figure out when I'd actually get to use the skill once I've practiced enough. I guess the banquets and balls happen pretty often? Could we host one here and invite all the arch-lords? That would be a good excuse to give *everyone* a chance to observe Ambrose and his people."

"I'm not sure he'd risk making any moves or revealing his intentions while in our territory," I say. "And Sylas may not want to give him the opportunity to do so in case he would after all."

"True. But one of the other packs might host one like Donovan did. The fae all know who I am now. His pack-kin might be less cautious talking about things when I'm around than they are with other fae since they won't expect me to be able to hear as well—or to use magic to enhance my hearing. If I can find some excuse to be kind of close to their carriage or somewhere else they might talk privately, but not close enough that they'd believe I could listen in…"

And if they caught her? My muscles have already tensed just picturing it. "You don't need to go that far," I say. "If the opportunity comes up, and you don't have to put yourself in danger to take it, that's one thing. You shouldn't go out of your way to have anything to do with Ambrose and his pack."

Talia returns her bright gaze to me. "But I might not get a chance if I don't go out of my way. I won't try anything *stupid*. They don't think I can do much of anything anyway."

"I just—" I grope for a different tactic. I love how Talia's strength and confidence have grown, but that strength and confidence are exactly what won't let her back down from a challenge, especially one that she thinks could help us. The last thing I want to do is diminish her abilities. She gets enough of that from the fae outside our domain.

"I've been training the whole pack," I continue after a moment.

"Whitt already has several pack-kin who know how to slip around and gather information for him. Whatever needs to be found out, we'll find it."

"But every little bit helps, doesn't it? There've been things I could do that no one else could before."

There have—and I've hated every one of those moments. When we had to stand back and watch Aerik and his cadre saunter up to her in that cage, when she held out her arm so Sylas could collect her blood in the Oakmeet kitchen… My hands start to clench at the memories. "If something like that comes up, then of course—but *we* should be the ones taking the risks until that happens."

The joy in Talia's face dims. She studies me, a furrow creasing her brow. "You don't want me to get involved."

I grimace. "I don't want you to get hurt, Sweetness. I'd rather take a thousand blows than see one land on you."

"But I still might get hurt if we can't stop Ambrose. Everything will be so much worse."

"And that's why Sylas and Whitt and I—and the rest of the pack—will make sure it doesn't come to that. You shouldn't have to face any of those threats."

"I *want* to. I'm part of this pack too. The whole reason I stayed here is—" She halts, her posture stiffening. "You've been acting a little strange since we talked about learning a new true name. No—you were tense right before Sylas talked to me the other day too… Are you upset that I didn't leave like he tried to convince me I should?"

My throat tightens at her obvious distress. "No, of course not. You have no idea how hard it was even making the suggestion to Sylas—"

She flinches. "Wait, it was *your* idea? You told Sylas that he should figure out a way to get me away from here?"

"Talia…" I can't deny it. I'd have to lie. But she's got to understand— "I only thought it'd be safer for you that way. It's my job to protect everyone in this domain, and Ambrose has already managed to hurt you more than once even with me so close by..."

I'm bracing myself for anger, but the reaction that comes over her is far worse. Her shoulders sag, her body withdrawing in on itself with a tremble of her chin. She clenches her jaw, blinking hard against a shimmer of tears. Agony wrenches through me.

I did that. *I* hurt her. The sight of her pain makes my fangs and claws ache to emerge, as if I could defend her from this offense with them. "Talia," I say again, my voice coming out hoarse.

"I got through Ambrose's tricks all right," she says before I can go on. She swipes at her eyes. "Do you really think I'm so useless that I'm better off not even in the same *world* as the rest of you? I thought— You've been training me so that I *can* fight, whatever ways I can—"

My hand twitches toward her, but I catch it, not sure she'd even want me touching her right now, as much as every impulse in me is hollering at me to hold her. "It isn't you. I think you're amazing. Heart help me, Talia, I love you, and I can't stand the thought that something might happen to you because I let you stay in harm's way."

She stares at me. "You're not 'letting' me do anything. It isn't your choice. I decide what I do. Isn't that—isn't that how it's supposed to be? You go off on plans that could get you *killed*, and I'm scared you won't make it back, but I don't tell you that you can't do it."

"That's not— I dedicated myself—" I stop, because I don't actually have a good response. I simply hadn't thought about it the way she put it before.

I *have* risked my life more than once since Talia came into it. No doubt I will dozens of times more over the course of that life, if it lasts as long as I'd like. If she asked me to hang back, I'd have to refuse. But as much as I'd say it's because I have a duty, because I swore to defend my pack and my lord with everything I have in me… that was my choice.

How can I say she should get to live freely and then try to hold her back? How can I tell her that her choice is wrong when it's the same choice *I* made?

"I didn't mean it that way," I finish weakly.

Talia's voice drops. "Being with you, with Sylas and Whitt, and with this pack is the only good thing that's happened to me in almost ten years. I love you, and I love it here. It feels *right* to fight for that every way I can. I know I can't contribute as much as you or any of the fae can, but I think I can offer at least a little bit…"

The hesitance creeping into her voice nearly kills me. I give in to the urge unfurling inside me, pulling her into my arms and onto my lap, enfolding her with my body as if I can hug the damage I've done away.

As hurt as she was, she leans into the embrace. I'm lucky she's not pushing me away.

I nuzzle her hair, my throat constricting. "I'm sorry. You've offered a *lot*. I shouldn't have tried to stop you just because I'm worried about you. That's really all it is. I—"

No, it's more than that, isn't it? The horror that stabs through me at the thought of Ambrose or his kin getting their paws on this woman echoes that other loss I try not to think about. The image flickers through my mind of my mother's crumpled body, and I close my eyes, tucking Talia's head even closer to me.

They might both have been human, but their situations aren't the same. I need to remember that. My mother never asked to stay among the fae. No one gave her any choice about it. What happened to her is on my father and all the other fae who failed to save her.

But Talia—Talia is sticking with us by her own will, devoting herself to this pack because she wants to.

I have to respect her choice, no matter how much it unnerves me. If I treat her like a victim, then what am I doing but turning her into one all over again?

I shift her in my arms and bring my hand to her cheek, holding her gaze. "You are so strong, so capable, and no one should make you feel like you're not, least of all me. Whatever you think of that you can do to help us against Ambrose, I'll support you. Forgive me?"

A glint of tears comes into her eyes again, but from her tentative smile, I think they're happier ones this time. "It's okay. I know you only wanted to protect me. I don't want to get in the way or make the situation worse."

"You won't do that. You wouldn't let yourself do that. I've seen how careful you are. I just have to accept that beneath all that sweetness there's quite a fighter in there." I brush my lips to hers, my voice softening. "I'm proud of you. For holding your own, for speaking up instead of giving in. I was wrong, and you had every right to say so. If I ever go off on a tangent like that again, feel free to wallop me upside the head as well."

An adorable little snort slips out of her. She runs her fingers into my hair, sending a delicious shiver over my scalp. "Somehow I don't think a wallop from me would have much impact."

I rumble and tug her mouth back to mine. "You *always* have an impact on me."

I don't know if there's any way I can melt any lingering hurt by cuddling her close and kissing her with every bit of tenderness in me, but I'm happy to try. And once I've started, it's hard to remember we had any other aims we meant to fulfill downstairs. My mind wanders to a very enjoyable time we had one other afternoon in the old gym, the first time Talia showed me she could conjure light.

Oh, right. As enjoyable as this is, I should probably get back to her practice with air. Otherwise I'll be keeping her from her intentions in a totally different way.

I kiss her once more, drawing it out and reveling in the softness of her lips, and then peck a trail across her cheek to her jaw. How can I resist taking a little nibble there? Talia's chest hitches with an eager gasp, and I nuzzle her neck, a grin crossing my mouth and the last of my guilt fading away.

"You know," I murmur against her skin, "there's probably some emotion or sensation that will help you master air, just like there was with bronze and light. Maybe we should experiment."

She hums with amusement. "An interesting plan." But she tips her head to the side to give me better access to her neck. I flick my tongue across the crook of her shoulder, feeling the giddy leap of her pulse. Unfortunately, that gives me another idea that doesn't involve staying quite this entangled.

I ease back and offer my hand to help her to her feet. "Let's see what happens if we can get you airborne—literally."

CHAPTER NINETEEN

Talia

It turns out the best way for me to connect with my sense of the air is to take a flying leap while I speak the true name. I'm really hoping it won't be long before I get to the point that I can just recall the exhilarating sensation of soaring through the air in those few moments before I come to earth, because there aren't a whole lot of ways to get a good lift when August is otherwise occupied.

I tried a few jumps on my own, but when I'm high enough to really get some wind moving around me, I can't land all that gracefully without help. My third and final attempt making use of the chair in my bedroom resulted in a jabbing pain in my warped foot that hasn't quite subsided.

I came outside thinking that the natural wind might give me enough extra sensation that I don't have to jump far. But I have to make sure I'm not too obvious, or the pack will wonder if I've gotten into the cavaral syrup and decided I'm a bird again.

If they heard me speak the syllables, they'd know just how much

August is teaching me. I've come to trust many of my pack-kin, but a human who can work true names might make a little too enticing gossip for every one of them to keep it to themselves.

I eye the shadowy line of the forest. I could probably find some logs to hop off there without being in full view. But of course while the men of the castle are busy, I have my sort-of bodyguard sticking close by, and Sylas hasn't thought it was wise to let even Astrid know just how much I'm capable of. Argh.

Can I come up with a reasonable excuse for wanting to jump off logs while muttering to myself—and is there any chance the warrior won't notice when I do provoke a little movement in the air? Or should I forget about magic for now and see how I can pitch in around the village?

I haven't quite finished my internal debate when Harper emerges from her house and heads toward me, her sleek, pale hair swaying around her face. She's hugging something to her chest, and her always over-large eyes look outright sad.

"Hey," I say when she reaches me, with a smile I hope comes across as welcoming. I was starting to get the impression that she'd decided a human friend was too boring for her adventurous tastes. It's been days since she said more than a brief greeting to me.

But then, I don't know what might have been keeping her busy. She could be getting orders for dresses from prominent fae from all across the summer realm already.

"Hi." She tugs her hair behind one softly pointed ear in a nervous gesture. "I'm sorry we haven't gotten to spend much time together lately. I—I'd still like to see more of the domain with you when we have the chance. It's just been a strange time."

Relief washes through me. "It has. That's all right. A lot's been going on."

"I made a new dress for you. I thought I should do something." Harper thrusts the folded fabric she was clutching toward me. "I hope you like it."

As I let the delicate fabric unfurl, she twists her hands together in front of her, her expression tensed as if she's afraid I'll throw it back in her face. Why would she be worried about that? Around the castle, I've been wearing plain dresses like the one I have on today—it's not as if my fashion standards are terribly high.

And her latest construction is as breathtaking as ever. Currents of aquatic teal ripple together with lacy stitching like seafoam, a line of tiny silver shell-beads ringing the neckline.

"It's gorgeous," I say. "Are you sure—you've already given me two dresses, and it's not like I'm getting that many opportunities to show them off. I know how important it is to you to catch the eye of people from other packs."

Harper shakes her head vehemently. "You deserve it. I mean, unless you don't like it…"

"I *love* it." But she still doesn't look happy. I gather the fabric in my arms, wondering if the hissing sound the silky texture makes is what ocean waves actually sound like, and study my friend. "Is everything okay? I really wasn't upset that we hadn't had much of a chance to talk lately."

"Oh, yes—yes, I'm just glad everything is good." She smiles then, wide and maybe a little tight, but I'm not sure if I'm reading too much into things now. "I'd love to see it on you whenever you want to wear it, to make sure it doesn't need any adjusting."

"Of course. I'll try it on right now." I don't have anywhere fancy to go, but if it'll reassure her that I appreciate the gesture, that doesn't matter.

I head into the castle, Astrid at my heels. She hangs back in the hallway outside my bedroom, turning to chat with one of the pack members who's been helping keep the massive building clean and orderly. At least Sylas trusts that I'm not going to meet some dire fate in my own room.

The dress shivers over my skin, cool like water too. When I

turn, the skirt appears to froth around my legs. I'll definitely have to wear this the next time I do have a special occasion.

On the way back downstairs, we run into August just outside the kitchen. He takes me in with an awed widening of his eyes that makes my heart skip giddily. "Look at you," he says.

As he steps closer, Astrid draws back through a nearby doorway to give us a little more privacy. August takes the opportunity to plant a kiss on me that leaves me even giddier.

"Are you sure you're not actually a sea nymph?" he teases. "You'd put the real ones to shame." Then he kisses my cheek and drops his voice lower. "How's your practicing going?"

To my relief, he shows no hint of any of yesterday's hesitation over what I'm trying to learn and why. I think we've put that behind us.

"Slowly," I say. "But it's coming along. It's better when you can help."

"Hmm. I bet I could fit in a training session after lunch."

I beam at him. "That would be wonderful if you can."

Sylas strides down the hall, back from whatever responsibilities he was attending to this morning. He slows at the sight of us, his expression warming. "All dressed up and lovely as ever. What's the occasion?"

"There isn't one." I gesture vaguely in the direction of the pack village. "Harper made it for me. I should probably get back to her. She wanted to see how it looks on me."

But even as I say that, something in me balks. I pause, turning over my memories of my friend's strange anxiety. Of the way she looked after she talked to the women from Ambrose's pack—of the fact that she was getting friendly with them at all.

My stomach twists. I'm probably being unfair, and maybe a little jealous that she's been more interested in chatting with other fae rather than me. But still… Something felt off. It's not as if she'll ever know if I simply ask Sylas— "Is there anything odd about it? I mean, it looks fine to me, but if there's any magic in it or something, I wouldn't be able to tell."

Sylas frowns and closes the distance between us. My face starts to heat, expecting him to say it's a completely normal dress and why would I think otherwise? But he pauses in his inspection, leaning in like he might if he were going to kiss my jaw, though his eyes are fixed on the dress's neckline.

He touches one of the silver shell-shaped beads and then another, a quiet word passing from his lips. His eyes narrow. His mismatched gaze jerks back to mine.

"What else did Harper say?"

My pulse stutters. "Not much. That she was sorry we haven't been able to spend much time together. She—She seemed like she'd been getting friendly with the daughters from that family from Ambrose's pack, but I never saw her do anything *wrong*."

A growl comes into his voice. "I suppose we'll find out how much of the wrongness she's aware of, then. First—"

He speaks another word. The shells all shiver and melt into shapeless blobs. The tension gripping his face makes my gut clench even harder. "What *is* wrong?"

"I think we'd better have the responsible party with us to get the full answers to that question." Sylas glances between me and August. "Did either of you say anything since Talia put on the dress that we wouldn't want Ambrose to know?"

I cross my arms over my chest, hugging myself. "I just came downstairs. We—" We talked about my magical training. But I knew Astrid was nearby—even though we were talking quietly, I was still careful. "We didn't say anything specific, I don't think."

August shakes his head. "It was only about the skills she's been practicing," he says to Sylas. "The self-defense?"

Which is technically true, since learning magic is part of protecting myself, and there wouldn't be any reason for Ambrose to think we meant anything else, right? I'm still not sure what's going on.

Sylas makes a brusque gesture toward the hall. "Go to the audience room, both of you. We'll have Whitt join us too—and I'd better see about Harper."

He stalks toward the entrance room, radiating lordly fury. I turn to August. "Do you have any idea what he found?"

August grasps my hand. "No, but it sounds like we'll find out soon enough. Come on. Have you seen the audience room before?"

"No. Was there one in Oakmeet?"

"We didn't bother. It's mostly for formality, and we weren't expecting to conduct much important business while we were there. If Sylas needed to speak with the pack-kin on a serious matter, he did it at their homes or in the entrance room—or in his study if he trusted them enough. But a lord is supposed to have a place that expresses his authority."

He guides me down the hall past the staircase to a room at the far end, a wing of the castle that didn't exist in Oakmeet's condensed replica. With a magic-tinged word from August, the door swings open.

I'm not sure the room has been used at all since we returned to Hearthshire, but Sylas has clearly ensured it was cleaned. The wooden walls and floor seem to gleam even more vibrantly than the rest of the castle. A thick red rug with a violet leaf pattern runs from the doorway down the length of the room to a tall seat of a darker wood. It's plated with gold panels with etchings of forest scenes, the seat covered with a layer of moss.

Crimson drapes tumble from the walls on either side of the throne-like chair. As we walk toward it, several glowing orbs gleam brighter on the high ceiling above us, set in a pattern like a petaled flower.

Several embroidered cushions like the ones Whitt sets out for his revels lie in a stack by the curtains. August grabs one and puts it on the floor near the throne's foot. He stations himself just behind it, next to the throne, and motions for me to sit on the cushion. He's put on a stern expression, but he caresses my hair as if to say he's still here with me, no matter what.

Thankfully for my nerves, it doesn't take long for the others to appear. Whitt saunters in first, shooting a quizzical glance our way, to which August offers an uncertain grimace. The spymaster takes in my dress and ambles over to the other side of the throne. He's just taken his spot there when Sylas marches through the doorway, nudging Harper ahead of him.

If my friend looked nervous before, now I'd say she's outright terrified. She's tangled her fingers in the strands of her hair just below her shoulder, and her back stays rigid as she walks along the rug to halt in front of the throne. Her eyelids twitch with frantic blinks. Any color her normally cream-pale skin used to contain has drained away. She clutches her hair tighter, watching Sylas settle himself on his seat.

The fae lord's dark eye blazes with contained ferocity. He keeps his usual steady tone, but there's an edge to it that demands answers. "Harper of Hearthshire, born of Oakmeet, do you know why I've called you here?"

"I—I'm not sure," she says faintly.

"Did you construct the dress that Talia is currently wearing?"

Her gaze skims over me. I think she stiffens even more when she must notice the misshapen shells. "I did."

"Every part of it, by your own hand? The fabric, the embellishments?"

She pauses, her mouth working. I know the fae don't lie if they can help it. It damages their connection to the Heart, the source of any magical power they wield.

Harper takes a quavering breath. "I made every part of it except —except the beads, my lord."

Sylas leans forward, his pose like a wolf about to pounce. "And where did you get the beads then, my pack-kin?"

"They were a gift. I thought they worked well with that fabric."

"A gift from whom?"

"From—from—" A quiver runs through her, and she ducks her head, covering it with her hands. Her voice spills out of her faster, just shy of a wail. "I'm sorry. They said no one would notice. They said it wouldn't really matter unless— I thought it would be fine. I didn't want to hurt anyone."

A chill trickles through me, pooling in my belly. She must have realized she *could* have hurt me. But she made the dress and gave it to me, encouraged me to wear it, despite that.

Sylas repeats his question, his tone even darker than before. "Who gave you the beads that were shaped like shells?"

"Lili and Irabel of Dusk-by-the-Heart," Harper whispers.

I knew Ambrose's pack-kin had to be involved, but my heart sinks farther hearing her confirm it.

"Did they tell you to weave them into a dress made for Talia?" Sylas asks.

"Yes."

"Did they say what those beads would do?"

"They said—they said the magic would pick up things people said and hold it inside. To prove whether Talia really is best off with you. That if she really is as happy here as you say, then it'll show that." She presses her knuckles to her lips, but a sound like a sob escapes her. "I thought it couldn't do anything harmful, then. It might even prove that she should stay here."

My hand rises to my neckline, to the tiny melted lumps of the beads. If we hadn't figured out the trick, if Ambrose had gotten his hands on them with whatever conversations they'd absorbed—he might have found out all sorts of things that could harm us that have nothing to do with me belonging here. Things about my magical power, about whatever plans we're making against him. The chill inside me prickles deeper.

Sylas pushes to his feet, looming even taller over the young fae woman. His voice reverberates through the room. "Really? You truly believed that the people who've proven themselves our enemies would give you the full measure of their plans? That it was safe to trust them with something you'd have your supposed friend wear at her *throat*? What in the world could have possessed you to take them at their word and go through with this plan rather than bringing it straight to me?"

Harper flinches. "I didn't know what else to do. I'd talked to them about my dresses, and they promised they'd wear them and tell the other packs around the Heart how they got them as long as I'd do one thing for them. I didn't know what it was. I—I took a vow. I know I should have asked more first, but it just seemed—I never thought— And when they told me, they said if I didn't, if I told anyone about it, they'd warn everyone against me instead. Say I'd broken my word to them, betrayed them, so none of the other packs would *ever* want me traveling to their domains."

"And what were you meant to do after? Find some excuse to take the dress back from Talia and return the beads to Ambrose's kin at some social gathering?"

Her answer is so weak I barely hear it. "Yes, my lord."

"I see. So you chose selfishness and your own gain over the safety of *your* entire pack." Sylas lets out a huff with a growl to it. "*Your* pack-kin shouldn't want you around. You have betrayed every one of them, including me, by putting your faith in these traitors rather than your own lord. Now you'll find yourself with no pack at all. I can't have someone in our midst who values what she has here so little."

My former friend's posture crumples with a shudder. Her head bows low. Her hands paw at her face. But she doesn't argue. She takes several gulps of air and then forces herself to straighten up again. When she does, she's looking at me, her eyes red-rimmed.

"I'm so sorry, Talia. I didn't *want* to, so I shouldn't have, no matter how scared I was. I shouldn't have let the things they said get inside my head. You deserve a better friend than that."

She turns to Sylas. "I—I accept your judgment. I understand why you can't trust me now. I wouldn't trust me either. I hope you know I never— It wasn't that— You've always been a good lord to us, to me. I'm so sorry. What would you have me do now?"

Even knowing what she did, my heart wrenches at the miserable resignation in the question. She *sounds* truly sorry. I've seen what the fae can be like, how they can treat people they think are worth less than themselves. She had choices, and she made ones that could have ruined us, but that doesn't mean it'd have been easy for her to go the other way.

I know what it's like to feel caged, how desperate you can get, the risks you become willing to take. I can see that anguish on Harper's face. Maybe she's never been caged anywhere as literally as me, but to have her dream within her grasp only to be threatened with seeing it utterly crushed for the rest of her long, long life…

I can't hate her. I'm not sure I'm even really angry. The chill has condensed into an ache I can only call sadness.

"You will go and collect your things, as much as you can carry by your own means," Sylas says. "I'll give you an hour to prepare and say your good-byes. You must leave this domain. You may no longer claim you're of Hearthshire. If anyone asks, you will tell them you've been banished for acting against your lord. Either you'll find another domain that will accept you, or you'll have to find your own way in the gaplands in between."

If she has to say she betrayed her former lord, I can't imagine any other lord will allow her to join their pack. The droop of Harper's shoulders suggests she's come to the same conclusion. She dips her head in acknowledgment. "Yes, my lord." Without a second's hesitation, she turns and starts walking toward the doorway.

She's taken three steps when I find myself on my feet, propelled by a rush of conflicted emotion. "Wait."

Both Harper and Sylas look over their shoulders at me, Harper startled, Sylas puzzled. It's Harper's expression that solidifies my unsteady burst of resolve.

She didn't expect anyone to stand up for her. She doesn't believe she deserves it, because she understands what a huge mistake she made.

"What is it, Talia?" Sylas asks.

I inhale sharply. "I'm the one she wronged the most directly. Shouldn't I get a say in her punishment?"

The fae lord eyes me. Anger still flares in his dark eye, but it's not directed at me. His tone gentles. "What would you say, then?"

"I think... Harper has never been in a situation before where she had to deal with this kind of conflict. That she did the wrong thing because she was scared and faced with enemies much more experienced at pushing people around. I don't think *she's* our enemy. She was the first person in the pack who really welcomed me and made me feel like I could belong."

"I recognize your points. Where are you going with them?"

I swallow the lump in my throat. "If there's some way we could give her a second chance, have her prove that she can be as loyal as she needs to be, then I'd like to do that rather than sending her away."

Sylas sinks back down in his seat, rubbing his jaw pensively. "I hesitate to give her another chance to betray the pack. Do you have some idea of an appropriate test that wouldn't put us at further risk?"

Do I? I think over everything Harper told us, everything we've already dealt with from Ambrose, groping for an answer.

A glimmer of inspiration sparks. "Ambrose doesn't know that

you found out about the beads. We could give him false information through Harper. You could cast the same spell yourself, couldn't you? We could decide what conversations we let them absorb, and then Harper can deliver the dress the way she was meant to. If she doesn't give away what we're doing, and Ambrose acts on the information we pass on, then we'd know she kept her word."

"In this one instance," Sylas says. "That wouldn't guarantee she couldn't turn against her kin if threatened in the future."

Harper has been gaping at me, disbelieving, this entire time. Now she spins toward Sylas. In a sudden swift movement, she throws herself forward on her knees, dropping her head so low her hair puddles on the floor.

"My lord, this is my home. I don't want anything as much as I want to stay with this pack. I'll do everything Talia said, and I'll give you my true name. You can command me never to act against you, never to even speak to anyone outside the pack, whatever you need to be sure of me—"

Sylas makes a rough sound, cutting her off. He stares down at her. "You're offering me your true name? You can never take that back."

"I know," she says, still bowed to the floor. "It would be worth it not to lose my family, my friends, everything that you provide for us. I'd offer it gladly. Nothing—nothing I ever wanted beyond this domain is worth it if I have no home to come back to."

There's a long silence. Whitt shifts on his feet but says nothing. I wonder if he's not supposed to comment unless Sylas asks for his opinion. I glance back at August, who inclines his head slightly to me as if in approval but stays quiet too.

Finally, Sylas stands again. "Up," he says, and Harper scrambles off her knees. He peers down at her, all incisive authoritative power, and in that moment it isn't hard to picture him standing among the arch-lords as one of their own.

He clears his throat meaningfully. "I don't want absolute control over you. I want pack-kin who believe in me, not forced into loyalty. But I recognize the sacrifice you were willing to make and what it says about your dedication to Hearthshire. As Talia has intervened on your behalf, I will revise my original judgment. You will deliver the beads to the conspirators according to plan without giving any sign of our awareness. You will never act in any way that could harm this pack again. My cadre and I will be keeping a close eye on you. If we see *any* sign you've betrayed your commitments again, it won't be banishment you'll face—it'll be execution. You can accept those terms, or you can leave."

Harper's face lights up as if he's handed over her greatest wish. "I accept them. Yes. Thank you, my lord. If anyone should ever ask me to act in any way that affects the pack again, I'll come straight to you."

"Then it will be so."

Sylas steps down from his seat and motions August and Whitt over to him. As the three men move off to the side to consult in lowered voices, Harper eases toward me. She snatches up my hands to clasp them in hers, and my shoulders stiffen.

"Thank you so much, Talia. I thought I'd really have to—I never wanted it to be like this—I really am sorry. The whole time after you went into the castle with the dress, I was all tangled up thinking about it—"

She moves as if to hug me, and I find that for all the compassion I've felt in the past several minutes, I've reached my limit here. I jerk back, my skin twitching. Harper blinks at me.

My voice comes out rough. "I didn't want you to have to lose everything over this. I know Ambrose's pack-kin put you in an awful situation. But you still—you could have put *me* in a situation that was so much more horrible. I think it's going to take some time before I can really be friends with you again."

Her face falls, which I guess at least means that my friendship was worth something to her. "All right," she says quietly. "That makes sense. I won't forget this—what I did or what you did. If you want someone to go roaming around with or just to talk with later on, I'll be here. I'm sorry."

She slips out of the room, leaving me wondering why, when I'm sure I did the right thing, now *I* feel all tangled up inside.

CHAPTER TWENTY

Talia

The faint rocking of the carriage leaves me unusually queasy. Tucking myself into the seat at the stern, apart from everyone else in the waning sunlight that reaches the uncovered spot beyond the canopy, I drag in several slow breaths.

I wasn't this nervous the last time we headed off to some fae party in another domain. Of course, last time it was at Donovan's palace, and this time we're being hosted by a lord whose allegiances Sylas isn't totally sure of. And last time I didn't know Ambrose was willing to have his people wound me and to bring my former tormenters around. I have no idea what to expect from him tonight.

At least he has no idea what we're up to either. At the other end of the carriage, Harper sits next to her mother, her own smile tight with nerves. She's carrying a small pouch at her hip containing the beads Sylas constructed that she'll say she removed from my dress after I'd worn it around the castle for a day. She's supposed to stop to chat with Irabel at this party and hand them over.

I haven't really talked to her since the confrontation in the audience room three days ago. I hope that carrying out this plan will loosen some of the tension I've been carrying in my gut. I don't *like* going around with a sense of betrayal twined through me.

Whitt drifts to the back of the carriage and props himself against the wall next to me, turning his face to the sunlight. "This is too nice a spot for you to keep it to yourself, mite."

"I wouldn't stop you from sharing it." I inhale in the crisply floral late-afternoon air and close my eyes. When I open them again, Whitt is studying me.

The question tumbles out, quiet but insistent enough that I can't hold it in. "Are you thinking that I went too soft on her? That I shouldn't have spoken up for her after what she did?"

Whitt shrugs casually enough that I believe he wasn't stewing over that subject. "No. Your compassion is part of what makes you admirable. You seemed clear-eyed enough about it—and about her." He pauses. "I do hope I won't have to act on Sylas's warning, though."

That if Harper's actions endanger the pack again, she'll be executed. A fresh jab of nausea prods my stomach. I glance toward my friend, taking in her pensive expression as she gazes at the landscape beyond the carriage. She looks as if she's taking the situation seriously enough. She offered Sylas total control over her.

But I never would have thought she'd turn against the pack in the first place, even under threat.

"What exactly happens if someone has your true name?" I find myself asking. "They can order you around, make you do whatever they want, just by saying it?"

"If the other party decides to be a tyrant about it, yes." Whitt drums his fingers lightly against the curved wood. "I've never experienced it myself. Most of us have the good sense to keep our true names to ourselves and not subject ourselves to masters who'd demand them. But from what I understand, it has some similarities to a soul-twined bond, only much more one-sided unless both parties exchange them. And not nearly as automatic, vivid, or immediate."

"But still pretty intense."

He nods. "Sylas would have had command over her entire being—he could have not just given orders but delved into her thoughts and emotions to whatever extent his magical focus allowed, cast his own thoughts into her head from afar if he wished to. Give someone your true name, and you can never escape them."

He nudges my ankle teasingly with his foot. "*You* don't have to worry about that, though, mighty one, seeing as you don't have a true name to begin with."

"Right. But I have essentially no magical defenses, so any powerful fae could probably do all of that if they really wanted to without needing any secret name."

Whitt pulls a face. "Touché. All the more reason to be grateful our lord is the type to refuse the power of a true name even over a traitor."

That's true. As my gaze slides to Sylas, who's speaking with Astrid and Brigit where most of the pack-kin joining us are gathered beneath the canopy, my queasiness retreats under a swell of affection. How incredibly lucky am I that I ended up with him and not one of the many other fae lords who'd be much less likely to care about a human's wellbeing, let alone listen to her opinions when they conflict with his own?

Whitt steps in front of me with a small smile, his tall frame blocking my view of the rest of the carriage—and everyone else's view of his hand moving to my face. He traces my lips with his thumb in a gesture so tender it feels like a kiss. "Careful you don't look at him like that when there are hostile parties around, or someone might realize he's more than just your keeper."

His tone is teasing rather than serious. I glance up to meet his ocean-blue eyes, lost for a second in their depths. "And how am I allowed to look at you?"

A smirk curls Whitt's mouth. "I'd like to say however you wish, but it's probably best you save the besotted gazes for August while we're among other packs. The rest of the time, I'll take as many as you care to aim my way."

He pulls away from me, swiveling to consider our progress. The sun has just dropped beneath the spiky treetops to the west. A violet glow stretches across the sky, and the shadows are thickening all around us. Amber lights glint in the distance, reflecting off a castle of spires that have a metallic sheen. I'm guessing that's our destination.

The event my fae companions called a "ball" looks an awful lot like one of Whitt's revels, only with a lot more people and a little more orderly. The lords and their pack-kin want to keep a certain amount of propriety around each other, I guess.

As we draw closer, I make out several low, gleaming tables made of what looks like the same rose gold as the nearby castle, spread with matching platters heaped with food and crystal goblets only a smidge less ornately carved than the ones at Donovan's banquet. Long velvet cushions and blankets lie across the grass around them, although no one is doing more than perching gracefully on them at a polite distance at the moment. Will the fae start to couple off into more intimate activities as the night goes on, or is that kind of merry-making reserved for private revels?

Most of the guests are still on their feet, spread out in small clusters around the tables and farther across the field. Their formal finery gleams beneath the glowing orbs. I run my fingers over my own dress—the first one Harper ever gave me, with strips of fabric melding together into what looks like a landscape of rippling treetops. Between my dyed hair and fae-styled clothes, I could almost pass for one of their own... but not quite.

Well, it doesn't matter what anyone from the other packs

thinks. My men, my pack-kin—they see me as a worthy presence. They're the only ones whose opinions I care about.

The carriage stops in a row between the castle and the area set up for the ball. As August helps me scramble out, my gaze darts over the meandering guests. There's Ambrose with his soul-twined mate, Tristan with a woman I assume is his, Celia lifting a goblet in toast, Donovan laughing at something his companions have said, various cadre members and other pack-kin around I recognize as well as strangers… but no sign of Aerik's or Cole's striking hair.

I exhale, tension flowing out of me with the breath. One small mercy. Of course, there are still a gazillion other things for me to be tense about.

I watch Harper slip into the scattered crowd and then jerk my eyes away. We have to make sure we don't look as if we're aware of what she's getting up to tonight.

Several of the other guests have already drifted over to welcome Sylas. A woman in a dress that glitters with streams of emeralds snatches Whitt's arm and tugs him toward one of the tables. Sylas beckons August, and Astrid steps into place beside me, staying within arm's reach in this company.

"Here we are," I say, suddenly wishing I wasn't. But this gambit was my idea. I should at least be here to see it through. And it looks better for Sylas's case the more I show I'm comfortable enough in his care to come with him to large gatherings like this.

I catch several of the fae peering at me and murmuring to each other, but no one approaches me directly. Whether they're more nervous of Sylas's claim to me or Ambrose's, it's hard to say. Maybe both in combination mean I at least don't have to field a bunch of prying questions.

Astrid and I meander over to one of the tables where she points out the "safest" foods for me to sample. The buoyant voices and vibrant giggles around us suggest that quite a few of the guests are getting tipsy.

Harper's parents have joined the other musicians who're attending the festivities, and within a few minutes they're playing a lilting tune that brings a bunch of the fae together in a clearer patch of field to dance, though with less abandon than I'm used to at the revels. They might be here to enjoy themselves, but they aren't going to forget themselves in the process.

I retreat to the fringes of the gathering with a pastry like a crumbly croissant clutched in my hand. At my nibbling, it dissolves on my tongue with a cloying buttery flavor. I can't see Harper now, although I don't want to search too obviously for her. I spotted Namior and Tesfira ambling by earlier, so presumably their daughters are around here somewhere too.

Astrid stands next to me, taking delicate bites of a shallow berry-filled tart that's as wide as her hand. She doesn't sway with the music winding across the field or appear the slightest bit put out to be stuck babysitting while everyone else parties.

"Do you like coming to these things?" I ask.

The warrior makes a neutral gesture with her free hand. "To be honest, I wouldn't come along if it wasn't to guard you. I'm much more comfortable in trousers and work shirts than this." She plucks at the skirt of her own dress, a subdued gray sprinkled with ivory embroidery, still way fancier than anything I've seen her wearing back in Hearthshire. "Don't worry yourself, though. It isn't any hardship. I'm happy to serve my lord, and you're not exactly difficult company."

The corner of my mouth quirks up. "So you're all work and no play?" I pause. I know she's old from the lines that have formed around the hollows of her face, but with fae, it's hard to figure out exactly what that means. "How long *have* you been working for Sylas?"

"His whole life," she says. "Well, as long as he's been established as a lord in his own right. I was part of his father's security contingent before that and his grandmother's before that."

"You left their domain to go with him?"

She nods and takes another bite of her tart. She takes her time chewing it as if chewing over the rest of her answer at the same time. "His father… wasn't happy about it. But he didn't own me. And he'd worked my mate so hard in the kitchens that he nearly lost his hand to an oven, so I wasn't all that happy with the old lord either."

The hint of snark to her voice with that last sentence speaks of a woman who's a lot more than just a devoted servant of her pack. And also— "You have a mate?"

She chuckles. "Don't look so startled. There was a time when these ancient bones had much lovelier flesh on them."

My cheeks flare. "I didn't mean—you still look totally—"

Astrid waves off my protests. "It's all right. You haven't seen me with him. That's because I *had* a mate. He was already a good century older than me, and his time under the old lord hadn't been kind on his body. I think the banishment broke something in his spirit. He passed within a few years of us going to Oakmeet."

"I'm sorry."

"Not your fault. He had a good long life. He'd have been glad to know we made it back to our rightful place." She gazes out over the crowd. "*He* liked these sorts of things. I used to come to humor him. I'm not usually the melancholy sort, but it does remind me of when he was still with us." She holds up her last bit of tart. "If he'd brought the baked goods, they'd have been twice as good."

Despite the trace of grief laced through her story, her critical tone in that last sentence brings a smile back to my lips. "He was quite the chef?"

"Oh, yes." She grins back at me. "I understand your taste in men. The ones who know their way around a kitchen are definitely keepers."

As if he's sensed that he's been mentioned, August emerges from the crowd. He beams at both of us, with a tip of his head to Astrid like a thanks for taking care of me. "You can't come with us to a ball and not dance," he says to me. "And if you're going to dance, I'd like to have the honor."

I take his hand when he holds it out to me, ignoring the nervous skip of my pulse at the thought of how many of the other guests may be watching us. "I guess I can't say no when you put it that way."

The musicians are playing a slower-paced song, which suits me just fine. August lifts our twined hands and sets my other hand on his waist, and we sway and turn with the music. I'm not anywhere near as elegant or smooth on my feet as the ladies around us, but from the way he smiles down at me, I don't think he minds.

They can speculate however they want. Right now, I'm his.

Some of the other ladies mind, though. Whenever my gaze slips away from August's, I catch narrowed eyes and subtle sneers aimed our way—and I'm sure it's not him they're resenting.

My fingers tighten around his, but I can't help wondering exactly how long I'll be his for. How long will he be mine before he finds a real partner among his equals?

A constricting sensation wraps around my lungs. A fae woman near us gives her hair a disdainful toss; one I notice farther off at the edge of the dancing area smiles but with a glint of fangs. I yank my gaze back to August's face, turned even more handsome with his fond expression, but I can't shake the impression that with every passing second I stay here in his arms, I'm painting a bigger target on my back.

My uneasiness must show. August's forehead furrows. "Are you all right, Talia?"

"Yeah. I—I think maybe I just need some space. I'm still not really used to big crowds like this."

The flash of concern in his eyes at my half-lie sends a pang of guilt through me, but he leads me through the other dancers and off across the field where I really can breathe again. When we've left the other guests far enough behind that their laughter is nothing more than a distant tinkling, my lungs relax.

I tip my head back to gaze up at the stars gleaming into view against the darkening sky. "Thank you."

August squeezes my shoulder. "Take as long as you need, Sweetness. You don't have to push yourself. No one expects you to be the belle of the ball."

No, but they wish I wasn't here at all. How many of the lovely lords and ladies and their kin back there think my proper place is in a cage?

At the hiss of boots through the grass, I turn to see Sylas and Whitt walking over to join us. "Was someone bothering Talia?" Sylas asks, his dark eye already glowering in anticipation of an appropriate target.

I can't tell them what really bothered me. It isn't even really the fae women's fault. How could they not consider me an intruder, an obstacle to their goals? They don't know me as anything other than the source of their cure.

"I was just feeling a little overwhelmed," I say, managing a smile. It does feel good standing here surrounded by my three men, even if I don't know how much longer they'll be completely mine. I feel totally sure in that moment that no matter where our romance leads or how it peters out, they won't stop caring about me. They'll still defend me and my place in their pack. That should be enough.

Whitt cocks his head with an arch of one eyebrow as if he doesn't totally believe my explanation, but before he can prod, we're joined by two much-less-welcome wanderers. Ambrose and Tristan are strolling across the field to meet us.

Away from the glowing orbs, shadows fall across the faces of the arch-lord and his cousin. The growing darkness can't disguise the menace that their every movement conveys. I force myself to keep my head up and my shoulders squared, but my hand gropes for August's again of its own accord.

Sylas and Whitt turn to face our enemies, drawing closer in the same movement so that I'm partly shielded by Sylas's brawny form. I can't imagine the arch-lord attempting an outright attack with so many witnesses nearby, but my heart thuds faster. Has he figured out our trick with the beads?

The two fae men stop a few feet away, their smiles haughty. "Where are you off to with our precious commodity?" Ambrose asks.

I'm not sure August has made any effort to disguise the growl in his voice. "She needed a moment away from the crowd."

The arch-lord hums to himself. "I suppose it's a good thing you've developed such an affection for the thing. It should make the logical next step easier. If she does end up remaining in Hearthshire, that is, which I very much doubt she will."

I'd like to bare *my* teeth at him, but I suspect he'd only laugh. I don't know what he's insinuating, though.

It seems Sylas doesn't either. "What 'logical next step' are you referring to, my lord?"

Ambrose lets out a chuckle that has a scoffing sound to it. "I would have thought you could put the pieces together yourself, Lord Sylas, with all the wisdom you claim to possess. The sage's words made it clear enough."

Whitt's smile is so sharp it could cut glass. "Why don't you pretend we're imbeciles and fill us in?"

"The largest flaw in our cure is the fact that she's dust-destined," Ambrose says in a tone that suggests he thinks both men *are* imbeciles. "But Nuldar said her connection to the curse was passed on to her from her grandmother. Indeed, that it has strengthened with each passing. In that case, she should also be able to pass it on, and her short lifespan won't be of consequence. I would recommend we breed her with fae of various status and with another human to determine the combination that results in the strongest carry-through—"

I flinch the moment he says the words "breed her," and August takes a step forward to come shoulder-to-shoulder with Whitt. The muscles in his arms have gone so taut I can see their bulge even through the thick fabric of his formal shirt. "She's not a brood-mare," he snaps.

Sylas holds up his hand to stop August from continuing, but his voice is no less harsh. "Arch-lord or not, *no one* talks about my pack-kin that way."

Ambrose snorts. "Your *pack-kin*? She's a dung-bodied human waif. And I will speak about her however I want. You know I'm right, Sylas. It's the obvious solution to all our problems, no more chasing after larger answers required."

My chest has clenched up again, my breath coming short. Dizziness whirls through my thoughts. If August wasn't still gripping my hand so tightly, I'm not sure I'd be keeping my balance.

Ambrose wants to force me to get pregnant, to have kids—kids with all different sorts of men, of *his* choosing rather than mine. Babies he'd take from me the moment they're born to test them and treat them like nothing but a container for the Seelie's cure, just like he sees me…

Every part of that idea makes me want to vomit. But even I can see the sick sort of sense it makes.

If I can pass on the cure, they *don't* need any other answers. They only need to keep my family line alive. As soon as I bear children who hold the cure in their blood too, as soon as there's more than one human with that power, none of us will be indispensable either. They won't have to worry so much about keeping me alive.

Even if the trio of arch-lords agrees to have me stay with Sylas, will they agree to order him to "breed" me?

Sylas leaves no doubt about how he'd respond to such an order. "I've claimed her as a member of my pack, and so she is. You will treat her with due respect or recognize that you insult *me* just as much as her. And I'm granted every right to defend my pack under the laws you uphold."

"I don't see why you're so offended about the proposition, Lord Sylas," Tristan says. "You'd have plenty of 'right' to her yourself. Unless you're concerned you're not up to the job, considering even your own soul-twined mate wasn't satisfied with you."

Ambrose shoots his cousin a glance as if he'd have preferred to do all the talking, but he doesn't interject. Sylas's body has gone perfectly, frighteningly still. His lips curl back, showing his full fangs. "What was that, Lord Tristan?"

A glimmer of anxiety flits through Tristan's eyes. He's not oblivious to the danger he's courting. But he appears to think getting this jab in is worth it. "Isleen got awfully restless, didn't she? Perhaps if the *right* lord had conquered her a few times as well as she needed it, she wouldn't have gone off making trouble and bringing retribution down on you all."

Sylas's stance tenses as if to lunge, and it occurs to me through my horror that Tristan might even *want* him to lash out. That would be an excellent piece of evidence for their claim that he's in no state to properly care for me, wouldn't it—if he attacks another lord over what they can say was only a little joking around?

Panic shivers through me, and my free hand flies up to clutch at the back of his padded vest. Not in any way that would look overly intimate—Whitt's warning is still floating through my mind—but enough that he has to feel the weight of my hold.

Stay with me, I plead silently. *Don't let them provoke you.* Even though I'd give anything to spring at these assholes and tear them to pieces myself if I had the ability.

Sylas shifts forward just enough to pull against my grasp, I tighten my grip with a lurch of my heart—and he stays there. His teeth are still bared, his fingers curled with the tips of claws protruding, but he must master his wolf and his temper, because no more of it shows other than a flare of anger in his dark eye.

"May maggots eat those who speak so ill of the dead," he says around a snarl, and fixes his gaze on Ambrose. "Put a muzzle on your cousin before he embarrasses your family any more by lowering himself past dust itself."

Ambrose hesitates. From his expression, I'm not sure he was in on whatever plan Tristan is carrying out. Maybe his cousin came up with that ploy in the moment. Before either of them can take it any farther, a few more of the guests wander our way, curious about what's happening.

The arch-lord doesn't want to look petty or hostile in front of impartial witnesses who might report back to his colleagues. He jerks his hand toward Tristan, and they both stalk off, leaving the four of us in shaken silence.

CHAPTER TWENTY-ONE

Whitt

*I*f Ambrose and his mangy mutt of a cousin had kept their mouths shut last night, today's news would count as a victory. As it is, I walk into Sylas's study at his summons feeling like I'm approaching a crumbling wall with only a speck of plaster to mend it.

The urge to take a gulp of some sort of fermented lubrication winds through my gut, but I ignore it. I indulged plenty at the last revel and wasn't terribly pleased with the results afterward. There's no smoothing the edges off of this horrible situation we've found ourselves in. I need to experience all the barbs at their full sharpness to navigate a way through.

Our glorious leader—who's been absent since I woke until now, not even showing up for meals—is braced in front of his desk rather than sitting behind it, which already doesn't bode well for whatever he's discovered that he means to share. August and Talia have already arrived, Talia perched on one of the armchairs and August next to her with a comforting hand on her shoulder. Despite the tension in the air, they both manage to smile at me on my entrance with genuine warmth.

To dust with it. I set aside thoughts of the troubles hanging over us for just a moment to walk over and steal a quick kiss from our lover. Talia grasps the front of my shirt to tug me even closer and extend the meeting of our lips, making my animalistic instincts stir more than is probably appropriate for this setting. I ease back half expecting a glower from one of the other two parties in the room, but August's smile has only widened. Even Sylas's expression has softened a tad.

At least we have this—this unity between us. A lord and his cadre and their lady. I straighten up with a little more confidence that whatever Ambrose intends, we'll crush those plans and laugh about it afterward.

"The musician's daughter fulfilled her end of the bargain satisfactorily, and our favorite arch-lord has started taking the bait," I report. "I heard from one of my people just before dinner that someone, presumably one of Ambrose's pack-kin, made a tentative foray to the spot at the edge of our domain we made a point of mentioning in the presence of those magicked shells. Nothing was done that we could pin on him as wrong-doing, but we'll see how the rest pans out."

Sylas inclines his head in recognition of that minor success. "I'm glad to hear it. He may be too cautious to extend himself far enough that we could collar him based on the false information we sent, but at the very least it should distract him for some time."

Talia looks down at her hands, now balled in her lap, and then up at Sylas. Her voice comes out steady but strained. "What he said about… about 'breeding' me." Her color turns sickly just saying the word. "Could the arch-lords force me to have kids like that?"

The fact that she even needs to ask makes my own stomach turn over. My claws itch to shoot from my fingers and then preferably sever Ambrose's head from his body. I grit my teeth, hating the answer I know Sylas has to give, wishing I had some way of shielding her from the worst the fae world would throw her way.

Sylas's face becomes utterly grim again. "I believe Donovan will stay on our side. But Celia would cast the deciding vote, and Ambrose has persuaded her on other matters. Even if I let Donovan take you in, their votes could overrule any decision he'd make for you." His tone darkens even more with a hint of a snarl. "But it doesn't matter what ruling they make. We won't let them dictate what you do with your life or your body. Whatever we have to do to stop it, we will."

It won't be pretty if we have to outright reject a direct order from the arch-lords. Everyone in this room knows that, including Talia. She sinks back in her chair, reaching to squeeze August's hand.

"I don't want you to have to defy your own rulers," she says in a small voice that tears at my heart. "They'd call you a traitor for that, won't they?"

"It doesn't matter. When a decree is unjust, the only just thing is to refuse it, regardless of who passes it down." Sylas lets out a rough breath. "But perhaps it won't matter at all. If Ambrose keeps up his attempts against Donovan and we can expose his own treachery soon enough, I may be the one holding that throne, and my vote with Donovan's will stop any further talk along those lines."

The ease with which he mentions that possibility prickles over me and dredges up an even stronger desire for the wine in my flask. I bite back any of the acidic remarks that want to spring to my tongue.

Such a great honor the youngest arch-lord is dangling in front of our lord. So much more glory for Sylas—and heaps more stress for August and me if we find ourselves the sole cadre-chosen of an arch-lord, the front line between him and every other schemer out there.

But no one would bother to ask the *cadre* how they'd feel about such a promotion, would they? Our sole purpose is to support our lord's ambitions.

I know my bitter thoughts aren't even fair. Sylas didn't ask for this, and he hasn't got much choice now that the honor has been offered, not without offending the man who's currently our key ally. If he *did* ask me, I'd tell him to accept the boon with all possible enthusiasm. So I swallow down the prickling sensation and focus on what's in front of me.

I'm about to ask if our actual favorite arch-lord has made any suggestions for exposing Ambrose when Sylas goes on, with a hint of vigor coming into his pose. "And I may have an opportunity to force Ambrose's hand. Tristan said more than *he* should have last night."

The memory of that lord's sneering remarks sets my teeth on edge all over again. "What do you mean?"

Sylas folds his arms over his chest, still grim but with a determined air. "I've given a lot of thought to the wording of his insults... and I believe I have grounds to call a formal challenge against him. Wolf-to-wolf, I'm certain I could beat him. Then we'll have him at the mercy of our yield. Ambrose won't stand by and watch his planned puppet be shackled by our demands. He'll have to make a move—a major one, and with much less time to plan than would be ideal. We'll be ready to catch him at it."

Grounds for a formal challenge... The queasy sensation that ran through me earlier rises up again, the dinner I abruptly wish I'd eaten less of starting to churn. "What grounds would those be?" He can't mean—

Sylas's jaw clenches. "You know that part of the reason I didn't pick up on Isleen's full intentions when she moved with her family against Ambrose was that I'd distanced myself from our connection because of tensions between us. It didn't seem relevant to mention at the time the exact, personal nature of those tensions… She betrayed our vows as mates with another man. Based on Tristan's remarks, *he* was the one who dallied with her. Interfering with a soul-twined bond and threatening the hoped-for family line is an undeniable offense."

Ah. There it is. August is nodding, his eyes widening—he clearly didn't know about the transgression. Talia bites her lip, looking pained on Sylas's behalf but not shocked. Had he already told her?

Those thoughts pass through my mind as if it's detached itself from my body, where my stomach is still roiling around and my veins have turned to ice. I'm not sure I could work my jaw if I wanted to. Every part of me seems to have shut down except this distant sort of awareness unspooling farther from the rest of me by the second.

I should have anticipated this development. It's my job to predict every eventuality. But some wretchedly naïve particle of me kept clinging to the hope that the reckoning was actually behind us.

"I would never have wanted to air the affair in any sort of public way," Sylas continues. "But if it gives us the advantage we need, I'll go out there tomorrow—I'll call Tristan before the arch-lords and confront him, and—"

Oh, no. The ice is seeping right into my chest now with a crackling of panic. I grab a hold of myself just enough to keep down my dinner and blurt out the words, "You can't know for sure it was him."

Sylas blinks at the interruption. "He all but admitted it last night. Those comments about her getting restless, about how she needed more from another man?"

"I assumed they were the most cutting insults his feeble mind could come up with, knowing that you and she had clearly not been on the best of terms at the end."

"I considered that, which is why I've been gone today tracking down a few leads. I've been able to confirm that on the evening when it happened, Tristan had departed from his castle with only one of his cadre-chosen, with plenty of time that he could have met up with Isleen by the time it happened."

With one of his cadre-chosen. Then beyond a doubt Tristan has a witness to his whereabouts. But even if he didn't, if questioned before the Heart, it'll clear he can't get away with lying.

I hurtle onward, scrambling for the most convincing argument. "Nevertheless, he said nothing specific. You can't know for sure where he went that day. If you bring him before the trio and make an accusation like that, and he's able to say it *wasn't* him, think of the consequences. Ambrose will spin it so you look unstable. Celia will resent the unnecessary imposition and be less inclined to take our side."

Sylas waves his hand dismissively. "I've endured taunts across several decades in regards to our fall from favor, and this is the first time anyone has raised the specter of my mate's lack of fidelity. And he'd be exactly the sort of dalliance Isleen would have chosen. A lord I've always clashed with, who I didn't think highly of and who had a low opinion of me in return—one with closer ties to the power around the Heart—who better to try to wound me with?"

I can think of a few.

"We have to make some kind of gamble," Sylas says. "There's too much at stake and too little time left to simply stand back and hope Ambrose makes a misstep. I'm certain enough. Unless you have any other reason to think this is a poor course of action, I'll begin making arrangements."

The panic that lanced through me is melting into a frigid pool of dread that saturates my innards.

I can't let him do this. There's no avoiding it any longer. I am his cadre-chosen, and I owe it to him and our pack to prevent this mistake—not least of all because it stems from the greatest mistake of my own.

"No arrangements." My voice comes out hoarse, and Sylas knits his brow. I force out the rest of the words I need to say. "I *know* it wasn't Tristan."

My lord frowns. "How could you possibly— Surely if you were aware of some betrayal that I hadn't acted on back then, you'd have told me before now?"

August and Talia are staring at me too. I swallow thickly. Of course there would have to be an audience for this moment. Of course it would have to be the two other people who matter most to me.

Well, why not? Perhaps they deserve to know the truth as much as the man in front of me does.

The words tumble out faster than before, a bitter pill I've been trying and failing to digest for far too long. "I know it wasn't Tristan because it was *me*. She came to me. I—"

I stop there, because the fury that flares in Sylas's dark eye is enough to kill a lesser man. Certainly my voice is no match for it. And it's not just fury but a deep, searing pain that draws the furrow of his scar deeper and twists his mouth. My wolf recoils inside me.

What a maggot-ridden fool I was to ever think I'd already faced any real reprisal for my crime. None of the coldness and the distance and the growled remarks held a candle to this. His expression flays me to the bone.

I deserve nothing less.

I've done what I need to do. I don't think it would make any of us feel any better in the long run if I stick around for him to literally flay my flesh. Feeling as tattered as if I've already been sliced open, I duck my head. My last statement scrapes my throat on the way out.

"There is no possible explanation or apology I can offer that would make up for my transgression. I'll remove myself from your sight and this domain immediately."

Then I stride out of the room and down the hall as if the Hunt itself were at my heels, with no thought penetrating the thunder of my pulse except that I make good on my final promise.

CHAPTER TWENTY-TWO

Talia

fter the door thumps shut in Whitt's wake, the silence that grips the room is so taut it practically pierces my skin. Sylas's hands open and close at his sides, every muscle in his body rigid. A flush has broken over his face deep enough to show against his brown skin. I've never seen him look so distressed or so furious.

"My lord," August says uncertainly, his formality revealing just how out of his depth *he* feels in this situation, and Sylas seems to snap.

"All this time—standing beside me while he—" The larger man cuts himself off with a growl fierce enough to shudder through my nerves and then lunges for the door as if to chase after Whitt.

My pulse stutters even harder than it did last night when I thought he might launch himself at Tristan. My mind is still numb with shock, but my body reacts, flinging myself off the chair and hugging his arm to hold him back. Sylas flinches at the contact, but he freezes as if afraid that if he keeps moving he might hurt me.

"No," I say raggedly, squeezing my eyes closed as I press my face to his sleeve. The past few minutes play out behind my eyelids. The agony threading through Whitt's voice as he finally made his admission, the shame written all through his stance as he fled the room...

It doesn't make sense. Maybe it explains a few things, like the occasional odd remarks the spymaster has made about Sylas's treatment of him, but I can also remember with vivid clarity that moment in his favorite glen when he told me about the envy he's struggled with over the differences in their status, the pleading note that came into his tone when he asked me not to tell his brother.

I've seen how vehemently Whitt will defend his lord and his pack. He nearly cost the entire Seelie people the cure I offer because it was more important to him to send me away when he believed my presence was wrecking the bond between Sylas and August. He might have felt resentful of Sylas's authority from time to time, but he *hates* that he feels that way. He'd rather hold it in than ever let Sylas notice.

He's held *this* secret in all this time, and he admitted it now not to save himself but to protect his lord.

I don't understand how he could ever have betrayed Sylas by sleeping with his mate, but I can't believe he just tumbled into bed with her without a thought to the consequences. There has to be more to the story.

"Talia." Sylas's voice comes out raw. He sets a careful hand on my head. "Duplicity on this scale—I can't let it go unaddressed." His bicep flexes against my cheek. He glances past me to August. "Take her to her room. No—better to the entertainment room downstairs. I don't want her to have to see or hear any of this."

The dark portent in those words only makes the alarm racing through my chest blare louder. I clutch the fae lord's arm in defiance, raising my head. "*No.* You can't charge in there all raging and tear into him. You don't even know why—he wouldn't have hurt you on purpose. You *know* that, don't you?"

Sylas sucks in a breath with a hint of a snarl. "I can hardly see how this could have occurred without him realizing the damage it would cause. I never would have thought—but I wouldn't have thought it of Isleen either until it happened."

"We have to at least find out exactly what did happen." But I don't think Sylas is in any state to sit patiently through an explanation. I meet his gaze with all the determination I can muster. "Let me talk to him first. *Promise* you'll wait until we know exactly what went on between them. If you still think he deserves whatever you want to do right now, then I—I won't stop you."

Sylas is silent for a stretch that feels like an eternity. At least my interruption has given his fury a chance to simmer down however slightly.

August speaks up hesitantly. "Whitt and I don't always get along perfectly, but I've never seen any reason at all to doubt his loyalty before this. Whatever retribution you'll have him face, you should be sure of the extent of his crime, don't you think?"

The fae lord sighs, swiping his hand over his face in a jerking motion. He peers down at me with his mismatched gaze, his jaw tight. "All right. You can have your talk. But on one condition."

Whitt's bedroom door is tightly shut, but I know that's where he's gone from the frenetic rustles and thumps carrying through it. He hasn't bothered with the lock. The knob turns easily under my grasp, and I slip inside.

At the opening of the door, Whitt's head snaps around with a wince as if bracing for an attack. An attack he assumed would be coming from Sylas. Even as his shoulders come down when he sees me, the ache of confusion inside me grows.

He might not be afraid that I'm here to savage him, but he doesn't appear to be particularly happy about my arrival. So much fraught emotion has tensed his normally breathtaking face that he looks outright haggard. I've seen him sleep-deprived and drunk and hungover, sometimes two of those at the same time, but never anywhere close to as shattered as this.

The blue of his eyes stands out starkly against the widened whites. His gaze darts to the bed, which holds a small chest and a greater than usual disarray of clothing and other scattered objects, only some of which have actually made it *into* the chest. Then he looks back at me.

"You'd better go," he says brusquely but without much real energy. "Whatever happens next isn't likely to be pretty."

It's the voice of a man who's given up. The ache creeps up my throat. I swallow hard and nudge the door not-quite-closed before crossing the room to the foot of the bed.

"I'm not going anywhere. I want to understand what happened."

He makes a strangled sound and returns to tossing things into the chest. "All there is to understand is that I fucked my lord's soul-twined mate, and that makes me the lowest wretch there ever was, and it'd be an immense mercy for him to even let me leave the castle alive."

He turns to grab a leather pouch off the bookshelf beside the wardrobe, and I take the opportunity to clamber onto the bed and shove the lid of the chest closed. Then I sit on it for good measure.

Whitt turns, taking me in with a wildness in his eyes that's more desperate and unsettling than I've ever seen him before. "Mite, this isn't going to—"

I hold my ground, crossing my arms in front of me. "No. Tell me what happened. Somehow I can't believe one day you just decided you had to sleep with her and then did it."

He bares his teeth slightly, and for a second I think he might lift me off the chest and chuck me back into the hall. I grip the edges of the lid, my pulse stuttering. As we stare each other down, the fierce light that momentarily flashed in Whitt's eyes fades. He steps back instead, leaning against the closed wardrobe and rubbing his forehead with the heel of his hand.

"No, it wasn't like that," he says. "But the details hardly matter."

"They matter to me."

"Fine." Somehow he sounds even more hopeless than before. He meets my gaze again, his expression hardening. "There's nothing all that complicated about it. My proclivities are far from secret, and she approached me precisely as any halfway sensible person would: coming to me with a bottle of some new vintage she offered to share while we discussed a matter she wanted to pass by me."

"What matter was that?" Had she thought she was going to convince him to join her rebellion?

"Either I don't remember, or we never got to that. It wasn't as if she typically came to me. You could never have called us friends. I'd have told her to bring whatever it was up with Sylas and leave me in peace, but I knew he'd *like* us to be friendlier, and the wine did sound excellent…" Whitt's eyes wander away from mine again. "And perhaps some small part of my ego liked that she might have thought I'd have better advice than Sylas did, or more sway with him than she had. She probably saw that in me too."

None of this sounds like a prelude to some kind of love affair. As far as I can tell, Whitt didn't like Isleen all that much more back then than he does now.

I frown. "And then…"

"I went with her, and she poured me some wine, and whatever she'd put in it was impressively potent stuff." He lets out a harsh chuckle. "I can moderate myself, but only when I know what I'm actually drinking. After that my awareness got pretty spotty, but the results were clear enough."

The ache from before contracts into something hard as a blade digging into my chest. "You don't remember *any* of it?"

"I remember bits and pieces. Enough to have no doubt at all

what we did."

The blade inside me cuts right down my center, and what explodes out of that gash is anger, so sudden and violent my shoulders shake with it. "She *raped* you."

Whitt's gaze snaps back to me. He blinks, so startled and confused that my hands tighten until my knuckles are throbbing.

"She didn't force herself on me," he says. "I was conscious; I participated." He spits the last word out.

"Because she drugged you so you were too out of your mind to fight her off."

"Talia—"

I stand up on the bed, which gives me a strange vantage point looking down at him when I'm so often looking up. "What would you call it if some lord fed me a bunch of faerie fruit, without even telling me what it was, and then had sex with me while I couldn't think straight?"

Just the suggestion brings a growl to his throat. "I'd call it someone just consigning himself to a slow and painful death. But that's not—"

"Did you *want* to sleep with her?"

"No," he bursts out. "But I didn't stop it either, did I?" His voice falters. "I wouldn't have touched her if I'd had my wits, but that doesn't mean— I can't say some small part of me didn't also take a smidgeon of satisfaction that she felt using me would hurt him the most, or that just once I had something that was supposed to be only meant for him. If it hadn't been for that, maybe it *wouldn't* have mattered what she'd put in the wine or any other way she set me up."

His head droops, and my hands ball at my sides. I haven't used my body for any meaningful violence in all the time I've been among the fae, but right now I almost wish Isleen were still alive so I could let this scream out of my lungs and throw these fists at her face.

What a horrible, vindictive piece of work she was, rampaging through this domain as if her desires were the only ones that counted, breaking Sylas's heart, destroying Whitt's faith in himself, bringing disgrace down on all of them.

I don't care what good things she might have done, what better qualities she must have had for Sylas to have even agreed to complete the mating bond. The venom she inflicted on these men and their pack left wounds that've lasted nearly a century. I don't know if there's anything I could ever do to seal them over.

But I can't shout or strike at her, and it probably wouldn't help anyone if I could anyway. So I do what I can, and slide off the bed to catch Whitt in an embrace.

The fae man stiffens as my arms come around him, but he doesn't push me away. I hug him tight and close, burrowing my head against his chest. Clutching him even harder at the shudder that runs through his tall frame.

"It wasn't your fault," I say firmly, turning my face so the words won't be muffled in his shirt. Maybe if I say them enough, in enough ways, I'll convince him. "*No one* could blame you for it, or at least no one should. She purposefully got you into a state where you couldn't make the decisions you'd have wanted to. If we have to take responsibility for every spiteful emotion we ever have, then I've become a murderer at least ten times in the last few minutes, so…"

A choked sort of laugh tumbles out of Whitt, and then he hugs me back, pressing his lips to my forehead. "Of course you would see it that way. I'm not sure Sylas would be so generous."

A low voice carries from the doorway. "Perhaps you should try me."

The door swings wide, and Sylas stalks into the room.

Whitt yanks himself away from me. I spin to face the fae lord, planting myself between him and his spymaster automatically. But as soon as I see Sylas's face, I know I'm not needed as a human shield. The rage that tensed his features earlier has waned. He looks weary and pained, but not vengeful.

Whitt steps to the side, closer to the bed, so I'm no longer shielding him anyway. He glances from Sylas to me and back again, his stance rigid. "How long have you been out there?"

An answer spills out of me before Sylas can answer. "I'm sorry. He said I could talk to you first as long as he got to listen too. At least—at least now he knows?"

The two men eye each other warily. Whitt brushes his fingers down my back as if to say he accepts my apology, but his attention stays fixed on his lord.

Sylas drags in a breath. "It seems I was even more unaware of my mate's schemes than I realized. If I'd known— Why didn't you *tell* me before now? You had to realize I didn't know it was you, that I had no idea of the full situation. If I'd set my plans today in motion before talking to you, we'd have had a wretched mess to pull ourselves out of. As your lord, as your *brother*…"

The betrayal in his tone isn't as potent as before, but the full explanation hasn't healed it completely. I guess that makes sense.

Whitt cringes. "I *didn't* realize. I thought… You kept to yourself for a few days afterward, and then you were distant and shorter with me than usual—I suppose you were with anyone, but I wasn't thinking about that. I assumed you *had* to know, what with the soul-twined bond. That you were simply making up your mind about what to do with me."

"But I didn't do anything."

"No. Because the assault on Dusk-by-the-Heart happened, and the banishing… I thought you must have decided it was better to pretend it'd never happened and keep me around to help the pack through those difficult times, despite how little you must have wanted me there. You have always been in the habit of putting their needs above your own."

"And all the times we've talked since then, all the things we've been through together, it never became obvious?" Sylas demands.

Whitt's mouth twists. "I *started* to suspect—and in the past few months, I became increasingly certain... But there were hardly a plethora of ideal times to bring it up, and there was still a chance you were intentionally sweeping it under the rug, and I—" He grimaces at the floor. "And I was a coward about it. For all the bitter little thoughts I've had about never being worthy of serving as anything higher than cadre, I couldn't bear to give that position up when I knew I might lose it. So there it is. I had no idea it would come back to haunt us like this."

Sylas's posture relaxes a little more, but his brow has furrowed. It takes him a moment to speak. "I didn't know you felt so ill-treated in your role here in general. If you *would* rather be free from my service and seek a different sort of life for yourself, I wouldn't hold you to your vow."

Whitt considers him. "Is that a polite way of ordering me to continue my packing and take my leave?"

My heart lurches, but Sylas shakes his head. "It's a roundabout way of apologizing for the crime committed against you, since the one who committed it isn't around to deliver that and so much more she'd owe you." He closes his eyes for a second. "If I hadn't shut her out to save myself pain, I'd have known how she violated you. I haven't earned as much of your trust as I should have as both your lord and your brother. If you have failed me, I can only see that I must have failed you as well."

"My lord." Whitt pauses to clear the rasp from his throat. His face has turned a fainter version of the queasy shade it took on before in Sylas's study.

He reaches out to give my hair a half-hearted tussle. "If we believe this one that I can't be held accountable for feelings I don't intend to act on, then it hardly seems fair that *you* should be held accountable for them either. And I'm not sure any of us were quite in our right minds during or after all the turmoil that led us to

Oakmeet. It would continue to be my wish and my honor to serve you and this pack if that is your wish as well."

"It is." The fae lord stands there, unusually awkward. I think this is the first time I've seen him utterly uncertain of how to proceed.

The anger might be gone, but plenty of tension still thickens the air. My stomach knots at the thought of how long it might take for their comradery to recover from this fissure. What if the initial injury has been left *so* long that it's already set wrong like my foot did, doomed to always be a little misshapen and prone to pain no matter what they do?

"Perhaps we could both use some time to ourselves to settle into this new understanding," Sylas says finally. He turns to go but stops when he reaches the doorway to glance back over his shoulder. "In case it needs to be said, I've never thought you deserved less simply because your blood didn't show as true."

The moment he's gone, Whitt slumps onto the bed. I reach for him, but he catches my hand, gives it a gentle squeeze, and returns it to me. "Thank you. For whatever you said or did that's meant all my limbs are still attached to my body. I'll thank you better later. For now… I don't think I'm going to be good company."

I'd insist, but even thinking of that reminds me of how Isleen imposed on him. Nausea wraps around my gut. But even if he wants to be alone, I want him to know he doesn't need to be.

"Okay. I'll be right down the hall if you change your mind. Even if you have to wake me."

He manages a flicker of a smile, a pale shadow of his usual grin. "Thank you for that too. Don't fret, mighty one. All's well that ends well."

As I limp down the hall, that remark sticks in my head, looming more ominously with each step.

It may very well be true. But the troubles we've been drowning in don't feel anywhere near their end.

CHAPTER TWENTY-THREE

Talia

"The Unseelie haven't attacked at *all* since the last full moon?" I ask August as the border comes into view ahead of our small carriage. The shimmering wall of gray fog rises from the distant grassy plain all the way up to the clear blue of the sky.

Is the sky just as clear in the winter lands on the other side where the raven shifters live? Or does everything become stormy as well as cold as soon as you cross that boundary?

August shakes his head. "Not even a small foray. At first I was glad that our response during their full moon attack made them back off, but it's starting to make me uneasy that they've been so quiet for so long. After our last clash, they might be waiting until they can launch an even stronger assault."

The summery breeze coursing over us is as warm as ever, but I shiver with a sudden chill. The Unseelie seem to be determined to slaughter as many of the summer fae as they can. They'd rather strike when they believe the Seelie can barely defend themselves than have a fair fight. But then, they clearly don't care much about fairness when they've been making grabs for land all along the border with no provocation at all from the summer realm.

It's been going on for something like thirty years, from what Whitt said, and the Unseelie have refused to even say why they've suddenly turned so aggressive. Before that, the two groups weren't friendly, but they left each other alone.

I hug myself, rubbing my arms. "*Someone* over there mustn't agree with the fighting, right? Someone who has access to the Heart on their side. The arch-lords got that note warning them about what was coming at the full moon, and only the Unseelie would have known what they were planning."

"Let's hope whoever that is can shake some sense into their companions," August says. "That note might have saved us a lot of lives lost, but I don't think a few secret warnings will be enough to end the conflict. But whoever it was might be regretting helping us now that they've seen how much bloodshed their side faced when we fought back."

My gut twists as much at that thought as at the hitch of the carriage coming to a stop by Hearthshire's camp of warriors.

The camp looks to be in better shape than when we came out to the border last month. During the lull in the fighting, the warriors stationed here have had time to fortify the rough wooden buildings they've been living in, and I can see signs that the pack's return from disgrace has made other squadrons more inclined to help out. The path between the camp and the nearby village of the lord who presides over this domain is much more trampled than before, and a greater variety of vegetables fill the storage bins than are growing in the camp's rough garden.

We've come bearing even more supplies. I stay in the carriage and hand the baskets and sacks out to August, who passes them on to the pack-kin who've emerged from their temporary homes.

Seeing one of the pack's cadre-chosen brings a smile to their weary faces.

It's been a lot of work for these warriors. With the pack's numbers dwindled during their banishment, Sylas had to send everyone he could spare out to help defend the border from the Unseelie, so they've had limited opportunities to return home.

Once we've unloaded the carriage, we sit around the fire pit with the warriors currently in the camp. A couple are off on sentry duty patrolling the border. August gets our pack-kin talking about the past couple of weeks here, and I mostly sit and listen.

My gaze keeps slipping over to the ominous glower of the fog that separates summer from winter. It's far too easy to picture a horde of ravens swooping through that insubstantial boundary.

August must notice my anxiety, because he tucks his arm around mine. He wasn't all that keen on me joining him out here in the first place, but I'm not going to get any opportunities to use my fledgling skills controlling air back in Hearthshire now that our enemies on this side of the border have returned home.

Ambrose and Tristan have squadrons stationed along the border too. The last message from our warriors mentioned that they'd noticed a few pack-kin of Tristan's visiting Aerik's camp that's just a short distance from ours. Maybe I'll get a chance to contribute something here.

"I can't wait to see Hearthshire again," a warrior named Ralyn remarks, poking at the leg of venison they've set to roast over the fire. A mild meaty scent laces the drifting smoke. "Lord Sylas must be relieved to have the pack home."

"I'm working on training up some of our other pack-kin," August tells him. "In another few weeks, we may be able to start a rotation so you all will have more of a chance to rest up where you belong. Lord Sylas will be glad to have you there as much as he can."

He pauses, a trace of a shadow crossing his face, and I suspect he's thinking about the subdued but obvious tension that's hung like a cloud over the castle since Whitt's confession a few days ago. Sylas and Whitt acknowledge each other if their paths cross but have been giving each other a lot of space. I've overheard the spymaster reporting on information his contacts have picked up— quickly and without his usual wry asides.

They're clearly still working through nearly a century's worth of hard feelings, and I don't know how much either of them has told August about what went on after Whitt left Sylas's study. Even if he knows the full story, I can't blame him for being worried. *I* am, and I was there for the whole thing.

But all of us have more pressing concerns. August leans back on the log we've been using as a seat, the muscles in his arm tightening against mine. He didn't want to launch right into an interrogation about Tristan's activities the moment we got here, since Sylas doesn't want the regular pack-kin any more caught up in that conflict than they have to be, but I can tell he's about to broach that subject before he even speaks.

"The last message we got mentioned some new activity at Lord Aerik's camp," he says carefully. "Would you fill me in on the details of that?"

One of the women grunts. "Not much to tell. We've been keeping a more careful watch on that camp since the trouble they gave Lord Sylas last time. Four days ago, I was coming back from patrol and saw a few unfamiliar soldiers just leaving; one of Lord Aerik's pack-kin told them to send his regards to Lord Tristan. We spotted the same bunch coming to visit once more since."

A man who just came back from his patrol a little while ago nods and jerks his head in the direction of the neighboring camp. "Make that twice. A couple of them are over there right now. I didn't get too close, but I'm pretty sure it's the same bunch."

August hums to himself. "And you don't know what all these visits have been about?"

"We know better than to make it too obvious we're keeping an eye on them," Ralyn says. "Don't want them finding some new reason to accuse Lord Sylas of anything. Could be nothing much, but I haven't seen Lord Tristan's kin around here before now. Second-cousin to the arch-lord's folk usually don't bother this far north."

Not until now. Ambrose and his cousin have obviously decided the enemy of their enemy makes a great friend. They must be hoping Aerik's pack can advance their cause in other ways.

I glance in the direction he indicated. I can only just make out several white shapes that are the buildings of Aerik's camp in the distance across the tall grass. It's definitely too far for any of us to overhear their conversations from here. But if Tristan's people are there right now—if *I* could get close enough for my magic to work but not so close that they'd be worried about a human listening in…

August is watching me. He can probably guess where my mind has gone. He thanks our warriors for their input, asks a couple other questions about activity along the border, and accepts a hunk of venison when Ralyn declares it done. I take a smaller piece and follow August apart from our pack-kin.

He stops by the carriage and turns to me, not yet having taken even one bite of his lunch. "You want to try your luck with Aerik's camp." His grimace tells me how little he likes that idea.

I swallow the morsel of meat I was chewing and draw myself up as straight as I can. "That's the whole reason I've been learning… everything I've been learning. The whole reason I came out here with you. They'll recognize who I am, won't they, thanks to my hair and the limp and, well, everything? I can head over upwind of them so they'll catch my scent too. They'd know the consequences if they attack me." Whether from Sylas or Ambrose—or all the arch-lords, if they damaged the source of the Seelie's "cure" beyond repair.

"I'm not sure how they'll weigh those consequences if they

realize you're spying on them." August lets out a little growl. "I should at least be close enough to jump in if they try anything."

"If you're that close, they probably won't say anything useful in case *you* hear them with those fae ears and your magic." I reach up to tap the side of his face teasingly, but a lump has come into my throat with the memory of our argument the other day in the gym. How hesitant he was to let me take any risks at all. How willing to send me completely away from his world and him if it meant I'd be farther from our enemies' reach.

I can't live like that.

"There's got to be a spell you can put on me that would protect me at least a little, and you can watch from farther away," I say, letting my tap turn into a gentle stroke of his cheek. "I've got my dagger and my salt for a little defense too. I need to do this, August. If I find something out, it could tip the balance in whether I stay safe in the long run. And I care about keeping me—and this pack —safe just as much as you do."

August leans in to nuzzle my temple, his fingers teasing along my jaw. Reluctance radiates from his stance, but he steps back with a dip of his head, his golden eyes darkened but determined. "All right. I won't hold you back, Sweetness."

The devotion in his suddenly gruff voice brings a swell of matching emotion into my chest. I tug his face to mine and meet his lips with a kiss I pour all my affection into. August kisses me back hard with a rough sound. I grip his shirt, holding him close, not caring at all what our pack-kin might think of this display.

He might be scared for me, but he believes in me.

When our mouths part, I brush mine to his cheek. "I love you."

He hugs me tight with a murmur by my ear. "If it's even half as much as I love you, then I'm the luckiest man in the summer realm. Let's get you ready for your mission. I want to make sure anyone who comes at you will regret it."

When he steps back, his gaze travels over my body with an

intentness much less heated than it'd usually get with this close an inspection. He speaks a few words, and a faint quiver of energy touches me through the fabric of my dress. Then he rubs his hands together. "That should buy you a minute or two if I need to get to you. And you remember the other training we've worked on."

"Jab 'em in the eyes, knee 'em in the balls," I say, and am rewarded for my cheekiness with a laugh.

"That's the spirit." August tugs me to him for another quick kiss and lets out a huff of breath. "You'd better get going before my wolf's protective side decides it won't be ignored."

"Hopefully I won't need to take very long."

Trying to look innocent and aimless, I wander in my limping way through the grass toward the neighboring camp, the tall strands swishing against my dress. As I run my fingers over the pale blades, I note the direction the wind ripples over them and veer so that it'll sweep over me on its way to Aerik's squadron.

Let them see a simple human girl passing the time while her keepers do the real work. A human girl whose ears couldn't possibly pick up any distant voices.

Thinner stalks jut up through the grass here and there with a sprinkling of pale blue flowers at their tips. I pluck some of them, gathering them into a small bundle. Watching how close I'm coming to the bone-white buildings from the corner of my eye.

Several figures are standing in a group next to one of those buildings, looking as though they're in the middle of an intense conversation. I start weaving the flowers' stalks together, reaching into my memory to summon the soaring sensation of leaping into August's arms and letting the rasp of the splitting stems cover the whispered syllables. "*Briss-gow-aft.*"

The air trembles but doesn't bend the way I'm willing it to. I concentrate harder on the impression of flight and the shape I want it to form, whisking the distant figures' words to my ears. "*Briss-gow-aft.*"

With a whooshing sensation, a current whirls against my cheek. Voices carry with it, faint but audible.

"—she doing here?"

"It's Sylas's pet human. Picking flowers, it looks like. His pack should keep a better eye on her. If she comes closer, we'll shoo her off."

"What were you saying about—"

The current falters, but I've heard *something* useful. They've noticed me and dismissed me like I hoped. I keep stringing the flowers together, making a necklace that would fit a giant, and murmur the true name again. The breeze swirls up.

"—whatever he needs."

"It took long enough."

"You can't hurry good work. He finished as quickly as he could. I suppose there's no point in asking—"

My effect on the wind fades like before. It sounded like they were talking about some kind of plan, but I'm missing it. Restraining a grimace, I meander a few more steps toward the camp and speak the syllables.

The voices return, but they've moved on to another subject.

"—that banquet. I'm looking forward to the next."

"Oh, he'll be hosting plenty. We'll see if your lord lets you off border duty for the occasion."

"It's about time I—"

And so the cycle repeats for several iterations. I only catch a few snippets before the current I've summoned drifts away. None of the scraps I hear tell me anything meaningful.

Frustration is starting to prickle at me by the time two of the figures step away from the others with hands raised in farewell.

Those must be Tristan's men. They're leaving. I won't have any chance at all to hear what they're up to once they're gone.

I grit my teeth for a second and risk drifting even closer to the camp, just as they also move toward me. Any moment now they'll shift into wolves and lope off. I say the true name as forcefully as I can while keeping the cadence August taught me. "*Briss-gow-aft.*"

The air tickles my hair, bringing their voices with it alongside the slightly more distant laughter from the warriors they just left.

"—sure the poison will do the trick?"

"That's why we came out here, isn't it? He's poisoned enough ravens to judge the dose. With enough on the blade, not even an arch-lord's magic could fend it off."

"That'd better be true, or Ambrose will be looking for scapegoats."

"We'll just have to point him toward the supposed expert in that—"

The sound dies, but I don't need to hear anymore. My heart is thudding so loud I'm not sure I'd be able to make out much more anyway.

I spin around and catch myself, remembering that I need to look as if I'm taking a casual stroll, not at all affected by anything Tristan's pack-kin said. No panicked thoughts racing through my mind. No swell of horror clenching around my stomach.

Just one foot in front of the other, slowly but surely back toward August where he's waiting near the edge of our camp, until the pressure in my throat aches to burst out.

When I'm only twenty feet from him, I let myself run at a lurching pace the last short distance, tuning out the pang that shoots from my warped foot.

August's eyes flash. "What?" he says before I've even reached him.

I wobble, clutching his wrist for balance. "I—I think it's even worse than we guessed. They're not just trying to frame Donovan for a crime now. They're planning to *kill* him."

CHAPTER TWENTY-FOUR

Talia

The carriage shudders with the strain of the pace August has urged it to. Wind roars past me where I've hunched in the lowest point of the floor, where the rushing currents still manage to whip through my hair. August kneels beside me, his arm around my shoulder, only lifting his head now and then to check our course.

It feels like we've been hurtling back toward Hearthshire for hours when his stance stiffens. He straightens up with a quick word to slow the carriage. I ease up to peek over the curved juniper-wood wall.

Sylas is sitting on horseback a short distance ahead of us on the beaten track through the forest, turning his steed now with a press of his heels to face us. The bay stallion is a massive animal to match its rider, with a glitter in its dark eyes that suggests it's something a little beyond the sort of horses I'd have encountered in the human world.

The fae lord casts a quick glance around with a few muttered words and then focuses on August. "I got called away for a hasty conference with Donovan—just returning now. We can discuss the rest once we're at the castle."

August's face pales. "I'm not sure we can wait that long. What did Donovan say?"

Sylas frowns. "Only that he's been invited to a luncheon at Ambrose's home tomorrow, one restricted to the trio of arch-lords, supposedly so they can discuss their private concerns. Celia will be there too, but no one else. Donovan suspects Ambrose will have some new gambit to try and wanted to make arrangements for me to act as a sort of witness."

My stomach flips over. This must be what Tristan's men were preparing for. I scramble to the bow of the carriage. "He isn't just going to try to trick him somehow. He's going to murder him if he can."

"*What?*" Sylas's posture goes rigid.

August nods, setting a hand on my back. "Talia was able to use her growing skill with air to make out a bit of conversation between Tristan's pack-kin and Aerik's. It sounds as though they came to Aerik's camp because he has a poisons expert there—someone who's doctored a blade that they expect to be potent enough to kill an arch-lord."

Sylas curses under his breath, and his stallion stomps its feet. "I told him it might be too much of a risk, that he should consider making excuses…"

"But if you'll be there with him, then you can help protect him, right?" I say. At least Donovan took that much of a precaution.

But Sylas shakes his head. "I won't be witnessing closely enough to stop a murder. Ambrose made it clear even cadre-chosen weren't to attend the luncheon. Donovan has given me a token magically charged so I can watch events through his eyes, so I can speak to what happens there. It's an immense gesture of trust—but it won't allow me to save him from physical harm."

He grips the reins, his mouth slanting as he seems to grapple with his decision, and then he shifts forward in the saddle. "I'll see if I can catch him before he makes it back to Blossom-by-the-Heart and bring him up to speed on this new development. We can't leave something so urgent and sensitive to messengers or charms."

Without waiting for our response, he taps his heels against the stallion's sides. It springs forward and dashes past us so swiftly I swear I see sparks lighting beneath its hooves.

I look at August, the uneasiness that's been coiled around my gut since I overheard the mention of poison winding tighter. "What if Donovan insists on going to the luncheon anyway? What kind of excuse could he give to back out?"

August squeezes my shoulder, his handsome face unusually drawn. "I don't know. Hopefully Sylas can work something out with him. But Ambrose has final say over who enters his castle and the magic to enforce it. Even Sylas wouldn't be able to force his way in if it came to that. Maybe Donovan can come up with some sort of protection he can wear or hold that would ward off the poison."

Difficult when we don't even know what kind of poison it is. As August starts the carriage gliding toward Hearthshire again, my hands clench. If only I'd been able to hear more details. I don't even know for sure that Ambrose *does* mean to carry out this plan tomorrow.

It's only a few more minutes before the massive gate of arcing trees comes into view in the distance. When the carriage soars through it, many of our pack-kin look up from their activities around the village. Several venture over to hear the news from the border.

The warriors out there are their friends—in some cases family. It probably bothers them that they aren't adept enough fighters to take on some of the responsibility of protecting the summer realm. I've seen how much many of them are itching to support Sylas more however they can.

That thought brings a flicker of inspiration with it. I follow August to our approaching pack-kin, turning the idea over in my head.

I can't see how it would hurt anything to simply have a discussion. Maybe Sylas will sort something out with Donovan, and whatever brainstorming we do won't matter. But I don't know how likely that is, and even if they manage to divert Ambrose's latest attempt, Donovan can't avoid him forever.

It'd be good to have a definite strategy up our sleeves. And if we're going to outthink a scheming arch-lord, the more minds we can put together, the better.

When August has finished speaking, I give a little cough before the pack-kin who've gathered can start to leave. "I think there's something important that Lord Sylas might need our help with. If there's anyone who'd be willing to talk through the problem and see what strategies we can come up with, you could join me in the entrance hall of the castle?"

I glance at August for his approval, since I don't really have any authority here, no matter what fond titles Sylas has bestowed on me. August hesitates but then tips his head. "This is important to the security of not just our pack but others too. What we do discuss can't leave those walls. And for now, it's only hypothetical."

Astrid steps up immediately. "You know you can count me in—and to see through this strategy too."

Brigit and Charce come forward, and then Elliot, Shonille and her mate, and a few others I haven't spoken to as much. August motions us all into the castle.

I limp across the thick rug and sit in the middle of the room, the others automatically sinking down around me to form a circle. All except one figure who hangs back outside that ring.

Harper's shoulders hunch when I look up at her, her body tensing as if she expects me to order her to leave. But she did come through with Ambrose the other day. She might have a better idea of his weaknesses than those who haven't had any dealings with him do. I exchange another look with August, who lifts his eyebrows as if to say, *It's your call.*

She can stay, then. I'm not going to say anything specific anyway. Sylas hasn't wanted them knowing the details of this conflict, and I can respect that. Besides, it's probably safer for all of us that way.

I set my hands in my lap and gaze around the circle. "Let's say Sylas needed to get into another lord's castle—one with magical defenses and guards so he couldn't just walk in whenever he wanted to. Because—because he needed to talk to someone inside urgently. It wouldn't have to be sneaky, just something that would let him come inside and find the right room without anyone managing to stop him before that. But he wouldn't want to hurt anyone either. Can any of you think of some magic or another sort of trick we could use to help?"

One of the men looks doubtful. "If Lord Sylas can't see a way…"

"Maybe he *will* figure it out," I say. "But he'd want to try to do it alone, because he doesn't like putting any of the rest of us in danger if he can manage it. You all want to do more than that, don't you? I want to fight for this pack and for everyone who's welcomed me, and I know some of you have wanted to step up too."

There's a moment of silence. Then Brigit speaks up tentatively. "Would all the possible entrances on the first floor—including openings like windows—be guarded?"

Astrid rubs her narrow jaw. "If this is a powerful lord, he'll have considered and secured all possible access points one way or another. The difficult part would be either getting past the guards or breaking a magical barrier where they're not around—and without alerting them so they'd come charging over right away regardless."

"If a bunch of us put our magic to work together," Elliot starts, and then pauses. "But we'd need to be close to the building to apply enough power. Maybe if we had the cover of night?"

August grimaces. "We'd need a technique that could work by day. We definitely wouldn't be able to bring even a small group close enough without being noticed and apprehended."

Shonille's mate drums his fingers on the floor. "Could we create a distraction that would draw some of the guards away and give Lord Sylas an opening?"

Shonille turns to him. "What could we do that would bring enough of them without making even more trouble for Lord Sylas overall?"

He rubs his mouth. "I don't know. Something to think about, at least."

A few more of the pack-kin toss out ideas that one or another points out a problem with. My spirits start to sink. I'd hoped that we'd be able to come up with something concrete so we'd have a plan in place if Sylas needs to rely on us.

I wish *I* could offer more in this discussion, but I still don't know all that much about how the fae world or its magic works— nowhere near as much as the fae around me do, at least.

But Donovan's survival, control over the Seelie realm, the lives of thousands of warriors—and my own safety—could all depend on what happens tomorrow. On whether Sylas can protect his arch-lord ally when it matters. We can't give up.

There are a lot of rules that've come into play in our past conflicts. The vows fae agree to when they're forced to yield, that they then must hold to. Cole breaking out of that obligation by pointing out a crime Sylas had committed against him. The two acceptable ways to displace an arch-lord.

What if what we need isn't magic or trickery but an appeal to some fae policy we can bend in our favor?

"Is there any law that ever allows fae to go into someone else's home without their permission?" I ask the gathering at large. "Or, like… if he had reason to believe something bad would happen if he *didn't* go in, would that be acceptable?"

"He'd have to be able to prove to the guards that there was a major threat first—one they believed they couldn't cope with, or they'd tell him to let them handle it," Charce says.

And Sylas doesn't have clear proof of Ambrose's intentions. So much for that.

But Astrid gestures for attention, her eyes lighting up. "There is one tenet that could force them to give him access. If any of his pack-kin are inside, he has a right to be allowed to go in to speak to them if they won't come out to him."

Brigit knits her brow. "But if they wouldn't let *Sylas* inside, why would they let any of the rest of us in?"

My pulse stutters. I can think of one person here that Ambrose would happily admit into his castle if he thought it meant he'd won: me. Not that he'd trust the situation if I came strolling up to his front door out of nowhere.

But I wouldn't have to, would I? My gaze rises to where Harper is still standing awkwardly at the edge of our group.

Before I've decided what to say and how much I should in front of the full group, footsteps rap against the floor behind us. I glance over my shoulder to see Whitt sauntering into the room.

The spymaster's air is as nonchalant as always, only vague bemusement showing on his face as he takes us in, but his eyes still look a little more sunken than they used to, the corners of his mouth tighter when it pulls into a smile. My throat constricts. It's bad enough we're facing this potential catastrophe at all, let alone while there's so much turmoil between two of the men who watch over this pack.

"Well, well, what's all this commotion about?" Whitt asks lightly. His attention settles on me. "Coming up with more schemes of your own, mite?"

It's a relief to hear him sounding so normal. I suspect he's not going to like my proposal one bit, though.

I push myself to my feet. "Actually, we are. But I think I should probably talk something over with you and August before we get further into it."

August doesn't need any more cue than that to motion to the gathered pack-kin. "Give us some time. Your input has helped us narrow down the possibilities. If we need to put a strategy into action, I'll make sure Lord Sylas knows he can count on you."

As the fae get up and head to the door, disappointment shows on some of their faces, but there's an equal amount of determination. The plan that's forming in my head has no chance of working without at least one of them participating willingly, though.

I raise my voice just enough to carry. "Harper, I need to ask you about something too."

Her gaze jerks to me with obvious surprise. For a second she stays frozen in place. Then she hurries over, a painful mix of hope and apprehension flitting through her expression. "What?" she asks quietly.

I wait until the last of the stragglers have slipped out. My heart is still beating faster with an edge of creeping panic. Do I really want to do this—to walk right into the lion's den?

But I could very well end up there anyway if I *don't* do something like this. I've gotten as far as I have by taking chances, taking my life into my own hands. I can't lie down and give up now.

Whitt and August watch, letting me take the lead. I inhale slowly to settle my nerves.

"It was risky getting those beads to Ambrose's people at the ball," I say to Harper. "Would you be willing to try something even bigger and riskier than that if it would mean protecting the pack—and all the rest of the Seelie—so much more?"

She blinks nervously, but it doesn't take her long to answer. "Yes. I—I want to make up for my mistakes. If it means stopping people who are trying to hurt us, I'll do it."

Then there's no reason this ploy shouldn't work. I turn to the fae men. "Okay. Here's what I'm thinking…"

It's almost dinner time when Sylas finally returns. I'm in the kitchen with August, drizzling icing over the tiny cakes that are our dessert, trying to let the normalcy of working alongside him drown out the jangling of my nerves. It'd be easier if he didn't stop periodically with a wince or a sharp inhale as if he's just remembered what I proposed all over again.

At least he isn't arguing.

Sylas finds us there. He stops in the doorway, running his fingers through his windblown hair, and catches the eyes of the official kitchen assistants. "Thank you for your work today. You can return to your homes—make sure August hands over some of those cakes."

August manages to chuckle as he fills a couple of small baskets, but when the other fae have left, he turns serious. "What happened with Donovan?"

Sylas presses the heel of his hand to his temple. "I managed to speak to him, but he didn't seem to appreciate the gravity of the situation. Or perhaps he can't imagine that Ambrose would truly go that far and believes our information must be faulty. Either way, he insisted on proceeding with the same approach we already agreed on, with me observing through his eyes from a distance. He reassured me very confidently that he'd be all right."

The grim dryness of his tone reveals none of the same confidence on his part. My lungs clench, but I put down the icing tube and ready myself as I swivel on my stool to face him. "We thought that might happen. So we've come up with a plan that should mean you can get into Ambrose's castle if things go wrong and you need to defend Donovan right away."

"Have you now?" Sylas folds his arms over his chest. "Go on."

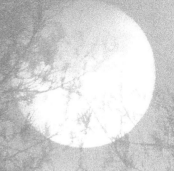

CHAPTER TWENTY-FIVE

Talia

When I wake up, it's fully dark out. I can tell from the glimmer of stars beyond my window and the mugginess in my head that it's still the middle of the night. I haven't slept nearly enough.

But when I close my eyes, my thoughts weave restlessly through my head, refusing to let my mind settle. After what feels like an eternity of tossing and turning, I get up and limp to the privy in case the walk and emptying my bladder will help me relax.

My nerves haven't calmed at all by the time I make it back to my room. I pause at the door, balking at the thought of lying there sleeplessly for much longer, and a faint creak reaches my ears from somewhere down the hall.

I might not be the only one having trouble drifting off tonight. Is August still up, stewing over tomorrow's plans?

I slip down the hall to where the men's bedrooms are, but the noise I hear next comes from *Sylas's*, not August's. There's a rough breath somewhere between a huff and a sigh, and another creak as he turns on the bed.

The fae lord wasn't exactly ecstatic about my idea for getting him into Ambrose's castle should he need to, but he's always so composed, I wouldn't have thought he'd let any worries get that much of a hold on his mind. I hesitate.

So much is on the line tomorrow for both of us. I might not get another chance to show him just how much his trust and affection mean to me. If there's anything I can offer that will set him more at ease, I want to—and I want to soak up any tenderness *he's* prepared to offer while I still can.

As I cross the floor to the bed, Sylas rolls to face me, his eyes open but his eyelids low. His sheet is tangled around his torso, revealing the sculpted planes of his bare chest. I know from experience that he usually sleeps in nothing but his undershorts.

He doesn't look startled—he probably heard me in the hall before I even reached the door. I'm not sure what to say, so I simply hop onto the bed and nestle myself close to him.

Sylas wraps his arm around me automatically, tugging at the sheet so that it covers me too. "Couldn't sleep, little scrap?"

I hum in agreement. "Neither could you?"

He sighs and tucks his chin over my head. "Tomorrow I may have to enter combat with one of the arch-lords I'm supposed to serve. The fact that it'd be in defense of another arch-lord doesn't make the possibility sit that much more comfortably. And all the while you'll be putting yourself under his power…" He trails off with a faint growl.

I slip my arm under his, my hand skimming his muscled back, and hug his brawny frame to me. "If it all works out, then I'll be right back out of his power quickly enough. If it doesn't… I was going to end up there anyway. At least I'll have done everything I could to stop it."

He pulls me closer to him, his heat washing over me. His voice roughens. "I hate the thought of what he wants to do to you, Talia. I look forward to the chance to tear him apart if it means he can never see any of that through. If that makes *me* a traitor to the Heart, so be it."

My throat constricts. "How can it? None of this would be happening if he wasn't scheming against his colleagues in the first place. You—you know I appreciate everything you've already done to protect me, don't you?" I raise my hand to trace my fingers along the side of his face, seeking out his mismatched gaze. "When all you have are awful options, it's not your fault that there's nothing you can do that feels totally right."

He gazes down at me, stroking his own fingers up and down my back through my nightie. "I do feel there was a thing or two I should have done differently the first time my people clashed with Ambrose. I can't see how I could be making a similar misstep now, but I didn't realize it back then either…"

Oh my passionate, honorable lord. My heart swells with so much more than appreciation. "Well, I might not be an expert on any of this, but I can't see any way you could be doing things better right now either. And I promise you that letting me go through with tomorrow's plan isn't a mistake."

"As if you would say anything else." He ducks his head to brush his lips to my forehead. "You know I believe in giving you your freedom, but I do dislike how often these plans of yours involve putting yourself in harm's way."

"I'd rather risk myself than ask anyone else to take the risks for me." I press a kiss to his shoulder in return. The smoky, earthy scent of his skin floods my senses, bringing out a headier heat that courses through me to pool low in my belly. I'm abruptly twice as aware of how little clothing there is between us, only a couple of layers of thin fabric. But I still have to point out, "You're risking more than I am."

"As is my job, as lord over my pack and loyal ally to the arch-lords who *aren't* committing blatant treason." Sylas lets out another sigh. "I suppose it's my fault for naming you our lady. I didn't mean for you to take on quite so many responsibilities to go with the title."

His tone has gone dry enough that a smile twitches at my lips. I scoot higher on the bed, compelled by a dizzying mix of love and desire. "It does seem to come with a lot of benefits too."

He meets me halfway, his mouth claiming mine with a demanding rumble. His tongue sweeps between my lips, hot and fierce, his hands molding me against his muscle-packed body. My skin sears everywhere we touch in the most delicious way.

I kiss him back hard, reveling in the urgency of his desire. He wants me this much. I *mean* that much to him, at least for now.

I want him too, so badly I'm already aching.

Sylas kisses me again, hunger thrumming through his chest, his fingers tangling in my hair. With a choked sound, he jerks backward. His breath stutters over my lips. Both his pupils have dilated, the dark one and the ghostly one.

"I promised you, when you'd come to me like this— There should be no expectations—" he says raggedly, calling back to the last time things got heated in his bedroom, when my feelings were much more muddled than they are now. But we already have a solution to that problem without any negotiation necessary.

I grip his neck and gaze back at him. My longing turns my voice husky. "Take me to the tryst room."

The words have barely fallen from my lips before he's scooping me up in his arms. He crosses the bedroom and then the hall in a few swift strides to the room he added to Hearthshire's castle like he did to the keep in Oakmeet—the one that's not mine or any of my lovers' but all of ours together, meant for moments like this.

Sylas is already planting a scorching kiss on my neck before we've made it to the bed. I whimper, gripping the thick waves of his hair. Need unfurls from my core all through my body, so intense it's almost painful. "Please," I murmur.

He makes a strangled sound and lifts me onto the bed, his body braced over me. His mouth recaptures mine, devouring me, drinking in every encouraging sound that quivers up my throat. He strokes my breasts, wasting no time in settling his thumbs over my nipples and drawing them to the hardest of points with giddying jolts of pleasure.

"Mine," he growls, nibbling my jaw, nipping my earlobe, as if he can't keep his mouth off of me for more than an instant. "*Mine.*"

The word feels less like a declaration of ownership than an adamant warding against the ones who'd take me away from him, like he's daring anyone to even *try* to rip me from this place. It resonates through me. I arch against him, wishing he could claim me so thoroughly that no one beyond this castle could ever even consider doing the same.

"Yours," I answer in a sort of prayer.

Another wild sound spills from his lips. He swipes his tongue across my neck and buries his mouth in the crook. His hand rakes down the front of my body, the tips of barely-emerged claws slashing through my nightgown down the middle.

My pulse hiccups, but only for a second before I'm enveloped in a flood of burning passion again. As fierce as Sylas's desire is, he didn't make one mark on my body, hasn't touched me to bring anything but pleasure.

I know right down to my core that this man would never hurt me.

He palms my breast, stirring another jolt of bliss, and then pulls back, his mouth branding my collarbone, my ribs, my belly in quick succession. Before I've quite caught on to where he's heading, he lowers his head between my legs.

The first urgent stroke of his tongue sets off sparks all through my sex and shocks a cry from my throat that's a plea for more. I press into his mouth.

Sylas works me over as if his life depends on urging every particle of delight he can from my folds and the sensitive nub above them. I cling to his hair, my hips swaying with each movement of his lips, each flick of his tongue. All I can do is ride the rush of sensation that sends me careening toward my release.

It comes with a burst of pleasure that knocks the air from my lungs. My head tips back into the pillow, a moan tumbling from my mouth. My body quakes as the aftershock tingles through my limbs.

Sylas kisses me once more there, firmly enough to propel the giddy waves even higher, and then prowls up over my body.

Yes. Every nerve inside me sings out in welcome. I grasp his shoulder and splay my legs, reaching to yank at his undershorts. He wrenches them off with the same force he applied to my nightie. His mouth collides with mine, tart with the taste of me combining with his potent flavor.

He slides his arm under my backside, raising me to meet him, and my knees clench around his hips. With a groan, he plunges right into me.

There's none of our first encounter's caution, but I don't need careful. It's thrilling to experience such intense desire from this man who keeps his fiercer emotions so vigilantly in check. To know that he could long to become one with me just as much as I long for him, at least in this way, in this moment.

My hips buck to meld with him of their own accord. Bliss flares from where he's filled me so perfectly to radiate all through my body. As our rhythm speeds up, our kisses start to fragment, as much panted breath and stuttered gasps as mouths embracing.

Sylas is so big, looming above me and penetrating me to my core. Power radiates off him with every thrust. But I don't feel small beneath him. With each caress, each clutch of his fingers pulling me closer and driving himself deeper, a sense of strength flows through me.

In this moment, I'm his and he's mine. I'm the woman he needs. I'm not a cringing victim or a fumbling human—I'm a fae lord's chosen lover, and I welcome every bit of passion he can pour into me.

The haze of expanding pleasure drowns out any further coherent thought. With a few more strokes, Sylas hits some perfect spot inside me, and my awareness shatters apart. I shudder and clench around him, crying out. He drives into me once more, and his shoulders go rigid as he follows me over that edge.

We rock to a halt at a much more tender pace than the one that brought us to our release. Sylas kisses me softly, drawing it out as I go slack beneath him, and then nuzzles my jaw. His own pose starts to relax, but when he gazes down at me, there's something unexpectedly fraught in the darkness of his unscarred eye.

His voice comes out quiet and a little hoarse. "Are you—all right?" His hand drifts to the shredded edge of my nightgown. "I didn't mean to let out so much of the animal with you. It was just the thought that I might *not* have you—but I should have—"

I interrupt him with a hand against his cheek and a smile so wide it brings an ache into my cheeks that matches the one around my heart. "I wanted this. I *asked* for this. It was my idea to come in here."

Suddenly I think of Whitt that evening when he first gave in to *his* desire, how he warned me against himself first and only accepted my advances when I told him I wasn't bothered by his supposed faults. I wouldn't have thought Sylas needed any similar assurances, but he is still a man as well as the stalwart lord. I know how deeply his emotions run beneath his controlled exterior.

I lift my head to press a fleeting kiss to his lips. "I'm not afraid of you—I'm *never* afraid of you. I know you'd stop if I asked you to. I wouldn't be yours otherwise."

An echo of a groan escapes him at those last words, and he leans in for a more thorough kiss. As I loop my arm around his neck and kiss him back, I can't help wishing that I could stay his just like this forever, as ridiculous as that hope might be.

At noon the next day, as I walk past the immense black stones that surround Ambrose's palace, the blazing heat of the sun makes me recall the gentler warmth of Sylas's embrace with a pinch of longing.

What I wouldn't give to be spending this day cozying with him in bed rather than marching toward a villain's house. What I wouldn't give to have him—or August or Whitt—walking next to me right now. But it's just Harper, Brigit, and Charce with me, making our way up the slope.

Even Astrid's presence would have been a relief, as much as I've sometimes chafed at her constant presence. We aren't sure that Ambrose's guards will admit us if we have anyone with us who looks like a warrior. Brigit and Charce were among those August has been training who volunteered to come along, chosen partly because of Brigit's past help and partly because Charce had the magic to control the carriage we supposedly stole for this trip.

We need every part of our story to line up for our best chance of seeing this stratagem through.

Another part of that story is making it believable that I'd have come along with Harper despite my previous insistence that I stay in Hearthshire. I let my gaze drift idly over my surroundings for the benefit of any watching sentries, lolling my head to one side and then the other, forcing a giggle at random moments. Drawing on every sensation I can remember from the time Whitt shared his cavaral syrup with me.

As we come up on the towering black form of the palace itself, my heart thumps faster. I will my expression to stay placid.

The luncheon was supposed to start at noon sharp. We're reaching the doors about ten minutes after the visiting arch-lords should have been admitted. We didn't want to leave Donovan unprotected for too long, but we didn't want to risk Ambrose having the chance to interrogate us before his guests arrived either. By now, he should be totally occupied.

Harper strides right up to the guards posted at either side of the main door. "We've come to give ourselves over to Ambrose's care." Hearing the steadiness of her voice brings a glow of pride into my chest. I know how nervous she was about this plan, but she's rising to the occasion.

Her statement isn't a lie—she's just leaving out how short a time we plan to *stay* in Ambrose's care. The guards eye us with obvious uneasiness. The woman on the right focuses on me.

"That's the human—the one with the cure in her blood."

Harper's head bobs. I make a point of humming to myself and tipping my head toward the sky rather than seeming to pay attention.

"I got her drunk on some good wine so she wouldn't argue," my friend says. "I've worked on Arch-Lord Ambrose's behalf before—his pack-kin who visited Hearthshire can tell you. We don't want to be on the wrong side if it comes to war. I thought the cure would make a good peace offering. He wants her, doesn't he?"

The guards clearly know their lord does. They exchange a glance. The man clears his throat. "The arch-lord is busy at the moment. He can't attend to you yet."

Harper shuffles her feet and ducks her head, looking sheepish and not at all threatening. "Could we at least come inside? It'd be easier to make sure the human doesn't wander off. And I'm not sure how long it would take for Lord Sylas to notice a missing carriage."

The woman makes a gruff sound, but after another silent

exchange between the guards, she motions for us to follow her. "You can wait in one of the sitting rooms. Just come along quickly."

Harper curls her hand around my elbow. Looking toward the cavernous doorway, my legs balk. For a second, I'm suffocating.

I think of Sylas's breath grazing my neck as we fell asleep entwined last night. Of August's tight hug before he watched me step onto the carriage. Of Whitt's final murmured reminders of details to keep in mind and the subtle squeeze of my hand as he moved to step away.

I will come back to them. I refuse to accept any other outcome. But to make sure of that, first I have to walk completely away.

My jaw tightening behind my dreamy smile, I propel myself into my greatest enemy's home.

CHAPTER TWENTY-SIX

Sylas

The warm breeze teases over my fur where I crouch amid the trees at the base of the Heart's hill. Farther up the slope, the stone wall of Ambrose's domain gleams starkly against the grass. Every muscle in my wolfish form is tensed around the urge to bolt across that distance and onward to the palace.

My pack-kin are up there. The woman I love is up there. They got out of their carriage just minutes ago to cross the rest of the distance on foot. Even now, Ambrose's warriors could be—

I clamp down on that line of thought and shove it aside, turning my attention to the more detached impressions trickling into my mind. I know exactly where Ambrose himself is right now. If his guards put out a call for his orders, I'll see it instantly.

When I focus on the faint pressure of the band fixed around my head and specifically of the enchanted gem resting right against my forehead, images and sounds filter into my mind as if I were seeing and hearing them with my own eyes and ears. But it's not my senses taking them in first but Donovan's.

I got into place here an hour ago and activated the gem's magic just before noon. With careful attention, I watched and listened as Ambrose welcomed Donovan and Celia into the palace, charted the route they took through the halls to the smaller, private dining room, and observed their innocuous small talk as the servants laid out the last preparations for the luncheon.

The three arch-lords are still standing next to the table. A woman brings out a carafe of wine, another arriving just behind her with a roast pig on a platter. The meal is about to start.

It's unnerving, experiencing two locations at the same time. Donovan's perspective affects my senses in a subtler, more distant way than the forest around me, but I can still smell the crisp meatiness of the roast, even feel the knot in his stomach as he and his colleagues move toward the table. He spoke about this encounter with confidence, but he *is* nervous.

I'm a little relieved to recognize that. He should be. Ambrose hasn't made any questionable moves yet, but I suspect it's only a matter of time.

My thoughts slip back to the after-image of his tormented face that filtered through my deadened eye all those days ago, the morning after the banquet at Donovan's palace. At the time, I assumed the distress I saw in that impression of him was emotional strain. But the young arch-lord has proven himself adept at conquering the stress of his situation.

Now, I'm more inclined to believe it was the physical agony of a man poisoned.

Was that glimpse a reflection of some future moment when I'll see his face so contorted in actuality? Is it a sign that I won't be able to protect him in time, whether today or on some later date? Do my fleeting visions *have* to show something true, or can what hasn't happened yet still be altered?

Those questions have been gnawing at me since Talia first

announced what she overheard from Tristan's pack-kin at the border. The magic that sliced through my flesh and seared my eye right through the socket left lingering traces I still don't fully understand so many years later.

By the Heart, let the risks that my lady, my pack, and I take today be enough to overcome Ambrose's malice.

In the dining room, the servants bow and scamper out at Ambrose's wave. No others have arrived to speak to him about unexpected visitors. The arch-lords move to take their places around the table, and Ambrose pauses, letting out a faint huff of irritation.

"It appears my staff have forgotten my wine glass." He glances around and makes a quick gesture to me—to Donovan, whose eyes I'm seeing him through. "There's one on the sideboard. Would you pass that to me?"

Donovan turns—the sideboard *is* right behind him, with a crystal goblet standing near the edge. It's an innocent enough request, but my skin prickles with more apprehension than I sense from the man I'm linked with.

However Ambrose means to carry out his plot, he would want every part of it to look innocent to both his victim and outside observers. He wouldn't want Celia raising any concerns about the events that follow.

Donovan hands the goblet to Ambrose. The other arch-lord inclines his head in thanks. "I trust we can all manage to pour our own wine and fill our own plates so that we can talk without disturbances from my faded kin."

"Of course," Celia says, regal and unruffled as ever, and takes the carafe first.

The conversation continues around the table without delving into any subjects I'd think warranted this level of secrecy. How would Donovan feel about my observing if it did? He must have decided his safety outweighs any such concerns.

I can only imagine how much Whitt would have enjoyed getting an exclusive surreptitious peek into the lives of the arch-lords behind closed doors. I thought I noticed a gleam of interest light in his eyes when I explained Donovan's contribution to this plan, although it vanished so quickly behind his new, more reticent manner that I could be wrong. He kept the remarks he made strictly to the practicalities of the business at hand.

Just remembering my last conversation with him—and other conversations before that—sets a prickling sensation unfurling through my chest. My claws dig into the earth beneath me.

I hate the strained wariness between me and my brother. I hate that I don't know how to breach it in a way that satisfies the full measure of my failures and expectations. I closed myself off from Isleen in self-preservation when with more fortitude I would have realized her crime and saved him so much anguish. Something in my behavior led him to believe he couldn't reveal her transgressions to me without my blaming him.

But how long has he held in the resentments he expressed to Talia, that he indicated dogged him long before Isleen's offense? How could he have served me so long behaving as if all was well?

There are no easy answers to those questions either. Right now, they can only distract me. Burying them under my more immediate apprehension, I stretch my legs to keep them limber and resist the urge to pace. Ambrose shouldn't have many if any sentries so far from the center of his domain, but I'd rather not draw the attention of any who might happen to pass by.

Surely Talia and the others have seen through the first stage of her plan at this point? Ambrose's staff had better be treating them kindly. My lips start to curl at the thought of the insults they might aim my lover's way.

Then Celia taps her fork against the side of her plate, drawing my and Donovan's attention.

The eldest arch-lord cocks her head. "This is a very satisfying meal, Ambrose, but I expected to find there was a matter of some urgency you wished to discuss. I can't imagine you called for this very private gathering solely to exchange pleasantries."

"Of course not." Ambrose leans forward with a clank of his plated vest. He takes a swig of wine, opens his mouth as if to launch into a speech—and shudders so hard the liquid sloshes from the goblet he's still holding.

What in the lands?

He tries to speak again but only manages a sputtering sound. A purplish cast is creeping over his broad face. He pushes to his feet and sways there, looking as though he might collapse at any moment.

His colleagues have leapt up as well. Celia's dark complexion has dulled with shock. "Ambrose, what ails you?"

He coughs and manages to spit out a few words. "I think— The wine—" He staggers toward Donovan and clutches the younger man's wrist. I feel the pressure of his fingers as if around my own foreleg. "I have something— The inner chamber— Help me?" He jerks his other hand toward Celia. "Find—bring my healer."

Celia whips around and darts through the doorway, leaving Ambrose and the man he wishes to kill utterly alone.

My heart lurches, and I'm springing through the trees toward the grassy slope without any further provocation. Whatever he means to do, he's setting it in motion now. I may have mere minutes before it's too late.

I may not get there in time at all.

I hurtle up the hill with every ounce of power I can summon from my straining muscles. Imposed against the grass and stones, another scene unfolds from within my mind.

Donovan glances toward the doorway Celia hurried out through, clearly aware of his vulnerability now that there's no one present to intervene. Ambrose sways again, and the younger arch-lord helps catch his balance. The apparently sickly man gestures toward another door at the back of the dining room.

No. Stay out of there.

But my thoughts can't carry into Donovan's head any more than his are into mine. As I sprint between the standing stones, my haunches and my lungs burning with the frantic pace I'm keeping, Donovan hesitates and says a few words that are drowned out by the pounding of my pulse and my panting breaths.

Ambrose grips his arm tighter and tugs him toward the door with another shudder—and Donovan moves with him.

Dust and doom. I fling myself past the last of the stones and charge the rest of the way to the palace door. The guards jerk to straighter attention, raising their weapons.

Heart bless us and let this gambit work.

I throw myself upright into human form so swiftly my flesh stings with the abrupt transition. My hair falls wild about my face; I can't imagine my expression is anywhere near as composed as I'd prefer it to be. But perhaps that will sell my story.

"I'm Lord Sylas of Hearthshire. Kin of my pack have come here. I must see them at once on a matter of grave importance."

The nearest guard's jaw clenches, but his gaze darts toward the doorway. "They didn't appear to wish to have anything else to do with you."

I glower at him with all the lordly authority I can bring to bear. "Have they sworn vows to another lord yet? I'm assuming not. I have a right to speak with them."

The other guard shuffles on her feet. "I'll ask them to come out." She ducks inside.

They'll refuse, and I'll be granted passage. I only hope the guard doesn't spend too long arguing with them.

In my mind's eye, Ambrose is shoving open the door to the chamber just off the dining room. He stumbles into what looks like a small office containing a rolltop desk, a matching cabinet with two narrow drawers, a few stacks of books on shelves carved into the dark rock of the wall, and a large clay vase in the corner. Donovan hesitates in the doorway, gripping the frame.

Raised voices reach my own ears through the door. The remaining guard shifts his weight, looking twice as tense as before.

Donovan steps into the study—

The first guard shoves the door in front of me wide. "They won't come," she says, frustration sharpening her voice.

I fold my arms over my chest. "Then I must speak with them where they are. *Now.*"

Her mouth twitches, but to my relief, she must decide she's better off skipping an argument when she knows fae law is on my side. She makes a brusque beckoning motion. "Come on then."

I follow her into the dark hall, only a sliver of the tension clutching my chest releasing at this minor victory. I'm inside—

Donovan is standing over Ambrose in the cramped room. The older arch-lord points to something on one of the shelves. I catch a glint of a metal blade—

There's no time left. I must act now.

"I've arrived," I call out, just loud enough to be sure the words will reach my pack-kin, and then I leap forward, releasing my wolf.

The guard who was escorting me gives a shout. I've already dashed as far as the bend in the hall where I watched Donovan take a right turn. A thump and a snarl behind me tell me that my pack-kin have sprung into action. Brigit and Charce will be holding back any guards who made to charge after me as well as they can, with Harper protecting Talia. If need be, my fierce little human will toss salt into the mix.

A pang of worry rings through me, picturing Talia so close to the fight, but she put herself in this position so I could keep going. If I can end this quickly, she won't be in danger for long.

I race around another corner, spotting the door to the dining room up ahead.

Donovan wraps his fingers around the wooden handle of the dagger Ambrose indicated. His confusion echoes into me with the hesitation in his movements, a twinge in his chest. He would have expected his colleague to aim a blade at him, not to offer one.

As he lifts the dagger, Ambrose snatches at his wrist. The older arch-lord yanks Donovan's hand forward with so much strength that Donovan's shoulder jars in its socket.

The dagger slams into Ambrose's chest, just beneath his armpit. Not a fatal strike by any means, but solid enough that Ambrose flinches at the pain, even though he must have been braced for it.

Donovan heaves backward, startled panic speeding his pulse. He flings the dagger to the side. It skitters across the floor to the vase. As I wheel toward the dining room door, he stares at Ambrose. "What game are you playing? Will you say I stabbed you—and perhaps poisoned you too with that cup? Do you think I won't speak up and tell whoever's judging us the truth?"

I barge through the dining room doorway, and Ambrose's lips stretch with a thin smile turned taut by pain. "You won't if you're dead."

My own blare of panic sends an extra burst of adrenaline to my feet. I burst past the study door just as Ambrose whips a needle-like blade from his sleeve and stabs it at Donovan.

I crash into Ambrose, slamming his arm to the side—not quite soon enough to totally deflect the blow. The narrow blade slices across Donovan's chest rather than piercing straight into it. A searing pain echoes from him into my own flesh.

I chomp my jaws around Ambrose's hand hard enough that his fingers spasm and drop the weapon. But as I kick it away, he shifts, wrenching his hand-turned-paw from my grasp. I manage to send the needle-blade spinning away into the dining room, but the door swings shut in my wake. I have to slam against it to avoid Ambrose's lunge.

Bracing myself against the frame, I rein in my wolf and stand tall while I draw my sword. When I brandish it in warning, the arch-lord backs up, muscles coiled through his shoulders and haunches. I don't want to skirmish with Ambrose any more than I have to. And Donovan—

The younger arch-lord has teetered and toppled onto his ass. Blood wells all along the thin line carved through his tunic into his flesh. Dizzyingly, I see both him and myself through his eyes. His vision doubles, turning my form into hazy twins. And his face—

His face is the image that swam before me those weeks ago in his office, contorted and shining with sweat. Ambrose might not have gotten the poison in as deeply as he meant to, but it's acting on the other man all the same.

It's acting quickly. A rattle has crept into Donovan's breath even as he murmurs the words of a spell that must be meant to protect him. I feel his lungs straining. As a green tint spreads over his face, his body slumps farther, his eyelids drooping, his voice failing. The hazy impressions cut off completely as he loses consciousness.

He's still alive. He didn't get the full dose of poison, and he had the chance to ward off at least a little of its effects. Healing has never been a particular skill of mine, but I can slow the flow of his blood, calm his nerves so the poison doesn't spread as quickly. Buy time for Celia to bring the healer.

If Ambrose will allow it.

I step toward Donovan, and Ambrose's dark wolf shoves me aside. As I raise my sword threateningly again, he rises back up as a man, gripping the hilt of the sword at his waist. Blocking my way to his dying colleague.

"So," he taunts with a sneer, "the great Lord Sylas shows his traitorous inclinations after all. Do you mean to run me through with that sword?" He pulls out his own.

The jab lands hard enough that I wince inwardly, but the sight of Donovan's sprawled body gives me all the resolve I need to hold my ground. *I* am not the traitor here.

I grit my teeth. "I don't want to. But I'd be betraying the arch-lord you've attempted to murder if I don't do all I can to help him survive."

Ambrose gives his sword a casual swing. "Is that what you're telling yourself?"

"It's what *everyone* will see. Fighting off someone who's attacked an arch-lord, even if he's an arch-lord himself, can never be treason."

"Hmm. That assumes that either of you will be around to tell your version of the story. Let me rectify that impression. Neither of you will leave this room alive, and I'll be sure your name and your pack go down in blazing infamy."

My gut twists with nausea, but an eerie calm settles over the rest of me. The memory of Talia's arms around me floats up through my mind alongside her soft voice, telling me with such certainty how much she trusts me.

I know she's right. I know *I'm* right. If killing an arch-lord is what it takes to defend the one who needs it, then as much as I abhor the idea, I'll do it. Not out of greed like Isleen and her kin. I don't care who becomes arch-lord when Ambrose is gone as long as he can't continue to risk all Seelie kind with his own lust for power.

And clearly that's what it's come down to: my life and Donovan's or his.

"Move out of the way, Ambrose," I say in one final warning.

He simply readies his sword. So be it.

I feint in one direction and lunge in the other. Ambrose parries, our blades clanging together. He pushes forward with a stab, a feint, and a swing, taking up every bit of the tight space in his attempt to press the advantage.

I dodge to the side, and he rams me into the shelves, books thumping onto the floor. Pain that's all mine splinters through my side. With a knee to the gut, I send Ambrose reeling backward, but only a couple of steps.

At my next strike, he smacks his blade against mine so hard the clash reverberates through my arms. As I swivel, he snaps out a word that turns my blood cold. "*Fee-doom-ace-own.*"

From Talia's lips, that true name can bend spoons, warp knives, and lift thin chains. She wouldn't be able to damage this sword in any significant way with its built-in enchantments specifically to prevent any ill effects in battle. But Ambrose is an arch-lord with all the power that runs in his family and that's built up in him with his proximity to the Heart. My blade sags from its hilt as if it's turned to melted wax.

I bash it at him from the side, but the lopsided mass throws off my balance. He dodges too easily. There's no chance my magic is enough to conquer whatever protections he's added to his own blade over however many months or years, especially when I've only been back from the fringes for a short while.

Sucking a breath through my clenched teeth, I make the best gamble I can.

I toss my ruined sword away. As the movement draws Ambrose's attention for the briefest of instants, I slam my hands at his sword-arm's wrist with a swift twist. The flat of his blade smacks my temple, but an instant later, bones crack.

I wrench the weapon from his fingers. It clatters to the floor. At a swipe of my heel, it skids across the floor behind me.

Ambrose doesn't waste any time bemoaning his broken wrist. He hunches into wolf form, already lashing out with his curved fangs. Thankfully I expected him to make the shift. As I spring backward, I unleash my own wolf.

I hurl myself at him, and he meets my charge. Our bodies collide, rolling over one another, claws scrabbling and teeth biting at every bit of flesh they can reach.

My tail brushes against Donovan's sprawled form, and my heart lurches. How much more time does he have?

I need some way to get the upper hand. As Ambrose attempts

to pin me down and we grapple against one another, my gaze flicks around the room. My sword is useless. I'd wager his is charmed to burn any hand other than his that attempts to grasp its hilt. The poisoned knife he cut Donovan with is out in the dining room.

But there was another blade he doesn't even know I'm aware of. I wasn't in the room when he forced Donovan to stab him with that dagger, not in any way Ambrose could observe.

Where did Donovan fling it to? It knocked against the base of the vase...

I manage to heave Ambrose off me far enough for me to hurtle toward the vase. My furred shoulder smashes through the pottery. Ambrose throws himself onto me, making the broken shards beneath me dig into my muscles, but I've caught the gleam of bronze.

There's no chance of demanding a yield. This isn't a fight for dominance but a desperate bid for survival.

I shift faster than I've ever changed before, snatch up the dagger, and ram it right between the arch-lord's eyes.

The blade slams home all the way to the hilt, shattering skull and slicing straight into Ambrose's brain. A groan and a spray of spittle bursts from his gnashing mouth. His wolfish limbs spasm and slacken.

The massive beast tumbles off of me, returning to the form of a man as he hits the floor on his back. Ambrose stares blankly at the ceiling, his body limp, blood dribbling from around the blade still lodged in his forehead.

My throat is throbbing where he dealt a shallow but broad gash, my torso aching with at least one cracked rib, but I don't pause to tend to myself or him. I spin toward Donovan. The younger arch-lord's chest is still hitching with erratic breaths, his eyelids quivering.

I press my hands over the wound on his chest, muttering the

true names for blood and muscle with all the power I can pour into them.

Slow the poison. Save his life. *Please.*

I'm not sure how many times I've spat out the syllables in the fading rush of adrenaline when a voice carries from the room beyond. "Ambrose? Donovan?"

It's Celia. "In here!" I shout hoarsely.

She flings the door open, urging a man who must be Ambrose's healer ahead of her. "I came as quickly as I could. I—"

They both stall in their tracks at the sight of the arch-lord's corpse.

I heave myself to my feet. "You can't do anything for Ambrose. He poisoned Donovan with a blade. Donovan's still alive, but he won't be much longer if he doesn't get proper help."

Faced with the death of his master, the healer wavers for only a second before dropping to his knees at Donovan's side. From his urgent incantations and his fumbling with his pouches of supplies, I don't think he has any interest in carrying out Ambrose's intentions now that the man is gone, if he ever would have.

Celia stays by the door, staring at the scene. As I take in her horrified expression, my heart sinks.

Ambrose may have his revenge yet. She has only my word that he was the one who attacked Donovan rather than me. She might very well accuse me of attempting to slay them both. I did burst in here uninvited under technically false pretenses; I had every reason to wish Ambrose dead for my own gain. Even if Donovan recovers enough to speak to his own injuries, she might claim the poison has addled his mind or see it as some conspiracy of our own.

She lifts her gaze to meet mine, taking in me as I was observing her. Her attention appears to settle on the band with its gem still pressed against my forehead. One corner of her lips slants upward.

"My young colleague was most thoroughly prepared," she says, and tips up the simple crown she's wearing to show a gem that matches mine fixed underneath.

Donovan gave her the means to see what happened too. Based on the fact that she's making no move to arrest me, I'm going to suppose that she heard Ambrose declare his intentions before the poison took hold. Thank all that is merciful.

I bow my head to her, the surge of relief mingling with the aches of my body. If I didn't have every muscle in my legs tensed, I'd sway on my feet. "Thank the Heart for that."

"It did no harm to accept his request, but I thought him rather paranoid." Celia considers the figures slumped on the floor again. "Clearly I was mistaken."

As if in response to those words, Donovan jerks to the side, folding over at the waist. With a quake of his abdomen, he spews yellow-green bile from his mouth onto the floor. The healer eases to the side, watching.

The young arch-lord coughs and gags again, but the sickly color is already fading from his face. He blinks, looking up at us with a dazed expression, and swipes at his mouth.

After a moment, a weak smile crosses his face. "Well," he says hoarsely, "this is not at all a respectable position for an arch-lord to find himself in, now is it?"

Celia snorts. "From the looks of things, you're lucky to be in the position of keeping your life. Worry about respect once we're sure you're doing that."

I sink down next to Donovan, ready to steady him if he wishes to sit up. He extends his hand, but when I grasp it, he doesn't make any attempt to pull himself upright just yet.

"I think you can count on this being the last time I don't fully heed your advice, Lord Sylas," he says. "Your conduct today should earn you rewards far better than becoming a colleague of mine, but I'm afraid that's the highest honor I'm capable of presenting.

Perhaps I should be kinder and send you on a century-long vacation instead."

I offer a small smile in return. "I served as I've sworn to, and as I'll continue to in whatever way you will it, my lord."

A thin hum emanates from his throat. "In that case… You'd better get your affairs in order, soon-to-be-Arch-Lord Sylas."

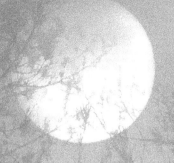

CHAPTER TWENTY-SEVEN

Talia

The Bastion casts a golden light over everyone within its walls, pulsing gently with the flow of energy from the Heart just beyond the building. Brilliant sunlight streams through the high windows into the huge central room with its vaulted ceiling. The gold ore laced through the warm stone gleams.

The expansive glow matches the crown Celia and Donovan are setting on Sylas's head together in the final stage of his initiation as arch-lord. The light wraps around him as if the Heart of the Mists itself is embracing him in his new role.

Which in some way it is. Even with my human senses, I felt the thrum of energy rising with the current arch-lords' words as they carried out the ceremony and asked for the Heart's blessing.

Whitt and August stand a few steps behind their lord, August beaming, Whitt sporting a crooked smile that's maybe not quite as enthusiastic but pleased nonetheless. I'm back by the edge of the circular room, where the spectators from the arch-lords' packs, Hearthshire's, and many other lords and their cadre-chosen have come to witness Sylas's ascension. The size of the crowd and the intensity of the moment make my nerves jitter, but Astrid's no-nonsense presence besides me keeps my anxieties in check.

"Welcome to the trio of the Bastion, Arch-Lord Sylas," Celia and Donovan say in unison. The crown on Sylas's head sparks with a brighter light. The arch-lords each take one of his hands, raise them in the air, and turn with him as if displaying their new unity to the entire crowd around them.

Sylas is smiling too—typically reserved, but there's no mistaking the awed pride in his expression. Just weeks ago, he wasn't even respected as a lord. Now he's one of the three most esteemed figures in the entire summer realm.

As I watch, so much affection wells up inside me that my chest aches with it.

When the arch-lords finish their rotation and lower Sylas's hands, a cheer rises up from the crowd. A smattering of applause grows to a deluge. I add my hands to the clamor, suddenly grinning uncontrollably.

The assembled fae stream outside to the grassy field that lies directly before in the vast, pulsing glow of the Heart, its light flowing over us and out into the hazy border that stretches into the distance on either side. Food and drinks have already been laid out on tables along the fringes of the field; several musicians strike up a rollicking tune.

The serious parts of the ceremony are over. It's time to revel.

Sylas makes his way through the crowd, shaking offered hands, acknowledging bows, responding to eager compliments. He stops when he reaches me.

"Congratulations, Arch-Lord Sylas," I say, aiming my grin at him.

He gives a low chuckle. "Maybe in a few decades that'll start to sound normal." He reaches to grip my shoulder, his dark eye speaking of all the things he'd like to say if we didn't have so much of an audience, but he's already said plenty over the past two weeks. "I won't forget how I got here and who I have to thank for that."

"I know." I rest my hand over his for a brief moment, and then the other fae draw him away into their midst again.

Several of the attendees begin to dance in the center of the field. August catches my arm and tugs me to join them. Gazing up into his joyful face, I tune out the stares I know are aimed our way.

Even a lord's cadre-chosen giving a human this much attention was unusual. An arch-lord's? It must be nearly unthinkable.

For a few songs, swaying and turning in his arms, it doesn't matter. But then pain creeps up my ankle from my warped foot even with my braced boot, and I can't ignore *that* discomfort any longer. August leads me back to Astrid before I'm outright hobbling, and in a few minutes he's been swept back into the festivities again.

I sit down on a cushion to watch. The flow of conversation and music carries on around me. The fae move from one partner to another, but none of my three lovers is ever without one—the women with their unearthly beauty, their feral grace, and jewels sparkling along the curve of their pointed ears. And when they pause to grab a drink or a bite to eat from the tables, they're surrounded by men as well, all seeking favor with the new power by the Heart.

Why wouldn't it be like that? It's all just a sign of how much favor my pack has gained since I joined them. Everyone is recognizing what a devoted and honorable leader Sylas is. I can't let myself see that as anything other than a good thing.

After I've rested my foot for a while, I venture to one of the tables with Astrid trailing behind me. My men are off among the dancers again; none of the fae around me pays me any mind. As I lean over to pluck a skewer of roasted fruit chunks from one of the platters, the voices of a nearby cluster of Seelie in low but audible conversation reach my ears.

"He'll be wanting an heir, though. He'll need a true-blooded mate for much chance at that."

"Oh, I've already seen a few widows positioning themselves. I'm sure he'll have plenty of choice even so."

"Too bad for you two, huh?"

A tinkle of a laugh. "Well, there's always his half-brothers. They're quite impressive too, and that heir will need a cadre, after all."

My gut clenches. My fingers tighten around the skewer, my gaze fixed on the fruit I'm no longer sure I can force down.

I carry it back to my cushion anyway and pick at the smoky, juicy bits for several minutes, doing my best to convince myself that I don't care at all about anything I overheard. That I already knew everything they said perfectly well.

It's just a little different hearing confirmation from outside my own head.

The music lilts on, winding through the chatter and laughter, but I can't will my spirits to lift again. I set down the half-eaten skewer and get to my feet, needing space from the bustle of the celebration. My gaze falls on the Bastion, the gold seams running through the rock glinting warmly.

"Can I go back inside?" I ask Astrid, tipping my head to it.

She shrugs. "I don't see why not. I'd imagine anything the arch-lords don't want messed with is locked away."

I wander across the grass and through one of the side doors. My uneven footsteps echo through the wide hall. Avoiding the huge central room where the ceremony took place, I veer toward a flight of stairs and limp up it to the second floor of one of the smaller towers.

In the landing at the top of the stairs, the small arched window gives a view over Sylas's new domain. He hasn't touched Ambrose's obsidian castle or wall yet, waiting until his appointment was official, but over the past week he and the pack-kin who are skilled with the right sorts of magic have been working on a new home to suit their tastes. Several immense trees already stretch toward the sky, not yet melded together or shaped into rooms, but giving a clear impression of how they'll make a castle like the one in Hearthshire.

Sylas told us he's changing the name of the domain too, to fully claim it and match our pack. Instead of Dusk-by-the-Heart, it'll be Hearth-by-the-Heart.

My fingers curl against the window ledge as I gaze out at it. That'll be my home too for as long as we stay here, which will hopefully be the rest of my life. I helped Sylas earn it. It can be a happy home, free from any fear of cages or other sorts of imprisonment.

And if it becomes too lonely once—once things play out as everyone expects, then I'm sure Sylas would allow me to make my way back to the human world if I asked to. He could send Astrid or someone to collect the blood they need every full moon until they find another cure, and otherwise I could let this all fade into a dream.

But I don't want to.

I close my eyes against the sudden burn of tears. I have to pull myself together. Soon I'll need to go back to the revel, and I have to look as happy as everyone else. I can't distract my lovers from the greatest triumph of their lives.

Apparently it's too late to avoid that, though. Footsteps rasp on the stairs below, and Astrid stirs where she's been leaning against the wall nearby. Her voice comes out wry. "It appears I'm no longer needed."

I turn to see her already slipping away down the spiral stairs—and Sylas, August, and Whitt emerging from the shadows.

I blink hard, but I'm too startled to hide my emotions that quickly. August's eyes have already widened with worry at the sight of me. So I start talking before they can. "What are you doing up here? You're supposed to be celebrating."

Sylas walks right up to me, the thin crown gleaming against his dark hair, and brushes his fingers over my cheek. "So are you, Talia. Whitt noticed you leaving and was concerned, and it appears he was right to be. What happened? Was someone unkind to you?"

A growl is creeping into his voice just at the thought. An arch-lord for only a few hours, and he's already preparing to use that authority to defend me. My gaze slips past him to Whitt—of course it'd be the spymaster who observed me slipping away—taking in the tensing of his shoulders and the dark flash in his eyes, equally protective. August comes up beside Sylas and grasps my hand, stroking his thumb gently over my knuckles.

"No," I say, willing my voice to stay steady. "Nothing like that. I just got a little overwhelmed by the crowd. I'm all right."

Whitt makes a soft sound, stepping closer while noticeably careful not to infringe on Sylas's personal space. "I may not have the occasion to hear many lies from my brethren, but I know one when I hear it. What's the matter, mighty one?"

"Whatever it is, we'll deal with it," August assures me, so firmly that tears prick at the back of my eyes again.

How can I explain that it isn't something they *can* deal with? That it's just my selfishness and nothing anyone's done wrong?

I resist the urge to hug myself. "I'm just being silly. Really, it's fine. You should go back to the party. People will wonder where you've gone."

A rumble reverberates from Sylas's chest. He wraps his arm right around my shoulders, tugging me to him. "If you're so concerned about me keeping up appearances, the fastest way to ensure I go is to tell me what's upset you."

I lean my head against his solid chest, clenching my jaw and clamping my eyes shut. But the familiar, delicious smell of him fills my nose, and the thought that I don't know how many more times

I'll get to be held by him like this chases after it. Before I can catch it, a sob hitches out of me.

All three men have circled in on me in an instant, August squeezing my hand, Whitt resting his hand on my back. The spymaster's voice turns fierce. "If someone said one nasty comment to you, I'll—"

"No." I pull back from Sylas, holding myself rigid as if that will seal in any other reactions I'd rather tamp down on. I guess there's no getting out of this. Embarrassed heat tickles over my cheeks. "I—I know this is stupid, and I don't expect anything else. I shouldn't be letting it bother me when there's so much to be happy for. I just—"

I can't look them in the eyes while I say it. I lower my head, my voice dropping with it. "The pack isn't outcast anymore. You've received the highest honor there is. So of course—of course you'll want to take proper mates now that you can. Maybe not right away, but— And that's *okay*. That's what you should do. You need heirs and all that. I promise you I'm not—"

"Talia," Sylas interrupts, his voice rough. He lifts my chin with his fingers, and then he's kissing me, so deeply and urgently I'm barely aware of anything other than the hot press of his mouth and his strong fingers sliding along my jaw.

August lets out a ragged sound and nuzzles my hair; Whitt plants a kiss on the shell of my ear. I'm completely encompassed by them, and in that moment I don't care what kind of future there is, I only want to lose myself in this feeling of shared devotion.

Sylas draws back, leaving me aching for more, but he stays close enough that his breath grazes my face. "I am *not* tossing you aside, no matter how many offers I get from the fae down there. *You* are the one I want, and I intend to spend every moment I can with you by my side. I have centuries to worry about heirs. I don't even need one of my blood if I choose to carry on my line by decree instead. There is nothing in this world or theirs I would give you up for." He pauses, and his voice thrums with emotion. "I love you, Talia. I should have said that the first moment I understood it."

I stare up at him, my pulse fluttering against my ribs like the wings of a frantic bird. I never expected to hear those words from August, let alone the fae lord. But the force of his declaration leaves no doubt that he means it. Still, I can't help saying, "You do?"

He kisses my forehead. "You own my heart. You've become my guiding light through so much turmoil, and as far as I'm concerned, there isn't a single woman in the fae realms who could hold a candle to you. And I don't think I'm alone in feeling that way."

He glances toward his cadre. August guides my face to him and steals a kiss for himself, all tenderness. "If I'd had any idea you were thinking that way," he says raggedly, and shakes his head. "You're everything I could possibly want or need, Sweetness. I can't imagine being happier than you make me. I'd sooner never set foot in a kitchen again then spend a day when I could have you without you."

My lips twitch with a smile at that last declaration, and then Whitt is turning me toward him. His mouth collides with mine, as fierce as his voice was a minute ago and searing with a passion much headier than just hunger. He lets the kiss linger on before releasing me, his fingers still teasing over my hair, and then tucks me against his chest like Sylas did before.

He hesitates, eyeing Sylas as if he's not totally sure whether his lord will object to his participation in this moment after all. The other man simply offers a slight smile and a dip of his head like a benediction.

Whitt hugs me tighter. "I may be a man of many words, but I'm not much of one for grand declarations. Let it just be said that I'm certainly not about to let these two lunks hoard you all to themselves. I expect we have many more adventures ahead of us, mite, and I wouldn't miss sharing them with you for anything."

Tears are filling my eyes again, but they're giddy rather than painful now. I hug him back and then turn in his arms to look at Sylas. "So what does that mean? We'll keep on the way we have been, with everyone thinking I'm only with August?"

"No," the fae lord says. "If you are ours and we are yours, it's only fair that we make that claim for all to see. You deserve that recognition." He frowns. "It's rare but not unheard of for fae to commit to a mate bond with a human. I'm not sure I've heard of any joint mate bondings where those sharing a lover made it quite so official all around. Perhaps our strategist can investigate an appropriate approach?"

Whitt grins, looking totally at ease with his lord for the first time I've seen in weeks. "It would be my pleasure."

"A mate bond," I repeat. The giddiness is spreading through my whole body. Can this really be happening? Can they really want— but how can I doubt it after everything they've said? I'm not totally sure what that means, though. The only thing I'm really sure of is— "It isn't like the soul-twined bond."

Sylas nods. "It's the formal exchanging of vows and entwining of magic that all those who aren't soul-twined mates can use to bind themselves to their chosen mate in love and loyalty. There would be none of the intense effects, but there's something to be said for a choice freely made."

Yes, there is. I remember the way he described the forming of a soul-twined bond. *It hits you like a lightning bolt straight down the center of you, like being suddenly burned through.* What I feel for these three men is plenty powerful enough without that, thank you.

Only one worry remains. "Wouldn't the other fae think it's strange?"

Sylas lets out a challenging guffaw. "They'll be welcome to tell me so to my face and discover the consequences. Let them gossip however they wish elsewhere. If my rule as arch-lord doesn't command enough respect to quell any disparagement, then I'm not doing my job well enough."

Whitt gives a lock of my hair a playful tug. "We'll remind them that you do have some small trace of fae blood in there somewhere, and you take to true-blooded coloring so well you might as well be one. Auggie can keep you in hair dye, hmm?"

August laughs. "I'll mash up a whole vat if it'll—"

"My lord!" Astrid's voice carries up the stairs with the thumping of hurried feet. She sounds rattled, so unlike her usual unflappable self that my body has already tensed before she hurtles into view.

She dips into a swift bow at the top of the stairs and straightens up, her jaw tight. "You're needed below, Arch-Lord Sylas. They— the arch-lords of the Unseelie have come across the border to parley."

Sylas can't rein in his shock. "They're here—*now?*"

Astrid motions for him to follow, and we all rush down the steps together.

My heart hitches behind my ribs. What could the Unseelie want? Astrid didn't say they'd attacked us—no, they can't. For any fae to cross the border near the Heart, they have to take a vow that they won't harm anyone on the other side.

The real question is, what could possibly have prompted the rulers of the winter realm to take that risk at this exact moment?

"They say they have magic on them that would retaliate if any of us attempt to hurt them," Astrid says breathlessly, filling Sylas in on the way down. "No one's dared to test it."

When we emerge from the Bastion, the musicians have stopped playing. The dancers have fallen back to the fringes of the field. Only seven figures remain in the clear span just in front of the Heart, outlined in its glow.

Donovan and Celia stand their ground before five fae in finery of pale gray, blue, and ivory—like the colors of ice. Silvery crowns gleam on all of the strangers' heads, and true name marks unfurl along their brows and jaws. Their expressions are coolly haughty. Broad wings rippling with black feathers stretch from their backs.

Apparently the Unseelie can use their wings in human form just like the Seelie can bring out their fangs and claws. And they have five arch-lords rather than three. I didn't know. I wonder if Sylas even did.

He strides through the crowd to join his new colleagues, his shoulders squaring. Whitt and August follow to the front of the throng, ready to leap in if called on.

Astrid tugs me to the side. We circle the clearing until we find a spot where the spectators are less densely packed and ease forward there to get a better view. She keeps one hand clamped around my forearm, the other on the hilt of her dagger.

When Sylas joins the other arch-lords, Celia is the one who speaks. I guess her age gives her the most seniority to speak for all of them.

"The three of us are before you now. What is the meaning of this visit?"

The Unseelie fae in the middle of their group is a woman so brawny even her tattooed neck bulges with muscle. She swipes her turquoise hair back from her face. "We heard there's been a changing of the guard in the lands of summer. Is it so strange that we'd want to see the new line of authority on the other side of the Heart?" Her chilly gaze skims over Sylas.

"Here I am," he says amicably enough, but his dark eye is wary.

I study each of the other Unseelie, searching for any clue of their true motives. There are three women and two men in total. I have trouble judging the age of fae, but they appear to range from a man with curly blue-black hair and bronze skin who looks to be as young as August to a slight, spindly woman I suspect is much older even than Celia.

They all stand straight and regal, their eyes fixed on the Seelie arch-lords, totally motionless—except for the young man, whose wings give a restless twitch behind him.

As I focus more intently on him, his attention slips away from the rulers in front of him to consider the crowd. He glances across the assembled fae so swiftly I don't have time to jerk my eyes away before our gazes collide.

And it truly is a collision.

The second his dark eyes catch mine, a wave of energy sears through me. As I hold in a gasp, it crackles into every nerve all the way to the roots of my teeth and the tips of my toes. It wrenches down the middle of my chest as if I'm being carved apart by a blade of fire.

As if I've been hit by a lightning bolt, straight down the center of me.

The bottom of my stomach drops out. My mouth falls open, but no sound comes out.

The Unseelie arch-lord stares at me as I must be staring at him, his own jaw going slack—and then a roar of sensation floods into the burned-out space where the energy blazed through me. The pinch of a belt buckled too tightly. The pang of a stomach too tensed to risk filling.

The image of a pale girl with vivid pink hair gaping at me—at *him*—from amid the crowd.

No. It's impossible. It *can't*—

I stumble backward in Astrid's hold, slamming my eyes closed, but there's no escaping the words that rise up in an unfamiliar voice that's somehow resonating from deep inside me.

How can— It's you. My soul-twined mate.

KINGS OF MOONLIGHT - BONUS SCENE

W *hat was going through Sylas's mind after Whitt's confession about Isleen? This bonus scene shows how he sorted through his thoughts with Talia's help later that night...*

Sylas

Over the decades, I've learned how to shut off parts of my mind as needed to ensure that I can fulfill my responsibilities with complete focus. Being at my best requires getting enough sleep. But this particular night, I can't stop the memories and imagined scenarios with different outcomes from whirling on and on through my head. Maybe because tuning out my uncomfortable thoughts is how we ended up in this horrific situation to begin with.

Finally, I push myself out of my bed and stalk down the hall to my office. If I'm not sleeping, I might as well attempt to accomplish something useful. Giving myself other tasks to think about might help settle my anguished emotions, if only temporarily.

Unfortunately, once I've reached my office and dropped into my chair, I find myself simply staring aimlessly at the documents and books spread out across it. What do I have here that I haven't already pored over that might give us a solution to our other problems? If the answer to protecting Talia and the security of our realm from Ambrose's ambitions were in this room, I'd have already located it.

As I'm casting about for some minor matter that might have escaped my attention and be at least possible to address, my keen ears pick up the uneven rhythm of soft footsteps beyond the door. My heart lifts and sinks at the same time, welcoming the company and saddened that the source of it isn't getting any more rest than I am.

When she knocks on the door, I've already turned my chair toward it. "Come in," I say.

Talia slips inside, her pale face drawn, her vibrant hair rumpled. I hold out my arms to her before she finds her words. With a choked little sound that cuts right through me, she walks over and lets me scoop her onto my lap.

I nestle her against my chest, holding her tight. An ache spreads all through my torso.

It's bad enough that the past has come back to haunt me and my cadre so viciously. Our sweet lover shouldn't have to bear any of the burdens of our past mistakes. But she's clearly been wrenched by the scenes she's witnessed.

Of course she has. The only heart I've ever encountered that's larger than hers is the one that glows and pulses in the center of our world.

"You couldn't sleep either?" she murmurs finally, tucking her head right under my chin.

I run my fingers over her hair as I keep my other arm poised in its firm embrace. "My mind is too full of regret and other turmoil."

She glances up at me with a flicker of concern crossing her face. "You aren't still angry with Whitt, are you? You said—"

"I meant what I said to him in our last conversation," I say. "Every word of it. But it's still..." I struggle for the words to explain my inner state when I can barely lay out my full feelings in my own head. "It's a wound we've been carrying for nearly a century. My assumptions about that incident have factored into so many of my decisions and interactions—and now I have to consider that they may have affected our lives in all sorts of ways I didn't even realize, seeing as I had no idea of how the situation involved or affected Whitt. It may take a while to untangle all of that."

"For him too," she says in a melancholy tone.

"No doubt." I lower my head to press a kiss to her temple. "But you don't need to worry about any harm coming to him from me. It's clear the only real villain in this situation was Isleen, and I suppose that fact makes it even more reasonable to say she met the end she deserved. Thank you for seeing through to the truth of the matter—thank you for appealing to the need for truth when my temper was getting the better of me. I should have thanked you earlier."

"It's all right. I didn't do it for your gratitude." She traces her fingers down my arm over my bicep, but I can tell she doesn't intend anything provocative with her touch. It's more as if she's feeling me out, making sure I'm the same steady presence I've endeavored to always be for her.

How did I ever deserve this little scrap who understands so much more than any of the rest of us managed to on our own?

"I know he cares about you a lot," Talia goes on. "I think he's been punishing himself for what happened over all those years because of how guilty he feels, more than anyone else could have punished him." She pauses. "That's probably a big part of why he was so hesitant to pursue anything with me once I was already with you and August, isn't it? He told me once… that he was afraid being with me would ruin things, or that he would, or something."

My throat constricts at the idea that my brother might have cut himself off from the joy I know he's found with our woman as some kind of self-imposed retribution for a crime that wasn't even his. "I'm glad you were able to eliminate that particular concern of his, at least."

Talia lets out a soft laugh. "I don't even know how I did exactly. But I'm glad too. I'm glad I was there today. I hope he can really forgive himself now that the truth is out."

While I may still be frustrated that Whitt didn't reveal his part in Isleen's ploy sooner, I can say without any hesitation at all, "I'll do whatever I can to see that he does."

My lover relaxes into my embrace more than she had before those words, which makes me even more committed to them. But it seems it's not only my feelings about my brother that have been concerning her. She hesitates for several seconds and then asks, "Do you ever miss her? Isleen? I know everything was awful at the end, and that you disagreed with her about some things before then too, but she was also your soul-twined mate. That's obviously a big deal. And you don't get to have another one, right?"

"Only the one." I take a moment to examine my reaction to the question, because I haven't asked myself it in a long time, and I want to be totally honest in my answer.

"I won't say that I never feel any sorrow that I couldn't have had a *better* soul-twined bond," I say finally. "For many true-blooded fae, it's the most fulfilling relationship of their lives, and I caught glimpses of what that might be like when she and I were getting along. But I have no wish at all to have kept her in my life. Now more than ever, I think both I and the pack would be far worse off even if she'd backed out of the attempted mutiny or survived it. Our goals and our values didn't align in so many important ways. The closeness we shared was always tainted by those conflicts."

Talia loops her arm around my chest in a hug. "I'm sorry. You should have gotten a better mate than that. You deserve it."

She speaks as if she doesn't know what *she* means to me. What a shining presence she's been in my life. But perhaps it would sound patronizing to compare her to Isleen when she's well aware that the soul-twined bond is something we can never replicate. I don't want to rub *that* truth in her face.

"I'm very happy with the company I get to keep now," I tell her, and nudge her chin up so I can claim her lips. She hums happily against my mouth, but I can feel the weariness in her, the lack of sleep weighing her down. I won't make any more demands of her tonight.

When our lips part, I incline my head next to hers. "Does that resolve all your worries, Talia? If there's anything else on your mind, you can always bring it up with me."

"I know. I think… I think that's everything." She presses her hand to her mouth against the beginnings of a yawn.

A fond smile crosses my face. I stand, lifting her in my arms. "Then I should be getting you back to your bed before I take another stab at making proper use of mine. Your presence has been a balm as it so often is, little scrap. We're lucky to have you."

Talia doesn't answer, only snuggling deeper into my encircling arms. She lets me carry her back to her room and all but collapses into her bed with obvious exhaustion. The last glimpse of her I get is a relieved if hazy smile as her eyelids droop. But as I walk back to my bed chamber, a slight uneasiness niggles at my gut.

Was there something she didn't say in that hesitation after I asked her what else she might be worrying about? And if there was, what else might be troubling the woman I love that she's too afraid to even mention?

ABOUT THE AUTHOR

Eva Chase lives in Canada with her family. She loves stories both swoony and supernatural, and strong women and the men who appreciate them. Along with the Bound to the Fae series, she is the author of the Flirting with Monsters series, the Cursed Studies trilogy, the Royals of Villain Academy series, the Moriarty's Men series, the Looking Glass Curse trilogy, the Their Dark Valkyrie series, the Witch's Consorts series, the Dragon Shifter's Mates series, the Demons of Fame Romance series, the Legends Reborn trilogy, and the Alpha Project Psychic Romance series.

Connect with Eva online:
www.evachase.com
eva@evachase.com

9 781990 338908